Love Hunt

FIONA WALKER

HODDER &
STOUGHTON

First published in Great Britain in 2009 by Hodder & Stoughton
An Hachette Livre UK company

1

Copyright © Fiona Walker 2009

The right of Fiona Walker to be identified as the Author of
the Work has been asserted by her in accordance with
the Copyright, Designs and Patents Act 1988.

A CIP catalogue record for this title
is available from the British Library

Hardback ISBN 978 0 340 82077 3
Trade Paperback ISBN 978 0 340 82078 0

Typeset in Plantin Light by Ellipsis Books Limited, Glasgow

Printed and bound by Clays Ltd, St Ives plc

Hodder & Stoughton policy is to use papers that are natural, renewable
and recyclable products and made from wood grown in sustainable forests.
The logging and manufacturing processes are expected to conform to the
environmental regulations of the country of origin.

Hodder & Stoughton Ltd
338 Euston Road
London NW1 3BH

For my beloved Gin and Scrap who are the gold at each end of my rainbow, and for their wonderful big brother who shines so brightly.

PROLOGUE

'It's a hoar frost,' Trudy breathed in an undertone to nobody in particular, watching her breath cloud and condense in front of her face like a small, steamy puff from a dragon. She'd always found the phrase amusing, imagining lots of very chilly trollops with goose bumps and pert nipples gallivanting around whitened flowerbeds pursued by Jack Frost's long, icy fingers.

Ahead of her, in the milky cold darkness, she could just make out the lace-edged skeletons of big, lonely trees scattered across formal parkland. Like a distant city that never sleeps, stars dotted the navy blue sky beyond them.

One was on the move – at speed. A shooting star.

Trudy closed her eyes and wished for freedom.

It was just past midnight at Eastlode Park. The Vale of the Wolds Hunt Ball was in full cry. All those who had gathered upon the frosty steps for a cigarette between courses agreed that it was proving to be a vintage year.

Yet to Trudy Dew it was a double-edged occasion. Upon arrival, the guests had quickly divided into youth and oldies, and husband Finn had kept her circulating with the oldies upstairs, not with the younger crowd in the cellars, where she'd longed to be all evening. Now that they were eating, the two age groups had at least reconfigured temporarily, but Trudy, seated between a yellow-toothed racing bore and her ungracious brother-in-law, was still isolated from her gossipy, irreverent, young-at-heart comfort zone and rapidly losing her sparkle.

As always, the huge Cottrell family into which she had married took up three tables with noisy aplomb, their many red-cheeked house guests relishing a rare prolonged spell of decent heating. Dinner talk was almost entirely taken up with antiques, gardening and racing, which made Trudy feel like a prematurely ageing relic going to seed in a one horse race to the exit.

Now, standing outside to cool her face and catch her breath, she drew strength and calm. Opening her eyes and looking at the stars, she rolled her head on her stiff neck and braced herself to return to the fray. She was damned if she was going to spoil a rare night out with her own bad temper.

Few had noticed her absence, but her very drunken brother-in-law Piers, who was always particularly raucous at hunt balls, had taken advantage by eating her main course, as well as polishing off his own and most of his wife Jemima's.

'I suppose it'll help the spring diet,' Trudy laughed magnanimously, although Piers made no attempt to apologise.

'You should have your stomach stapled,' he suggested, showering her with a light splattering of port *jus* from the venison that she should have enjoyed. 'Pickle Mainwaring had it done last summer – she was an absolute heifer, bigger than you, Tru – and now she's out hunting three times a week with thighs like a Russian gymnast's. Marvellous sight. Where the devil is she? *Pickles!* He was on his feet, scanning the room and bellowing, much as he did when standing up in his stirrups on horseback in search of a stray hound

Jemima reached up a slim arm and hooked her husband back down by his soup-splattered lapel. 'She's not here, Piers. Skiing in Klosters, I think'. She turned to Trudy, china blue eyes glittering with a malicious challenge to engage in a little bitchy banqueting badinage. 'But I'll give you her number, if you think it might help. I know she'd tried everything, too – diet, drugs, personal trainers, lipo.'

'Thanks.' Trudy's stiff smile matched her stiff neck as she feigned polite gratitude and turned away to join in a conversation about Cheltenham hopefuls. Taking on Jemima – or any competitive Cottrell – in a verbal spat was a blood sport she no longer participated in. She preferred, instead, to nurture the younger family crowd.

Yet when she finally joined them in the mass exodus to the cellars after dinner to listen to two local bands play live sets, she still felt alienated, this time too old and reactionary to blend in. Her sense of unease was not helped by Piers, who followed her down in the hope that she might be harbouring narcotic substances to go with his third port. Even after all these years, Piers still believed that Trudy scattered Es on her breakfast muesli, ate hash brownies for lunch and freebased crack cocaine all evening, simply because she had once been a part of the music scene. Consequently, when very drunk, he reverted into a reckless adolescent and badgered her mercilessly to share her 'goodies'.

'Here.' She fished a couple of supermarket paracetamol from her handbag and pressed them furtively into his sweaty palm. 'Don't tell anyone.'

'You are a darling girl.' He gave her an oleaginous kiss before knocking them back with a dash of Dow's 1983 and loosening his bow tie. 'Let's dance – can't have you being a wallflower all night.'

He started manoeuvring her around the packed cellar dance floor with a vigorous technique that was part ballroom, part rugby ball control and entirely at odds with the throbbing, hypnotic beat, so they looked like two left-footed breakfast TV stars in the first round of *Strictly Come Dancing*.

At this point, Trudy was forced to laugh and join in his high spirited fun for fear of crying. She wondered what the hell had happened to her. Ten years ago, she'd been chic, cutting edge cool, ultra fashionable and idolised by many. Now she was a nondescript Cotswold housewife who was in serious danger of losing her ability to pull out all the stops and put on a show when she chose to. The vintage oyster silk dress that had looked so understated in the shop, emphasising her curves and her wonderful golden skin, now made her feel pale and sallow. Her strappy kitten-heeled shoes – hardly skyscrapers compared to the harlot four inch trotters she'd once adored – killed her ankles and pinched her toes.

At least the music cheered her. It was vibrant, sensual, life-affirming stuff and reminded her of how much talent was out there and how much fun it had been working at this level, hoping for a big break. She'd already sent a demo tape of one of tonight's bands to some contacts in the industry and she knew that they were eager to set up a meeting. She tried not to dwell upon the fact that her own lack of original material was of more immediate concern to those contacts. Only this week, her agent had warned her that she was losing touch with 'bankable sounds'.

Grateful at being released by Piers so that he could return to his duty dances in the ballroom upstairs, Trudy turned to watch the beautiful young bodies writhing so effortlessly to the hypnotic beat, and felt like a ghost from another age.

And when, much later, she limped to the loo, she found that her make-up was an inch lower than she'd originally applied it, and her normally sexily dishevelled curls had gone so flat and static in the heat, she looked as though she'd been working as a motorcycle courier all day. Trudy rarely dressed up these days – opportunities were few and far between – but when she did, she was loath to let herself down.

Her familiar face gazed back at her from the mirror; those knowing hazel eyes seeing a self-conscious thirty-something caught on the painful cusp between youth and middle aged spread.

In the great scale of things, she reminded herself firmly, she didn't look half bad. She did, after all, possess her mother's enviable bone structure with a smooth, high forehead that many women her age spent a fortune on Botox to achieve; wide cheeks with beautifully sculpted hollows beneath them that no amount of cookie munching filled out and that other women had to have teeth removed to achieve; a similarly lucky genetic inheritance from her father had shaped her face to an exquisite heart and gifted her a classic profile without a hint of a double chin, with a long enough neck to balance her broad shoulders, and with enough height in her long-backed, athletic body to carry extra pounds without looking fat. A perfectionist would claim her ankles were a little thick, her bust a little heavy and her nose a little wide, but to criticise her looks with undue self-hatred was wasteful. So what if she had once been regularly compared to Debbie Harry and Michelle Pfeiffer, and now – on the rare occasions that she was talked about in the media – was more commonly aligned with Anna Nicole Smith or Jayne Mansfield? The latter two had still been complete sex sirens, although both had conducted torrid love lives and met decidedly sticky ends.

To be judged purely physically, as Trudy had been so often thanks to her career, regularly left one in a state of perpetual dissatisfaction, blaming lacklustre nights such as tonight on bad hair, an unflattering dress or unfair genetics when the truth was much more deep-rooted. If beauty was only skin deep, then happiness went through to the marrow of your bones.

Trudy was wised up enough to know that her size fourteen curves, topped with a fabulous and still buoyant cleavage, tailed with a pert bottom and shapely legs, centred with an hourglass waist and crowned with a pretty face, was an enviable package. She didn't need to lose weight – she needed to gain self-esteem. Had she once been a tongue-tied, breathless size twenty whom nobody had noticed, she'd love her shapely, seductive body and outward serenity now. But she had been an effortless size eight with fan clubs, lookalikes, acres of press coverage, a personal stylist and boundless mischievous verve. That was a hard act to follow. No wonder she so often shunned dressing up and putting on a public face these days.

Outside the loos, she bumped into a very overexcited Dilly – lead singer of local band, Entwined, and a young, blonde bombshell who had already been compared to Trudy in her heyday.

Radiating a glowing, healthy, sexy energy that could light up a neighbourhood grid, Dilly danced from toe to toe as she kissed Trudy on the cheeks.

'Did you hear us play? Wasn't it *amazing*? I thought we'd flunk it, but Mags was fantastic and pulled it all together. Thank you *so* much for all your help. You're the *biz*.'

Trudy shook her head. 'You're the ones with the talent.'

'You encouraged us so much. I hope you don't mind my saying, but we all think of you as "Mummy" now.'

Trudy laughed, although she did secretly mind; she minded a lot. The original members of Entwined – Dilly, her talented boyfriend Magnus, and Trudy's own in-laws Flipper and Nell Cottrell – were all in their twenties; it made her feel prehistoric to be thought of as their mother. She was only thirty five.

'You are *the* coolest chick ever,' Dilly said breathlessly, making her feel marginally better – although when the *Cotswold Life* photographer dashed up to capture them both, she still found herself vainly edging her bottom behind an ornamental colonnade, turning her body three-quarters away, lifting her chin, sucking in her cheeks and pressing her tongue to the top of her palate as a model friend had once taught her before flashing the very expensive veneers that her fortune had bought her a decade earlier. Beside her, Dilly just grinned goofily and still looked twice as gorgeous.

'Could you move a little closer to your mother, darling?' the photographer called, then lifted his chin to study Trudy over his camera. 'Didn't you used to be Trudy Dew?'

'That's right,' she muttered through the clenched, artificial smile that she had once perfected through a thousand magazine shoots.

'She still is!' Dilly defended hotly.

'No I'm not,' *Trudy* kept the smile rigid. 'I'm Trudy Cottrell. I usually drop the Dew.'

'A dewdrop!' Dilly giggled as the photographer fired his rapid shutter, capturing her looking ravishingly happy and Trudy looking haunted.

'"'Tis of the tears which stars weep, sweet with joy,"' she sighed.

'Is that a line from one of your songs?' asked Dilly, as the photographer wandered off.

'Just an old poem my father used to recite.'

Her father had been absurdly fond of *Festes*, the epic verse written by the absurdly young, absurdly handsome nineteenth century poet, Phillip James Bailey. Kit Dew had often quoted that line, along with another: 'Dewdrops, nature's tears, which she sheds in her own breast for the fair who die. The sun insists on gladness, but at night when he is gone, poor nature loves to weep.' Nowadays Trudy understood its bittersweet truth far better and longed to tell her late, great father so. But unlike Bailey – who had never replicated his first great work in a long lifetime of disappointments – Kit Dew's life had been too short, leaving the world with far too little of his talent and legacy.

'I think it's a shame not to call yourself Trudy Dew any more,' Dilly was saying. 'If I ever become famous, I'll keep my name forever, even though Dilly Gently is bloody awful.'

Still thinking about her father, Trudy nodded. 'You're right. Perhaps I'll resurrect it.'

'You do that. After all, you're much more successful than Finn. Why should you take his name?'

Trudy smiled as Dilly dashed off to rejoin Magnus – so in love that five minutes apart felt like a lifetime. After ten years of marriage, Trudy was only too grateful that Finn had given her some free rein tonight. Like many married couples, they worked best socially if they parted company at the door upon arrival, along with their coats, only to be reunited when they left. And yet these days, for all her gratitude that he left her alone to party with the children while he networked with the grown-ups, she couldn't help wondering if he did so because he was embarrassed to be seen with her.

'There you are! We should have left hours ago. The Vesteys' taxi hasn't turned up and I've promised them a lift home. They're dead on their feet.'

He stalked up to her on long, stiff Basil Fawlty legs with his handsome jaw set disapprovingly like a cartoon character. He handed her a cloakroom ticket, waggled his car keys, jerked his head to the door, tapped his watch and stalked outside. It was his shorthand marching orders. When Finn wanted to leave a party, he preferred to do so without ceremony and with military efficiency. To avoid his wife's usual protracted and jolly leave-taking of friends and family, he would have already made farewells on Trudy's behalf, heavy with the apologetic insinuation that she was too dizzy and socially inept to make them herself. Now she had five minutes to gather the coats and the mysterious Vesteys – to whom she couldn't even remember being introduced – and stand obediently in line for collection, or risk the full force of his wrath.

Wandering outside instead, she rejoined the smokers enjoying a final cigarette with their brandies on the magnificent front steps of the hall beneath the grand, classical stone portico. The hoar frost had hardened to a sharp, nose-biting night of bitter chill, dusting every stone in the gravel sweep ahead of them with shimmering white.

Shivering, Trudy looked up at a cluster of stars and vowed that she would make a supreme effort to overcome self-doubt and vanity next time she was out on show – an occasion that was only just around the corner.

The annual Auctioneers' Ball was traditionally held at the end of March. Every year, the Cottrell family sent a representative. This year the task fell upon Trudy's and Finn's shoulders to uphold the Cottrell auctioneering, estate and land agency dynasty.

Pretentious, formal, and ridiculously expensive, the ball was among Finn's favourite social events and Trudy's least. But that was about to change. This year, in a smart country hotel in the Surrey hinterlands, a convenient gavel fall from London, Trudy Dew would pull out all the stops and bring the house down. She had a month to get her act together.

As if on cue, summonsed by her own silent cry for an ego boost, a low voice purred her name and a warm arm reached round her shoulder, at the end of which a perfectly manicured hand sporting a gold signet ring initialled 'H' swirled a vast cognac in a balloon glass.

'You look absolutely heavenly, tonight, Trudy,' purred Giles Horton, local roué, as he lit a cigar, blond hair gleaming in the frosty half-light.

'Thank you.' She took his brandy glass and helped herself to a long, warming sip. 'Where's your date?' Giles had been ostentatiously parading a staggering blonde all night, letting off sparks of newly forged sexual energy.

'Gone home to her husband,' he sighed. 'Finn?'

'Fetching the car.'

'Damn – I can't sneak you away and ravish you, then?'

'No,' she laughed. Giles was always refreshingly lecherous. Suddenly the oyster silk didn't seem quite so drab.

'Another time?' he kissed her bare shoulder where her stole had slipped.

'Of course.'

It was their standard patter. Trudy had never imagined that time would actually come. Now she wasn't so sure.

Blue eyes twinkling, Giles growled, 'I'll hold you to that.'

Catching sight of the kiss so casually and intimately dropped on his wife's bare shoulder as he turned his Range Rover on to the gravel sweep, Finn Cottrell narrowed his eyes and drummed his fingers on the leather steering wheel. The irritation was not at his cousin Giles's customary libertinism. It was that Trudy was not wearing her coat and had therefore clearly not bothered to queue at the cloakroom yet.

Finn bristled. He had worked hard on the Vesteys to persuade them that he should play chivalrous chauffeur instead of ordering another cab – they lived quite some distance from him and Trudy and had a babysitter to get back to, now well into 'extra hours'. Finn had been hopeful that Gavin Vestey, a hugely successful hedge fund manager he had been buttering up most of the night, would co-invest in some projects he was working on, but Trudy had just blown that prospect. Now the Vesteys were no doubt furious, exhausted and unlikely to show any further interest. It stood to reason that if Finn couldn't control his own wife, how could he hope to control Gavin's money?

With a sudden blast of cold air from the open passenger's door, Trudy flopped into the car beside him, smelling of cigar smoke, gratefully kicking off her strappy shoes and reaching for the heater controls on the dashboard.

'The *coats*?' he hissed apoplectically. 'The *Vesteys*?'

'Oh yes! Oops!' she replied brightly, reaching for the door handle, her feet stabbing around in the footwell to relocate her shoes.

'Don't bother – I'll go!' he snapped, snatching back the cloakroom ticket which was still crumpled in her hand. 'If you embarrass me like this again, you'll be sorry,' he hissed, leaving Trudy wondering quite what she had done to embarrass him. They had barely been in the same room since dinner, and she hadn't dribbled, spat or crashed face-down into her pannacotta during that.

'I'll hold you to that,' she sighed, echoing Giles's words as she settled back into the heated seat and closed her eyes, thinking about the Auctioneers' Ball and her determination to feel better about herself. 'I'll hold you to that.'

I

These days, Trudy looked forward to trading a night in her scruffy Oddlode home for the anonymity of a hotel.

There had been a time when she had been practically living out of them, and had become increasingly disillusioned, despite the luxury. After a while, one five-star hotel with its artificially lit corridors, its mirrored lifts, its marble-heavy, leather-sofa-ed foyer, became very like another – she would wake in the night not knowing which country she was in, let alone which city or hotel. She had craved home, safety, continuity. But now that hotels had become a novelty once more – she and Finn hadn't been on holiday for almost two years – the prospect of even the humblest Travelodge or B&B was exciting.

A night at Crawbourne Hall, a very luxurious and chichi new country boutique hotel that was a great rival of Eastlode Park and beloved of sports stars, socialites and WAGS, was a great incentive to look and feel fabulous upon arrival.

Determined to make the grade, Trudy booked herself in for a rare hair appointment. Having made do with home products to keep the odd grey hair at bay and the blond lights in her curls, her hair was now more raffia than silk and in desperate need of a cut. On a good day, she might fantasise herself Farah Fawcett meets Julie Christie, but on a bad she looked like the bastard child of a Fraggle and Don King.

Long gone were her days of being on first-name terms with the faces behind the trendiest shampoo brands, of getting fast tracked to the VIP chair in the most exclusive salon in London where that household name would pander to her split ends on a weekly basis. But this time she did splash out, forfeiting the cosy, perm-smelling delights of the blue rinse brigade's favourite, Cut Above, in local town Market Addington, for the minimalist intimidation tactics of ultra-trendy Urban Roots in Oxford.

The young gay stylist with unlikely pink sideburns shaped like scimitars obviously found Trudy far too ordinary on first impressions to place in the window seat, and whisked her to a private area behind a fibre optic screen to start slapping goo on long foil strips that he sliced through her hair like an explorer through a jungle.

'This hasn't seen any loving care in a while, has it?' he carped.

'None of me has,' Trudy admitted, too excited at the well-thumbed salon copy of *Grazia* to take his criticism personally.

Within half an hour, having bonded over bitchy comments about reality TV stars and Amy Winehouse's tattooes, Trudy and Pink Sideburns were giggling away like best friends, and he was raiding the staff biscuit tin to accompany her cappuccino. Trudy's innate curiosity had already elicited his life story and he was well on his way to confessing his hopes and dreams; she, meanwhile, had not even revealed where she was planning to go on her holidays this year. Once her colour was rinsed out, he moved her proudly into a window seat and set about cutting in an elaborate, scissor-swivelling, hip-jutting dance that was one part Cossack, another part eighties robotic.

The end result was close to miraculous. Urban Roots didn't disappoint. Her curls – still shoulder length but wondrously glossy, round and rumpled again – gleamed in rivulets of gold, copper, ash and chocolate like a stream of caramel and treacle tumbling and bubbling over shiny honeycomb pebbles at sunset. It took years off her.

'You come back soon, do you hear?' Pink Sideburns insisted as he handed her a card with his name on it at the tills and crossed his arms over his chest to watch her leave with his head cocked, now as indulgent, proud and protective of his charge as a mother hen. '*Lovely* woman,' he murmured to one of the juniors in an undertone. '*Fab*ulous hair – very thick and forgiving.'

'Like your boyfriends,' the girl giggled.

He gave her a withering look before turning to watch Trudy's retreating back. 'I bet she's an actress. I should have asked.'

'Stace says she used to be a pop star.' The girl manoeuvred her gum from one cheek to the other.

'Really? Then quick – sweep the hair from around her chair into a plastic bag. Could be worth a tenner on eBay. What d'you say her name was again?'

Hugely cheered, Trudy had emerged from the salon tossing her head like a shampoo model and danced her way towards Little Clarendon Street to search through the vintage clothes shops.

She had always preferred second-hand clothing, even in childhood when she had raided her mother's wardrobe or spent her pocket money at jumble sales. She relished the feel and comfort of something pre-loved, the sheer workmanship of well-made clothes in quality fabrics dating back to seamstresses and regular made-to-measure wear, before disposable mass-produced high-street fashion became the norm.

Finn, who was a great devotee of designer labels, had been thoroughly disapproving of this passion until the recent trend for Hollywood stars to wear 'vintage' made the practice acceptable, if not wholly comprehensible.

In a tiny antique dress shop off a side alley, more of a front room than a retail unit, with rails so crammed with clothes that taking any out required a crowbar, she tracked down 'The Dress'.

Infinitely better than the oyster pink silk – what she had imagined she was doing buying that she had no idea, although she vaguely recalled being half cut in Portobello Market after a lunch with her agent in Beach Blanket Babylon – this was her colour spectrum, her shape and a perfect fit. It could have been planted there by a helpful fashion fairy. She even had the ideal shoes, bag and shawl to go with it at home. It was fate.

The builders who were renovating Church Cottage wolf-whistled when Trudy got back home, downing tools to admire her new look as they sweet-talked their way towards their first freshly brewed mugs of tea of the day. They missed her if she went out, especially when like today they were left with the sour-faced, disciplinarian Finn who acted like project manager, foreman and local squire all rolled into one. Trudy, who flirted, gossiped, made endless mugs of tea and asked after their families by name, was their treasure. They might be increasingly unhappy with the renovation project, which was turning out to be a loss-making nightmare driven by Finn's unrealistic demands, but they loved Trudy.

'You look like Nell McAndrew,' sighed Gaz, who thought Page Three models the pinnacle of beauty.

She tracked Finn down in his study at the far end of the house, typing self-importantly into his laptop. Trudy was no technological whiz-kid, but even she could see that he had three internet gambling sessions minimised on his bottom tool bar with give-away names like Poker, Casino and BetOnline.

'Had fun?' he asked with loaded disdain, looking up.

'Yes, thanks. I had my hair cut.'

'So I see. Very nice.'

'Nice' was one of those words that, if said in the right tone, meant something entirely different. Today was one such occasion, but Finn wasn't feeling generous enough to elaborate, leaving the word hanging pompously in the air with an echo that could convey anything from 'ridiculously expensive' to 'very pretty' to 'what a mess'.

Trudy was accustomed to his verbal meanness and still felt elated from her trip. Finn rarely gave compliments these days and made no further comment about her transformation now beyond suggesting that taking a day off work when she was so behind on all her projects was a little indulgent.

Nonetheless, in the coming days, as his Gieves and Hawkes dinner suit went off to the cleaners and '*The* Dress' stayed hidden in one of her many wardrobes, Trudy felt better about herself than she had in weeks. Feeling that she had to live up to her hair she started to dig into those crammed wardrobes for smarter clothes and slap on some mascara and lip-gloss. She was complimented by neighbours at the village store, on the village green walking the dogs, and even by the postman.

Trudy's increasing cheeriness by-passed Finn who was approaching the forthcoming night away like a military operation and found his back-up squad lacking. In the fortnight leading up to the ball, he alternated between increasingly sullen sulks and massive hissy fits as he tried and failed to locate his favourite diamond-studded cufflinks, his patent leather shoes, his white silk scarf and his newest designer dress shirt; unlike the recent Hunt Ball, the Auctioneers was black tie rather than white, and Finn was a stickler for etiquette. Blaming Trudy for their disappearance, he took himself off to buy new ones, even though he had plenty of other cufflinks and white shirts. Being something of a Beau Brummell, Finn loved retail therapy, and his mood briefly lifted as his new designer purchases were laid out on the bed. Trudy wasn't the only one who deserved new togs for this occasion, he decided. They would both cut a dash. The Cottrells might struggle through their down time together, but they could still put on a good public show, and Finn was determined to be bandmaster as always.

For all Trudy's pride in being organised for the occasion, Finn was now leagues ahead of her – his Vuitton suit-carrier already packed and hanging on the back of the bedroom door four days before the event. Which was when he discovered that Trudy hadn't yet booked them a room at the hotel. Rounding on her as if she were a negligent employee, he shouted so loudly that the dogs hid behind the sofas and Mildred the cat took refuge on the fuse cupboard.

'Instead of calling me every name under the sun, why not just call the hotel?' she suggested with a shrug. The only thing guaranteed to accelerate Finn's legendary petrol fire anger was not to take it seriously.

In the end Trudy called Crawbourne Hall with Finn's hot, fiery breath on her neck, and discovered that they had to choose between a twin-bedded broom cupboard in the attics or an ambassadorial suite at ten times the cost; Trudy booked the broom cupboard, Finn phoned straight back and changed it to the suite. He then looked it up on the internet and made Trudy stand at his shoulder and admire the 360-degree tour of the three rooms and balcony. Like the purchase of the new dress shirt, the luxury splurge cheered him up briefly. Trudy hastily arranged for the village's resident house-sitter, Hayley Gates, to come and stay the night to look after dogs, cat, horses, bantams, temperamental boiler and even grumpier builders.

'If they disappear for more than an hour, will you promise to call me personally?' she asked.

'Are we talking your animals or builders here?'

'Well – both, really.'

The following day, Finn sacked the builders, so that was one less thing to worry about.

'You've done *what*?' Trudy howled when she returned from slogging round Tescos on a freezing, rainy day to find the drive devoid of the usual vans, rusting estates and pick-ups, and the cottage silent and abandoned.

Finn was full of bristling indignation. 'Neil invoiced me for an unscheduled interim payment, although they're on a fixed fee. He wants another eighty grand! He claims it's client changes. I told him I'd see him in court.'

'Couldn't you negotiate?' pleaded Trudy, who knew that Finn had indeed made a lot of changes to the specification in recent weeks.

'I only negotiate with businessmen,' he said pompously. 'That man is a pleb.'

Neil had been one of the most skilful, reliable and tightly budgeted builders they had ever hired. He was also one of the few willing to tender for the job in the first place, and was now the last in a long line of contractors that Finn had fired over the years. Getting a replacement would be incredibly tricky as his reputation for changes, arguments and bad payment spread yet further.

Whether he privately realised the rashness of his actions, Trudy couldn't tell, but Finn instantly became foul-tempered and uncommunicative once again, the forthcoming ball now seeming to serve only to irritate him more.

'We can hardly bloody afford it after this. The company will pay our expenses, of course, but the time away is equally precious. *You* have to work your socks off to make up for lost time right now, after all.'

He sounded alarmingly like a pimp.

Hiding in her study, Trudy phoned Neil to beg him to consider coming back on the job. 'I can talk Finn round, I promise. And then we'll look at this interim payment together and I'll see what I can do.'

'Sorry, Trudy – you are a diamond, but there is no way I'm coming back.'

Guessing that Trudy had pleaded with Neil behind his back, Finn went into a livid sulk.

That same evening, man flu struck Church Cottage.

It was barely more than a passing head cold – Trudy, similarly afflicted, had already taken double doses of vitamin C and echinacea, knocked back some supermarket cold capsules and quickly chased it away with red wine and will power.

Finn took to his bed, drew the duvet over his head, ordered that the curtains be closed and announced that he was dying.

For the ensuing forty-eight hours, bowls of home-made chicken soup, hot Lemsips and ice-cool bottles of his favourite designer Italian mineral water were whisked regularly to and from the room without any perceptible change. The little television in the corner was constantly on ('I'm too ill to really watch it, but it's company'), the heating turned up to max, tissues topped up twice daily then crumpled randomly around after use (they had to have aloe vera in them and had to be placed in exactly the right spot on the bedside table beside the handbell), copies of newspapers and magazines procured ('I'm too ill to read them, but the pictures help take my mind off my splitting headache'); feet were massaged, menthol candles lit and cool, fresh Egyptian linen pillowslips fitted. But nothing helped. He just felt worse.

Trudy, run ragged and only slightly feverish, had to take his plight seriously lest she incur his legendary wrath by daring to suggest he should attempt to 'fight it off'. Of course, poor Finn was too weakened by the near-fatal encounter with killer virus cells to fight. Had it been a broken bone, a machete wound, a severe muscular sports injury or a bullet hole, then naturally he would have fought – but this silent, deadly killer was dragging the life from him in sweaty paroxysms of agony.

He demanded that a hot bath be run for him, foaming with *Cartier pour Homme* bubbles and sprinkled with Olbas oil; he insisted that she make him hot toddies to his mother's exacting recipe with best Irish whiskey, cloves and butter (she never got it right); he groaned and snuffled and tossed and turned and rang his bell constantly, complaining of every symptom known to man, from cold sweats to hot shakes, from delirium to migraine to cramps, stiff joints and even lockjaw. If sympathy was not forthcoming in exactly the right weight and measure along with those more practical ministrations to his ailments, he grew louder, sicker and more martyred.

Trudy just stopped herself offering to put him out of his misery with a saucepan over the head. The thought of the jaunt to Surrey cheered her along.

Then the day before the ball, deciding that he had really not punished her enough for failing to come up to his mother's standards in Florence Nightingale duties, Finn announced he was far too ill to go.

'Call my father and see who can deputise for us,' he instructed brusquely with a long-suffering cough. 'And please close that window. It's freezing in here. Do you want to bloody kill me?'

As she trailed back downstairs for the twentieth time that morning, a thought dawned on Trudy like a fresh spring day. *She* could still go – *without* Finn. Her inadequate nursing skills were clearly starting to irritate him, so the break would do them both good. His adoring mother would happily take over for twenty four hours.

Trudy shamed herself with the glib ease with which she danced down the bottom steps and called her father-in-law.

'Finn is far too under the weather for the Auctioneers' Ball, so I thought I could take Johnny, instead?'

Johnny would love it, and the thought of seeing her brother again, away from the Cottrells and Oddlode, lifted her spirits like a compliment from a stranger. It had been far too long. While waiting to get through to her father-in-law on the land line, she'd already sent a text to check out Johnny's availability, and a cautious reply had come back that he'd be more than happy to change his plans for her just so long as Finn was definitely not going to be there. The atmosphere between the two had become quite hostile in recent years.

But Finn's father, a stickler for protocol and a total homophobe, put a spanner in the works. 'Johnny's not a Cottrell. Need a family representative at these things.'

'Yes, but *I'm* a Cottrell, Piggy.'

'Hmph. Leave it with me.'

She already knew that most of the family were unavailable. Finn's older brother and his wife were wrapped up in a big charity event of their own that night; his middle sister was on holiday with husband and children; Piggy himself was suffering badly from his recurrent gout and would never last the evening; the twins would flatly refuse to go. That left Trudy – and brother Johnny, who was dapper and good-looking and knew more about antiques than most of the Cottrells put together.

But, like a mad medieval matchmaker with no heed for the consequences just so long as the family line remained intact, Piggy procured an official Cottrell date within hours.

'He'll pick you up tomorrow after lunch,' he barked with pugnacious vigour when he called her back. '*Do* be ready. I know what you girls are like.'

'Who is it?' she enquired worriedly, wondering whether he'd need a hotel room too. But Piggy – always terse to the point of rudeness on the phone – had already rung off.

Breaking the news that she was still going to Finn took great tact and courage, neither of which Trudy had ever possessed in much measure. Hearing a great wild boar roar coming from upstairs minutes later, she guessed he had found out through one of the many gadgets that he had lined up on his sick bed.

'Who's taking you?' he spluttered consumptively when she crept up to verify the news that had just been broken by his mother, eagerly planning her meals on wheels menu.

'I don't know, your father didn't say.'

'Well bloody well phone him up and ask.' He dissolved into death-rattle cough, turning as red as a beetroot and almost falling off the bed in very Dickensian fashion.

But according to the Cottrells' reception staff, Piggy had now disappeared in his chauffeured Bentley with his phone switched off. Trudy suspected he was visiting a mistress.

Now a normal colour once more but wheezing alarmingly, Finn moved downstairs to access the satellite television so that he could watch the last of the day's races from Cheltenham Festival and keep an eye on his wife at the same time – an exercise which took twenty minutes of descending a dizzy step at a time, propped heavily against Trudy, with the duvet over his shaking shoulders.

'Who has the old bugger bribed into taking you?' he demanded hourly, in between inhaling Friar's Balsam over the coffee table. He made Trudy sound unflatteringly like a simpleton maiden aunt whose companions had to be paid to take her bath chair around the park.

'I haven't a clue,' she said cheerfully, hoping it wasn't one of the smarmy, chinless estate agent staff, but deciding that anything had to be better than staying in the plague-ridden, doomed House of Influenza a moment longer. 'You never know,' she added as she danced upstairs to pack, 'whoever it is might know the name of a good builder.' It was a cheap jibe, but she didn't care. Married life was getting more and more expensive these days; insults were the only things they traded freely.

The next day, Finn watched furiously through the window as his wife jumped into the very flashy silver Aston Martin belonging to his cousin Giles and, waving excitedly, they reversed in a great swoosh of gravel before accelerating from the drive, leaving an arc of deep tyre ruts.

Relieved to be able to drop the pretend cold symptoms at last, Finn was initially more annoyed by the disturbance to his beautifully raked gravel than by the fact that the most notorious womaniser in the Lodes Valley was taking Trudy for an overnight spin. He was, at least briefly, grateful that she was gone – even accompanied by Giles. All that fake coughing had given him a sore throat, and he was fed up of her sanctimonious attitude about the builders. He had every right to sack them. They were disrespectful. She should have backed him up from the start. It was a matter of loyalty.

He phoned Hayley Gates and put her off. He hated interruptions. His mother, primed to deliver soup and medical succour at regular intervals, would at least have the courtesy to call beforehand.

Then, casting off his duvet, he headed upstairs to shower and dress, singing along to his favourite radio station, Kerrang. Finn's taste in most things was deeply reactionary and lifted directly from his parents – he read the *Telegraph*, watched *Newsnight*, ate fish on a Friday – but with music, he remained a top volume rock, air-guitar thrashing teenager at heart.

Dressed and refreshed, he sent the first of many texts to Trudy.

Hot and cold shakes still. Having difficulty breathing. Keep blacking out. Please advise.

The reply was swift.

Take paracetamol. Drink fluids. Sleep. If worsens, call your mother.

'Hmph.' He looked at his phone grumpily as he grabbed a lager from the fridge and headed towards his laptop to look up the rest of the afternoon's live odds at Cheltenham.

He'd have to increase the pressure.

It was only now that the niggling doubts started to eclipse his home-from-school feeling of rebellion. The thought of Giles and Trudy together unsettled him. True, Trudy had always treated Giles's obvious admiration as a huge joke – as did all the family – but she had never been put under this sort of pressure before. Giles was a smooth operator, as his reputation bore witness.

Suddenly Finn remembered the kiss his cousin had dropped on Trudy's bare shoulder at the Hunt Ball; a gesture more intimate than any he had shared with his wife in many months. Giles was a breed apart from his cousin. He treated all women as objects of pleasure, whereas Finn differentiated between those he respected, such as wives, mothers and sisters, and those he saw as disposable, like junior staff, bar girls and escorts. It might have once taken a young Finn six weeks of courteously formal dates to kiss Trudy properly (or, in truth, for her to get frustrated and kiss him), but Giles would have no hesitation in asking for a spot of dropped-napkin fellatio beneath the dinner table on a first date.

For the first time in three days of claiming extreme changes in body temperature, Finn felt a genuine cold sweat spring to his brow.

He trusted Trudy to behave herself, albeit not always soberly, in almost all circumstances, but he didn't trust Giles one bit. Tonight's ballsed-up Auctioneers' Ball scenario – which he refused to admit was of his making – was potentially critical. Having exaggerated his illness somewhat, he was now not only left home alone, but powerless to prevent Giles from making a play. He felt hugely hard done by.

To cheer himself up, he elbowed Trudy's fat, sleeping cat sharply off the back of the sofa and watched it scrabble for dear life, as wide-eyed as a bush baby, before losing its grip and landing on its backside, shooting across the room in a puffed-up state of panic, rucking up the rug edges and finally losing its back end on the quarry tiles around the corner to the stairs like a badly driven rally car. Satisfied by the result, Finn leaned forward over his laptop to lay a huge online bet on the Gold Cup. If it came in he'd win enough money to pay off Neil the builder whose solicitors had already issued a formal written warning that the disputed invoice would be pursued through the courts if not honoured.

'Aggressive little pleb,' he hissed, adding another thousand to the bet before picking up his phone once again to text Trudy.

Trudy received roughly one text per half hour as she and Giles belted along the back roads between West Oxfordshire and leafiest Surrey.

Fair and sporty as a Ralph Lauren ad, Giles was very much a type, and it wasn't Trudy's. In some ways he was laughably anachronistic; having once been told he was a dead ringer for Robert Redford in *Butch Cassidy and the Sundance Kid*, he had kept the look ever since. Floppy blond hair and moustache complemented the tanned skin, happy crow's feet and devilish blue eyes. He dressed like a glitzy eighties soap opera hunk: all Italian chinos, hand-made loafers, open-necked shirts and cashmere sweaters slung round the neck. He was a dinosaur, albeit an extremely attractive one with a refreshingly self-aware sense of humour to soften the endless chat up clichés. Emotionally, he was a lot more complicated and far more in touch with his female side than his sports-car-driving, cigar-smoking, wife-seducing, heartbreaking façade would ever care to admit. He knew how to talk to women, to coax truths and secrets, and to massage fragile egos along with delicate, shy bodies that responded deliriously to his touch. He was a pro at infidelity.

'Are you still seeing the ravishing blonde from the Hunt Ball?' Trudy asked with customary inquisitive charm.

'Regrettably not,' he purred over the big cat roar of his car. 'Husband is a jealous type – and was an Oxford boxing Blue, I gather. As darling C was only trying to make him jealous, I thought it best to back off soon after the threatening phone calls started.'

'Very wise.' She admired the blossom-heavy blackthorn hedges that they were racing past, bracing herself for a Leslie Phillips chat-up line, full of double entendres, insinuating that tonight was her lucky night.

But he was too busy playing with his toys to lay siege to Trudy just yet. He knew that she required far more delicate handling than his car, which he treated with the same adoring, distracted disrespect he had all his wives.

Giles liked to throw the vintage Aston around the lanes, engine alternately purring and roaring, jazz belting out of the high spec stereo system at full volume. His many married lovers, who required obvious discretion, had demanded a more inconspicuous vehicle over the years and so he drove a dull luxury Jaguar estate most days, rarely ever using his beloved 'Italian Job' DB4 with its silver birch livery and seductive black leather. Given that his legal practice was based just three miles from his home – with fitting irony, Giles was a divorce lawyer – and the courts he frequented mostly lay within a fifteen-mile radius, the Aston was enjoying its longest outing in almost a year.

So was Trudy, although she already felt uncomfortable trying out enjoyment for size.

'What qualifies you to go to an Auctioneers' Ball any more than my brother?' she grumbled, still hurt on Johnny's behalf that he had been cast aside as her chaperone.

'I am on the Cottrells' board,' he pointed out. 'And I have control of Mother's voting shares as well – so in fact, I have more clout in the company than anyone except Piggy.' Just for a moment, the familiar Cottrell arrogance resonated through his Home Counties drawl.

'Wow. May they shake at your feet tonight, Squire Horton,' she said in a wholesome wench accent, casting him a mock-coy look.

There was a pause and, watching his manicured fingers drumming on the leather steering wheel, Trudy wondered if she'd overdone the teasing. She didn't really know him that well, although they had alternately flirted and scrapped like Beatrice and Benedick for years.

But jovial, wolfish, seductive Giles was firmly on course.

'I'm the one who'll be doing all the shaking tonight,' he purred as he turned to look across at her. 'I can't believe I have you all to myself at last, gorgeous Trudy.' The Cambridge blue eyes were full of sweet sin.

Despite the fact that both her heart and libidinous pulses had started deliciously thrumming, Trudy lifted her chin and gave him a stern look.

'You'd better behave,' she said, talking to herself as much as to Giles.

Crawbourne Hall was a vast, sand-blasted white Georgian pile sitting in thirty acres of manicured grounds, with matching modern white wings containing fitness suites, pools, spas and conference facilities. A nine hole golf course cut an artificial swathe into the old parkland along with a state-of-the-art sports training centre, an ultra-posh riding stable and a five-star crèche. Its air of neutered, neutralised, naffed-up historic architecture was curiously enticing.

As soon as they arrived – leaving the Aston with an unimpressed-looking valet who parked footballer's wives' Ferraris, Astons and Porsches as a matter of course – Trudy begged an extra room from the supermodel-style staff at the vast marble reception desk. They surely still had a broom cupboard in the attic free for Giles?

They didn't. The hotel was now fully booked.

Trudy's heart began hammering in true French farce manner until one of the models looked up from clicking away at her concealed computer and beamed victoriously at her. Much, much better, 'madam'; they had the second bedroom adjoining her pre-booked suite, unexpectedly vacant after a cancellation.

'Auctioneer's flu – a lot of it about, I hear.' Giles winked, taking his key card and joining a reluctant Trudy as they followed a porter who ostentatiously trolleyed their meagre luggage along to the lifts in a high-sided, gilded rack.

Trudy's suite was ridiculously OTT with vast six-man white leather sofas parked on cowskin rugs in the sitting room, a plasma television the size of a double bed on one wall, a bed the size of an entire master bedroom, and a zinc-tiled bathroom with sunken Jacuzzi and separate wet room so huge and high tech that Trudy had to call room service to ask how to turn the shower on.

Emerging wrapped in the fluffiest white towelling gown and matching towelling turban known to man, she found Finn had texted saying he was dry-vomiting and covered with a red rash that didn't disappear when pressed with a glass. Trudy texted back suggesting he fill the glass with water and use it to take more cold capsules.

Her phone rang.

'Want to throw open the gateway to untold pleasures?' Giles, growled seductively just a few feet away. 'I've opened my side.'

'Nope,' she said firmly, looking across at the discreet door which led from her sitting room to his bedroom and which both parties had to unlock from their respective sides.

'Fair enough. In that case, I'll knock on your door at about seven to share a sundowner and admire you in private before I'm forced to show you off.'

'Make it seven fifteen,' said Trudy, unwilling to miss *The Archers*.

Giles, a fitness fanatic, made a beeline for the gym. Trudy, a exercise-phobic, looked through her vast Condé Nast magazine selection, her complimentary toiletries, minibar and wide 'treat' drawers at great and indulgent length. Amongst hosts of goodies ranging from jelly beans and goji berries to hypnotherapy CDs and funky designer flight socks, there was even a selection of sealed pampering kits containing oils, herb teas, face masks, aromatic candles and assorted delights, each individually branded with names like 'Bag Bag', 'Sag Bag', 'Lag Bag' and 'Nag Bag'. One was for hangovers, one for jet lag, another was for de-stressing and, to Trudy's amusement, one named 'Shag Bag' was for intimacy, containing condoms, scented lubricant, feather ticklers, blindfolds and – baffingly – mints. As ever, the expensive and alluring packaging was more appealing than the contents. It was one of the lessons that Trudy had learned throughout her career and life: packaging was nine-tenths of the attraction of impulse. Wait for the urge to pass, and you were far better placed to know if you wanted what was inside. Despite registering this valuable philosophy, Trudy remained hugely greedy and impulsive in most things.

Turning on MTV and marvelling at the energy bursting from the screen, she ate her way through all the jelly beans in the jar from her treat drawer. It was bliss to be away from home, on her own and ridiculously pampered. For a brief spell of sugar-coated self-indulgence, she could almost forget Finn's texts, the tempting door that led through to Giles's room and the horrific price tag that this trip was racking up.

She took the bottle of vodka that she had craftily packed in her case and slugged some into a glass of Coke from the fridge as she started the long and leisurely task of readying herself for that evening. She rarely spent more than five minutes on her appearance so this was an unheard of extravagance.

'The Dress' worked its magic like a spell cast over her long-neglected, much-maligned body. She'd forgotten how stunning it was, how well it suited her.

A full length thirties gown in heavy Titian satin, the colour of a fox, it matched the copper lights in her eyes. It was pure Jean Harlow glamour, cut perfectly on the bias to emphasise her curves whilst ironing out any bumps. Daringly backless for its day – thank heaven for modern bra technology and expensive fake tan treatments – its halter neck was a row of thick old gold ropes that dropped from her shoulders to cross over beneath her breasts, creating a plunging neckline, and then curl round her waist and meet at the base of her back in flattering silhouette.

Matched with a rope of pearls that she wound several times around her long neck like a choker before letting it drop down her back to a snaking pendulum knot at the base of her spine, wide pearl cuff bracelets, absurdly high gold heels hidden beneath the sweeping fishtail of skirt, a tiny vintage sequin clutch bag and a hand-painted cream organza shawl that her brother had given her years ago and which kissed her shoulders as lightly as a breath, it was a knockout look.

She'd kept her make-up simple but dramatic: smoky eyes, golden skin, lusciously glossy lips. She parted her hair at the side and coaxed the curls into sculpted waves that framed her face perfectly.

Twirling in front of the mirror, Trudy temporarily gave in to vanity. It had been a long time since she'd gazed at herself with pride, rather than quickly checking for spinach on the teeth, loo roll on the shoe or buttons on the loose.

She almost wished Finn were here to admire her. Almost, but not quite. Giles would have to do. Tonight wasn't about male admiration, after all. It was about self-esteem. She had to crack through her own criticism, not anybody else's. And, fuelled by jelly beans, vodka, MTV and freedom, her heart was so aflame it could melt any inhibition she possessed.

2

In Oddlode, having failed to recoup his day's Cheltenham gambling losses on the online poker games and casino tables where, under the user name 'Shark Finn', he dwelt in the strange world of cyberspace gamblers on a regular basis, Finn flicked dispiritedly through a few television channels and found an old repeat of *Top Gear* to distract him. But his feet still tapped the carpet, his fingers drummed on the sofa arm and his tongue made repeated tappety-suck noises against the roof of his mouth.

He checked his watch. Trudy would be dressing now. She was always ready in no time these days, which he thought rather a shame. Women should spend hours prettifying without compromising on punctuality, like his mother did. His mother did everything with a perfect mix of lady-like delicacy and super-efficient practicality.

He reached for the white oven dish at his side and finished off the last few forkfuls of the delicious fish pie that she had lovingly created just for him that evening, dropping it off fresh from her Aga sealed in a foil-lined bag so that he didn't even need to reheat it. The premier cru Chablis that Trudy's agent had sent them for Christmas (as an incentive to pull her finger out and do some work, no doubt) went with it beautifully and – mindful that he would have to hide the evidence – he had already finished the bottle.

He sent another text complaining of more dizzy spells, blurred vision and headaches. When she didn't reply within the requisite wifely five minutes, he started to feel twitchy, firing off another text about blackouts, vomiting and possible concussion/broken bones.

Five minutes. Ten. Twenty. A fresh episode of *Top Gear* kicked off. No reply.

Heartless cow. Even his mother had texted him to ask after the fish pie, and she took longer to write an SMS message than a mason carving it on a stone tablet.

Having now worked himself up into a state of high dudgeon about Trudy's disloyal desertion that evening, with Giles of all people, Finn couldn't settle at all. More and more vile thoughts were clouding his head. Giles was notorious. He was completely led by the groin. If Trudy got drunk, God knows what might happen.

Not normally much of a drinker himself, Finn hadn't realised quite how much he'd shipped during his long, self-indulgent afternoon and evening. Mixed with all the cold capsules, Lemsips and paracetamol-laced hot toddies that Trudy and then his mother had forced down him, the net result was a groggy, paranoid state of jumpy-legged inertia that was almost unbearable. He was sicker than he had been all week.

'That bastard's going to bloody well try everything to get into her knickers tonight,' he hissed, seeing black dots dance in front of his eyes.

On screen, Jeremy Clarkson was raving about an Aston Martin.

'Shut up, you bigoted buffoon!' howled Finn, throwing a cushion at the television. It bounced back neatly into the remains of his fish pie, proffering an embroidered slogan that read: My husband and I were happy for twenty five years. Then we met.

Giles stepped back into the corridor when Trudy opened the door to him, turned pale beneath his winter tan and whistled under his breath.

'I hope Finn's kitted you out with a chastity belt under all that,' he purred, eyes trailing up and down in sheer delight before he stepped forwards again to kiss her chastely on the cheek.

'Better still, he's kitted me out with a guilty conscience.' She waggled the mobile phone she was holding. 'He's just texted to say that his mother hasn't brought him any supper and he passed out in the kitchen when he tried to get something out of the freezer. He's only just come round.'

'Bollocks.' Giles headed for the minibar and extracted the half bottle of champagne. 'He's just come round to the realisation that you're here with sexy old me, and he's there on his own.' The cork popped and he tipped the foaming contents into two glasses.

Already flying along quite merrily on the back of several vodka Cokes, Trudy took her glass and reminded herself to behave that night.

'Let's prove that he can trust us, huh?' She raised it high.

'How insufferably dull.' Giles smiled roguishly, but he raised his glass too, knowing that Trudy was a prey worth hunting with supreme, watchful skill; she was a deer he had stalked for years, after all. If he frightened her off, he might never get another opportunity.

'I warn you not to try to get me drunk.' She watched him over the rim of her champagne flute. 'For one, I am perfectly capable of getting drunk by myself. For another, I can outdrink any man I meet.'

'I don't doubt that.' He secretly planned to get her very drunk indeed. He knew from family gatherings of yore that Trudy was a happy, carefree drunk who loosened up deliciously when correctly blootered.

'So you promise to behave for Finn's sake?' She gave him a mock-stern look that he found vampishly erotic.

'Promise.' He refilled her glass to the rim and raised his eyebrow with Clark Gable aplomb.

But when she popped into the bathroom for a final pee and preen before they went down, he picked up her little mobile phone from beside her handbag and – hurriedly dropping his dress trousers – took a shot of himself mooning, bollocks to the fore, to send Finn.

When Finn received the picture text of a naked male arse and nuts medley from his wife's phone, he did something that he hadn't done in over twenty-five years. He wept.

Usually a fortress of rigid self-control and masked emotions, he cried like a baby for a few minutes, striking Jeremy Clarkson from the screen in front of him in shame, as though the testosterone-filled zoo at the *Top Gear* studio had a live feed from the Church Cottage snug.

He blamed his illness. The flu must be worsening to the delirium tremens he had falsely claimed earlier. He was, in fact, really, really ill.

Groping for the phone, he rang Trudy urgently, determined to order her home.

But twenty minutes earlier, Giles had inserted her phone skilfully between two of the big white leather seat cushions on the vast sofa in Trudy's suite and now – thinking that it was already in her little gold bag – Trudy was taking the lift with him down to the ballroom oblivious to her husband's plight.

★

The Auctioneers' Ball was, as always, a spectacularly artificial, snobbish and cliquey occasion that had to be taken with a vast pinch of salt and large quantities of alcohol to ensure survival. Tequila slammers were the perfect accompaniment.

Giles and Trudy escaped to the bar between courses for these, lamenting the fact that their table was crammed with bores.

'If I have to pretend to be interested in twentieth-century Treen for a minute longer, I will spear him with my fork,' Trudy sighed of her neighbouring diner, a man obsessed with all things small and wooden, apart from his wife, who had been boring Giles to death about her love of amateur dramatics in Bishop's Stortford.

After dessert, the awards started, a long-winded roll call of droning auctioneers who filed up to the stage one by one to collect a golden gavel, usually accompanied by a deadly speech prepared on note cards that they kept alongside their reading glasses in the inside pockets of their dinner jackets.

Giles and Trudy sloped away to the bar again, this time for vast cognacs. Leading her out on to a terrace that was spired with patio heaters for the nicotine addicts, Giles lit a cigar, blue eyes crossing in front of him as he focused upon the match flame dipping and flaring amid plumes of smoke.

They were already very drunk, and the dancing had yet to start.

'At least there's not a bloody Auctioneers' Ball auction,' Giles pointed out, resting his elbows on the balustrade in very Noël Coward fashion. 'Can't stand all these black tie dos where one's forced to bid for a week at some other sod's ski lodge.'

'How ungenerous of you,' she teased, lighting a cigarette.

'You need a long holder for that – match the Dietrich dress.' He was unable to stop his admiring eyes going for a long, lingering walk around her body. 'You really do look sensational.'

She smiled, grateful not to be receiving the customary lecture on smoking that Finn always dealt out. She had cut right down in the past year – especially socially – but she still stubbornly clung on to her vice.

Looking up, she saw that the stars were once again out, just as they had been at the Hunt Ball. In their midst, a little glimmer raced across the sky.

'Make a wish.' Giles was looking up too.

Although Trudy was fairly certain that it was a jumbo jet heading towards nearby Heathrow and not a shooting star, she still closed her eyes and thought fleetingly of her many unfulfilled wishes: children, a successful career again, a better marriage, true love.

But she was high and tight and holidaying too far away from her homely guilt complex to dwell on them. Instead she wished for freedom, just as she had a month earlier.

Then she jumped as Giles's warm lips made contact with her shoulder.

'Stop that,' she said gently, the wish still fresh in her head.

'Do you realise how much fun you're denying yourself?' he drawled.

Trudy shrugged, not trusting herself to speak in case she gave away how tempted she really was.

On paper, Giles was categorically not her type. He was too blond, dapper, sporty and way too obvious. She did love his cockiness, a trait that had also attracted her to Finn and, before him, to the other great love of her life, rock singer Pete Rafferty. In fact, Giles and Pete had a lot more in common than first appearances might indicate: Giles was the same age now as Pete had been when he'd first seduced her, possessed the same driven sexual energy, self-assurance and smell of success, yet tempered that overpowering masculinity with an empathy and generosity which was hard to resist. Both had terrible reputations, yet they could make you feel like the only woman in the room . . . the country . . . the planet, and that their single-minded mission was to win your heart and access all areas. It was a tough act to resist.

'Well, if you're going to fight me off, I need another drink.' He handed her his cigar and took her glass. 'Same again?'

Aware that she was seeing even more shooting stars after so much tequila, wine and cognac, Trudy asked for a vodka Coke – a drink she could take all night.

It was a wise move. One more cognac and the rest of his cigar later, Giles was losing the plot. On their way back into the ballroom, he veered dramatically off-course and ended up sitting on the lap of a pre-eminent expert in eighteenth-century snuffboxes.

Shot through with a sugar caffeine rush, Trudy remained clear headed and, despite a hefty dose of foot-shooting regret, knew she'd stay in control.

Far too drunk to dance, Giles lounged listlessly at their table, flirting half-heartedly with the Hertfordshire amateur dramatics devotee.

Trudy danced without break. There were no age divides here; she was in her element. Never short of partners, she jived, jitterbugged, moshed, waltzed, discoed, salsaed and cha-chaed to the music, laughing and whooping, her heart on parole for once, far from its gilded cage yet still protected from the temptations of the flesh. A couple of her more determined and lascivious dance partners tried to monopolise her, ply her with drinks and conversation, but she held firm.

After an hour, she took pity on Giles who was lounging at the table with a glazed expression, blue eyes half-closed and starting to cross.

'I think I'll go up,' Trudy told him as she gathered her shawl and bag. 'Would you walk me to my room?'

Giles was up and off his chair in a flash, hand grabbing hers as he lurched gratefully for the exit.

'Careforamoonlitwalk?' he slurred, reeling towards the terraces.

Trudy tugged him back in the direction of the lifts. 'I meant it. I am going to bed.'

'CanIjoinyou?'

'No.'

'Fairenough – feelabitwoozy – oops!' He pitched sideways into a waiting lift.

Up on their floor, Giles cannoned along the corridor like a pinball, knocking all the pictures to jaunty angles.

''S'mazing! Nevermetawomanwhocouldoutdrinkme,' he slurred.

Trudy deciphered this as she parked him outside his door and felt through his pockets for his key card while he tied to thrust his Amex into the slot.

'I *did* warn you that I can outdrink any man,' she pointed out gently, locating his key card in his breast pocket and stepping back as he interpreted her jacket grope for a cue to kiss her.

'Nightcap?' He reeled around a moment longer.

'No.'

'Bath?'

'Got my own.'

'Nightofpassion?'

'Not after the amount you've downed.' She kissed him on the cheek. 'Sleep it off, huh? I'll see you at breakfast.'

He nodded, glazed blue eyes managing to glimmer with a moment's lucid admiration and good humour. 'I'mabloodyfool – lettingyougo-likethish. Could'vehadsushgoodfuntogethertonight.'

She patted him on the arm and posted him inside, firmly quashing her own secret, matching disappointment.

In her suite, her phone was bleeping furiously from deep within the white sofa. She leaped guiltily on it.

There were twenty-eight missed calls from Finn and seven furious texts demanding a reply. His voicemail messages sounded dreadful, the fake coughs and sniffs replaced by genuine fear. There were three further voicemails on the room phone.

It was past midnight, but she still called the house. He took forever to answer.

'You got me out of bed. I was sleeping it off. I could have bloody died for all you care,' he snapped, sounding completely normal – his standard-issue, just-woken-up, grumpy self.

'What happened? Are you OK?'

'Fine,' he hissed sleepily. 'I think it was the worst of the fever coming out.' He cleared his throat and then managed a couple of forced coughs.

Trudy explained about the phone mislaid in the vast sofa. 'It's bloody enormous. You could lose a dead body in there.'

'I know,' he muttered possessively. 'I showed you a virtual tour of that room online, remember?'

'Of course. You booked it.' She bristled.

'What's Giles's room like?'

'No idea. Why don't you look online?'

'I'm in *bed*.' He let out a resentful huff. 'Is he still partying?'

'Crashed out already – completely off his face,' she reported more happily.

Finn didn't swallow it for a moment, but he gave nothing away. 'You off to bed now, then?'

'Yup,' she yawned. 'As long as you're sure you're OK now?'

'I'm still bloody ill,' he corrected pompously, 'but I'll try to sleep as long as I know I'm not going to get any more interruptions.'

'You do that. I'll leave you alone. Night.'

'Night . . .'

She braced herself.

'. . . love you,' he said, so leadingly that there was almost a question mark at the end.

'Love you, too,' she parroted obediently.

As soon as she put the phone down, it rang again.

'Sorry.' Giles's deep, drawling voice sounded more sober than it had a few minutes earlier. 'I have just stood under a cold shower for five minutes, and I can't apologise enough.'

'For what? Cooling your ardour?' She curled back into her vast sofa and pulled off her shoes.

'Failing to look after you properly tonight – leaving you at the mercy of all those dance-floor letches.'

'I had a lovely evening.'

'It's not over yet.'

'It is,' she said firmly, the smile on her face hidden from her voice.

'I'll leave my door open this side – that'll leave your options open.'

'My legs remain closed, Giles.'

'We can work around that,' he growled teasingly. 'I know the most marvellous position where one—'

'Goodnight Giles.'

'I sober up terribly quickly. It's a Horton attribute, short recovery time – be it from indulgence, from exercise, from sex; I am back up and at 'em in no time. Try me. Talk to me.'

She couldn't help but laugh. The temptation to take this further, even just this phone call, so easy and sexy and relaxed and carefree, was crazy. Phone flirtation would be all too easy, as would opening her side of that dividing door. Neither was tantamount to adultery, but both were accessories to the crime and she knew it.

'Goodnight Giles,' she repeated.

'I'm here if you change your mind.'

'Thank you. Sleep well.'

Her system still flooded with caffeinated sugar, Trudy paced her rooms, the dress swishing and swaying, satin heavy and sensual against her skin.

Again and again she passed the dividing door, trying to imagine what lay beyond it. Another's body alongside hers, intimacy and eroticism, feeling wanted, desired, respected and adored tonight rather than taken for granted and used night after night. The thrill of new sexual awakenings and explorations laced with long-lost, familiar sensations of pleasure and climax.

Getting hotter and hotter, she threw open the double doors to her balcony and stood outside, breathing deeply into a sharp frost.

The tang of cigar smoke immediately hit her nostrils.

'Changed your mind?' A soft purr from the neighbouring balcony.

Trudy trembled, although the cold air barely registered against her skin. She couldn't see him, the high wall that divided their balconies assuring complete privacy.

'What are you doing out here?'

'Sobering up. Thought I might head back down for a bop shortly. Scotch any rumours that Cottrells can't take their drink.'

'That legendary recovery time serving you in good stead?'

'Absolutely. They'll be dancing for hours yet. Lots of attractive totty on show.'

Shivering, Trudy felt the cold very suddenly, like a smack on the face with a freezer door. Why did she feel as though Giles had just insulted her? She could hardly be possessive after all. Perhaps it was just the swiftness with which he could move on, before she had even registered the true nature of her desire and found her feet to walk a straight line towards it.

'How's Finn?' he asked.

'Much better.'

'Good.'

'I'll wish you goodnight.' She turned away.

'Open the door, Trudy.'

It was fifty fifty and Giles knew it. And Trudy would have done it. She would have opened the door to temptation had it not been for the most prosaic of things. Heart and groin thumping, adultery in her veins and nostrils, and desire coursing every sweet manner of lubrication between her legs, she caught sight of her face reflected in the glass of the balcony door. Those wise, familiar hazel eyes looked back, rebuking her, reminding her that she was just Trudy. She was nobody special. A pretty dress and a palette of warpaint couldn't steal the sadness from her eyes.

She went back inside and straight into her bedroom, unthreading the long pearl necklace from around her throat.

After a warm bath, she once again wrapped herself in the fluffiest robe known to man and padded into the sitting room to turn out the lights.

Now in darkness, she stood staring at the dividing door, willing herself to take the risk, live a little, make the first leap towards hedonism and liberation.

But she turned back to her bedroom.

Accustomed to insomnia after years of working nocturnally, she lay awake all night, alone in a bed the size of a boardroom table, hating herself for her cowardice.

At breakfast, Giles was very late and very grey, his dark glasses failing to disguise the hungover pallor.

'Did you go back down, then?' Trudy asked as he battled to drink an orange juice, leaning back from the table to stop himself gagging at the sight of her indulgently huge pile of treats from the grill.

He nodded.

'Get lucky?'

He nodded and then shrugged, managing to splutter between clenched teeth, 'Depends how you view it.'

Trudy was too circumspect to ask more, but later, when they were checking out side-by-side at reception and declaring their minibar quota, her modest jar of jelly beans and bottles of Coke and champagne were nothing to Giles's binge:

'The champagne, the red wine, the white wine,' he told the receptionist, 'two Tia Marias, the Baileys, the Scotch, the cognac . . . and, er, the "Shag Bag".'

The model-like receptionist didn't even flicker an eyebrow as she tapped it all into the computer to add to his bill.

Trudy, meanwhile, had to turn away to hide her laughter. A moment later, she kept her face averted from both Giles and the receptionist to conceal her horror at her own room bill. Even with a modest bar tab, it came to as much as a week's family holiday in France. She put it on her personal savings debit card, certain that the joint account wouldn't stretch – Finn always kept that lean. Of course, he had planned to claim the expense from Cottrells', but knowing that the company was in dire straits and that the outing had hardly done much for their corporate image, Trudy didn't have the heart to charge it to them. The night away had been her treat to herself, after all; – although she suspected that staying in the attic shoebox room would have been much easier on both purse and conscience. She might even have managed some sleep.

To make up for her restless night, she slept most of the way home in the car, lulled into unconsciousness by the beautifully pitched drone of the vintage engine – a sousaphone that swallowed her up and hugged her tightly in its comforting curves.

Beside her, squinting to concentrate on the roads through his hangover, Giles drove the return stint at a leisurely pace, regretting that his brief window of opportunity was closing so fast. Occasionally stealing glances across to Trudy, he felt disappointment at the way things had panned out the previous night. His 'consolation' conquest, a rather stringy blonde from Leicestershire whose cuffs had most certainly not matched her collars, had left a sour taste in his mouth. He never found one night stands particularly satisfactory, especially with single women who then plagued him with calls. She had already sent three suggestive texts.

Next time, he vowed, he would be better prepared. He wouldn't give up this chase; Trudy was a thrilling quarry.

At Church Cottage, the reception awaiting Trudy was as dark, unwelcoming, anaesthetised and antiseptic as a recovery ward. Finn, sulking furiously, might have cast off the more extreme fake symptoms of man flu, but he was not about to let her get away with such wilful husband neglect. He now had very real symptoms to exploit.

He was in fact just as hungover as his cousin, his drug and drink binge of the previous day leaving him with a dry mouth, thumping headache, shakes, a tightly knotted belly and diarrhoea.

He'd been up since dawn, unable to enjoy the promised wife-free, Radio-Five-Live-filled lie in because his whirling head had turned, his belly churned and his bowels evacuated their fish pie contents with rapid fire gusto against the loo porcelain. He blamed Trudy completely for his affliction, and deliberately hadn't flushed so that she could see just how ill she had made him. Marching angrily around the house all morning in between loo stops, he'd worked out a plan.

His instinct to confront her as soon as she got back, to throw every accusation at her, to shout her to the ground, had swiftly been cauterised by his pride. He simply couldn't admit his very real fear of being cuckolded. She would, in any case, deny it – and without concrete proof, he would be left to play the jealous fool who cared too much.

The thought of punishment without explanation was far more tempting, but he knew he wouldn't follow through because he feared that she would just run away if pushed too far. She already seemed to live dangerously close to self-destruct.

Instead, he decided to set his wife a test, to lay a trap.

If Trudy had indeed spent the previous night wrapped round Giles as Finn suspected, he would prefer to make her suffer slowly and painfully. He'd hit her where it hurt most: her clever head and her fragile ego. He was certain that she had failed him, but he needed to prove it once and for all. This way, she would be caught in her own net.

Feeling very pleased with himself and his genius, he had spent the past few hours at his laptop, plotting Trudy's downfall.

So when he heard the car tyres on the gravel outside, he carefully switched off his computer and bit down on his dry lip with a satisfied sigh. Closing the door to his study behind him just as she walked into the house, he was able to face her without red mist descending.

'What have you been up to?' she asked as he walked listlessly along the back lobby towards her, still wearing his old sleep joggers and T-shirt, his handsome head low.

'Working,' He looked up at her through long-suffering, curled brows, his voice still cracking with dryness. '*I* can't afford to be off sick – let alone party day and night.'

She took the dig on the chin.

'Well, let me fix you some lunch and a hot drink,' she offered magnanimously.

'I'm not hungry.'

'Not even a bowl of soup?'

He shook his head, closing his eyes as the headache clutched his temples.

'Poor you,' she soothed, stifling a yawn. 'Perhaps you should have a lie-down?'

'Will you join me?' he asked sullenly, more of a cantankerous jibe than a tempting suggestion.

It was her turn to shake her head. 'I should take a leaf out of your book and do some work – make some calls. As you say, neither of us can really afford to party, can we?'

In her study, listening to the floorboards groaning and the small television droning overhead as Finn banged about, apparently watching 'Flog It!', Trudy laid her face on her desk and stared across at the corner of a box file wishing she had dared to open that hotel dividing door after all.

Later, when Finn was safely in the bath and Trudy trailed upstairs to unpack her beloved dress and change into the usual scruffy comfort layers that enabled her to work and run the house and animals, she caught sight of herself in the mirror, stripped to her lacy underwear and socks. It was not a pretty sight. The fake tan had already started to go patchy and the light through the window behind her caught her cellulite at the most unflattering angle.

Her mind's eye, having travelled so hopefully in recent weeks only to arrive back where it started, was looking at a completely different view. She felt like the wicked stepmother in *Snow White* who, having trusted the beauty in the looking glass, suddenly found betrayal staring back at her as it revealed old age and ugliness.

'Come back,' she begged her reflection, those wise hazel eyes that just for a few hours the previous night had greeted her as a stunning woman full of confidence and joy.

But only anxious, unhappily married Trudy looked back. The brutal truth of her reflection taunted her. Gone was the siren of the night before, along with her infectious, delighted self-confidence. She already missed her alter ego more than she could say.

'She *was* here,' she reminded herself with a pinch to her chest. 'You *were* here, Tru.'

'Who was here?' Finn wandered in, lobster red from the bath, muscles gleaming as he towelled his dark hair.

'Nobody.' She hastily sidestepped him and backed from the room to the landing. 'Just a ghost.'

Finn let out a disparaging hiss and narrowed his eyes.

He would lay a trap all right. And the first hair wire would be just outside their front door.

3

When she heard a car engine in her driveway, Trudy lifted her cheek from the piano keys and blinked sleep from her eyes, panic starting to rise as she peered through the dusty windows to see a large off-roader parking behind the abandoned builders' skip. Out jumped Liv Wilson, a willowy brunette in immaculate riding gear who then made her way cautiously along the path to the front door, weaving through a slalom of pallets and cement bags. The dogs started to chorus furiously at the letter box in greeting.

Trudy's elbows crashed out two jarring chords while her fingers raked her wet face. She'd completely forgotten that Liv was coming this morning. She'd been crying for over an hour now – she must look like sin. Tear-clogged lashes stabbed at her puffy, stinging eyelids. One cheek was creased and striped from the piano keys. Her nose and upper lip felt like a flaky, snotty, throbbing inferno. She was still wearing the ancient jogging bottoms that she had put on first thing to muck out the horses, walk the dogs and feed the chickens. There was straw hanging off the dog-eared sweater of Finn's that she had flung over her sleep vest, and more still decorating the greasy blond tangles that were scraped back with a cheap plastic hairclip.

For a moment, she thought about hiding, but she couldn't do that to Liv. Super-sensitive Liv would know. It would cut her down.

So she grabbed a pair of sunglasses, pinched her cheeks hard to drag some colour to them, mopped her face on the arm of her sweater and took a deep breath as she threw the door open.

'Sorry, Liv my love – been working all night. Quite lost sight of the time. I must look a fright.'

'You look . . . lovely and dishevelled and creative,' Liv said kindly, but was unable to stop her eyes darting briefly around the mess that greeted her. Rather surprisingly, it came across as glamorous mess; just as everything about Trudy struck Liv as larger-than-life and enviably glitzy. She was almost pathologically tidy so that her own mess appalled her, and yet half-renovated, shambolic, dusty Church Cottage was as unexpectedly appealing as its smiling, tousled hostess.

Trudy batted away the vast pack of dogs that were crowding round her immaculately breeched and booted new friend and ushered her hastily through the open reception hall with its grand piano and large-scale debris, past the kitchen which was a total bombsite, and into the study 'snug', which at least had a sofa, even if the table in front of it was playing host to ten dirty mugs, three full ashtrays and a month of Sunday papers.

'Wait there – I won't be a moment. Just have to change. I'd make you a coffee, but we're out. I can offer you gin and tonic or Finn's herb tea?'

'Oh – really, I don't mind. I'd hate to be any trouble . . .' Liv's voice trailed away.

Trudy had already rushed out, tripping over a paint pot because she couldn't see very well in her dark glasses.

Upstairs, she quickly examined the damage in the bathroom mirror and groaned. It was worse than she'd feared. Her eyes were half closed, she looked as though one cheek had been branded. Stinging tears pricked evilly at the back of her eyes, as familiar and uncontrollable as ever. It was the same old pattern; robbed of sleep by a racing heart and thoughts, she had stayed up most of the night trying to work, drinking too much and totally forgetting that Liv had asked for her help. Now, hardly able to think straight, she was the one badly in need of help just to pull herself together.

Without a therapist, Prozac and total body detox to hand, there was only one thing for it . . .

Closing her eyes, she started to hum.

'Mmmm . . . mmm . . . hmmm-hummm-hmmm . . .'

No, it wasn't working. Bugger it. Desperate measures were called for, Trudy realised. It was a big house, and Liv was tucked in the far corner of it. She'd never hear.

Opening her mouth, she let out a full blast chorus.

'The sun has got his hat on,
Hip, hip, hip, hooray!
The sun has got his hat on and is coming out to play.'

She opened her eyes and smiled at her own reflection as she sang, watching the creases melt from her cheeks and a glimmer of the old, familiar sparkle pick out the gold streaks in her eyes.

On the medley raced, not giving her pause for thought as she sang the refrains from all her favourite cheery-day songs to combat depression – 'Oh What a Beautiful Morning', 'Wonderful World', 'Sun is Shining' and 'Sweetest Feeling'.

She sang through a toothpasty gurgle as she lashed a brush against the teeth she had been grinding all night. She sang her way to the bedroom and searched through the piles of clothes scattered on the dusty floorboards for something clean and capacious enough to fit. With so much unwashed laundry piled up downstairs, her lingerie drawer was reduced to a few pairs of big knickers with faded gussets and detaching elastic waists. They'd have to do. She slid her thumbs into the waistband of her tattered joggers and pulled them down.

A small voice came from the doorway behind her.

'Sorry to interrupt – Oh!'

For a moment, Liv Wilson was confronted with a Rubenesque, pale bottom resplendent with a jaunty tattoo of what had once been a songbird but, thanks to the ravages of weight gain and cellulite, now resembled a club-footed toucan.

'Jesus!' Trudy hitched her joggers back up.

As Liv turned hastily away to face the opposite wall, both women pretended that the moment hadn't occurred. 'I . . . um . . . couldn't help hearing you sing,' she blurted hurriedly to cover the gaffe. 'It sounded lovely.'

'Thanks.'

Blushing furiously, aware that she had just committed a serious faux pas by seeing her hostess moon – however glamorously – Liv stared at the floor in front of her. 'I just thought I'd better pop up to remind you that you said you'd ride him too?'

'I said I'd do what?'

'Otto the horse. You said you'd have a sit on him today? Only I'm really quite a novice.'

Trudy's sleep-deprived brain raked together a few facts. Liv wanted to buy a horse. She had offered to help out. They were looking at one this morning. Had she offered to ride it? She must have been in a state of self-denial. Or drunk. Probably both.

'Yes – of course.' She gushed apologetically. 'Thanks. I *had* forgotten. I'll put on some breeches, although I'm not sure he's really up to my weight.'

'Of course he is. You're not that . . . um . . . big.'

Trudy smiled, touched by any small flattery and by Liv's desperate awkwardness which had a calming effect. Having someone to buck up always bucked her up in return. With her huge, dark eyes and slender nerviness, Liv reminded Trudy of a whippet she had once owned who had quivered all over with happiness if you so much as stroked her head. She was desperate to be liked, and being with her provided instant gratification.

'You'll probably get so carried away enjoying him that you won't need me at all,' she reassured her. 'He is a lovely creature. You'll suit each other.'

Liv looked thrilled. 'You don't think he'll be too much for me?'

'God, no. Dilly's only a slip of a thing and I'm sure you ride a lot better than she does. Just give me a moment . . . have a look round the rest of the house if you like. You can see what we're up against. Unfortunately, my husband sacked the builders last week, which won't help. God knows where we'll find replacements. Mind the floorboards in the bedroom with the arched window – and don't go up to the attic. It's lethal.'

After Liv had disappeared again, Trudy went in search of her long-neglected riding gear. Her only clean breeches wouldn't do up at the waist and had a hole appearing in the crotch where the stitching had been strained to the limit. A few extra pounds were very unforgiving in riding wear . . .

'I will not cry,' Trudy told herself firmly, starting to sing again, but quietly, so that Liv couldn't hear.

She wrestled with a sports bra, clamping it round her back like string round a pork joint, then covered the trussed torso with one of Finn's fleeces and went in search of a safety pin to secure her waistband. It was weeks since she had ridden. Her own horses were just growing fat and idle in the field, stuffing their faces with spring grass. Arty, the old white mare, was entitled to her life of Riley; she was well over twenty and relishing her fifth year of retirement, despite Finn's occasional dark threats of euthanasia, bandied about to wind up his wife on black marital days. But the younger of her two mares, Tara, was as unfit as her mistress.

She had a vague recollection of offering Liv some sort of DIY livery deal – a bit rash as they had only just met, but now that she thought about it, that could be just the motivation she needed to get in some riding. If Liv *did* buy the Gentlys' gelding and keep him here with her own horses, she might be motivated to start working Tara again, enjoying some companionable hacking and conversation. It would be lovely to have a new chum on tap. The more she thought about it now, the more the idea appealed to her.

Nurturing this friendship was important to Trudy. She had lost too many friends throughout her marriage, and craved company.

Once again ensconced on a lumpy chaise in the snug downstairs and chewing nervously on her nails, Liv was thinking much the same thing.

She craved friendship, and Trudy had been one of the only truly welcoming people she had met since moving to the village three lonely months ago.

And yet she was also fighting a thudding chest and a huge lump in her throat that begged her to run away. Trudy Cottrell was too intimidating to be her friend, a small voice told her. She had always found friendships awkward to forge and harder still to hold on to, battling her timidity, sensitivity and – since her marriage – her husband Martin's snobbish criticism. Yet he was the one who had been nagging her about her lack of new 'social alliances' locally. He clearly wanted her to befriend smart, Home Counties yummy mummies, and Liv had no idea what he would make of childless Trudy's bohemianism. It took a lot to unsettle Martin, but Liv had a feeling Trudy was far enough removed from Martin's safety zone to rattle him. In a small, rebellious way, it was one of the reasons she wanted the friendship to work out.

She stayed glued to the seat while Trudy hummed and sang upstairs, listening to the beautiful sound, feeling increasingly like a fish out of water, yet unable to flee.

Martin was several thousand miles away, manning his company's Singapore office, to which a last-minute management reshuffle had summonsed him just weeks before the family relocated from the London suburbs to the Cotswolds; too late to stop the move, but urgent enough to take Martin away for the first few critical weeks of settling into the new village life he had claimed to crave. Liv tried not to resent the fact that he had consequently enjoyed luxurious ex-pat living while Liv struggled to oversee the move alone. Shy, socially awkward Liv had found the changeover daunting without a husband to back her up and lend her much-needed validity in what she saw as a hostile, alien new community. Isolated, lacking direction and acutely self-conscious, she struggled through a day at a time, missing her Croydon friends at the gym, the children's school and the yard where she had shared a horse; the routines she had built up there over several years; the easy way in which she had eventually filled her free time. Here, the Cotswold yummy mummies had ignored Liv at the school gates for a full term now – or sent their nannies to ignore her.

Her attempts to cheer herself up and find distractions had ultimately cost a lot of money and given her little pleasure: a newly decorated, freshly furbished house into which she had no friends to invite, endless pampering and exercising at the salon and gym to keep trim for a husband who was residing on the other side of the planet, cheering little 'me' treats like aromatherapy and crystal healing that ended up making her feel more guilty than rewarded, fun clubs, outings and after-school classes for the children which, having inherited their mother's timidity, they cried through and came away from friendless.

Three months after relocating to idyllic Oddlode, Liv was bored and lonely and becoming increasingly depressed. Meeting Trudy had come in the nick of time.

A week earlier, she had been idling by the noticeboard at the village stores, rereading an advertisement which for more than a fortnight she had gazed at daily with the eager eyes of a child rather than a thirty-six year old mother of two.

For Sale: 16hh 9-y-o strawberry roan gelding. Warmblood X Anglo Arab. Great all rounder. Competed usual pc activities, SJ, XC & Devil's Marsh race. Easy hack, shoe, clip. £4000 inc tack.

It was an advertisement that made Liv's heart race so fast that she hadn't noticed somebody studying the postcards over her shoulder.

'Christ – fifteen people are now advertising for a cleaner on this board. Don't tell me you're one of them?'

Liv had stiffened and narrowed her eyes. 'A cleaning lady?'

'No, of course not with a lovely Kelly bag like that,' the voice behind her had laughed. 'I mean an advertiser. Then again, given the hourly rates they can get away with charging around here, chars are probably the only ones able to afford Kelly bags. Old Dot Wyck, who charges me a small fortune to come and muck us out once a month, probably has a small stash of crocodile Birkins at home. And if you *were* a cleaner, I might just have to kidnap you. Mine's the advert written in blood there.' She tapped the window beside a yellowing postcard, peeling at the edges with age. It simply read 'Squalid, short-sighted couple seek cleaner. Any standard. Good rates paid.' And there was a mobile number.

Giggling and peering shyly over her shoulder, Liv had been confronted by a glamour-puss in cream fake fur and dark glasses. A tousled, streaky blonde with high cheekbones, a curly-cornered smile and glowing, golden skin scattered with freckles like sesame seeds on a toasted bagel. Very scruffy around the edges, admittedly, but there was no mistaking the wow factor. She'd also looked distinctly familiar, and Liv suspected she had seen her on television or in a magazine.

She'd sneaked a look at the woman's advert again, but there was no name.

'Actually I was looking at this advert for the horse.'

'Oh, that. Classy roan the Gently girl's been riding for a couple of years. Nice sort.'

'You know about horses?'

'A bit,' the glamour-puss had smiled, holding out a hand covered in biro marks. 'Trudy Cottrell. You must be new to the area?'

Liv was gratified by the firm grip and the bloodshot but sparkly toffee-coloured eyes that had studied her cheerfully over the dark glasses.

'What makes you say that?' she'd asked after she'd introduced herself.

Trudy had huddled closer in a conspiratorial fashion, a heady waft of Versace Blonde surrounding them both.

'You want to buy a horse. That's always the first thing the bored, neglected Cotswold wife does. Reliving our pony-mad youth. It never lasts – we soon find we ache all over and don't like smelling of horse any more.'

'Oh yes?' Liv was entranced by her laughter-laced, husky voice and intimate, confessional manner.

'After that, most give up on trying to fall in love with Dobbin and just cut to the chase and look for a real lover.'

Liv was shocked.

'Oh, I know you're not *nearly* there yet,' Trudy had reassured her with a playful pat on the arm. 'Much better to try horseflesh first. I have two of my own and not a lover to my name. Honest. And this one,' she had pressed a finger to the roan's advert, 'is a very good-looking beast. Why not give them a ring? I'll come with you if you like. Here, take my number.'

With overwhelming gratitude, Liv had fed both numbers into her phone and skipped home to do some detective work. At last, she had something to look forward to and a project to get her teeth into.

And so it had begun, an unlikely friendship between two very different characters, drawn together through boredom, loneliness and a mutual love of four-legged fun.

Having introduced herself by her married name, Cottrell, rather than her professional one, Dew, Trudy had sidestepped the risk of immediate recognition, although it took Liv very little time to get to the truth with the help of her hairdresser, Google and a couple of the friendlier yummy mummies who swapped notes at the school gates. Trudy Dew had been quite a big hit in the early nineties, albeit briefly. More excitingly as far as Liv was concerned, Cottrell was a far more infamous name locally than Dew: Trudy was part of the auctioneering, land management and estate agency dynasty that had for decades dictated the price of everything from houses to straw to silver to ironmongery. Well-trained by Martin, Liv had been quick to do her homework and was impressed by what she learned.

Acting quickly, before she lost her nerve, and buoyed up by a succession of increasingly large G and Ts, Liv had called the roan gelding's vendor to arrange to view him. After a stilted conversation with a woman who could hardly hear her over the wail of a baby crying and a belting cacophony of classical music, Liv had eagerly dialled Trudy's mobile. She couldn't have been nicer, although Liv had an uncomfortable feeling that she didn't really remember meeting her at the post office. Yet, within minutes, Trudy was warmly agreeing to come and see the horse, and even offering her a place to keep him in the fields with her own. Having heard that Trudy's auctioneer husband, Finn, was something of a local god – by all accounts a cross between Mr Darcy and James Bond – Liv was thrilled at the idea of befriending the Cottrells.

Martin would surely approve of her getting in with the hunting and shooting set? He might have grumbled about the expense of her riding hobby when they were in London, but now that they were living in the Cotswolds, horses were a vital lifestyle accessory, and it was high time she had one of her own – soon to be joined, she hoped, by ponies for Lily and Jasper, and a brace of Labradors to follow them on family hacks.

Yet now, sitting alone in Trudy's huge, chaotic cottage, Liv wasn't sure it was a friendship that she could really cope with. Something about it, and about Trudy, frightened her.

She caught sight of a wedding photo on the mantelpiece. In it, Trudy looked stunning and radiantly happy, slim as a waif in luxurious cream satin. Beside her was quite the best-looking man Liv had seen in a lifetime of teen pin-ups, action-hero movies, chick-flicks and flipping through Martin's copies of *GQ* in the loo.

Like a child poised on a roller coaster, Liv gripped the arm of the chaise longue and chewed her lip with apprehensive excitement.

Upstairs, the far more straightforward fear of falling off a horse was concerning Trudy. It was more than a month since she had ridden Tara; the two mares in the field outside lived increasingly for ornamentation these days. Along with her beloved Bechstein piano, they were her comfort blankets – a holy trinity of happy memories from another lifetime, as precious as family, of more sentimental than practical use as the years passed by.

Watching them through the window as she stalled for time, Trudy wished she had made an effort lately rather than sleeping, drinking, lying and crying her way through the indifferent hours that separated day from night.

She could easily come unstuck on a hot-headed character like Otto as soon as he rumbled how rusty and unfit she was, exposing all her boastful exaggeration. Yet now that she was potentially about to be humiliated, she still couldn't bring herself to tell Liv that all her friendly confidence was a sham.

With her huge, eager brown eyes, slim figure, polite manner and neat, flicky brown hair, Liv reminded Trudy of the sort of girl she had always longed to be, the sort who did well in the Brownies, progressed through school without ever starting fights or getting bullied, did well without being branded as a square or a show-off, had a steady boyfriend, never had 'issues' or 'trouble at home' and, of course, never got involved in anything as seedy as sex, drugs and rock and roll. Liv was a good girl, a nice girl, the conventional sort of girl – even all grown up as she was – who made Trudy feel good to be associated with.

Trudy remembered that weeks ago local gossip, Gladys 'Glad Tidings' Gates, had held forth several times about the Wilsons, who had moved into one of the big, new executive houses in Coppice Court just after Christmas. Gladys thrived on scandal and was only too happy to impart that 'she' (Liv) was a 'pretty thing, but quiet as a mouse and a bit stand-offish', that the 'kiddies' (one of each) were 'lovely little creatures with perfect manners' and 'he' (still no name to hand) was 'never there – she says he works abroad, but for all we know he could be *inside* or something.' At this, Trudy had happily let her imagination run riot, suggesting fraud, embezzlement, gold heists and hustles until Gladys had gone positively pink in the face with excitement. They enjoyed rumour-mongering together, happily discussing broken marriages, affairs and strange behaviour in the village.

Now, having met Liv in person and registering that she was very vulnerable and really rather sweet, Trudy felt guilty at all her idle banter those weeks ago.

Drawing a bolstering breath, she took one last look at her horses through the window, hoping that she could pull this thing off.

She wanted to impress Liv, like a teenager showing off. Liv liked and needed her, and it had been a long time since Trudy had felt liked and needed.

Even though it was just a few minutes' walk from Church Cottage to the field beside the river Odd where Otto the horse lived, Liv insisted on ferrying them in her very shiny 4x4.

'The horse's owner, Ophelia, said she and her daughter Dilly might be late,' Liv explained as they set out on the short drive. 'Someone called Giles will meet us, apparently.'

'Oh God, that's all we need.'

'You know him?'

Trudy nodded. 'My husband's cousin.'

'So he's a Cottrell?'

'In a manner of speaking. In manners, mostly – bad, mad and dangerous to women.' Trudy tried not to grip too obviously on to the seat belt as they lurched around the turning into Goose Lane, passing between high Cotswold stone walls and verges bursting with daffodils. The village had started to put on its Easter show at last after a long, mist-swathed winter and bitter spring of alternate frost and downpour, like a khaki-clad dog-walker wearing a jaunty new headscarf. She perked up at the sight, grateful to be out of the house.

Equally grateful, Liv, who loved the idea of the Cottrell family from all she had ascertained so far, was looking forward to meeting one of its legendarily good-looking men.

Giles was no disappointment. Waiting for them at the head of a long gravel drive was a tall, tanned vision in sports casuals with wild licks of greying blond hair, a heroic moustache and the naughtiest blue eyes Liv had ever seen. His smile was pure hedonism.

She tried not to feel too affronted that this smile was directed entirely on Trudy as he made a gallant dash for the passenger door and helped her out.

'Trudy! My God, you are a welcome sight!' He gathered her up into a very thorough hug. 'Where have you been hiding?'

'Just working.' Trudy extracted herself from the embrace and introduced her companion.

Giles's blue eyes sparkled as he turned to Liv, taking a customary scenic tour of her body before he stepped forward in welcome.

When he took her hand, she quivered at the bolt of electricity which raced through her. He really was incredibly flirt-making.

'Enchanted.' Giles kissed her hand, admiring the whopping solitaires to either side of her wedding band. 'I gather you are interested in this magnificent beast?' He waved over his shoulder at what appeared to be a small, muddy donkey in a paddock behind him, although his eyes didn't once leave Liv's as he added in a drawling undertone, 'I do hope that if you buy him, you'll continue to keep him here? I charge very little field rent and am always on hand for help.'

Liv nodded with mute delight, her fingers still resting in Giles's big hand, her eyes trapped in his unblinking blue gaze, her anxious smile mirroring his knowing one.

Trudy sighed, seeing her plans of companionably sharing her own fields with Liv sliding away. She had seen Giles work his magic many times before, although never perhaps quite so close to hand.

As surely as the spring sunshine was bursting from the clouds overhead and lighting up the puddles, Liv had fallen for Giles Hornton's spell. Otto was as good as sold by simple virtue of the fact that he was a sitting tenant in Giles's very private, tree-lined paddock – scene of many an illicit liaison over the years.

Despite being the cliché bounder, Giles had a fearsomely successful reputation when it came to bedding women, especially married ones. With four marriages of his own behind him, he had abandoned attempts at wedlock and finally settled for seducing other men's wives instead, finding himself cornering a niche market. The lonely, neglected wives of the Lodes Valley blossomed under his manly attentions, responding to his old-fashioned wooing, his flattery and ministrations like frost-nipped tender perennials transferred to a hothouse.

The fact that he was so open about the whole thing eased his passage rather than hindered it. Admittedly, the perfectly straight nose had been expensively recast a couple of times after being broken by irate husbands, and some teeth were porcelain in place of the shattered ones that had encountered the knuckle of a flying fist, but on the whole he got away with his adulterous antics with surprising ease.

One thorn in his side was his ongoing inability to bed Trudy and his attempts to woo her had become something of a running joke between them. Since the Auctioneers' Ball, a deepening fondness had set in, but there was no real progress towards mutual, stripped bare seduction – much to Giles's regret.

As he chatted up Liv, Trudy wished she could respond as other women did, but Giles was just too transparent to her, yet equally emotionally closeted. He was all artifice and guile, and he had an awful lot of baggage.

A piece of this baggage was currently making her way breathlessly along the drive. Not spotting the approaching danger, Liv laughed delightedly as Giles described what a wonderful paddock landlord he would make, promising to put up jumps and bending poles and have a hip-flask ready at all times.

Ophelia Gently, with four month old baby Basil strapped to her hip, sped up progress on her damp, silver ballet pumps as she spotted Giles locked on target. Bloody man!

If it wasn't bad enough that Trudy Cottrell was smouldering against a post-and-rail fence, bursting out of too-tight breeches and a shrunken sweater with her hour-glass waist and her huge cleavage, there also appeared to be a stick-thin, Desperate Housewife type flicking her lowlights around under Giles's chin and muscling in on the act.

Pheely waded into battle with a charm offensive, flicking her own metre-long, teak-brown corkscrew curls like Medusa's snakes and thrusting her H-cup, milk-filled bosom into the fray.

'You must be Olivia! Sorry, sorry! I was waiting for my daughter to get back from London – Otto is hers, you see – but there's been a change of plan. Here, Giles, bond with your *son* for a moment.' She untied the papoose and thrust its dribbling contents at Giles's camel-coloured chest before turning to beam at Liv. 'I'm Ophelia – Pheely. We spoke on the phone.'

Liv swallowed in disappointed surprise as her Mills and Boon moment was shattered and she realised that Giles and this loud, forceful siren were not only an item but the parents of a small, bug-eyed baby as well.

'Call me Liv,' she said faintly as she took in the cloud of glossy brown corkscrews, the myriad curves, the layers of purple velvet and the very green eyes – in more sense than one. Giles is mine, they told her firmly. Back off.

Two solitaire diamonds were no match for the armoury of amethysts and garnets set in silver on Pheely's fingers that crushed their way into Liv's bony knuckles as they shook hands.

Behind them, in Giles's arms, baby Basil let out a big slug of milk sick from his mouth, screwed up his face and started to bawl.

'Just jiggle him!' Pheely snapped as Giles immediately tried to hand him back. Her eyes didn't leave Liv's, smile still beaming out threateningly. 'Otto is a *wonderful* character. Everyone in the village loves him – don't they, Trudy?'

'Huh?' Trudy was trying to help Giles calm Basil, who had amazing lung capacity and was already drowning out any other noise for miles around. 'Oh, yes. Lovely. What are you doing about the donkey?'

'Oh, Bottom comes as a part of the deal – BOG OFF, *you know*?' She raised her voice to be heard above the baby's screaming so that she was almost shouting at Liv.

Gaping at her, Liv wondered if she had just been given her marching orders.

'BOG OFF – BUY ONE GET ONE FREE,' Pheely yelled. 'Buy the horse and we'll throw in the donkey.'

'Donkeys don't like being thrown,' Trudy commented idly, winking at Liv. She had now relieved Giles of baby Basil, whose frantic crying immediately dissipated to an uncertain mewl as he looked up at her freckled, wide-cheeked face and ready smile.

'They might land on their ass!' Giles bellowed with amusement.

Pheely glared at him. 'Why don't you get us all a lovely, big drink while we look at the horse?'

He nodded cheerfully. 'Bottle of wine?'

Liv hardly drank in the mornings except at Christmas and longed for a cup of coffee, but was too frightened to ask.

'Isn't he absolutely gorgeous?' Trudy sighed, cuddling Basil's chunky warmth as Giles walked away. 'You just want to squeeze him all day.'

'Utterly divine – all Dilly's girlfriends want to take him home,' agreed Pheely, fishing in her pockets for Polos, 'but he'd walk all over them.'

Watching Giles's tight buttocks moving beneath the cream chinos in the distance, Liv nodded dreamily.

It was a moment before she realised that they were all at cross purposes. She was thinking about the blond hero; Trudy was talking about the baby; and Pheely was pointing at an amazing pink horse that had appeared beside the donkey and was whickering greedily for attention and mints. With huge, limpid eyes that gazed passively from a white face, framed with a neatly parted forelock as streaky as a raspberry ripple, he completed Liv's perfect daydream. The emerald green paddock beside the little white cottage owned by the dashing blond hero, overlooking the curling little Odd river, near which a pink horse grazed with his little brown companion – just a hundred yards from the lovely golden house in which lonely Liv paced restlessly, awaiting her neglectful husband. It had the makings of the fairy tales she told the children. She wasn't sure where Trudy and Pheely fitted in – that complication ruined the daydream a bit – but she already knew that if Trudy was too fairy godmother-magical to be a safe friend, then Pheely was too pure witchcraft to make for an easy enemy.

Right now, Pheely's serpent-like green eyes were running over her like microsurgery lasers.

'Horses are such lovely creatures, aren't they?'

Liv quailed.

'*Much* better than the men around here,' Trudy gurgled, bouncing Basil. 'I've already told her that, although this one is to die for,' she kissed Basil's nose, making him gum and grin happily. 'It's once they're all grown up that they start to get wayward, and we girls have to return to the far more trusting and faithful love of four-legged friends.'

'Hmph.' Pheely didn't seem very taken with Trudy's theory. 'You have the best of both worlds, darling – horses *and* the "loveliest man in the Cotswolds".'

'Aren't I lucky?' Trudy said smoothly, deliberately not reacting to the line that was so often quoted back to her. Calling Finn 'the loveliest man in the Cotswolds' was a silly throwaway comment she had made to a journalist years ago. It had ended up forming the shout-line for a double-page spread in a dreadful glossy Sunday supplement and become legend in the village ever since.

'Have you met Finn?' Pheely asked Liv darkly.

'Not yet.'

'Oh, he'll bowl you over, you wait. He's gorgeous.'

Liv was struggling to imagine a man lovelier than Giles and, having seen Finn's photograph, thought him far too tall, dark and scary.

'Why don't we catch Otto and tack him up?' Trudy suggested.

'Good idea,' muttered Pheely, who had seen Liv ogling Giles's bottom (rather than donkey Bottom). 'Oh bugger. Slight problem.'

'Being?' Trudy handed back Basil as she prepared to catch the horse.

'Forgot the tack,' Pheely apologised. 'It's at home. I'd better go and fetch it.' Giles reappeared from his house carrying champagne and four flutes. 'Let's all just have a little drink first.'

Liv, soon tight as a tick after just half a glass of champagne, bucked up by Trudy's reassuringly lovely presence, willing to do pretty much anything to avoid any confrontational situations with Pheely, and more stimulated than she had been in many weeks, made a sudden announcement as she gazed across the magical field beside the river with its two tail-twitching companions.

'I'll buy the horse!' she squeaked triumphantly.

4

That evening, after putting the children to bed, Liv broke the news of her four-legged purchase to Martin via email. It was easier communicating with him that way, and made up for the time difference, she convinced herself. Carefully glossing over the fact that she had barely set eyes on the beast before agreeing to part with her husband's hard-earned cash – let alone been brave enough to ride it – she added the exciting news that Pheely had thrown in a donkey as a freebie, which 'will be such fun for the children!' What's more, the two animals could stay in their current field very cheaply 'of which you will no doubt approve!' The field was owned by a very nice chap called Giles who, she hastily added, was Pheely's boyfriend, although she didn't mention his reputation. Instead she told Martin about the baby called 'Basil – named after the herb, not the hotelier, I'm told!!!'

Liv always used a lot of exclamation marks when emailing Martin. She hoped they cheered up what was usually rather dreary news. Today's was far more action-packed: new friends, new hobbies, new directions.

He had better come home soon. She wasn't sure she liked what was happening to her, but she was too excited to want it to stop just yet. The last week had opened her eyes to a whole new range of possibilities. All Trudy's talk of adultery made it seem possible, above board and within her reach. Most of it was just idle talk, and yet . . .

'We all miss you so much!' she typed with unusual tenderness and then, tapping her cursor keys back through the sentence, replaced 'we' with 'the children'.

Why, she wondered, did a woman married to 'the loveliest man in the Cotswolds' come across as so cynical about men and so open to the possibility of infidelity?

Since her marriage, Liv had never really had a true, three-dimensional opportunity to be tempted by the flesh – her timidity and Martin's bullish possessiveness had precluded any flirtations – but temptations of the mind were another matter, and Trudy had planted a seed in very fertile ground. By day she might be a home-maker and wannabe yummy mummy, but by night Liv fantasised herself a far more sensual soul. Neglected by Martin, finding herself with long, lonely evenings to fill, and existing on a diet of scurrilous television, racy women's fiction, internet chat rooms and glossy magazines, Liv had started to suspect that there was a lot of fun out there if one was just ballsy and brave enough to go out and get it. She didn't want the years to keep sliding past, stealing away her looks and coquettish wiles as she remained hidden in her domestic Rapunzel's tower, not daring to throw down her hair. Trudy was ballsy and brave and had acres of amazing hair that she was forever tossing about with flirtatious abandon. Being married to 'the loveliest man in the Cotswolds' didn't stop her talking about extramarital affairs as though they were as therapeutic as shopping for shoes. Perhaps that was what kept her marriage alive. Trudy and Finn could both have lovers for all she knew. It was what the upper classes did, wasn't it?

She found the idea of high-octane Cottrell immorality hugely distracting, and pictured the Abbey as a Cotswolds Southfork, with Piers Cottrell as J.R., Finn as Bobby, Trudy as Pam and Giles as Cliff Barnes, perhaps. Liv longed to fit in somewhere, and secretly already imagined herself on Cliff Barnes's arm at the oil barons' ball, all smoky eyes, shoulder-pads and stretch satin. Her own husband was the one pushing her up the social ladder, after all . . .

'You'll have to watch out,' she added by way of a postscript to her message to Martin, 'because I hear that there are local bounders who prey on neglected wives around here! I might be tempted to stray if you stay away much longer!'

She chewed her lips for a long time before deleting the last two sentences and asking if he had yet confirmed with the office that he would be coming home for Easter. His parents had already invited themselves to stay for a great chunk of the children's school holiday, and the thought of entertaining her in-laws without Martin around was terrifying. She envied Trudy the Cottrells; they sounded much more entertaining than Edna and Gordon Wilson with their non-stop talk of sciatica, the caravanning club and gardening.

But at least she had Otto to look forward to – and Giles Hornton.

Both terrified and intrigued her in equal measure. If it weren't for Trudy and her bewitching chutzpah, Liv wouldn't have the nerve to walk up the River Cottage driveway again. As it was, she was already girding her loins. She suspected that Trudy was far more involved with Giles than she let on. Finding out more, and being a little part of it, was the most exciting thing that had happened to Liv since she'd moved to the area.

With any luck, her in-laws could babysit while she spent as much time as possible with her new horse.

'I can't wait for Easter!' she told Martin now. 'Hurry home!'

Trudy was also describing her entertaining morning via email, camping up the details and distorting facts like mad to entertain her brother, Johnny.

Johnny was well aware of Giles's reputation so would appreciate the effect that Oddlode's notorious adulterer had rendered on sweet, vulnerable Liv. Also familiar with Ophelia Gently from Trudy's emails, Johnny would love the way she had swept in, velvet wraps at full sail, and claimed *droit de seigneur* via Basil. It was a classic Oddlode scene.

Buoyed up by new friendship and by a rare outing, Trudy took a brief break from her computer to splash a healthy measure of vodka into an icy pool of diet Coke and then, carefully not mentioning her home life at all, she reminded Johnny exactly what he was missing by selfishly not paying her a visit in so long. It was almost a year since he and his then new boyfriend Guy had crossed her threshold. On that last visit, Finn had been away, and they had all got very drunk in his absence, ending up having a stupid brother/sister row because Johnny had got dangerously near to exposing just how close Trudy was to the edge, probing her about her marriage and their failure to start a family, and asking whether there was some sort of problem. It was always like a red rag to a bull with Trudy, who guarded that part of her heart like a snarling sentinel at the gates of hell, unconsciously knowing that to reveal the truth would be to breach the dam on a boiling tidal wave of repressed emotion. Unable to glibly joke the topic away as she did with most friends and family, she had turned the tables and started to pick away at Johnny's own relationships, notable for their brevity and a long-established pattern of flirtatious betrayal on his part.

At this, her brother's gaydar had gone on to full sensitivity alert, thinking that she was somehow judging his sexual persuasion rather than his fidelity. The truth couldn't be more different, but the row had festered for weeks and normal service had only recently been restored, although not yet physical contact.

He had better come to see her soon, she thought distractedly as she described how wonderful the village was looking now that it was spring, how much better their mother had seemed last time they had spoken, how well the horses and dogs were, how brilliantly the house was coming along and how well work was going.

All her usual lies tumbling out. It was easier to write make-believe these days than to write music, or pen her ridiculous memoirs. And a silly, childish part of her, the part that still wanted to prove Johnny wrong, took a twisted pleasure in telling these easy, see-through lies.

Johnny had been right, she realised as the happy bubble she'd created popped and tears started almost without her noticing. She was claustrophobically trapped, longing for escape. He'd seen it all those months ago, before the dividing line between her fake and real lives became as impossible to cross as it was now. He'd seen her overwhelming urge to run long before she had, and now she was too deeply entrenched to seek help, too embittered and self-loathing and much, much too frightened. That's why she needed Liv. Because Liv's life seemed so refreshingly black and white, so simple: a bored wife looking for a fantasy life, which Trudy could provide in spades, only too happy to spoon out the flattery and conjecture and gossip and scandal to keep them both safely entertained. Trudy could live through Liv.

'Live through Liv,' she said aloud, giggling at the word-play. 'After all, Finns can't get any worse.' The punchline was a very bad, old joke which cheered her up all too briefly.

Trudy's capacity to pull herself together, to smile and laugh through her tears was legendary – dating back to early childhood, when she had quickly learned that if one laughed off a tumble or a fall it earned far more respect than ranting and wailing. Later, she had forced herself through a long battle with the crippling paralysis of stage-fright by harnessing her capacity to smile and pretend all was well. She could even fool herself, albeit briefly – increasingly briefly these days.

Only now did she mention Finn in her email to her brother, saying that he was well and that he would love to see Johnny and Guy, too.

In fact, she added – exaggerating as always – he sent his love and had earmarked some retro lots in forthcoming auctions for the couple to check out if they did come down.

Please come and see me, Johnny, Trudy pleaded silently as she signed off with a carefree 'lots of love and hugs and the usual'.

Hearing Finn arrive home, she immediately set about hiding her tears and her drink, now such a customary cover-up ritual that she did both without really thinking.

'Hi! You working?' he called as she crouched in the gloom of her study, praying he wouldn't come in.

'Yes – absolutely in full flow!' She hastily switched her computer to the programme she used for composing and switched on the spotlamp above the electronic keyboard.

'I'll leave you to it. Want a drink?'

'No, I'm fine! Need to keep a clear head.' She had brought the vodka bottle through with her, so had a good couple of hours' worth of anaesthetic.

Both their voices were brittle with the falsetto of forced cheer.

'Oh – before I forget!'

Trudy tensed as his voice came closer, but he remained in the hall.

'Next weekend – the family party. Can Phoney's in-laws stay in our bit?'

Trudy groaned silently. The Cottrell Easter knees-up. She had been pushing it deliberately out of her mind.

'Yeah, sure, whatever. As long as they don't mind the damp.'

'Our bit' referred to the wing of the Cottrells' sprawling, crumbling house that was kept for Finn and Trudy. It consisted of a few huge, formal rooms in the Abbey that Trudy was convinced were haunted. Finn's siblings all lived on the estate with the family; it was considered a divine right and, by flouting it, Trudy and Finn were rowing firmly against the tide. But Trudy had no desire to live so close to Finn's family and, thankfully, Finn saw no profit in renovating their section of the old house, which could never be sold on separately, so 'our bit' mouldered emptily for most of the year, occasionally being opened up for the Abbey's house guests to brave the cold, the damp and the ghosts.

As she listened to Finn's footsteps fade away, Trudy was shot through with the familiar twin pinches of guilt and relief.

Idling her way through some junk emails sent on to her by far-flung girlfriends as she put off the moment when she would have to put in an appearance to cook supper and cheerfully act her way through it, Trudy came across a link to a website.

'How to Have an Affair' it announced in triumphant flashing true-type.

As she scrolled through the bullet points of the guide, Trudy found herself cheering up. There was lots of material for Liv here. It even had a diet and exercise plan.

Repentant cramps squeezed her lungs and she quickly struck the website from her screen and returned to Outlook Express to reply to the old music college chum who had forwarded the link. As she wrote a ridiculously long email to a distant friend, full of hyperbole and false cheer, Finn waited on the opposite side of the house flicking from the sport to the motoring channels, stomach grumbling, sulkily hoping that he might get supper before midnight for once.

In front of him was his own personal gadgetry that linked him to the outside world and, in some ways, created just as false an impression as his wife. Far more technically adept and far more addicted to the latest gizmos than Trudy, Finn had Blackberries, iPods, palm-tops, mobile phones and laptops galore, all linked together and to the outside world via Bluetooth and WiFi. Like shiny black familiars to his warlock skills, they beeped and pinged and whirred.

He was using his laptop to check through all his gambling interests, irritated that none of the horses he had backed that day had won him any money. He was tempted to cheer himself up by taking a turn on the tables of his favourite virtual casino, but his credit was in question and he preferred to keep an eye on Trudy's email.

Unbeknown to Trudy, he had set up her computer so that he could use his laptop to access her internet and email folders directly through the wireless network, reading her personal files and checking up on her work in progress. This was, he justified, essential for her well-being. She had become dangerously idle lately, devoting less and less time to songwriting, losing direction.

At a time when the family firm was in crisis and progress on the restoration of Church Cottage had become hamstrung by technical issues, he needed her to pull her finger out more.

Over the years, Finn had tried his best to guide her into a more businesslike structure, but she resisted like a child being told to play by the rules when their imagination had rewritten them entirely. It frustrated him enormously, especially when it impacted upon their joint finances. She still preferred to 'talk' than to 'do', although thankfully she had long ago called a ceasefire on the tearful tantrums that had featured early in their marriage and now seemed satisfied with endless, time-wasting emails to friends and family.

Bored with her current email, which had moved on to long, fluffy recollections of the good old days, he checked both his own and then Trudy's Facebook pages, smarting as always that she had more than ten times the friends he did. Having used her password to edit it, he tweaked a couple of lines in her latest blog to make them read better, and noted that among the plethora of recent messages was one from a very attractive local point to point trainer who had met Trudy at the races a fortnight earlier and now had the cheek to ask her if she wanted to get together for a drink. Finn deleted it and blocked the sender.

Seriously hungry now, and growing rattier with his slatternly wife, he blocked a few more of her male 'friends' and removed the more attractive photographs from her gallery.

As his stomach growled loudly, he pressed a few buttons and angrily wiped her email from under her nose, hoping that she would think her computer was playing up again and abandon it in a tizzy. But his plan backfired as, after a furious squawk from her study, she just started to write the damned thing all over again.

Pheely, by contrast, sent just a short text to daughter Dilly that evening. *Have sold the horse and ass. Will take commission.*

She then settled by her own computer and spent an hour looking at internet dating sites.

Giles was about to stray again – not that he had ever exactly stayed faithful, and nor had he promised to. Since Basil's birth, however, he had at least shown a degree of discretion. And she was damned if she was going to stand back and watch it happen without creating a little distraction for herself. With Basil just four months old, Pheely had to steel herself to act so fast, but she was spurred on by a combination of wish-fulfilment and desperation, mixed with a hefty dose of jealousy that daughter Dilly, so long in the shadow of her gregarious mother, was currently madly in love and getting far too big a share of fun.

Already halfway through a bottle of her favourite white plonk, CWW, she idly replied to some adverts that appealed to her, concocting a few choice lines to describe herself, wrapped in the comforting hug of a lifetime's self-delusion. She was just describing herself as 'a Penelope Cruz lookalike with a wild and wanton streak' to a thirty-five year-old history lecturer from Gloucester when her mobile rang.

'You will never *guess* what happened to me today.' It was her close friend Pixie, calling from her bungalow beside the market gardens on the opposite side of the village.

'Aliens landed in your potato patch?'

'Worse! I took your advice and went to have a bit of a pampering at that salon in Maddington. The stylist persuaded me to get rid of the blue dye.'

'*No!*' Pheely feigned shock, although she had been secretly hoping Pixie would ditch the jokey statement blue hair colour for months.

'Oh *that's* not the awful thing – I was getting rather bored of it to be honest, and I know Sexton *hated* it.'

'All the more reason to keep it, surely?'

Pixie's long-term partner had recently left her for a very silly blonde.

'Not if I want him back, darling. No – *don't* argue. Anyway, there I was under a heat lamp with my head covered in ruddy foil like a Dalek, not a scrap of make-up on and every wrinkle positively shouting out in the ghastly halogens when who should come and sit beside me with a towel on her head?'

She left a suitably theatrical pause.

'Jacqui!'

Pheely balked. 'Bloody hell.'

Jacqui was the aforementioned very silly blonde.

'Exactly. Poor little me was positively *trapped* there with a metal arrangement on my head and twenty minutes left to cook. You'd have thought she'd have the grace to make an excuse herself, but oh no – she just got stuck into *Heat* magazine while her very grubby tidemark of roots was anointed with trollop blond and, shooting me sideways looks, she proceeded to tell the stylist that she and Sexton are going to Barbados after Easter with their kids. I am practically *bankrupt* here, my kids are bursting out of their school uniforms, and he is going to Barbados!'

'Poor you,' Pheely sighed, helping herself to more Cheap White

Wine and deciding that perhaps Giles's silly flirtations weren't so bad.

'At least,' Pixie consoled herself after ranting on for a few more minutes, 'I now look a million dollars. The hair is divine. Takes years off me.'

'What colour did you go in the end?'

Pixie let out a trademark gruff giggle. 'Full-scale trollop blond. If you can't beat 'em . . .'

'Good for you. Now that you look so hot, you should try internet dating. I am.'

'God, no!' Pixie snorted as though her friend had just suggested swimming with slugs. 'All those weirdos and perverts.'

'Suit yourself.' Pheely peered at James, forty-four, a businessman from Cheltenham who looked far from perverted. Clicking her mouse, she blew him a virtual kiss. 'Times have moved on, you know – there are millionaires and playboys all over the net, but it's your loss.'

'I'm a gardener, darling. I like to see the plant in the soil, check out its root structure and feel its foliage, not buy it over the internet.'

'Well, if you're aiming no higher than vegetable life forms . . .'

'I'll have you know I've had a lot of fun with vegetables over the years,' Pixie teased.

'Ugh – you really do need a date.'

'No, darling, I just need a jolly rogering – as do you. Forget all this looking for love in the cyberspace sea nonsense. Pop on your fishnets and we'll go hook a couple of tars for a night of fun.'

'Pixie, I am not interested in meaningless sex.'

'Of course you are. We all are. I'm certainly planning to take a dip soon. Why should Sexton get all the action?'

Pheely, who was far less sexually experienced than her much-married friend with the racy past, was secretly envious that Pixie seemed to find it all so effortless. Just attracting a man in the first place was a very hit-and-miss exercise for Pheely, whereas Pixie took it as read.

'With whom are you planning this dip?' she asked rather piously.

'The secret of really fun meaningless sex,' Pixie replied, 'is to be terribly, terribly discreet.'

'It sounds too sordid for words,' Pheely snapped, finding her friend's philosophy uncannily like Giles with his alley-cat morals and endlessly roving eye. 'You should aim higher. I want an *affaire de coeur* – a true love affair.'

'And I've already told you, I want Sexton back,' Pixie said stubbornly, 'if only to make him squirm. I'm not interested in a "love affair" with anybody else, just sex. Sexton's my main man, God damn him. Anyway, what's wrong with Giles? I thought you two were having a purple patch.'

'Only purple patches will be his bruises if he keeps flirting with Trudy Dew.'

'Trudy? That's old news – he's been after her for years, but it's just play-acting. Besides, Trudy's a good egg. She'd never take him off you.'

'Her new friend would.'

'Friend?'

'Tall, skinny thing with Bambi eyes and expensive taste in cashmere. Pretends to be all bashful and respectable, but you can tell she's inwardly burning with licentious desire.'

'Ah,' Pixie sighed, recognising Giles's weakness as described. 'Still, might never happen.'

'We both know it probably will, especially as she's just bought Otto and is keeping him on at River Cottage.'

'Doesn't Bambi have a big, protective stag of a husband?'

'Works overseas.'

'Poor sod. I only worked out in the fields and I couldn't see what was going on.' While Pixie was digging over winter beds by shortening day and curling up with good books by lengthening night, Jacqui's and Sexton's affair had been raging on unobserved.

'What should I do?' Pheely implored.

'Don't fight for him, darling. You know he hates that.'

'You said that about Sexton, and he's hardly come running back to you,' she pointed out brutally.

'He will.'

'Hmph. I must go – Basil's crying.' In fact Pheely was the one who was going to start crying and it irked her to reveal how much she cared about Giles and his philandering. Hanging up and leaning across the desk to plug her phone back into the charger, her heavy breasts pressed down on her computer keyboard and she inadvertently sent three more kisses and a cyber-wink to James the businessman.

Giles had better come to his senses soon, Pheely told herself firmly as she logged off and threw a purple silk scarf over the screen, with a crackle of sucked static.

Taking the remainder of her bottle of CWW through to the main body of the cottage, where her sculpture works-in-progress sat on stands beneath wet sacking and plastic like wintering shrubs, she pulled the covering from a bust of Giles that she had been idly playing with as a potential birthday present for him later that year and stuck a pen up each of his nostrils to cheer herself up. Not entirely satisfied, she drew up her working stool and reshaped his nose like Gene Hackman's, his eyebrows like Vincent Price's and his mouth like Cherie Blair's. Then she gave him two horns and pointy ears. Finally, she sliced the bust from the stand and threw it into the big, lidded drum in the corner where she kept waste clay to reuse or turn into slip.

Even though she had sworn that she wouldn't be the first to call, she gathered her phone back from the charger and dialled Giles's number. She wasn't going to fight for him, she reminded herself firmly. This was just a reconnaissance mission.

The inevitable jazz was playing in the background at River Cottage when he answered, although she was gratified not to hear Trudy Dew or her fawn-eyed little friend whispering sweet nothings over his shoulder.

'Darling!' He sounded surprisingly pleased to hear from her. 'How are you? How's our beautiful child?'

'I'm about to run out of battery. Can you come round?'

'D'you need recharging?' he chuckled, his voice husky with Scotch and desire.

Pheely's eyebrows shot up. Perhaps there was hope after all.

In the five minutes it took Giles to lock up his house, saunter along the lane and fight his way through Pheely's garden to the Lodge cottage, she managed to throw herself beneath the lukewarm shower, hurriedly douse herself in Dilly's posh Molton Brown shower gel and scrape a razor over her legs and armpits.

Still sticky with soap suds and scented body cream, she pulled on her sauciest underwear: a strapless purple bra from which her vast, milky boobs rose like soufflés from shallow ramekins, and matching French knickers that strained over her post-pregnancy belly with a worrying ripping sound, but seemed to remain intact. She then dragged on a long, stretchy green velvet dress that had fitted her body like a slinky evening glove before she was pregnant and now fitted more like one of O J Simpson's gloves. Walking with a curious wiggle because it practically bandaged her legs together, she lit a few candles and opened a fresh bottle of CWW.

They had only made love half a dozen times since Basil's birth, all of those occasions at River Cottage in a snatched few minutes while the baby was napping, and each time Pheely had been too self-conscious about her pregnancy weight and too tense in case the baby woke to enjoy it. At least here Basil stood a chance of staying asleep for longer; and she was always more relaxed on home turf, where she could set the scene.

She killed the lights just as Giles opened the door.

'Darling!' he squinted into the gloom.

'Come in – have a drink. Basil's asleep.' Pheely wiggled her way to the spot that she had deemed most flattering, with her back to the fire and one arm draped on the mantelpiece.

With only a couple of dim, guttering candles and the glow of the wood-burning stove to light his way across the cluttered room, Giles shinned himself several times on the furniture, tripped over the nappy pail, got prodded on the bottom by the clothes airer, banged his head on a beam and only just made it to the sofa intact. When he did, he found he was sitting on a huge pile of unironed laundry crammed up against Hamlet the Great Dane, who yawned widely and let out a volley of very acidic farts.

'This is – an unexpected treat.' He cast around in the darkness to locate Pheely in the shadow of the chimney stack. She was a mere murky outline against the wall, but it was a very enticing outline.

'Isn't it just?' she purred, deciding not to waste any time on preambles. Basil could wake at any moment and Giles needed claiming as her own. She would see off the competition with some mind-blowingly meaningless sex if that was what it took. Tonight was her golden opportunity to strike while the iron was hot and trump the opposition.

'Come here, you gorgeous creature.' He held out his arms, his white shirt providing a clear target point in the near darkness.

Needing no more invitation, Pheely let out a throaty, passionate growl of which Pixie would be proud and launched herself towards the sofa. Given that her thighs were trussed so tightly together by the velvet dress, making a wild leap seemed both practical and novel.

But as she landed rather more heavily than intended, there was an almighty ripping sound, followed by a muted wail from Giles and a louder howl from Hamlet. A split second later, the entire sofa toppled over backwards and crashed on several bags of discarded clay, piles of books, the clothes airer and the nappy pail. Like a ship capsizing against rocks, its human, dog and laundry contents were spilled unceremoniously on to the cluttered flagstone beach beyond the wreckage.

The smell of dirty nappy and wet clay was too overpowering for Giles's aftershave or the subtle tang of Molton Brown shower gel to take on. It hovered around Pheely and Giles like a stink bomb.

'Are you OK?' She cautiously flexed her toes and fingers in search of broken bones.

'Yes – yes, I think so – a bit winded. But I think you may have killed the dog.'

'No!' Pheely sat up groggily and found her bare bottom resting on the cold flagstones. Before she could register why, an equally cold and reassuringly wet nose was suddenly thrust against the back of her neck and Hamlet, very much alive, gave her a reassuring lick.

Giles groped his way on all fours towards the wall and located a light switch before turning back to survey the scene. 'I say!' He stared at Pheely in amazement. 'Your clothes have fallen off.'

Pheely looked down. He was right. During her leap, the straining velvet dress had burst its stitching on both shoulders and along the entire back seam so that it was now around her knees. Equally, her strapless bra had popped open, catapulted away and was now dangling from Hamlet's back like a pony saddle, and – most shamefully – her knickers had split apart along both side seams and were resting in a grotesque twist of overstretched satin on top of the squished clay 'bust' of Giles that had rolled from the kicked over scraps barrel.

'Oh, God.' Pheely covered her face with her hands in shame.

Giles, who would normally have been more sensitive to her plight, had consumed rather a lot of Scotch that night and found his fight with laughter an impossible one to win. Biting his lips, blinking back tears, he started to snort, then cough, then guffaw, until finally he let out an uproarious howl.

'Pheely, darling, you are such a scream,' he spluttered in between wails of mirth. 'Only you could undress in mid-air. Glorious! Like an exploding Zeppelin.'

Sitting in a pool of wet nappy water, naked from the waist up, Pheely wailed too, but not out of shared amusement; she singularly failed to see the funny side. She had never felt so unseductive in her life. Giles would never fancy her again, let alone stay faithful. She was so angry – with herself, with unsympathetic, heartless Giles, with Trudy Dew's stupid pop-eyed friend and with life in general – that she wanted to scream herself hoarse.

Hamlet, who liked nothing more than a little choral work with his friends, sat back on his haunches, raised his great head towards the ceiling and howled along with them both.

Only baby Basil, tucked tightly into his Moses basket in the tiny bedroom behind the chimney stack, failed to join in the group wailing. Sleeping soundly, oblivious of the deafening affray, he stayed conked out for another hour and a half – long after Pheely had sulkily locked herself in the bathroom and refused to let Giles in, long after he apologised through the door, long after she had told him to leave and never come back, long after she had called him every name under the sun in his absence while clearing up the mess from the upturned sofa – and long after she had collapsed back into that sofa to snivel into a succession of tissues feeling very, very sorry for herself.

Basil stayed asleep so long, in fact, that his parents could have enjoyed a very leisurely bout of meaningless sex without fear of interruption.

But Pheely could never have meaningless sex, especially not with Giles. He meant everything to her. And now she had pushed him even further away with her display of domestic squalor. She suspected that half the reason Giles was so hooked on married women was their innate mystique. The adulteress's lover rarely saw his mistress in the context of her home, her kids and her conjugal chores. But that was all he ever saw of Pheely these days. And today, she had etched the image forever in his mind by posing naked in a sea of baby poo.

Pixie was right. She couldn't fight for Giles. She had to let him come to her of his own free will. She was equally aware that she couldn't bear to just sit back and wait while he sniffed around for a new scent to distract him from the lingering pong of nappies. Unlike

Pixie's utter conviction that Sexton would return, Pheely had no real trust that Giles *would* ever come back to her. But she was determined that if he ever did, he wouldn't find her lounging against the mantelpiece in a too tight dress, scrubbed and perfumed and desperate to please. As she wasn't allowed to fight for him, *he* would have to fight for her.

Pheely would damn well find her love affair, whatever Pixie said about all the cruel, sex-crazed perverts out there in cyberspace. They couldn't be any more cruel, sex-crazed or perverted than the man she loved.

5

Getting Liv on board Otto was quite an undertaking. Had Trudy not felt so responsibile for the horse's purchase in the first place, she might have given up on the challenge. But she was convinced – rightly – that Liv's nerves could be overcome with patience and lots of positive back-up.

Like a little girl, Liv liked to 'play' horses without actually risking her neck, so she was more than happy to groom and feed Otto, to shop extensively and expensively for his wardrobe and to spend hours at his field getting to know him (especially if that also meant bumping into Giles). But riding him was a very frightening prospect.

Eager for distraction from the demon work, Trudy checked on her progress daily with texts and calls, encouraged and cajoled, offered to help, to keep her company on a ride, to lead her from the ground, but Liv maintained a strong resistance, repeatedly using Jasper and Lily as an excuse.

'I can't possibly leave the children,' she said.

'But surely they're at school during the day?'

'Easter hols,' Liv explained airily, 'Mungo House break up terribly early.' The cliquey little prep was renowned for having longer holidays than the Blair family.

'I thought you said your in-laws were coming to stay for Easter?'

'Not until next week.'

'We'll go out for a ride together then, shall we?'

'Hmm – yes. Maybe.'

Trudy named a day early in the week. Gentle, persistent and dogged, she managed to talk Liv out of every hollow excuse until the allotted hour when – miraculously – she found Otto tacked up in his expensive new German leatherware and ready to be mounted when she rode Tara along Giles's long drive.

White as a sheet and flapping around so much that a startled Otto

flinched and started to dance away from her at rein's length, Liv was
visibly shaking. 'I've given him a double dose of herbal calmer and
half a bottle of Rescue Remedy,' she confessed when Trudy came
within earshot.

'What about you?'

'I had the other half of the bottle.'

Liv would have used any excuse to avoid the inevitable moment
when she had to ride the horse that her nightmares had now turned
into a cross between a wild stallion and a rodeo bull, but she'd been
driven to take to the saddle by the disapproving, stalking presence
of her in-laws. Even risking her neck on Otto was infinitely preferable
to getting it in the neck from Gordon and Edna Wilson.

But still she faltered at the final hurdle.

'There's no mounting block,' she fretted. 'I can't get on without
one.'

'Use the fence.'

'I've tried. He won't stand still.

'In that case, let's get you on, shall we?' Realising she had to act
quickly to avoid another confidence catastrophe, Trudy jumped off
Tara and legged Liv aboard the surprised strawberry roan before
either could protest.

Once in the saddle staring down at Otto's pink ears for the first
time, Liv seemed to gather some much-needed wits about her.
Clutching tightly on to a fistful of mane with one hand and the
martingale neck strap with the other, she looked around her in
wonder, like a child in an aeroplane gazing rapturously out of the
window after the trauma of take-off.

'You must think I'm *such* a wuss. I do honestly get a lot braver
once I trust a horse.'

'Not at all – I'm just the same with new horses, ditto new
hairdressers, accountants and lovers.' Trudy hauled herself back
aboard Tara and led off at a smart walk.

'Would you mind if we just go once round the Green and back?'
Liv bleated as Otto, unridden for several weeks, snorted along in
Tara's slipstream, pogo-ing from one side of the drive to the other.

'Great idea. I can give you the low down on all your neighbours
as we ride past their houses. I love spying over garden fences from
horseback, don't you?'

Trudy could cram an awful lot of confessional chatter and gossip into twenty minutes. Liv so adored their little excursion that long before they passed the scary bollards outside the village school, she had almost forgotten her riding nerves. This was helped by the fact that the herbal calmer had rapidly turned Otto into a spaced out hippy who could barely focus on anything including the newspaper boards outside the Post Office stores flapping in the wind.

'Of course, you've met the Lubowskis who run the shop?' Trudy was chattering away happily. 'She rules him with a rod of iron. He's not even allowed to flirt with the female pensioners, poor sod. You watch next time you go in – he leaps a mile if an attractive woman smiles at him. I think she has him wired to electrodes behind that counter like a laboratory rat.'

'I know how he feels. I leap a mile if a good looking man smiles at me.' Liv surprised herself with her openness.

'Does Martin have you wired to electrodes, then?'

'No, of course not!' She stared down at Otto's streaked mane. 'In fact, I think he's rather flattered if another man finds me attractive. He likes me to dress sexily.' Her face coloured as she confided beyond her usual comfort zone, a strange effect that Trudy had on her.

'Ah – the man showing off his racy sports car. Look but don't touch.'

'Hmm, I guess.' Liv couldn't think of a suitably witty retort.

'Finn's sports car is always covered with mud and tarpaulins,' Trudy laughed. 'He'd love me to have a full wax polish, but until I do he keeps me parked in the garage and only uses me for short trips. My engine's so neglected that every time he starts me up, we're both almost asphyxiated with carbon monoxide fumes.'

Liv giggled. How cleverly Trudy phrased things.

'They say marriage is like a bird cage,' Trudy went on. 'Those on the outside are dying to get in for the seed and shelter but those trapped on the inside are equally desperate to get out.'

Liv was starting to suspect that things were not as rosy between her new friend and 'the loveliest man in the Cotswolds' as popular myth would have her believe. Trudy might be cheery and amusing, but there was a brittle quality to her quick-witted asides and anecdotes which struck Liv as familiar. It took one to know one.

'The awful thing is, I think I married for the wedding party first and the lifelong commitment second.' Trudy was laughing at herself now. 'All my friends got married within a very short space of time, which coincided with my dating Finn – there was one summer he and I spent every Saturday eating poached salmon in a marquee; his friends were at it too. Quite often we did two weddings in a day. Before long, it felt like going to a succession of dinner parties and being under an increasing obligation to issue return invitations. "They've had us to their wedding, darling, we really *must* have them to ours." Now half of them are divorced and it all seems silly.'

'I couldn't wait to get married,' Liv admitted. 'Martin was my first serious boyfriend.'

'You must have been very young?'

'Twenty-two – I was a late starter romantically. But we were married by the time I was twenty-four.'

'So the children came a bit later?'

'Six years.' She nodded. 'Martin would happily have waited even longer, but I was worried I'd lose my chance if I left it until after I was thirty. My mother was forty-five when she had me after my brother, who was Down's. They said she was mad to try for another. The statistics get so much worse – complications and disabilities and so forth. Mum always said I was a miracle.'

'She must be very proud of her grandchildren.'

Liv stared at her white-knuckled hands again. 'Mum passed on five years ago, just after Lily's fourth birthday. But you're right – she adored the children. I miss her.'

'I'm so sorry. How about your father?'

'Oh, Dad died when I was a teenager. That's the sad thing about having older parents, you lose them when you're still young. It's why I wanted to start earlier. I'd hate to be in my fifties or sixties looking after teenagers, wouldn't you?'

At which point Liv realised that Trudy, already well past thirty herself, might still be planning a family.

She hastily changed the subject. They'd both had similar childhoods, Trudy's in a hidden corner of the West Country, Liv's in the hinterlands of rural, coastal Kent. Although Trudy's upbringing was a great deal more Bohemian and academic, both women came from very secure, close families and had been brought up within idyllic time-trapped bubbles – Trudy in her Cornish commune, Liv on the marshes, her schoolteacher parents determined to bring her up far from the contamination of bright lights and popular culture.

Now that she was a mother herself, Liv well understood that urge.

She might once have longed for the excitement of the city, discos, boys and life in the fast lane. Yet for her own children, she aspired to recreate her childhood of sunny summer days at fêtes and gymkhanas, of cycling along quiet lanes and playing free-range around the safety of a small, friendly village. She wanted to don a gingham pinny and bake with them, make handicrafts, and plant a garden together. In truth, she often longed to be a child again herself, far from the responsibilities and trials of adult life, and without a time-travelling device, the closest she could come was to recreate the best of her childhood memories for Lily and Jasper alongside such modern indulgences as PlayStations and Cartoon Network, which she wished had existed when she was seven.

'A very wise man – my late father, in fact – once told me that the secret of achieving harmony in adulthood is to recognise that one never actually grows up at all.' Trudy turned along Goose Lane towards the river and raised an arm to thank a motorist who had slowed down for them. 'It's all a myth.'

'But we all get older,' Liv countered.

'More's the pity,' Trudy laughed. 'But we still keep the children we once were inside us. Some hide theirs better than others, but they're always there: like an invisible friend.'

Liv was amazed to find how true such a simple statement rang through her life. It had shocked her that so much about herself and Martin remained naively childlike – both the moments of pleasure and the furious times of discord. Martin could behave like a spoiled little boy, but she often felt like a lost little girl. And now the little girl had a wonderful new friend, she didn't feel quite so lost any more . . .

She was so engrossed in thought that she didn't notice they had turned into the River Cottage driveway until Bottom woke her from her stupor with an indignant bellow through the hedge.

'That was such fun!' she gasped in amazement, turning to Trudy with bright eyes and a soaring heart. 'Can we do it again tomorrow?

Riding away, Trudy shook her head with a wry smile and told herself off for banging on about the 'child inside'. She must have sounded like Kate Bush in search of new lyrics. Her line in clichés and truisms would make a whole new range of embroidered cushion mottos for her sister-in-law, Jemima, who specialised in naff interior gifts.

★

Liv returned home as high as if she had ridden round Badminton Horse Trials on cross-country day.

Shot through with adrenalin and beaming from ear to ear, she was completely impervious to her in-laws' carping complaints.

'The water was too cold for a morning bath.'

'That big Aga thing is just impossible to grill bacon with.'

'The children say they can wear what they like when they're on holiday and play computer games, which can't be right, can it?'

'You haven't arranged for the *Daily Express* to be delivered.'

'Those leather sofas play havoc with my sciatica.'

Letting this customary grousing wash over her, Liv scooped up her bored, fractious children from in front of the thousand piece jigsaw of a steam train on the Romney, Hythe and Dymchurch railway and challenged them to the console game of their choice upstairs in the playroom. Thrilled, nine-year-old Lily set up a snowboarding race, at which her mother was only fractionally less useless than her younger brother.

Shrieking delightedly, Jasper tucked under her arm, Liv fell off her board amid macabre splats of blood on snow, but had no fear of real pain, unlike that morning when climbing on to Otto.

Her children were perfect fusions of herself and Martin. Lily, nicknamed 'Savage', had her mother's fine frame, dark glossy mane and huge, limpid eyes, but was a tough tomboy with a stubborn streak, a mechanical mind and huge inner reserves of willpower. Although both children were shy, Lily could tough out most situations with deadpan pragmatism. By contrast, Jasper – two years his sister's junior and known to the family as 'Carrot' despite his father's mousy hair – was a sensitive soul who adored music and art. He was as easily intimidated and moved to tears as his mother, and had yet to recognize the amazing strength he held in his little lion cub heart, a lesson that had taken Liv herself almost forty years. Liv's heart went out to him; she knew how harshly life could bruise him. She felt that Lily, with her robust and practical ingenuity, would find it easier to crack the local under-tens network, even though she struggled more academically.

She didn't know how she would survive without her children, leaning up against her now, riotously urging on the snowboards to a thumping soundtrack while their grandparents pointedly listened to Melody Gold downstairs in the kitchen, sharing the *Express* that they had resentfully bought from the village shop. The love that she felt haemorrhaging out of her was something she had never counted upon before embarking on motherhood.

Her love for Martin was more structured and controlled, more subject to external forces; her love for her children was absolute: constant, reassuring and self-affirming.

Alone with them, she was at her most joyful and extrovert. She played exuberantly, unembarrassed to be imaginative and enthusiastic. Equally, she could be a tough disciplinarian, could arbitrate arguments and offer wise advice that she found impossible with her own peers.

With her children, Liv had a confidence that she rarely found with adults, yet Trudy came close to bringing it out of her, too. In the past few days, she had given Liv a taste of that sort of self-assured mutual relationship. Trudy simply refused to countenance Liv being intimidated by her – disarming, self-deprecating and flatteringly interested in her, she radiated such easy enthusiasm for the friendship that Liv was bowled over. She had never met a woman who made such a concerted and exhilarating effort to befriend her. What was even better, Trudy encouraged Liv to feel more relaxed and confident around Otto and, perhaps inadvertently, around sexy Giles too. It was an addictive combination.

Of course a part of her remained wildly envious of Trudy. She wanted to be more like her. She longed for that *joie de vivre*, that popular charm and fêted life. But she knew that she could keep this green-eyed ogre in check, because she knew she had two of the most prized assets that Trudy lacked. She had her children. Lily and Jasper were precious beyond words.

Racing them once more along the blood-splattered ice banks of what they assured her was a 'tube', she laughed aloud, snowboarding the adrenalin crest of new friendship, of riding her own horse, of being a trainee yummy mummy. As she started to view life through Trudy Dew's sparkling, mischievous and occasionally cynical thrill-seeking eyes, she saw her horizons widen dramatically.

Trudy's sparkling eyes were glued shut as she stood beneath the shower's blasting jets, rinsing shampoo foam from her head and singing Babooshka.

Like Liv, she was feeling surprisingly elated. She had forgotten how much camaraderie, idle banter – and riding darling Tara – lifted her spirits; that, and the knowledge that Finn was in Cirencester until at least eight o'clock that evening.

Medleying effortlessly through 'Wuthering Heights' and 'Hounds of Love' to embark upon 'Don't Give Up' – how *did* that middle eight go again? – she suddenly realised that the water had turned cold.

Typically, there were no towels on the bathroom rail and her dressing gown was missing from the hook on the back of the door.

Dripping everywhere, still trying to hum the missing heart of the Kate Bush, Peter Gabriel duet to satisfy her curiosity, she trailed wet footprints along the bare floorboards to the laundry cupboard. But then, just as she was poised to reach inside, she remembered the chord sequence with a victorious whoop.

Bounding nakedly downstairs pursued by dogs, she was gratefully reunited with her piano and the half-drunk, pre-shower vodka and Coke that she had abandoned on top of it. Sitting down on the stool in a shaft of dusty, setting sunlight, she played first the elusive middle eight, and then launched into the song from the beginning, singing along, wet curls sending out tiny rainbow rivulets as she threw back her head and melodically pleaded with herself not to give up.

Outside, shaded by the tall yews, Flipper Cottrell glanced in the direction of the last, bright needle of red sunlight reflecting off the dusty glass mullion arches of Church Cottage. Having just meandered along the drive after a long, flirtatious lunch with a pretty veterinary pharmaceuticals rep in the Duck Upstream, he stepped towards the porch and reached for the door knocker. At that moment, he spotted the naked songstress sitting at a grand piano in the dark, honeyed shadows of the house. Taking his hand from the wrought-iron fox head, he smiled and turned away.

Like Liv and like Trudy, he felt absurdly uplifted that day – and it wasn't just from the change in weather.

'Don't give up,' he reminded himself cheerfully as he vaulted the paddock gate and sauntered back through the fields towards the pub to sleep off his lunch in his car without the aid of one of his sister-in-law's sobering triple espressos.

6

Pixie Guinness surveyed the plots in her upper field anxiously, counting the serried ranks of freshly sown earth mounds that cushioned her future livelihood – beetroot, carrots, Swiss chard, summer cauliflower, lettuce, leeks, turnip, spring and pickling onions, radish and peas. Alongside these lay new experiments: salsify and scorzonera, which she knew the local gourmet housewives would try out, inspired by Hugh Fearnley-Whittingstall, *Masterchef* and occasional trips out to the Duck Upstream which was basking in the reflected glory of its first Michelin star.

It had been back-breaking work; four solid days of crouching and shuffling had left her stooped like an old crone. Now she was unsure how much of her new planting to cover with fleece – the beetroot were certain to bolt, for a start. Equally, a harsh night or two could halve her future yield. Sexton would know; he'd always had a natural feel for these things.

It hit her afresh, like a snake whipping down from a branch to sink its fangs into her neck – a shocking, bewildering, frightening snap of pain, so unfamiliar, yet certain and mortal: Sexton had gone. She was on her own.

Yet, typically, she mocked her self-pity as quickly as she registered the pain.

'Poor little Pixie,' she scoffed affectionately. 'All alone in the world.'

Practical, unerringly positive, fortified by life's hard knocks and unable to gaze at her navel for long, Pixie didn't dwell upon the pain. She simply registered it and moved on. Gathering her tools into her belt, she decided to fleece the veg crops the next day with the children's help. They could be blackmailed with a DVD hired from the village shop if necessary.

Pursued by her pack of dogs, she squelched back to her bungalow to take a quick shower. It was barely midday, yet it was as dark as dusk overhead.

The weather had been foul and unpredictable that spring. A cold, dry winter had been followed by an almost relentless deluge from late February through March, temperatures soaring above average and everything rushing to sprout at once with buds and blossom all bursting forth overnight like fireworks. The spring bulbs had given spectacular early colour, fat, juicy blooms dancing from every verge.

Then, quite unexpectedly, in early April, the temperature had plummeted once more, a week of harsh frost stripping blossom from every hedge and shrub, gale force winds ripping the colour clean out of the beds and verges, two days' thick snow covering anything that was left alive, freezing it tight with another bout of frost which turned the blanket to a crust of ice and finally washing away the corpses with a huge, wet thaw that swept melting snow into the already flooded water courses along with several inches more rain.

Such weather was a complete catastrophe for gardeners. A fortnight later, the colour was creeping back into some beds and verges, but lifeless, mud-brown gardens still abounded, making for hours of heavy work and damage limitation.

Pixie's small plant nursery and market garden had taken a massive blow. Equipped with vast tracts of poly-tunnels and heated glasshouses, she had possessed better equipment than most, but her manpower was severely depleted. Sexton had always done the work of two men. Tough, hardy and a grafter, Pixie had struggled on without back-up. Her children were either too surly or too young to help out much and her friends (whom she was loath to ask) were not a hardy bunch – Pheely had just had a baby; Anke was setting up a new business; cousin Jemima was far too pampered to get her hands dirty, and Diana had been largely incommunicado since rekindling her love affair with old flame Amos. The ageing allotment crowd, who adored Pixie and liked to lend a hand at their neighbouring market gardens in their spare time, were often more of a hindrance with their non-stop chatter, assortment of arthritic ailments and inability to master the computerised till in the shop. Alone most days, trying to work at three jobs at once, Pixie was shredded with exhaustion. Her cosy bungalow – once a love nest of relaxation and pleasure – brought little joy.

She stepped out of her plastic trousers and work boots at the door, hooked her sodden coat above the chest freezer, stepped over piles of boots and dog paraphernalia and opened the door to the small shower that Sexton had installed to wash away their working mud. Discarding the rest of her clothes beneath the tiny handbasin, she stepped into the creaking, plastic pod and started the jets.

While she washed – a practical, non-sensual process involving a lot of nail- and hand-scrubbing, a quick and vigorous scour through her recently highlighted hair with cheap shampoo that would make her stylist weep, and a perfunctory top and tail with a cracked Imperial Leather bar and a scratchy flannel – Pixie contemplated her afternoon.

As she stepped from the shower, she wrapped herself in a towel nicked from a smart hotel many years ago when she had frequented smart hotels, and padded through to the kitchen for much-needed hot tea and local weather reports on the radio. The news that the sun was going to try to break through that afternoon cheered her enormously.

Leaning over her breakfast peninsula, an eighties eyesore that she and Sexton had never got around to ripping out, she recalled her recent chat with Pheely about dating. Her friend would have her dancing around her Mulberry in a Cirencester nightspot giving any passing blood the glad eye.

It was far, far too early. She only wanted Sexton.

Yet she was aware that the cobwebs were already threatening to turn her into a black widow. It was high time she dipped her toe in again and enjoyed an erotically charged frisson. She was not a woman who liked to stand still in any aspect of her life, be it family, home, work or sex.

Pixie had never been a romantic. Her many relationships had toughened her up over the years, but she had never started from a dewy eyed perspective in the first place. The only daughter of an old-fashioned gentleman farmer, the youngest of five children, Pixie had looked to her older brothers for guidance in matters of the heart. Her mother, supportive, nurturing and practical as she was, had remained tight-lipped to the last, never sharing a single confidence abut such things even when Pixie's many affairs and subsequent marriages had all failed dismally. A woman who had dedicated her life to the Pony Club, English Springers, the Church and her family, in that order, Pixie's mother's fifty year marriage had seen her to the grave without a word of complaint. Had she been alive today, Pixie was certain that her only advice regarding Sexton would be, 'Buck up, could be worse. Go for a ride and you'll get over it in no time.'

Pixie's friendship with Pheely was a rarity. Tomboyish and stoic, it was unlike her to share emotional confidences, although she had always been open-hearted and straight-talking. But her friends were normally far more no-nonsense than Ophelia Gently; her friends were normally male.

Yet from the moment Pixie and Pheely had first met out dog-walking, when they had been forced to separate Hamlet from a hopeless gay shag with Pixie's oldest collie, Humpty, and had both ended up on their knees in tears of laughter, they had been like the sisters both had always longed to have. They sometimes scrapped, they bitched, they entertained stupid rivalries and they were chalk and cheese, but they adored one another.

Since Pixie's split with Sexton, however, relations had become more strained. She had once regarded her friend's messy little cottage as a bolthole to which to escape for a few hours' succour and wine, a comfortingly feminine enclave which she could take in small doses – like deliciously sweet Turkish Delight – safe in the knowledge that life was generally far more savoury and sensible. But since her life itself had become so traumatic, she was finding Pheely's neurosis too much to take in tandem. She craved the company of selfish, logical, matter-of-fact men.

In fact, Pheely had invited her to the Lodge cottage that afternoon to share wine and wisdom, but the prospect of a long diatribe about Giles and internet dating hardly filled Pixie with glee. She needed action, not analysis.

'Go for a ride,' she muttered now, imagining her mother at her side, patting her firmly on the shoulder with a liver-spotted hand.

'You know,' she replied to the imaginary ghost as she went to raid her wardrobe. 'I might just do that. Put my toe back in the stirrup, so to speak.' She pulled a pair of old breeches out of her chest of drawers and then slid open another drawer and studied her underwear. 'Dip my toe in the water and ride the white horses as surfers say.' She dismissed several trusty sports bras and tunnelled her way to silk and lace. 'Time to dip my toe in.'

Although a battered Land Rover with *Oddlode Organics* emblazoned on its side and dogs barking furiously from within was hardly James

Bond stuff, Rory Midwinter could be forgiven for thinking that Pussy Galore had rolled up at his rundown little riding centre high on the Lodes escarpment.

'Rory, darling – it's been too long!' Pixie gurgled as she walked towards him, arms outstretched.

Rory had long harboured a soft spot for older women, especially glamorous blonde ones.

Pixie Guinness, until recently a make-up free, mud-splattered and blue-haired Oddlode oddity whom he had only ever really espied clutching gardening equipment or vegetables, was today looking decidedly Honor Blackman in tight suede-bottomed breeches, long Dubarry boots and a fitted quilted jacket. The ensemble showed off her perfect size eight figure, unchanged in twenty years. Her blueberry eyes sparkled mischievously from her pretty, tanned face as she took his hands in hers and reached up to kiss him on the cheeks.

'Forgive me turning up unannounced, but Diana said ages ago that I should just swing by if I ever fancied a quick canter.'

She sounded like Pussy Galore, too, Rory realised: that laughter-laced voice, the creamy vowels, every sentence seemingly loaded with flirtation and double entendre. Part jolly hockey sticks head girl, part kinky mistress, it was wholly aphrodisiac. Normally he would curse his older sister for telling her friends that they could come and ride at the yard any time for free; it drove him mad that she treated his business as a freebie. But Pixie was different. She made him feel like Sean Connery on a mission.

'By all means.' He grinned, leading her towards the big American barn that housed his office and tack room alongside his classiest horses.

Before she'd arrived, Rory had been about to head sulkily into his cottage in search of Scotch to cheer – and warm – himself up. He was having an awful day thus far. His teenage yard helper, Faith, was on a college field trip leaving him with all the mucking out; two teaching clients had cancelled blaming the threatening weather – even though it was sunny now – and girlfriend Justine had just blown him out for the evening saying she had to work late. Justine, who had got a new job with local estate agents, Seatons, and whom Rory suspected harboured a bit of a crush on her hunky boss Lloyd, had been working far too many late nights recently.

'Isn't this marvellous?' Pixie was admiring the set up as she passed stalls of horseflesh. She paused by an open bay housing shavings, straw bales and fresh hay. 'I bet you've given the prettier girls a good roll in here in your time. Eh?'

Pixie couldn't help herself. She was always full of innuendo when let loose with an admiring young man and Rory's admiration was flatteringly, tongue-lollingly obvious. The dashing, floppy-haired wild man of local equestrian circles had always been a bit of a pushover by all accounts, despite his many female admirers. He was as soft as putty – as sweet and roguish as a hound puppy. Pixie knew his type.

'So you'd like to take a horse out?' He headed into the tack room, his cheeks high with colour.

'If that's OK?' Collecting a riding crop from a rack by the door she tested it out playfully against the palm of her hand. 'Something nice and easy. It's been a while . . .'

'You can give Magpie a whirl.' He reached for the saddle belonging to his trustiest black and white cob. 'She'll look after you.'

'Going to keep me company?'

Rory glanced at his watch. He didn't have a client for hours. How could he resist? She was twirling the crop now, framed in the doorway, pure Pussy Galore.

Wrapped up in an extra coat that Rory had lent her to keep out the chill of the harsh northerly wind, Pixie and her handsome young escort set off at a spanking trot along the track which led directly from the yard towards the old Gunning estate – for years out of bounds and unwelcoming, but recently rediscovered by horse riders and dog walkers.

Pixie chattered happily and easily about the dreadful weather playing havoc with the market gardens and nursery, about being desperately short staffed yet unable to afford more paid help, about her aching bones. She didn't complain – her manner was upbeat and self-mocking – she simply stated facts and made light of her woes with a hefty dash of humour.

Rory completely empathised. His business also existed on a shoestring with margins as narrow as a printer's bleed. Like her, he was completely weather-dependent, this year struggling with hoof infections, cracked heels, thick muddy gateways and lack of spring grass. And he too was a constant victim of aches, pains and a bad back.

'We must swap tips,' Pixie gurgled. 'I have lots of amazing lotions and potions I've picked up over the years – and I know the most fantastic back man near Stroud who can put you right with a click of his knuckles.'

In turn, he told her of his latest body blow, delivered that morning by a client who he had hoped would turn his fortunes around once and for all.

'I've been teaching this chap to ride for a few months – had to be very hush-hush because he's a bit of a celebrity and didn't want the press popping out of bushes taking photographs and frightening the horses.'

'Oh, who is it?'

Rory courteously but firmly deflected the question with some generously heavy hints. 'He lives very near here – has a big farm. Quite a local hero. You'd know him if you saw him.'

'I would?'

But he didn't give her any more clues.

'I like him. He's down to earth and a thoroughly nice guy. Plus he's a quick learner and fearless, with natural balance, which always helps. He's been coming here three or four times a week and recently he's started to bring his friends at weekends, too. He has these huge house parties where they all troop down from London to stay at the farm. It's all very rock and roll. They come here to ride off their hangovers, sometimes six or seven of them, almost every weekend. It's made a huge difference to the yard financially. Kept me afloat, to be honest.'

'I can imagine.' Pixie knew his sister Diana had left him in the lurch quite recently.

Rory's handsome sandy brows knitted together as he went on with the tale. 'My client wanted me to look out for a nice horse for him to hunt around the farm and do some jumping on, so I've been trying a few out – something with a bit of class, but a sensible head; a true schoolmaster. They're not easy to find.'

'Absolutely not,' agreed Pixie, who had been around horses most of her life and knew the pitfalls of trusting something that weighed half a ton, only five ounces of which was brain.

'It's been taking a long time and my client apparently got a bit impatient,' he sighed. 'What I found out this morning was that he's gone ahead without my help and bought a little ex-racehorse out of the sales. I have a few here which I produce for eventing and so he knows they can be good sorts. But as I'm sure you appreciate, there are as many bad as good and without knowing what you're looking for it's easy to cock up.'

'And he cocked up?'

'God, yes,' he groaned, rolling his eyes. 'His new purchase took off with him at home yesterday morning and ditched him big time.'

'Ouch,' Pixie winced. 'Thank goodness the ground's soft at the moment.'

'He fell in a concrete yard – up against a set of tractor harrows.'

'Jesus! Not so soft.'

Rory shook his head. 'The poor sod called me from hospital where they are about to operate on his femur. He has every type of bloody fracture you care to mention – complete, oblique, comminuted, spiral open fracture. He'll be lucky if he's walking again in six months, let alone riding.'

'Oh, the poor man.'

'Which on a thoroughly selfish level for me means no more private lessons three times a week, no more big rides out with his friends at weekends and no commission for finding him the sort of horse that would no more ditch him than Whitey here.' He patted the neck of his big grey thoroughbred, a proven event star and positive equine head of house among schoolmasters.

'How much are we talking?' Pixie cut to the chase.

'About a thousand pounds a month regular income with another couple of thousand for finding the right horse.'

'You can't afford to lose that, surely?'

'I just have.' He looked across at her with a rueful shrug.

'That's the equivalent of all my veggies floating away in another flood,' sympathised Pixie, thinking about her rows of delicate, newly planted seeds. 'I'd go under.'

'Quite.' Rory cleared his throat and then cast her his boyish smile to show he wasn't sulking. 'Still – never look a gift horse in the mouth, they say. I'm getting the rogue ex racehorse to sell on. I may just have lost my best client and his multitude of rich friends, but I've gained another neddie worth cat food money. You know the saying, "If wishes were horses, beggars would ride"? In my case, if horses were beggars, Rory would earn a hell of a lot more from sending them round the Circle Line for an hour rattling their feed bowls than a year in the Cotswolds.'

Pixie laughed.

'Hard to get a horse down the escalator at Paddington,' she mused.

'They don't like the downdraughts,' he agreed.

'There's an Arabian saying that the air of heaven is that which blows between a horse's ears.'

'I like that.'

On they chatted, barely noticing the hour that sped past as they completed a long loop around the outskirts of the famous Gunning woods, cantering steadily back through set-aside and along the headlands of ploughed fields before finding themselves back on Rory's land where they cooled off the horses at walk for the final leg to the yard.

'You are an absolute *darling*, letting me do that,' Pixie said gratefully as she jumped off, wincing as her cold feet hit the concrete below and sent shock waves up along her aching legs. She might be as fit as a flea, but riding used a completely different set of muscles from dog walking and gardening, and she knew she'd pay for this.

Her face was burning from her exertions and from the wind, her cheeks bright pink and her eyes smarting, although her teeth chattered.

'I knew you'd get cold,' Rory apologised, slinging Thermatex rugs over his horses' quarters and then finding a spare one to wrap round Pixie. 'There's a tiny slug of Scotch left in the hip flask on my desk through there – go and knock it back to warm up while I untack these two. I insist.'

'I shouldn't, or I'll be the unbridled one. Spirits absolutely do me in,' she protested, but she was too shivery to refuse.

Since Sexton had pushed off, she found the cold penetrated her bones far too quickly. As she located the hip flask, she fretted about her seedlings out in the chill wind. It felt as though there was going to be a late season frost tonight; she'd have to fleece the plots, after all. That meant getting back to work soon or she'd be doing it in the dark.

The wearying thought distracted her so much that she didn't notice Rory's 'tiny' slug was about a third of the flask until she had tipped her head right back and emptied most of it into her mouth.

Eyes bulging and watering, she held it there for a moment looking around desperately for somewhere to spit it out. There was no sink in sight.

Nose pinching and throat burning from the rough spirit, she closed her eyes and swallowed.

'Lord!' she shuddered as a furnace of heat immediately ignited inside her. It felt glorious, warmth running through her like a hot spring, from throat to chest to belly.

Pixie had never possessed a head for hard liquor and today, her body fuelled by just one slice of toast eaten six hours earlier, it acted like a petrol bomb in her system. Backed up by the adrenalin of a fast ride and attractive company, the Scotch blew off her cobwebs faster than a Dyson at full throttle.

'Wow!' With ill-advised recklessness, she took a second swig. This time the heat crackled along her veins to the most unexpected of places: fingers, toes, pert nipples and recently neglected pink bits.

She felt an overwhelming urge to high goal flirt for the first time in years. Sexton, hugely jealous in his heyday and broodingly possessive to the end, had always resented the slightest hint of flirtation on her part to such a degree that she'd got out of the habit, although up until his departure he had still accused her of shamelessly chatting up tradesmen, young men, old ladies and dogs at every opportunity. Such grateful, easy targets were her only solace.

She weaved back out of Rory's office in time to see him manfully carry two saddles into his tack room, followed at heel by his Jack Russell, Twitch.

Perfect! A young man and his dog . . .

'You must have to be frightfully strong in your line of work,' she admired, settling on an unopened shavings bale in the open bay opposite the tack room. 'Almost as strong as a gardener, I'll bet.'

The voice was spiked with honey and molasses, sweet and moreish. She could see from the way he paused for a beat as he put down the saddles that Rory felt a long finger of lust trail up and down his backbone.

'*Much* stronger than a gardener!' he scoffed, re-emerging and shouldering the door, as sunny as an Abyssinian cat stretched out on a hot Cotswold wall.

'Rubbish – I have shoulders like a body builder,' she boasted.

'I have thighs like steel girders.'

'I can imagine,' she gurgled. 'I went out with a jump jockey once – you could reshape diamonds in his legs.'

Rory raised a tawny eyebrow.

'Let me have a feel.' She beckoned him forwards.

He walked up to her and let her feel his thigh muscles through his breeches. They were as hard as metal, with glorious long, smooth planes of definition, and felt enticingly warm against her cool hands.

'Bloody hell – that *is* impressive.' She gazed up at him, berry eyes mischievous. 'I bet you look glorious stripped.'

It was a very Carry On moment, camped up beautifully but with a hefty enough dash of real spice to tempt them both away from collapsing into fits of giggles. To his credit, Rory held her gaze steadily, grey eyes matching her challenge.

When two super-fit people whose wayward partners are letting them down share too much idle conversation and adrenalin, it's a lethal cocktail. Pixie – whose many affairs had invariably started via winter field sports and fast riding – was too wise to let the moment pass without seizing the initiative. She had no doubt that Rory's past was as littered with deliciously unstable, stable-bed relationships and straw-scattered, stalled couplings in horse-stalls as her own. Event riders were notorious for testing the suspension in their horseboxes whenever they were competing away from home.

She knew Rory was a soft-hearted romantic, and she didn't want to hurt him or his relationship; but at this precise moment, she fancied him rotten. Pixie hadn't had a roll in the hay since the eighties. The nostalgia would be glorious.

He was staring down at her, as hypnotised as a Burmese python in the clutches of a snake charmer, at once potent with power and yet helplessly in a trance.

Slowly and deliberately, Pixie slid her hands up from his thighs to his waist and started to undo the buckle of his belt.

Rory's other eyebrow shot up and his handsome smile sprang into life at the same time as his eager cock – instantly as hard and muscular as his thighs.

Opening the buckle, zip and buttons to newfound treasure, Pixie was pleasantly surprised. Unlike Sexton, who was equipped like a priapic donkey, Rory was quite modestly hung, but what a beauty of smooth proportions and symmetry. His manhood was no veiny, knobbly, dark-hued craggy peak that required a small mountaineering team to scale. It was a sleek-sided, tawny-skinned pillar of perfectly honed weight and structure, like a Rosa Portogallo Estremoz marble column or a glossy sandstone obelisk.

'How absolutely beautiful,' she sighed, 'a flawless Calla lily spadix.'

'It's never been called that before.'

She slid her hands beneath his sweater to pull it over his head, taking in the sinewy chest, wide shoulders and the shadowy hint of a six pack across his abdomen. He was built just like Euan the jump jockey, she realised fondly. It would be fun to relive that fast, thoroughbred lovemaking.

'You really are quite perfect.' She discarded the sweater and reached up to run her fingers through the tousled blond hair that she'd just swept into a frenzy with her impatient undressing. 'Do you mind my ravishing you?'

'I consider it an honour.'

'Good. Because you must say if you think I'm going too fast,' she cooed in her most teasing, throaty voice as she ran her finger across his pectorals and around the little tattoo of a horseshoe on his right shoulder. 'The perils of being a bolter, you know.'

Standing in front of her with that glorious hard-on, stripped naked to the knees where his long boots still gleamed beneath his crumpled breeches, he knew he was at her mercy. Even walking a few steps would be impossible – running was out of the question. Not that he wanted to run anywhere right now . . .

Unbuttoning her layers of coats, gilets and shirt with swift dexterity, Pixie revealed a very jaunty black satin plunge bra covered with red poppies. Its wispy lack of support had given her hell when they were cantering, but the expression that crossed Rory's face now he saw it made the pain worthwhile. She had once hunted in nothing but lacy Janet Regers for just the same purpose.

She pulled an old striped Witney horse blanket across from one of the bales and, spreading it out behind her with an expert flick of the wrist along with the quilted Thermatex from her shoulders, sank back on them both to lean against the highest bank of straw and wriggle out of her breeches.

'Come on – let's be unbridled!'

Rory whooped and leaped aboard.

It was a gorgeous, giggly half hour of breathless, bouncing copulation. Pixie delighted in every carefree, irresponsible moment of it, especially Rory's grateful smile when he learned that she had a condom zipped away in her breeches pocket.

'My mother always used to send me out hacking with two pence in my pocket for an emergency,' she giggled as she helped him gild the lily spadix with shiny sheer rubber – Pussy Galore dressing her

Goldfinger. 'Nowadays one takes a mobile phone, GPS and a Durex Featherlite.'

She just hoped he didn't clock the sell-by date; the condom dated back to her pre-Sexton gallivanting days. Soon she was too distracted by the thrill of the chase to care.

The perfectly honed marble obelisk slid effortlessly and very pleasurably into her soft, welcoming depths. As Pixie had predicted, he went at a great gallop almost throughout, as fit, fast and enthusiastic as one of his horses let loose in open countryside. He rode every furlong flat-out, as he probably always had. They made a fantastic team for this one-off ride; she wanted it as fast, furious and straightforward as possible. In another lifetime, she would take him in hand and teach him a thousand precious tricks to pleasuring a woman, of becoming a true staying chaser with any number of clever tactics stored up to tackle his jumps without a peck or fall, and thrill connections at the finish. But that knowledge would be for another to bequeath to lovely Rory Midwinter, his beautiful body and his bountiful stamina. Pixie was determined to stay selfish and take her pleasure – her great pleasure – from him in its raw state.

He would be far too easy to fall for if one hung around, she realised, and incredibly hard to resist once he was hooked, too. It was vital for both their sakes that she walk away from this encounter without looking back.

The thought made her feel mouth-wateringly rash and immoral – and that rare streak of the old Pixie coursing through her fire-stoked veins also made her body light up like a Roman candle, shudder deliciously and climax with quick, easy abandon. It was nothing on the high-octane combustive scale to which Sexton was capable of driving her, but it was nonetheless heavenly in its self-contained perfection.

Rory followed hard on her heels to the quarry, fast and furious, rewarding her with the most wonderful husky, breathless, sweet-moaning finale during which he not only cried out her name twice but also told her he loved her. For that second she believed him.

They slumped back on the straw-flecked, scratchy blankets afterwards, staring up at the cobweb-laced hollow of broad-span barn roof overhead, its dusty skylights letting in the last of the fading sunlight as fast-moving clouds scudded past in a blue sky.

'That was quite the most perfect tonic to a truly dreary old week.' She stretched across and kissed him lightly on the lips for the first time. 'And I will adore you forever for it.'

He wiped the beads of sweat from his brow, colour high in his cheeks as his almond-shaped eyes blinked long lashes then slid their silver hearts across to study her. 'Can we do it again some time?'

She adored his eagerness, but shook her head with a regretful smile. 'I doubt that would be wise.'

'You call the shots,' he said quietly, tracing the line of her breastbone with his finger. 'But can I ask why not?'

'You have a very sweet girlfriend, I believe.' She picked strands of straw and hay from her glistening thighs. 'And I have a rather grisly and very jealous partner with whom I hope to reconcile differences before long. I'd call that a very, very long shot.' She let out that addictive, golden-syrup laugh. 'But I never say never again.'

Rory closed his eyes and smiled rapturously. He was lying back in the hay with Pussy Galore after the most fantastic, strings-free frolic imaginable. His childhood fantasies had come true.

'Just call me whenever you fancy another canter,' he sighed dreamily, reaching across to squeeze her hand.

The gesture was at once so childlike and so reassuring that Pixie was amazed to find a lump choking her throat.

'I will,' she croaked. 'I do like to keep my toe in.'

'Don't you mean your eye?'

'No, I mean my toe.' She grinned contentedly to herself, hoping Sexton was experiencing impotence problems and had a bout of crabs. This old girl hasn't lost her charms yet, she thought happily. He'll be back for more, the silly sod.

That evening, as she battled to pin fleece and plastic over her new veggie rows in a howling, ice-cold wind, Pixie remained warm inside, fuelled by the knowledge that she still had the power to attract young blood and enjoy its euphoric excesses.

Pheely might be sampling the dating wares of the World Wide Web with its rapid data transfer, digital photos, Skype calls and virtual sex, but Pixie knew that her pipe-opener today was more than equal to modern technology.

'You can't beat good old-fashioned meat and two veg,' she mused as she pinned plastic sheeting over her baby carrots.

★

In Upper Springlode, Rory was feigning delight at a surprise change of heart from Justine who had turned up straight from work, reeling with guilt that she had dared to take him for granted lately.

In truth, Justine had experienced a minor epiphany that day. She had suddenly realised that Rory was twice the man that her boss, Lloyd – whose new Latvian girlfriend, Svetlana, had come into the office that evening looking like a Wonderbra model – would ever be. He was better looking, classier, kinder to women and probably better in bed. Justine hadn't had much sexual experience, and sometimes wondered whether it wouldn't be nice if he would take more than thirty seconds to undress her and start pumping away, but she knew that Rory – who had infamously been to bed with all the prettiest girls in the county – was far higher-ranking in such matters, and so she always took his lead.

This evening, she was gratified that he went more slowly than usual, asking her lots of questions about her day, giving countless compliments, plying her with wine and suggesting that they curl up and watch a DVD as opposed to going straight to bed together as usual.

Thrilled, and feeling even guiltier about her misguided boss-crush, Justine curled up beside him on the sofa and shuddered happily as the opening credits of *Cold Mountain* came on screen. She'd bought him the special boxed edition weeks ago and he'd shown no interest until now.

But she had barely laid eyes on Jude Law (who reminded her of Rory) before the snoring started up noisily in her ear.

Tucking her lover into a more comfortable position in her armpit, Justine watched dewy-eyed as Nicole Kidman elicited the sort of lifelong, life force love from Jude that she had always craved from easy-going, boozy Rory.

She knew that she would never achieve anything close to it. He was still playing ladies man Alfie whenever they were together. He knew no other role. As if in acknowledgment, his sleeping hand now rested on her right breast, jolting occasionally against her nipple in unconscious spasms.

'Little pixie,' he muttered in his sleep. 'Unbridle pixie. Might bolt. Fancy a canter.'

Justine felt her heart soften. He was working too hard, trying to run the yard single-handedly, teaching endless kiddie lessons that he loathed.

She pressed her lips to his sleeping head now, drew in a shaky breath and consoled herself that, even if she couldn't be his Nicole Kidman, at least she wasn't the weird little Renée Zellweger character, Ruby. That was a part reserved wholly for teenaged Faith Brakespear who stalked Rory with frightening adoration.

'You watch out for those pixies,' she smiled as she stroked his hair and watched Nicole proffering lemonade to a thirsty Jude. 'They'll trick you with their magic.'

From beneath her armpit, Rory snapped open a wary eye, rolled it around for a moment, established that it was a false alarm, and lapsed gratefully back into sleep.

7

Trudy looked at the notepad into which she was scribbling ideas for her autobiography. Already written down were the headings suggested by her publisher – 'Childhood', 'First Love', 'Career', 'Sex, Drugs and Rock 'n' Roll'. 'Marriage and Happy Ever After'. The final heading blurred in front of her. She wiped her eyes angrily and uncapped her pen with her teeth, adding 'Adultery', as she reached for her vodka and Coke. Drinking before midday. Her mother would have a fit.

Trudy glanced at the 'Childhood' heading, thinking guiltily about her mother in the Dorset cottage where she and Trudy's retired stepfather Jim tended a garden perfect for grandchildren and had redecorated one of the spare rooms so that it was ideal for youngsters. Johnny was hardly likely to provide those longed-for grandchildren. He and Guy lived in a flat in Battersea crammed with delicate *objets d'art*. Their child was a Bengal cat called George, whose sister Mildred now lived with Trudy because the siblings had fought so much that they had to be separated – rather like Trudy and Johnny as children; rather like all her nieces and nephews by marriage.

She took another swig of her drink at the prospect of the Cottrell grandchildren squabbling later.

They were due at the in-laws by midday for the annual Easter lunch, an occasion Trudy always dreaded. The whole clan would be gathered by mother hen Dibs – in-fighting, bragging, bitching, marauding – and that was just the adults. There would be children everywhere, screaming, bratting and scrapping their way through the traditional Abbey Easter Egg Hunt. Patriarch Piggy would zealously embrace his duty of orchestrating this mission in military fashion, along with a host of other games, and would no doubt later drunkenly demand that Trudy sing for her supper, like a performing seal.

The word 'Career' glared up at her from the pad. Songstress, sometime pop star turned ballad writer beloved of producers. It had been a fabulous career, especially in the early carefree days, blessed with good luck and hard work. But she hated singing for her supper these days. One reason she had given up her chart-topping career was because of the crippling self-consciousness that made singing in public torture. Another was that she hadn't written a decent song for years, and the old ones made her cry too much to perform them; they reminded her that she'd been bloody talented once.

She lit a cigarette, her last drug besides alcohol to accompany the sex and rock 'n' roll. Except she no longer had sex very often, and rocking and rolling involved hauling rocks out of the overgrown garden and rolling the pitted paddocks in which she kept her horses. That was because she was living her Happy Ever After, married to 'the loveliest man in the Cotswolds'.

She found the notion of writing an autobiography faintly ludicrous; after all she had been out of the limelight for well over a decade. Yet her agent was adamant that there was a market. When she'd approached him to see if she could generate some more income – Finn was overspending as usual, and January's tax bill had taken her dangerously overdrawn – it was all he would talk about.

'"Where are they now?" is all the rage, darling,' he had insisted. 'Besides which, if you name names, we're guaranteed a media furore even today. We both know *who* I'm talking about here.'

Trudy's reaction had been far from positive, especially at the prospect of revisiting one of the most painful episodes of her life. But with no other sources of income on the horizon, she let herself be talked into it, promising to do her best to satisfy the public thirst for erstwhile stars to humiliate themselves in the media spotlight for another fifteen minutes.

A publishing deal had been struck and, while the advance was modest, she was too cash-strapped to refuse. She had yet to even begin to dish the dirt on her past, however, and one ex-lover in particular – the one name guaranteed to create a bidding war for serialisation rights – was already haunting her dreams with shame and fear of kiss-and-telling after all these years. Finn, who loathed her talking about him publicly, was extremely edgy about the idea. If Trudy hadn't pointed out with uncharacteristic anger that it was his fault they needed this money in the first place, she suspected he would have banned her from writing a thing. She avoided confrontation as best she could, but when forced together he had been more bullying than ever recently, wound up by their continual lack of money.

She drained her drink, determined not to cry. She didn't want to look foul for the Cottrell Easter torture. It was going to be tough enough without pretending she had conjunctivitis again, or wearing dark glasses which led her sister-in-law Phoney to accuse her of being 'starry'.

On cue, the loveliest man in the Cotswolds arrived home in a hurry, almost flattening two of their bantam hens which were pecking thoughtfully on the driveway. His new Range Rover had a freshly waxed gleam; he must have run it through the car wash in his parents' honour, and because he wanted to one-up elder brother Piers who never washed his inferior, older Discovery.

'Aren't you ready yet? We're going to be late. Come upstairs and we'll change together. I can have a quick grope – heugh heugh.'

Lately, he'd been fashioning a 'dirty old man' act, based on a very laddish comedy sketch show he liked on BBC3. It involved a gravelly voice and gurning face.

She shuddered. 'I am ready. This *is* what I'm wearing.'

He wavered at the foot of the stairs, eyes narrowing as they assessed her, that masked Cottrell face giving nothing away. His pretty pop star accessory – once so fashionable and must-have like all his gadgets and snazzy suits – now scruffy and dysfunctional.

She was wearing her usual uniform of old jeans, a big polo-necked sweater and cowboy boots, streaky blond hair curled up in a crocodile clip at the back of her head. It was what she wore every day. It was all she ever wore.

'Tru – it's my *parents*,' he goaded, with an attempt at a half laugh, deliberately keeping his tone light to avoid a scene.

'So? Your mother always says I suit brown.'

'You look as though you're about to muck out the chickens.'

'I did muck out the chickens. It's OK, I have drenched myself in the Versace Blonde you gave me for Christmas, and I'm wearing eye make-up – look.' She batted her lashes at him, almost gluing them together because she had gone a bit wild with an old, clogged mascara wand.

'Have you been drinking?' He cast a judgmental eye on the tumbler sitting amid the ring-marks on the piano top in front of her.

'Just Coke.' She picked up the glass and headed towards the fridge. 'Hurry up, darling. Don't want to be late.'

Listening to him thudding around on the bare floorboards overhead, Trudy pressed her forehead to the fridge door and sighed, eyes crossing as she tried to read the Post-it note in front of her nose.

'GFFA'. She'd put it there the day she'd gone with Liv to look at the Gentlys' horse, and later seen the website advising would-be philanderers. It stood for Get Fit For Adultery. When Finn had asked her about it, she'd told him that it stood for Go Find Food Alternative. Accustomed to her many attempts at dieting, he had simply raised a derisive eyebrow and told her exercise was far better than starvation, pointedly reminding her that the gym membership he'd bought her for her last birthday was still in effect.

Trudy's diets never worked. In her heart, she knew why. She was a misery eater. The secret of losing weight wasn't to remove the food, it was to remove the misery.

She wasn't even really overweight, although Finn – who had initially fallen for the stick-thin Trudy he'd first met when she was reeling around with a broken heart, too suicidal to eat at all – preferred his women, like his own rather bland diet, completely fat-free. A rebellious part of her longed to tell him to get stuffed while she happily stuffed her face – but she secretly agreed with him on this one point. She longed to be slim again; to look at her reflection and recognise herself.

At the Auctioneer's Ball just a month earlier, she distinctly remembered looking in the mirror and seeing a curvy, sensual sex siren smouldering back. Now, if she looked in the mirror she saw a hideous, distorted porpoise with her familiar hazel eyes peeping out of its face. Her weight hardly yo-yoed, but her self-esteem swung through polar extremes. Without knowing where to start to remove the cause of the misery eating, she was left with the old habit of removing the food. Diets might not work, but they were a habit that she clung to – like smoking and drinking too much.

She hadn't made much progress in the GFFA plan, although today she had cut out breakfast in favour of a little liquid refreshment, which felt like skipping a meal.

Nor had she made much progress in her fitness campaign. A week of driving rain had put paid to plans to ride out again with Liv. Feeling glum and antisocial, she had hidden away in her study instead, making notes about her childhood that had made her cry.

Today, she knew she had to put on her Happy, Bubbly Trudy Show for Finn's family and the prospect terrified her, although she didn't doubt that she could pull out all the charisma stops and smile her way through the occasion as she had so often in the past.

She slugged some vodka from the freezer straight into the lip of a half full can of Coke and took it to the window to look out at her horses. Still wearing their woolly winter coats with Billy Goat Gruff beards and muddy legwarmers, the mares didn't look like the glamorous duo with whom she had posed for publicity shots in her heyday. Kept in a smart London livery then, they had been polished to within an inch of their lives. Tara, the rangy liver chestnut with the golden highlights in her mane, had shone like a freshly minted penny coin when Trudy had posed side-saddle on her in a field full of poppies, wearing nothing but a sea green bikini and long chiffon shawl. And Arty's white coat had been painted with love-hearts and flowers for an album cover, while Trudy had sat bareback on her, naked body painted with matching whimsies – a shot later deemed too 'hot' for the final version. The body artist had told her she had the best breasts she had ever had the pleasure to decorate.

Looking down at her drooping brown knitted bosom now, Trudy took a determined swig of Coke. Today was going to be hell.

Piers Cottrell was, as usual, doing three things at once. Very few men could multi-task like Piers, but he had long perfected the art of trading horses and networking while out hunting, flirting with a pretty dealer and glancing through the *Telegraph* while hosting an auction or driving, talking on his mobile and studying a map simultaneously. This morning, he was texting a mate in Ireland with one hand, pleasuring his wife with the other, and keeping an ear on the *Archers* omnibus at the same time.

The one task Piers could not juggle enjoyably alongside anything was working for his father's company. And, while today was a family gathering that had been going on since his childhood, this year the business was in such dire straits that even the deliberately distanced Piggy Cottrell – patriarch and autocrat turned second childhood retiree – would be unable to avoid mentioning it. Getting brothers Piers and Finn together under one roof was a rarity these days, and certainly hadn't happened at Cottrells' head office in Morrell on the Moor for several weeks, although the two men were technically both heading the company since their father's retirement eighteen months earlier. Both had interests elsewhere: Piers in the training, hunting and dealing of horses, and Finn in property development. Sister Phoney, a recent recruit to the office, working part time since her children had started at school, was more aware of the flailing fortunes of Cottrells' Auctioneers, Chartered Surveyors and Land Agents than either of her brothers.

The oldest of Piggy's children, Piers felt a degree of guilt and consequently a reluctance to be cornered by his father that day, yet not enough to take the problem seriously. The company had been through similarly bad patches before and it had always survived. After all, what did they pay a host of high-salaried staff and consultants for if not to see them through such crises?

Piers' wife, Jemima, perhaps aware of his distraction, yawned and wriggled away from his ministrations. 'It's not really going anywhere, is it, darling? And we are going to be awfully late if we don't get dressed soon. Poor Nuala has been trying to keep a lid on the children since breakfast.'

Piers accepted this with a reluctant sigh and, kissing his wife's pink nipples, rolled from the bed and headed for the bathroom.

Jemima reached back to retrieve her gold watch from the bedside table and, seeing that Piers had left his phone there, quickly scrolled through his recent texts to make sure there was nothing suspicious. It did no harm to check.

Married for twenty years, most of those reasonably happily, Jemima was under no illusion that she had her husband's undivided attention these days; just as he no longer fully held hers. They rubbed along reasonably well, seldom argued and were a good team parentally and socially, but their interest in one another had dwindled to a vague familiarity. She herself had enjoyed a very refreshing series of short affairs a few years earlier, and was in no doubt that Piers occasionally sought distraction elsewhere, although she hated it when he lazily did so under her nose, developing inappropriate interest in the nannies or grooms – a succession of pretty young things the family brought over from Ireland.

Thankfully, Nuala, who currently looked after the Cottrells' two adopted Chinese children, was carrying two or three stones extra weight and a large amount of excess facial hair, so Jemima had enjoyed a brief resurgence of Piers' sexual affections of late. This occasional interest made little impact on her libido, alas, but it did make her feel more secure.

However, she remained on alert, and was certain that – despite there being no classic signs of adultery – something was not right. There had been a few too many hushed phone-calls and hang-ups recently, although each time Jemima had managed to 1471 or 'recall' them, they had revealed the numbers of family members, most often Finn. Piers, typically taciturn, refused to admit that anything was awry, but Jemima planned to quiz Trudy about it later that day.

Trudy, with her blowsy good looks and her earthy self-assurance, so alienated the more prudish, conventional Jemima that something of an unspoken rivalry now existed between them. At the heart of this polite, frosty rift lay both women's deep-rooted insecurities, natural by-products of marrying into a family like the Cottrells. To Trudy, Jemima was uptight and disapproving. To Jemima, Trudy – who eight years earlier had snatched Finn from the arms of his childhood sweetheart and fiancée (and Jemima's dear friend), Hils – was not to be trusted. As well as an incomprehensible sex appeal, Trudy possessed that most suspicious of all assets: a career.

Despite disapproving of married women working, Jemima had recently made an almost accidental foray into a little part-time pin money enterprise, with a surprising degree of success, thanks to amazing contacts and natural aptitude. A genteel course in embroidery, started as a worthy recreation to fill the hours when the children were at school, had quickly become an obsession as she had crafted embroidered gifts for friends and family, soon finding her witty phrases stitched on to anything from sweatshirts to handbags to bell pulls in great demand. This had flourished into a profitable sideline as she designed very exclusive cushions, doorstops, curtain tie-backs and throws with bon mots sewn into them – as varied as love poetry, pro-hunting slogans and naughty puns. Within weeks, her order book had been so crammed that she was forced to employ staff.

A year on and she no longer made any of the items herself, employing instead a small army of local women to manufacture and then sell these exclusive interior gifts and accessories through craft fairs, rural sporting events and chichi local boutiques. Perhaps cruelly, she called her workers 'DIVS' because they were all divorcees from the surrounding villages.

Mention the word 'retail' to Jemima and she would recoil in horror, but she was secretly rather proud of her achievements and therefore doubly offended that, a lone voice of dissent among her husband's supportive family, Trudy seemed to treat the whole thing as a huge joke. She clearly had no sense of interior style because she had confessed that the embroidered pieces weren't really her 'thing'. The cushions which Jemima had given her for Christmas with quotes from her song lyrics stitched on to pretty Laura Ashley fabric had soon ended up on the dogs' sofas at Church Cottage, although, when confronted, Trudy claimed that everything ended up on the dogs' sofas. Last time Jemima had popped in, they had been conspicuously moved to the window seat in the study, where they'd been mauled and ripped to shreds by Trudy's neurotic cat.

Although Trudy always seemed willing to gloss over their chalk and cheese differences with an easy charm, Jemima still couldn't trust or like her. A part of her resented Trudy's slatternly self-confidence. She would never dare let herself go like that – not with Piers to keep in check. Yet Trudy still had a baffling hold over men, not least among them her husband; Finn seemingly doted on her for all her scruffy excesses.

As she dressed for the big lunch, she studied her small, oval face with its big, baby blue eyes and neat blond Eton crop, and congratulated herself on still being the best looking woman in the Cottrell family, barring Piers' little sister Nell, who at twenty-three was practically a generation removed.

The thought of Nell made Jemima stall, eyes narrowing. Another thing that made her jumpy was the fact that Nell, like twin brother Flipper, was close to Trudy. And Nell was pregnant, purportedly expecting the first true Cottrell blood grandchild. Only Jemima knew differently . . .

It was important for Jemima to feel that she had an edge. For, while looks played an important part in Cottrell family standards, it was breeding that really counted for everything: horse-breeding, game-rearing, animal husbandry and, above all, well-branched family trees. Progeny was destiny. Despite being incredibly well bred, Jemima had never been able to produce children herself. In a family like the Cottrells, that was a huge failing.

Ironically, this failing was one of the few things that Jemima and Trudy had in common, Jemima's own precious brace of children having been adopted as babies from China. And, despite having the big-breasted, wide-hipped hourglass Nigella Lawson figure of a home-baking earth mother, Trudy had yet to bear a child. Jemima was unsure whether Trudy and Finn had simply decided against children or fallen foul of the Cottrell infertility curse – the sisters-in-law weren't close enough to discuss it, and Cottrell men would never dream of talking about such things. Over the decade of her tenure in the family, Trudy had shown no obvious signs of broodiness, although she did appear to have adopted the twins as substitute children. Since their teens, Flipper and Nell had idolised her, treating her as confidante and counsel – part fairy godmother, part big sister, and part wild role model – and sought her out above anybody else in the family.

Both twins had lived away from home in latter years, leaving Trudy further out in the cold, but their reappearance on the scene in recent months had drawn Finn's renegade wife back in and now threatened Jemima's status as favourite imported daughter and family backbone.

The closeness between her sisters-in-law bothered her, particularly now that Nell was pregnant. The younger generation were rising up to join the older married ones like Piers, Finn and Phoney; and Trudy held the key to spanning the two camps. It was therefore very important that Jemima not only kept Piers in check, but also that she allied herself more closely to Trudy.

Not that Jemima was particularly concerned if Piers had an affair for sexual gratification. But if, God forbid, he were ever to produce a natural heir, she wasn't sure she'd survive the fallout.

That was why she policed him so closely and carefully, why she strove to remain slim and desirable and beautiful and why she still laid out all his clothes on the bed now, ready to wear. In twenty years' marriage, Piers Cottrell had not once needed to get a pair of underpants out of a drawer for himself. Just like his mother, Dibs, Jemima knew how to look after a Cottrell man.

Whatever crisis he was facing now, she would take no blame for it.

Resolve hardening, she smothered herself in her favourite Chanel – adding a quick, possessive squirt to Piers' boxers for good measure.

Trudy, meanwhile, had never selected a pair of pants for her husband in their eight years together, although as they drove up the winding, hilly lane from Oddlode to Fox Oddfield, she did begin to wonder if somebody had put itching powder on those designer jockeys of his as he fidgeted and wriggled in the big leather passenger's seat beside her.

'Will you stop doing that?' she snapped.

'I wish you hadn't insisted on driving,' he winced as she clipped the verges with the Range Rover's wings. 'This car takes lot more handling than yours.'

'You know I get sick when you drive me in this thing,' she pointed out, squinting into the sun and wondering vaguely whether she was over the limit as she groped around in the dashboard cubbies for some dark glasses.

'Watch out!' Finn grabbed the wheel and wrenched it left just in time to avoid driving headlong into an oncoming car.

'I saw that coming!' she snarled.

'You weren't even looking at the road.'

'I was. Just butt out and play with your air con or something.'

'Don't be childish.'

'Fuck off.'

'And please don't swear. We're about to spend the day with my family.'

'I never swear in front of your family, you know that.' Although God knows, I have provocation, she added silently.

'Why are you in such a foul mood?'

'Oh, you know. Hormones, period due, the usual . . .' she muttered, barely disguising the sarcasm behind the lie, knowing that he would be happy to accept her explanation. Finn had always seen women as strange, exotic aliens ruled by chemical imbalances and faulty wiring.

There was no point attempting to explain that she found his family's big gatherings increasingly traumatic, that the children upset her, his mother's pitying stares, his father's jollying flirtation and his siblings' superiority set her teeth on edge, that she felt bereft whenever they all gathered, and she didn't really know why – just that she did, that it hurt and that Finn's embarrassed, angry awareness of her unhappiness simply compounded it.

There was no point in ripping away the mask of lies, excuses and platitudes. Because the many, many times in the past that she had tried to explain, groping her way towards an understanding that even she had yet to fully grasp, she had never succeeded. Finn would look at her as if she was completely mad. He would get angry and shout. He would then withdraw and sulk and punish her with festering silence. Making any attempt to go over that old ground again, minutes away from his parents' home, was destined to fail.

Reaching deep inside herself for her cheery, happy-go-lucky mask, she mustered a smile and stuck it firmly on her face.

'Let's not scrap,' she said cheerfully, practising her gurgling, joyful voice that would ask after health, hobbies and hunting as she chatted to each of the Cottrells in turn. 'I will be a happy Easter bunny, I promise.'

As always, Trudy fell for her own façade, albeit briefly, the fake dopamine taking hold. Driving on towards the Abbey she almost started feeling enthusiastic, although that was probably at the prospect of another drink.

When Trudy had married into the Cottrells, she had known very little about marriage as an institution, or the family with whom she had just signed a lifelong pact. All she had seen was what appeared to be a safety net after her ungainly trip along a tightrope in her twenties, leading her away from the stage-struck limelight that she loathed and out through a trapdoor to freedom. Little did she know that 'trap' was the operative word.

Her own parents had never married; quite a daring rebellion in their day. They had met on the hippy trail, eventually settling to bring up children amid a small community of artists and free thinkers in the West Country. Raised free-range in this remote corner of Cornwall, Trudy and her brother had evolved with a curious mixture of bohemian sassiness and naivety. Home educated until they were in their teens, far from television, computers and mainstream culture, encouraged to be creative, expressive and empathetic, the siblings had found the wider world an alien place. Trudy still did, despite her apparent early success and the image of streetwise street-cred that had been foisted upon her. She'd met Finn on the rebound. Adoring, old-fashioned and attentive, he had romanced her like no other. The prospect of escaping London into the safe, cosseted warmth of a strong family community again had seemed irresistible.

But the Cottrells, it transpired, shared nothing with the close knit, laid-back egalitarian society in which Trudy had been raised. The snobbish world of the upper-middle-class country set was almost as suffocating as the fast, furious competition of London's media-ville. And married life was just as political, dominated by the most demanding ego – in their case Finn's.

At first, Trudy had assumed that he was the expert on marriage – he had grown up with shining examples throughout his life, after all. She had been happy to play follow-my-leader, to allow him to set the pace and the rules, to take almost childish delight in 'playing house'. Now their play-acting had become a habit and – like all Trudy's addictions she clung on to it like a prop. Even her surly, rebellious side was an act, hiding the true hurt and confusion that raged ever-closer to the surface.

Their first nicknames for one another had been Roo and Kanga, one living in the other's pouch. Nowadays Trudy saw herself as Eeyore the grumpy malcontent, and Finn was Owl, a pompous character pretending to be far wiser than he was. They were still play-acting children trapped in a fictional world.

Trudy hid behind half-truths and assumptions in order to survive. Now she was happy to let Finn to believe that her current black mood was a result of working too many all-nighters, premenstrual stress and general dieting grumpiness. It spared a scene and Trudy trod a fine line between registering her constant frustration and actually voicing her true dissatisfaction.

Marriage, especially marriage into a family such as the Cottrells, provided a terrific defence barrier against the world, obliterating outward signs of unhappiness. Link two names together – Hillary and Bill, Elizabeth and Philip, Terry and June – and they become a single entity, a brand. Add a third name like Clinton, Windsor or Cottrell and the brand becomes household, a corporate product. It didn't matter that the constituent ingredients had separated inside the bottle, they were still expertly packaged and identifiable as one unit. So it was with Finn and Trudy. They were a married couple within the Cottrell clan. To locals, that made them part of a dynasty.

Not that the Cottrells' high social standing was entirely merited. Self-made in the previous century, patriarchal, opinionated, arrogant and more than a little crooked, the Cottrell family might be popularly hailed as one of the oldest and most respected names in the fields of property and auctions, but its real heritage was far more ruthless and prosaic. They were, as Piggy Cottrell was proud of announcing *en famille* after a few too many clarets, nothing more than a bunch of lucky Irish horse-traders who had won both their fortune – and the means with which to make it – in a gamble.

And now they looked set to lose it all through neglect and ill-will.

Trudy, whose own fortune had been entirely sucked up by Finn's profligacy over the past few years, could easily see how the family had reached its current crisis. She wished that she had it in her to care, but years of having her opinions ignored or overruled had left her immune, almost grateful that it had come to this. Something was going to have to happen, and it seemed that today would mark the beginning of it. The whole family, despite being national champions at putting their heads in the sand, had been restless for weeks.

Having been restless for much longer, Trudy felt a mix of fear and excitement alongside the usual discomfort at attending a Cottrell gathering. As she drove along the familiar, high-hedged road to Fox Oddfield, she stole a glance at Finn, whose handsome, set profile was the usual rock-face. He never gave anything away, but she knew that even his usual insouciance was under threat.

'You will at least *try* to be cheerful today, won't you?' he demanded peevishly.

'Of course I will,' she placated, reaching across to give his knee a pat and almost driving into a ditch. 'I'm sure today will be *great* fun, as always.'

Her sarcasm was lost on him as, seemingly contented with this, he checked his reflection in the sun visor mirror, eager to retreat into the vanity of self-denial and his mother's unconditional love.

'Great fun,' Trudy repeated hollowly as Fox Oddfield Abbey at last loomed over the horizon, a big slab-like slice of Regency cake, mouldering around the over-sugared, fanciful edges.

8

Contrary to all the family's expectations, Piggy Cottrell was in ebullient mood. That morning, while planting Easter eggs amid the overgrown topiary walks and rose gardens of the Abbey's formal grounds, he had come up with a last-minute idea to save his family business. In a moment close to epiphany, it had suddenly struck him how to attract customers back to his old auction house.

He could hardly wait to gather his children and make the announcement.

Wife Dibs, with her usual unquestioning support, had already agreed wholeheartedly that Piggy's idea was a stroke of genius. Not having a grain of business acumen in her make-up (much like her husband), it didn't strike her as remotely fanciful or ill-advised to pursue such an unsophisticated option. Like a pair of Easter ostriches, they plunged their heads back into the sand with great relief.

Piggy was unstoppable.

'We are going to host a treasure hunt!' he boomed, waving his walking stick around like a majorette's baton.

Now in his seventies, Peregrine Grenoble Algernon Finbar Cottrell still bore the trademark Cottrell characteristics that gave all the family's men such a heroically charismatic and convincing air. He could persuade a crowd that black was white, up was down and fact was fiction. It was what had always made Cottrells such naturals in their field of selling houses, managing land and auctioning goods – if only they could be bothered to put in a decent day's work.

And Piggy, a thwarted ringmaster in another life, loved nothing more than regaling a crowd. He milked it mercilessly now, deepening his already bass voice, rolling his 'r's and striking the floor regularly with his stick as he went on to explain the idea.

'Cottrells Auctioneers will set a series of cryptic clues throughout the next season of sales, each leading to a magic lot number. Put the lot numbers together and you have a combination code. The final clue will lead treasure hunters to a safe where, if they enter that right code, the door will open to reveal a huge cash prize for the winner!'

Armed with champagne cocktails and fighting for space closest to the roaring fire in the Abbey's long hall, Piggy's children were equally taken with the fanciful notion. Whoops and cheers followed his announcement.

Piers and Finn, relieved that they were no longer required to find a 'get out of jail' card for Cottrells', were more than happy to lend their approval. Nell and Flipper couldn't care less as long as their trust funds stayed secure. The only voice of dissent was ever-sensible middle daughter, Phoney, backed up by banker husband Harry, who pragmatically pointed out that with the bank poised to foreclose and creditors circling, it might be wiser to continue to asset-strip and simplify the company rather than embark upon some far-fetched marketing campaign.

'Nonsense!' Piggy cheerfully overruled them, red cheeks flaming. 'The bank will love it! I'm taking old man Hewitt fly fishing on Joss Oare-Witt's lake next week – the chap's never tickled a brown trout, can you believe? – plan to run it past him then. Bound to put up a fat prize for us. That'll turn everything around, you'll see.'

Hewitt was an ancient fossil who still held great sway at his family's private bank, the only reason Cottrells' was still able to trade at all these days. A lifelong crony and former school-chum of Piggy, he was amazingly tolerant of the company's increasing progress into the red. Somehow, despite the rest of the bank's partners kicking up a fuss of late, Piggy had managed to use this old school tie and his considerable charm to keep the funds coming.

Watching her father-in-law from the sidelines, Trudy grudgingly admired his lofty, broad-shouldered swagger, and the great lick of thick peppery hair that had only recently succumbed to the greying of age. Those high cheeks were streaked with sharp rose hips of colour, a trait all the family shared when excited, and one that offset their olive colouring. His animated brows were still as dark as ravens' wings above the searing grey-green eyes.

As her gaze slid from father to sons, she couldn't deny that the gene pool had been unfairly benevolent to the Cottrells. Their mask-like beauty both fascinated and appalled Trudy. It meant they could get away with murder. She had learned through bitter experience that wearing your heart on your sleeve around the Cottrell clan was asking for it to be punctured. They never betrayed a flicker of emotion and, although the turbulent grey-green eyes always seemed on the verge of meltdown, one couldn't read anything into that at all. She had studied Finn for years and his eyes were as stormy when he was watching mindless television as they were when he was shouting in anger. It was what made him so frightening.

He was now pointedly ignoring her after their scrap in the car, swaddled by his rowdy family, childlike and cocky. Trudy found it hard to see him objectively these days, although however bad things got, his beauty could still set her shallow aesthetic belly aflutter. Taller than Piers – more of a rower to his brother's rugger player build – he shared the same thick pelt of black hair, high colour and dark-lashed eyes. Flipper and Nell were the real show-stoppers of the family, with a more self-aware sexuality and flirtatious edge, yet Finn was the one that people always remembered, for his aloofness, his almost threatening stillness. The fact that he made no effort to stand out made him all the more distinctive.

Nobody could accuse Nell of being aloof, although she possessed the family volatility and arrogance in spades to compensate. Right now she was green with morning sickness and livid that smoking and boozing were not only *verboten* but – even if she could have sneaked an illicit fag and a drink – made her throw up on contact. Despite this uncharacteristic sickliness, she still looked sensational in a figure-hugging blue wool dress, her short black hair swept off her temples and not an inch of pregnancy bulge yet showing at eleven weeks. Always the black sheep of the family, Nell had already split up with the father of her unborn child – an amicably mutual decision by all accounts – and picked up with a married ex-boyfriend of whom the family disapproved. As if this wasn't enough in an allegedly Catholic family, Nell had recently announced that she planned to bring up her child as a Buddhist.

'Isn't this ghastly? I know you loathe it as much as me,' she said now, having wandered up to deposit scented kisses on Trudy's cheeks, speaking in an undertone because her father was still in full flow. 'Watch out for Flipper. He's in a perfectly vile mood because he was press-ganged into coming, but, being a boy, he can't see the funny side. He was supposed to be watching the Boat Race today with some old college chums, enjoying free champagne on a plush penthouse balcony by the Thames and being set up with a Latvian model.'

The twins had successfully avoided about half the obligatory family gatherings in the past few years; while Nell had been living in the family's London house, now sold off like so many other assets, Flipper had been away at university and then in his first veterinary post in Suffolk. But now that they had returned to the fold as permanent residents, they found it impossible to escape the compulsory attendance.

'He only agreed to come at all because you'd be here,' Nell muttered through a stiff smile as her father cracked a bad joke about buried treasure and the family plot.

Trudy forced a smile as Piggy stared expectantly at her, flattered but doubting she was much compensation.

Flipper was a rare Cottrell because he had actually knuckled down and forged a profession for himself as an equine vet. Nor did he take himself as seriously as the others. In other ways, he was a typical family product. He was arrogant, impatient, detached and occasionally downright cold just like the rest of them; yet Trudy liked him much more than most. He let his mask slip sometimes, revealing a puppy-like playfulness and innocence, traits that she had glimpsed in his older brother years earlier but now seemed to have lost sight of.

Catching Trudy looking at him now, Flipper gave her a wholly inappropriate wink. Had she been drunker, it would have had the desired effect of making her giggle, but she just looked away and, from frying pan to fire, her focus landed on cousin Giles's lascivious gaze. Feigning a theatrical yawn, he blew her a kiss from behind his hand.

Beside Giles, his mother, Aunt Grania, stood with Dibs Cottrell, two contrasting matriarchs, like different species of flamboyant dahlias thrust into the same pot. Elder sister to Piggy and therefore a Cottrell by birth, Grania cut an eye-catching figure. Like Piggy, she possessed the amazing aquamarine eyes and olive skin, although her hair was dyed a rather unlikely copper blond and, having put on a lot of weight in recent years, she had taken to wearing jogging suits for 'comfort'. Today's was baby blue with orange stripes down the sides, and had been matched with a pair of neat gold ballet pumps, a cream pashmina and her pearls to mark the occasion. Already

thoroughly merry on gin and It, she beamed at Piggy, not taking in
a word because she had sensibly left her hearing aid in her private
rooms upstairs. In crueller moments, the Cottrell children referred
to their Aunt Grania as 'the Free-Loader' because she had arrived
from London a couple of years ago for the shooting season, a great
family passion, and was still living with them, even though the estate's
shooting rights had all been sold on for much-needed cash. Nobody
dared ask her to leave and, as Giles showed no filial inclination to
look after his impoverished mother, she rattled around the house
getting in everyone's way and occasionally causing a panic when she
let loose a few shots in the garden to keep her eye in.

Dibs couldn't have been more different from her sister-in-law. Slim
to the point of gaunt, she was a tall, fine-boned Irish gem who wore
the distant expression of a mountain hare. Far paler than her children,
yet with the same peat-black hair, hers bearing a distinctive streak
of white at the crown, she had an unintentionally vampiric air about
her not helped by today's blood-red velvet dress and black shawl.
Dibs's aloofness and beauty made her intimidating to those who met
her. Many had jumped to the wrong conclusion that her coolness
stemmed from Gothic arrogance, a classic Cottrell trait. But Dibs
was as shy and gentle as a fawn; she had few social graces and cared
little for small talk. She lived for her family, her beloved kitchen and
her operas. Trudy had hoped that their mutual love of music would
draw them closer, but Dibs had no taste for anything as modern as
Trudy's creations, nor the softer classics, choral and jazz music she
liked to listen to. It was full-on Wagner or nothing, and she remained
as distant towards Trudy as she did to any who were not her blood
relatives.

Had Trudy borne children into the family, things would be
different. Dibs adored children, fussing around them with endless
patience. Her grandchildren were all adopted, and Trudy had long
suspected that this was something Dibs found difficult with her
staunch Catholicism. That Nell was now pregnant should have been
a great cause for celebration, but with Nell unmarried and with the
baby's father in another relationship, the joy was muted. The onus
had always been upon Trudy to produce a true grandchild – one
that she feared would be swamped by the force of Dibs's special
love.

After Finn had been born, a succession of miscarriages, ectopic pregnancies and ultimately the tragedy of a still-born child had led to Dibs being advised not to try for more children. Desperate for a girl, she and Piggy had taken in a newborn baby, in what appeared to be a private adoption. With her dark skin and eyes, strongly African features, amazing plume of hair and sharp mind, Persephone could never have been fooled into thinking that she came from the same gene pool as her siblings, and her parents had sensibly made no secret of her birth from the start. Then, ten years after adopting Persephone, Dibs had fallen pregnant at forty-three and the twins had come along. By then, their 'dark' daughter was known to all as 'Phoney'.

This nickname had struck Trudy as somewhat callous, but Phoney was emphatic that she herself had coined it, shortening the rather lumpen 'Persephone'. All Cottrell children were given names beginning with 'P', although only Piers had stuck to his; Finn had been shaped from Phineas'; Flipper was 'Phillip', and Nell 'Penelope'. Piggy himself was a 'Peregrine' and had gained his rather unflattering pet name not because he resembled a pig, but because he squealed like one when he laughed.

And he was wheezing and squealing now as his older sons back-slapped and congratulated him on his brilliance, and started to help plot the great Treasure Hunt that would reverse Cottrells' fortunes.

'Isn't this super news?' Jemima gushed as she trotted up to refill Trudy's champagne glass. 'I'm sure you've been as worried as me.'

Trudy eyed her sister-in-law warily, immersed in a cloud of Chanel, which Jemima applied like her horse's fly-spray. Ballerina petite and pretty, with an upturned nose and the bulging eyes of a chihuahua, Jemima's little-girl mannerisms and sweet surface belied a lioness heart. Capable of social climbing the north face of the Eiger on her husband's behalf, the little blonde was as close to Dibs as it was possible for a married-in stranger to get. Trudy knew that Jemima thought her self-indulgent, idle and trampy; they had barely spoken in weeks. Any approach was cause for suspicion.

'From what I hear,' she said carefully, 'it might take a bit more than this to turn the company around.'

'Oh, I'm sure Piggy knows what he's doing. We girls would be best to offer our wholehearted support, doncha think?'

'Hole hearted?' Trudy repeated listlessly, at least grateful that her glass was once again brimming. Anything to anaesthetise the pain of a pep talk from Jemima.

'The boys must be *so* relieved. I gather they've been chatting about this thing for weeks.'

'I wouldn't know.'

Jemima tucked back her chin. 'C'mon, Trudy dear. They are *always* on to each other. You must have noticed?'

'Nope; I have no idea what Finn's up to most of the time,' Trudy tried not to react to the fact that Giles had placed himself in her eyeline and was miming a rope strangling him in sympathy with her plight. Giles thought Jemima poisonous, although that never stopped him flirting with her.

'You really owe it to the family to pay more attention. I mean, what with the hiccups in the company and the worry over Nell's pregnancy, we all have to do our best.' She flipped her neat blond hair back from her Botoxed forehead and gave Trudy an insincere smile consisting of part Betty Boop, part overexcited Pekinese.

'What worry?' Trudy noticed Nell was now missing from the room.

Jemima's voice dropped to a hushed breath, 'I think the general consensus is that she should be encouraged towards adoption.'

'Surely not?'

'She's not remotely maternal.'

'But Dibs will help.'

'Oh, quite, quite – we're not talking external adoption. Lord, forbid!' she let out a little tinkle of laughter. 'We're talking *in house*.'

'In house?'

'The family needs to pull together right now.' Jemima laid a little hand on Trudy's freckled arm.

'What are you driving at?'

Jemima gave her a wise look. 'The boys might not say it aloud, but the company needs a *huge* cash injection if it's to survive. You are by far the wealthiest, so perhaps we need to think about what the family can do for you in return for help. Finn can be extravagant, so you've been understandably reluctant to invest in the company; Piers was quite profligate at one time too, you know. Of course, now the onus really is on him and Finn to keep Cottrells' alive. They must *both* knuckle down. It made a huge difference to Piers when we adopted. You and Finn would be wonderful parents, and I personally feel that a child is just what he needs to stop him being quite so directionless. Can't you see?'

It was taking a long time, but scales were starting to fall from Trudy's eyes.

'Are you suggesting I *buy* Nell's baby?'

'Good God, no! Whatever makes you think that?'

'You seemed to be implying: give us a bung and have a newborn and some company shares; you're a true Cottrell now.'

'That's *dreadfully* unfair! I am simply trying to enlighten you to the state of internal family politics,' Jemima tutted, making it sound as though she was advising how best to iron a shirt. 'You really should be taking an interest in Finn's livelihood, you know.'

Trudy bit back the urge to point out that Finn never took the remotest interest in *her* career, just as long as she paid the bills and covered the more lavish elements of their lifestyle. 'Oh, Finn's fine. He prefers me hands off.'

A smooth arm slid its way warmly round her waist, 'Does that mean the rest of us stand a chance of getting you hands *on*, darling Trudy?'

She looked up to find Giles's wicked blue gaze sparkling into hers with its usual uncensored message of carnal need and adoration. For once, she was grateful for the attention.

Even Jemima was not immune, letting out a little shudder of pleasure as he gallantly stooped to kiss her hand. 'Piers is a damned lucky man.'

'Thank you,' she replied with a smirk. 'I was just reminding Trudy how important our back-up is at the moment.'

'I agree.' Giles nodded emphatically. 'You are second to none in the back-up stakes, Jem. Backs up all the way, eh Trudy?'

Jemima missed the double entendre entirely and beamed at him.

'Must check on the children – excuse me.' She had a distinct skip in her step as she trotted away.

'What d'you really think of this treasure hunt idea of Piggy's?' Giles turned back to Trudy.

'I don't give a toss.'

'God you are such a sulky cow, it's sexy as hell. You're always gloriously vile when you're in this house – quite unlike your usual self.'

'My usual self?'

'Dazzling, joyful and desirable,' he growled wolfishly.

'You must be mistaking me for someone who still has a pulse.'

'You really mustn't get too depressed, you know. I can always cheer you up.'

She checked they were out of earshot 'You really think that shagging you behind my husband's back will make me happy?'

'Immensely. I recommend you give in to temptation as soon as possible. I will make you happy. I am quite hopelessly in love with you, as you know.'

'Given your narcissism, doesn't that make for a conflict of interest, Giles?' drawled a soft voice as Flipper appeared, looking down his nose at his dissipated older cousin.

'Just cheering Trudy up,' Giles snarled, old stag to young pretender.

Not even bothering to lock horns, Flipper refilled his sister-in-law's glass and pointedly ignored Giles' half-empty one as he studied Trudy carefully.

'Are you OK?'

'Delirious,' she muttered, knocking back the drink and holding out her glass again. Whether it was the sight of the champagne, or Flipper, she did feel better, her whole body relaxing.

A smile flickered on Flipper's beautiful, petulant mouth. 'Funnily enough, Giles always has that effect on me, too. Like malaria.'

Giles gave him a scornful look, begrudging his cousin's youth. The two men had more in common than he cared to admit, and therein lay far deeper foundations for Giles's strong disapproval than simple resentment of the younger man's charms. But he refused to dwell upon it. It was a family secret which, like so many in the Cottrells' vast and clattering warehouse of skeletons, had to be endured through a lifetime's silence. In another lifetime he had the power to turn Flipper around, to make him a more worthwhile human being than the arrogant little shit who had returned to the Lodes Valley from his years away, but that was impossible the way the cards had been dealt and so it was easier to treat him as an irritation.

'Bugger off, Flippant,' he warned him now. 'I hardly ever get to chat up Trudy as well you know.'

'Actually, Giles, your mother is asking for you. She's lost her top teeth somewhere in the shrubbery.'

'How on earth did she do that?' Giles huffed.

'Egg hunting. Pa has hidden some toffee-filled ones this year. Extraordinarily sticky.'

'Oh for God's sake – will she never learn?' Giles muttered, stalking off.

Trudy eyed Flipper. 'You made that up.'

'So?' He didn't smile. 'You wanted rid of him.'

'Who says?'

'You always want rid of him.' He scuffed his shoes against the edge of the threadbare Persian rug, looking up at her from beneath black brows.

She closed one eye thoughtfully. 'You know, he was starting to cheer me up a bit.'

'My God, you *are* low.' He lowered his forehead to her shoulder in despair. 'Me too. Shall we end it now?'

'I'm just not drunk enough yet. Are you low because you had to trade the Boat Race and a model for this?'

'Nell told you?' His laugh was muffled in the wool. 'Lucky escape. Bashka is probably a spotty heroin addict with a body like Meccano.'

Trudy smiled into his dark, sweet-smelling hair. 'So why are you low?'

'The usual. Nobody loves me. My sister's up the duff with her future career in tatters, and is acting as though it's this year's black. My family are pissing away their fortune and my father thinks the answer is to give more money away.'

'Nothing too drastic, then?'

'I'm amazed Pa isn't asking you to trump up this prize money. Aren't you the family's golden goose?'

'Oh, Finn's already spent all my money,' she said idly.

'The golden goose is cooked?'

'Something like that.'

'Is that why you're mad at him?'

'I'm always mad at Finn. Thankfully, he just takes it as a general sign of my overall madness.'

Flipper was one of the few people with whom Trudy ever came anywhere close to the real truth, although only disguised as trademark flippancy.

'Finns ain't what they used to be,' he slurred the well-worn joke now. 'Giles is lucky, really, despite being a plum idiot. He just does happy all the time, non-stop like an English setter – untempered and un-neutered. It must be great to be like that, huh?'

'It's worked for an awful lot of his conquests in the past,' she agreed as, in need of fresh air, she wandered out to the terrace to watch the egg hunt.

'Not for you, though,' Flipper insisted as he followed her. 'You're worth more than that.'

'I told you, I'm not the goose that lays the golden egg any more. In fact, I'm a lousy lay these days – too much of a chicken.'

'You're the Cottrell family treasure.'

'There's nothing left on deposit.'

'Yes, there is. You've just buried it so deeply, you think you've lost it.'

On they pattered, bucking one another up by saying it all while admitting nothing.

'So how do I find it, this lost treasure? Can you set me a series of clues with a map?'

Flipper looked out across the formal gardens. 'Your treasure is far too precious to risk it getting found by a marauding pirate like Giles.'

Trudy looked at him in amusement, the brooding set of his shoulders reminding her of the troubled youth she'd first met ten years earlier – an angry, opinionated rebel with a tongue so sharp it could draw blood, and a rare charm. He'd reminded her of Johnny at that age, hiding his vulnerability behind steel armour. Breaking through had taken skill; she'd quickly realised the depths of his teenage crush on her and had trodden carefully to convert lust to trust, but as the years passed they'd become firm friends.

Their mock flirtation, part Noël Coward, part *The Graduate*, had started when Flipper had returned for holidays from school and then veterinary college full of thwarted desire, usually for a completely unavailable woman. He did that a lot as a teenager. Talking and laughing with Trudy had loosened him up and had provided her with a much-needed distraction at the interminable Cottrell celebrations.

That had changed after college, where a few one-night stands had been the sum total of his romantic track record, despite so many of his fellow students adoring him without acknowledgement. Living alone in Suffolk, working as a large animal vet, he had launched upon a dubious mission to work his way through as many local beauties as possible, annihilating hearts en route. Totally unable to commit or engage emotionally, he was a lethal philanderer.

Flipper was very much a spoiled child and treated most women like new toys at Christmas – after an initial burst of obsessive enthusiasm, he'd either break them or tire of them within a week.

Yet for all his arrogance and cruel wit, Trudy knew that Flipper was ragingly sensitive and very mucked up – he had confessed enough of his secrets to her to reveal his vulnerable flip-side. Part mother figure, part big sister, and a little bit of an ageing pin-up to him, she knew that she was one of the few people in his life to whom he really listened.

His behaviour had not improved much since returning to the Lodes Valley.

He had recently conducted a short and heated affair with Dilly Gently that had blown up in his face. She had moved swiftly onto new pastures, falling in love with local musician Magnus Olensen – the father of Nell's unborn baby – leaving both the twins with eggs on their faces, and Flipper with an even surlier attitude.

Trudy tried to keep him in check, and their flirtatious repartee had become more muted recently, crystallising into a more genuine friendship as Flipper regularly called at Church Cottage for breakfast when out hacking or coffee when on his rounds, sharing his love troubles and his wicked humour in equal measure.

'I suppose we should go and hunt for eggs,' he drawled half-heartedly. 'Join in the fun.'

'Let the kids have them.'

My eggs are all shrivelled now, she found herself thinking illogically – like so many of the random thoughts that assaulted her out of the blue these days. Flipper's right: I have lost my treasure. My libido is the ultimate treasure hunt.

Stupid tears sprang to her eyes and she had to look away to hide them from him. God, she was drunker than she had imagined. She could feel her balance starting to go. The fresh air, far from clearing her head, had made it spin all the faster.

'You're not really contemplating having an affair with Giles, are you?' he muttered in an undertone.

Trudy rubbed her eyes with the cuff of her jumper.

'Of *course* I won't have an affair with Giles.' She put an arm round him and head-banged his chest disparagingly, unable to resist adding, '*Far* too close to home.' Her words were starting to slur, too, she realised.

Flipper pushed her to arm's length. 'So you *are* planning to have an affair with someone?'

Certain he was teasing her, she smiled enigmatically.

'Fuck.' His eyes darted warily and he licked his lips, party to a secret confession he didn't want to hear. She was his brother's wife, after all.

'Calm down, Flips. I'm not the unfaithful sort.' She realised that she had read him wrongly and struggled to think soberly. 'Sorry. Finn's cool. We're cool. Honest. I wouldn't do that to him.'

But Flipper shook his head, not taking his stormy sea-green eyes from hers. 'I wish you would.'

'You what?'

'You heard.'

'You want me to be unfaithful to your brother?'

'People have affairs all the time.'

'Not me.'

'Why not?'

She laughed, trying to break the tension. 'Maybe I haven't got the nerve.'

'You've got too much nerve, you mean. Cowards go for the instant gratification of infidelity, of feeling wanted and desired with quick-fix, junkie love and sex. You're brave enough to try to cold turkey from love for the long-haul. That takes guts.'

'Want to bet?' Trudy fought to clear her head.

A smile pulled at Flipper's mouth.

'Unlike the rest of my godforsaken family, I don't really gamble much, but I'd be willing to lay any odds that you'll share another man's bed before any bloody treasure is found.'

'What man?'

He ignored the question. 'This coming summer, maybe sooner.'

'What makes you so sure?'

'The odds are narrowing,' he said cryptically, 'to evens. And it's time you got even.'

Trudy looked across to where Finn was helping one of his nephews find an egg among a thick crop of daffodils. He looked such a perfect father-in-the-making. From the moment they married, people had been commenting on what wonderful parents they would make, what a terrific daddy Finn would be, how much love they both had to give. Only Trudy knew different . . .

She longed for love again, for its taste and feel and sleepless obsession. She had thought that children would provide that love, but the idea became laughable these days, her fast-track to old age guaranteed. She wanted to jump off it into the arms of love, even quick-fix junkie love like Flipper described.

Looking at Finn now, she remembered loving him so fiercely that their future seemed guaranteed. She wasn't going to take the coward's way out. Infidelity was too thorny, too hurtful. She was determined not to go there. She was far too vulnerable, her self-esteem too low.

'How much?' She turned back to Flipper.

'What?'

'How much do you bet that I'll have an affair?'

He took a long time to answer as both of them watched Finn snatch up the foil-wrapped egg from his nephew and dance around the garden while the little boy chased him, both laughing uproariously.

The first time Flipper said it, Trudy thought she must have heard him wrong.

'I'm sorry?'

'I bet my soul,' he repeated.

'Isn't that a bit Faustian? How about hard cash?'

'You told me you didn't have any.'

'I am pretty broke,' she admitted. 'I'll have to sell my body at this rate.'

'OK then. You can bet that.'

'This old thing?' she snorted.

He nodded. 'You lose this bet, we go to bed together. That's the deal.'

'If I have an affair, then I sleep with you too? Are we talking orgy here? Surely that's a bit debauched even by your standards?'

'Well, you could always cut out the middle man, and have an affair with me in the first place. I'll even throw my soul in for free.'

Trudy stared at him in amazement. 'You want that?'

There was a long pause. Flipper tapped his foot rhythmically on the ground in a gesture that could equally convey mocking impatience, or unbearable suspense.

'Only if you wanted to sleep with me, and yes – I've never wanted anything more in my life. I've wanted it since the day I met you.'

As unexpected as an axe swinging through the thick, impenetrable wall that she had built up around herself, Trudy felt a hot buzz of sensation leap between her legs.

'You were fifteen when you met me,' she scoffed.

'Exactly. That sort of loyalty deserves a pay-off. My soul's on the line here, remember.'

Trudy gaped at him.

His stony profile, so like Finn's, gave nothing away.

I'm making a fool of myself, she though wretchedly. His family are all around us, for Christ's sake. My husband's yards away. What sort of farce is this?

'You're supposed to be cheering me up here, not offering your services as my gigolo,' she grumbled petulantly.

He flared his nostrils, a muscle hammering briefly in his cheek. 'I rather hoped that telling you I am absolutely hooked on you, that I'm probably in love with you and that the reason I screw up with every woman I try to form a relationship with is because I am unable to see past you might just cheer you up.'

'Wait a minute.' She held up an unsteady finger. 'You didn't tell me that. You told me you wanted to shag me at fifteen. Most men your age wanted to shag me at fifteen.'

'Lucky for them you didn't go on to marry their brother then,' he snapped.

Finally losing her fight with sobriety, Trudy lurched sideways and was only saved an ungainly descent down the terrace steps by the intervention of a potted bay tree. From it, a single egg, wrapped in golden foil, dropped straight into her hands.

Holding it up to Flipper, she whistled in squiffy amazement. 'Now that's what I call an easy lay.'

'Unlike you,' he pointed out sulkily, before the faint curl of a smile once again hit his lips.

Tension drained away.

'I prefer laying bets.'

'Not with my odds.'

'Your soul is far too big a stake for a night with me.'

'I thought it was a good line,' he defended, eyes shining. 'I've been working on that line for ten years. You've just shattered my fantasy. I'll have to go back to the drawing board. Slay a few dragons, perhaps,' he muttered, starting to laugh. 'Climb a mountain or two and visit a secret soothsayer for a love potion.'

'We've been through all this before, Flipper,' she told him. 'Women don't expect you to gallop in on a white charger. You have to take it slowly.'

'But I *have* taken it slowly – ten bloody years. You obviously needed cheering up, so I thought I'd kill two birds with one stone.'

He'd been winding her up all along, Trudy realised with relief. Finally letting the laughter Heimlich her chest, she swept him into a tight hug. 'Darling, darling Flipper, you bloody well *do* know how to cheer me up! Thank you!'

'Nothing like an unrequited love to get them rolling in the aisles,' he drawled.

'Nothing unrequited about our love, Flips. I love you too. Giles might make me feel a smidgen better by being an old lech, but only you can always tickle my funny bone. Thank you, sweet thing.'

Watching her later as she flitted around the party, transformed by a few more drinks and the self-confidence he'd inadvertently injected into her bloodstream, Flipper wished Trudy would take herself seriously for once, instead of constantly looking for the punchline and making sure that the joke was on her.

Only today, he had a feeling that for once the joke was on him.

Buoyed up by booze and Flipper's cheering Lochinvar moment, Trudy sang for her supper without the usual reluctance.

She didn't attempt her standard repertoire. Instead, smiling rather manically, knowing that she had drunk far too many champagne cocktails to trust her piano playing, she launched cheerfully into Ain't Misbehavin', her smoky voice still packing more than enough punch to silence the room into spell-bound wonder despite the odd fluffed lyric. Wildly sensual, gurgling with sexual potency, an unhurried purr that had seduced listeners for years and which now more than ever vibrated with erotic undercurrents, her voice suited the song perfectly.

Smiling with wanton abandon at Giles, who had brought her more champagne and was leaning on the piano smoking a cigar in very David Niven fashion, she gave one of her all-time electric performances.

Finn, who had never been willing to co-star in her recitals, even in their most loved-up days, stood with his back to her in a far corner, talking in an undertone to his mother.

But Giles seemed happy to play Noël Coward to her Gertrude Lawrence, so when the family demanded an encore, she struck the first few chords of one of her favourite party pieces. It was years since she had played it – her pre-Finn London days of riotous, boho music industry parties and lost weekends in country houses whose locations and guests she had long forgotten. She'd sung it with primitive abandon then, knowing that it could propel half her audience up to the bedrooms in search of sexual relief.

'Love for sale,' she sang in her rasping, husky counter-tenor. 'Appetising, young love for sale . . .'

Across the room, Flipper visibly flinched, sitting up to watch more closely.

Even Giles blinked in surprise and she wondered if she was going too far. But she was too drunk to care as she sang on, her voice hypnotising in its lost soul shamelessness.

Finn steered his mother out into the back hallway like an old reactionary finding the young things' hip-hop too risqué.

It wasn't the song itself that was disturbing, nor her deadpan, heavy-lidded eyes and blank face, a trick she had learned from miming to a hundred Blondie tracks as a teenager. It was her voice that was so unnerving, a tool once described by *NME* as 'one part vodka, one part nicotine and three parts pheromone'. It had a power that hot-wired groins, set free rebellious hearts and sent minds spinning. She hadn't let loose its full power for years.

As she sang, reliving a delicious electric charge of her old chutzpah, she found herself looking at Giles with an almost detached sexual appetite.

He sidled along the piano afterwards and breathed in her ear. 'Do me a favour and sing a couple of verses of "Chick-chick-chick-chick-chicken" to help me out? I have a massive bloody hard-on to hide here.'

Bursting out laughing, her brief torrent of mischief replaced by a greater sense of fun, Trudy did as she was told, ensuring that all the Cottrells, young and old, joined in.

She then took an exaggerated bow and made to exit as swiftly as possible, cheered and clapped riotously as she swept out of the room.

'Bravo!'

Giles cornered her by the double doors to the inner hall, cleverly engineering a kiss so close to her mouth that for a second she felt a champagne-tasting slither of tongue between her lips.

She pulled away, eyes darting nervously over his shoulder.

'That was very . . . rousing.'

'Recovered?' she asked casually.

'Never.' He shook his head, dissipated blue eyes crinkling as his blond brows curled together. 'You are an incurable disease, my darling.'

'Drop her, Giles.'

They both jumped as Finn loomed large around the double doors, carrying a fresh bottle of bubbly. Rather than appearing angry, he simply seemed mildly bemused as he walked past them and towards the main party without another word.

'Caught goosing again.' Giles cleared his throat and let out one of his waggy-tailed randy Labrador growls before cheerfully backing away, blowing Trudy a regretful kiss.

9

'You were on good form today,' Finn commented as he drove his very tight wife home.

'I love your family,' she giggled, hiccuped, leaned across to stroke his cheek and nodded off, hand lolling into his lap. At that moment, it was true. When she was drunk, Trudy loved everybody.

Finn pressed his foot hard on the accelerator, eager to get her home and cash in on her good humour.

But by the time he had finally managed to prise her out of the car at Church Cottage, drag her past the pack of eager dogs and man-handle her upstairs, her sleepy, loved-up mood had changed to one of irrepressible giggles.

'You won't find any treasure down there!' she shrieked delightedly as he wrenched off her jeans, hard-on poking from his open trouser fly. 'X marks the G-spot and all that. It's long gone. Sorry.'

'What?' he snapped, fingers pulling at her knickers, already angling himself above her for a quick entry.

She watched his head – several heads in fact – spin round, 'Like Davy Jones' locker.'

He started jabbing away with the fat tip of his cock, like a maddened cave bear trying to find the entrance to his hidden lair among the bushes at the base of a mountain.

Suddenly, Trudy stopped laughing.

Knowing she would be as tense and dry as a tiny fissure in the rock face, she braced herself for the pain, unwilling to reach down and help him, but equally reluctant to give in to her instincts and fight him off. They had reached this point too many times before with sulks and fights and tantrums. Easier to let him get on with it and hope he was quick.

His right hand reached down and felt around to open her up. His fingernails were too long, tearing at her pubic hair and snagging across her soft labia.

Then, with an almighty grunt, he was in.

Trudy bit her lip as his weight cranked her hips like a rough osteopath, his left shoulder was thrust under her chin and his cock forced its way as deep as it could, pushing past desire-parched resistance.

As he started shunting away slowly, a steam train waiting to get up to speed, his right hand reappeared and grabbed her breast, kneading it with the tenderness of a pizza chef with a rush on in the restaurant.

The steam train was accelerating: faster, faster, deeper, deeper, grunts getting louder.

Bang, bang, bang. She felt him crashing against her cervix now, the pain starting to register in her head. Bang, bang, bang. A baton on a drum.

She closed her eyes tightly, willing for it to be at an end soon.

'Does that feel good?' he breathed, depositing a trail of saliva straight into her ear. Her involuntary shudder led him to interpret her reaction as affirmative, even though she didn't dare open her mouth, nausea rising too fast to counter.

Silence fell as he concentrated on the final push for victory – a strange anomaly about Finn's sexual technique. Whereas most men got louder and louder as they approached orgasm, he got quieter. She hadn't noticed when they were first together because she herself had been such a loud, giggly exhibitionist, but these days the silence haunted her on the very few occasions they had sex.

With an efficient, almost clinical series of high-speed thrusts and a low groan, he terminated his journey at last.

Finn let go of her numb, bruised breast and raised himself up on his forearms to look down at her, eyes gleaming in the dark.

'How was that for you?' he asked smugly, dipping his head to wipe his sweaty brow on her belly.

Trudy felt her hollow chest, stomach, head and vagina contract simultaneously with shame and self-loathing.

'Oh God,' she blinked up at him. 'I think I'm going to be sick.'

She only just made it to the bathroom in time.

While Finn started to snore loudly next door, Trudy leaned over the toilet basin, her belly performing back-flips as it fought to evacuate a stream of vodka, Coke, champagne, roast chicken and chocolate all at once and at great speed.

As the spasms finally abated, she sank back on the floor and pressed her hot cheek to the cool glass of the shower cubicle, closing her eyes to stop the room spinning.

Already the events of the day were fading into a comforting blur. Soon she would hardly be able to remember a thing about her conversations with Jemima and Giles, about Flipper's extraordinary way of trying to cheer her up, about Piggy's treasure hunt announcement, her stupid singing display and, most soothing to forget of all, Finn's own personal hunt for long-lost treasure.

Soon the heavy cosh of a drunken sleep would steal away every poisoned chalice that the day had given her, an intoxicating sip at a time, replacing them with vague snatched memories that her mind would eventually edit into a neat, slightly embarrassing order.

But when she dragged herself up to the sink to splash water on her face and clean her teeth before she passed out, just one conscious thought clung on in her thumping head, repeating the same image in her mind's eye. And it wasn't Flipper's turbulent eyes staring at her, nor Finn's alarmingly similar gaze.

It was a smiling, blue-eyed face that had a message so simple even Trudy's addled mind could remember it.

'I *will* make you happy.'

That was a treasure worth hunting, surely?

10

When the Cottrells' treasure hunt was announced in the local paper, Pixie Guinness couldn't wait to rush round to friend Pheely and enlist her help.

Hidden amid a garden as impenetrable as a box of tangled green wool, Oddlode Lodge Cottage was a little landlocked, upturned hull of Cotswold stone and sagging tile, barely big enough to house a couple of tidy hobbits, let alone a hugely messy hoarder of a sculptress, her grown-up daughter and baby son. As usual, having fought her way from the hidden gate in the garden wall to the cottage with the aid of her secateurs, Pixie then had to put her shoulder to the swollen back door, trip over a week's worth of recycling and slalom through the laundry skips and clay bags to find her friend and break the news.

'We must team up on this,' she enthused, 'two minds being better than one and all that. God knows, we're clever old birds and we need the dosh.'

'Less of the old,' Pheely grumbled, peering at the headline LOTS OF LUCK – *Local Auction House lets Public Bid for Ultimate Prize.*

As she reread the newspaper feature, she was almost tempted out of her gloom by the prospect of cryptic clues and treasure maps. But her lacklustre ennui refused to lift quite so easily.

The normally astute Pixie was very slow to pick up on her friend's bleak mood because, in a rare role reversal, her own was so unusually ebullient.

'Rather!' she agreed as she flicked a hand through her magnificent, newly highlighted short blond mane. 'I feel younger and racier than I have in an age.'

Since her hair make-over from rebellious blue streak to new 'trollop' blonde, Pixie had enjoyed a much-needed ego-boost. It had been years since men had looked at her in the admiring and frankly carnal way that they did now. She had not missed the attention, but now that it was back, she found it surprisingly uplifting.

Her recent canter with Rory Midwinter had rejuvenated her far more effectively than a spa week with chemical peel and brow lift thrown in.

Completely without vanity, and yet once so exquisitely pretty that her childhood nickname had permanently replaced her given Christian name, Pixie's looks had always been at odds with her tough, tomboyish nature.

Capricious, playful, easily bored, Pixie had left each of her first three marriages for the greener grass that she perceived over the fence. None had been easy decisions, particularly with young children involved, but such was her ability to attract – most especially determined, domineering men who would not take no for an answer – that she had developed a rather fatalistic attitude to life. Largely disowned by her disapproving family and erstwhile high society contacts, she was a loose cannon who had, at one time, seemed destined to ricochet from one disastrous affair to another.

But Sexton had been different. Ten years her junior, obsessive, jealous and deeply emotional, he had seemed unlikely to be unfaithful. Previous husbands had conducted discreet affairs just as she had, but she had never been abandoned for a younger model before. It hurt. Being betrayed by Sexton, whom she still foolishly loved, had annihilated her self-confidence. This faltering anxiety affected every corner of her life, from running her business to parenting her children and even presenting her usually brave face to the world.

Left with a clutch of confused children with no father-figure, a business that had relied upon the two of them working like Trojans, a mountain of debts and a very bitter taste in her mouth, the past few months had been hell. Yet Pixie salvaged positivity wherever it was to be found, whether in a new hair colour, a roll in the hay or a distracting treasure hunt. Today it was such heaven to be playing hooky from the market garden and contemplating an exciting new challenge that she barely registered Pheely's un-characteristic gloom.

'Aren't you going to get dressed?' she asked now, noticing that Pheely was still wearing a pilled purple satin dressing gown covered in baby sick and a pair of matted grey slippers shaped like monster claws. Her amazing dark curls were held back from her face with a makeshift Alice band fashioned out of a pair of tights.

'I suppose so,' Pheely sighed. 'One gets so slipshod when there's nobody around to admire the great work.'

'Basil and I will admire you.'

'Huff.'

Pheely had always been vain and was secretly a dark soul. She relied upon praise and flattery to keep her going, loved the fripperies of femininity, the attentions of men. To her, despite looking like a fecund goddess, motherhood was not a natural state and she envied Pixie her ability to have dropped six children on the hoof, raised them effortlessly, retained her figure and carried on working throughout. That Pixie, through her various ill-fated divorces, had turned her back on a world of great wealth and privilege amazed her. Pixie seemed to thrive on work whereas Pheely loathed it and dreamed of being a kept woman. New baby Basil exhausted her too much to work on her sculptures, and money was fast drying up. Thank goodness for daughter Dilly who, despite a deranged upbringing, had remained devotedly loyal to her mother and, knowing how many sacrifices Pheely had made, was paying her back now that she had finally started to earn a living.

Yet the fact that Dilly looked poised to rise to giddy heights in the recording industry with songwriter boyfriend Magnus made Pheely feel even more of a failure; a left-behind, empty-nest mum facing another long slog at motherhood with Basil with no reliable father to support him or nurture her frail ego. Giles was adorable yet hopeless, and cutting her heart open for him again and again made Pheely wretched. Life, love and adventure had passed her by and she wasn't yet forty.

'Spectacular!' Pixie exaggerated when Pheely reappeared from her bedroom wearing a shapeless mauve sweatshirt and clashing red wraparound skirt. 'Those wretched computer chaps have no idea what they've overlooked.'

'Oh they looked me over, all right. It seems my looks *are* over.'

Recent forays into internet dating had compounded Pheely's current self-loathing. Last week, she'd arranged to meet James, the dishy Cheltenham businessman, at a wine bar, and from the moment they met he had made no secret of his disappointment and boredom. Not even stretching to a bottle, he had stumped up for a mediocre glass of Merlot and, looking at his watch a lot, pretended that he was running late for an appointment. Having spent all day pampering and glamming up until she felt a million dollars, then forking out for a babysitter and a taxi, Pheely was home by eight thirty feeling suicidal. Two days later, in the City Art Gallery in Gloucester, the history lecturer to whom she had described herself as a 'Penelope Cruz lookalike', had gaped at her as though she was a particularly offensive piece of Brit Art lingering alongside the Turners and Gainsboroughs.

Trying to ignore this, Pheely had wafted winningly around beside him as he bored for England on all the Roman and medieval exhibits. She'd longed to get to the art, and when they did was rewarded by finding one of her late father's sculptures amongst the twentieth century exhibits. It was a delightful, frolicking naiad cast in bronze.

'He used to base all his female figures upon me,' she had boasted happily.

'Really?' He'd barely hidden his disbelief as he compared the svelte little glossy-shanked water fairy to Pheely's current rolling, earthy curves.

'Of course, I was a lot younger then.'

'Yes. Quite. I must say, you're not at all what I expected,' he had managed to splutter eventually, his breath smelling of blue cheese.

'You mean I'm much fatter than you thought I'd be?' she had suggested bluntly, fed up with the fake courtesy.

'No – I mean, not exactly – that is . . . larger than life, perhaps . . .'

'And you're shorter than I expected. And balder. And boring.'

He'd crawled away to lick his wounds in the natural history section; Pheely had stalked off to the café and consoled herself with a large sugary cappuccino and a Danish pastry.

Despite her sweet consolation, the final bitter twist was that she knew she had wanted to punish him as much for not being Giles as for anything. He had not called since the disastrous night her dress had burst apart, and she was damned if she was going to call him, although she had seen his car parked in his drive when she had walked past, along with a very shiny 4x4. He clearly had other coverts to flush out; ones containing Bambi-eyed housewives, no doubt. She would bide her time.

As she reread the newspaper feature about Cottrells', she supposed that distracting herself with a little treasure hunting might be no bad thing – although she couldn't resist flipping forward to the Personal Section while Pixie was busy opening the bottle of wine she'd brought.

Among a frightening number of adverts for new escorts and private

massages was a large block advert of Dial-a-Dates. Casting her eye
through 'Men for Women', she counted the number of times 'slim'
was listed as a requirement in a potential partner.

Twenty out of twenty-three.

She threw the paper furiously to the floor.

'Isn't it wildly frustrating as well as exciting?' Pixie enthused as
she carried over two mugs brimming with cheap plonk because all
the glasses were languishing dirtily in the sink. 'The first clue will be
released a week before the Spring Horse Fair, where the first lot
number is hidden. I can't wait!'

'I hate the Horse Fair,' Pheely grumbled.

'But it's such a tradition – all those wonderful coloured cobs and
the Romany girls in all their finery looking for husbands.'

Pheely, who had been mistaken for a gypsy maiden at the fair
several times in her youth, and on one terrifying occasion almost
found herself married off to a toothless horse-trader in exchange for
three piebalds and a goat, wasn't keen on the famous Morrell on the
Moor gathering.

Twice a year since time immemorial, travellers from all over the
country had converged on the little Cotswold market town to trade
horses. It was an anarchic, chaotic and occasionally law-breaking
affair, spilling over several days and into several fields and lanes
surrounding the medieval market square. In recent years, the police
and local authorities had attempted to wrest back control by enlisting
the help of Cottrells' Auctioneers to organise the horses, ponies and
harness into lots which could be sold through an official sales ring.
Although this lent the occasion some sense of order, it was well known
that the majority of the buying and selling still took place behind the
scenes, along with frantic trotting races, partying, flirting and fighting.

'Fifty grand to the winner.' Pixie marvelled at the prize on offer.
'God knows, you and I could do with that. Just think of all the clay
you could buy.'

'I was thinking more along the lines of a radical course of Botox
and a stomach staple.'

'Don't say you're still beating yourself up about the Halitosis
History Man?' complained Pixie, who had found tales of the
disastrous internet dates hilarious.

Pheely got up to gather a mewling Basil from his Moses basket
into a hug.

'Darling girl, you have ten years on me and the most glorious face and figure,' Pixie insisted. 'Be grateful for it, and be absolutely certain that whoever is attracted to you – and there are many – will be so for all the right reasons, and not be some snivelly little academic with a hang-up because he's got a small prick or whatever.'

Pheely snorted. Pixie could always cheer her up.

'Perhaps *you* should advertise?' she suggested now. 'That way *you* can be the choosy one; pick off the duds.'

'You think so?'

'Defo! Just be honest.' She gave her a wise look. 'Less of the Penelope Cruz.' Seeing Pheely's furious face, she added hastily, 'you are *far* more classical looking. More like . . .' She scrunched up her face, desperately trying to dig herself out of a hole.

'Like . . . ?'

'A Pre-Raphaelite heroine. What's that wonderful Rossetti portrait? La Donna della Finestra?'

'Lady at the Window? That's a study of Jane Morris.' Pheely pouted. 'I always thought he made her look like Brian May on steroids compared to the frail beauty of Elizabeth Siddal.'

'Rubbish. She was stunning – as are you, my dear.'

Pheely, who would rather look like Penelope Cruz than a Pre-Raphaelite, changed the subject. 'Have you asked Anke to be a part of our treasure hunt team?'

She was referring to the third member of their unofficial friendship trinity, elegant Danish dressage rider turned bookshop owner and über-wife, Anke Brakespear, who had moved into the village the previous summer.

'I rather thought – not,' Pixie said as lightly as she could. 'She's bound to want to take part with her family and she can be a bit overbearing, doncha think?'

Both women nodded with relieved agreement. Anke, while wonderfully supportive and clever, could come across as rather disapproving, plus uncomfortably bossy. Recently, her tendency to bluntness had veered alarmingly towards rudeness, and she made little secret of the fact that she thought both Pixie and Pheely's naughty senses of humour and rather scarlet pasts smacked of depravity.

'Besides,' Pixie added, 'she hardly needs the money. Graham is absolutely loaded.'

'Loaded,' Pheely agreed. 'Let the needy amongst us be first in the queue. You know, I'm sure I was *this* close to getting the *Masquerade* hare as a teenager.' She pinched finger and thumb together.

'Hard as finding a good man these days,' Pixie sighed.

'You don't really want Sexton back, do you?'

'Put it this way – it would be wonderful for the battered ego to know that I *could* get him back if needs be.'

Once the bottle of cheap wine had been plundered and Pixie had rushed off to save her children from one another, Pheely settled at the computer to compose her advert. Opening the window, she lit a very weak spliff to get her in the mood, apologising over her shoulder to Basil. Halfway through it, she put on an old Carpenters CD and closed her eyes as she contemplated the best way to describe herself both temptingly yet truthfully.

Stunning classical goddess trapped in curvaceous body armour seeks determined Svengali to liberate me . . . she started.

As the words started to flow, she failed to notice that the wine and dope were littering her typing with errors and, forgetting Pixie's warning words, she quickly abandoned honesty for hyperbole.

Soon, she was entering her Switch number to access three months' membership and post her advert live.

'There, boys!' She threw the purple shawl over her computer and turned back to baby Basil and Great Dane Hamlet, both of whom were fast asleep in their respective baskets. 'I think we can safely guarantee that you two will not be the only male influences around here for too much longer.'

But later, unable to stop obsessively checking her profile to see how many times it had been viewed that night she was disappointed to find that it hadn't been looked at once.

It took a while for her to notice that she had failed to fill in a section of the profile relating to her height and build. Instead of her usual tall story that she was five feet seven and an average weight (showing a head in the clouds and three stones lost in translation), her profile just displayed the form's start defaults of four foot six and very heavy build.

Livid at the waste of time and money, Pheely stomped off to bed. As she did so, her page received its first virtual kiss.

Flipper rode out at first light, stealing the best of the early dawn before the valley awoke, catching wildlife on the hop, dew intact on the fields, birds still exchanging pillow talk and a misty spring sun bursting over the horizon.

He had traditionally ridden out at this time with old chum Rory Midwinter, but nowadays, with a yard to run virtually single-handed, and a bigger drinking habit than ever, Rory rarely ever made it out.

Flipper missed his company; the companionship and rivalry had been cheering.

Now he had to rely upon the supportive charms of Olive, the one female in his life to whom he was unequivocally devoted. A gangly, dappled bay mare with a big white splash across her nose and one wall eye, Olive was pretty special. She had been bred at home at Fox Oddfield Abbey, and Flipper had seen her born in the big honeyed stone foaling box beside the archway in the yard during his school's Easter holidays. He had been in his first A level year at the time, undecided upon a career, still wavering between his secret dream of veterinary work and the obligatory pull of the family firm. The sight of Olive, slithering from her mother, fighting her way from the translucent birthing sack on to her wobbling feet, all big joints, wet fur and drooping ears that opened to look like a tortoiseshell butterfly within the first hour of her life, had made up his mind.

It had been unconditional love at first sight, and a career path had been embarked upon.

Eight years later, and Olive was a seasoned hunter and chaser. Unlike her fearless, bullish older full brother, Popeye, who belonged to Nell, Olive was a cautious soul who needed coaxing. But such was her trust in her master that she would jump any hedge or ditch for him, however unsighted the landing side; she would pass through fields of half-wild stock, wade through deep plough, trot along dual carriageways and ford a torrential stream. She trusted him with her life, and the feeling was mutual.

Until recently, their morning routes had inevitably taken in Church Cottage so that he could stop off and beg coffee – and often breakfast – from his sister-in-law. It was usually just Trudy in evidence, still awake from working all night, half cut, giggly, gossipy and irreverent. Finn, slumbering upstairs, rarely showed his face. In recent months, Flipper had even taken along girlfriend Dilly, sharing his most intimate time of day, his favourite places and people. She had rewarded him by dumping him just a few weeks earlier.

'We're best off without her,' he told Olive, whose tortoiseshell butterfly ears twitched in response.

Flipper was a natural on a horse, long legs wrapped easily round a saddle, thighs like steel, shock-absorber buttocks, gentle hands and an easy balance that glued him securely in place whatever country they were crossing.

Today, in the first steely light, he rode along the edge of the Gunning Woods as they hugged the spine of the ridge to just above Oddlode, the valley brightening in front of him so that he could now make out the pointed outline of the church spire, the roofs and chimneys and the lush triangle of Village Green with its steely mirror of a duck pond – a scaled-down toy village of model perfection when seen from a distance.

Dropping down through a small coppice and out into a cold breeze as he trotted a length of headland alongside newly planted linseed, he finally caught sight of the roof of Church Cottage appearing behind its neighbouring pair of church yews.

A light was glowing in the window of Trudy's study, and the small chimney above it was puffing out a thin line of smoke, indicating that she had her wood-burning stove blazing away. She worked in tropical heat, flicking her cigarette butts into the flames. Flipper joked that it was a very expensive ashtray.

Reining up by a gateway, he could see right down through the neighbouring field beyond the cottage paddocks. If he squinted, he imagined he could see Trudy's shadow against the far wall of the study.

He longed to thunder down there and knock lightly at the door, alerting her without waking Finn, but self-preservation held him back. He had lost too much face with Trudy as it was. Every time he thought about their encounter at the Easter family party he was drenched with a cold sweat of shame. She'd think he was a serious loser. Besides, he was due in early at work, having been offered the opportunity to assist one of the senior partners in a lengthy and delicate tendon operation that had only ever been attempted half a dozen times. It was a specialist area Flipper was keen to pursue, and participating in the operation was a great career bonus.

He kicked Olive into her effortless canter back up the hill.

Trudy's handsome chestnut, Tara, looked up and nickered as she recognised another horse so close by. Her field-mate, old half-blind Arty, let out an excited roar and started trotting towards the fence, grey head high.

But Flipper, with the devil at his heels, paid no heed as he hastened Olive to a gallop, eating up the miles to Fox Oddfield.

'You might have cooled her off a bit,' Sean the groom grumbled as Flipper handed over a sweating, breathless Olive.

'Stick her on the horse walker for ten minutes . . .' He dashed towards the house, almost tripping over his dog Mutt who had trotted out in delighted welcome.

'It's broke again . . .' Sean called, but Flipper was already out of earshot, racing inside to shower and change in time to for the clinic.

'Bastard!'

Despite the occasional moments of kindness – an offer of a lift to town on rare days off, a slug of brandy after a long frozen wait with second horses out hunting, an extra twenty quid in the pay packet as thanks for a sleepless night during foaling season, an enquiry after family – Flipper was as bad as the rest of the Cottrells under the skin, expecting to be waited on hand and foot. The family undoubtedly knew their horses, rode like cossacks and were as brave as lions, but they were also legendry for their reckless neglect.

Huffing irritably, Sean took Olive to rub her down.

He had barely thrown a sponge of warm, soapy water over her flanks when Nell appeared over the half door.

'Is Popeye in?' she enquired after her own long-forsaken mount, whom she hadn't ridden since falling some weeks earlier when first pregnant.

'Out with the brood mares,' Sean told her, blushing the shade of his hair and nose. Even five months pregnant, Nell was gallingly beautiful. 'You'll find him in the field by the gulley. Piers said to rough him off now you're – expecting,' he finished awkwardly.

'Has he got shoes on?'

'Not if he's out with the mares – Piers wouldn't allow it.'

'Damn! What's in that I can ride?'

'Nothing in at all today, apart from the lame ones on box rest.'

'Well, I'll take Olive out, then.'

'Flipper's only just got off her. She's awful hot.'

'I'll walk her off for him, cool her down. Save you slopping all that water about. Tack her up will you?'

'Are you sure you should . . .' He glanced involuntarily at her belly.

'Of course I can! My aunt was hunting a week before she gave birth.'

Given the opportunity to please Nell, and to slope off for an early tea break, Sean did as he was told, although he hoped she'd be true to her word and stick to walk, both for the sake of her baby and for poor, tired Olive.

Flipper was still in surgery when Piers called close to midday, leaving an urgent message. The tendon op was a long and delicate undertaking, presided over by Ross Dent, a vet Flipper idol-worshipped for his mind and skill, if not his manners. Brusque, short-tempered and unforgiving, Ross was lucky that his professional skills so greatly surpassed the limits of his personality. He was not a man you left hanging to take a call.

So when Piers called again, this time relaying an urgent message through the reception staff to say that Olive was colicking, Flipper sent word back to give her some Bute and get Sean to walk her round.

They had changed hay at Fox Oddfield recently, having run out of the home crop from the previous summer, and the new bales bought in from a local supplier to tide them over were upsetting some of the horses' stomachs. Several had suffered with the runs, and mild colics. Given Olive's sensitivity, she was bound to be among those affected.

It wasn't until Piers turned up in person and made a hullabaloo outside the operating theatre that Flipper realised there was something seriously wrong.

'GET OUT HERE!' he yelled at Flipper, sounding like their father in the days when he had demanded all his children run three miles every morning, a short-lived Piggy fanaticism that had driven them all demented.

Piers had brought Olive with him in the horsebox to the clinic.

'We might have lost her already,' he muttered through gritted teeth as he, Flipper and one of the veterinary nurses rushed round to the ramp.

The sight that greeted Flipper wrung out his heart.

Olive had gone down in the box, her sides drenched in sweat, steam rising from her coat. She was still putting up a fight, her eyes rolling, teeth bared and legs thrashing, but she was exhausted and in great pain.

'Jesus. Oh, Olive. I had no idea.'

For the first time in his professional career, Flipper froze.

Piers had rudimentary bedside manners, but he knew what to do in a crisis.

'Let's get her up!' He marched urgently up the ramp and reached for a long coil of rope on a high rack.

With little time for gentleness, but with an insistent level of persuasion that would have shifted a concussed rhino, Piers and the veterinary assistant got the mare to her feet, where she wobbled dangerously, trying to lash out with both hind legs. She was only persuaded to exit the box with the aid of a lunging whip, a broom and a lot of shouting.

Flipper stood rooted to the spot, helpless in his shock and guilt, watching as his greatest ally staggered into an observation stable.

Piers came back outside, threw an arm round Flipper's high, square shoulders and bunched him close, muttering in his ear.

'You *can* make a difference here.'

'I should put her out of her misery.'

'Give her a chance. You owe her that.'

Flipper looked across at his brother, a wise man who had worked around and loved horses all his life, who might have a mercenary streak that meant he'd sell any horse at the drop of a hat, but who would never willingly see one suffer. If Piers thought it was worth trying, then he couldn't refuse.

Rushing to scrub up, he tried to clear his mind completely. In order to function professionally, he knew that he'd have to imagine that he was back at college, working with a horse he had never seen before, his attitude purely clinical. The only difference was he had no expert help on hand here – no senior veterinary surgeons to observe, to advise and take over if necessary. This looked to be one of the most advanced colics he had attempted to treat, way beyond his realms of experience; he'd only have textbook examples to work by.

It was patently obvious that Olive needed surgery. Everything pointed towards a twisted gut – fatal without hasty intervention. The state of the art operating theatre at the clinic was still occupied by the irritated, abandoned Ross. Yet, without its specialist hoist and anaesthesia equipment, there were huge risks involved in opening up the mare in a makeshift alternative.

'You can't afford to wait,' Piers said as Flipper raced around, ham-fistedly setting up a drip to get some fluids into her.

'I'll give her some more Buscopan.' Flipper's teeth had started to chatter despite the relative warmth of the day. 'Ross'll be finished inside the hour.'

'Look at her! She doesn't have an hour. I haven't brought this bloody creature here to watch her die while you make whimpering noises. Just fucking well get on with it.'

Flipper did as he was told, knowing that Piers would probably punch him if he vacillated longer and, while he could stand the blow, it wouldn't help sharpen his eye for a painstaking operation. He went to scrub up again, his throat so tight it felt as though it was being garrotted.

They anaesthetised her in one of the padded recovery rooms, but his hands shook so much he could barely open her up.

Internally, Olive was a very complicated mess. Almost a third of her large intestine was unsalvageable, black with oxygen starvation where the torsions had segregated it from its life support. There was no choice but to cut it all out. The two ends of gut would then have to be attached together, but they were almost impossible to match up. The mare's defences were weak; she had been fighting this onset for a long time. That she had worked so willingly to her limit that morning without complaint, until she had literally dropped, made Flipper determined to save her.

At last, in his final stages of patching up what was left of the large intestine, help came to Flipper's aid in the form of Julian Goose, one of the clinic's longest-serving vets. A partner of the old school, who reeked of his liquid lunch with his racing cronies, he was a fearful snob and reactionary, but he did know his horses, and had performed more colic ops than most.

'Bloody lucky for the adoring owners that you're in charge on this one,' he commented after a good look, 'I might have been tempted to tell them there was nothing I could do. What did Ross say?'

'He's in surgery.'

'No he's not. He's having tea in the office with that pretty new receptionist – told me you were in here.'

'Bastard!' Flipper hissed.

His idol leg man had feet of clay.

But nor was Flipper particularly grateful for Julian's opinion when, after they had finally patched her up, he asked how he rated Olive's chances of recovery.

'Fifty-fifty if I'm generous. Haven't seen many lose that much gut and survive a week, let alone long term. Personally, I'd have put the beast out of its misery as soon as it got here.'

Cancelling his day's appointments, Flipper stayed with Olive all afternoon and through the night, monitoring her on the hour – much to the delight of the two veterinary nurses who lived in staff accommodation on site and had him to themselves for once. But he barely said a word to them, hardly acknowledging the cups of tea, biscuits and sandwiches that they lovingly laid before him.

Olive's limpid eyes watched him passively as he ran a hand over her skin, checked her abdomen and heartbeat, her breathing, her gums and her fluids.

But she never really recovered. Later, looking back, he wished he hadn't put her through it, that Julian had been around to advise earlier, or that he had listened to his own instincts. He had known she was a lost cause, yet his head had refused to go there, allowing him to be swept along in his brother's determined tide.

By late morning the following day, it was all over. An unshaven, creased and defeated Flipper shook hands with the kennel-man who had come to fetch the mare's body and then walked to the back of the surgery building where he wept like a child.

He drove up to Broken Back Woods, where he stared out across the valley that he and Olive had so often criss-crossed like a spider's web, and he wished her farewell. A part of him, in the darkest corner of his secret soul, wished that he had gone with her. It was better than the daily pain he had learned to endure these recent months.

Several sympathetic texts came through from colleagues, offering a shoulder to cry on over a drink if he needed it. But there was only one person he longed to speak to. Her mobile was switched off and he was too choked to leave a message. He tried the landline and recoiled as a horribly familiar voice answered with a smug 'hello.' The conversation was brief, the reaction down the line unsympathetic.

In the end he went to see his mother.

Like many women once possessed of spellbinding beauty, Dibs Cottrell had struggled with her desire to be an 'ordinary' mother to her three boys. Her sons could never find an equal to her, their friends (and their friends' fathers) fancied her, their girlfriends were intimidated and wildly jealous, their wives treated her like a simpleton as a defence mechanism. She was isolated time after time.

So when her youngest son turned up, as white as a sheet, looking like a car crash, she was ecstatic to welcome him into her arms.

Despite a lifetime of longing, poor Dibs was unpractised in the art of succour, and turned out not to be a natural at all. After stiff hugs and rejected offers of tea and cake – a point which she laboured far too hard, listing multiple baking options – she spent too long on the seating arrangements as she relocated her son from the kitchen to the smallest sitting room, then fiddled about arranging some of Jemima's embroidered cushions around him as though he were an invalid before fussing that he was wearing muddy shoes on her Turkish rugs.

Finally satisfied with the practicalities, she sat back with an expectant expression on her beautiful face, waiting to be told the reason for Flipper's distress without actually asking him. For a taciturn man like Flipper, brought up to hide his emotions, this led to an uncomfortable silence of several minutes.

The story finally came out in a stilted, confusing series of staccato sentences – his fault entirely, colic, might as well have got up and killed her with a bullet that morning, not worthy to be a vet, lost her forever, never deserved her . . .

When she discovered the source of her son's distress was just a dead horse, Dibs exclaimed in relief: she thought he had lost the love of his life.

'She *was* the love of my life!' he howled, already on a third glass of his father's best malt.

Dibs had a brief panic. She had mistakenly seen Peter Shaffer's *Equus* once and found it quite unsuitable for her taste.

She told herself firmly that Flipper was absolutely not that type.

He was still rambling on about the horse being more faithful than any woman, about losing his heart too many years ago to count.

'Don't be silly, darling.' Dibs patted his shoulder stiffly. 'You are far too young to have lost your heart.'

His troubled, dark-lashed eyes fixed on hers.

'I swear, mother, it's lost for all time.'

'Well you'd better set about finding it, then,' she said briskly, sounding like the tough-line nuns who had educated her in her native Ireland.

Flipper studied her face for a moment – her distant, watchful eyes, her amazing sculpted bone structure, and her ethereal beauty.

'What if somebody has taken it?'

'Nobody can steal a heart. We give them willingly, son.'

'*Hers* was stolen.'

Dibs disliked talking in metaphors. Plumping up the cushion at her elbow that read *Insanity is hereditary – you get it from your children*, she cleared her throat.

'Are you saying that you are in love with somebody who is already in a relationship?'

He nodded, relief already softening his taut features as he realised that he could confide his lifelong secret. 'She's married.'

Dibs pressed her lips together before reaching out to take his hands in hers, genuinely concerned. The lost horse was nothing to this; this was deadly serious. At first she had hoped that he'd been referring to his recent ex-girlfriend, Dilly (although secretly Dibs had been delighted when the union ended; the Gently girl had always been a Jezebel; her mother was just as bad).

But her beloved youngest son had just confessed that he was in love with a married woman. Dibs almost certainly knew who this woman was. She squeezed Flipper's hands very tightly and stared into his turbulent eyes, trying to reach for his poor, tarnished soul.

'In that case you must put her out of your mind, do you understand?' Her voice was low and earnest. 'You must *not* threaten the sacrament of marriage – the sacred bond. Oh, my poor boy, my poor boy.'

'But I love her,' he croaked.

'If you love her, let her go.'

It was a cliché so hackneyed that it should have come with a drum-roll and a cymbal clash, but Flipper didn't register the platitude. He was as low as he had ever been, all the fight drained from him.

'Promise me?' she entreated.

He kissed the soft knuckles of her fingers. They smelled of Pears soap and shortcrust pastry.

His own Catholicism had long since deserted him, but he knew how important the faith was to his mother. And he knew that if a sign was ever to be heeded, it was losing Olive today. There would be no more cosy breakfasts at Church Cottage. He had no right to be there, interfering in his brother's marriage and embarrassing Trudy. It was time to leave them alone.

'I promise.'

12

'It's so beautiful around here, isn't it?' Liv called over her shoulder as the horses climbed the bridleway towards the ridge that overlooked the Oddlode Valley, just hours after Flipper had regarded the same view, lamenting his loss.

Trudy followed her gaze.

After a slow, thwarted start, the landscape was starting to froth and fizz with blossom and spring flowers, with everything arriving at once. The cherry and hawthorn were both out in foamy splendour, along with yellow splashes of gorse matching the last of the wild daffodils, the ever-cheery primroses and the first cowslips. The Odd valley stretched beneath them like a vast green bedspread which had just been bounced upon by a host of rowdy spring toddlers eager to wake up their parents after the long winter sleep. Furled with creases and folds, scattered with new lambs and piped with hedges of lacy blossom, it was a wonderful, verdigris muddle of awakening life.

'I suppose I've just got used to it,' Trudy sighed, acknowledging it was indeed stunning, burnished with low, late afternoon sunlight.

'Oh, I don't think I'll ever take it for granted.' Liv watched a buzzard soar high overhead, screeching plaintively.

Despite the fact that her white-knuckled fingers were still clamped into Otto's mane and her top teeth were stapled nervously to her lower lip, she was starting to enjoy herself at long last.

They had hacked out daily for a week now, grateful that the rain had finally passed and enabled them to gossip and giggle on horseback. Liv was still nervous; it took her several slugs of Rescue Remedy to mount up, twice as much if Giles was around, but she was beginning to relax more as each day passed. So far, they had stuck largely to the village lanes, where she felt safest, but Trudy was determined to break that habit. The local tracks and field margins were drying out; there were hills to gallop and hunt jumps to fly.

As well as her tactic of distracting her friend with village gossip and witty criticisms of marriage and fidelity, she had pulled out another trick: the boozy lunch. After a couple of glasses of wine, Liv had the nerves of a jump jockey. They admittedly only lasted about fifteen minutes, but that was long enough to get her in the saddle and off-road.

Today, bolstered by a shared bottle of Pinot Grigio over open sandwiches in the Duck Upstream, and the fact that she had cut Otto's oat ration to calm him down, Liv had been persuaded to take the safe, circular route along the ridge, a cart-track avenue with high hedges and sturdy rails to funnel the horses along. Having reluctantly promised to stay in walk at all times, Trudy was now quite grateful because the safety pin had given way on her broken breeches' zip, rendering anything faster likely to cause a serious wardrobe malfunction. Besides which Tara, still monstrously unfit, was already steaming.

'That makes two of us,' Trudy murmured to her mare, patting her hot, wet neck.

She was more than happy to idle along, anyway. Finn had decided to work from home today, so anything that kept her out of the house was a bonus. The dogs bounded along behind them, happy for the long walk. The sun, staining the clouds on the horizon an eye-watering saffron as it fell lower, cast a wonderful, slanting yellow light across the fields, bringing out the high relief of the ridges and furrows.

Talk at lunch had been dominated by the treasure hunt, about which Liv was highly excited.

'It's such a shame you can't take part,' she said for the umpteenth time.

'Well, it would look pretty shabby if a Cottrell won the money,' Trudy pointed out. 'There's nothing stopping *you*, though.'

'People might think you're giving me the answers,' Liv fretted.

Despite the relative newness of their friendship, the two already worked like foils together. Trudy was externally positive and impulsive yet riddled with self-doubt; Liv was outwardly cautious and pessimistic whilst inwardly volatile and occasionally irresponsible. Quick to criticise others if they behaved in a way she thought selfish, Trudy was equally quick to forgive if they redeemed themselves. Secretly swift to damn others, and deeply unforgiving, Liv could nonetheless be a magnanimous and thoughtful devil's advocate. She also worried endlessly about what people thought of her whereas Trudy, apparently, couldn't give a stuff, especially when it came to the Cottrells' treasure hunt.

'Let them think what they like,' she said now. 'You could get Martin to help.'

'But he's in Singapore.'

'So?'

'Mmm, I suppose he could still take part – he's a whiz at crosswords and such. I'm going to email him the first clue.'

Appearing on posters for the Horse Fair throughout nearby villages, and in a large advert in the local press, the first of the clues was a dreadful poem written by Piggy after too much port.

The treasure hunt irritated Trudy, being a classic example of the Cottrells sticking their collective heads in the sand again. She wanted no part of it. It was all Finn talked about, making her all the more allergic to it.

'When is Martin coming home?' she asked now, to change the subject.

Liv sucked in her pale cheeks. 'Well, he was really frustrated not to make it back for Easter and he gave his bosses a *very* hard time, so he promises he should be able to get a decent break soon. Oh, God, a pheasant!'

She let out a panicked shriek as the big, golden bird flapped from the hedgerow and squawked off into the sunlight. Beneath her, Otto barely gave it a second glance, far more focused on trying to snatch mouthfuls of sugary cow parsley and wild cherry blossom as he passed them.

'There – he's pheasant-proof,' Trudy reassured Liv, who was still shaking.

Liv rode as upright as a cavalryman; head forwards as though wearing a neck-brace, stiff shoulders clamped anxiously to her ears and hands clinging on to leather and mane for grim life.

'What does Martin think about you getting your own horse?' Trudy asked now, knowing that keeping her companion talking was one of the secrets to relaxing her.

Liv was no more keen to talk about Martin than Trudy was to discuss the treasure hunt. Martin had, in fact, said nothing about when he was due home from Singapore and meanwhile, Liv was giving houseroom to his boorish parents, who insisted on eating supper at six o'clock, watching all the soaps, hogging the hot water for their baths and leaving the landing light glowing as they creaked and puffed to the loo four times a night. If Liv started letting off steam about her husband or his family right now, she was in danger of not knowing when to stop.

'Oh, he was all for it,' she lied. 'I've emailed him lots of pics of Otto, and Martin even says that he might have a go when he gets back. He wants the children to have lessons again, too.'

Martin had actually grumbled about how much it was going to cost him, commented that all horses looked the same to him, and made pointed remarks about the smell of manure. But he did want the children to start, seeing it as another rung up the country set social ladder.

'Take them to Rory Midwinter at Upper Springlode,' Trudy suggested. 'He starts most of the little ones off around here. The place is chock-a-block with patterned-welly mums at weekends, most of them dolled up to the nines for young Rory, who is something of a dish. He thinks they're dreadful, but he's great with the kids. He'll love you because you're different.'

'I have patterned wellies,' Liv admitted.

'Perfect disguise! You have to wear them if you're to fit in with the yummy mummies, but Rory will think you're heaven after all those pushy three-wheeler buggy bitches he has to fight off with a yard broom.'

Trudy was great for bolstering the ego.

'So the local mummies don't have much luck?'

They were heading back to their favourite risqué topic of Oddlode flirtation and adultery.

Trudy shook her head. 'Not as far as I know. He's one for the single girls, not a specialist like Giles. I'll text you his number later,' she promised. 'I even have his mobile number – what the local Boden Brigade wouldn't give for that! You should offer it for sale at the school gates. That would get them crowding around you.'

Liv had been complaining about the arrogance of the local yummies, her tongue loosened by the wine. With the children back at school after the Easter break, Liv was once again enduring the cold Joseph shoulder pad at the school gates. It might be a bore that her in-laws were still in situ, but at least she could dispatch them to brave what Trudy variously referred to as the 'Boden Brigade',

'Patterned Welly Parents' or, at her most cruel, 'Hildas', which stood for Husband in London Doing Adultery. Liv didn't like to dwell on what Trudy thought husbands in Singapore got up to.

Trudy's witty, sarcastic way of rendering the local community into a series of cartoon vignettes for Liv's entertainment made her paranoia and sense of inadequacy melt away.

'I'll give this Rory a call,' she promised now, and then added, 'what – er – did you mean by saying that Giles is a 'specialist'?'

'Oh, just that he has an eye for married women – I've told you as much. Has he been hanging about, then? I sensed a frisson last week.'

Trudy couldn't help herself. Like a child that keeps edging too close to a fire and poking it with a stick, even though it knows it'll get burned, she was fuelling the flame of Liv's crush on Giles. A part of her hated herself, yet this prurient performance was providing her greatest kicks right now as she lived the vicarious thrill of a crush alongside her new friend.

'Oh, he's been really lovely, terribly helpful. I had no idea he knew so much about horses.'

'Only when it suits him,' muttered Trudy, surprised by the stab of jealousy that dug its way between her shoulder blades. 'You watch out there.'

Rory Midwinter was teaching his last lesson of the day: Jemima Cottrell's children, Bartleby and Georgia. Aged ten and eight, they were already fiercely competitive Pony Club stalwarts, well-known at local shows for their unusual Chinese looks and their foul language.

'Get off my fucking line, G!' Bartleby shrieked now as he thundered around the short side towards a little upright jump and almost ploughed into his sister.

'Just like his father,' Jemima sighed as she watched from the sidelines with teenage stable hand Faith Brakespear, who worked for Rory when her A-level commitments allowed.

Faith had bunked off college that afternoon to spend time at the yard, riding her horse Rio and hanging out with Rory. His company was infinitely preferable to an afternoon of Geography, and it was lovely to get him to herself for once . . . well, almost to herself.

She glanced at her watch. The lesson was overrunning.

'It's past four!' she called out.

He glanced across and nodded, a ghost of a grateful wink touching one grey eye, making her belly concertina like a squeeze box.

'Rory always gives mine extra time because they're so talented,' Jemima boasted, aiming her words six inches over Faith's head despite the height difference that placed her at chin level. 'It was Rory who suggested extra coaching on top of the Pony Club rallies he runs – he spotted their talent a mile off.'

He needs the money, more like, and spotted your indulgent streak, Faith thought irritably. She gazed across to Rory who was putting up the jump, sliding the rusty metal cups up the wooden wings with their peeling paint. Everything at the yard needed replacing or doing up.

Having as Faith saw it been let down by his family, Rory was permanently strapped for cash, his talent with horses forever overshadowed by the long hours he worked, his ongoing debts and the way that everybody took advantage of his kind, easy-going nature.

Tawny and blond, with a permanent sleepy smile, almond-shaped silver-grey eyes with long, sooty lashes, a mane of unkempt hair the colour of eucalyptus bark and high, slanting cheekbones, he was better looking than any male model, actor or rock star Faith could hope to pin up on her wall. Still boyish enough to bound around Tigger-like with the children he taught, yet more than manly, stubbly and feral enough to set their mothers' hearts racing, he was the ultimate Home Counties heart-throb – a talented horseman, a party animal, a renowned seducer, a total charmer, and a part of the almost extinct Constantine clan to boot. If only he didn't drink so much, he might survive long enough to make something of himself. At just twenty-five, he was already in danger of self-destructing, just another thing that made him so irresistibly attractive to women, and teenage girls.

Faith and Jemima admired Rory's bottom in silence for a moment. It was one of the best sights in the Cotswolds.

'How's your lovely mother?' Jemima asked eventually. 'I'm so excited about the little bookshop reopening. It's perfect for gifts.'

'Hmph.' Faith had no interest in her mother's business venture, taking over the reins of her grandfather's antiquarian bookshop in Oddlode.

'Do pass on my regards,' Jemima quacked on.

Faith nodded. Her mother, Anke, was hugely popular locally, fetêd almost. Much as she loved her, Faith found her mother austere, blunt and sometimes socially awkward because of her Danishness. Yet, as well as attracting academics, arty types and culture vultures through her bookshop renovation, the glamorous horsey and hunting set like Jemima Cottrell were also all over her. Faith supposed it was because Anke had once been quite a famous rider; she'd won an Olympic gold, after all. In addition, she belonged to all sorts of local groups, from gardening to history to music appreciation to literature, along with sitting on an enormous number of charity committees. Anke was a 'doer', with a kind heart and a wealthy husband. She also looked stunning in an icy, blond cashmere-and-pearls way, with her shiny bob and her wide-cheeked, symmetrical bone structure.

Faith, who wished she had inherited more than just her mother's height and skinny legs, was neither a doer nor a looker. Resentfully studying for three A levels when all she wanted to do was ride professionally, she was going through a prolonged awkward, gawky phase that had started at puberty and, at sixteen, showed no signs of blossoming into swan-like beauty. She still had running braces on her goofy teeth, her shoulders sloped, she had yet to develop breasts or a waist, she towered over other girls, had size nine feet and dreadful, frizzy hair the colour of a used tea bag. She loathed the way she looked. To make matters worse, she was going through a very difficult patch with her mother who, fearing that Faith was developing body dysmorphia syndrome, had recently been making unrealistic attempts at bolstering her daughter's confidence by buying her hideous new clothes, telling her she looked wonderful and suggesting they attend dance classes together 'for fun'.

Faith put up a dogged resistance: mother and daughter's matching stubborn streaks were dividing them.

At last, Rory was wrapping up the lesson. If Faith had timed it right, Jemima Cottrell would get her brats' ponies in the trailer and go home with at least a clear hour before Rory's horrible new girlfriend Justine Jones arrived.

But Jemima hung about chatting to Rory for an age.

The old bat was flirting with him, Faith realised furiously. Once a very successful three day-event rider, Jemima still had the firm thighs and trim waist of a regular athlete, matched with ridiculously big blue eyes and a toothy smile. She was, Faith acknowledged, quite attractive in a leathery, starched, poppy-eyed sort of a way. And she was still very well connected in the horse world, dropping so many names that Rory couldn't help but hang around and watch them fall, knowing he was being thrown tempting scraps. Struggling on the lower rungs of eventing himself, he was aware that being allied to Jemima Cottrell was a very good thing. With her contacts, husband Piers' constant influx of top-quality horseflesh and the Cottrell family money, Jemima was just the sort of patron he dreamed of.

'Had Hugo and Tash Beauchamp to sups last week,' she was braying.

Faith snarled jealously into the top of her broom handle. The Beauchamps were all-time sporting heroes of hers; Jemima Cottrell didn't deserve to know them. Her love for Rory made it easy to hate anyone that monopolised him.

When Jemima finally made to leave, Faith resisted the urge to whoop with relief and sweep her and her spoiled children up into the Land Rover. At last, she could talk to Rory about her plan.

But before Jemima had even started her engine, Faith heard another car heading their way from the village and looked to the driveway to see her mother's big, shiny off-roader turning in from the Oddlode lane.

Jemima fell on Anke like a long-lost friend, which at least gave Faith a chance to corner Rory as he sloped off to the tack room to locate his hip flask in an abandoned jacket.

'Have you read about the Cottrells' treasure hunt?' she demanded quickly as she panted after him.

He looked blank, sagging into the ancient leather armchair in the corner, which was heaped with rugs and numnahs. A moment later, and a furious yard cat leaped out from beneath him to be unceremoniously chased from the room by Twitch, the Jack Russell.

'There's a fifty grand prize up for grabs,' Faith pointed out.

The sleepy pewter eyes gleamed with interest. That would buy a very decent event horse – and repair the elderly horsebox.

'What do you have to do to win it?' He swigged back the contents of his hip flask.

She explained breathlessly.

'I thought we could do it together; with my brains and your local knowledge, we'd be brilliant.'

Rory smiled that wide, crooked, white-toothed smile that reached right into the corners of his eyes and which always flipped over Faith's heart like a pancake. 'Us?'

'Yes.' She tried to sound cool by adding, 'I had been going to team up with my brother and Dilly, but they're too busy. I thought you'd enjoy it instead. You're always saying how clever I am.' She blushed to her gingery roots.

'You *are* clever. But I'm as thick as two short planks. I'd only hold you back.'

'I need you!' she bleated, and then, realising that she sounded far too eager, cleared her throat and shrugged casually. 'You've got local know-how – hunting and all that. The Cottrells are bound to focus on that.'

He looked uncertain.

'I've already worked out the first clue,' she badgered, watching her mother shake off Jemima Cottrell and make her way towards them. '*Please* Rory,' she went on urgently. 'We can split the profits.'

'I'll think about it,' he murmured unenthusiastically. 'Maybe I'll talk to Tin Tin and see if she wants to join in? That could be more fun.'

Faith groaned. The last thing she wanted was Rory's chesty, giggling girlfriend Justine joining in. But she'd lost his attention.

'You look wonderful, as always!' Rory was kissing Faith's mother on the cheeks, bounding around her like an enthusiastic puppy. She had been an idol of his for years.

Tall, athletic and blue-eyed, Anke was a flawless specimen of womanhood, if not particularly mumsy-looking, warm or sensual. Today, she was immaculately turned out in spotless, well-tailored white jeans, a striped Breton top and navy loafers.

'I thought I might find you here,' she said to Faith.

'She's been a great help this afternoon.' Rory slapped Faith on the back with chummy vigour.

Anke smiled frostily. 'I'm sure – but she is supposed to be at college this afternoon.'

Faith scuffed her toes against the gravel underfoot. 'The afternoon's last lesson was cancelled.'

Anke gave her a disappointed look. 'I was waiting outside when it came out, but your friends said that you left after lunch. I was going to take you out to tea.'

Faith could have died. Only her mother would do something as humiliating as turning up on campus to offer her a cream tea.

'Still, I've found you now,' Anke went on, not wanting to cause a scene. 'I'll give you a lift home and we can have a chat there.'

'I've got my bike,' Faith pointed out irritably, feeling about six. 'Besides, I haven't finished here.'

'Yes we have – everything's about done,' Rory assured her. 'And I need to hop in the shower before Tin Tin turns up.'

Faith scowled into her fleece collars. Any mention of blowsy Justine with her dark curtain of perfectly straight hair, tiny waist and 36DD assets, made her feel physically ill.

'In that case we can put your bicycle on the car rack.' Anke patted her daughter's back so that she almost swallowed her zip tag. 'I want to talk to you about the auction treasure hunt.'

Faith glared.

'Have you heard about it, Rory?' Anke ignored her daughter's black look.

'Faith was just telling me. She even knows what the answer to the first clue is, clever thing.'

'Well that's wonderful, *kaereste*! For some reason, I thought you might not be interested.' Anke was delighted at the opportunity to share some valuable mother–daughter time.

'But I'm doing it with—'

'Great idea!' Rory saw a way of getting himself off the hook. 'You'll both have a ball and are bound to win it; you're so clever. I'm too busy anyway.'

'But I—'

Anke cut across her, taking the baton from Rory. 'Let's hurry home for tea before Graham and Chad get back and steal all the cake – I bought your favourite from Oddford Delicatessen. Coffee and walnut.'

Faith, furious at being hijacked from treasure hunting with Rory and faced with a cake guaranteed to blow her diet, travelled back to Wyck Farm in a glowering sulk.

Her only consolation was that if she won the money – and she supposed having her painstakingly pedantic mother on board was some sort of asset in that department – she was definitely going to blow her winnings on cosmetic surgery. She had it all planned: rhinoplasty, liposuction and lip augmentation just for starters. She also wanted eye laser surgery and teeth whitening. But most of all she wanted a boob job. Rory was a breast man, and she was determined to have the best breasts in the county, however much they cost. Her mother couldn't stop her. In fact, it gave Faith a certain macabre pleasure to realise that her mother was, in fact, going to help.

Beside her, totally unaware, Anke smiled contentedly and looked forward to the weeks ahead in which they could at last share a common interest.

Negotiating the narrow lanes from Upper Springlode to Fox Oddfield with the pony trailer hitched behind her husband's big Discovery, Jemima Cottrell was enjoying an equally contented glow as she rode the wave of her lovely chat with Rory, one of her favourite local young bloods. He could be wild, and known for drinking too much and partying too hard, but he was undoubtedly one of the greatest unsung riding talents in the county. Piers often commented that the boy could have become an international star by now were it not for his love of hell-raising. Still only in his mid-twenties and running the business that he had inherited from his uncle, Rory lived on a shoestring, yet continued to show such untapped potential that it was a source of constant frustration to those who knew and loved him.

Jemima felt rather protective towards Rory for all his faults, and longed to help him out, however much Piers resisted the idea. She rather liked the idea of mentoring young talent, becoming an owner and a coach in the eventing world that she missed so badly now that she was a dedicated wife to a hunting-mad auctioneer. And Rory certainly needed the help. He was also gratifyingly easy on the eye, eager to please and hugely sexy.

She had found herself fantasising about him while Piers was doing his conjugal duty one recent Sunday morning, although the outcome hadn't been entirely satisfactory when Piers had lost his erection. He blamed a hangover, but she was unconvinced. In the past, any short-lived impotence had been a sure-fire sign that he was playing around. This time, she was too deflated to feel angry; she simply felt numbed by the familiar sting of his lack of respect. Turning her head away in disgust, and her mind back to Rory, Jemima had spent a consoling half-hour contemplating ways in which she could cultivate the young eventing star for both business and pleasure – and a little sweet revenge on her philandering husband.

Recently the return of his elder half-sister, Diana, had seemed to augur a change in Rory's fortunes. But, with a reputation even wilder than Rory's, Diana had been quickly distracted by a love affair and had now lost all interest in the stables; local rumour had it that she was expecting a baby. Jemima thought her an infuriating waste of time, far too like Trudy, if somewhat better bred and considerably more fecund.

Jemima's mistrust of her sister-in-law had escalated since the Easter party. While not exactly ignoring her, Trudy had been infuriatingly vague that day and Jemima suspected she had been extremely drunk, or on drugs. Why the men in the family always crowded around her so attentively baffled Jemima. Trudy had looked awful. Maybe they saw her as 'one of the lads'. After this most recent attempt to extend the hand of friendship across the divide, Jemima felt rejected, although she wasn't exactly sure why. She supposed Trudy's brush off just added to a catalogue of little snubs on previous occasions – the failure to return calls or lend her useful name to Jemima's charity events, and the forgotten birthdays, especially the children's.

Jemima had always felt superior to Trudy. She had a better background, was better educated, better turned out, more socially adept, far better at running a household and far more skilled at dealing with the Cottrell egos. Yet Trudy failed to acknowledge this, or even rise to the competitive challenge. Friendly, effusive, embarrassingly demonstrative yet curiously uninterested in Jemima, she drifted around as though in an animated dream. Jemima was jealous of Trudy. It made no sense, and yet there she was, envious and resentful, in a state of mind that was eating away at her.

Head full of irritable thoughts, she belted the car too fast over the blind hill at the top of the ridge, the low sun looming directly into her eyes. Suddenly, from nowhere, she found herself facing two riders on horseback.

Forced to brake too fast, she cursed under her breath as her children screeched from the back seat and the ponies in the trailer behind started thumping disapproving hooves against the rubber-coated mats of the ramp.

'Bloody imbeciles.' Jemima squinted into the sun where the two riders were clattering across the road, holding their crops up in gratitude and apology. For a moment, she was so blinded by the light that all she could make out was the closest one, slouching like a cowboy and smoking a cigarette.

They were probably gypsies heading towards the forthcoming Horse Fair.

Hot-headed with adrenalin from the near miss, and not stopping to think, she buzzed down her window and shouted: 'That was a bloody fool place to cross the road!'

A familiar gurgle of apologetic laughter greeted her and she winced in recognition.

'You are absolutely right, Jemima! Forgive me. We were so wrapped up talking that I didn't think. My fault entirely.'

'I could have flattened you, Trudy,' Jemima quacked, realising that her sister-in-law was the culprit, lounging indolently on her tall liver chestnut mare. Some sort of bad karma had to be at play here. The kids were ecstatic, buzzing down their windows to greet 'Aunty Tru' with enthusiasm.

'Isn't that the Gentlys' gelding?' Jemima cut across their banter as she peered at Trudy's companion on the striking roan.

The woman nodded, frozen with fear, like a field mouse in the path of a hay baler.

'Olivia Wilson, this is my sister-in-law, Jemima Cottrell,' Trudy introduced them, explaining, 'Liv bought Otto from the Gentlys a week or so ago.'

Jemima nodded approvingly. 'Haven't we already met? Were you at the Fulkingtons' drinks party last week?'

Liv shook her head.

'Elderly Care Aware fund-raising lunch?'

Again, Liv shook her head.

A little voice behind Jemima piped up, 'She's Jasper and Lily's nanny.'

The penny dropped. 'Oh – forgive me. Sweet little things. You must work for the parents. My two go to the same school. You must chum up with my nanny, Nuala. Lovely girl.'

As Liv's eyes filled with mortified tears, Trudy waded in to save her. 'Olivia is Lily and Jasper's mother, Jemima. They are *her* children.'

'Oh, Christ – how ghastly of me to jump to the wrong conclusion!' Jemima apologised profusely.

Overcompensating for the gaffe, Jemima found herself issuing an unheard-of spontaneous invitation.

'You must come to late lunch one day. Next week, perhaps? Nuala can collect the children and they can all play together. Might that suit?'

Liv nodded.

'Super! I'll call you to arrange the day. Trudy can give me your number. In fact, Trudy *must* come, too.'

'Gee, thanks.' Trudy tried to visualise herself in amongst the yummy mummies and 'divs' that Jemima inevitably gathered at such events.

Jemima smiled insincerely, gave both riders a curt nod and, checking in her wing mirror, set off again with a regal wave.

It was only when she was halfway home that it occurred to her that Liv Wilson hadn't uttered a single word during the encounter.

'What are her children like?' she asked her two now.

'Shy.'

'Quiet.'

'A bit boring, really.'

Jemima sighed. 'Oh, dear.'

She was already dreading lunch. It had nothing to do with Liv and everything to do with wanting to trounce Trudy.

Trudy was still laughing as they rode out from the last wooded stretch of the bridleway and onto the lane that led back towards Oddlode.

'She *has* to want to gather you into her posse,' she assured Liv again. 'Believe me, she has no interest in me. We're like chalk and cheese – we're polite enough, but from different planets. She disapproves of my humble origins and wicked past,' she giggled. 'Her family are incredibly top-drawer. She even went to finishing school. When I was lurching about Penzance with my mates drinking too much scrumpy and comparing love-bites, she was learning to arrange flowers in some Austrian *Schloss*. Imagine that!'

Common sense could have told Liv that Jemima Cottrell was from just as different a planet from herself, but her latent snobbishness temporarily blinded her to this. Trudy helped keep that daydreaming wool pulled comfortingly over her eyes as she pandered to Liv's social climbing streak.

'You're *definitely* in with the yummy mummies now,' she uttered the sacred phrase. 'Jemima is their head girl. You wait and see.'

Liv flushed. Martin would be thrilled when she emailed him later to say that she'd been invited to a girls' lunch with the local MFH's wife.

It had, she reflected, been a wonderful afternoon – having her ego massaged and her sense of humour tickled by Trudy was far better than an aromatherapy session. Otto was starting to scare her a bit less. She even had the makings of an extra-curricular social life with other mothers.

And best of all, in the gathering shadows of the long, tree-lined drive to River Cottage, she could make out Giles Hornton.

'Good ride?' he greeted them with a blue-eyed smile.

'Super, thanks,' Liv managed to croak.

'Liv and Otto are getting on superbly.' Trudy patted her own mare's sweaty neck. 'They'll make a great team.'

'Good for you.' Giles carried on twinkling at Liv as he held her reins so that she could dismount. 'Can I offer you two girls a drink?'

'Not for me.' Trudy turned Tara back towards the lane, although the suggestion of much-needed alcohol made her tongue hang out. 'I have to get home before it gets any darker.' With no fluorescent riding gear and the dogs following loose, she was already running risks by riding through the lanes in the fading light.

'Shame.' Giles hid his disappointment behind a big, come-hither smile. 'Still, you'll share a glass of wine with a lonely chap while you untack, won't you Liv?'

While Liv nodded eagerly, Giles gave Trudy a private and very hot look over Otto's back. It was like a shot in the arm, better than any stiff drink.

'I'll call you about that – other matter, shall I?'

'What other matter?'

'The matter you and I were talking about at the Easter party. Our unfinished business from the Auctioneers' Ball – I told you I had a *Semillon* I promised you could sample.' He emphasised the wordplay.

Trudy screwed up her face in concentration, wishing that she could remember more of the Easter party, but apart from the usual mild flirtation with Giles, and his promise that he could make her happier, it was all a bit of a blur.

'Yeah, sure. Best to text me, maybe?' That way, she could try to remember details at leisure.

'Text?' Giles swaggered with bravado in very Leslie Phillips fashion: 'I don't text, darling. It's common.'

'You don't text because you don't know how,' she teased. 'It'd help you no end with all those illicit liaisons. Leaving notes *d'amour* rolled up in dry stone walls and trees is a bit old hat don't you think?'

To do him credit, he laughed. 'I'm more of an email *d'amour* man these days.'

'So widen your repertoire and text *d'amour*. It's great for making the thumb flexible.'

'You're right. I've got to learn sometime, particularly as I've just got a snazzy new phone: unlimited texts.' He waved something tiny and metallic at her. 'It even takes videos and plays a five-act opera in perfect stereo through a headset. 'Mazing stuff. D'you want my new number?'

She shook her head, eager to get away from all the innuendo. 'No time – I must go. Just text me later and I'll save the number. Enjoy your drink. See you!'

Trudy hoped, as she trotted away, that Liv would be safe. Giles was radiating testosterone, making her suspect that he was between affairs and getting restless for new blood. He was always at his most persistent when in that state. She cursed herself for almost flirting back. There was a wanton reek of adulterous intention in the air and she knew it didn't come from squeaky-clean Liv.

But Trudy was quite wrong. At River Cottage, Liv was fragrant in her flagrance, wafting out the honeyed pheromones of temptation. Bolstered by her lunch invitation from Jemima Cottrell, Liv was in rare, flirtatious form, eager to eke out the day before returning to her disapproving in-laws who were showing no signs of returning to Kent while they could enjoy Martin's Waitrose account, satellite movie channels and under-floor heating. For once, Giles's unadulterated testosterone-and-sin eyes didn't frighten her, nor did his suggestive one-liners and distractingly masculine, toned and tailored physique. For once, as soon as they were alone together, she didn't run coyly home to lie in her room and fantasise about him. She stayed for another drink. And, as Trudy had discovered, after a couple of glasses of wine, Liv had nerves of steel. Before she knew it, they had finished the bottle. Liv didn't hesitate to accept his offer to open another.

'Marvellous! I have a particularly fine Semillon I'd like you to try,' he purred, steering her in through his French windows. 'I was going to save it for Trudy, but I've a robust, full-bodied red already laid down that I think will much be more appropriate for her.'

13

At Church Cottage, Finn was wearing a boiler suit and pointedly banging about with paint pots, brushes and dust sheets under the five-hundred-watt glare of several metal-caged work lights. But his hands, face and hair were suspiciously free from paint-flecks, the television was tuned to a satellite horse-racing channel and the squashed, messed-up cushions on the sofa in front of it were still warm.

He still hadn't hired a new team of builders to replace those that he'd fired, and decorating was a pointless gesture in the light of the vast amount of construction work still to be done. They both knew it, but neither would mention it until the situation got critical – in the same way that Trudy said nothing when Finn made a big show of paying the milkman or window cleaner in cash when he owed tens of thousands elsewhere.

'Any calls?'

'A few. Nothing important. Why, were you expecting any?' he snapped, stirring some congealed paint with what appeared to be a brand-new screwdriver.

'Just my book editor. She said she'd catch up by the end of the week.'

'She didn't call.'

'So who did?' She resented the fact that he never, ever passed on phone messages – even urgent ones from her mother, agent, friends or doctor – and she was hoping to hear from Johnny.

'The electrician, crying off until next week. I sacked him,' he reported with satisfaction, then added as an afterthought. 'And Flipper rang about a dead horse.'

'What horse?'

'No idea.' He scraped the screwdriver loudly on the side of the pot. 'It didn't sound important.'

'Did he want me to call back?'

'I hardly imagine so. He's *my* little brother, Trudy.' He banged the lid back on the paint and straightened up, wiping his hands on his boiler suit.

Trudy clenched her teeth at his petty possessiveness over his family. He very pointedly wanted nothing to do with her family, so considered his own to be out of bounds unless she was under supervision.

'You know Flipper's sick sense of humour. It was probably just a joke.'

'Not a very good one by the sounds of it,' she muttered, realising that she hadn't spoken to Flipper since the drunken Easter party. That had been a strange day; no wonder he was resorting to ringing up with Mafia jokes. She really should pull out of her bad mood soup and call him to clear the air. It was easy to instigate quick, cheery chats with friends and family when she was on good form, but in her recent rundown and disheartened state she had let things slip, Flipper included.

Finn was following her around as he always did when she had been out, more bodyguard than companion.

'Did you have a good ride?'

'Great thanks.'

'Did you go out with your new chum? Liz, isn't it?'

'Liv – yes.' She re-tied her pony tail, wrapped up in thoughts of neglected friends, and new ones. 'She's a really sweet person, very shy and apparently superficial, but incredibly complicated underneath. I think she's probably a lot tougher than she realises.'

But Finn was only interested in practical details, as though staging a military debrief. 'Where did you go?'

'Oh – just the short ridge ride. I hope it helped Liv's confidence. I think having her husband so far away has knocked her self-esteem.'

'What does he do?'

'Something in telecommunications, I think.'

'Successful?' Finn judged people by their salaries.

'Well, that barn conversion must have cost over a million.'

'We should have them over to supper when he's back.'

Trudy glanced around the room, which was mostly swathed in dust sheets. 'Yes – we can all eat off a wallpaper pasting table,' she joked.

He shot her a withering look. 'I've been making headway.'

Resisting an urge to point out that that they needed builders not paint effects, Trudy determinedly avoided conflict. Finn rarely exploded these days, preferring to snap and snipe, or sulk silently, but tonight his safety catch looked suspiciously hairline. Trudy was fairly certain that his day at home had nothing to do with wanting to work on the house, and everything to do with wanting to avoid the Cottrells' office and adult responsibilities.

'It was a fun afternoon,' she said lightly, 'but I should really be making headway, too. I have lots of ideas and a much clearer head, so I might work this evening if that's OK?'

'Sure, we can work together. I'll listen to you "creating" at the piano.' He made it sound like she would accompany him at his labours with a few background arpeggios like a hotel lounge entertainer.

Trudy felt suffocating fingers clutch at her temples. He would check she wasn't drinking too much, comment on everything she was doing, cajoling and criticising like a teacher encouraging a dim-witted pupil. It was the way he controlled her, a long-established pattern that had once been comforting. Sitting at her piano with the cat asleep on top and Finn lounging on a fireside sofa behind her had once been her ultimate domestic tableau. These days it was a living nightmare.

'I'll be at the computer with the headphones on,' she muttered. 'You know I can't concentrate if there are interruptions.'

'I won't interrupt.'

She smiled stiffly, knowing that just having him breathing over her would kill her creativity. 'I have to put some stuff on disc. Then I really need to get on with these memoirs – just a few notes. It shouldn't take long.'

'If you insist.' He shrugged grumpily. 'What's for supper?'

'Posh Waitrose ready meal. You can cook it, if you like – it just needs microwaving.'

He looked affronted, as always when she suggested he lift a finger in the kitchen. It was as if she had asked him to don a pinny featuring fake bare breasts, sport a hairnet, clingfilm his manhood between his legs for health and safety reasons and then whip up a cordon bleu extravaganza involving miniature soufflés, wild garlic *jus* and truffle foam.

'Say about eight?' she pressed, knowing the meal was an idiot-proof prick and ping.

'It's all right, I'll leave it to you.' He gave her a condescending look. 'I really need to crack on this evening even though I didn't have the luxury of an afternoon off.'

Trudy went to mix herself a drink, uncapping a beer for Finn while she was about it because she felt guilty for the involuntary, skin-tightening way that she always reacted to him. His bossiness and superiority were just defence mechanisms, she was certain, and yet they triggered fear and paranoia in her.

But he didn't accept the peace offering, glancing pointedly at his watch and setting the bottle of beer to one side.

Feeling rebuked, Trudy sloped to the study with the dogs, quietly shutting the door behind her and then topping up her weak vodka Coke with the bottle of Smirnoff she kept hidden in her stationery cupboard. Hooking her headphones over her head, but keeping them away from her ears so that she could hear if Finn was coming, she brought up all her songwriting programmes onto the screen.

Then she connected online to take her usual tour around Facebook and MySpace and pass time checking her emails until the anaesthesia of alcohol kicked in enough to work

There was still no news from her brother, but her agent and her publisher had both sent polite reminders, chasing work that was well past deadline. She'd write them apologetic replies later, claiming a heavy cold or similar.

Opening new browser pages, Trudy surfed her way on to her newest distraction: property search engines and estate agents' websites. Lately, she had taken to idly wondering what she could get if she and Finn sold Church Cottage once it was completed and split the assets. It wasn't as though the plan had fully formed in her head, but the fantasy of running away was a great comfort. All she needed was a little cottage with a couple of acres for the horses. She wouldn't mind being rural. She liked her own company, and found it a strain keeping up an act with other people. If only a fat royalty cheque would land unexpectedly in her lap, she could buy a 'writing bolt-hole' – a long-held dream of hers of a seaside cottage where she could compose and create uninterrupted. But Finn spent her royalty cheques before they were even earned. She had stopped looking at their bank statements because they frightened her too much. He claimed to be in control, to have strategies and plans; Church Cottage would make them a mint, he promised. And so Trudy had started to mentally spend her imaginary share, but instead of investing it in another joint project, she visualised escaping from all her demons, including Finn.

'Planning the next move?' he asked suddenly over her shoulder.

Trudy almost leaped out of her skin.

'Just having a quick look for something Liv mentioned that she'd seen,' she lied clumsily, staring in a blind panic at the remote stone cottage close to the Cornish coast, being marketed with stamp duty paid and no onward chain.

'I thought they'd only just moved here?'

'They have, but they're looking for a holiday cottage,' she managed to spin the lie further. 'An investment, you know – and great for the kids in summer.'

'*Mug's* game. No long-term benefit these days, no capital growth,' he harped back pompously. 'They won't make any money doing that.'

'More than we do,' she couldn't resist muttering.

He hovered over her shoulder, staring at the screen.

'Ridiculous lay-out. No scope to enlarge. And it's listed. I suppose you could sell the paddock for development, but it's doubtful in that area. Tell her to steer well clear.'

'Tell her yourself – I'm sure she'll appreciate your expert advice.'

'I will,' he said smugly, 'when they come to supper.'

Trudy felt the skin on her back creeping with tics and itches.

'Here, I'll show you something.' He leaned further across her to grab the mouse and take over, his breath hot on her ear.

Seconds later, they were looking at the Cottrells' website, a surprisingly state-of-the-art piece of design for such a disorganised and old-fashioned company, largely because Finn had insisted on his father paying for an expensive and pretentious pair of web designers called Chad and Brad to create it.

The treasure hunt was all over the home page, along with the first clue, now as recognisable to Trudy as one of her naffer song lyrics:

A Country Seat, or an Army Post?
With a stirrup cup, drunk by a ghost.
Pommel high and a cantle wide
Full leather hides to either side.

'What do you think?'

'It's a saddle,' she sighed. 'Obviously. A military one, probably with some provenance. It'll be listed among the leatherwork and harness lots at the Horse Fair.'

'Who told you that? Flipper?'

'It's just obvious.'

'Aren't you the clever one?' he hissed, more irritated than impressed.

'I was always good at things like this.'

'Good job you're not eligible to take part.'

Yet again biting her tongue, Trudy tried to be placating.

'I'm sure your father has deliberately made the first clue quite easy,' she soothed. 'That way the public will really bite.'

'Of course he has,' Finn snapped, grabbing the mouse again. 'Anyway, I'm not asking you to solve it. I just thought you'd like to see it.'

'It's – impressive,' she nodded, desperate to end the virtual tour so that he would leave her alone. 'Well done. I wish I were eligible. I'm sure it'll be great fun.'

'It's not just about *fun*. It's a marketing ploy to increase footfall revenue.'

She nodded with fake enthusiasm, hoping he wasn't about to embark on one of his jargon-filled lectures. But he seemed content to hog her mouse, breathe stale air down her neck and take her through every page of the website, condescendingly pointing out each new element from indexes to online catalogues, pop-ups to enquiry forms, all the time barking out rhetorical questions. 'Isn't this ingenious?'; 'Have you ever seen anything so smart?'; 'Guess whose clever husband thought this bit up?'

Her replies were monosyllabic, but they seemed to satisfy him. Eventually, he stepped back and glanced around her study, his husbandly authority restored sufficiently to cast a critical eye around the domestic lair.

'This place is a tip. There's dust everywhere.'

'I'll clean it when I've got some work done. Talking of which . . .'

Trudy shut off the internet connection and clamped her headphones to her ears, trying to stop the scream from forming in her throat. *Go, go, go,* she wanted to yell. *Go away!*

When she finally looked over her shoulder, he'd left the room.

Sinking her face into her hands, she raked her bitten nails across her forehead and groaned. The mixture of guilt and relief was like a bittersweet balm – part the hot oil of shame that she could not bear to have her own husband in her space, part the sweet soothing consolation of knowing that she was alone.

In her pocket, her mobile phone started to vibrate, still switched to silent from her hack. It was a text, the number hidden, registering on screen simply as 'Unknown Caller'.

'*Guess who?*'

Despite the lack of a return number, her phone still flashed up a 'Reply?' option alongside 'Save/Delete/Forward'.

She tapped the option buttons idly one by one, not pressing hard enough to commit.

It had to be Giles playing with his new gadget, taking her up on her challenge.

The thought made her smile fondly at the shared joke, but also started an uncomfortable jump in her heartbeat which combined guilt and trepidation.

Draining the last of her drink, she switched off the phone and found that she could work.

Dedicating the evening to her now very overdue memoirs, she moved on from her childhood years to writing about her 'overnight' success. Press cuttings traditionally referred to it as such, although she had been gigging since her schooldays, floating around for half a decade on the fringes of the folk and indie scenes with her mates, supported by part-time jobs and amazing, laid-back parents who saw no reason for her to get trapped into a career so young when there were dreams to be chased and creative passion to vent. Then, talent-spotted at twenty-three at a rustic arts festival on the Cornish coast by a holidaying record producer, she had been fast-tracked to the A list so rapidly that it would have been easy to forget her Ps and Qs. She'd been groomed, styled and synthesised for success by a mainstream label who put vast tracks of cash behind her to create a brand that was part Dido, part Kylie, part Blondie, an alchemy of blondes, contrived entirely to appeal to as mass a market as possible.

Her first single, backed up by a massive marketing and publicity campaign that sent her on the road for dizzying weeks of green rooms, press suites and radio studios, had gone straight into the Top Ten. The upbeat, cheekily insolent track – her own song, 'Play With Me' – had ultimately borne as much resemblance to the soulful, folky number that she had once sung in seafront pubs for tourists as sushi to stargazy pie, but at least both had once shared the same seas; it had been hers and that pride had kept her focused. Her melodies and the bittersweet truth hidden in the lyrics were all she really cared about. She had no great vanity. Stylists could treat her like a mannequin and she posed as happily as a little girl with a dressing-up box; she was confident and tireless – no shoot was too long, no night too late; she would talk to anybody about anything – the press ate her up; she existed on fresh air, strong tea and endless cheese and pickle sandwiches – far from her vodka-swilling, Marlboro-puffing, java-glugging addictions of late. Paranoia, self-consciousness and fear had yet to creep up on her; it was all an adventure.

How she envied her young self now. Lucky, lucky Trudy. So pretty and fun and witty. So doomed to failure.

To the record company, however, she could do no wrong and came surprisingly cheap, although she saw it as a fortune at the time. Unusually for a new signing, she'd brought with her a small mountain of highly commercial material, written throughout her late teens and early twenties and by far her greatest asset. And thanks to her father, who had spent hours on the phone trying to ground her, she'd at least had the sense – and wise counsel – not to sign away the rights to her work. Her subsequent singles and first album had gone Top Ten too; she became a pin-up, a chat show favourite, a national treasure and a red carpet regular within six months. Europe fêted her with gay club anthem mixes; Japan miniaturised her with Trudy dolls; America idolised her. Her smoky, sexy voice soon haunted the airwaves and music television on both sides of the Atlantic. It was that easy, and it spiralled upwards from there.

Her second album went platinum; her accompanying European tour sold out overnight, her coast-to-coast American publicity cavalcade grew from one bus and a couple of gigs to three luxury Winnebagos, two stadiums and David Letterman's people fighting Jay Leno's for first dibs. 'I Hate Loving You' smashed records for staying on top of the charts in seven countries. Her face was on the front of *Marie Claire*, *Cosmo* and *Vanity Fair* the same month, much to their fury. A teenage Prince William was said to be besotted with her; a sixty-something Hollywood movie star sent red roses every day; a young grand slam tennis ace flew from South Africa to Holland between matches to wine and dine her. She still preferred talking to her mates and reading thrillers. She sang of love and dreams and ambition and loss, but she knew nothing of them.

Now that she had taken so many punishing body and head blows from life, she was amazed to look back at her own lyrics and feel them hitting a nerve with every perfect note. She had been wise beyond her years. If she was jealous now of her erstwhile energy and artless beauty, she was positively spitting with green-eyed resentment at her effortless composing talent.

Staying up all night writing about a young, cocky girl enjoying those first whirlwind years as a rock chick was cathartic. She now saw that she had willingly signed away her free will. Her unquestioning, hedonistic outlook had condemned her. She had remained passive, spirited along by the great oiled machinery of the record industry and her mentors, trusting their combined ability to look after her like the family she had left behind.

And her label had certainly safeguarded their investment. They had been a phenomenal merchandiser and she was a dream product. Tonight, typing so fast that every other word was misspelled, she'd described it the best way she knew how.

> It was as though I'd laid my head on a pillow as a naïve child and wished with all my heart that I could be a superstar. So many girls do it, but I was the one who actually awoke to find I'd arrived in Neverland. Some have suggested that being propelled to stardom made me grow up very fast, but I beg to differ. I didn't grow up at all – and while I lived and breathed the dream, I didn't wake up back in reality for a very long time either. When I did, the world looked completely different.

Reading this last paragraph back after pouring herself another drink from her secret stash, finger on her computer power button and glass on her lips, Trudy splattered her monitor screen with vodka.

'Christ that's schmaltz,' she laughed, reaching for a tissue to wipe the dripping screen, and wishing she could mop up the sugar-coated fantasies from her writing as easily.

Whether her short taste of fame had been a nightmare or a dream, Trudy had never really decided. At the time, she had been too busy working at full pace to contemplate. It was only when she had made the biggest mistake of her career that she had blurred the boundaries between dreamland and real life enough to start waking up and smelling, tasting and feeling again.

She had fallen in love with Pete Rafferty.

But that was a story she couldn't begin to write down yet. She wasn't sure she ever would, for all her publisher's demands that she either substantiate or refute one of the music industry's greatest rumours. There was no way to sugar-coat that story, or downplay the devastating effect that it had wrought on her life. She rarely allowed herself to think about Pete these days.

Tonight she dared, but only briefly. It was like holding her hand over a flame. She could do it for a nanosecond and feel no pain. Any longer and it was excruciating.

It was after ten o'clock by the time she and Finn shared the burned ready-meal and a bottle of wine, sitting in front of the television news so that they didn't have to talk, apart from the odd self-important comment that Finn directed at the small screen, telling politicians how to run the country.

Afterwards, he left his dirty plate on the coffee table and went grumpily to bed, telling Trudy not to stay up late. Plonking the washing up in the sink, she ignored his command and headed back to her desk, steadily making her way through a second bottle of wine, a cafetière of coffee and a lot of mindless, screen-staring attempts at getting her work back off the ground, all of which failed in the wake of such a depressing hiatus.

She simply couldn't get past the chasm of personal narrative that yawned between the early success she had just catalogued and her premature escape into married life and relative anonymity. Because that gap could only be filled with writing about Pete, and the death of her father, Kit. And that was beyond her pain threshold. In one of the last serious conversations that they'd had before his stroke, her father – who as a poet had always taken a great interest in her songwriting and in the emotional meaning it conveyed – had said that a lost love could only ever be replaced with an equal or greater love. Anything less simply shrivelled in the wake of its superior, like a fire starved of oxygen in the wake of a greater blaze.

Losing the two men that she had loved most in short succession had extinguished the flames of a great furnace of fire in Trudy. Any hope that she could kindle the spark between herself and Finn was inevitably doomed.

Now, after so many years, the burned out hollow where those flames had once raged craved to be filled again, even if it was just with another brief spark, a comforting blaze from a homely hearth or a nostalgic bonfire that smelled of woodsmoke and wet leaves and reminded her of a happy childhood.

As dawn began to break, she switched on her mobile phone, unable to resist checking whether Giles had sent another text. Instead she found a voicemail from Jemima, left the previous evening, asking for Liv's telephone number.

Aware of the anti-social hour, Trudy sent it by text, and pondered replying to *'Guess who?'*

She fiddled with her phone's settings for a while, trying to make it show the number that had texted her, but unlike her husband, who bought and mastered every Blackberry, iPod, palmtop and mobile phone the day it came out, she had never been very technical and failed to get past the 'Unknown Caller' message.

'Bloody thing.'

Her customary mental state after staying up all night was always strangely serene, despite all the stimulants, lending her a what-the-heck daring that she seldom exploited, although she often shared her most outrageous jokes with Flipper when he hacked over for breakfast, almost certainly the reason he did so. This morning, in that familiar half-hour wind-down cushion of time between turning off her computer and hearing Finn start to get up, she decided to take advantage of her dawn devilry, selecting the 'Reply' option.

'Give me three clues . . .' she texted back.

Not long after Finn had left for work, and Trudy and the dogs had conked out on the still-warm, creased sheets on the big marital bed that husband and wife so seldom shared these days, three separate text replies came through to her phone, ready to greet her when she awoke.

The first read simply *'I'*.

The second *'Love'*.

'You,' said the third.

14

Jemima hosted her lunch party the day before the Horse Fair, guaranteeing that Piers would be well away from the house finalising the details of the auction and the launch of the treasure hunt. She hated it when he sniffed lasciviously around her girlfriends.

'Cottrells' have had some wonderful press coverage,' she told her guests as they gathered around the breakfast table for one of her famously 'informal' lunches. 'Piers has been giving interviews all week. The local television news teams are coming tomorrow, as well as the papers.'

Intimidated and excited, Liv was staring around her, impressed.

Jemima, Piers and their children lived on the Cottrell family estate, occupying the grandiose Home Farm, half a mile from the main house. Built from the same mellow Cotswold stone as Fox Oddfield Abbey, it was a mini replica of that great house's classic proportions – an attractive mix of Georgian and Victorian with the former era's perfect symmetry and huge paned windows presenting its best face to the world in front of the formal gardens, and a jumble of mismatched annexes and craggy roof-levels belonging to the latter era hidden far behind, alongside stables, coach house and garages.

It was in one of these annexes that the kitchen and breakfast rooms were situated, where Jemima had decided to host her 'girls' gathering'.

Both rooms were huge, at least twice the size of Liv's own state-of-the-art breakfast diner, with its slate floors and granite worktops, steel splash-backs and island unit. And, although this was more state-of-the-Ark, it was stylish and smacked of old money.

Jemima had a very practical eye for decoration, which Liv found refreshing and calmingly minimalist compared to Trudy's messy shabby chic. Unlike Liv's own super-modern house, the old farm was furnished with battered, serviceable antiques and family heirlooms, but these were placed sparingly and well. The walls of the breakfast room were painted in pale eggshell tones with a few simple hunting oils and watercolours hanging from the picture rails. A huge, scrubbed oak table with ladder-back chairs and carvers sat upon a faded, threadbare Afghan rug that was being pegged down by springer spaniels at three corners.

'Pedlar, Cobbler and Tanner,' Jemima introduced them as they thumped their short tails politely against the rug.

'Piers likes to name his dogs after old-fashioned trades,' Trudy explained. 'Unfortunately, Hooker met a sticky end on a Boxing Day shoot.'

Trudy was not on her best behaviour. Up until dawn again, lacking sleep and perspective, she was rattling from so much caffeine, and furious that she hadn't succeeded in crying off. Jemima had brusquely swept aside any suggestion that Trudy was coming down with a cold that morning. Immediately after taking Trudy's thwarted cry-off call, she had clearly primed Liv to give Trudy a lift as she was feeling 'off colour'. It was a conspiracy.

At least her abstracted mental state gave her a glorious immunity from Jemima's usual yakking crowd of acolytes.

As predicted, it was a mothers' meeting, with two other yummy mummies from Liv's and Jemima's children's school, plus Phoney, and Jemima's cousin Pixie.

Trudy was grateful to see Pixie, with whom she had always got on. Today, despite being dressed in her 'Sunday bests' of inky jeans and a crocheted jumper, her newly styled blond hair freshly washed and her berry eyes sunrayed with mascara lashes, she still ranked as the scruffiest guest along with Trudy, who passed muster thanks to rumpled sex appeal, great skin and hair from the daily dose of fresh air, and the fact that her oversized Nicole Farhi polo neck, bought in her London days and stretched beyond belief, was now ancient enough to count as vintage.

The two immediately ensured that they were seated next to each other.

'Thank goodness – someone I can pop outside with to smoke a ciggie,' Pixie said. 'I won't feel such a pariah.'

'I always feel a pariah here,' Trudy confided. 'Can I borrow a child?'

'Be my guest. Three of the ones I brought are Sexton's. He might not be talking to me, but he has no compunction about thrusting his children on me for a day.'

Trudy pulled a sympathetic face. 'How's that going?'

'Pretty hellish,' she admitted. 'I just wish we could *talk* – it would help enormously. Not deep "why I did it" stuff, although God knows, he owes me that too, but simple communication skills. I know he feels guilty, and he obviously has grievances, too, even though he was the one who pushed off. But it's murder on the kids, who all adore one another. Then there's the whole money thing . . .'

Pixie's confessional mood, which she later referred to as her 'ancient mariner bender', got Trudy through lunch.

It helped Pixie too, who had found Pheely rather self-obsessed lately, barely listening to her grievances. Talking to Trudy was heaven.

'Oh, God, I'm completely monopolising you!' she apologised when she caught Trudy sneaking a glance across the acres of smoked salmon and rows of langoustines dripping in home-made mayonnaise to check on Liv.

'Not at all!' Trudy insisted, satisfied that Liv was nose-to-nose with a yummy mummy. 'You were saying something about furniture?'

'Yes – bloody Sexton and the trollop were renting a swanky barn conversion, but the owner's coming back from America or something, so they've found an unfurnished cottage on the old Dedcote estate. That means Sexton wants all his bits of furniture although, God knows, that's just a few ghastly flat-pack cheapies. All the decent stuff is mine. I hate the idea of breaking up the house. The children will probably react badly – and it all seems so *final* somehow. At least I'm not remotely attached to any of it, but it compounds his physical departure in a way I haven't had to face yet. I mean, his socks are still in the drawers and his photographs from travelling around India are all over the loo walls. It's as though he's just popped out for a minute.'

'And is that how you feel?'

'Sometimes – although I am so mad at him, I'd be waiting by the door with a cosh for his return. Another part of me has already cut him off like a truncated limb, trying to put him in the same place as my other exes, and there are rather too many of them.'

Trudy remembered that Pixie purportedly had a very racy past. 'You've been married more than once, haven't you?'

'What a polite way of putting it! Thank you. I have hitched and ditched a shameful number of times, my dear, not to mention the in-betweenies.'

'Were the others like this?'

'Well it certainly hurt like mad, even though I was walking out on them rather than vice versa, especially when there were children involved. I went through the mill – but a friend once explained that if you leave a marriage it's rather like thrusting your hand into the naked flames. There will be great pain at the time, and for a long time afterwards. But eventually, when the burns heal, new skin will grow looking younger and softer and better than before, a complete rejuvenation. After all, a phoenix can never rise from the ashes without getting at least a little singed.' She tilted her head thoughtfully, a phoenix of many incarnations. 'This time, unfortunately, feels nothing like those occasions. I'd absolutely made up my mind to go then, you see, without looking back. And *this* wasn't my decision.'

'Do you think Sexton has made his final decision?' asked Trudy.

She closed one sloe blue eye in contemplation. 'I doubt it. I think he feels as confused as I do; but perhaps I'm just fooling myself. He's already got someone else to comfort him, after all. When I walked out on each one of my marriages, I had someone else on the go, I fear – and it makes a huge difference, although it's probably terribly cowardly. He's the big bad wolf this time, the one being held up to blame.' She rubbed her forehead with suntanned fingers which, despite a good scrubbing before lunch, were ingrained with dirt from long hours in the veggie patches. 'But the end of a marriage or a long-term relationship under any circumstances is devastating, whoever is to "blame". It's never that simple.'

'Isn't it?'

Pixie shook her head. 'You are very lucky. Your marriage is firmly glued and happy. But if there's someone else involved, it's all too easy to cast it as a pantomime playbill of cowboys and Indians, goodies and baddies. The adulterous ones are baddies – the poor long-suffering one left behind is the goodie.'

'Not so?' Trudy chased a piece of rocket around her plate, vaguely aware that the chatter around them was of skiing holidays and Eastern European au pairs, Common Entrance and piano tutors, and Rory Midwinter's tragic Byronic descent from dreamboat to washed-up lost cause.

'Not at all so.' Pixie was waggling her fork emphatically, shooting a crab-stuffed cherry tomato into the mouth of an eager spaniel. 'It's jolly hard to face up to one's marriage and admit defeat, and takes a braver woman than me to do so alone. Far easier to be what Nancy Mitford called a "bolter", preferably with someone holding your hand. I endured years of bloody unhappiness, absolute daily torture, with at least two husbands. I'm talking unimaginable bullying, in one case physically, as well as dreadful, deliberately cruel neglect. Then of course, when I finally plucked up the courage to walk out on the bastards, I got it totally in the neck because I *dared* to do so with somebody else rather than alone. I was seen as a weak, sexually depraved harlot with no sticking power. It's a terrible double standard.'

'And Sexton?' Trudy buttered a great hunk of French bread, eager for comfort food to fill a stomach which was churning as Pixie touched raw nerve after nerve. 'What about his double standards?'

'Oh, he's a man. They all have to run off with someone else, even if they just want you to promise to never tape *ER* over *Top Gear* again.'

Trudy noticed that Jemima was eyeing them both closely while at the same time doing a big sell on her new range of food-themed curtain tie-backs, which were gracing the windows of the breakfast room with very subtle embroidered lines from Elizabeth David.

'We're launching them at Badminton, along with my new line of equestrian draught excluders,' she announced.

'Sexton will come back,' Pixie said, clearly with a great deal more confidence than she felt, her hand shaking as she helped herself and Trudy to yet more Chablis, much to their hostess's horror. '*Then*,' she went on in an undertone with a naughty laugh, 'I can always have my revenge by buggering off with somebody else and giving him a dose of his own medicine.'

'You wouldn't?'

'Of course not,' she scoffed cheerfully. 'Been there, done that, learned from my mistakes; I was absolutely *desperate* in my bolting days – talk about frying pans and fires. I just craved the feeling of being wanted, being loved. A marriage without love is pure purgatory – *Huis Clos*, *Ship of Fools*, Room 101. If someone wants to hold your hand down there, it's almost irresistible. It helps one find the exit.'

Trudy nodded, the words echoing her own late-night sleepless thoughts so accurately that Pixie must have been eavesdropping on her dreams.

'How did you meet these other men?'

'Hunting, mostly. It's the perfect social gathering for adultery. Giles Hornton should really learn to ride.'

At the mention of Giles's name, Trudy jumped. Across the table, so did Liv.

Jemima pricked up her ears once again. 'What are you two whispering about in such a clandestine manner?'

'Oh, just bedding arrangements,' Pixie said smoothly, shooting Trudy a wink. 'Trudy needs some advice for planting out the front garden at Church Cottage.'

After Liv, her shy children and Trudy had left, Jemima waylaid Pixie in a quiet corner where she was polishing off the last open bottle of Chablis.

'So what did you make of her state of mind?'

'What?'

'Don't tell me you've forgotten? Trudy! I asked you to sound out Trudy?'

'Oh, she's such a sweetheart, and a hoot to boot.'

Jemima rolled her eyes impatiently. 'Do you think she's happy?'

Having talked about herself non-stop, Pixie wasn't entirely sure, but her imagination had always been as active as her social life and she let the best part of a bottle of wine fill in the gaps.

'God no, poor thing, but bloody good at hiding it. Reminds me of myself when I was with Jerry, just before I had my breakdown.'

Jemima shuddered at the 'breakdown' reference, uncomfortable with anything that smacked of mental abnormality.

'Is it babies?' she asked now, eager to get to the hub of Trudy's psyche, and the key points that would help her manipulate her sister-in-law.

'Maybe – but I think it's more about wanting love. Whether a baby or lover comes first is immaterial. Yet she feels she has no right to either, which is terribly sad.'

Pixie wished she had the time to help more, but right now, with pests already on the rampage and the weeds growing as fast as the crops, she needed friends with strong backs, iron constitutions, no dependants and top-notch horticultural know-how.

'Do you think she'll leave him?'

'Not sure. She's got a lot of fibre. I suppose it rather depends on him. And on who else is out there.'

'*Is* there someone else?'

'Not yet. Just the usual suspects lining up, I would imagine. I don't think she's really aware that she has that option. She's terribly humble. Not a big-headed flirt like you and me.'

'Pixie, do try not to sweep me into your sub-section.'

'Oh, come on, you flirted your way through every meet last season. Thankfully, the fact that you and Piers both do it rather cancels one another out, like both eating garlic or voting for opposing parties.'

Jemima was appalled. 'Piers and I *always* vote Tory. And you have no idea what you're talking about. Trudy is a *dreadful* flirt. You should see her with Giles – I'm amazed Finn puts up with it.'

'Oh, he's probably far too busy flirting with his own ego to care,' murmured Pixie. 'He and Piers are terribly alike in that department, aren't they?'

Thanking Jemima for lunch, Pixie left her cousin in slack-mouthed, pop-eyed shock.

As soon as she recovered her composure, Jemima reported back to her mother-in-law.

'She's definitely pining for children,' she reported confidently. 'And if Finn doesn't hurry up and do something about it, she'll be off.'

'Oh Lord, d'you really think so?'

'Absolutely. I don't think we have much time.' Jemima cleared her throat and lowered her voice earnestly. 'The timing is right, and the solution is right under our noses.'

Dibs Cottrell's soft, Irish voice was thick with emotion. 'I will work on Nell. That baby deserves the best chance in life, and could be the answer to all our prayers. Our little saviour.'

Satisfied, Jemima replaced the handset and listened to the contented little shrieks and splashes coming from upstairs as Nuala supervised evening baths.

Trudy had always been a trendsetter. Like the myth of lemmings, Jemima sensed that if one jumped the whole Cottrell clan would start free-falling. And even she was only holding on by her fingernails. Therefore Trudy the family wild card had to be kept in check. Giving her a baby would be the perfect solution, keeping her in the Cottrell clan, but not allowing her too much power. She could not escape, could not be let loose to humiliate them. Neither could Jemima risk her producing a beloved heir to be favoured by the inflexible Cottrell rules of patrilineal birthright. Nell's child was no more true blood

Cottrell than Phoney's brood or Jemima's own beloved little Chinese children – of that Jemima was supremely confident. Because she knew the secret that very few others were a party to.

Flipper and Nell were not Piggy Cottrell's biological children. They were the result of an affair between Dibs and a secret lover, known only as H. Jemima knew this from the diaries and love letters that she had found in the secret panel behind the mouldering bound Dickens collection in the library of the main house. Dibs had always been a prolific and very secretive diary keeper, and Jemima had always been a great snooper, the two creating a perfect cocktail for family secrets tumbling from closets, and indeed floorboards, attics and meat safes. Dibs's diaries were hidden all over the Abbey, unearthed by her daughter-in-law during long bouts of house-sitting when Piggy and his wife took their annual pilgrimages to Ireland.

They were the source of great solace to her, and had brought her closer to her reserved mother-in-law than Dibs would ever know.

They were also a reason to feel fairly certain that the likelihood of Piers and Finn producing their own heirs – while possible – was remote. It seemed that Cottrell men largely fired blanks; an irony amid such a shooting-mad family. A genetic disorder had given them very little potency, despite being wholly enthusiastic and tremendously good shots. There simply wasn't much lead in their cartridges, and those that could be discharged were not in great shape.

That Piers and Finn had been born at all was close to miraculous. Both had taken a long time to be conceived. A third son had been lost shortly after birth. After that, the long fallow period had led to the adoption of Phoney, and Flipper and Nell had finally appeared when all hope seemed lost. Poor Dibs had been driven close to insanity, blaming and hating herself for years before the truth was uncovered. The diaries had followed the whole saga, containing a secret that had never been told within the family and almost certainly not outside either. A private consultant who had eventually diagnosed the condition had been instantly dismissed, his conclusions never discussed. In a family that still stood by primogeniture, it was an ironic and terrible inheritance.

It now seemed that both Piggy's natural sons had inherited their father's problem. Yet Piers, like his father, refused to accept that the lack of fertility he and his wife had experienced could have anything to do with him. Both father and son considered that if anyone was to blame it was the woman, not themselves. The fact that it could be her husband's problem had never even occurred to sweet-natured, self-deprecating Dibs thirty years earlier when she had castigated herself for her shortfalls. Jemima, made of sterner stuff, knew that she was not at fault. She also knew that, with no true male blood heir among Piggy's grandchildren, her own children's futures could be assured.

Nell's child, even if it turned out to be a son, was equal amongst its generation, because Nell was not a Cottrell. Her father was 'H', a man about whom Jemima knew frustratingly little except that he had written letters of incredible tenderness and passion, begging Dibs to run away with him. The letters had even made a toughie like Jemima cry, and she had remained dry-eyed throughout *Atonement, Cold Mountain* and *Titanic*.

If Trudy took on Nell's child – H's grandchild – then it might just turn round the family fortunes. She was wealthy; she would lavish her money upon it, keeping her riches in house along with the trust fund assets and property that would be kept safe from creditors by being divided equally amongst the Cottrell grandchildren when the family ship went down, like stolen Nazi war art thrust into attics. Trudy would be bound more tightly into the family fold, alongside Dibs and Jemima. They would regain control.

The ultimate conspiracy theorist, Jemima thrived on such detail. And she intended to use it to achieve her best ends. Georgia and Bartleby must remain at the top of the tree, children of the oldest son, groomed to become supreme high achievers. Piers must be kept on a tight curb rein, provided with enough family funds to keep functioning but not so much that he played fast and loose.

Trudy was intrinsic to these plans. All Jemima had to do was stay one step ahead.

Overstimulated from lunch, with her children on sugar highs from Jemima's nanny's home-made cakes, and with Trudy snoozing on the passenger seat, Liv stopped off at Otto's field on the way home. She was thrilled to see that Giles's car was parked outside River Cottage.

He was out in a flash, wearing his jogging gear and feigning surprise to find them all there, blonde brows beetling attractively over his blue eyes, white teeth flashing.

'What a wonderful treat! How can a man run away from this? I can see I'll have to stay a while and chat you all up.'

When Liv dashed off to stop Otto savaging her children as he jealously guarded Bottom the donkey, Giles jogged up to the passenger window and indicated for Trudy to wind it down. Without the key in the ignition, however, the electric button didn't work and she was forced to haul the door open, almost breaking his nose in the process.

Giles took it in good part.

'Let's run away together.' He waved a hand towards the end of the drive, bounding from one leg to the other.

'Jog off.' She grinned sleepily and shut the door against the chill, closing her eyes again.

That evening, Trudy received another text from the Unknown Caller.

'Still looking for clues?'

She imagined Giles lounging on his leather chesterfield with a large cigar and a malt whisky on the go, laboriously improving his text life, cleverly hidden behind an expensive veil of technical anonymity to protect him from jealous husbands and suspicious Trudys.

Sneering slightly to detract from the fact that her heart was hammering, she replied. *'Yes.'*

'Inside the hollow oak. Tomorrow morning.'

There was a famous hollow oak on the grass triangle in front of the church, just along the track from Church Cottage.

'A note d'amour?' she texted now, wondering why her fingers were shaking so much that she kept making mistakes.

'An old fashioned challenge,' came the eventual reply, making her squeak with involuntary excitement.

Trudy tried to stay up working again that night, but after almost forty-eight hours without a decent stretch of sleep, fatigue finally overcame her despite a vat of coffee and wine, and she conked out in the early hours on the tatty old sofa in her study, curled up with the snoring dogs.

It was only when the first steely fingers of dawn slid through the slats in her window blinds and tickled her eyelids that she sprang awake, head throbbing, and dashed straight outside, pushing her feet into Finn's huge wellies by mistake.

It wasn't yet six, but she could hear hooves thundering along on the tarmac through the village as the gypsies who had been camped on the Green headed off to the Fair.

Today was the big day when the Cottrells' treasure hunt started.

And, in the hollow of the oak, heavy with dew, Trudy found a curled piece of parchment tied with a yellow ribbon. On it, in an old-fashioned printed font, was a poem:

> Seek lion hearts
> On well-heeled feet
> With steel-toed boots
> In a poorly shod place
> Not under the hammer
> Gavel never falls
> Elves fire bad cobblers
> Remember Ignis Fatuus

She clutched it to her chest and ran back to the cottage, pausing to greet her horses at the paddock gate where they were waiting with velvet muzzles and warm, pasture-sweet breath.

'I don't know what treasure I'm hunting,' she told them breathlessly, 'but I have a feeling it might be worth a lot more to me than fifty grand.'

She had her own quest – a personal adventure to drag her out of her rut of ennui and depression and into uncharted territory. It was exactly what she needed. Whoever was challenging her was a soul after her own heart.

15

The Morrell on the Moor Horse Fair was always well attended, but this year it was set to be legendary.

News of the treasure hunt had spread far and wide, not just among the potential clients and customers whom Cottrells' hoped to attract back to their failing business. The gypsies and travellers were keen to participate, too, along with professional competition entrants, tourists, the press, curious locals and – for publicity reasons of their own – the entire cast and crew of a local amateur production of *Treasure Island*, dressed in full costume.

With the ranks of onlookers on the pavements and around the auction ground massively swollen, there was barely room to take in the scene, let alone navigate one's way through, and despite the traffic diversion in place it was a dangerous place to be walking along the roads themselves.

Horses thundered back and forth across the market square at a fearsome elevated trot, some in harness, others being ridden bareback. Most were coloured, dramatic splashes of black and white and chestnut, with full, thick manes and tails and flying feathers on their legs. None took much heed of the passers-by, or of anything directly in their way.

To Faith, who had never been to the Fair before, it was a spectacular sight. She marvelled at the poker-faced youths – some seemingly no older than six or seven – who rode the little vanner cobs at such breakneck speed with no more tack than a head-collar and binder-twine reins. Some shared the broad, hairy backs with amazing-looking girls sitting sideways, dressed up in traditional cosumes. They looked, to Faith, like Spanish flamenco dancers, with dark hair piled up in intricate high-rise confections of curls, pins and even tiaras, skirts and sleeves layered with lace like the tiers of wedding cakes, tight, brightly coloured bodices showing off tiny waists and magnificent boobs.

Faith was very aware of boobs right now. She was almost tempted
to take a few discreet photos with her mobile phone to show to her
surgeon once she'd won the prize and could start buying some
reconstruction.

Her mother was less impressed by the spectacle. Anke's pragmatic
eyes saw only the horrors: the thinnest of the horses, the lame ones,
the injuries and scars; the nicotine stained teeth and fingers of their
vendors, chewing at cigars and counting out notes; the litter being
swept along the little streets; the noise and the cheap tat for sale and
the swearing; the unruly children and uncouth adults with their trust-
no-one eyes and secret codes.

The Morrell streets and lanes, usually awash with the Barbours
and Puffas of the locals as well as the Burberry and Goretex of
tourists, was an exotic bustle of clashing colour, lace, satin and old
corduroy.

Then, amid this strange sea, Anke spotted two welcome lifeboats
bobbing her way, a vision in dapper Paul Smith and Tommy Hilfiger,
lost castaways like herself.

'Hello!' she called across.

The two men, who had been bickering, swung round anxiously
before great smiles spread across their faces.

'Anke Panky!' they cried, rushing to greet her with hugs and noisy
air kisses.

Faith, who had been admiring their slick hair cuts, trendy sideburns
and neat bottoms, curled her lip. Her mother had very camp taste
in male friends, and these were camper than most. They must be
dressage riders, she guessed.

'Faith – meet Mark and Spencer,' Anke introduced them. 'This is
my daughter Faith.'

The men waved in unison, bearing the customary polite surprise
that someone as stylish as Anke could have a daughter as
unprepossessing as Faith.

Faith was equally surprised that two slick Cotswold peacocks could
bear such silly combined names.

'As in M and S? You *are* kidding?'

'No, dearie.' Mark, who was darker, almost Italianate, with a neatly
trimmed little beard and very long eyelashes, gave her a
condescending smile that showed off his expensive veneers. He
dropped his voice to a deep, seductive rasp. 'Creamy, smooth

Antipodean mixed with meltingly dark Italiano. This is not *just* Mark
and Spencer. This is Mark and he is Spencer.' It was obviously a
stock response, hammed up like the store's television advertising
campaign.

'The boys run a lovely antique shop just along Sheep Street.' Anke
pointed to the opposite corner of the Market Square. 'I adore
browsing there.'

'It's not actually called Mark's and Spencer's, is it?' Faith giggled.

'We wanted to, but we weren't allowed,' grumbled Spencer, who
was whippet-thin, with floppy, highlighted blond hair and a slight
accent, possibly New Zealand or South African. He let out a squeal
as he was shunted from behind by the hurrying crowd. 'This is a
nightmare, isn't it? I still think we should go back to the shop and
batten down the hatches, Marco.'

'The hatches are battened.' Mark patted his partner's arm. 'We're
trying to win a fortune, remember?' He turned to Anke. 'Spencer
doesn't want to leave the shop unattended, but the only businesses
that do any trade in this town during the Fair are the chip shop and
the police station.'

'It must be very hard,' Anke sympathised.

'It can be – but today is rather fun,' Mark admitted. 'We are dying
to win this treasure hunt, and we think we know what the first clue
is.' He patted a finger against his tanned Roman nose.

Anke tapped her own perfectly straight nose. 'Good for you.'

'You'll have to beat us if you bid for it, too.' Mark started to back
away, as though he were prepared literally to race for it.

'I didn't think one actually had to buy the thing?'

'Better safe than sorry,' Spencer explained as Mark started to skip
away in the direction of the main Cottrells' ring. 'My only concern
is where we keep the damn thing.' Before he could explain further,
he had dashed off in pursuit of his partner, eager not to lose him in
the crowd.

'Aren't they fun?' Anke turned to Faith, but she was gazing
forlornly in the direction of the small triangular grass green that
separated the Market Square from the church, upon which were a
cluster of tents and trade stands. Nosing their way through one were
Rory and Justine.

'Oh – we must say hello.' Anke started towards them.

'We must *not*,' hissed Faith, grabbing her mother's arm and steering her towards the Corn Exchange, in which the lots of saddlery and harness were due to be sold. 'We are going to get to this treasure before anyone else.'

'All right,' Anke capitulated, grateful that her daughter was showing such enthusiasm.

Pixie was in her element as she marched around the Fair, a terrier amid ferrets – quite a breed apart, but with the same end goal and the same ferocious determination to flush out her quarry.

Trailing behind her, with her hair crammed into a beret, chest flattened by baby Basil in a papoose, and luscious curves covered by a hideous mackintosh coat, a reluctant Pheely was determined not to risk kidnapping by amorous Romany folk.

'Come *on*,' Pixie urged as she flipped through the auction catalogue at the same time as jogging eagerly through the crowds towards the sales ring. 'We have to get a good position.'

Pheely wished she hadn't come.

Their friendship was on the drift. As in a stale marriage, they were starting to irritate one another. Hurt, neglect, rejection and possibly even infidelity were inevitable. Pheely had an unpleasant feeling that she was about to be replaced, but she couldn't possibly have any notion of how soon that would happen.

Both women were unaware that they were being tailed. Several paces behind, a strange figure in layers of sackcloth and crochet was chewing a cheroot that threatened to set light to the lowered brim of a frayed flat cap, pale blue eyes tracking the duo through the trails of smoke. Staying in the shadows, moving with heavy-booted determination, the figure never let them out of sight.

Trudy texted Liv as soon as she arrived at the Fair.

They met furtively behind the war memorial, like a couple of spies.

'I mustn't be seen,' Trudy insisted, eyes darting around.

'We mustn't be seen together,' Liv agreed anxiously. 'I'll be accused of cheating.'

'Quite.'

'So what *are* you doing here?'

'Read this.' Trudy handed over the printed clue.

Liv tried to shove it straight back. 'I shouldn't be looking at that.'

'Why ever not?'

'It's the second clue, isn't it?'

'No – not at all.' Trudy, too keyed up for discretion, was unable to resist talking about her mystery texter, albeit as vaguely as possible.

'So you have no idea who left this in the hollow tree?' Liv gasped, eyes on stalks as she handled the clue like a sacred scroll.

Trudy shook her head, certain that mentioning Giles's name would be a mistake, just as it would be a mistake to repeat the 'I Love You' texts. That made it all too serious, and this was her magical mystery quest, an upbeat challenge to perhaps rashly share with a new friend; not a serious moral quandary.

'It could be anyone. And the clue's hardly love poetry. Whoever it is is probably knows I can never resist a game.'

But Liv was still agog. 'Wow! It's just – just *amazing*. Who d'you think it could be? You must have an idea?'

Trudy shrugged, again wary of saying too much, and wondering if telling Liv at all had been a wise idea; Liv's crush on Giles seemed innocent enough, but she had no wish to upset that apple cart. Yet it was bliss to share the secret, to have a mate on side. She'd always been a terrible blabbermouth.

And Liv embraced the secret challenge with gusto, as though they were two Brownies sent on an underground assignment by Brown Owl. 'We must work out what it means. Gosh. It's even harder than the official treasure hunt. Whoever set this is *very* clever. What's "Ignis Fatuus"?'

'Will-o'-the-wisp.' Trudy enlightened her.

'Oh.' Liv was clearly baffled as she reread the clue.

'I think we're looking for shoe buckles.'

'Shoe buckles?'

'The bit about cobblers, well-heeled and poorly shod,' she explained.

'I should have seen that – I *love* buying shoes,' Liv sighed. 'Where are you supposed to find shoe buckles around here?'

'From someone called Sowinger.' She pointed to the first word on each line of the clue. 'That's what the initials spell, see?'

'Wow! I wish I could solve the Cottrells' treasure hunt clue as easily. I think it might be a saddle, but Martin says it's definitely a horse.'

'I think *you* might be right,' Trudy said carefully. 'And you'd better hurry up and find it. The lot number is the solution, but the next clue is hidden around it, and once it's gone under the hammer it disappears, or at least that's the theory.' She was in no doubt that the second clue would be all over the internet by dusk. 'And the quicker you get both written down, the longer you can help me look for shoe buckles.'

'I'd better dash,' Liv agreed. 'I'll text you when I'm done and then I can help with this.'

'Thanks.' Trudy peered over her dark glasses at the crowd. 'I have no idea where to start to look for a Sowinger, except by asking around, but I don't want any of the Cottrells spotting me.'

'Why not?'

'They'll suspect something is up – I never come here. I hate it. We'll have to work separately, Comrade Wilson.' She hammed up a Russian accent. 'They have spies everywhere.'

'Of course,' Liv giggled, thrilled to be a part of the action.

'Text me.' Replacing her dark glasses, pulling up her cowl neck and squashing the floppy hat lower over her face, Trudy set off to seek her own treasure, hugely cheered to have an ally.

Anke and Faith had already sought out the saddle in the thronging Corn Exchange, and were copying down the lot number, along with the next clue which was written on the reverse of a large luggage tag attached to one of the D Rings. A bored Cottrell clerk had been paid to lurk nearby to ensure that nobody removed the tag entirely, thus scuppering the hunt for anybody else.

'I wonder where Mark and Spencer got to?' Anke gazed around in concern.

Faith, who couldn't care less and wanted to get away before Rory spotted her with her mother, hustled her out of the building and straight into the tracks of Pheely and Pixie.

'Ah – Anke, hi.' Pixie feigned delight, although she was clearly caught left-footed. 'I wondered if you would be taking part in this lovely tomfoolery.'

Pixie refused to look guilty, even though it was obvious that she and Pheely had excluded Anke from their team.

Anke, who never bore grudges and was genuinely pleased to see them, suggested that they all grab a cup of coffee.

'We've only just got here,' Pixie pointed out. 'Got to find some treasure first. Later?'

'*Muuuuum*,' Faith groaned in an undertone. 'You said you'd take me to the yard to ride Rio.'

'Well, I will,' she promised. 'Later. Shall we say twenty minutes by the sales ring?' she suggested to the others.

Pheely and Pixie both secretly dreaded the idea of plastic coffee and horse dealing, but both nodded eagerly nonetheless.

'I look forward to it!' Anke said brightly, marching Faith away in the direction of a stall selling lace doilies.

'I see the mother–daughter bonding is a little strained,' Pixie whispered to Pheely as they finally escaped into the old market building.

'At least it got us off the hook. Imagine having Anke *and* that grumpy daughter of hers on our team?' Pheely started to relax now that she was away from the thoroughfares of trotting horses and lascivious Romany menfolk. 'Mind you, they're bound to scoop the loot – we're far too thick.'

'Speak for yourself.' Pixie donned her half-moons as she started to pick her way meticulously through the piles of saddles that rose from long bench-like stands all around them like strange brown ducks flying in formation. 'We're looking for a military— ah! This must be it, doncha think?'

But Pheely was frozen to the spot. Just a few feet behind them, breathing deeply down their necks, was the oddest-looking character she had ever seen.

'Don't look now,' she hissed. 'But I think I'm being stalked by a gypsy admirer, and this one is even scarier than last year. Looks like a Red Indian. Either he has a huge hard-on, or a totem pole up his trousers. Help!'

Pixie swung round and gaped at the figure over her half-moons.

Draped in crocheted ponchos and indistinguishable brown layers, greying ginger hair in long braided plaits, flat cap glittering with political badges, cheroot smoke swirling around a freckled nose and very slight five o'clock shadow, the character stepped forward with a clank of clog against flagstone.

'Pixie Guinness?' came a gruff enquiry.

Peering closer, Pixie shrieked suddenly, 'Sioux Denim!'

The character gave a brisk nod.

'It's been years!'

'I'd know you anywhere.'

'You haven't changed a bit.'

Opening her coat, the weird figure who, it seemed, was female drew a large cream ferret out of a pouch attached to her belt and held it up.

'I named my best jill after you.'

'I am honoured,' Pixie gurgled, turning to beam at Pheely. 'Darling, this is Sioux – we knocked around together in the eighties. God, those were the days. This amazing woman was like a guru to me. She knows absolutely everything one could hope to know about living off the land like a true nomad. She can make a bivouac and a five-course meal out of nothing more than the clothes she's standing in and a few essentials gathered from the ground around her. Sioux, this is Ophelia.' There followed a brief pause in which Pheely expected her credentials to be inserted – 'talented sculptress, amazing raconteur, brilliant mother, invaluable friend' – but they weren't.

Regarding her in that pregnant pause, Sioux's pale blue eyes didn't blink. They were, Pheely realised as she clutched Basil closer and feigned a polite smile, distinctly hostile.

Skulking about like a spy with her hat brim low, her collars high and her dark glasses pushed firmly up her nose, Trudy darted amongst the crowds, as self-conscious as in her heyday when the public regularly recognised her in the street.

Her search for any member of the Sowinger family was not going well. So far, she had been pointed in any number of directions, all of them drawing a blank. If she had been looking for members of the Cottrell clan, however, she would be close to double figures already. Acutely aware of the high number of Cottrell family and employees in the vicinity, she was becoming increasingly jumpy.

It was easy to cast Finn's family as the 'enemy' at times like this, when she was feeling lonely and silly and outnumbered.

Liv hadn't made contact again, and a part of the thrilling adventure that Trudy had perhaps rather childishly felt swept away by just an hour earlier had descended into adult dilemma. To compound her loneliness, her phone was rapidly running out of charge so she couldn't even risk looking at the '*I*' '*Love*' and '*You*' texts to cheer her on.

Who was she trying to fool? she asked herself. The texts were probably just a joke at her expense; as was the clue.

A panic attack was starting to take grip. She had to get away.

But as she turned to make a dash for her car, she walked slap into Giles.

Waiting for Pixie and Pheely by the snacks van, which was doing a roaring trade from the wide grass verge besides the main Morrell Road, Anke tried not to feel hurt that Faith deliberately stood several paces to one side, not wanting to be associated with her. In truth, Anke was almost relieved not to be seen as closely associated with Faith, either. Her dress sense had been going a bit haywire in recent months, and today was a regrettable example, matching extremely baggy jeans that were falling off her hips and wrinkled around the ankles with a shrunken sweater that strained across her padded bra, a very unsavoury duffle coat that had once belonged to her stepfather, a dreadful striped woolly beanie hat and heart-shaped dark glasses. Anke, who was rarely embarrassed by anything, felt an un-characteristic prickle of shame cross her skin whenever she looked at her daughter.

Instead she cast her eyes right and blinked in shock as she spotted Mark and Spencer walking up the High Street leading a large black horse.

'I'm sorry, we got there first!' crowed Mark. 'Meet Undertaker, today's treasure.'

'We're renaming him Steve McQueen,' Spencer giggled. 'Much better, don't you agree?'

Anke was speechless. The horse – a threadbare, much-neglected pensioner with old white scars around his mouth and poll, his withers, belly and knees – eyed her benignly and let out a rip-roaring fart.

Stepping closer to her mother, Faith's first thought was for the welfare of the animal. 'Where are you going to keep him?'

'There's a very big garden behind the shop,' Spencer said brightly.

'And we're going to grow our own carrots,' added Mark.

Anke closed her eyes in horror, although whether this was because of Mark and Spencer's ignorance or because her daughter had just drawn breath to let out a tirade of sanctimonious criticism was uncertain.

'You pair of bloody idiots!' Faith raged. 'Have you no idea the responsibility of horse ownership! This isn't a lap dog you know. This is a creature of flight and fear weighing in at almost a tonne that lives on its wits . . .' On she raged, barely pausing for breath as she quickly attracted a small band of onlookers and a very red-faced mother.

Mark and Spencer stepped back, cannoning against the black horse, who regarded both them and Faith sleepily.

She might look like a pale, ugly, frizzy imitation of her mother, but when roused she was a force of nature all of her own making.

Liv was proud of herself. Without any help from Trudy, she had located the first 'official' treasure and copied down the lot number and the second clue. She had also, inadvertently, stumbled upon the Sowinger family straight afterwards.

They were traditional Romanies, telling fortunes from a highly decorated wooden caravan parked a little way apart from the main action, on the cobbles beneath the wide archway that led to the quiet, pedestrianised shopping court at the rear of the Corn Exchange. With all the shops closed up for the day, and the walkway leading nowhere but a private back alley, it was getting very little attention. Liv only ventured there because she was looking for somewhere quiet to text Trudy.

The caravan, lurking deep in the shadows, was surrounded by signs offering palm readings from Marie-Rose. It was only when Liv – a sucker for such things – approached to try to see if there was a price list that she spotted another, smaller sign advertising ornamental silver buttons and buckles for sale.

Marie-Rose was shut off behind a curtain in her caravan tending to a customer, but someone Liv took to be her daughter, a poker-faced girl of about fifteen, answered her enquiries in monosyllables.

Granted leave to forage in a wooden box of buckles, Liv excitedly found two shaped like horseshoes, tied together with red ribbon. At the centre of one was a heart, the other a lion.

As she fingered them, the girl's eyes flashed. 'You interested in those two?'

'Yes. How much are they?' Liv thought how pleased Trudy would be with her.

There was a long pause. Eventually, unable to bear the tension, she looked up. 'Please. Name your price. I really want them!'

'They're not for sale.' The girl made to snatch them back.

'But they're in the box!' Liv clutched them to her chest and thrust out her chin stubbornly.

'I'll have to ask Mum.' The girl glanced warily over her shoulder and then turned back to eye Liv suspiciously. 'What's your name?'

'Why d'you want to know?' Liv blustered. 'I'll pay in cash.'

'You're not . . . what I was expecting.'

'How not?'

The girl shrugged, black eyes and blank face giving nothing away. 'Things ain't always what they seem, I guess.'

'Like a will-o'-the-wisp?' Liv asked faintly.

The black eyes flashed again, and a toothy smile spread across the thus-far impassive face. Fishing in a crocheted bag beside one of the caravan wheels, she drew out a small paper bag with string handles and reached out her hand.

'Give 'em here – I'll wrap them for you,' she nodded.

Hardly able to breathe for excitement, Liv waited until the little string handles were in her shaking fingers before daring to ask again after a price.

'No charge. You can have them for free.'

Liv nodded, thanking her.

'Good luck,' the girl's face was masked again. 'Be careful.'

Liv dashed back towards the market square. Inside the bag was an envelope, and she was certain it contained another clue.

But before she could find somewhere quiet to take a look and text Trudy she was hailed from the side.

'Olivia, my dear – what a treat!'

Jemima Cottrell executed a perfect side-sweep like a prize collie gathering a stray ewe. Liv felt a gratified rush of in-crowd exclusivity and special privilege.

Jemima knew an opportunity when she saw one, and Trudy's little friend was looking as shifty as a first-time shoplifter sidling out of M & S Food Hall with a side of smoked salmon tucked in her undies.

Meanwhile, Trudy's cover was also well and truly blown. Giles, with his come-hither smile and hip flask, would not let her pass easily. He was in playful chaperone mode, a warm arm instantly curling round her shoulder, a comforting smell of expensive cologne and cigar smoke drifting from his tweed collars. He was like a big, creamy cat that had her trapped between his paws and relished the sport.

'What are you hunting today, my treasure?' he teased, blue eyes inches from her dark glasses.

'I'm sure you know why I'm here.' She was too disconcerted to play along.

'To find me,' he agreed with a heartier bellow, offering her his hip flask, breath warm on her ear. 'Why not cut out all this fickle nonsense, and let's head back to River Cottage, eh? It'll be lovely and quiet in Oddlode this afternoon. We can make merry.'

Taking a swig of sloe gin, she shook her head. 'What's the fun in that when I have a mystery to solve?'

'A *mystery*, indeed?'

'Yes.'

'What fun! Let's do it together, darling creature. I'm sure I can help.'

Trudy wavered, questioning her own judgement. Were they playing some sort of courtly *Dangerous Liaisons* ritual here – all innuendo and façade? Or were they just at complete cross purposes?

Whichever, she couldn't match his enthusiasm. 'I think not, Giles. You know you'd cheat.'

'Sometimes cheating is the best fun.'

'Not today,' she said firmly, knowing that she was wrecking her day by being unable to control her emotions long enough to play along.

Giles seemed to know it too. 'Spoilsport. Meet me for a drink, later instead? Celebrate solving your "mystery".'

'I might not be able to solve it,' she muttered.

'*Course* you will. Clever girl like you.'

Suddenly his strong hand gripped her shoulders and that cologne and cigar smell enveloped her like a comfort blanket. His voice, softer and huskier than the usual bass drawl, spoke with mesmerising conviction.

'You are capable of anything, Trudy my darling, and the sooner you realise that – with or without my help quite frankly – the better. I am always here to help, but I know when to bugger off, too. That's one of my many – *many* – good features.'

With that, he let her go and stepped away into the crowd with a rueful smile and an old-fashioned, gentlemanly wave.

Trudy reeled, certainty returning.

That was it. He *had* to be behind the secret texts and the clue.

Less than a minute later, she got a text from the Unknown Caller.

'*Hurry up, my beauty. I am an impatient soul. Tell me what you find.*'

Her heart skipped, confidence heating up her blood. Bloody Giles! If he thought he could whisk her straight back to River Cottage to have his wicked way, he was mistaken. She was on thin enough ice as it was, and, being a slow burner, needed to generate an awful lot more heat before she had the confidence to melt away her inhibitions and dive into an affair.

And yet he knew exactly how to raise her spirits. Despite her reservations, she set out with renewed vigour to find a family called Sowinger.

But when she was finally pointed in the direction of the arched courtyard behind the Corn Exchange, the family's caravan was long gone.

'Flipper! *Here!*' Jemima called out with the shrill, demanding cry of a gun ordering a Labrador to retrieve pheasant.

Her brother-in-law reluctantly but obediently made his way around the crowded sales ring, a cigarette dangling from his mouth like a rogue dealer rather than a country vet.

Liv, clutching her paper bag tightly to her chest, cheeks flaming from the subterfuge she was being forced to undertake, allowed herself to be introduced to the infamous local heartthrob.

The youngest Cottrell son, Flipper, was as handsome as everybody said – like a young knight in a medieval tale, with a beautifully chiselled face, wide shoulders tapering to narrow hips and long, lean legs – and an expression of distracted hauteur.

Although he shook her hand with bone-crushing intensity, his eyes barely flicked over her face as he scoured the sales ground.

'Looking for anyone in particular?' demanded Jemima.

'I thought a friend might be here.'

'Rory?'

'No – I've seen him.' He finally remembered his manners and pecked his sister-in-law on the cheek. 'How are you, Jem?'

'Same old, same old. Isn't this place ghastly on Fair day?'

'Good crowd, though.' He seemed miles away.

'Oh, yes, great for business. Piggy must be thrilled.'

Taking the auction himself, Piggy was knocking down lots from the rostrum at the head of the ring with terrific gusto, Piers at his side pointing out bidders and checking the catalogue as the sale progressed.

Liv admired father and son's ruddy-faced, tweedy command of the bidding.

'He's in his element,' Flipper muttered, eyes narrowing as an evil-looking pony entered the ring, cow-kicking furiously to try to get away from its handler. 'Shame the quality of the stock doesn't get any better year on year. This one's been grabbed straight off a moor by the looks of it.'

'Thank goodness Trudy's not around – she'd be buying them all out of pity,' giggled Jemima. 'Is that why you're here?'

'I'm sorry?'

'To buy a horse? I heard your mare went down. Jolly bad luck.' She made it sound as though he'd lost a favourite sock.

Flipper shook his head, too choked to speak.

'What a relief. Dreadful place to buy a horse – they're all crooked. Piers says he'll look something out for you next time he's in Ireland.'

Flipper nodded briefly, colour mounting in his hollow cheeks.

'She's stayed at home today then?' he asked casually.

'Who?'

'Trudy the one-woman horse charity.'

'Finn always insists on it, I believe. Besides, she hates it here. Hardly going to support the family cause today. Isn't that right, Liv?'

Liv knew that she should try to contact Trudy again, but she was rather enjoying being monopolised by Jemima. For the past twenty minutes, the little blonde had towed her around like a new pet, hailing friends and family from all directions to introduce them. It made her feel popular and special. Never more so than now, when they were joined by the Cottrell matriarch herself, the saintly Dibs, resplendent in a navy moleskin Puffa and matching Alice band raking her grey-streaked raven's hair back from her pale, watchful face.

'Dibs, darling, *do* meet Olivia.' Jemima hooked her arm companionably through her mother-in-law's. 'She is such a find. Just moved to Oddlode from London, and has two terribly sweet children.'

'How *wonderful* to meet you, Liv.' Dib's soft, Irish voice was pure cream. 'Jemima was telling me only last night how much she hoped that you would become a good friend.'

Dibs Cottrell had a strange effect on other women with her mixture of gentleness and stillness, succour and Gothic chill. She was a mother superior in plain clothes, an undercover agent for God's highest order, and a woman so well connected that everyone feared and courted her.

Liv took the cool, smooth hand in hers and felt blessed, all thoughts of Trudy forgotten.

Taking the cue to slope away, Flipper pulled his phone from his pocket again, and checked for messages; but there was nothing.

Soon ensconced in the 'sponsor's tent', a grandly named marquee besides the temporary horsebox park on the playing fields, emblazoned with Cottrells' logos, a place where Cottrell associates could escape the unwashed throngs and quaff champagne, Liv felt the warm glow of the family's inner circle close around her. Dibs wanted to hear all about Martin and the children; Phoney, whom she'd met at lunch the day before, was as chummy as a new room-mate.

Then, striding into the tent like a dashing officer arriving from the front line, came Finn Cottrell.

Liv gulped. He was by far the most mesmerising son: taller, leaner and better-looking than Piers; older, craggier and less boyish than Flipper; a classic hero with a cruel arch to his brows and a passionate flare to his nostrils.

He marched up to their table without introduction. 'Have you seen my wife?'

The phrase struck Liv as odd – not 'Trudy', but 'my wife', like a possession. But there was no denying the Mr Darcy appeal of his hauteur.

The question was directed at Jemima, who quacked, 'I thought you wouldn't let her come? She hates the Fair.'

'I'm sure I've just seen her.'

'Ask Liv – they're bosom buddies.'

Liv raised her eyes as far as Finn's broad waxed cotton chest, cornered and terrified.

'You're Liv?' His tone was hardly welcoming, although he thrust out a hand to shake hers.

Forcing herself to look him in the face, Liv encountered a cool smile and scorching gaze.

'I poked you last night,' he said drily.

Jemima shrieked with laughter. 'You did what?'

'On Facebook,' he added witheringly. 'Trudy suggested you might need my professional advice.'

'Oh, really?' Liv couldn't imagine why she'd need his advice, but she found the whole notion of being poked by Finn highly stimulating.

'So is Trudy here?'

Liv gulped and gave a small shake of her head that could be a yes or a no depending on the angle of interpretation.

'Must go to the loo!' she squeaked and dashed off.

'And that's the last we'll see of her,' Finn muttered suspiciously as he watched his wife's new friend tripping hurriedly out into the Fair.

'Lovely woman – terribly shy.'

'She's left her shopping.' Dibs noticed the paper bag on the table beside the empty champagne flute. 'Do you think she's coming back?'

'If she doesn't, we'll leave it with the girls behind the desk here,' said Phoney. 'One of us is bound to bump into her later to tell her. It always amazes me at this Fair how one sees an extraordinary array of friends despite the crowds – better than a point to point. I've been trying to track down Diana Henriques for weeks and I've just bumped into her by the faggot stall.'

'You should have just poked her on Facebook!' Jemima honked.

Finn shot her a withering look and stalked to the champagne bar.

Pheely was livid. Something, or rather someone, had bewitched Pixie. And it was no kindly, white witch, but an evil great hippy of a hairy bad witch, the sort that lured small children into gingerbread cottages to eat them.

Sioux Denim smelled like an old house cat, smoked endless evil cigarillos all over Basil, swore constantly, spat a lot and had a disconcerting twitch that made her look as though she was winking lewdly – yet she also seemed to have an unending capacity to reduce Pixie to gales of laughter as they reminisced.

They had, it transpired, originally met by the perimeter fence at Greenham Common in the early eighties, when Sioux had lived there as a permanent protester and Pixie had marched there as a rebellious teenager running away from boarding school. She had stayed three months, nurtured by the extraordinary women's collective, of which Sioux had been the moustachioed matriarch.

It seemed she had once been some sort of high-flying lawyer before trading it all in for a life on the road, and had remained largely nomadic and highly political ever since. Pheely suspected alcoholism, drug addiction, professional malpractice or all three were behind that life choice.

The two women had formed a bond which had continued for years after Pixie's rich, domineering family had gathered her back into its fold. They had only lost touch relatively recently, when Sioux had embarked on a long stint of overseas travels to remote destinations.

'Lived with the Mongols for six months after that,' Sioux was saying now after a seemingly endless list of adventures.

'How *thrilling*,' Pixie was agog.

'Then I travelled through Albania, along the Dalmatian coast – picked up with true Romanies.'

'Wow!'

'Wow,' Pheely muttered, pressing her lips to Basil's head and looking around for Anke.

'Looked up the same vibe when I got back here. I love the travelling way. It's like no other. So pure. So raw.'

Kent, Pheely decided. That accent was definitely Kent.

'And where next?' Pixie asked.

She lit another cheroot. 'Not sure. I might pitch my tent around here for a bit.'

'Most of the campsites around here don't open until late May,' Pheely pointed out.

'I was talking figuratively.' Sioux's cold eyes glared at her from beneath the flat cap. 'I'll look for some work, find some digs.'

With a sinking heart, Pheely knew what was coming before it happened. Her friendship was about to be usurped; Pixie was so quixotic, always on the lookout for entertainment, for magic tricks and circus acts to sate her lust for danger.

'Stay with me – I insist!' Pixie gushed. 'I could really use some help around the nursery with summer coming. Your knowledge and skills would be a godsend. I'm flat out. And the kids will love you – they're having a tough time with Sexton gone. We all are. I crave adult company at home. Won't take no for an answer.'

'Won't get it,' Sioux cackled, shooting Pheely a victorious look.

Pheely forced a smile around gritted teeth. The woman was obviously a freeloader. It was written all over her.

Her only consolation was that compared to the huge, hairy Sioux, Pheely looked like a svelte temptress. Her body-obsession was all-consuming now. After months of sizing up so badly in comparison to tiny Pixie and athletic Anke, that, at least, was some solace.

'I'm going to get my fortune told!' Pixie announced, hooking her arms through each of her friends'. 'I've *always* wanted to have my palm read, and they might tell me something about bloody Sexton.'

Pheely reluctantly allowed herself to be dragged along to the market square with the cheroot smoker broadside, but the old gypsy caravan that Pixie had spotted in a quiet corner earlier had gone.

'Rats! I was going to ask what my future held,' Pixie huffed.

'I tell fortunes,' Sioux muttered in the sort of voice that hinted at incantations to raise devil spirits and blight whole villages. 'Passed on to me by a true Romany I met in Kosovo. I still have her cards.'

'Oh, goody – can you tell mine?'

'Soon.' Sioux drew her to one side so that Pheely felt deliberately excluded. 'In fact, at the fair this coming autumn I'll take over a little fortune-telling caravan business from a contact I met up with here today. It's my retirement plan. We've shaken on the deal, but I need to earn his asking price in the interim . . .'

'Of course.' Pixie didn't need to be told more. 'I'll pay you whatever I can as a wage.'

Sioux gave her a grateful slap on the back that had such unwitting force, Pixie was propelled back into Pheely's arms.

'Has she been telling your fortune then? Pheely muttered resentfully, having been unable to glean a word of the recent exchange.

'Not quite.' Pixie avoided her gaze like a guilty husband fresh from his mistress's arms.

A foul-smelling ferret lover has just walked into your life to cause trouble, Pheely predicted silently as Sioux let out a flurry of bronchial coughs and suggested they repair to the mulled cider stand.

Having almost walked straight into her husband twice in ten minutes, Trudy retreated to her car and smoked a cigarette twitchily, wondering what to do.

Finn had been marching self-importantly around the Market Square, drumming up interest in the tack and harness auction and dropping heavy hints to the very few treasure hunters who had not solved the first clue that it was about to go under the hammer.

Trudy's clue, meanwhile, appeared to have vanished.

In despair, she texted the Unknown Caller.

'*Sowingers left before I could buckle my shoes and run after them.*'

The beep of the reply made her jump so high that she hit her head on the roof of the car.

'*Never trust a gypsy.*'

That was typical Giles.

Another text.'*Second clue will be waiting for your return.*'

As soon as she got home, Trudy took the dogs and raced out to check the hollow oak. But there was nothing there.

She trailed home, trying Liv's number again, but still getting no reply.

Hanging from the wrought iron knocker on the cottage door were two silver buckles tied together with red ribbon.

Trudy rushed to gather them up, glancing over her shoulder, but the drive, and the gardens and paddocks, were deserted.

A rolled piece of paper was tucked into one buckle. The message read:

> Oh, you went through the Dark Corner
> Licking the password to your lips
> Even Tittle Tattles couldn't stop you then
> Seeking life beyond the Lilac Mist
> Expecting the grass to be greener
> Now the Jostlepots have you, Pippin
> Search the shelves for an escape, in bits.

Trudy closed her eyes. Somewhere in her deepest memory, bells were ringing – but she was too far away to make the connections.

She was so busy trying to remember that she didn't notice Finn standing behind the piano.

'Jesus!' she yelped in shock when he stepped forward from the shadows.

'Sorry – didn't mean to alarm you. I'm only dashing in and out. Been walking the dogs?'

She nodded, trying not to look too guiltily at the dogs, who had been outside barely five minutes and were in a state of high confusion.

'What's that?'

'Oh, nothing. Just a note from the milkman.' She thrust it into her pocket, keeping the fingers of the other hand tightly closed over the buckles so that he couldn't spot them. 'What are you doing back so early? I thought you were needed all day.'

'Just popped back for this.' He gathered his laptop case from the piano. 'Forgot it earlier – it has the next Cottrells' press releases on it.'

'Oh, right.' She scuttled past, unable to look him in the eye. 'See you later, then.'

'It's going very well,' he called pointedly.

'Good.'

'The treasure hunt has really got the crowds in.'

'Great.'

'See you later then.'

'See you later!' she called cheerily from the fridge in the distant kitchen, already pouring herself a stiff drink.

Guilt crawled all over her skin like a plague of insects. She dropped to her knees in front of the fridge, pressing her forehead to it and swallowing a great glug of vodka Coke.

It wasn't until she went back into the main hall to sit at her piano and reread her clue that she realised she had something stuck to her forehead.

It was a Thelwell fridge magnet one that her brother had given her years earlier as a stocking filler. It was shaped like a fat, hairy pony.

'Of course! *Silver Snaffles!*'

16

'. . . I tried to persuade them to let me help, but they are convinced that they can cope,' Anke was chatting away cheerfully to Trudy as she searched through the shelves of her antiquarian bookshop in Oddlode's Orchard Court, still in its first few weeks of business. 'Apparently, the catalogue entry said something like "Broken to ride and drive. Friesians are believed to be the oldest breed in Europe, always jet black and lauded amongst seventeenth century cavalry officers and Dutch artists." Mark and Spencer latched on to the army connection in the Cottrells' clue. It was a red herring, of course, but they convinced themselves that this poor, wretched horse Undertaker was the treasure *and* they thought they had to buy him to win the first round.'

'Why Undertaker?'

'He used to pull hearses. They've renamed him Steve McQueen.'

'Does that mean they want him to ride a motorbike now?'

Anke looked blank.

The Dane, who was cool, forthright and took most things literally, was never one to humour her customers unnecessarily. She reminded Trudy of her mother-in-law Dibs, and she consequently found her quite a tricky, humourless character although she knew that she was popular locally. They really should be introduced.

'Poor thing. I can't imagine M and S making very responsible owners,' she mumbled.

'Exactly.' Anke turned back to scour the shelves. 'Ah! Here we are. Primrose Cumming. Is this what you're looking for? It's a first edition, too. I think it only came in this week.' As she handed the book over, a piece of paper fell out.

Their foreheads clashed painfully as both women stooped to retrieve it.

Trudy got there first, recognising the cream paper of another clue.

'I'll buy it!' she announced cheerfully, reuniting book and clue.

Later that afternoon, Anke greeted another new customer through her doors.

'It's Olivia, isn't it? You live in Coppice Court?'

Liv nodded, amazed that after so long in the Oddlode social wilderness, she now appeared to be almost famous. It must be because she was so close to the Cottrells.

When Anke found out what title she was looking for, her blond eyebrows shot up.

'That's the second time today I've been asked for the same book. I sold one earlier to Trudy Cottrell. I don't think I have another.'

'Really?' Liv asked in a strangled voice 'What a coincidence. Never mind. I'll get one from eBay. Thanks!'

'Strange woman,' Anke told Pheely later when she popped round to the Lodge to cuddle Basil and enjoy a chat. '*Very* nervous.'

'You have that effect on people sometimes.'

Pheely was not in a great mood. Pixie was completely incommunicado now she had Sioux in tow.

And Pheely was on the horns of a dilemma.

She had a virtual admirer. A very persistent admirer, who – despite believing she was dwarf-height and weighed as much as a small family hatchback – wanted to meet up. She badly needed confidence-bolstering advice and daredevil encouragement. Pixie would be the ideal supplier. Somehow, Pheely knew Anke's advice would be far too sensible. Yet she had to tell someone.

'So who exactly *is* he?'

'I don't know. He's out there, through the ether.' Pheely waved her hand vaguely about. 'On the internet.'

Anke shuddered. 'Then leave him well alone. They're all murderers and paedophiles.'

'He sounds lovely – his emails are so articulate.'

'Many psychopaths are highly intelligent.'

'He's even called Sven, can you believe it?'

'Sven?'

'I asked for "a Svengali".'

'Then he is lying to win your trust.'

'He's Danish.'

Anke paused. 'Really?'

'Yes.'

'Ah,' Anke settled deeper into the sofa. 'In that case, tell me everything – from the beginning . . .'

Trudy read *Silver Snaffles* from start to finish, briefly magicked back to a childlike time where worries had been tiny passing clouds that any breeze could blow away. She felt optimistic and yet more tearful than ever.

Finn was out of the house all day, valuing an elderly lady's collection of Minton, so Trudy could howl and scream and chuckle at will.

The book, which she had first read at about seven and which had belonged to her mother as a child, told of an impetuous pony who travelled from life in horse heaven to a world beyond the 'mist', a cruel place where people had no horse sense and treated her appallingly until her friends came across to rescue her. The parallels with Trudy's own life seemed uncanny.

Starting to worry that she was going mad, she poured a huge drink and paced her way to her computer. There she began typing furiously, writing two thousand words of the 'childhood' chapter of her autobiography without thinking, the mental link to her youth faster than conscious thought, the quickest of broadband connections, an instinctive reunion of sensation and emotion rather than specific memories.

She wept as she remembered the security of her Cornish upbringing, the unquestioning love that had surrounded her, the laughter, play and stimulation as well as edification and ethics. She thought of her father's warmth, eccentricity and openness, her mother's wicked humour, imagination and patience, her brother's mischievous adoration and their mutual trust.

It was in this state of nostalgia that Flipper found her when he called in for one of his habitual afternoon coffee breaks – the first time in weeks – obviously in a dark humour.

'I wasn't going to come and see you again,' he announced at the door.

'So why did you?'

'I hate being told what to do.'

'Who told you not to come?' She stepped back as her pack bounced around underfoot welcoming his mongrel, Mutt.

'God, apparently. Have you been crying?'

'No.'

Dressed for work in a light blue shirt splashed with iodine and purple spray, and green moleskins with mud on their hems, Flipper still had the ability to look as though he'd just walked from the pages of a glossy *Tatler* advert for high-end Swiss watches.

He took in Trudy's red nose, watery eyes, jumpiness and curious high with his cool, grey-green eyes mocking.

'Christ – don't tell me you're dabbling with the Class A's again?' he remarked drily, stalking past her into the kitchen.

'You know I only dabble with sixth formers,' she snapped. 'Class A is far too young.'

'Kids grow up fast these days.' He put the kettle on to boil. 'Look at me.'

'You're still a child.'

He peered at her thoughtfully over the coffee grinder. 'So what's up? You look hellish.'

'Thanks!' she snarled. 'I've been cultivating the hellish look for a while, I'll have you know. It's very this season.'

'What's up?' he repeated.

Trudy sighed, staring him out for a few seconds before snorting with laughter. She couldn't help it. Seeing Flipper always cheered her up, even when he was vile. It was all an act. And the feeling was mutual.

Within seconds, they were grinning at one another.

'I'm just mad because I've missed you,' she hammed. 'Where have you been this past fortnight?'

'Busy,' he lied. 'And don't change the subject. Why are you in such a state?'

Unable to explain, despite her tapping feet and red eyes, Trudy went for the customary brush off: 'Just the usual – underpaid, over-deadline. You know. Stress.'

This wasn't a total lie. She had been unable to play a single note since receiving the mystery clues, her concentration shot to pieces. Her mind distractedly raced through romantic escapist daydreams and conspiracy theories, she was hopelessly jumpy and shifty around Finn, and yet she still couldn't sleep. In this heightened state, she should be at her most creative, but she was barely able to play a short refrain without a bum note creeping in.

So she hadn't really registered Flipper's absence over the past ten days.

And if she had been less distracted, Trudy would also have noticed that for all his customary cool, Flipper was unusually uptight.

'Given you're so stressed, you probably don't need a coffee.' He hooked the kettle back off the range. 'In which case, I vote for a bloody big drink.'

Trudy didn't need asking twice.

'I have the rest of the afternoon off thanks to a cancelled wolf tooth extraction near Worcester,' he announced cheerfully as he poured himself a vast measure of Finn's best malt. 'No need for a sharp eye and a steady hand now, thank goodness. You can tell me how wonderful I am instead.'

Trudy wasn't entirely sure she liked him when he was like this, however cheering his company. 'You're wonderful. Now you can go home.'

'I need more reassurance than that, Tru. A "bloody marvellous" or two and a "handsome, talented bastard" wouldn't go amiss.'

'The bastard bit I endorse.' She led the way through to the snug. 'I don't exist purely to pander to your ego, you know, Flips. You need a good therapist, not a jaded old sister-in-law who sees your good side where others fail to.'

'Ha ha. You know it's my bitter and twisted side that secretly fascinates you. Anyway, you said you'd missed me.'

'Rather like one misses a bad habit.'

'Like you and your Class As?' He settled beside her on the sofa, two sets of feet propping up on the coffee table at the same time.

'You're in the detention class.'

'That's only because you want me to stay behind after school.'

This patter was classic Flipper and Trudy. He adored her ability to take the piss out of him, something women very rarely did, or got away with if they tried. Trudy was one of the rare exceptions who could sneak effortlessly under the wire – and under his skin.

Equally, she could pander to his ego like no other. She was no sycophant, but she had a natural, ebullient way of cheering him up. And today, Flipper needed cheering up.

'To Olive.' He raised his glass in a belligerent toast.

'To Olive,' Trudy followed suit with amusement. 'Has she done something particularly splendid, then?'

'Made a good supper for hounds.'

'What?'

'Haven't you heard? She pegged out last week. Colic.'

Trudy's shock was eclipsed by bitter sadness that something so unfair could happen, and a deluge of pity for Flipper who had worshipped the agile, fleet-footed mare.

'Oh, Christ, Flips, I had no idea.' She reached across to hug him.

For a moment he wanted to drown in her embrace and weep like a baby, but he managed to keep the upper lip stiff and the jaw quilted.

He pulled back. 'I opened her up, but it was hopeless. Should've put a bullet in her as soon as I saw her, poor girl.'

'I wish you'd called.'

'I did,' he said flatly.

From the drunken dregs of her memory, she recalled Finn passing on a message about a dead horse.

'Oh, Christ, I'm sorry.'

'You have your own life.' He shrugged. 'As my mother said at the time, she was only a horse. The family is far too obsessed by treasure hunts to notice she's gone. I think I could chuck myself over the Abbey ramparts and they wouldn't bat an eye.'

'Is it that bad?'

'The atmosphere at home is ghastly. We're all faking Happy Families, while avoiding one another at all costs, as per.'

'I thought the treasure hunt had united the clan?'

'Hardly,' he snorted. 'Of course, the party line is that we're all wildly excited by it, but Pa's the only real believer. Everyone knows the company's in its death throes come what may. Only Phoney's brave enough to stick her neck above the parapet and say it, but they all just ignore her.'

'What about you?'

'Not really my business – I'm just a country vet. What do I know?'

'Don't be such a flake. You're on the board.'

'I try to forget that. We might as well be stuffed dummies for all the influence we exert.' He took a swig of malt and let it linger in his mouth, wincing appreciatively at the punch to his taste buds. Finally he swallowed, watching Trudy over the glass rim. 'Jemima is getting worse. Mother's completely under her manicured thumb, as is old Phoney, Piers of course – and Pa. *She* might as well run the bloody business.'

'Jemima? I had no idea she was so involved.'

'All completely backstage – but that's her speciality. Machiavelli Puddle Duck. She loathes you, by the way.'

'Does she? But she invited me to lunch last week.'

'You know what they say: keep your friends close, but your enemies closer. And she hates poor Nell even more. In fact she's really got the knives out at the moment – Nell's convinced she's going to snatch her baby from her arms as soon as it's born.'

'She might not be far off the mark.' Trudy told him about the strange conversation that she'd had with Jemima about the baby staying *en famille*.

'Bloody hell, that woman's a stirrer.'

'It'll never happen.'

'Of course not. Queen Herod, she ain't. She just can't bear the idea of anything taking attention away from her own spoiled little brats.'

'So why does she hate me?' asked Trudy. 'I don't even have kids.'

He shrugged. 'You're high profile – the most glamorous member of the family. I guess she's jealous.'

'We're hardly running on the same turf.' Trudy laughed in confusion, 'I rarely ever see her outside the family. Although funnily enough she *does* appear to have stolen my new friend.'

'Really? Very schoolgirl. Is she a timid brunette? Big eyes and great legs?'

'Liv Wilson. You know her?'

'Jemima introduced us at the Horse Fair; I think she mentioned you. They were certainly hanging out together very chummily.'

Trudy tried not to feel hurt as she remembered their so-called pact that day. 'Liv can be friends with whoever she likes.'

'I got the distinct impression that she was terrified of Jem – and of poor Ma, come to that.'

'Your mother was there?' Trudy realised that she'd had a narrow escape that day.

'Jemima insisted on dragging along the poor old duck, even though she hates the Horse Fair almost as much as you do. Family women showing a united face, I guess.'

'They didn't ask me.' God, how stupid to be jealous over something she would have pulled out teeth to avoid.

'Jemima's two faces more than make up the deficit,' Flipper said scornfully. 'I think she's up to something, don't you?'

'Like what?'

'You should know better than me. She's obviously piss bored being married to my feckless brother.'

They pondered this for a moment; Flipper sipping his malt, Trudy trying not to think about the aspersions he was casting upon her own marriage.

'You know she made a pass at me once?'

'Jemima?' Trudy almost choked. 'No way!'

'It was after my third year at vet school. Boxing Day – we'd all been following hounds, and she'd been overdoing it on the sloe gin. I think she wanted to make Piers jealous; he'd been shagging the nanny for weeks, and driving Jems mad. She pretty much chased me all over the house. It was very Benny Hill.'

'Did you succumb?'

He shook his head. 'I *was* tempted, more to piss off Piers than anything else. He's so bloody pompous. Plus, she is incredibly fit – must have thighs like nutcrackers. Thankfully sense prevailed, and anyway she passed out after a couple more drinks.'

Trudy was seeing a whole new side to Jemima. 'Do you think she's strayed with anyone else?'

He studied her thoughtfully. 'Are you thinking that maybe you two *are* on the same turf?'

'Meaning?' she bristled.

'Both looking for a little extra-marital relief?'

'You're the one who started laying bets on that front,' she reminded him. 'At the Easter egg hunt.'

'Cluck, cluck. As I recall, I just wanted to lay you. And I offered very good odds – my soul each way.'

'Lay off!'

'It's true! You have no idea the things I used to get up to in my bedroom once, listening to your CDs.'

'Ugh!' Trudy shifted uncomfortably. Suddenly the sofa felt very small and Flipper felt disturbingly, teasingly close.

'When you were a teenager,' she reminded him.

'A Class A. Shame you weren't such a user then.'

'I had a natural high in those days.'

'That's fresh air for you. You should get out more.'

'So why are you keeping me indoors now?'

'Well,' he said scrutinising her face, 'I have to check up on you; make sure you haven't got Giles stashed naked in a cupboard.'

Trudy choked on her drink.

'Whatever gave you that idea?'

'Everyone thinks you two are having an affair.'

'Ker-ist! Who exactly? Your mother? Finn?' she gulped. 'Do you discuss it over supper, or at board meetings?'

He tipped his head to one side, unwilling to commit to a name, more interested in her reaction.

Trudy was genuinely pole-axed. 'I can't believe you really think that.'

'I didn't say me – I am not everyone.'

'But . . . but we're not,' she blustered, thinking guiltily about how tempted she had found herself in that direction since the clues had started arriving.

'Giles should leave you alone, then. He's been sniffing around you too much lately.'

'He's all right. He just can't help himself.'

'You like it!'

'It cheers me up occasionally.'

'How does he do it? I mean, why do women fall for that?'

'He has a certain charm.'

'So you *are* tempted?'

She sighed. 'Oh, I don't know – men like Giles are always a little tempting because they are so gloriously, flatteringly straightforward. He's like a waggy-tailed, sexually rapacious golden retriever that comes bounding right up and gooses one between the legs. It's refreshingly up front.'

'Compared to what? Finn?'

'I guess.' She didn't want to talk about him.

'How come?' Flipper clearly wanted her to talk about Finn very much indeed.

But Trudy knew how to divert him. 'Finn is much harder to read – all you Cottrell men are. You frighten some women. Call it the Cottrell effect. *You* more than any of them.'

'Me?' Flipper fell for her bait.

'Yes, you. Don't deny it.'

'C'mon, am *I* really frightening?'

With the vodka loosening her tongue, Trudy was happy to ramble on any given topic, excluding Finn. Teasing Flipper, while at the same time pandering to his ego, was easy. Yet, *in vino veritas*, she still inadvertently revealed far more about her marriage than she realised.

'You don't frighten *me*,' she snuggled back amid the cushions, 'but

I do wish you'd loosen up a bit. Vulnerability is like a bad smell to you, but it's the scent of attraction to most women.'

'Bollocks! We weren't all brought up in a hippy commune like you.'

'It would have done you the world of good.'

'Women like tough guys and bastards, not drippy star-gazers. It's clinically proven.'

'Maybe – at least at first glance. But you have to be prepared to take off the hero's armour at home. You can't make love wearing a big fuck-off codpiece and chain mail. Women like to see the fragile ego behind the chest-beating bravado.'

'I always take off my chain mail for hot dates. Food gets caught in the metalwork otherwise.

'Yeah, yeah – you still sport one of the biggest codpieces around these parts, buster,' she jeered.

He inclined his head with mock modesty. 'Bigger than Finn's?'

'It's all relative. Your ego is *far* more fragile.'

'Meaning?'

When she didn't answer, he nudged her knee.

'Actually mine is bigger than Finn's,' he boasted. 'It's a fact.'

'I assume you're talking egos here?'

'You were the one bandying around codpiece comparisons and marking me highest. Wouldn't Finn be upset by that claim, especially coming from his wife?'

'I was talking metaphorically.'

'It's pretty big metaphysically too.'

'Metaphysics is a concept of abstract thought.'

'I'm a vet, not a philosopher.'

So they sparred on, revealing secrets in between bitching and insults, but then losing them as the drink stole the memory of the conversation. Getting tipsy together on a windy afternoon seemed completely normal after the third drink, as did scrapping, bitching and occasionally even flirting.

Trudy saw Flipper as a little brother, not unlike Johnny with his acid humour and camp asides; his relative youth and openness with her made him easy to joust with, if not confide in. She would not reveal the secrets of her marriage, but she revelled in his admiration, his ability to gossip and tease.

'Finn used to scare me rigid as a kid,' he revealed after pouring another brace of drinks. 'More so than Piers, who everybody thought was the family bully. Sure, Piers put me up on horses that were far too big and strong for me, shouted at me a lot and gave me hell on the rugby field. But the old cliché of "doing it for your own good" rang true. He was always ready to defend me, or keep schtum with the parents if I got into scrapes. Finn just didn't give a shit, you know?'

'How do you mean?'

'Well, he could play the doting big brother if it suited him, but he never backed it up. Mostly, he ignored me. I remember once he came back to the school to collect a prize on Founders Day – he'd gone up to university by then, and I was in my first year as a boarder. I was just eight, and desperately homesick. I was so excited that Finn was coming, I didn't sleep the night before. Younger boys didn't attend the Founders Ceremony, so I waited by my house gates for him to visit me. I stood there for hours, turning into a block of ice. Eventually my housemaster took pity and sent for him. But it turned out he'd left hours earlier. He just hadn't bothered to come and see me.'

Trudy recognised the behaviour pattern.

'Of course he could be amazingly generous, too,' he went on. 'At Christmas or birthdays there was sometimes a big gesture to Nell and me – a lavish gift that completely overshadowed anything else we got. But as often as not he completely forgot. It depended on his mood. You never knew where you were with him.'

Trudy bit her tongue, knowing that to cry 'touché' was to give too much away.

'And he could be bloody cruel,' Flipper went on. 'He'd think nothing of selling a favourite pony of Nell's to turn up some petty cash, whereas Piers wouldn't dream of it – it was one of the reasons they stopped trading together and Finn went into property. Selling a house has less emotional value than selling a horse.'

'Unless it's your home,' Trudy muttered under her breath.

'I used to think it was because he didn't like kids. Having a brother and sister ten years younger than you could be pretty burdensome; but he hasn't changed. I still can't read him. The only really genius thing he did was bag you. That won him some admiration.'

'Gee, thanks. I'm so glad I added to his kudos.'

'Why d'you marry him?'

'Why does anybody marry?'

'Big white dress?'

'I didn't wear a big white dress. Neither did Finn.'

'Of course. Ma was in spasms when you refused to take the Catholic mass, and when you turned up for the wedding wearing red velvet, it almost finished her off.'

'It was a bit of a pretentious dress,' she sighed, remembering her beloved vintage Vivienne Westwood frock with its corseted wasp waist, cleavage-enhancing whalebones and saucy bustle.

'You were the most beautiful woman I'd ever seen.' He whistled, sounding like a cocky kid again, 'and I had posters of supermodels all over my walls at the time.'

'You'd never actually seen a supermodel in the flesh though, had you?'

'True.'

'That's why I didn't invite any to the wedding. Couldn't stand the competition.'

'Oh, you'd have made their skinny knees knock in fear. Nobody could be more beautiful than you that day. I was so bloody jealous of Finn.'

Trudy swallowed back a curious lump in her throat and patted his knee affectionately. 'When you marry, perhaps it'll be Finn's turn to be wildly jealous of you?'

'Only if I marry you.' He grinned, hooking his feet up on the coffee table and casting her a classic sideways look beneath his lashes. 'But of course, I'm *way* too frightening.'

'And I'm way too old, too married and too addled. Now bugger off. I have work to do.' The conversation was getting dangerous, and she was too drunk to trust her reactions.

'Of course – cause of all your "stress".'

'Exactly. I now feel gloriously de-stressed and ready to tackle the load,' she lied. 'Thank you.' She stood up unsteadily.

'Any time. Can I have a kip on your sofa? I need to sober up before I drive back.'

She was suddenly desperate to be alone with her thoughts. 'Finn'll be home soon.'

'So? He'll hardly think his little squirt of a brother has been squiring his wife in his absence. Now if it was *Giles* snoozing on the chesterfield . . .'

'Don't start that again!' she snapped, gathering up glasses. 'I meant that if he sees you here, Finn will know we've been drinking; *I've* been drinking. You know how disapproving he gets. I can't face another row.'

'*Another* row?'

'Oh, just get your head down.' She stalked to the kitchen, made a sloppy attempt at washing up the glasses then retreated to her study.

As she tried to work, head pounding far too much to concentrate, she envied Flipper his afternoon sleep. Like a dog in search of companionship, she longed to stretch out beside him on the cracked leather and share body warmth.

It had turned cold, dark clouds clustering in front of the dropping sun, the wind switching from easterly to northerly and carrying a bitter chill.

Shivering, Trudy stood up to close her window, noticing that the silver linings to the clouds were shooting long fingers of light through the yew trees by the church and casting even longer shadows in her direction. She squinted at the horizon, certain that she had just seen a figure running between the trees. But now she could see nothing except the leering gargoyles on the corners of the church tower, and a perky-looking squirrel shooting up a trunk.

Headache now gripping as tightly on to her temples as a damsel in distress hanging from a cliff by her fingernails, she went to fetch a painkiller and found the house deserted. Flipper had disappeared, along with his coat and car keys, although the mud-splattered Audi was still parked in the drive, blocking in Trudy's rusty old Alfa.

She picked up her recently thumbed copy of *Silver Snaffles* again, leafing through it and extracting the clue that had been left inside.

> You were never Sapphire to my Steel;
> Only New Avengers raided my heart,
> Now peppered with shot.
> Go seek out your namesake,
> Every bit as broken as me.
> Dark corners exist here too.
> You know the password
> My lifelong friend who betrayed me;
> Offer the value of a shattered heart.
> Keep the last cartridge for me;
> Ending this pain could taste no sweeter

Again she shivered, although this time it wasn't because she was cold. In direct contrast to the joy with which she had greeted the cryptic verse that led her to the Primrose Cumming pony story and then lapped up the familiar tale afterwards this clue gave her no pleasure whatsoever, and she was in no hurry to seek out the treasure. Her treasure hunt was turning as sour as the hungover acidity already furring up her tongue.

She knew where to go. Yonge and Dymoke were notoriously snobby sporting gun dealers trading out of an old Georgian town house in Idcote over Foxrush. One was only allowed to view their stock by invitation, or by use of a discreet password given out to the elite client mailing list.

Trudy knew she was on the hunt for a Purdey – or a part of a Purdey. Joanna Lumley had played the character in *The New Avengers*, during that late seventies era of high camp action drama series, when she had also played the title character in *Sapphire and Steel*. If this clue was set by Giles, then he was bound to have been a great fan; it matched his *Magnum PI* moustache and *Tales of the Unexpected* twisted humour. Yet the clue was very dark, hinting at shattered hearts, betrayals and even suicide. Hardly the mating call of the wife-seducing loins of Oddlode.

She folded the verse and tucked it into her jeans pocket before checking her mobile, but there were no new messages in the in box.

She was in the bath when Finn came back that evening.

'Why's Flipper's car in our drive?' he bellowed through the bathroom door, miffed that she had locked it.

'He popped in for coffee.'

'Where is he now?'

'Not sure.'

Hugely dissatisfied with this answer, Finn stomped about, turning a few power tools on and off to make it seem as though he was working on the house, although he was in fact watching the rugby highlights.

When, later, they briefly shared the same space – and a microwaved Tesco's Finest meal – in front of the familiar distractions of the television news, Finn treated her to sulky silence, fiddling with his laptop in between sniping at Hugh Edwards.

Relaxed by her bath, and a couple of glasses of wine, which took the edge off her hangover, Trudy decided to be conciliatory.

'Find anything interesting at today's go see?'

'It's a valuation, not a "go see" – and yes, there were some items of note,' he said pompously, failing to enlighten her as to what they were.

Trudy couldn't be bothered to ask.

Yet, after a few more minutes of mastication and non-communication, during which they watched Jeremy Bowen in a flak jacket reporting staccato through a satellite link, Trudy found herself trying to bridge the gap again.

'How's the treasure hunt going?'

'Moderately well. I've been too busy to check the details.'

Which meant that there were problems, Trudy realised. He was already showing the classic Finn behaviour of dissociating himself from anything that smacked of failure. Last week it had been his baby. Now he was too busy to keep tabs.

'All set for the next clue being auctioned?'

'The fine art sale in Morrell-on-the-Moor next week, yes. Father is rather tiresomely insisting that I take the podium, although I have a stack of work on my desk, not to mention trying to make some progress on this place.' He waved his fork around, all the dogs' eyes following the progress of the small piece of meat resting there. To their frustration it stayed speared on its silver point until it was inserted into his mouth and chewed at great length.

Trudy sat out the pause.

'Father devised the clue again, when he'd expressly stated that we would each take turns to set them. It's far too obscure; nobody will solve it. People will lose interest.'

'This is the clue to the painting?' Trudy was surprised. 'I thought it was easy, given the provenance of the saddle from the first clue.'

'Yes, well you are privy to inside information.'

'Nobody told me – I solved it for myself.' She reached across to one of the crumpled piles of paperwork that littered every surface in the house, leafing through it for the official second Cottrells' clue. 'It's not hard, but it is quite clever I thought. Here it is: "Take your treasure and oil it well". Well, the first treasure was a saddle, but "oil" means something else here, as does "mount" in "Mount it high on the Morrell", which becomes obvious when you read on – "Stretch the canvas, peg in tight. Subject set, in perfect light." It's a painting, and one look at the fine art catalogue for the next Morrell sale shows

a portrait listed of a Major Hamish Curruthers on his hunter Bugle
– the same Major Curruthers whose saddle was sold previously.
Bingo!'

Finn forced a smile. 'Clever old you.' There was no admiration in
his tone, simply exasperation. 'I doubt the great unwashed will be so
quick-witted.'

'Don't be such a snob. I'm sure plenty will get it. And it'll probably
sell for twice its market value.'

'Rubbish. You have no idea how these things work.'

Giving up on any further attempt at conversation, Trudy wolfed
the last of her congealing luxury meal, washed down with the rest
of the wine, intent on retreating to her study to raid her chocolate
drawer as soon as she had finished.

But before she could escape Finn dropped a casual comment,
guaranteed to wind her up just enough to make her linger.

'I thought Liz Wilson was your new riding chum?'

'Liv,' she corrected lightly, 'and yes – we've been out on a couple
of hacks together. Why?'

'It's just that I've seen her riding out with Jems the last couple of
mornings. Didn't you want to go along?'

So Jemima and Liv were *really* chumming up.

'I've been too busy working,' she murmured vaguely, smarting that
she had not been asked, trying not to feel hurt at Liv's defection and
her own exclusion from Jemima's outings. Of course, Finn knew that
there was no love lost between his wife and sister-in-law; but he was
far too sly to say anything directly. His digs often worked by
insinuation, picking her apart far more subtly than a surgeon, playing
to her lack of self-confidence.

'It's not as if I have the time to ride every day,' she said brightly.
'I'm lucky if I manage once a week. I work; Jems doesn't – neither
does Liv.' It was her opportunity to turn the screw. 'They both have
a lot more free time than me, kids allowing. It must be fun to be a
rich wife.'

'And you're not?'

'I was.' She collected the plates together, keeping her tone
deliberately chirpy. 'But then my poor husband spent all my money.'

Whisking the plates into the kitchen, she dumped them on top of
the dishwasher and grabbed another bottle of wine to take to her
study. Bugger the chocolate drawer.

'Don't you mean you drank all the money?' he called, matching her sing-song voice. But the tight throat behind it made it clear that the trip switch was perilously close to flipping.

One further comment from Trudy, and she knew he would come storming after her for a full-blown row.

Trudy couldn't face it. These days, rows saddened her as much as they frightened her, and she knew Finn would rather fight to the death than let her have the last word. She was happy to let him have it just so long as she had the last drink – and her escapist fantasy Facebook world of domestic bliss, along with make-believe emails to old friends.

Darling Carrie, she wrote to one now, an old riding buddy from her London livery days, with whom she had once been as close as a sister. *Life in the idyll is as heavenly as ever. Sorry I never get time to return your calls. Finn sends his love. We are madly busy . . .*

Looking back over her marriage with increasing detachment, Trudy could see Finn's weaknesses more clearly, especially when it came to money. That she had once so trusted in his dependability, strength and invincibility – relied upon it even – was her own weakness. He still frightened her with his rigidity, his utter self-belief and his bullying, but she no longer had faith in those seemingly bullet-proof, domineering assurances that he was in control and that all would be well.

Covering up the financial mess he left behind him was a practised art, and he had been better at it in the early days. There'd been a lot more money, for a start, and more projects on the go to wish it away. He felt it important that they have a 'London base', so not long after they married he bought a little pied-à-terre in Chelsea which they never used because leaving the dogs and horses became such a logistical nightmare. Finn loved buying dogs and horses. Not long after the arrival of the couple's first brace of Labradors, Percy and Petra, two miniature Shetland ponies that looked like mini-me replicas of Trudy's horses had been decanted from a trailer sporting satin bows and heart-shaped helium balloons; dogs of various shapes and sizes burst out of boxes on each of her birthdays for several years; a parrot came and then swiftly went when it started attacking him and crapped on his new lambskin coat. After she banned him from buying more animals for her to walk, feed and train, he bought majority shares in several racehorses named after Trudy's best loved tracks. All cost a small fortune to keep in training, but were complete failures, prone to injury and barely raced.

They ate well, holidayed well, partied well and drank well. Trudy, in particular, drank very well, finding herself more and more reliant on the bottle to get through each day. She felt the onus was on her to work harder. Finn had so many irons in the fire and tried so hard. She had taken to working overnight to make up for occasional wasted days.

It was around this time that she stopped speaking to friends and family on the phone, turning instead to the more measured and distant art of emailing. Websites like MySpace and Facebook were still in their infancy, but Trudy was amongst the first to get a dedicated page and invite friends along. Other media figures were slower, but she was delighted to find that fans as well as friends wanted to communicate regularly and that – with the wonder of lots of vodka and wishful thinking – she could make it sound as though her life was a fairy-tale happy ending.

. . . so you see it's all go, go, go here! She was finishing off her message to Carrie now. *We absolutely love hearing your news – please do keep it coming and yes, I agree it would be great to meet up sometime very soon. Leave it with me and I'll fire some suggested dates your way when the diary starts to clear of work commitments. Can't wait! Heaps of love, as always. T xxx*

Burying her head in her hands after she had pressed 'Send', Trudy knew it wasn't work commitments that she had to clear from her diary. It was emotional ones.

17

For all her frivolity, Pheely could be a stubborn and secretive soul.

Alone late at night, while Basil dozed close by, she exchanged long, excited messages with Sven – a man with whom she already daydreamed a sunset happy future. Peppered with literary quotes and show-off cultural name dropping largely based on her father's boho set and her conversations with Anke, she felt she was just about keeping up with his repertoire of scholarly references and his academic life story. His mind was wildly attractive, although the blurry picture that he had emailed was less revealing. If she squinted at it from the right angle, he looked slightly like a young, balder, ash blond Brando, pouting moodily. Squinting at it from another angle, however, he just looked like a hairless Boris Johnson. Without squinting, he was a haze of pixels approximating the head and shoulders of a bald man.

Yet Pheely liked to fantasise that he was a dashing, charismatic force of nature whose personality and charm filled a room; rather like her own. She just knew they would be magical together.

He claimed to be a specialist in contemporary furniture design, a part-time university lecturer, occasional composer, music critic and archivist. He had been married twice and had four children, two of whom still lived with him. His first marriage, in his native Denmark, had ended in divorce; his second, to an English musician, had ended with her death from cancer ten tears earlier. They had moved to the New Forest to be close to her parents in her last months and Sven had stayed there after her death, although in what Pheely thought was an impossibly romantic gesture he had been unable to bear living in the cottage that they had shared beneath the shadows of sweet chestnuts of a private wood, so had razed it to the ground and built another in the clearing deep within the fortress trunks and magical, dappled light.

That description reminded her of her own little upside down boat of a cottage hidden in the tangled gardens of the grand Lodge. It was Oddlode Lodge that her father had bequeathed to her and which she now found too expensive to run, although she stood guardian over it as did Sven with his late wife's beloved woods.

They had an enormous amount in common. They were both creative souls, both artists who felt the quality of their work superseded the need for commercial gain (Pheely, a great self-editor, conveniently forgot the naff glazed water nymphs that she regularly churned out for Pru Hornton's Oddlode gallery when she needed the cash). They both believed in the supernatural, although not in God. They both loved Copland, Bernstein and Barber (OK, so Pheely preferred Clannad and the Carpenters, but she'd seen *West Side Story*), as well as Shostakovich, Britten and Bartok (these three heavyweights being a new discoveries for Pheely after Sven mentioned them in an email, but she definitely liked them *now*, or was learning to). She drew the line at Stockhausen, despite Anke enthusiastically lending her a CD of what sounded like a gang fight in an orchestra pit, but she agreed wholeheartedly with Sven that he had a very valid place in the annals. They both also had teenage daughters who drove them to despair and delight in equal measure.

In fact, Dilly knew nothing of her mother's preoccupation. Away in London with Magnus most days, she dashed in and out on a cloud of self-obsession when she did visit, dumping dirty clothes and collecting clean ones, talking excitedly with a slice of toast in her mouth and a text message on the go, squeezing Basil and making him gurgle and giggle before handing him back to her mother and racing off again.

Sven sympathised. His eighteen-year-old daughter, Dorte, came and went in the same manner, currently commuting between home and the South Wales coast where she was madly in love with a man called Flute who lived in a camper van under a derelict pier and made dream catchers. Sixteen-year-old Mette, obsessively mugging up for GSEs, would only communicate with her father via webcam or SMS. Despite this, both appeared to dote on him.

'As could I,' Pheely sighed, reaching for her *Dictionary of Quotations* to spice up her message. Something on the theme of 'curves' perhaps . . .

Best of all, Sven – who appeared to love the company of women far more than his own sex – was a man for whom curves were mandatory. He wanted Pheely to describe her every buried crevice and concealed valley, her Rubensesque folds and plumptious bulges, her softness and roundness and ripe, overspilling, milkily maternal excesses. He made it sound gloriously erotic.

Pheely got into the spirit and went wild with the adverbs and quotations. He made her feel desirable. She couldn't wait to meet him.

And yet, deep inside that luscious, fecund, voluptuous chassis that she described so well, hid a secret.

She didn't want to be fat and adored. She wanted to be thin and adored. She couldn't help it.

So when Sven invited her to come and visit him, offering lunch and alfresco music with a small crowd of friends, two things nagged at her conscience and snagged the edges of her happy daydream.

Did she really want to get it together with a fatty-fetishist?

And should she have mentioned Basil?

The lunch was a part of a local Spring Arts festival of which Sven was patron, and included a musical recital which he hosted annually. It was the perfect opportunity to size him up and stake out the joint without feeling pressurised into getting intimate. If he was truly hideous, she could be back on the journey home before coffee.

And if she expressed plenty of milk in readiness for the day, she could always pretend Basil was a friend's.

'My little chaperone and bouncer.' She looked at him guiltily as he slept, long lashes dusting his cheeks. Snoring lightly, he let out a series of farts.

'Just like your father,' Pheely sighed.

Which led to her third daydream-shattering doubt; was she really only doing this to get back at Giles?

Not for the first time, she cursed the malodorous Sioux for stealing away dear Pixie and her wise counsel.

Such was her hurt at Pixie's defection that Pheely hadn't really paused to question her dislike of the ageing nomad. Pheely, despite being self-obsessed to the point of narcissism, was a surprisingly good judge of character. She had disliked Sioux on impact.

On the opposite side of the village, unaware of her friend's late-night dilemmas, Pixie was thrilled to have Sioux for company. Despite the endless cloud of cigar smoke and continual whiff of ferret, she was a breath of fresh air. She was already proving of huge help at the market garden, propagating and planting as fast as a machine, weeding more efficiently than a dose of glyphosate and mastering the electronic till in five minutes. Pixie's only regret was that she couldn't afford to pay her more. She couldn't really afford to pay her at all, particularly as Sioux was already eating like a horse and drinking Scotch like its lonesome cowboy rider at Pixie's expense, but knowing that Sioux was saving up to buy her 'retirement caravan' she gave her what little she could. But it was obvious from Sioux's sharp intake of breath each time a small roll of notes was handed to her that the cash bungs were considered lacking. It must be terribly difficult, Pixie realised, to reach Sioux's age with no nest egg or fall-back if times got hard. No wonder she wanted her caravan so badly.

Sioux seemed equally invaluable in bringing order to the chaotic home life in the bungalow. Childless as she purportedly was, the great erstwhile matriarch of East Gate Peace Camp was brilliant with the children, telling the younger ones fabulously imaginative, just-scary-enough bedtime stories that had them scrabbling for their pyjamas earlier and earlier each night. The teenagers forgave her the bizarre clothes and brown teeth because she knew more about drugs than they could ever hope to, she helped them with their homework and knew how to download bootleg music on to their iPods. Even Pixie's disapproving grown-up daughter, Julia, who was staging a rare visit from Edinburgh where she was a trainee solicitor, sat at Sioux's feet in awe when she learned that this strange-looking, strange-smelling woman had once been a pre-eminent human rights barrister, working alongside Helena Kennedy, Mike Mansfield and Geoffrey Robertson.

'What's your real name then?' Julia demanded. 'Not Sioux Denim, we all know that. I'm bound to have heard of you.'

'I'm sure you have.' Sioux smiled mysteriously, pale eyes glinting like coins.

'Mum's real name is Clodhilda,' Julia offered indiscreetly, earning her a horrified look from Pixie.

'After my grandmother, bane of the Ruskin-Wests,' she explained feistily, accustomed to the laughter. 'She was rather magnificent, actually – explored most of the Middle East on a camel before marrying some sort of sheik. I inherited a lot of this furniture from her.' She nodded at the ornate pieces which littered her tiny bungalow, looking out of place in the modest rooms, like tigers crammed in hamster cages

'That one is rather impressive.' She pointed to a vast chest, peppered with ivory and pearl inlay, as tall as the ceiling and as wide as the room.

'How on earth did you get it in here?'

'Sexton took the wall down,' Pixie remembered with inadvertent fondness. 'He's good like that – put in the RSJ himself, then fitted the French windows to fill the hole. He called that piece "Diana Dors" because it's a huge chest with lots of front, and hidden depths.'

'Giant doors with big drawers.' Sioux nodded approvingly.

'Yes, many doors and many drawers.' Pixie tapped her nose with a knowing smile. 'Some more obvious than others.'

'Meaning?' Sioux was only half interested. Over her many years on the road, she had focused her curiosity about items of value on those that could be easily carried, and was not averse to pocketing the odd treasure, despite her legal past.

'One can hide a multitude of sins in this beast – including people. I remember a marvellous game of sardines . . . but that's another story.' Pixie forced herself to swallow the huge lump that had welled up in her throat thinking about the fun she and Sexton had one shared. 'Now let's all jump into work boots and hit those poly-tunnels. You have to earn your lunch around here.'

Pheely was determined to earn her lunch with Sven in the New Forest.

The normally chaotic Gently roadshow underwent a temporary transformation to one of military precision as she planned her trip and shrouded it in secrecy. Not that this was easy.

'But you don't have any friends,' Dilly pointed out when her mother casually mentioned a trip to Hampshire in support of some chums who were hosting a Spring Arts Festival event.

'Darling, I have lots of friends.'

'Not beyond the boundaries of this village.'

'*Old* friends. It may come as a shock to you, but I did have a life before you were born.'

'You were a teenager.'

'So. This is an old school friend.'

'I thought you were educated at home?'

'I had a brief spell in formal education,' Pheely fudged. 'Anyway, that's all water under the bridge. Will you look after Hamlet while I'm gone?'

'Can't, sorry. Mags and me are going to New York next weekend.'

'Hang on a minute! I can't go to the New Forest without getting the third degree, and you're planning to swan off to New York without mentioning it?'

'I'm mentioning it now, aren't I?' Dilly had been deliberately keeping her plans from her mother to protect her feelings, afraid of the envy it would trigger. Instead, she found Pheely spitting because she hadn't got a dog-sitter to cover her own escapades.

'If it's only a lunch thing, surely Ham can stay here. You can ask someone in the village to let him out.'

'I – no – it might be longer – hm – I may stay overnight. Might want a drink, you know.'

'How are you going to get there?'

The Gentlys only had a moped and a clapped out 2CV between them.

'I'm hiring a car.'

Two days later, Pheely and Basil set out for Hampshire in a rented Micra with a Great Dane sprawled in the back seat, plus a case of CWW and an overnight bag discreetly tucked into the boot.

That same day, Sioux took Pixie to have her aura read by a women's collective she knew based in a tepee village near the Forest of Dean.

The day was a disaster from the start.

Just as they joined the M5, Sexton texted Pixie to announce that he would collect his furniture from the bungalow that morning. Firing a reply straight back to put him off and point out that she would not be there, she was furious when he responded that he was happy to let himself in with the spare keys, and could he have last winter's pheasants he had shot out of the freezer while he was there?

'The bastard!' she hissed. '*I* bagged those birds – just because Geezer the retriever brought them back to his master's heels, it makes no odds. He bribed the beast with Smarties.'

Pixie was far from happy with the idea of Sexton raiding the house unmonitored and, after several terse texts had passed between the exes, she tried to persuade Sioux to turn the car round.

Handling Pixie's beloved little van like a Sherman tank, rattling on and off the hard shoulder as she squinted at the road signs, Sioux ignored her and cranked up the volume on the cassette player.

'What *is* this music?' Pixie yelled above the din.

'"Womb Beats",' Sioux explained. 'Recreating the mother–child heartbeat exchange as the baby passes through the birthing canal, using nose flutes and ancient percussive instruments. It's very soothing.'

'You can tell you've never given birth.' Pixie sent Sexton another text, demanding that he hold fire for an hour, cursing herself for leaving the spare key amongst the tomato plants as always. Why hadn't she changed the locks?

Having worked her way through half her phone book with no joy – where in hell was Pheely when she needed her? – she called Jemima in desperation.

'Darling – huge favour, you know I hardly ever ask. Can you just drop by and check Sexton isn't taking all the seedlings? And he *must* be gone by the time the kids get back from school. Too upsetting for them. I've sent them texts, so they already know the house will look a bit different.'

'Leave it with me,' Jemima promised reluctantly. 'I've got to be in Oddlode today for Lady Belling's summit meeting about the hound show, so I can divert on my way home.'

'Oh, you are a star!'

In the New Forest, Pheely was aware that people visiting glasshouses shouldn't arrive stoned. On balance, the swift spliff she'd had while crouching behind her parked hire car in a New Forest lay-by had been a mistake. For one, she had trodden on her skirt and rolled over backwards into a pile of nettles. For another, a passing minibus full of teenagers had screamed out of the windows 'We know what you're doing!' Totally paranoid that they were going to report her to the local fuzz for taking drugs in a National Park, she'd stubbed out her half-smoked spliff in an Evian bottle and buried it in an overfull litter bin, covering her hands in ketchup and ash. It was only later that she'd realised they just thought she was taking a pee. But by then the paranoia refused to budge. Rather than relaxing her as usual, the home-grown sinsemilla made her feel extremely uptight. She was now convinced she was going to walk straight into an architect-designed glass wall.

Sven's den, rather grandly named Kronborg, was a maze of interconnecting clear cubes, and was almost entirely see-through, like a stack of shiny Perspex containers laid out in a wooded clearing for a picnic, although Pheely worried that this observation was far too suburban to pass on to Sven. And Sven was anything but suburban.

For a start, he would never fit in a traditional house. He was a huge man, at least six feet four, and wide as a wrestler. He was not conventionally attractive, but he had a tremendous, charismatic life force. His blue eyes seared through one like blowtorch flames; his big, pneumatic laugh drew eyes and feet like jungle drums; his skin was tanned the colour of teak, and his big, white smile was as dazzling as his shiny, bald head. Paying no heed to fashion or the weather he was dressed in bright orange Bermuda shorts, purple Crocs, and a baggy linen shirt matched with a blue waistcoat that revealed a lot of tanned chest and white chest hair. He radiated charm. And he was surrounded by admirers.

Pheely was reminded of Picasso. This suited her, appealing to her artistic bent and her vain fantasy that she resembled the artist's first wife, Françoise Gilot. Just like Picasso, Sven was flirtatious to the point of licentiousness, and quixotically demanding.

Having shared so many intimacies in cyberspace, Pheely found that meeting him in the flesh was like finding oneself naked in public. The urge to hide behind trees – and there were many – was overwhelming.

Her paranoia rendered her tongue-tied and as shy as a teenage virgin at her first barn dance, mumbling, not making eye contact and dashing about with dog leads and changing bags to avoid direct conversation and scrutiny. Unable to get within six feet of her for the first twenty minutes after her arrival, Sven stood back and watched her, his party circling around him. Far too flustered to take this in, Pheely convinced herself that Sven was keeping his distance because he had clocked Basil and didn't want to know. Or, worse still, had clocked her and didn't want to know.

In a way thinking this was a huge relief. It meant she didn't have to try. Nor did she have to compete.

From the moment she arrived, she had been conscious that she had many female rivals and she had been forced to to battle a childish urge to turn tail and stomp home in childish rage. Having spent a lifetime telling people – and herself – that she was non-competitive,

Pheely was unaware that she was so fiercely competitive that she had developed a self-preserving pattern of avoiding any direct contest. If opposed, she could well fight to the death. Seeing so many challengers gathered in one place made for very unsafe territory and her instinct told her to flee.

She stayed put for several reasons: Basil was red-faced and fractious after the long car journey and needed feeding and changing; Hamlet immediately disappeared into the woods and looked set not to return until he had sniffed and marked every tree stump in the New Forest; she had hired the little Micra for two days, paying up front, and had no intention of returning it early; she had splashed out almost a hundred quid on a new dress, and most of all she fancied Sven rotten. Besides, she reminded herself that she had never been invited on a formal one-to-one date. This was just a fun day out. He was allowed to invite as many other attractive women who fancied him rotten as he liked.

'Ophelia!' He finally managed to corner her by a weeping willow, bowing his head to kiss her cheeks while long, feathery branches danced around them like a green waterfall. 'You could never do yourself justice in print, of course – all the Romantics combined could not do you justice. You are quite the most beautiful creature and very, very welcome. Now, you must sit still so that I can admire you properly.'

Barely batting a long white eyelash at Basil, he parked her on a modern, woven steel interpretation of a swing chair that shot backwards and forwards rather alarmingly. Then he hoofed off to fetch her a vast glass of Petit Chablis (the only *petit* thing about Sven, she decided) and finally beckoned a select clutch of guests over to introduce them.

'You have plenty of time to find me boring, I hope, so I will give you interesting people to entertain you first, like a beautiful queen arriving in a new court, huh?'

When Sven clicked his fingers, people jumped, she noted, wishing she didn't feel quite so like a specimen in a jar as his adoring harem was examining her.

'Pamela – Monique – Carla – Gwen – Lisel, meet my beautiful new friend Ophelia.' The names came thick and fast as perfumed hands were thrust into hers and insincere air kisses rained around her face.

Amongst the coterie were various women from the Arts Council
– all woven shawls, ethnic jewellery and mascara starfish eyes behind
ugly tortoiseshell specs; there were also a pair of stalwarts from a
local charity supporting single HIV mothers in opera or something
like that (Pheely didn't catch the detail); a tall woman wearing
unflattering salmon pink with a matching turban who appeared to
be a neighbour (although Pheely hadn't passed a house within two
miles of approaching the place), and a very sulky bottle blonde whose
sagging, freckled cleavage in her little black dress revealed an even
littler red bra. This, Pheely sensed from the bristling attitude and
death-wish grey eyes, was her major rival.

'I hear you sculpt?'

'Yes,' Pheely returned a wary smile.

'Your baby?' she barked.

'Well, not yet, although I have cast his feet in—'

'I mean is this your baby?' she corrected.

So much for any cover story; Pheely was far too proud to lie about
Basil.

'Yes,' she agreed.

'How old?'

'Five months.'

A greying eyebrow shot up beneath a bottle blond fringe. 'I thought
Sven found you on the internet?'

'He did.'

'You are brave – advertising so soon after the birth.'

'Why wait?' Pheely lifted her chin defiantly. 'Post-partum social
dating is far less exhausting than trying to keep a marriage together
after one's baby's born.'

In fact, sitting in state, with Basil much admired and the Petit
Chablis starting to sink in, she began to relax. Quite apart from the
drooping boobs and saddlebags, Saggy Blonde was decidedly
scrawny.

Under the excuse of changing Basil at last, she went for a snoop
round the house, but it was very difficult to have more than the
swiftest of furtive sweeps, given that the glass walls exposed all her
movements to the gathered crowd. Also, Sven appeared to be totally
minimalist. There were no framed photographs, barely a book or
picture in sight, let alone sculpture. The kitchen was a vision in slate;
the bathroom a stone sacrificial chamber. The only bedroom she

espied had a platform bed the size of a helipad and a huge marble bath in one corner. She wondered how on earth he contained two rampant teenage girls in such uncluttered perfection.

Outside, musicians were gathering on the rostrum that had been set up at the far end of the shady garden, in front of a large lake from which rushes and reeds stabbed a hundred spears like a protective underwater army awaiting orders to charge. In a haze of midges and pollen, a hay-fevered conductor was blowing his nose, eyes bulging nervously above his handkerchief.

'What's the repertoire?' Pheely asked one of the bespectacled Arts Council women, hoping she was phrasing it correctly. Apart from a couple of low-key Cotswolds music festivals, and the regular live music nights at the Oddlode Inn, she hadn't experienced anything approaching a recital since her father had died.

The Arts Council mogul threw her silk scarf from one shoulder to the other and pushed her glasses up her nose.

'A Lyndhurst composer called Fidelis Gardner is showcasing the overture to her new opera, *Roundheads Ruling Hearts*,' she said in reverent tones. 'It's based on a homosexual love affair during the Civil War. Of great local interest; Sven has been particularly supportive.'

'I'm sure,' Pheely enthused, worrying that Sven was bisexual. Surely he'd have mentioned it? Then again, she had failed to bring up the topic of Basil . . .

'The second half of the programme, after lunch, is a mixed bag,' Silk Scarf was still droning on. 'Mostly Tippet and Maw, with a lovely lesser-known Britten choral piece to finish.'

'How marvellous.' Pheely sagged back into her modernist metal swing chair and inadvertently flew back and forth a few times before settling to a more sedate, if equally uncontrollable sway. Basil shrieked delightedly.

The singers were milling about behind the rostrum, batting away the midges with their folders of music. The musicians had already taken their seats to tune up. Despite being dressed in the standard uniform of black bottoms and white tops, they sported individual touches at ground level – the flautist had fishnet tights on; the clarinet player twinkled in gold ballet pumps, and the second violin was flashing Bart Simpson socks beneath a lot of hairy leg.

The overture to *Roundheads Ruling Hearts* was excruciating. Two overweight tenors, sweating heavily, spent twenty minutes trying to out-moan one another, accompanied by a very stertorous bass chorus making lewd gasping and grunting noises. Meanwhile the principle violinist stabbed her strings with discordant vigour, and the clarinet player blew so hard she split her reed. In front of them, the hay-fevered conductor let the sweat fly as he thrashed his baton, nose streaming.

Pheely buried her mouth in the top of Basil's head and fought giggles.

Across the shade-brindled lawn, she caught Sven watching her, his eyes hidden behind a rather alarming pair of mirrored aviator sunglasses.

I don't really care what he thinks of me, Pheely decided. I have escaped for the day. I am away from Oddlode. That's what counts.

She would stay away that night, come what may. There were lots of B&Bs in the New Forest; at least one was bound to be willing to accommodate Hamlet and a baby.

Almost tempted to cut her losses and run now – if it weren't for finding the missing Great Dane and negotiating her way out of the garden seat, Pheely would have been out of there – she shot Sven a beaming smile over Basil's head and listened as the tenors panted at one another adoringly while the flute player did a lot of suggestive tonguing.

At that moment, Basil stumbled across the opening in her new wraparound dress and, nosing his way eagerly past her nursing bra towards the familiar milky smell, he appreciatively latched on to a nipple for an unscheduled snack.

As the tenors grunted and gasped, Basil slurped along with abandon, letting out contented moans.

Pheely finally let the suppressed laughter ripple through her chest. Pretty soon, it had taken hold and she was shuddering with hysteria, tears plopping from the corners of her eyes.

'You found it moving, huh?' Sven pounced on her afterwards, just as she was simultaneously loading her plate and her mouth with goodies from the long lunch buffet. 'I saw tears in your eyes.'

Greed had overcome her, despite her overpowering urge to leg it. A similar urge had, it seemed, overcome Hamlet, who was hugging her knees and drooling eagerly as she passed along the line of music lovers poring over the white-clothed trestle table.

Mouth overflowing with coleslaw, she made a non-committal shrugging gesture.

'So you *were* crying, huh?' His slightly sing-song, sonorous accent reminded her of his fellow-Dane, Anke. Yet the 'huh?' after each sentence made him sound Antipodean.

He was so big, she was completely eclipsed by shadow, enabling her to study him closely at last, despite the sun shooting ray-gun blasts through the trees behind him.

His tanned skin was blotchy, peppered with pigment and red patches after a life in the sun. Pale laughter lines radiated out from the sides of his mirrored glasses like tie-dye streaks. The big, fleshy mouth was moving, talking to her, but she was too transfixed by the sheer scale of him to listen. He must have been as blond as Giles once, she decided, wondering how much older Sven was. Giles was notoriously cagey about his age, but Pheely guessed it to be early forties. He had a good fifteen years on Sven. Yet there was something far more up to date and youthful about Sven and his avant-garde, devil-may-care eccentricity compared to Giles's dapper, sports casual country convention.

She crammed a slice of quiche into her mouth, vaguely aware that she had probably drunk far too much Petit Chablis to risk driving, especially now that she had lost her powers of speech.

'Where is your baby?'

She nodded to Basil, slumbering in his car seat under the shade of a sweet chestnut tree, surrounded by admiring women.

'I'm not afraid of admitting that I'm extremely annoyed,' he said directly.

Mouth still full of quiche, Pheely coloured awkwardly.

Sven leaned closer, that sing-song bass voice teasing, 'He's clearly far more attractive to my female guests than I am.'

'Oh, they don't stand a chance,' she assured him, finally swallowing enough quiche to risk talking. 'Basil's a one woman man.'

'And you?' He raised an eyebrow as white as a gull's wing.

The ambiguity of this question threw Pheely. 'I'm not a man at all.'

'I can see that.' He admired her body with lingering pleasure. 'I meant, are you a one man woman?'

'Oh, yes.' To her shame a mental image of Giles popped up in her head, smiling at her with blue-eyed devilry.

'What about Basil's father?' He seemed to read her thoughts.

'Off the scene sexually,' she said airily. 'But we're still great mates, and he's there for Basil.'

'I approve.' Sven dropped his voice intimately. 'I have slept with almost every woman at this lunch and, as you can see, we are all still cordial. They are my friends, huh?'

At a quick guess, Pheely estimated there were thirty women present.

She swallowed, pastry crumbs catching in her throat. She really, really should leave.

A sudden thought stopped her.

In a room of thirty local women, Giles could probably also pick out at least half as ex lovers.

Sven and Giles, while miles apart socially and intellectually, were hewn from similar base rock. And she had sought them out as surely as a geologist with a yen for aragonite.

The more women Sven had seduced, the less it mattered. She was looking for fun and diversion, not ever-lasting love.

Sven had a hand resting on the back of her neck, idly stroking the downy curls of hair there. The gesture made all the other hairs on Pheely's body stand to attention.

'Can you stay for supper?' he asked now, squinting over his shoulder into the sun as the musicians started to settle back into their places.

'How many women who you've slept with will be there?' she joked.

'None, although I very much hope that will change between courses.'

She gulped.

He nodded, bending his head to breathe in her ear. 'Tonight it will be just you and me, Ophelia – and Basil, of course, as guest of honour.'

Thank God she had come.

In the Forest of Dean, Pixie's aura revealed itself to be a worrying shade of goose-crap brown, signifying trauma and doom.

Sioux's tepee friends reassured her that this was only a transient state, and that things would look up. They didn't elaborate as much as Pixie would have liked on this, however, as they were too absorbed in sharing a foul-smelling clay pipe with Sioux and cackling. The soothsayers seemed more interested in Pixie's noble past and exploring the wealth and fortune which that might bring her, although she assured them that she wasn't expecting any windfalls apart from the usual ones in her fruit orchards. Quickly boring of their stoned obsession with inheritance, life savings and fine jewellery – she had always thought hippies to be beyond such mundanities – she couldn't wait to leave.

Pixie insisted on driving home, belting her little van along the fast lane at a shuddering ninety all the way, but it was late evening by the time they returned to the market gardens. The bungalow was in darkness.

'Shit – he's left the French doors open!' Pixie leaped from the van, dogs surging around her.

Then it hit her. 'He's *taken* the French doors.'

As Pixie stayed rooted to the spot in horror, Sioux weaved her way past and through the empty space where the doors had been, still wired from the contents of the earlier pipe.

'That's not the only doors he's taken,' she pointed out.

'Oh, no!' Pixie rushed in her wake. 'He's taken Diana Dors. The bastard!'

Basil was very contented with his lot. For the first time in his short life, he was not sleeping in a Moses basket in the dark, damp, messy and clay-dusted cottage of his birth, but instead found himself in a magical, clean paradise which was dappled with amazing shadows as the floodlights which Sven had placed through the surrounding trees sliced dappled light into his glass house like a fairy grotto.

His eyesight was not yet sufficiently developed to see his mother and the big bear of a man who had made him giggle all evening cavorting naked in a vast bath in the far corner of the room. Instead, he was transfixed by the pretty lights as he yawned gummily, eyes drooping, about to nod off.

Nor could he hear them shriek and laugh as the amazing choral music – Per Nørgård's *Wie ein Kind* – seemed to collect up the sounds of his mother and her new lover and make it a part of the magical lullaby.

He was a very happy baby. Curled up beside his car seat, stuffed full of the big steaks Pheely and Sven had been too preoccupied to eat, burping contentedly, Hamlet was the second most contented Great Dane in the house as, across the room, Sven entered Pheely with a great splash of foamy water and a victorious choral bass note.

'Calm down, Pixie!' Jemima quacked down the phone at her cousin, who was babbling incomprehensibly. 'Sexton may have got some of your beloved furniture, but he has *not* taken the kids, *or* the dogs, They are all here. Listen.' She held up the receiver.

True enough, there was a familiar cacophony of screaming, shrieking, swearing and barking in the background at Home Farm.

'Why didn't you tell me earlier?' Pixie wailed. 'I was going demented.'

'Henry said he would text you,' she explained, referring to Pixie's most unreliable teenager.

'Never trust a thing he says. Why didn't you stop Sexton, Jems? Or at least call me? He's taken half a conservatory.'

'I know, I know. The hound show meeting dragged on and on. Sexton was long gone by the time I arrived to find your place ransacked. I didn't want the kids to see it like that, so I loaded up the loose dogs, lurked in wait for them at their school bus stops and brought them straight here.'

'Oh Jems, you are a treasure!' Pixie was stifling rare tears.

'Why on earth did he do it?' Jemima was baffled. 'He is the one who left you, after all. Why loot the place like that? And as for Clodhilda's stuff? It's *yours*. He has no right.'

'He always had a chip on his shoulder about Diana Dors,' she sniffed. 'I think he knew that I'd hidden . . . Oh, God! I never, ever told him. I tried so hard to keep things equal. He was always so spiky about the fact that he was a humble gardener, whereas I am supposedly from "noble stock". So I hid the papers. I didn't imagine I'd ever need them. But when times are tough, they always make me feel safe and now he's . . . Oh, God!'

'What *are* you going on about, Pix?'

'I can't explain,' she sobbed. 'But when he took Diana, he *knew* he was hurting me. He knew she held my secrets. And if he finds them, I am pretty certain we'll *never* get back together.'

With that, she rang off.

'Was that Mum?' Henry was peering out from beneath his long, scruffy hair and hoodie.

'Yes, that was your mother, Henry.'

'Cool. Can we go home now?'

'Not just yet,' Jemima said tersely, hoping her cousin would pull herself together by *The Archers*. This was very inconvenient.

'I'm hungry.'

'Well ask Nuala to fix you something on toast.'

'It's boring here without Sky.'

'We all have our crosses to bear.'

To cheer herself up, she called Rory Midwinter, but he was teaching a new client, he explained and wanted to make a good impression by not talking on the phone throughout.

'Pretty girl?' she teased.

'Gay antique dealer,' he said under his breath. 'Pretty horse, though. C'mon, Spencer!' he called out to his rider. 'Let McQueen know who's boss!'

'You tell him,' Jemima giggled, then dialled Liv Wilson.

'Hack tomorrow?'

'Yes, please!' Liv sounded pathetically grateful to be asked.

'D'you think Trudy will come along this time?'

'I'll see. I think she's busy right now.'

'Well, tell her those mares of hers are getting far too fat. Say, tennish on the Green?'

Hanging up, she auto-dialled the number she had listed as 'Dandy'.

'Darling, I need you,' she rasped.

'God, what perfect timing! I was just thinking naughty thoughts. Meet me at Guy's cottage. They're away. I have a key.'

'And I have a houseful of children and animals.'

'So? You have staff to look after them. Is Piers around?'

'He's in Ireland.'

'Then what are you waiting for, woman? I'm dying for you.'

Jemima caught her reflection in the mirror: pink-cheeked and pretty in a cream silk shirt and designer jeans, her throat reddening with desire. She was wearing new silk undies. He would love them.

'I'll meet you there in ten minutes.' It was high time she kicked up her heels – what black sheep cousin Pixie always referred to 'dipping her toe in' – and she also had a little detective work to do while she was about it, having finally figured out a suspect for the mysterious lover 'H' in her mother-in-law's diaries.

When Pixie finally arrived at Home Farm to collect her children and dog pack, Jemima wasn't in.

'Visiting a sick friend, I think she said,' Nuala declared loyally.

'Oh.' Pixie was too tired to doubt this.

'I've deflea-ed them, by the way.'

'Dogs or children?' Pixie asked.

'Both.'

18

The tall, tweed-sporting snob who opened the door at Yonge and Dymoke, the Ibcote over Foxrush shotgun dealers, regarded Trudy as though she had rung the discreet customers' bell to offer him some clothes pegs and home made lacework.

'Yuss?'

'I've come to look at guns,' she told him confidently. 'I rang ahead.'

Brogues parallel parked on the top step of the grand entrance to the Georgian townhouse, he studied her down his long and bulbous nose, which resembled a tapir's, and narrowed his buggy eyes.

'Name?'

Trudy, who knew Yonge and Dymock's reputation of old and had for once bothered to dress the part in a shooting waistcoat, a pair of moleskins that cut into her waist, her two hundred quid Dubarry boots and one of Finn's rugby shirts with a pro-hunting slogan on it, felt like saying 'Bin Laden', but she knew that her married name was almost as sacred as the silly password that the company insisted upon for admittance to their special collection.

When she said 'Cottrell', Tapir-Nose stepped back reverently but still reluctantly to allow her access.

Looking like a private house from the outside – there was only a very small brass plaque to reveal the company name, plus the suggestion of treasure with cast iron grilles over the lower windows – inside, the gun shop resembled a colonial Kenyan gentleman's club. Grazing like buffalo in random pairs on the acres of faded Persian veldt were battered leather chesterfields, looked down upon by a canopy of wooden blinds, incongruous ceiling fans, cigar smoke and more stuffed game than the Natural History Museum.

Trudy got straight to the point.

'I'm looking for a pair of Purdeys.'

There was a disparaging snort.

'Can you help?'

'Ha!'

He sounded like a walrus with a fish spine stuck in its throat.

She glared, politeness quickly vanishing. 'I suppose you want the password?'

'Ha!'

'It's "Dairy Maid".' She had gleaned it the previous evening from Lady Belling, a shooting stalwart and Oddlode near neighbour, by pretending that she wanted to buy Finn a very special shotgun as a surprise for his birthday. A lifelong Yonge and Dymoke customer, Hell's Bells had been only too glad to help.

He balked. 'How d'you know that?'

'Would you mind showing me the guns now?'

'No.'

'Sorry?'

'The password is out of date.'

'It was valid yesterday.'

'We change them monthly.'

Today was the first of June. Trudy bristled.

'Oh, for God's sake. I'm here now. Lady Isabel Belling gave me the code – she offered to make a personal introduction, but I am in a dreadful hurry.'

'We *only* work from personal introductions.'

'So call her.'

'*Written* introductions.'

'How ridiculous!'

Tapir-Nose was already walking towards the door to see her out. 'I'm afraid it's company policy.'

'Do you have any Purdeys in stock here?'

'Not on display, no.'

'In the private room?'

'I couldn't possibly comment.'

Exasperated, Trudy stood her ground, crossing her arms across her shooting waistcoat and facing him combatively, determined to find his weak spot.

His small eyes flicked involuntarily towards her chest, swelling rather obviously above her crossed arms.

Gotcha!

Once a consummate flirt, digging deep into her coquettish reserves was no easy call for Trudy these days. Faced with a lusty male, she experienced the same frozen fear as she did when faced with a keyboard. She knew how to play it by heart, but her heart was no longer in it, her confidence tattered, her head muddled with doubt, and the button on her self-protect mechanism so sensitive that she could completely shut down before striking a single chord.

But today she was determined to get what she wanted. And boob men, being fairly low down the food chain, were usually a push-over.

Bracing herself, she ran her tongue across her teeth, uncrossed her arms and, discreetly lowering the zip of her waistcoat, leaned towards him across the back of a chesterfield so that her chest was gloriously shelved upon its curved leather undulations.

'Don't be so stuffy,' she purred, looking up at him through her lashes. 'Surely I can have a quick look? There's nobody around to tell tales.'

'I am extremely busy,' he bristled.

'C'mon – it won't take long. I really *am* a serious customer you know.'

'It would be most unorthodox.'

'*I'm* unorthodox.' She pressed her elbows closer together to increase her cleavage. 'It doesn't make my purchase any less valid.'

He was wavering, nostrils flaring, pale eyes glued to her chest.

Trudy felt empowered for the first time since the Auctioneer's Ball. A mini-fix of endorphins charged into her bloodstream and raised her game.

I am still attractive, she realised in amazement. I may not be the babe I once was, but I can thrill a Hooray Henry with floppy hair and a vaguely Hugh Grant air to him. I am still in business.

'C'mon,' she coaxed in a voice that was pure raunch, 'just two minutes.'

Within a minute, she was inside Yonge and Dymoke's hallowed private gun room. A surprisingly understated space, more like a large walk-in wardrobe than an exclusive retail chamber, it brought her unpleasantly close to Tapir-Nose's briny armpits and liquorice breath, but gratifyingly within reach of the next clue.

The only Purdeys in evidence were a pair of nineteenth century duelling pistols.

'How apt.'

'Exquisite pieces,' he enthused, his long nose-tip just inches from hers. 'Converted from flintlock to percussion by Purdeys themselves. Mechanically perfect, with very fine engraving to the plates, you'll see. We have several collectors interested.'

'At what price level?'

Tapir-Nose visibly shuddered at the uncouth mention of money.

'About twenty,' he said in measured tones, looking from the pistols to her cleavage.

Trudy said nothing, afraid that she might squeak. Her treasure hunt suitor was losing the plot. Twenty thousand pounds was so beyond her budget, it beggared belief.

'May I see the case?' she asked.

He looked confused.

She nodded sagely. 'One can tell so much about guns' histories from the original cases, don't you find?'

Ignoring the beautiful workmanship of the pistols, Trudy huddled over the case and studied it minutely, pulling out the loading tools, bullet mould and powder flask, poking into all the niches and crevices.

There was no sign of a hidden clue.

She handed it back in defeat. 'These aren't quite right. Are you sure you have no more pairs of Purdeys?'

'Must it be a pair?'

'Yes. It's a – um – romantic anniversary present for my husband,' she lied. 'The *pair* is significant.'

'Why? Are you planning to shoot one another?'

For a brief moment, the joke made him quite attractive. His eyes were a charming shade of faded denim blue, and he had remarkably good teeth.

Picking up on this momentary lapse faster than a hound on fox scent, he stepped towards her.

'Your husband is a very lucky man,' he drawled, breathing liquorice over her.

'Isn't he just?' She cast her eyes around desperately for ideas.

Which was when she noticed the pictures on the wall: mostly rather grizzly Landseer prints or jokey Bryn Parry cartoons. Amongst them were several rubbings of gun plates. One, which stood out because it was rubbed in some sort of glittering silver pastel on crimson paper, was clearly marked 'Purdey Pair'.

She bounded towards it.

'Is *this* for sale?'

'What?'

The framed rubbing showed ornamental rose and scroll shotgun lock plates, plus carved breech ends featuring perky spaniels, and a completely OTT trigger guard dripping with pheasants, each silver rubbing beautifully labelled by hand in fine black pen, the same pen having carefully picked out the most ornamental details within the rubbings themselves. It was exquisite and painstaking draughtsmanship

'Oh, old Foths did that when he worked here – he liked to keep a record of the best guns we handled. Think those two sold for as much as a small cottage.' He was breathing down her neck now as he peered over her shoulder. 'But that was before my time.'

'Is "old Foths" not still around?' she asked.

'Dead.'

'How sad.' She discreetly peered to the back of the frame where, sure enough, there seemed to be a piece of paper taped to the backboard. 'I'd really like to buy it.'

'Not for sale.' He was breathing heavily. 'Lovely scent.'

'Thanks,' she muttered. 'Surely you'll give me a price?'

'Hmm,' he chortled salaciously. 'How much would you say it's worth?'

'Fifty pounds?'

'Now that is *very* offensive.'

'It's only a rubbing.'

'Some men value rubbing very highly.' He was clearly hoping for payment in kind.

'One hundred,' she offered. 'Take it or leave it.'

'If it means that much to you . . .' He pressed her up against the wall as he hooked down the rubbing.

Feeling his lean, tweedy length up against her, the strangest thing happened; a series of small, sizzling explosions in her solar plexus. The sheer weight of his body, the insistent bulge of his crotch and the hot breath on the nape of her neck aroused and uplifted her. Being desired by a stranger was thrilling after all these years in self-imposed, married isolation.

Finn had long treated sex with her as a nuptial right, not a thing of any great worth. Giles's indiscriminate lust was mandatory locally; Flipper's admiration had always been a juvenile shaggy dog story with nowhere to go. Tapir-Nose, while initially as charismatic as a gatepost, was gloriously carnal. And quite funny in a dry, understated way. If there was one thing guaranteed to breathe a little life into Trudy's long-quashed libido, it was laughter.

'I think,' he crooned into her ear now, 'that this little rubbing is worth rather more than three digits.' He had a very sexy voice when he wasn't barking like a walrus, not unlike Nigel Havers playing a roué in a rom com.

'Surely not?'

'I think we're talking telephone numbers here.'

Her heart hammered as his lips brushed her neck. 'Some telephone numbers are three digits – the operator and nine-nine-nine for example.'

'I was thinking *your* telephone number.'

'But I'm married.'

'No married woman as desirable as you gets through life without at least one contact number of which her husband is unaware.' His lips merely teased the tips of the tiny hairs standing to attention on her skin.

Trudy quivered with unexpected jubilation. She could feel moisture beading on her forehead and between her breasts.

'And if I can't pay?'

'We at Yonge and Dymoke are very gentlemanly about recovering our debts,' he assured her gallantly.

Outside in the main offices, the phone began to ring with an echoing peal. It broke the spell irretrievably.

Trudy turned to face him, looking down at the picture with its delicate, dusty silver impressions of engravings etched out as clearly as the little hotspot on her neck that had been kissed by a stranger.

Then, as if shaking himself from a daydream, he cleared his throat and handed her the picture with an almost bashful dip of the head. 'A gift.'

'I don't deserve—'

'You do,' he assured her emphatically, floppy hair sweeping across his long face as he did so. 'I just hope you will call again.'

'Of course I will.' She meant it for a brief moment – just as she meant to lean across and kiss him lightly on the lips. It was only as she said the words and felt the slimy-centred, dry-edged texture of his lips that she regretted both sentiments immediately. It was like sitting in the car, stuffing back a hot, greasy deli counter sausage after doing the weekly supermarket shop – a quick fix that repulsed as much as the desire had enticed in the first place.

She turned and fled.

Out in the drizzle of Idcote High Street, she was so wrapped up in her own hot-cheeked shame that, dashing into a tiny side street and crossing towards the opposite pavement, she didn't notice the muddy off-roader roaring out of a narrow driveway behind her until its bull bars made contact with the backs of her knees and tipped her on to the bonnet.

Luckily it was moving so slowly that, apart from an ungainly pose that was definitely not out of the glamour model's car show guidebook, Trudy was unharmed and the big car ground to a steady halt with her still aboard. The only casualty was her Purdey picture, which rattled to the tarmac with a crunch of smashed glass.

Slithering stiffly from the car, Trudy turned and looked at the driver. She did a double take.

Jemima was glaring at her red-faced, clearly torn between fury and embarrassment. It wasn't quite the reaction Trudy would expect in the circumstances. Nor was the fact that Jemima merely buzzed down the window a fraction and, through a cloud of familiar Chanel, quacked. 'You OK? Good. Sorry – frightful hurry. Speak soon.' She drove off, running over the Purdey rubbing for good measure.

Trudy prised its squashed remains from a gravelly, glass-filled puddle and straightened up, just in time to come face to face with another car racing far too fast out of the same arched driveway. It was a familiar, shiny Jaguar. At the wheel, looking unusually unkempt, was Giles.

He beamed when he saw her and opened his window.

'Darling Trudy. What a treat! Need a lift?'

'My car's parked just along here, thanks.' She noticed that a sign above the driveway read 'Strictly Private – Inglenook Cottage'.

From Giles's heated car came a waft of hot leather, hot bodies and illicit liaisons. He smelt more strongly of Jemima's perfume than she had.

'You look damned choice today.' He admired the waistcoat's low zip and her long boots, blue eyes suggestive as ever. 'Been shopping?'

Trudy clutched her wet, broken picture to her chest, trying hard to cover it up. She didn't want to give him the satisfaction of knowing that she was running around after his stupid clues while he was clearly squiring Jemima. 'Just browsing.'

'Got time for a drink?'

'Must get back to work.'

'Me too, I suppose,' he said pulling a face at his watch. 'I was supposed to be in a meeting with clients half an hour ago. Call me!'

It wasn't until she was back in her car that she peeled the sodden, muddy clue from the back of the picture.

> Why not seek out Dot?
> You know her feather dusters well
> Could she hold another clue?
> Keeping our secrets warm like a broody hen?
> Maybe she is showing them off
> Openly displaying her little clutch
> Ready to hatch out all our truths
> Ripened for that special day
> Easter's egg hunt goes public
> Like the family treasure trove
> Lavishly lauded beneath its canvas canopy

She immediately scanned the first letters along the lines. WYCK-MORRELL.

Dot Wyck – she of the feather duster – was Trudy's occasional cleaner, who bred bantams in her spare time.

Trudy cast the clue aside, unable to get her mind off Jemima and Giles appearing out of the same driveway. It was pretty obvious what was going on.

On impulse, she called Liv's mobile and caught her buying groceries at Waitrose.

'I'm so glad you've called,' she gushed. 'I've been meaning to call you. Please let's meet up. Are you free for coffee? I've just bought a box of luxury Tiffins and need someone to stop me eating them all by myself.'

Put like that, Trudy couldn't resist. For once, she was well dressed and in good spirits. Coffee and gossip was just what she needed.

Liv looked amazing. Gone were the straight jeans, loafers, white shirt and navy blue sweatshirt, replaced by inky skinny jeans, long brown suede boots, a clingy velvet top and fur-trimmed gilet.

'What happened?' Trudy hugged her, surprised by how cheered she felt. 'You're dressed like a yummy mummy!'

Liv blushed. 'If you can't beat them . . .'

'Wow! You look fabulous.'

There was a new-found assuredness to Liv that Trudy immediately picked up, yet she still edited herself. Congenitally unable to keep a secret for more than ten minutes, Trudy would normally immediately spill the beans about seeing Jemima and Giles leaving the same cottage driveway seconds apart. Instead, she kept it in reserve and tested the water.

Liv had been hacking out with Jemima every day, she said. They had been for a few lovely lunches, and to the cinema and exhibitions. Jemima wanted her to join all sorts of committees.

In fact Liv was gibbering with guilt, but she kept this firmly hidden. She knew her defection from Trudy to Jemima was disloyal – and in large part spurred on by Martin who had kept tabs on her developing friendships by email. He thought Jemima a 'good' thing and Trudy a 'bad' one. Liv missed their daily, intimate, giggly chats, but she was uncomfortable at how much Trudy already knew about her – about her marriage, her secret desires, her inner frustration. Jemima, who knew nothing of this nor cared to, was easier to be around and willing to propel her up the Cotswold power wife network with lunchtime nosebags, endless charities and after school pow wows.

'Lily and Jasper have joined Bartleby and Georgia at the Wolds Fencing Club.'

'Are we talking wicker hurdles or épées and foils, here?'

'Fencing, silly – it's terribly exclusive. Several Royals are members.'

Trudy rolled her eyes, but Liv seemed delighted. She had been asked to join the Mungo House PTA, was helping organise a summer wildlife walk, and now shared the school run with two other 'yummies', giving her bags more free time 'to do all sorts of selfish things!'

'And what would they be?' Trudy teased. 'Not skinny dipping in the Odd with Giles Horton, I hope?'

'As if! I've hardly seen him. Jemima keeps me far too busy.'

Trudy should have picked up on the tell-tale signs that Liv was covering up a secret: the way her hands fluttered to her face, one finger rubbing her lower lip, the other playing with an earring, and the way she crossed her legs more tightly, tucking the toes of her upper leg behind the calf of her lower.

But Liv was a surprisingly good deceiver, from years of extravagant shoe-shopping behind Martin's back. Turning the tables and going straight for the gossip jugular, she asked about Trudy's secret admirer.

'Has he left any more clues?'

'I think my admirer might have other fish to fry.'

The natural intimacy between her and Liv that had so quickly built up over their hacks together was now on more fragile ground and Trudy felt wary. Unspoken mistrust and jealousy were at play here. Trudy, more hurt by Liv's defection to Jemima than she let on, felt she was being grilled as much on Jemima's behalf as Liv's.

'So you know who he is?'

'Possibly.' Despite knowing it was wrong to start rumours, despite knowing that she was saying it to belittle Jemima-who-could-do-no-wrong in Liv's eyes, she shared her Ibcote adultery sighting. It was the impulse to show off; she wanted Liv to know that *she* was the one with news hot off the press. She didn't really think about the consequences. And she certainly didn't expect Liv's reaction.

Liv had turned white beneath her ultra-subtle, professionally applied fake tan.

'Are you sure?' she breathed.

'Absolutely, it was so obvious – somewhere called Inglenook Cottage. Very Cotswolds leg-over.'

'Off Sheep Street in Ibcote. I know it.'

'You do?' Trudy was amazed. 'How come?'

'He took me there last week.'

'He *what* . . . ?'

'It belongs to a friend of Giles who only uses it about three times a year. He holds the spare keys. He told me it would be our s-special p-place. Our s-special s-secret.' She burst into tears, unable to hide her big secret a moment longer in the face of such overwhelming evidence that it was more sordid than special.

Trudy dashed forward to hug her.

'Oh God, Liv, I had no idea. I am so sorry. I shouldn't have said a thing.'

'Of c-course y-you should!' she wailed. 'He's m-made a fool of me. And p-poor M-M-Martin.'

Deciding that it wouldn't be very helpful to say that from what she'd heard so far, selfish Martin was probably shagging the bargirls of Singapore left, right and centre, Trudy gave her another hug.

She tried to make amends. 'Giles is an incorrigible bastard. Most of his conquests are well aware of that. He should never have picked on you – however beautiful. You are too fragile.'

Liv stopped howling. 'I'm not beautiful.'

'You are. Now mop up and open some wine. And, after we've drunk it and cheered ourselves up by discussing how pathetic Giles is, I'll go over there and give him a piece of my mind.'

'But I love him!' Liv sobbed. 'Jemima is a complete bitch!'

'God help us.' Trudy went in search of tissues and wine in the immaculately tidy house. She thought about the hundreds of song lyrics that she had written about love over the years, about how easily the word slid from one's lips without thought – a daily parlance, a favourite of advertising slogans and London cabbies.

'Right,' she said as she sat back down beside Liv. 'Let's get one thing straight. You are *not* in love with Giles. You love the way he makes you feel about yourself. Welcome to the Cotswold Adultery Club, of which Giles is a founder member. It's less exclusive than the fencing club, but there has been at least one Royal member over the years.'

Liv looked glum, but at least she had stopped crying, and seemed to be listening.

Trudy handed her a fresh hunk of tissues. 'You are not the first and will not be the last woman to feel the way you do about him, and he has just taken you through the very basics at entry level, believe me.'

'He makes love a thousand times better than Martin!'

'He probably only needs to touch you to make you feel on fire whereas Martin needs an hour with sexy music, a massage table, every essential oil and a battery operated device.'

Liv snorted with tearful laughter.

'That's the way your libido's directly wired to your imagination. It's adultery you've just discovered, *not* Giles,' she went on. 'Men's libidos tend to be wired from eyes to dick, bypassing brain entirely.'

Liv giggled, grateful for Trudy's damning humour. 'Martin's like that,' she agreed. 'I thought Giles was different.'

'Most of Giles's conquests are pretty thick-skinned and know what he's about. You're more sensitive, and he shouldn't have taken advantage, the bastard.'

Half an hour later, mildly tight, sucking a mint and sufficiently mopped up and bolstered for her kids' return from school on the yummy run, Liv gratefully waved Trudy off at her gate.

'Promise you won't tell him you know about us?' she begged for the tenth time.

'Promise.'

'And you won't forget to check on Otto. I can't face—' Her features started to crumble.

'Promise,' Trudy agreed. 'You just forget about it for now. I'll sort it.'

Sounding far more reassuring than she felt, she drove in the direction of River Cottage.

19

Giles was napping on his sofa in front of an antiques programme, Scotch at his side, clearly sleeping off his exertions. The French windows on to the riverside deck were open. Walking up there from the garden bank, Trudy gained entrance into the house unchecked, perched on the sofa arm at his feet and woke him by prodding his socked feet.

He screamed and fell off the sofa.

This was a rather more extreme reaction than she'd anticipated.

'Jesus! My arches!'

'Your what?'

'My collapsed arches – the slightest touch is torture.' He struggled to his knees, clutching his feet. 'All that jogging – they're agony.' He finally registered who she was. 'What are you doing here, Trudy darling?'

'I thought I'd take you up on that offer of a drink.'

'Of course, of course, how welcome.' Mustering dignity, he got to his feet squinting with pain as he limped to the drinks cabinet. 'You've caught me literally on the hop – ha ha. I know you drink vodka and Coke, but I have no cola. Orange?'

'Fine.' Trudy needed a bolstering drink, but didn't want to fall upon his hospitality too readily.

Fast regaining composure, Giles managed to skilfully pour drinks while tucking in his crumpled shirt, straightening his hair and revving up some seductive Cole Porter on the stereo.

By the time he handed Trudy a vodka and orange so strong it was the colour of horse pee, the sexy smile was back in place and the blond lion was ready to play. He slid into the sofa beside her, a hand already stroking her arm.

'You look quite ravishing today.'

'So you said,' she pulled her arm away, 'when I caught you driving off after shagging Jemima in your chum's holiday cottage.'

'Steady on!' He was clearly rattled by the accurate and concise summary of events.

'Don't pretend.' She took a big slug of drink. 'And before you tell me that it's no business of mine, I quite agree. I wouldn't dream of passing comment were it not for the fact that you're also shagging her new best friend, and that *really* isn't cricket, Giles. Women talk, you know.'

'Which little bird has been singing loudest, I wonder?' he snapped, all affability forgotten. 'We all know who's the biggest blabbermouth around here, Trudy.'

'Liv is sensitive. She can't take your sleazy duplicity.'

'She's tougher than you think.'

'You'll destroy her.'

'You think she's never done this sort of thing before?'

'Of course not!'

'Christ, Trudy, you can be naïve. Bored, pretty housewife seeking distraction, abandoned by career-mad expat husband. She has it down to a fine art. She was all over me from the start – Princess Di eyes and giggling fits. I hardly had to lift a finger to get her. She's a consummate flirt, even if she is about as original in bed as a cup of cocoa and a Georgette Heyer.'

'Don't be so bloody patronising!'

'At least she's having some fun.'

'It didn't look much fun when I left her.'

'Blame the messenger.'

Trudy was aware of an unpleasant taste in her mouth – her own hypocrisy. He was right. She *was* stirring, however she justified her actions as defending her friend and exposing Giles's sham. But the bitter taste just outraged her even more as shame mixed with self-righteousness.

'And *Jemima*? What are you thinking of? Piers would kill you if he ever found out.'

'He hasn't for the past decade.'

Her eyebrows shot up. 'I thought you despised her?'

'Good camouflage, huh?'

'You utter shit.'

'Jealous?'

'Of *what* exactly? Your inability to keep your dick out of the family?'

'Jem and I have a long-standing arrangement.'

'Shouldn't that be long-lying?'

'She knows what we have isn't exclusive – and she wouldn't want that. It's no secret that Piers shags around, and isn't too fussy with whom. Jemima prefers a more exclusive arrangement with someone she knows and trusts. I am there when she calls – and can always be relied upon to satisfy.'

'Why doesn't she just go to Ann Summers and buy herself a Rabbit?'

He shot her a withering look. 'We haven't actually got it together for many months, a year possibly, but Jem called out of the blue this week – and has been very eager, I must say. I rather suspect she wanted a little pipe-opener or two to stop her feeling ring rusty.'

'I'm sorry?'

He studied the last sliver of ice melting in his drink. 'She's obviously thinking of taking a new lover. Why else come to me for a tune-up?'

'I have got to be dreaming. Strait-laced convent girl, charity stalwart and all-round brown owl, Jemima Cottrell, who so disapproves of *my* wanton rock and roll ways, is in fact wrapping her horse-hardened legs around the infidelity course and distance champion so she can try jumping a new mount?'

'Very pithily put.' He drummed his fingers on his knee. 'Jemima would approve of the analogy, if not the character reference.'

'You're a pair of self-seeking, selfish bastards.'

He nodded thoughtfully. 'Of course you *are* right, Trudy . . .'

'Too bloody right.'

'. . . all this *is* none of your business.'

The taste in her mouth was as bitter as battery acid.

'So I'll bugger off.' She hopped furiously off the sofa arm, but he caught her sleeve and pulled her back.

'Stay for another drink.' He took her empty glass back to his bottle collection. 'Let's not part enemies, darling one. I must say I am very flattered by your jealousy.'

'For the last time, I am *not* jealous!'

'So why are you here?'

She cast her eye around the room, asking herself the same thing. She had been on a mission when she arrived on a sanctimonious charge, sure of her incorruptibility. Now she felt wrong-footed.

'I'm worried about what you're doing to my friend.'

'So go and hold *her* hand.' He handed her a fresh drink, pushing her gently back on to her sofa perch. 'Don't lecture *me*; because you're wasting your breath. As far as I'm concerned, we're all grown ups; we have free will. Liv knows what she's doing, just as Jemima knows what she's doing just as I know what I'm doing. You're the only one in denial here, Trudy darling.'

'Don't give me that! You'd have me join your bloody harem here and now if you could.'

'No offence, but I don't have the energy this evening.'

To her own embarrassment, Trudy felt affronted, tempted to make her exit after all. Her bile and hackles rose.

'Hallelujah!' she snapped, standing up victoriously. 'So stop sending me stupid bloody love notes and treasure clues.'

He drew back his chin incredulously. 'I beg your pardon?'

'It might have seemed funny at first – and I admit, they did get me going, but the novelty has worn off.'

'Am I supposed to understand a word of this?'

'You know damned well what I'm talking about.'

He stood up, his nose level with hers, blue eyes concerned. 'I suggest you take a deep breath, park your beautiful arse back down somewhere out of reach, and tell me what you mean.'

When she did, it was abundantly clear that he knew absolutely nothing about the secret treasure hunt that she had been set in tandem with the main event.

Trudy felt sick and silly: sick that she had spilled the beans to yet another acquaintance she didn't entirely trust; silly because it all sounded so childish in the cold light of day.

Yet Giles seemed delighted by the distracting little side-thriller. 'So our mystery man – or woman – texts you anonymously or leaves clues hidden in the foliage, so far leading to shoe buckles, an old book and a silver rubbing. *Why?*'

'Well, I suppose it does seem rather odd. The clues are very personal. It's somebody who knows me well. And it's quite romantic, I suppose.'

'So whatever made you think it was me?'

The atmosphere between them had started to warm towards mutual understanding. Vodka was loosening Trudy up, along with a splash of mistaken-identity shame.

'Yes, I forgot that you're really only interested in getting to know women carnally. Their minds are forever off limits.'

'Oh, that's a bit unfair. I am capable of holding a conversation over dinner. But poetry really isn't my thing.'

'Then who . . . ?'

'I would have thought that was patently obvious.'

'Meaning?'

His blue eyes widened theatrically. 'Come *on*, Trudy. Don't be thick. The boy's been in love with you for years. He makes little secret of the fact. You might treat him with contempt for it – as does Finn – but it isn't such a joke to him. Sometimes he can barely function as a result. Christ knows how he'll end up if he carries on beating himself up, unable to move on. Like me, probably.'

Trudy tucked her feet beneath her as she watched Giles, surprised by his sudden outburst. For once, someone was actually several drinks up on her.

'I was there, don't forget.' He waggled a finger. 'Easter.'

'What about Easter?'

'Christ knows, I understand his plight. I have been married to three women, but never loved them the way I did and I still do the one I can never have. He should never have come back to live here. If he has any sense, he'll move away, far away. I should have bloody done that, but I couldn't bring myself to leave her, especially after . . .'

'After what?'

He shook his head, springing up to fetch the bottles and tripping over the edge of the rug on his return.

He was jumpy and blundering, not his usual insouciant self at all. Something had rattled him, and Trudy had stumbled upon the fall-out – the unique sight of Giles, three parts cut, indiscreet, uptight and for once unable to see the funny side.

'She doesn't believe the way I feel, either. Her confidence is shot to pieces, married to that bastard all these years, steam-rollered by his ego, putting on the show of the good wife, the good mother, the most true of friends while all the time dying inside. She just sees me as a bloody fop, a joke – a plaything.'

'She still lives nearby?'

'With her godawful family,' he snarled, 'and that egomaniac of a husband.'

He poured more drinks with hands that shook, his jaw taut, hair dishevelled, eyes blazing. He was far more attractive in the raw like this. At last the front was down and he was absolutely genuine.

She guessed he must be talking about Jemima. It was why the affair had lasted ten years when he bored so quickly of others. He loved her.

'Have you asked her to leave him?'

'A thousand times,' he laughed bitterly. 'Although not recently. What's the point? She'll never go. The time to go was obvious, and she stalled too long then. It's long past.'

'Does she love you?'

'She certainly *did* – but perhaps she loved the fruits of my bloody loins more than my heart and soul. Ironic given that *I*, as you so rightly point out, am really only interested in women carnally these days. What goes around comes around.'

'But that's why you always pursue married women, isn't it? Because of her.'

'Maybe. I can certainly spot the unhappy ones.' The corner of his mouth twisted in a rueful smile. 'Like you.'

'We're not talking about me.' She ducked the topic swiftly and set her glass of unadulterated vodka to one side knowing it would tip her into a stupor.

Showing no such restraint, Giles drained half his glass in one. 'Of course we're not. And you're not like her. But Liv is. Very like. That's why I can tell she's a lot tougher than you think.'

'Liv is nothing like Jemima!'

He took a couple of beats to catch up. 'Who's talking about Jemima? I'm in love with Dibs,' he sighed, his voice mournful.

'Dibs?' Trudy gasped. The Loins of the Lodes loved her shy, frosty mother-in-law.

He nodded wretchedly. 'I have adored her since I was a boy. I fathered children for her, for Christ's sake. Now I would never do that for Jemima, or even you, my darling Trudy.'

'You fathered children for Dibs?' Trudy was unable to stop the frantic mental calculations. 'But that means—'

'The twins.' He nodded. 'I was nineteen. I loved her with all my heart.'

'You're Flipper's *father*?'

'Like father like son. And darling Nell, of course.'

'Do they know?'

'Hell no! Dibs would never countenance that.'

The enormity of the confession seemed to linger in the room like smoke.

'Best-looking pair of Cottrell kids, though, you have to admit,' he boasted with a nervous, self-mocking smile that plucked Trudy's heartstrings.

'And Flipper's got a far better brain than the rest of the family, so would Nell if she applied herself and spent less time on her back, but I suppose she gets that from me, too.'

'Heavens, Giles, you know this means you're going to be a grandfather?'

'God,' he barked with laughter. 'I can't possibly be old enough.'

'Goes with the collapsed arches.'

'And the lifetime of regret,' he sighed, but only half-seriously as his hand closed tightly over hers. 'You know, I really feel quite invigorated after our chat. I've never told anybody all this. Most refreshing. I don't suppose you'd like to come to bed with me now?'

'No, Giles!' She reached for her abandoned drink, heart hammering. 'I need to get my head round this.'

'Christ alone knows why I have told *you*,' he groaned, rubbing his brow. 'I've just bared my soul to the most godawful gossip I know. You fool, Giles! It's those bloody great big hazel eyes of yours. I can't resist them. Like truth drugs. Or the best fudge.'

'So people say. Does Jemima not know?'

'She seems to have rumbled something – kept asking all sorts of strange questions today about Dibs. Of course, I put her off the scent, but she knows *something*.'

'Could Dibs have told her?'

'Christ, no! Dibs is the soul of discretion. *Nobody* knows.' He pulled his temples up with his fingertips as he stared at her, temporarily rearranging his laughter lines. 'Except you. How on earth can I trust you to tell nobody?'

'You have my word.'

'If Flipper or Nell find out about this—'

'Surely, they deserve to know?'

He shook his head. 'I left that decision to Dibs.'

'So talk to her about it again. They're grown-ups now. She can't live a total lie.'

'We all do, Trudy darling. You of all people should know that.'

20

Pheely lay back against the navy blue Egyptian cotton sheets and shuddered with pleasure. Sven might be minimalist in most things, but lovemaking wasn't one of them.

It had been three days since she had first walked into the magical clearing in the New Forest to find the giant silver Dane guarding his glass house.

For a transparent dwelling, it hid a surprising number of secrets. The basement, its walls tangled with tree roots that Sven had incorporated into the decoration like veins and arteries in the backlit glass-block walls, was as messy as Pheely's beloved lodge cottage. Running the full length of the house, with a high gallery above that let in a stream of heavenly light from its opaque glass walls, it was filled with teenage clutter, music players, gaming consoles, computers and a vast television, along with oversized furniture, musical instruments including a grand piano, stacks of unhung paintings, piles and piles of books and, perhaps rather incongruously, a vast array of state of the art gym equipment.

'I didn't realise you were so keen on exercise.'

'I'm not. The girls use it. They are very body conscious.'

As Pheely had found out the following day when meeting two ash blonde bombshells with bodies like whips.

Such close-to beauty and slenderness would have depressed her had it not been for their instant unguarded warmth towards her, and total adoration of Basil.

'He is such a little peach!' Dorte, the eldest, had cooed.

'You must let us look after him while you and Dad spend time together!' Mette, her younger sister, had insisted.

Uncertain how long she should stay, Pheely had muttered awkwardly about not outstaying her welcome.

'Rubbish!' Sven had boomed. 'I am going to keep you prisoner here. You want me to find the classical goddess trapped within those stunning curves, don't you?'

Hearing this – her own internet plea repeated back to her – Pheely had swooned.

Now, three days later, she was shamelessly enjoying her captivity, despite the strict exercise routine. When the sex was this good, both the calories and the midnight oil were worth burning. Whether burning her boats was quite so wise, Pheely was not so certain.

Sven made no secret of his admiration of her body, despite her carrying at least two stones' surplus weight on her hips, belly, bum and boobs. He adored curves, creases, dimples, wobbles and even cellulite, he claimed. He certainly spent hours admiring them from every angle, stroking, fingering, tasting and kissing.

Yet he also claimed he would enable her to shift it all, and fast.

'That's the deal,' he'd explained simply. 'I enjoy you while I can, and once you are approaching the size you desire, I liberate you both from your shame and from this lover.' He patted his big, hairy, tanned chest where his shirt was unbuttoned. 'It suits us both. I have no desire to commit, yet I want you all to myself – but only *this* you.' He had stroked her breasts and trailed his hand down to her pot belly. 'I will not want the new you. Therefore I will get exactly what I want, as will you.'

When Pheely had asked how long this Svengali transformation would take, he'd replied about a fortnight or so. It seemed remarkably quick and easy, and also very logical in a left-field way, if rather unromantic.

She needn't have worried about romance. Each night, he massaged her from head to foot, bathed her in the deepest of bubbling baths, wrapped her in the softest of towels and then hand fed her from the mountains of fresh, healthy food that dripped from his table like a harvest banquet. Not that Pheely was hungry. Desire had stolen her greed right away; it was all she could do to force back a glass of champagne and a sliver of poached salmon.

His lovemaking was legend. While, two stories beneath them, Basil snored contentedly in a makeshift cot between the two sisters' basement dens, lovingly checked and monitored, Pheely had every extremity sucked and licked, much to her shame at first. Her feet had not seen a chiropodist in years and were armour-plated with scaly skin and thickened nails; her buttocks read like a Kama Sutra in blocked-pore Braille; her bikini line had become more of a trunk-line of shame, and her labia hadn't seen any attention since the labours of Basil six months earlier. Some women rubbed in olive oil and rejuvenating avocado pulp post partum. Pheely, who preferred her avocados and olive oil on a plate with balsamic and a few king prawns, had paid scant attention to her private parts.

But Sven lavished attention on them, nightly rubbing in oils himself; trimming and shaping her pubes during long, hot baths together, even revelling in exfoliating her arse and moisturising the toes that he had just pumiced for hours, until all were as smooth as marble. Then, in bed, he savoured every newly colonised area with a long, indulgent tasting session.

Pheely found it remarkably easy to give into him in every aspect. He so obviously derived pleasure from his actions and such was the force of his personality that resistance was hopeless. The pleasure that he gave, once she abandoned herself to his whims, was unprecedented. Never had she orgasmed so spontaneously, so forcefully and so joyously – utterly without effort on her part. Even with Giles she often stretched and strained, helped him along with a little self-stimulating fingering, held her breath until her temples throbbed and – on bad days – closed her eyes and imagined he was Brad Pitt. And Giles was a consummate lover: considerate, passionate, funny, fiery and impulsive. But Sven was a virtuoso.

The trade off was the daily workouts in the basement gym. To deafening and incomprehensible modern music, Pheely was forced to run marathons on the treadmill, climb several Empire States on the Stairmaster, lift warehouse loads of weight on the bench press and cross the Atlantic solo on the rowing machine.

Sven's regime was merciless.

He was the ultimate taskmaster, marching around her with a stopwatch, barking out orders and encouragement, watching her like a hawk in case she tried to slacken off (which she did, regularly), and pausing from his vigil only to change the music or take a call.

'Don't you have to work?' she grumbled on the third exhausting day. 'I thought you lectured?'

'I'm taking a sabbatical. And I'm lecturing you. This is a very short-lived arrangement after all; I get ephemeral tyranny, you get endorphins and hunger, and we both get off on it. Next month we will have moved on completely.'

Somehow, the short lived promise of the situation, the deadline and its guarantee of going separate ways made the physical torment bearable by day, and the physical pleasure unbearably tender by night. They were intimate straight away, totally trusting, sacrificially devoted and yet destined to part. It added a frisson like no other. Pheely had never known that emotions and physical sensation like this existed.

When, on day four, she realised that the skirt she had brought with her was already sliding off her hips, the gratification became almost insufferable.

She was so wrapped up in her new world of pain and pleasure it barely occurred to her that her absence from Oddlode might be causing worry. The only person she had contacted was Dilly, texting her to say that she was extending her stay. Dilly had texted back happily from New York to say that she was staying on there longer too, and did Pheely want any new shoes?

Who needs shoes when you're walking on air? Pheely replied cryptically.

It was perhaps a good thing that Pheely was too distracted to dwell upon her empty place in Oddlode because, in truth, nobody had really noticed her absence.

Anke was very concerned about Faith, who she was certain was truanting regularly from A-level studies at college to spend hours at the stables with Rory. Not that it could be technically defined as truanting, as Faith's course tutor pointed out when Anke put through a worried call to him. She was a voluntary student in further education now, after all. But it was a shame, he agreed, that she was wasting her chances by missing so many lessons. She was a bright girl; she had every chance of straight As if she knuckled down. At this rate she would be lucky to scrape basic passes.

Anke couldn't blame Rory. He had no real idea what was going on, but neither was he willing to back her up and tell Faith to get back to her missed classes.

'It's her choice,' he told Anke when she called him privately to discuss it. 'I don't pay her; I don't even talk to her much. She has no incentive to come here.'

Apart from love, Anke had thought sadly.

She tried to encourage Faith to focus on the treasure hunt and the imminent fine art auction at which the next clue would be hidden behind the magic lot number but, while Faith was vaguely interested, she hardly engaged. Nor did she want to get involved in looking after their new field guest.

To add to Anke's load, she had felt beholden to help out antique dealers Mark and Spencer, who had struggled from the start to look after their impulse buy, the Friesian horse Steve McQueen. Their back garden had proven completely inadequate for the big, black gelding and he had trashed the decking, the pond and several ornamental stone cherubs within days. The neighbours complained; Steve became increasingly hard to handle; the boys were frightened of him. Rory's livery prices were too high.

Feeling sympathetic towards two innocents out of their depth, and motivated also by a basic concern for animal welfare, Anke offered Steve temporary refuge with her own two retired horses at Wyck Farm.

Faith was critical from the start and, far from showing an interest, took every opportunity to slate Anke for being a soft touch, criticise Steve's long back and shaggy mane and berate his owners for their gullibility and ineptitude.

Anke had no idea how to get through to her daughter. Fiercely independent, private and uncommunicative, she reminded her mother of herself at that age.

Amidst all the worry about Faith, Anke completely failed to notice that Pheely wasn't in evidence.

Nor had Pixie noticed her friend's absence. She was too embroiled in attempts to recover her 'stolen' chest from Sexton, ably assisted by Sioux.

Sexton claimed that she had given him the chest or, more precisely, that he had won it during a drunken game of poker during their earlier, happier years.

'He might be right,' Pixie confessed to Sioux. 'But the awful thing is, I can't remember a single one of them. I have always been a dreadfully forgetful drunk.'

'In the eyes of the law, he doesn't have a case,' she pointed out. 'Just appoint a good family solicitor to thrash out a separation agreement, and you'll have it back in no time.'

But Pixie refused to take that route, considering it too antagonistic. Instead, she surprised Sioux by announcing that Sexton could keep the chest.

'I don't want it. Strictly *entre nous*, I've always rather hated it. It's what's inside it I want.'

'But Sexton emptied the contents before he took it.'

'Not entirely, there's a hidden compartment he doesn't know about.'

'And what's in that?'

'Hundreds of thousands of pounds worth of bonds that Daddy left me. It's all my inheritance, really – and my kids'. I kept meaning to put them in the bank for safekeeping, but our family are rather hopeless about such things. Daddy kept them in a secret lining to his fishing flies box.'

'Jesus!' Sioux reeled back. 'Then we have to get our hands on that chest, don't we?'

'Oh Sioux, I'm glad you're here. Your clever mind can track it down.'

Sioux gave her a beady look. 'If I do find it, I don't suppose you could see your way to cutting me in?'

'Cutting you in?'

'My caravan . . . a little nest egg to see me and the destiny wagon rolling off to green pastures.'

She started to laugh. 'Darling Sioux – your fortune telling is costing me a fortune, but of course I will. Yes. Take it as read. If you can get these papers back for me, I'll buy you that caravan and a crystal ball to go with it if you like.'

Sioux patted Pixie the ferret in her pocket and lit a contented cheroot, already planning her line of attack.

Several days after hearing Trudy's revelations about Giles, and having neglected Otto completely by avoiding River Cottage, Liv had sulked sufficiently to start cheering up.

She no longer hated all men. Just Giles.

Martin had sent quite a caring email for once; at least it said he was missing her and he asked her to email him a photograph of herself in her underwear to put under his pillow, which she thought sweet after ten years' marriage. He had also been very helpful with the latest Cottrell treasure hunt clue, doing all sorts of research on the internet his end to identify a painting in the forthcoming fine art sale.

Liv had been distracted from any matching research by a rather exciting number of messages flying to and from Finn Cottrell via

Facebook. He seemed to think she was looking for a Cornish holiday cottage and, while she'd never dreamed of such an extravagance, she looked forward to his rather abrupt but terribly well-written and occasionally very funny messages so much that she didn't enlighten him and they happily exchanged opinions on original features, courtyard gardens, off-street parking and coastal versus inland.

It said in Finn's profile that he had an upper second degree from Durham – much better than Martin's third from Loughborough – and listed fast cars, yachts and polo amongst his hobbies. His favourite music was a band called the Pigeon Detectives which she had never heard of. She went out and bought a CD and found it incredibly sexy, dancing around the house to it when the children were at school. She envied Trudy enormously, that familiar overlapping of resentment and approbation.

She couldn't understand why Trudy had been so sarcastic about him when he came across as so kind, witty and charming. Her own complicity in that bitchiness about men and marriage, and Trudy's husband in particular, was starting to compound Liv's ever-increasing guilty conscience. Her feelings towards Trudy grew even more ambivalent.

To cheer herself up, she stopped off in Morrell on the Moor en route to collect the children from Mungo House and checked out the new, exclusive boutique that had opened on Sheep Street, tracking down a host of goodies there, including a pair of exquisite navy blue suede Italian loafer mules that would be perfect for summer.

The high that the purchases gave her enabled her to just about maintain her composure and hold back a blush when she bumped into Jemima at the school gates, collecting Georgia and Bartleby in place of Nuala.

'She has an aunt visiting from Ireland – they're "doing Cheltenham" this afternoon,' she told Liv as she air-kissed her cheeks. 'How *are* you? Haven't seen you in an *age*. Up for a hack tomorrow morning? We can have lunch at the Duck Upstream afterwards.'

'Gosh. Lovely. Yes.' Liv nodded nervously.

'Think Trudy might come along? Will you ask her?'

Why she couldn't ask her sister-in-law herself mystified Liv and she chose to meet the request with a vague smile, already planning to wear her Italian loafers to lunch.

When she'd finally gathered her children and strapped them into the 4x4, Liv realised that the encounter has passed better than she'd dared hope and she was still the favoured one. Knowing about Jemima and Giles made surprisingly little difference to Liv's feelings for the queen bee of the county set. She was almost as envious of Jemima as she was of Trudy, but found Jemima's schoolgirl bossiness easier to read. Trudy's complexity and honesty made the truth too funny and painful to deny, whereas Jemima hid behind platitudes and cushion slogans. That was safer territory for Liv, particularly in current circumstances. She and Jemima had a great deal in common. Despite an initial flash of hurt and anger, she didn't blame her for falling for Giles; they both had, after all. In a way it made her feel their friendship was more evenly matched. She even had an element of one-upmanship because she knew about their secret, whereas Jemima had no idea about Liv's.

The main difference between her affair and Jemima's, Liv decided smugly, was that she had got over Giles already.

In the same way that she could swap friendship allegiance so quickly – or so she thought – Liv believed that her sexual affections could return to their default position with barely more than a hot bubble bath, a few of her favourite episodes of *Desperate Housewives* on DVD and giving herself a stern talking to.

She sent Martin a photograph of herself in a frilly white basque taken with the digital camera on self-timer balanced on the dressing-table mirror. She hoped he didn't notice the shoeboxes spilling from the Morrell boutique bag on the bed in the background.

Feeling suitably purged of Giles, she finally plucked up the courage to go to see Otto on a weekday mid-morning, certain that her ex-lover would be at work.

But he was at home, sitting on a plantation chair on his river deck in dark glasses and a panama, still in his dressing gown, looking like death. When he saw her car pulling up, he accidentally upended a jug of iced water from the chair arm over himself. Jumping up in alarm, he clutched on to the deck railings for support.

Fickle heart hammering, Liv raced to his side. 'Are you all right?'

'Food poisoning,' he managed to splutter, swaying dramatically.

He was in fact suffering from a prolonged and noxious hangover, probably involving mild alcohol poisoning and salmonella, having consumed an entire bottle of Scotch the night Trudy had visited, followed by six prairie oysters and two Bloody Marys the following morning in an attempt to drink himself sober. He hadn't managed solid food in the intervening forty-eight hours.

'Oh, you poor darling.' Liv felt his forehead. His big blue eyes were as helpless as a Weimaraner puppy's. 'I can see you need looking after.'

He nodded mutely.

Liv was still too intimidated by Jemima to call her in person, but she was now able to text her fairly easily, even to tell a blatant lie.

Otto lost a shoe & lame, she tapped out cheerfully. *Sorry! Trudy busy, too. Another time? L x*

She turned back to Giles. 'Let me make you some chicken soup and fetch you some cool compresses for your forehead.'

'You are an angel,' he croaked gratefully.

He was in fact ferociously bad-tempered after his indiscreet ranting to Trudy. He was furious with himself, and with Trudy for possessing one of those faces, bodies and, most pertinently, that drinking buddy stamina, that always made him uncharacteristically careless. Just as she had at the Auctioneers' Ball, she had proven she could outdrink and outthink him, and those were traits he found deeply disturbing in the fairer sex.

Being tended to by an attractive woman who could do neither was a welcome distraction in his current malaise, allowing him to put his feet up and try to remember what the hell he had said.

Unaccustomed to being stood up – even by a girlfriend – Jemima mounted her volatile young event prospect, Lord Haw-Haw, and, fuming to herself, contemplated hacking straight down into Oddlode and nonchalantly clip-clopping past River Cottage to check out Liv's alibi.

Jemima didn't trust her one little bit, for all her doe-eyed fragility. There was an iron will there, along with an occasional wanton streak born of many years living with an insufferably selfish man – it took one to know one – and Jemima suspected some duplicity at play.

Warming to the idea, Jemima planned a swift circuit of the village, dropping casually in on Trudy as she knew Flipper did regularly for coffee and gossip. But that would be too shaming, especially as Lord Haw-Haw was prone to having the last laugh, and had almost had her off a few times recently. She had no intention of losing face by appearing on Trudy's driveway covered with mud.

Instead she took the bridle path that speared away from Fox Oddfield through the pheasant coppices and then climbed towards the ridgeway, running directly alongside Rory Midwinter's land in Upper Springlode.

Luckily Rory was riding and she could look across the hedge quite casually to find herself almost at eye level as they both trotted along, her on the track, him in the adjacent field, schooling a little dark mare over fallen tree trunks.

'Hi!' he called cheerfully.

'That looks like fun – mind if I come round and have a go?'

'Be my guest.'

It was that simple. Rory, kind-hearted, half cut as always (even in the morning), affable and a great admirer of good horseflesh, horsemanship and womanliness, was an eager fly in her web. With her blond pertness and her honeyed, cut glass accent, she had echoes of her cousin Pixie which always reminded him of their roll in the hay earlier that year. Jemima was primmer and bossier, but she had a certain sexy schoolmistressy quality.

When Faith cycled up the drive half an hour later, puce from scaling the Ridgeway, she saw that Rory was riding an unfamiliar, flashy chestnut over the practice 'coffin', a depressingly named combination of rails, steep bank down to ditch and then bank up to more rails. The horse, obviously young and green, was giving it huge amounts of air and firing out volleys of excited bucks afterwards, but there was no denying the quality of the jump or the boldness of the attitude.

'This is some beast!' he called over his shoulder.

For a moment, Faith thought he was talking to her and she threw down her bike to dash through the gate. But then she slithered to a halt as she saw Jemima Cottrell – the 'poisoned Sloane' – stepping out from behind a hedge to approach the horse with a Polo and a pat.

'You ride him so well. Really, he's too wilful for me. I've had great fun hunting him last season, but he's ready to go to a pro now. Piers wants me to send him to Hugo.'

Faith bristled at her insensitivity. Hugo Beauchamp, while admittedly on top of the sport and an all-time hero of hers, had more potential four star horses than an entire Olympic squad. Rory just had old Whitey who was practically drawing his pension, and a small string of dirt cheap hopefuls that he would have to sell if they showed so much as a glimmer of talent. Jemima should offer him the ride.

But Rory was as magnanimous as ever. 'Hugo'd do a great job,' he agreed. 'This is just his sort. A bit sensitive perhaps, but Tash is good at nursemaiding the youngsters through the lower grades, and this chap doesn't lack confidence.'

'Of course, I'd love to keep him closer to home,' Jemima purred. 'That way I could still hunt him occasionally. I am ridiculously possessive over my home-breds.'

'Plenty of good riders around here,' Rory said with a nod, totally oblivious of the huge hint being dropped.

Don't be thick! Say you'll do it! Faith wanted to scream as she clambered over the gate, but she was still too out of breath from cycling.

'So there are.' Jemima caught sight of Faith. 'Hello there, it's Anke's girl, isn't it? Here to do a shift? Perfect timing. Could you be a duck and pop Haw-Haw here in a box with a bite of hay while Rory makes me a lovely cup of coffee?'

'Oh, hi Faith, you OK with that?' He kicked out his stirrups and looked down at her.

Faith nodded grumpily, casting Jemima a dirty look, but not wanting to say anything that might jeopardise Rory's chances of getting a decent horse at last.

'He can go next to Whitey. I think I've got some instant coffee in the tack room, but I can't vouch for the milk.'

'What *would* your mother say?' Jemima laughed with artificial prissiness. 'I insist on being invited into the house, Rory. I want to talk business – *privately.*'

'It's a bit of a mess,' Rory apologised as he jumped off the big chestnut and threw the reins to Faith. This was, in fact, something of an understatement. The cottage was awash with pizza boxes, beer cans, dirty crockery doubling as ashtrays, and Justine's very frilly underwear that Rory had taken to ripping off with such abandon that G-strings dangled from several light fittings and the antlers above the wood burning stove.

'I'm sure it's not that bad,' she quacked, leading the way at indecent speed.

Watching her admittedly very shapely bottom encased in tight, clean cream breeches weaving up the garden path, Faith hoped it was a very quick coffee. She didn't trust Jemima Cottrell with Rory at all.

But 'coffee' lasted over an hour and Rory was red faced when he finally emerged with a smug-looking Jemima, her blond hair suspiciously ruffled, one collar standing to attention and her customary bright pink lipstick missing.

Faith, who had only just resisted peering through the windows, rushed into the American barn and tacked up the chestnut again so quickly that when she led him outside he almost fell over his own feet in amazement, blinking goofily.

'How extraordinary – he usually takes great pieces out of Sean when he saddles him, and getting a bridle on is a two-man job.' Jemima looked grudgingly impressed as Faith angled him beside the mounting block.

'I guess I just took him by surprise.'

Rory would normally level a joke at this point but, his high cheeks still stained with a red blush, he gave Jemima a leg up and patted her thigh with far too much familiarity.

'Think about it,' Jemima said cryptically.

'Oh, I will,' he gulped. 'I'll find it hard to think about anything else.'

'Atta boy.' She blew him a kiss, nodded curtly at Faith and rode off.

'Think about what?' Faith demanded.

'Can't talk about it,' he muttered, turning abruptly on his heel and disappearing into the tack room, where he conspicuously closed the door behind him. Rory *never* closed the tack-room door.

For the rest of the day, Faith couldn't get a thing out of him, despite barging in and out of the tack room on the pretext of collecting every manner of unnecessary item from stud spanners to drop nosebands. Drinking his way through black coffee and Scotch in equal measure, Rory looked punch drunk long before his eyes glazed over with the familiar affability of mid-afternoon inebriation.

She then overheard him leaving a message for Justine, telling her that he was feeling really rough and thought it best to have an early night alone. Rory *never* cancelled a date.

Loitering in the aisle of the American barn outside the tack room door, she gnawed on her nails. Justine was threat enough, with her huge boobs and big, baby eyes, but at least Faith could console herself with the fact that she was a hopeless rider, not very bright and liable to bore Rory within a few months. Jemima, despite being ancient and married, was a sensational rider, flirty and well connected, witty and charming – and probably amazing in bed. She was Rory's dream woman. He had never made any secret of his adoration for older women; he had posters of Sophia Loren, Catherine Deneuve and Lucinda Green in the stables loo.

Smarting and confused, she ignored the fifth text that her mother had sent her that day demanding to know whether she was still in college, and stalked into the loo to glare at Sophia Loren before turning to stare at her own reflection in the very dusty, cracked mirror. A fresh-faced, wide-eyed child stared back with hopelessly frizzy mouse hair, a bulbous nose and vile braces on her teeth if she tried to smile.

At this rate she would be the first patient to ask her plastic surgeon to be made to look twenty years older. And she was definitely going to use the prize money to buy Rory a top class event horse and lure him away from Jemima Cottrell's chestnut and associated sexual favours.

She *had* to win that treasure hunt. Which, she supposed, meant that she had to start talking to her mother again, because she hadn't figured out what the latest clue meant and the auction was in just a few days' time.

Grudgingly, she texted back Anke, saying that she had just popped in to see her horse Rio, not mentioning that she had been in the yard since mid-morning.

Anke was drinking tea in Pixie's kitchen at the time her daughter finally made contact, watching in amazement as her friend's odd houseguest enacted some sort of ancient Wicca ritual.

Sioux was muttering incantations over a noxious pile of smoking leaves in a metal bowl on the pine table, wafting her hands around, flickering her eyelids and flaring her nostrils like Kenneth Williams in a brothel.

'What *is* she doing?' Anke asked.

'Trying to focus her thoughts on my chest.'

'Chest? Have you got a cold?'

'No – a piece of furniture Sexton made off with. We've just been to his shag pad to reclaim it and it's not there. The trollop wouldn't tell me where it is or, indeed, where Sexton was, although I strongly suspect he had hidden in the bathroom.'

'You confronted "the trollop"?' Anke was impressed.

'I gave her what for,' Pixie said proudly. 'Not that it got her to spill the beans about my missing chest, but I felt rather cheered up calling her a cheap, thieving tart. I've been longing to say that since I saw her in the hairdresser.'

'Good for you.' Anke was still watching Sioux, who had picked up her smoking bowl of twigs and was waving it around overhead, moaning tunelessly. 'And can your friend there really help locate this missing chest?'

'So she says.'

They both watched as Sioux circled the kitchen, a ferret peering up out of her coat pocket. After a little more moaning and some grunting, she dumped the smouldering bowl in the sink and gave a long, mournful sniff. 'He has sold it.'

'No!'

'Most certainly.'

'Who to?'

'That, the spirits will not divulge, but I saw a black horse and heard some very rousing music.'

'Lloyds Bank?' Anke suggested.

'Squire Gordon?' Pixie laughed despairingly. 'Oh God, I *have* to get my hands on it, just for a few minutes in private. It's desperate.'

Anke gave her a sympathetic pat. The English, particularly very well bred ones like Pixie, were full of eccentricities and became sentimentally attached to the most unlikely inanimate objects. Saying a quiet farewell to a piece of furniture did seem rather unnecessary.

But Faith was resolutely not interested when her mother later recounted the story of Sioux's soothsaying in what she hoped was a witty fashion.

'What do you know about Jemima Cottrell?' she asked.

'Jemima? Not a lot.'

'I thought you two knew each other really well?'

'We sit on a few committees together. She invited me to lunch once, but I couldn't make it I think.'

'What's she like?'

'Very pleasant.'

'Hmmph.' Faith had always disapproved of her mother's dispassionate fair-mindedness.

'Not really my sort of person.' That was as far as Anke would be coaxed.

'I hate her with all my heart,' Faith muttered unexpectedly.

Anke's blond brows shot up as her daughter charged from the room.

The following day Jemima was at the yard again when Faith arrived, this time watching her children having a lesson with Rory. She was dressed in a ridiculously flimsy summer dress with flowery flip-flops and a tight cashmere cardigan. While not remotely Sophia Lorenish, she looked formidably attractive and cocksure.

To Faith's fury, she and Rory disappeared into the cottage 'for coffee' again after the lesson, leaving the children running riot under Faith's supervision.

'Why don't you go and find Mummy in the house?' Faith suggested evilly when she caught them trying to dress the yard cat in a tail bandage.

'Mummy said that if we interrupt her, she'll take away all our privileges and ground us for a week.'

'Pretty radical.'

When Rory and Jemima reappeared, he was bright red and she had her cardigan on inside out. She supervised her children loading their ponies into the trailer while practically attached to Rory at the hip, whispering in a very flirty and secretive fashion. She kissed him a lingering farewell on the cheek before getting in her huge car with a lot of flashing bronzed thigh and driving away with a jaunty wave,

'Are you having an affair with her?' Faith asked bluntly.

Rory swung round in alarm.

'What in Christ makes you say that?'

'It's pretty obvious.'

'It isn't obvious and it isn't true!' he blustered. 'God, you can be weird, Faith. Bugger off.'

Justine called the yard as Faith was about to cycle home. She picked up the call on her way out because Rory was teaching an evening lesson to a large, middle-aged housewife with whom, she noted, he was *not* flirting.

'Why don't you try his mobile?'

'I have been trying all day, but he's not answering,' Justine said in her silly, babyish voice. 'Has he lost his phone again?'

'No.' Faith chewed on the word thoughtfully, jealousy and spite curdling in her belly. 'He's been chatting away on it as usual. Seems in a really good mood.'

'Oh,' Justine let out a shocked puff of air at this. 'So he's not unwell?'

'No – in great form.'

'But . . . he said he was ill. We were supposed to be going to see the latest Harry Potter film tonight.'

'Oh, well – yes. Maybe he is,' Faith lied as unconvincingly as she could. 'I mean he would have to be *really* ill to miss out on that, wouldn't he?'

'I suppose so. Faith, you know him really well, you would tell me if something was up, wouldn't you?'

'What do you mean?'

'If he's avoiding telling me something.'

'Like what?' She knew she was being infuriating, but anger and resentment were driving her blindly forward.

'If you thought, maybe he wanted to end it. With me?' Justine's voice wobbled with tell-tale tears, the frustration of twenty unanswered calls bursting out unstoppably.

'I don't think you should be asking me that.'

'But I can't ask Rory! I can't get through to him.'

Listening to her sniffling away on the other end, heart hammering, Faith noticed the old copy of *Horse and Hound* on the desk in front of her, its cover thick with doodles. Rory always went mad with a Bic when he was on the phone.

Along the length of the big white blaze of the featured show hunter was one word repeated in indulgent swirls and loops and even hearts. It was even more schmaltzily done than the hundreds of 'Rorys' that Faith herself had written throughout her diary and her rough exercise books. The word was 'Jem'.

'If you can't ask Rory,' she spat down the phone, 'Why don't you try asking Jemima Cottrell?'

She hung up and burst into guilty, angry tears.

Rory was furious. It was the first time that Faith had ever seen him truly angry and it was terrifying. He was pacing around the kitchen at Wyck Farm when her mother called her down. At first, when she saw him inside her own home, her faithful heart leaped in customary welcome, but his thundercloud face stilled her.

'What did you tell Justine?'

'Nothing.'

'You told her I'm having an affair with Jemima Cottrell.'

'I did not!'

'You bloody did!' he stormed over to yell at her.

'Did you, darling?' Anke asked more gently at his shoulder, big blue eyes full of sympathy.

A huge lump of shame and injustice rose in Faith's throat, threatening to choke her as she spluttered that she had not said that, she had merely mentioned Jemima's name to Justine when she'd called and it was all a big mistake.

'Too right,' Rory snarled. 'A big mistake that means my girlfriend turned up in a hysterical mess and now doesn't ever want to see me again. A mistake that means should she breathe a word of this, I'll lose half my bloody clients and quite possibly my jaw, given Piers' temper. A mistake that means the horse Jemima was going to place with me will probably go to Hugo Beauchamp. A mistake that means you are no longer welcome on my yard as a helper or a client. I want your horse out by the end of the week.'

His dramatic departure was somewhat hindered by the fact that his ancient banger refused to start, stranding him on the Wyck Farm drive with a groaning engine until Faith's stepfather Graham went out and gave him a jump start from his Lexus.

Upstairs, sobbing into her pillow, Faith ignored her mother's warm hand stroking her frizzy head.

'I know you are very passionate and easily hurt, my darling,' she soothed. 'But this is what happens when you tell lies motivated by love and longing.'

'I didn't lie!' she howled.

'Rory says Jemima was offering him a horse.'

'And the rest!'

'I really think you have got it wrong, *kereste*.'

'What does it matter anyway?' Faith wailed. 'I have lost him forever, *Forever!*'

'Oh dear.' Anke was not good with histrionics. 'I think I should make some supper.'

'I am never eating again!'

'If you say so.' Anke stood up. 'It's only roast lamb, parsnips and redcurrant sauce.'

Red eyed and silent, Faith made it through two helpings. Only, she told herself, to gather her strength. Tomorrow, she would set about proving that she was right.

Liv Wilson danced around her spotless kitchen to the Carpenters on Radio Two feeling on top of the world. Forget the Pigeon Detectives and all that loud, rocky youthfulness – *this* was real music. The children were in bed asleep, she was on her second large G and T and she had just emailed Martin telling him that life was really so wonderful here, he could stay away as long as he liked – why not forever? His only comments about her basque photo had been to ask if she'd put on weight and to point out that there was a piece of skirting board missing by the bed. But she didn't care. Nor did she care that Finn Cottrell had completely ignored her when she waved cheerfully at him from outside the village Post Office as he passed in his big, sexy car.

That afternoon, she'd experienced her first full-blown orgasm for over a decade. She still shuddered occasionally from the aftershock.

She felt so full of beans and self-confidence that she even put a call through to Trudy.

'I feel so *awful* that I haven't been in contact after you were so kind the other day. How are you?'

'Fine,' Trudy said bleakly. 'You?'

'Oh, much, *much* better!'

'Great. I'm glad – sorry, I should have called.'

'You – um – had a bit of a go at Giles, I take it?'

'Yes.'

It wasn't like Trudy to be so reticent but, fresh from Giles's creased sheets, Liv was well aware that she was top of his list, so whatever Trudy had said had done no harm. Quite the reverse.

'And the treasure hunt?'

'The Cottrell Hunt is going great guns from what Finn tells me.'

'No, not *that* one,' Liv whispered, as though she was in danger of being overheard in her big, clean, lonely house. 'Are you any closer to finding out who's setting the clues?

'Wild goose chase.' Trudy muttered. 'Waste of time.'

'Oh that's a shame. I'm still dying for a catch up over a coffee, properly this time. I have so much to tell you. Are you free tomorrow evening? The kids are going straight from school to a birthday party. I don't have to collect them until eight.'

'Why not?' Trudy agreed. 'But forget coffee. Buy me wine and I'll run eagerly towards the sound of a cork coming out.'

'I thought I'd pop into the fine art sale preview first – look out for the next clue. Is six-ish OK?'

'Perfect.'

Liv hung up feeling that warm hug of exhilaration that always overcame her after talking to Trudy. She couldn't help herself. She would never previously have dreamed of confiding in another soul – not even her diary – and yet she couldn't wait to tell Trudy about her orgasm.

21

It was the first viewing for the fine art sale at Cottrells' auction rooms in Ibcote over Foxrush and the bustle was ten times that normally expected this early on a Friday evening. Generally only the trade would be milling around getting an early peek at the goods – the commuters and tourists were still struggling west in the rush hour traffic and the wealthy wives and amateur 'doer uppers' were busy settling children or stripping wallpaper. But today was different. There was barely room to open an auction catalogue, let alone step back and admire a painting.

'It's hideous,' Faith commented when she and her mother finally tracked down the oil of Major Curruthers aboard his favourite hunter, Bugle. 'The fetlocks are all wrong – and look at the rider's lower leg. He should be shot.'

'I think he was – in the Boer War,' Anke said, reading the catalogue.

A hand tapped her on the shoulder with a triumphant, 'Great minds think alike!'

It was Pixie, looking very foxy in a bias cut white skirt and a clingy cashmere T-shirt, although her strange-looking friend rather ruined the illusion with her pork pie hat, great coat and biker boots. The smell of cheroot and ferret was overpowering.

'Did you use your magical powers to find the hidden lot?' Anke asked her politely as Pixie and Faith searched around the painting for the next clue.

'No, we saw you come in and followed,' Sioux cackled. 'Pixie said you'd lead us straight to it.'

Anke had to smile.

Meanwhile, Faith was interrogating Pixie.

'Jemima Cottrell is your cousin, isn't she?' she asked as they located the laminated clue attached to a long ribbon hidden behind the picture.

'She is. Why?'

'No reason.' Faith studied Pixie's face closely, looking for familial signs. Pixie was older, but definitely prettier, and kinder-looking, with sparkly eyes and lots of laughter lines. Rory had always liked her – she was just his 'older woman' type. He harboured stupid erotic fantasies about ravishing, middle-aged vixens coming to seduce him in his hayloft. Faith knew because he rambled on about them sometimes when he was too drunk to remember who he was talking to and so treated her like one of his bloke friends. These rambles made Faith depressed, especially now that Jemima had seemingly fulfilled his desires, although she would almost certainly never lower herself to the hayloft, and Faith thought she was about as sexy as a snappy lapdog. Pixie, at least, was the real deal.

Aware that she was under scrutiny, Pixie glanced up at Faith's mother, who shrugged in bewilderment. She certainly had no intention of explaining Faith's latest obsession to Pixie, who would take it straight back to her cousin – and probably to half the village as well. She had promised utter discretion to Rory and knew it was vital to keep her word if Faith was to stand any chance of ever getting her trainer and stabling back.

Anke suspected that Rory, for all his fury and pique, was secretly relieved to be rid of Justine and her bouncy cleavage. She was equally suspicious – and very hurt – that Rory might be similarly relieved to find an excuse to get rid of poor Faith. Even though this played into Anke's own hands, she felt great indignation on her daughter's part: Faith was such a good rider and worker that Rory was mad to abandon her for all her teenage crush and prying ways.

Anke was also certain that Jemima Cottrell was not having any sort of affair with Rory. The idea was ludicrous.

Jemima stretched a glossy, waxed leg up from the bed and admired her perfectly manicured coral pink toes.

Beside her, Rory was napping contentedly, his dark lashes sweeping towards those high, tanned cheeks that were dusted with golden freckles, the long nose as straight as a Grecian hero's, the wide mouth relaxed and curled into a sleeping half smile. He really was the most exquisite creature. Drunk rather too often, admittedly, and somewhat gauche; but what he lacked in finesse, he more than made up for in enthusiasm.

Today was a rare treat because, with the children going straight from school to a party, she had all day with him and had told the family that she was visiting a girlfriend in Wiltshire.

Getting him alone was the one problem. At least Rory had, at Jemima's behest, dispensed with the dreadful teenage hanger-on but the yard was often peopled with his friends and family. Rory's crowd was a large, loud and close-knit one. At its centre was the unholy trinity of the valley, Rory and his hell-raising cousin Spurs along with Jemima's own brother-in-law, Flipper. The three had known one another since childhood. As vanguards were half a dozen Hooray Henry types, local young bloods who hunted, team chased and made merry, usually with a clutch of attractive, leggy Sloane Ranger girls in tow.

If they weren't cluttering up the yard and cottage – or, more often, luring Rory away to the village pub, the New Inn – then his dreadful mother Truffle was picking her way round the garden with a gin and It stealing cuttings, or sister Diana and her riotous children were galloping around the manège and Rory's little cross-country course on half-wild ponies laughing manically. It was a madhouse.

Jemima had been forced to impose a curfew on Rory two mornings and one evening a week so that she could have him to herself, coinciding with morning hacks when she brought Lord Haw-Haw for schooling, and the 'art class' that Piers and the children still believed she took in Market Addington.

But despite clearing the human clutter from Rory's environs on those occasions, she could do nothing about the canine one – and he wasn't her biggest fan.

At the foot of the bed, Twitch the Jack Russell curled his lip, showing off a rather yellow set of ground-down teeth. Unimpressive as his raised hackles were, they still made Jemima uncomfortable. Unlike her exhibitionist husband who liked nothing more than making love with the curtains open or risking being caught while having an alfresco quickie, Jemima was very private about her lovemaking, and even being scrutinised by a dog was off-putting.

She got out of bed and, shooting him a dirty look, put on one of Rory's shirts so that she could go down to the kitchen and make herself a cup of tea. Sunlight streamed in through the low, dusty windows, fighting its way past overhanging honeysuckle and wisteria to form strange shadows across the floor.

It was a very pretty cottage if you ignored the mess. In daydreamier moments, she fantasised herself as a glamorous Mrs Tiggywinkle in a Cath Kidston pinny – wafting about with a feather duster, beeswax and lavender oil, clearing away the grime and clutter to reveal a heavenly love nest that she would share with Rory to raise a small team of junior riding champions; Georgia and Bartleby were joined in her fantasy by another brace of her own and Rory's. They would live frugally but happily, ruddy-faced and full of *joie de vivre* from fresh air and organic home grown veggies.

Of course she knew it was all poppycock, but she had nonetheless never fantasised about Giles in this fashion, nor indeed the other discreet lovers who had passed through her life since her marriage. Nor had she ever pursued a lover, having always been content to sit and wait. She had long seen that Rory found her attractive, but to act upon it had taken a very decisive change of heart.

For all her sterling work at staying sexually attractive to her husband, efficient, organised, scintillating, titillating, a glorious hostess, perfect companion and marvellous mother, Jemima had experienced a recent epiphany.

Her marriage was on the rocks.

Piers had conducted countless affairs. He took her entirely for granted. He didn't respect her or love her any more. He would probably have left her years ago were it not for his family and religion.

She no longer loved him.

Things were going to have to change.

While she told herself firmly that she had no intention of leaving him for Rory, the affair was giving her the much-needed boost and confidence she needed to begin to tackle the situation.

And now, suddenly feeling inspired, she decided to go home early and do just that. Ignoring Rory's sweet, sleepy protests that he wanted to massage her all over, run her a bath then cook a special meal, she gathered her things, got dressed and drove through the hammering rain to Home Farm.

The sight that greeted her there changed her mind about everything.

At the fine art viewing, the crowd had reached unmanageable proportions. Finn was cursing his brother for not turning up on time to help him oversee the event.

Treasure hunters scrabbling for the laminated clue attached to the

Curruthers were literally coming to blows and were threatening Sir Hamish and Bugle's frail stretched canvas with their antics.

His pregnant sister Nell, who had just arrived with her married lover Milo in tow for a loved-up Cotswolds weekend, was adding to Finn's hot-headed indignation because he knew that the local scandal-mongers would spread the word that dark, exotic Milo was the unborn baby's father, complicating the smear on the Cottrell family name yet further. But Nell simply thought that, and the unruly crowd, were a hoot.

'It's like Sodom and Gomorrah!' she giggled as a sales catalogue flew past overhead and two women nearby started tussling over a small cameo they thought was the treasure.

'Fetch Piers!' Finn ordered through clenched teeth as he physically restrained a stout, bearded man in a beanie hat who was waving an antique, hand-tinted framed map at a tall man in a Pacamac. 'I don't care what he's doing – get him here *now!*'

Nell and Milo drove to Home Farm to track down the recalcitrant Piers who was not answering his mobile phone or land line.

What greeted them was a scene even more soap opera than that in the sales room. Piers, wearing nothing but silk underpants covered in hunting whips, and a dressing gown that appeared to be dripping with spilled red wine, was slumped at the kitchen table with his head in his hands and his anxious spaniels at his feet.

Nuala the nanny – crying openly and emptying the dishwasher on autopilot – was dressed in a strange combination of jeans, see through top and too much make-up and gibbering to nobody in particular that she would have to collect the children from their party later if Jemima was leaving, and what were they going to do about tomorrow's polo picnic with the Boland-Wrights?

Meanwhile it sounded as though the house was being trashed by burglars as a series of thumps, crashes and stomping footsteps came from upstairs.

'Go away, sis!' Piers howled when Nell explained Finn's predicament. 'About time he learned some gumption. Can't you see I have a crisis of my own, here?'

Realising that they weren't about to be offered a drink, Nell and Milo drove to the local pub, running whooping through another sudden downpour from the car park to the bar.

'You know, I think my brother's marriage might be on the rocks,'

Nell mused, sipping a weak Pimms. 'I always thought it would be Finn's that fell apart first.'

'It's certainly highly charged around here,' agreed Milo, who had found Nell's family rather staid on a previous visit. 'I thought they were like the Archers, but in fact it's more like the Borgias.'

'You haven't even *met* sex siren Trudy yet.' Nell got out her phone and started texting. 'Now she is a cat among the pigeons – or a beater among the pheasants. I adore her.'

'Are you asking her along for a drink now?'

'God, no, she costs a fortune to fuel. Drinks vodka like a fish. I'm just passing on the goss to Flipper.' She looked across the table at Milo, her slanting grey-green eyes gleaming. 'He's madly in love with Trudy, you know. Has been for years.'

'This gets better and better.'

'I think it's rather sad.' Her pregnancy hormones were lending her emotions that she had never experienced in a lifetime of devil-may-care self-confidence. 'They'd be perfect together.'

'So tell them.'

Smiling naughtily, Nell's thumb danced across her little phone.

22

Having successfully avoided him all week, Trudy literally bumped into Flipper on her way to Liv's that evening.

It was raining stair-rods, a sudden summer downpour that bounced the drops back off the hard ground like hail, darkening the skies overhead as though sunset had come early and dragging a thick, warm mist down to cloak the hills.

Trudy decided at the last minute to take the car rather than walking, avoiding the rain and making up for lost time because she was running late as always. Speeding away from the house without her lights on, she leaned across to eject the CD in her stereo and find Radio Four for *I'm Sorry I Haven't a Clue*.

With her head dipped towards the car stereo, she didn't even see the big Audi swinging in through the entrance gates from the church track under the shadows of the high rhododendrons, and she was speeding towards it so fast that the driver had no chance to react before the two cars slammed into one another. Trudy felt a sudden lurch forwards into halt and a great jolt of the seat belt knocking all the air from her lungs at the same time as she heard a loud, metallic crunch. Gales of laughter arrived on cue through the car speakers as Tim Brooke-Taylor and Jeremy Hardy came over the airways playing 'Bat Out of Hell' on the swannee whistle and the kazoo.

Straightening up and peering through the windscreen, she saw Flipper staring back at her through the driving rain, also gripping on to his steering wheel in shock, but in his case from behind a huge white marshmallow of an airbag. Mutt was barking furiously out of a rear window, seemingly none the worse for wear.

Not thinking straight, Trudy put her car straight into reverse and found it rooted to the spot, spitting up gravel and roaring furiously. The cars' front bumpers appeared to be stuck fast.

Flipper signalled hurriedly for her to stop, jumping out on to the driveway.

'Shit!' She was almost certainly, she knew, over the limit, having chased down an early glass of wine with a couple of family sized vodka Cokes to get her in the chatty mood. But she wasn't on a public road. And she wasn't in any mood to argue the point.

He was waiting by her driver's side window.

Seeing Flipper made her feel hopelessly uptight, prang or no prang. Like all incorrigible gossips – particularly those who are innately incapable of keeping a secret for more than a few minutes – she could barely look him in the eye, knowing what she knew. Had Giles wanted to warn her off Flipper completely, he couldn't have done a better job. She wanted to bolt as fast as she could, not caring that their cars were entangled.

She even eyed the passenger door to her left, wondering crazily if she could slide across to it, leap out and run.

He tapped on her window, his voice muffled. 'Jesus! I didn't see you, Trudy. Are you OK?'

She couldn't look him in the eyes.

'Fine!' she yelped, staring straight ahead.

Inside the cocoon of the car, Humphrey Lyttelton was setting the panel the challenge of finishing greeting cards poems.

Outside, Flipper's breath left a small, steamy cloud on the window. 'I tried to brake, but you were going so fast . . .'

'I'm in a hurry.'

'Are you hurt?'

'No.'

Humph was reciting a poem: '"You are my love, my Valentine, my soulmate and my spouse; Husband, you are a real good man, head of our happy house. Our family are so close, when you're far away it's sad . . ."'

Flipper tapped lightly on the window.

'Are you going to get out?'

'In a minute – I'm listening to *I'm Sorry I Haven't a Clue*.'

Graeme Garden was finishing the verse: '. . . so I go doggin' with your brothers and play hide the sausage with your dad.'

Flipper crouched closer to the door. 'You what?'

'It's almost finished.' She carried on watching the raindrops bouncing from the bonnet.

He leaned back, rubbing his wet hair and clearly thinking she was in deep shock. After a few moments, he bent down to open her door and found it locked.

Trudy had pressed the 'lock all' button inside. She gnawed at a nail, cursing Giles under her breath. How could he expect her to carry around a family secret of this enormity, to shoulder it effortlessly and say nothing to those involved? Flipper was her friend. He deserved to know. And, as for his feelings towards her being more than just a crush he had grown out of, she wouldn't even go there. She just wanted his car detached from hers and far, far away – with him in it.

'Trudy, I think you're hurt. You have to open the door. I need to get you in the house.'

To riotous applause, Humph announced that the teams would be playing 'Cheddar Gorge'.

Her mobile started to ring inside her handbag. It was Liv, checking where she was.

'I've had a bit of a mishap. Nothing serious, but I'm not sure I'll be able to make it before you have to set out to fetch your kids. Another time?'

Trudy hung up and stared mindlessly at the phone.

Flipper was banging insistently on the door now.

Trudy ignored him, listening without hearing to the radio, head full of Giles and Flipper – and Dibs and Nell – and the secrets she just couldn't hold on to any longer than she could stay locked in her car in the rain blocking her own driveway. She felt like a child with a Rowntrees Fruit Pastille trying not to chew.

A text came through from 'Unknown Caller', making her jump guiltily as she fumbled hurriedly to read it.

Get out of the car, Trudy.

She gaped up at Flipper through the steamy window, her eyes like saucers.

He held up his phone from which he had just sent the message. 'It seems the only way of getting through to you . . .'

She was out of the car in a flash and towing him by the hand to the house.

'Steady, we need to check you out. You might be a bit concuss—'

'I'm fine,' she hissed, unlocking the front door and falling over the dogs. 'I didn't hit my head.'

'So why do you have blood all over your forehead?'

She turned to stare at the mirror propped over the fireplace. He was right. Trickles and splashes of drying blood ran from her hairline to her eyebrow and a big red mark foretold a bruise to come.

'My airbag didn't go off.'

'You drive a vintage car. It doesn't have an airbag.'

'Or brakes,' she agreed, heading for the vodka bottle that she had abandoned on top of the grand piano.

He took the bottle out of her hands. She wrestled it back.

'Stop it!' he snatched it away, sounding so like Finn in a fury that she sat down on her piano stool with a jolt. 'You have a head injury. You mustn't drink – besides, you've had enough already.'

'I have not been drinking.'

'You reek of it. When you opened your car door it was like you were walking out of a pub.'

'Rubbish!'

'Trudy, you're a drunk. Admit it.'

She shook her head violently, 'I am a heavy drinker, but I am *not* a drunk, an alcoholic or any other sort of wino.'

Shaking her head had not been a wise move, she realised, as several Flippers towered over her giving her a hard time.

'I don't care how you define it,' he raged. 'I just thank God I stopped you setting off along public roads on this occasion, even if it meant stopping you forcibly with my car. You have to clean up your act or you'll wind up dead, or in prison.'

Her head pounded. The room span. 'Don't be so bloody judgmental!'

'Trudy, I care about you!'

The room was flying up and down like a fairground ride. Flipper was spiralling round and round overhead.

'I know, Flipper. You love me.'

'Steady on.'

'You love me, and I love you. I love you, but you are my beautiful young friend. I am old and fat and past caring. I *am* in a prison, and I might as well be dead.'

She was finding it hard to breathe, gulping for air with shallow gasps, the walls closing in on her.

'Calm down.' Flipper crouched down beside her, reaching for her hands.

'My husband's brother – half-brother, my brother, my lover, my mystery unknown caller, not Giles at all, not him. Your father. Bloody hell.'

Without warning, the big, intricately patterned Afghan rug beneath the piano came up to meet her.

'You should have bloody caught me,' she managed to mutter before passing out.

When Trudy came round she was on the sofa beneath the mullioned window that overlooked the churchyard, the one usually reserved for the dogs. It stank of wet fur, half-chewed roasted bones and cankery ears.

'Ugh!' She lifted her face. Then, as the delighted dogs who were lined up on the floor below decided it was safe to join her, she batted them away with a series of furious 'Get down!' wails.

'Thank God. You've only been out about thirty seconds.' Flipper dashed back from the kitchen with a bag of frozen peas. 'I think you need to go to A and E to be checked out.'

'Rubbish. I'm fine.'

'Head injuries are serious. The brain can swell up and—'

'You know as well as I do that any hospital will tell me to go home, get some rest and make sure someone is close by to observe me for any signs of dizziness and nausea in the next twenty-four hours.'

'Do you feel dizzy or nauseous?'

'No,' she shook her head and then abruptly stopped. 'As long as I don't do that.'

He handed her the peas.

'Thanks, I'm not hungry. But I'd love a—'

'No vodka!'

'—cup of tea.'

He disappeared back into the kitchen, allowing Trudy to struggle to her feet and examine her head again. It wasn't really very impressive – the cut in her hair barely the length of a matchstick, the red mark already hardly visible. Apart from a very faint, dull ache, she couldn't feel it. She was more alarmed by way the red cable knit polo neck seemed to give her four breasts, emphasised her double chin and brought out the broken veins on her nose and cheeks.

Reluctantly, as he squeezed tea bags from mugs and threw them in the bin, Flipper asked if he should call Finn.

'Why?'

'He'll want to know.'

'He can wait.' She sat wearily at her piano, her familiar safety zone, stroking its keys. 'He's tied up today, anyway. He won't be back until nine or ten.'

'What's he doing?'

'Holding the fort at the fine art viewing.'

'I heard there was a bit of a rumpus there earlier.' Flipper carried the tea through. 'Nell said a fight broke out over the treasure hunt lot. The police were called.'

'God. High drama – thanks.' She took the tea and stared into its comforting brown surface. 'What happened?'

'Not sure. Nell was on the phone to me as I turned in here, so I had to ring off.'

It took Trudy a moment to register this properly.

'You were on the phone?'

'Er – yes.'

'So it's your fault!'

'I'd hardly say that.'

'Not that it matters,' she sighed. 'Our cars are tangled up. I guess I'd better call someone to come out and separate them.'

'Hank will sort it.' Flipper pulled his phone from his pocket and started dialling; Hank did all the handy-work and mechanics at the Abbey. 'He's a godsend.'

Another lucid memory came back to Trudy.

'Why does your mobile phone flash up as "Unknown Caller" when you ring or text someone?'

'Does it?' He didn't look up. 'This is the clinic's phone. Mine got trodden on by a horse last week, so I'm waiting for a new Sim. They have a couple of spare mobiles for the vets to use in emergencies— Piers! 'Sme – you all right, there?' He spoke into the phone, suddenly looking perplexed. 'No, it's just that you sound a bit strange – sure, if you're in a hurry. Have you got Hank's mobile number handy? Cheers . . .'

She eyed him suspiciously while he fumbled for a pen, uncapped it with his mouth, scribbled the number on the back of his hand and then called through to Hank.

He looks like Dibs, she realised, but nothing like Piggy. Unlike Piers and Finn, who bore their father's jutting jaw, high hairline, rugby build and slightly stooped gait, Flipper, and Nell, had always been finer and more athletic with wider cheeks and small, slightly beaked noses as opposed to their siblings' wide, Romanesque ones. She had put the disparity down to the wide age difference, assuming the twins would age into the thicker set features, but the truth was far simpler. They were genetically different from their older siblings.

She tried to see Giles in Flipper, but there were few points of reference. His colouring and bone structure were wholly his mother's. Squinting, she visualised him with a moustache, but the vision was so disturbing that she blinked to rid herself of it.

'He'll be here in an hour,' Flipper announced, hanging up. 'Are you OK? You look a bit faint again.'

Trudy knew that the secret was about to spill out unless she did something drastic. Shaking her head, she dropped it down into her hands and raked her fingernails into her hair, wincing as her palm pressed against the emerging bump.

Flipper put a warm arm against her cheek and she leaned into him, briefly comforted.

'It's all right,' he said in a low voice, stooping to speak into her ear. 'I know some of what's going on in your head. You ranted a bit when you were about to pass out.'

'I did?'

'Best you spit it out. A half truth is always so much worse than the reality.'

'I don't even know what I've been told is true. It's just a complete hornet's nest – but it's your hornet's nest, not mine. You deserve to know.'

'Know what?' He gently prised her fingers from her mouth. 'Don't chew your nails. You're a pop star.'

'*Was* a pop star. Briefly, before falling.' She started humming 'Catch a Falling Star', watching his long-fingered, ink-stained hand closing round her pudgier, freckled one.

'You'll always be my pin up.'

'Don't start that.' She snatched her hand away.

'What?'

'The kid crush thing.'

'But you love me too. You said so.'

'When?'

'When you were delirious.'

'I always say I love people when I'm delirious – or drunk, which thankfully is most of the time.'

'Funny.' He ducked his head away. 'I just say it when I love them.'

Looking down at the top of his head, she automatically reached out to stroke the soft, dark hair at the nape of his neck, her heart turning over like a kid's butterfly toy being wound up on a rubber band, knowing that it was about to be released to spin at a hundred rotations a minute.

Tell him, tell him, tell him, she urged herself. Tell him what Giles said. Tell him before you burst.

But as she opened her mouth he turned and kissed her.

Her trapped butterfly heart was released in an instant, beating its wings frenziedly, flying so high the air thinned and there was nothing but sunshine flooding in all around her.

She tried to stop herself, but she had no choice but to kiss him back. Her hands found his face, soft finger pads touching stubble, feeling the angle of his jaw, the soft curled folds of his ears, the wide tautness of his neck, the cotton crease of his collars behind which the heat of his body rose like a furnace.

He was down on one knee by the piano stool, pulling her towards him. Gravity and dizziness had her beaten almost instantly as she tumbled beside him on the Afghan rug, laughing in disbelieving elation. Drunkenness had nothing on this. This was pure rapture; her entire body was trembling with gratification; it was like taking the wrong turning from six degrees of separation and stumbling into seventh heaven.

His body rolled over hers as they kissed beneath the belly of the piano, a weight of such thrilling possibilities that she felt the floor fall right out from beneath her for a moment, free-falling dizzily through the layers of rug, oak board, foundations, earth and granite beneath her to the hot core of the earth.

I want to make love with Flipper, I want to make love, I want to make love right here, right now, her uncensored mind screamed deliriously. Somewhere, very faintly, in the back of her head a tiny voice was squeaking 'Stop it, Trudy!', but the blood was pumping through her ears too loudly for her to hear.

Flipper kissed her with such desire and tenderness that she wondered why, how, for what possible reason she could have resisted him for so long, overlooked her knee-jerk response, her cleaving need for him and the passion they both triggered. The rug was going to combust in a moment.

Clothes were coming off at an alarming rate. Who was undressing whom was uncertain, but layers flew in all directions.

Trudy felt his skin against hers – smooth, naked planes sliding together, uniting warmth and anticipation and pure craving.

They didn't hear the Range Rover's engine because it couldn't get past the two cars jammed together at the head of the drive.

Had the dogs not gone into a frenzy of excited whimpers and barks at the door, they would have had no warning at all. As it was, Flipper looked up to see a shadow fall across the small square of glass in the front door and reacted with the speed of an SAS assassin. Rolling off Trudy, he grabbed any clothes within reach as he tumbled away from the piano, springing up and diving behind the dog sofa with a hissed order: 'Get in the shower – now!'

The downstairs wet room shower was through the utility room. Trudy staggered upright, hitting her head on the edge of the piano as she heard the latch lift in the door. Thankfully the dogs leaped so excitedly against the door that they slammed it shut. She could hear Finn cursing them from the far side.

Tripping and stumbling because her jeans were round her ankles, bra dangling from its straps, boobs bouncing and polo neck still round her throat with its empty arms dangling to fore and aft, she hurtled into the wet room, which was only ever used for the dogs and damp laundry. Hitting all the buttons of the high tech shower Finn had insisted upon having fitted, she was immediately blasted backwards into the handcrafted Italian marble tiles, feet slipping on the accumulated scum of dog hair and mud beneath.

Heart hammering, she pulled off her increasingly sodden clothes and squished them beneath the big pile of wet dog towels by the door. She heard Finn's footsteps outside, leaping back as he hammered on the door.

'Trudy, is that you?'

'Yes, out in a sec!'

'What the fuck is going on?'

'What d'you mean?'

'That twerp of a baby brother of mine trashing your car. Where is he?'

'Um . . . I think he's . . . hang on . . .'

She was forced to wrap herself in an inadequate, dirty, dog-smelling towel because there were no clean ones to hand.

Finn had retreated to the kitchen to fetch a beer from the fridge. Drinking this early was unheard of. Trudy felt panic rise in her throat. He must have guessed everything.

Her heart thumped harder.

'You're back early,' she said, feeling like a crazed adulteress in a Ray Cooney farce.

'Had to shut the saleroom – total bun fight for this treasure hunt lot. Things got completely out of hand.' He opened the beer with a hiss and drained half the bottle in one gulp. 'What a day! Just when I thought it couldn't get any worse and the police were slinging out mad treasure hunters hand-bagging one another among the oil paintings, Piers calls me saying that he's in a spot of bother, and then—'

'What bother?'

He waved the question away, still in his rant. 'And *then* I come home to find your car wrapped round Flipper's.'

She waited for him to add, 'And you wrapped round Flipper,' but he didn't. He just stared at her, green eyes cantankerous and condescending.

She was too twitchy to reply.

'Where d'you say he was, by the way – and why were you using the dog shower?'

'Because I was using the upstairs one,' drawled a voice from the doorway. 'Trudy very kindly insisted. We got soaked out there trying to get those bloody cars apart. Had to give up and get warm, scrub off the dirt and oil.'

'You should have called Hank.'

'I have – he's on his way.' He came into the kitchen, wrapped in the frilly chintz dressing gown from the back of the spare room door and with a pink towel on his head, deliberately camping it up.

'What happened?'

'I was on my mobile driving too fast, Trudy was changing a CD and driving too fast – crunch! No real harm done.'

'Bloody typical. Beer?' Finn offered.

'Thanks. Now, talk to me about Piers.'

'You know?'

Flipper nodded. 'That's why I'm here. I knew you'd be the one to take charge.'

Finn loved that, an officer about to command troops.

'Good man.' He dismissed Trudy with his eyes before turning back to his brother. 'I'm heading off to see him in a minute, although he insists he's fine; sounded quite cheerful in fact. Nevertheless, I closed the viewing early. Piers is in no state to help out and the rest of the staff is hopeless. I've just popped back here for a change of clothes.' He loosened his tie like Clark Kent about to leap into a phone box and lycra.

It was, Trudy realised as she crept upstairs for fresh clothes, that disingenuous. She and Flipper had just stepped back from the tracks with half a second to spare before the express train came hurtling past, and yet Flipper was acting as though nothing had happened at all. Perhaps he was more like his real father than she had accounted for.

Walking into the bedroom, she closed the door quietly behind her and grabbed a pillow, stuffing it into her mouth so that she could finally release the emotional tidal wave and scream. Her body was in a complete state of riot: drenched in cold, guilty sweat, heart still racing, nipples electrified, head pounding and pink bits on red alert. She was so slithery between her legs that she had to wedge a handful of tissue there while she found a clean towel with which to dry herself, aware that every stroke of soft fabric against skin was sending a charge right through her. She had to get a grip.

Turning on the radio, she found a very boring local phone-in about changes in council tax and forced herself to listen very hard.

When she went back downstairs twenty minutes later, dressed in her fluffy brown and cream cover-all layers, Finn and Flipper were on their third beers, passing another to Hank, who was dressed like a dodgy poker playing saloon extra from a spaghetti western, in Stetson, leather waistcoat, checked shirt, a bootlace for a tie and faded hipster jeans with a rodeo buckle on the belt, over which his beer belly spilled like loaf crust over a tin.

'You lose control of that fast little car of yours again?' He assumed it had to be Trudy's fault given that she was the female driver.

Finn smirked as he sauntered out of the utility room clutching a change of clothes fresh from the tumble dryer.

'I'll have to leave you to it, Hank,' he apologised smoothly, avoiding any physical labour. 'I promised I'd go and see Piers.'

'What is this spot of bother?' Trudy demanded.

'Flipper will explain.' He fetched a bottle of malt from the drinks cupboard. 'Don't wait up – I'll probably crash there if you'll pardon the pun.' Blowing a kiss, he was gone, leaving Hank noisily slurping on his beer and making small talk about the weather.

'Wet as a fish's nads this evening, huh?'

He looked from Flipper to Trudy, expecting laughter, but they were frozen in silent shock. Finn had left them together without a suspicion in the world. He had even told Trudy not to expect him home that night.

Hank drained his bear. 'Let's get these beauties apart – I'm in a hurry; taking the missus line dancing tonight.'

Flipper nodded. 'I'd better get dressed.'

Trudy fought the urge to tell him not to bother.

With nonchalant ease, he ducked behind the sofa for his jeans, collected his shirt from under a cushion and bounded upstairs, returning just seconds later, buckling his belt. His jockey shorts were still on the stairs; he stepped over them as he passed.

Trudy tried not to quiver at the realisation that he had gone commando as he pulled on his shoes and grabbed one of Finn's coats from the rack to fend off the hammering rain.

The two cars came apart easily if noisily with the help of Hank's old pick-up and a length of rope. The only apparent damage was to Trudy's racy old banger – a dangling bumper, smashed headlight, the odd dent and some lost paint. The Audi was unscathed.

Flipper gave Hank a twenty-pound note for his efforts and he doffed the rim of his Stetson in thanks before driving away in a cloud of diesel fumes.

Standing side by side in the driving rain, waving him away like a pair of grandparents seeing off the kids after Sunday lunch, neither Trudy nor Flipper knew what to say or do. Both were drowned rats.

Eventually, Flipper turned towards the house.

'I need a drink.' He hooked his arm beneath hers, towing her inside.

But Trudy shook her head when he picked up the vodka bottle and turned questioningly.

'You're right.' She peeled her sodden mac from her shoulders and shook out her wet curls. 'I am a drunkard. I need to cut down.'

'Not now, surely?'

'I've had a bump on the head,' she reminded him, squeezing drops from her hair and watching as he searched for a decent whisky. 'Finn took it, remember? You'll have to make do with Teachers. We've nothing else in the house.'

He wrinkled his nose. 'I'll make more tea then.'

'You do that.' She felt more relaxed, the urge to rush forward and strip his clothes off tempered with a little self control. 'What is up with Piers?'

'Jemima's left him.'

'*What?*'

'Caught him in bed with the nanny, apparently.'

'Nuala?'

'Is that what she's called? Then yes, Nuala. He's been up to those tricks for years, of course, but I don't think Jems has ever caught him in flagrante before. She was *livid*. Apparently she found rather a good bottle of Saint Emilion open beside the bed and deposited it over him to cool his ardour, screaming that as it was only the nanny he should have stuck to Blossom Hill, which I thought was quite witty in the circumstances.'

'But – Nuala! Nuala? She's just so . . .' She trailed away, realising that she had meanly been going to say 'fat'.

'Young,' he finished for her. 'I know, but Piers likes young girls. Fewer opinions. If they don't speak English, that's an even bigger bonus.'

She tried to imagine how she would feel if she found Finn up to his balls in nanny. 'Jemima must be livid and . . .' *I'd* be livid, she realised in surprise, having thought she'd be immune to Finn straying, her feelings for him now so deadened by ennui. It would be the indignity of it, she acknowledged, not unaware of her hypocrisy. She would also be terribly relieved despite her fury. It would be her exit pass. '. . . and devastated for the children,' she added lamely.

'As far as I'm aware,' Flipper was musing, 'she was waiting for the excuse to go.'

'I'm sorry?'

'Don't tell anyone this came from me, but she's been shacked up with Rory most mornings this past fortnight.'

'Rory!'

'We had a drink a couple of nights ago. He tried to be all secretive about it, but he's a crap liar. I saw right through him.'

'But he's so . . .'

'Young?' he suggested sardonically.

'Yes.'

Oh the parallels! Trudy reeled back to her comforting piano stool to regroup, fighting the temptation to bang out a quick verse or two of 'Tempted by the Fruit of Another' or perhaps 'Me and Mrs Jones'.

Instead she crossed her arms and legs tightly in front of her and stared at a glossy red toenail poking out of a hole in her sock. 'So how does Rory feel about Jemima?'

In the kitchen, Flipper was searching for clean mugs. 'Besotted, scared, sexually obsessed, imagines he's in love, the usual.'

'Did he ask her to leave Piers, d'you think?'

He shook his head, dousing two tea bags in steaming water. 'I doubt it. They've barely been lovers ten minutes. If she rolls up on his doorstep with a suitcase and two children tonight, he'd freak. His own sister did that last year and he barely survived. Jemima will eat him alive.'

'You should call him.'

'He'll call me if he needs me. The fewer people involved in this the better.'

'What if Rory and Jemima are genuine? What if it's love?'

'Bollocks it's love!' He propelled the used tea bags into the sink at furious speed. 'She's just done it to prove a point to Piers once and for all. He needs pulling into touch and fast. He'll crawl and grovel and beg her to come back, and she'll concede. That's what this is all about.'

'But what about Rory?'

'He's good at being heartbroken. It's an art form.'

'I can't believe she would go this far – would leave Piers, would ride roughshod over Rory, without being serious.'

'She's *not* left Piers. It's a gesture.'

'The kids?'

'With Ma, Finn thinks.'

'So your parents know about this?'

'Fully briefed as far as I know; Jemima was on the phone to the main house before the poor nanny had pulled her pants up. When she told Ma what she'd found her son up to, she was completely supportive and has offered babysitting services for a few days while Jem goes off to make Piers sweat and repent his sins. Like any good Catholic grandmother, she's helping out in a crisis and consulting the priest on an hourly basis, although she's obviously not aware of the Rory element. Neither are Piers and Finn. Only you and I know that.' He reappeared from the kitchen.

'Christ.' Trudy blinked as she took it all in.

Flipper settled a tea mug on a pile of manuscripts above the piano, standing beside to her.

Realising how close this brought them back to the moment where all hell had broken loose earlier and libidos had been unleashed, she leaped up, took the tea and paced her way to the window.

'Why leave him for Rory?' she pondered. 'Why not Giles?'

'Giles?'

Dangerous territory. Trudy checked herself. But the compulsion was too strong.

'He's a regular refuge for married women on the run, isn't he? He wouldn't be hurt, like Rory could be.'

'Might be a bit surprised, given that he and Jem aren't lovers.'

'They are, though. Have been for years. I mean, who isn't being squired by Giles around here?' she looked at him over her shoulder.

The rain had made it so dark outside that she could barely make out his expression.

'You?' he suggested carefully.

'Liv is,' she laughed hollowly. 'He's like a drug guaranteed to make you look slimmer and younger; women can't resist. That charm, the cockiness, the total assurance that he'll make you feel better.'

'He rarely does, I gather, like most drugs. The comedown is shocking.'

'Maybe. But *he's* the one with the real addiction, you know. He does it to dull the pain – like some of us drink.'

'Is that a fact?' Flipper sounded bored, but she knew that he was fascinated. 'Are you sleeping with his therapist, too?'

'We talked.' She looked out at the black horizon. He has secrets he can't hold on to any more.'

'Naturally. He's getting to that age where the memory goes – and there have been a *lot* of women.'

'Only one woman he's ever loved.'

'Don't tell that to his three ex-wives.'

'Before them. He was younger than you. Younger than Rory. She was married.'

'Surprise, surprise . . .'

'You need to know who she was, Flipper.'

'Why?' the feigned boredom was turning to irritation now. 'Giles is knocking on so this woman's probably decrepit. I'm not interested. The only one I want to know if he's shagging or not is *you.*'

'They had a child together.' She kept her face turned away so that he couldn't see the tears in her eyes. 'Two children.'

'So what? Giles has about ten children. Two more hardly count.'

'They're grown-ups now, but they don't know he's their father.'

'This is all marvellously sordid, Trudy, like a daytime soap, but I really don't give a shit.'

'You should!' She wiped her face with the back of her hand, not hearing him approaching her from behind.

'Why? I only care that he might be telling you all this while you're in bed together. I couldn't bear that . . .'

Lifting her hair at the nape, he started to kiss the back of her neck.

Trudy fought not to black out with the headrush – and body kick – of lust.

'Please stop that. I'm trying to tell you something.'

'I love listening to you talk,' he said between kisses. 'I have loved listening to you talk for years, which is a good thing because you're one mouthy bird. This evening, however, I wish you would shut up for just . . .' he kissed her cheek '. . . one . . .' he kissed her damp nose '. . . minute.' He kissed her mouth.

Trudy shut up. For a moment nothing mattered but this unexpected, magical, irresistible mutual feeling. The door to seventh heaven flew open and she fell through it willingly. But her foot caught on the Welcome mat and hooked her back.

She pulled away.

'Flips, this is all wrong.'

'Why? I love you, you love me.'

'Don't say that!' She let out a moan of uncertainty. 'I have to tell you something, I have to explain.'

'*Not* about Giles! *Please!* I know all about Giles. Don't break the magic, don't ruin this. I know. And *I don't* want to talk about it. Now, don't argue,' he put a finger over her mouth. 'I'm going to take you to bed.'

Trudy quelled the tremor of blissful apprehension that coursed through her.

He took her hand to lead her upstairs like a little girl.

Every step gave her an opportunity to turn tail and run, but she allowed herself meekly to be led to her room. There, Flipper sat her on the edge of the bed and, stooping to stroke her cheek, looked at her gravely.

'You don't need me right now. I'm going to go.'

'But I—'

'I want you to try to sleep on this – on everything.' He played with the fingers of her left hand, tracing the calluses to either side of her wedding ring from riding with it on. 'I don't want to be some sort of Rory to you.'

'But I—'

'*Or* a Giles. You are worth more than either of those could offer. You have to choose what you do next from your heart. My offer is totally serious and genuine.'

'But you—'

He covered her mouth again.

'Forgive me, I just can't talk this through right now. I'm finding it hard enough to walk away as it is. You need to know what you're doing. Find me tomorrow.'

'But tomorrow we'll be cowards again!' she pleaded, reaching out as his fingers slid from hers.

'You'll find me.'

'But—'

'But, but, but,' he pressed her finger tips to his chin and looked at her over them. 'You butt like a doe goat, my darling Trudy – always fighting.'

She longed to quip that she also screwed like a rabbit, but her confidence was fading.

'Butt off!' She gripped his hand, willing him to stay and scrap at least.

'Butt *on*,' he rubbed her knuckles along his lips. 'Butt*on* it, in fact. Just for now. You could talk me in or out of anything, but it's you who needs to give herself a talking to.'

'But—'

'*Butt*on it, he repeated, laying her hand gently back in her lap. 'You press every one of my buttons, Trudy. You always have. Tonight you'll trigger nuclear meltdown if we let this carry on. I want you to press these buttons very slowly and willingly, not out of some sort of self-destruct mission. Remember my offer isn't for one night only. It's for keeps.'

With that, he was gone. She heard him dash down the stairs two at a time, slam the door and then crunch over the wet gravel. A moment later, his car engine was roaring away.

Trudy fell back against the pillows, the memory of his kisses still on her lips and throat, his hands on her skin, his words jumbled in her head. 'Offer – genuine – serious. You choose.'

'But you haven't made me an offer,' she groaned aloud at the empty space where he had just been.

Then she remembered. On the day of the Cottrell egg hunt, he had offered her his soul.

The next morning, Dot the cleaner staged a rare professional visit to Church Cottage after some interesting rumours had circulated at her line dancing class the previous evening.

Letting herself in with the key hidden beneath the loose saddle-stone, she found her employer absolutely dead to the world. This was not unusual, although unbeknown to Dot, Trudy had usually only just gone to bed when she arrived at half past eight in the morning. On this occasion, however, Trudy had slept soundly through the night for the first time in months, surrounded by a pack of duvet-hogging dogs and one Bengal cat who was purring luxuriously on the pillow beside her. It was the first night in years that she had known Finn would stay away, ensuring total blackout.

Dot was no respecter of Trudy's odd hours, which she considered unhealthy, and so commenced hoovering around her at ten past nine.

'Brought you them banties you wanted,' she said when Trudy sat up in bed and the Miele was finally stilled. 'Silver Wyandottes. They're in that old run a yours out back, but I think a fox'll get 'em less you fix up them holes in the wire. That or your dogs. I can get Reg to fix it up if you like? Quote a price?'

But Trudy wasn't listening. Instead she was staring in alarm at the foot of the bed.

'Mutt!'

'I beg your pardon?' Dot blinked in surprise, thinking that Trudy was casting aspersions on her handyman husband.

'He's left Mutt.' Trudy stared at Flipper's scruffy little dog – one part collie, one part terrier and two parts Brillo pad, who was watching her from the depths of the duvet, warming himself between the two adoring whippet bitches.

That's how he had known that she would find him. He had left his dog as bait. She found herself grinning from ear to ear, now rested enough to think straight, those thoughts going straight to Flipper, to his love, patience, passion and touch, and staying there. Nothing else mattered. Flipper had kissed her and it had unlocked her heart.

Her spirits soared and she beamed at Dot. 'You are too kind. Did the chickens come with any paperwork?'

Dot looked at her as though she was mad.

'Never mind – I'll go out and admire them now. Coffee?'

As she bounded out of bed and headed for the door pursued by dogs, Dot noticed that she was fully dressed.

Peculiar girl, she thought to herself as she turned on the vacuum again. Not that being married to a Cottrell wouldn't make anyone behave strangely. Many years ago, before the 'incident with the Meissen soup tureen' that gave her nightmares to this day, Dot had house-kept for Piggy and Dibs Cottrell at their then home of The Manse in Oddlode. The children had still been tiny ones – the twins not even born – and quite wild; indulged by their rich, distracted father and cosseted by their meek, unhappy mother. The comings and goings in that house could have turned a more innocent soul than Dot's black with shame. It was a wonder any of the children had grown up sane.

Outside, Trudy raced to the old hen coop and greeted its new residents eagerly, hunting high and low for another clue. But there was nothing.

Oddly disappointed, she guessed that the hunt was off now that Flipper had revealed his hand. She had to play it openly like a grown-up: adultery or bust.

With a heavier heart, she turned back to the house.

The clue was behind her windscreen wiper, flapping around in a plastic bag to protect it from the rain:

> Happy are those who rise at dawn
> Under a mackerel sky;
> Nothing better to do that day
> Than chat and sell and buy.
>
> But on some very special morns
> Objets d'art appear;
> Only those who can hunt like swine
> Take their quarry, I fear.

She dashed into the house to find Dot making the promised coffee in her absence.

'You and Reg go to car boot sales, don't you?'

'Regulars, we are.'

'When's the next one?'

'Depends – them's all over.'

'The closest one to here? This week, next week?'

'There's one up near Maddington next weekend, at the old Enscombe Air Base out on the Odd Norton road.'

'What time does it start?'

'Early as you can get there if you want a bargain. What are you after?'

'Happiness,' she laughed, splashing far too much milk in her coffee. 'Happiness.'

23

The fine art auction was a ragged state of affairs, with a very hungover auctioneer and a far too full saleroom, most of its occupants having no interest in bidding for a single item.

'I knew this treasure hunt idea was doomed.' Finn cursed at his assistant, conveniently forgetting that he had been all for it initially.

Unlike Piers, who was wont to swagger around behind the rostrum, keeping the masses entertained with his dry and witty repartee, Finn's technique was dour and domineering, wringing every last bid from the room like a demanding teacher taking assembly. Today, however, he just wanted to get through the lots as fast as a Texas cattle auctioneer, not caring whether that meant sacrificing a few pounds of commission.

Through the catalogue he flew, his mouth dry, his porters dashing from lot to lot like footballers undergoing circuit training at the start of the season.

He barely noticed the oil of Major Hamish Curruthers come and go, although he did register that the price was unusually high for a piece of mediocre portraiture. Trudy's words echoed in his ear when he finally let the hammer fall: 'It'll probably sell for twice its market value.'

It had. Almost to the penny.

He ground his teeth and announced the next lot. At least he had been right on one point. Most of the public had no idea of the solution to the clue – many were still frantically leafing through the catalogue and fishing around inside boxes of loose prints in search of it. The laminated cryptic verse had already been discreetly removed from the back of the sold Curruthers' portrait by the porters and handed back to him.

Irritated that his saleroom was teeming with so much human detritus, Finn announced regally that the second treasure lot had now gone under the hammer, so all those who had not located it in time could leave the sale because they would no longer have access to the next clue.

There was a lot of moaning and cat-whistling, but his words had the desired effect. The room emptied by almost two thirds.

The prices being bid for lots suffered a similar fall as bidding dried from a steady flow to an intermittent trickle, with many lots not reaching reserve.

'You bloody fool,' Piers berated his younger brother when he turned up just before lunch to find the saleroom deserted. 'Getting a mob here is what this sodding event is all about – the crowds are here to *buy*, not just hunt, whatever they may think. You know what auctions are like. People can't resist putting their hands up. Thank God Father isn't here to see witness this.'

'He's the one who set the clue nobody could solve.'

'Well I've devised this next one, so we're bound to get back on course.' Piers yawned. There were big bags under his hooded green eyes, and his usually ruddy cheeks were distinctly grey.

'Have you heard anything?'

He shook his head. 'I expect she's gone to her mother's, but nobody will take my calls. Ma is quite happy minding the children, thank goodness. Meanwhile, Nuala headed back to Ireland this morning.'

'Good.'

'Practically flooded my car upholstery on the way to the station. Can't stand women that cry.'

'Agreed.' Finn shuddered.

Piers didn't like to admit that he was particularly annoyed by Nuala's admission that she would miss the children more than she would miss him. He plucked the laminate from the rostrum and read the four lines proudly. 'Much better than Pa's efforts.'

'Very good,' his brother admitted grudgingly. 'When is the next lot coming up?'

'Next week, upstairs at the Lodes Inn – the standing straw sale for Foxrush Holdings and the Gunning Estates. Father's taking it.'

'Not much room up there. He certainly doesn't want too many random members of the public swanning around the place – they may be happy to bid on the odd small picture while they're waiting, but they're hardly going to trump up for eight hundred bales of wheat straw.'

'True.' Piers raised a smile for the first time in twenty-four hours. 'I'm not sure he's really thought that one through.'

'It seems I've done him a favour today.' Finn nodded towards his empty saleroom, emptier now that everyone had dashed out to fuel up during the half-hour lunch break. 'We needed to reduce the field a little.'

'Hmm.' Piers looked at him sceptically. 'You might try to come up smelling of roses, but there's still a lot of shit to hit the fan and you know it.'

'Manure makes the best fertiliser. I'm just adding some shit to the roses to make them smell all the sweeter in the long run.'

The brothers exchanged conspiratorial looks laced with just a slight twitch of fear before heading out to grab a sandwich from the overpriced organic delicatessen across the road from the Cottrells' offices.

The previous night, they had spent less than half an hour talking about the Jemima situation. Sharing the bottle of malt and a lot of memories, they had talked about the future of the family firm into the early hours, carefully glossing over their personal contributions to its downfall while at the same time silently acknowledging the bond of culpability. Together, they had accelerated the auction house's fall from favour, along with failing business for the land and estate agency and near-annihilation for the small surveying arm which had been the only profitable wing of the firm. Like two senior cabinet members desperate to hold on to their ministries, they were happy to blame everybody but themselves for the collapsing house of cards. Together, they were a tour de force of denial.

Both agreed that it would be best to sell Cottrells' as a going concern as soon as the treasure hunt was through – earlier, if discreet advances to other major players in the industry were positively received, and a buy-out could be arranged; the family name held a great deal of sway that younger, more profitable agencies might wish to cash in on; the client base was impressively blue-blooded; the land assets were significant. Equally, selling Fox Oddfield Abbey would release much-needed capital that could be distributed amongst the family, while ridding them of the astronomical running costs. Piers, Phoney and Finn had second properties in Ireland, London and Oddlode respectively; the twins needed to find their own feet and Aunt Grania needed to go into a home, the brothers agreed. Their parents would benefit greatly from living somewhere smaller and warmer like a renovated farm or a barn conversion. It all made perfect sense.

Having thus sorted matters to their mutual satisfaction, the brothers had lost all interest in the treasure hunt – to the point that when one particularly irate competitor came up to them in the deli queue, complaining that the lot had been too hard to find, Piers handed him the next clue.

"'It wanes but it never waxes when the police are around,'" the man read aloud in a nasal whine.

'It has Isle Of Wight pointers that are hidden underground
It will stand and deliver by the wood of splintered spines
That's bound by local legend and a knot of golden twines.'

'Moon? Police?' the man suggested, pulling off his orange cagoule hood to scratch his bald head. 'Isle of Wight pointers? Some sort of coloured sand ornament in a glass vessel the shape of a moon – or a truncheon? Am I right?' He looked up eagerly.

'Oh for Christ's sake, it's bloody easy!' Piers huffed as his brother sniggered. 'It *wanes* but it never waxes. *Wane* is the first clue, along with *police*.'

'Rooney?' the man nodded eagerly. 'He's been in a few scraps on the wrong side of the law. A signed shirt, am I right?'

'No!' Piers snapped. '*Wane* – wain – what other famous *wains* are there?'

'John Wayne?'

'No – no, think more laterally – in conjunction with a police *constable*, maybe?' Piers was spoon feeding him hints.

'Yes, yes!' The man held up a finger. '*Rio Bravo* – the Duke played a sheriff, am I right?'

'Forget wane for a minute,' Piers said through gritted teeth. 'Let's look at the next line: The Isle of Wight is famous for which promontories? Pointed promontories?'

'Piers!' The man nodded happily, pointing at the auctioneer in front of him.

'Needles!' he hissed.

'Oh. So – moon, Wayne, needles. Are we talking rock and roll memorabilia by any chance?'

Finn howled gleefully.

Piers took a deep breath. Voice rattling with contempt, he spelled it out. 'Wane is "*Hay*wain", as in Constable's famous painting. The Isle of Wight pointers are the Needles as in "needle in a *hay*stack". The wood of splintered spines is Broken Back Wood on Parson's Ridgeway, where Bob Turner of Hill Farm currently has seven hundred small bales of meadow hay entered in next week's sale, all stacked ready for the buyer to collect. It's the only hay we have in the July standing straw sale – freshly baled and nicely bound up in yellow binder twine, Bob tells me. The only access is along a narrow track through the wood. Local legend has it the track was frequented by highwaymen once.'

'Quite ingenious.' Finn beamed at his brother before turning to order two beef and horseradish bloomers.

The little man in the orange cagoule shook his head in bafflement. 'Well, if you don't mind me saying. I think you'll struggle to get anyone to work this out. Really struggle. It's a *standing straw* auction, not a *hay and straw* one.'

'We often sell new hay with standing straw in summer,' Piers said witheringly.

'How am I, a layperson, supposed to know that?'

'Look it up! You don't win fifty grand for nothing, you know.'

'I don't much like your attitude, my man.'

'Oh, get lost, you ungrateful little prick. I gave you the clue.'

'Don't you take that tone with me!'

'Fuck off,' Piers snarled, turning his back on him.

'"*Much* simpler than Pa's clue",' Finn scoffed when the man had gone, handing Finn his beef bloomer.

'He was a simpleton,' Piers muttered.

'He *does* have a point. How the heck is anyone supposed to know about Broken Back Woods and hay being sold at a standing straw sale?'

'Anyone who hunts knows the place – it's one of the best Vale of the Wolds coverts.'

'Hardly anyone bloody hunts these days.'

'More's the pity. Adulterers know it as well; they all go up there to shag their mistresses in the back of their Mercs.'

'I'm surprised you didn't allude to that in your poem – so much clearer!'

'Anyway, it's a clear enough clue to get them looking at the standing straw catalogue online, from which it's pretty obvious.'

'Just so long as they don't trespass all over Bob Turner's land in search of hay bales.'

'Of course they bloody won't.' Piers pulled out his mobile phone to send Jemima another furiously apologetic text demanding that she come home to talk this thing through. 'Bloody women,' he grumbled, still in the mood for a fight to clear his head. 'No sense of timing. I wish she'd waited until after this wretched hunt to make her stand. Trudy still behaving herself?'

'Mmm.' Finn was reading his own phone messages, falling into step as he and Piers headed back to the sales rooms. 'You know Trudy. Head in the clouds, happy making music.'

'Not about to do a runner, then?'

Finn bristled. 'Whatever makes you ask that?'

'Tactless of me, sorry. One becomes pretty cynical at a time like this. I always thought it was your marriage that would come unstuck, not mine, but I was obviously wrong.'

The words came spitting back like gunfire. 'Very wrong. We're fine. Working bloody hard as usual. Trudy hardly leaves the house.'

'Good girl.'

There was a telling silence.

'Giles keeping his distance?'

'Yes,' came the terse reply. Finn's suspicions from the Auctioneers' Ball, along with that dreadful text of the mysterious male buttocks and balls, remained a strictly private matter.

'Good. Used to sniff around Jemima too. Soon saw him off.'

'Quite.' Finn cleared his throat, immensely uncomfortable. 'That must be a great relief.'

'Certainly is. Too many bachelor hounds in our family.' Piers was warming to his topic. 'Flipper's the one to watch. Had a crack at Jem as soon as his balls dropped, I shouldn't wonder – but she can't tolerate milksops. Been after your wife since day one, too.'

'He was practically in short trousers then.'

'Not now.'

'Trudy doesn't notice. She thinks of him like her brother, Johnny.'

'The poofter?'

'Yes. Flipper's a substitute.'

'Think Flipper's a poofter?'

'God, no.'

'Thank Christ for that. It'd finish Mother off.'

'According to Nell, he's quite lost his heart to some busty blonde village girl,' Finn drawled, 'grand-daughter of that batty sculptor, Norman Gently. Very pretty. Enormous tits.'

'Thought that was off?'

'He wants her back; bends poor Trudy's ear about it all the time. God knows how she has the patience to listen.'

'Stupid boy,' Piers tutted. 'Glad Trudy treats him like a poofter.'

Finn reached into his pocket and glanced at an incoming text, eyebrows shooting up, along with an involuntary intake of breath.

'Business?'

'Personal.' Finn read the message again, colour rising in his cheeks.

'Ah.' Piers was a master of assumption and had already interpreted that one hissed word as tantamount to a mistress in a love nest in Chelsea. 'You dipping the wick elsewhere then?' he asked as matter-of-factly as if enquiring whether his brother's Range Rover was meeting its fuel consumption targets.

Finn almost dropped his phone. 'Am I *what?*'

Piers slapped his younger brother on the back. 'Men are far better at keeping it all at trouser level, you know. It's the girls who get all tearful and silly about it.'

The uncomfortable conversation had taken them as far as the private rear doors into the Cottrells' saleroom and offices. Hanging back, Finn looked gratefully at his watch. Piers had been digging too close to the bone on all fronts, and he was eager to escape.

'If you're happy to take the podium for a couple of hours, I've got some projects that need chasing elsewhere.'

'Sure, leave it with me. You get on with whatever – or whoever – it is you're chasing.' With a Terry-Thomas guffaw and another brotherly slap on the back, he went inside.

Trudy squeezed Mutt and the rest of her pack into the back of her battered car and set out for Broken Back Woods. She had already texted Flipper, announcing that she was walking the dogs on the Ridgeway and seemed to have a stray in tow, a body on fire and a heart in limbo. Then, remembering his trampled sim card, she added the unknown caller number to the message recipients.

Pulse racing and belly tumbling, she drove up the winding hill from Oddlode to the ridge, the sun in her eyes and her heart in her mouth.

Several cars were parked on the wide verges alongside the lane that ran beneath the skirt hem of the woods. Although dog walkers often took the bridleway, famous for its stunning view of the escarpment at the far end, it was unusual to have so many here at once. She didn't recognise Flipper's Audi amongst them.

Trudy huffed in frustration as she unleashed her pack of dogs from the car. She and Flipper were hardly going to be able to have a discreet tête-à-tête here, let alone another kiss, fantasies of which had been bringing her out in cold sweats of guilt and anxiety.

It soon became apparent why there were so many cars parked in the normally secluded spot. People were crawling all over the hay bales stacked in a field adjacent to the path in search of clues.

Trudging past in an increasingly foul temper, Trudy headed out on to the Ridgeway proper and, looking down into the valley from her sunny standpoint, watched a rain cloud tipping its contents on Oddlode in a dark grey torrent.

Her phone was vibrating in her pocket – a text from Unknown Caller.

'Tied up here. Can't stray. Soon.'

It wasn't until she turned and headed back to the car that she realised Mutt was no longer amongst her pack.

At Church Cottage, Flipper peered forlornly through the windows and knew, from the lack of dogs barking and the deserted appearance, that Trudy was out, not just taking one of her daytime naps. His heart sank.

He hadn't heard a word from her, and now had no idea where she could be.

He was standing in the pouring rain again: a second day of being drenched, water running beneath his coat collar and down the back of his neck as it tipped from a clogged gutter above the porch.

He moved further beneath the little roofed shelter and, scraping a couple of gnarled geraniums along the stone bench beside him, made enough space to sit down, propping his feet on the bench opposite and taking his phone from his pocket to text her. It was a laborious process on the unfamiliar veterinary clinic phone.

He had barely pressed send when he heard tyres on gravel and jumped up, a stupid smile plastered across his face.

But the smile dropped with a clank. It was Finn, and his face behind the wheel of the Range Rover was a mask of brutality.

Trudy was racing around the woods in ever-decreasing circles, calling Mutt until she was hoarse.

When her phone chimed insistently again, she read the message as she ran, confused by what she saw: *Where are you? Where is my dog? Am waiting. Flip.* As before it had come up as from an Unknown Caller.

'Mutt!' she howled, pocketing the phone. '*Muuuuuttt!*'

But the little dog was nowhere to be found.

Finn eyed his brother distrustfully as he let himself into the cottage and emptied the contents of his pockets on to the lid of the grand piano – keys, loose change, sweet wrappers and a couple of grubby tissues.

'Doesn't Trudy hate it when you do that?' Flipper had followed him inside, dripping water all over the floor boards.

'None of your business. Stand on the mat,' Finn ordered, pulling off his tie and gratefully discarding it over the dog sofa arm along with his jacket. 'What do you want?'

'My dog. I left him here last night.'

'I think Trudy's dropping him back at the Abbey. Didn't she call?'

'No.' Flipper felt a nervous tick leap to his jaw.

'Well, he's probably already there.'

'OK. Thanks,' Flipper turned back towards the drumming rain.

'Wait a minute,' Finn hailed him inside again, like a schoolmaster. 'Don't you want to know how Piers is doing?'

Flipper looked surprised. 'I didn't think I was privy to that sort of brotherly information.'

'I'm not going to tell you his innermost thoughts.'

'Fine. How is he?'

'Pretty fucked up, actually. Thinks she'll coming running back as soon as her mother starts getting on her nerves.'

'And you don't?'

'Depends if she's *at* her mother's.'

Flipper forced a laugh.

Finn watched him silently, as always possessing the ability to make Flipper feel adolescent and cornered.

'Shut the door a moment, Flipper.'

He swallowed uncomfortably, reaching out for the latch. As he did so, his phone started shrilling, some stupid ring-tone that one of the other vets had downloaded when it was in his possession, a comedy version of the *Lone Ranger* theme tune.

'Ignore that.' Finn stepped forward, rolling up his shirtsleeves.

Flipper waited until the call transferred to voice mail, jumping as the phone shrilled again to tell him he had a message.

Finn was directly in front of him now, nose just inches from his, eyes direct and unblinking.

'I'm not going to say much,' he breathed in an undertone as threatening as the loudest war cry, 'but I am going to make myself understood. Trudy finds your attentions more than a little embarrassing. You have put her in an incredibly awkward position and we both – we *both* – want it to stop right here. She's asked me to tell you to back right off. Do I make myself clear?'

'As day.'

'And you agree?'

Flipper ran his dry tongue along his teeth. 'No.'

'I'm sorry?'

'Trudy can ask me herself. Then I'll agree.'

This time the full war cry was unleashed. 'For fuck's sake, she's my wife!'

Flipper refused to stand down or raise his voice. 'She's not your possession.'

'Don't be so fucking naïve! Your sick little puppy love aggravates the hell out of her, but she's a sweet girl and she hates hurting people.'

'So she kindly sent you to do her dirty work?'

'Just leave her alone!'

'I love her.'

As Flipper's phone started ringing cheerfully again, a set of tightly beaded knuckles struck him hard across the cheekbone.

He reeled, but a second blow caught him firmly on the jaw, this time with a very audible crack that sent a shard of pain straight up into his head. Moments later two more strikes completed the attack, a nose-breaking smack from a forearm into his face followed by a knee to the groin so hard that he almost blacked out.

'You stay away from her,' Finn hissed as he bent over his brother. 'If you don't, I'll kick out every one of those straight white teeth.'

Flipper ran his tongue across the jagged edge of his front tooth, defiant in defeat. 'That's up to Trudy.'

'How *many* times? You give her the creeps,' Finn's voice was so thick with testosterone and bile that it was bloodcurdling. 'I swear if you come here sniffing around her again, you'll find her horses joining yours in the big glue factory in the sky.'

'You what?'

'You heard. She needs you out of her life. If you're not, those bloody useless horses are. Your choice. Your conscience.' With that, he hauled him up by the collar and threw him out.

Flipper was on his knees outside, rain hammering down on him, red drips of blood mingling with the puddles on the gravel drive to form jewel-like pools. The *Lone Ranger* theme tune was still tinkling insistently.

His hands shook so much that he dropped the phone when he tried to turn it off. But as soon as the ringing transferred the call to answerphone, it started up again – the caller redialling continually now.

He peered at the screen and groaned as he recognised Trudy's number.

Hobbling and scrabbling to his car, aware of Finn's eyes boring into him from the Gothic arched hall window, he reversed from the drive at speed and made it out on to the village lane, parking up in the gateway to the allotments.

Trudy was sobbing so much that he couldn't understand what she was saying at first. Eventually, however, he managed to piece it together.

'Mutt's g-gone,' she wept. 'It's all m-my fault. I've searched and searched. Oh, Flipper. I think he's d-dead.'

Flipper drove as fast as he could towards the ridge. He made it as far as the Upper Springlode turn before his blurred vision became so bad that he couldn't judge the corner over the narrow bridge. Braking too late, he felt a series of crashing jolts as his car hurtled through the narrow rails beside the Cotswold stone walled bridge and nosedived into the brook.

The passing motorist who found him reeling around beside the road dripping water and blood a few minutes later understandably assumed that the broken nose, smashed cheek and split lip came from the crash. So did Flipper's family when, refusing to let an ambulance be called, he accepted a lift to Fox Oddfield Abbey.

He had pleaded with his Good Samaritan to take him to Broken Back Woods instead, but was ignored, partly because his swollen lip and broken tooth made it sound as though he was asking to be taken to 'Brixton Backwards', and partly because the kind soul on whose car he dripped blood and muddy water was a local do-gooder who recognised him as one of Piggy Cottrell's wayward sons.

As soon as he arrived home, Flipper found himself clamped in his mother's vice-like nursing grip, flattened on to a day bed and trapped beneath warm wet flannels and wads of TCP, force-fed cake, sweet tea and brandy, and told under no circumstances to leave the house until the family doctor arrived. She even removed his mobile phone like a nun confiscating contraband tuck. Dr Garrotty – an ancient, tobacco-smelling charlatan whom the Cottrells favoured because he still made house calls – set his nose, diagnosed a mild concussion and recommended bed rest.

Flipper could have put up a fight, but it had drained out of him. Finn's words echoed in his head: 'You give her the creeps'. He just wanted to escape to his attic apartment and sleep for a week.

24

Everybody told Trudy that the dog would turn up, that it could have happened to anyone, that it wasn't her fault. But when Mutt hadn't reappeared after a week, she blamed herself totally. Every day she drove or rode up to Broken Back Woods to search. Every day she trailed back again defeated. It became an obsession, pacing out lonely hours among the tall, scrawny pines on the ridge, stumbling down the steep slopes, wobbling over the springy pine needles, and all the time calling until she was hoarse.

The woods started off busy with treasure hunters trespassing on to farmland in search of the hay pile, until Cottrells' were forced to put up a sign explaining that there were no clues to be found there. Still they came, and were sympathetic to Trudy's plight when they encountered her, some helping her search until they grew bored and became distracted by their more urgent, fiscal hunt. She put up signs herself with her number to call in case anyone spotted him, and offered a hefty reward, even placing an advert in the local paper to say so. Several false sightings were reported, but no true sign of Mutt.

After the standing straw sale at the Lodes Inn – by all accounts a farce of overcrowding and confusion, greeted with delight only by the landlord who tripled his takings for the night – the woods fell quiet as usual. Trudy preferred her solitary hunts, her daily vigil of calling and then stopping to listen. It was easier with no chattering distractions, no car radios, mobile phone tones and footfalls on mulch. Yet she heard nothing but the echo of her calls and the shuddering fear in her own intakes of breath.

Refusing to help search, Finn was blisteringly unsympathetic. 'You have to accept the fact the dog is long gone, either stolen or more likely dead in a trap or a fox's den somewhere. If he does by some miracle reappear, it won't be as a result of you traipsing around in the bracken.'

But still Trudy haunted the woods. It stopped her thinking about anything else; it stopped her feeling so raw with guilt about Flipper.

There had been no contact since the first, awful call she'd made. When she tried him again, his mobile phone was switched off. The next day, that phone was back behind the desk of the equine hospital and she was told that Flipper was taking a few days off, but that he would be checking in occasionally. She left a message there for him to call her. He didn't.

She called the Abbey several times, but the phone line into the attic flat which the twins shared just rang out. News filtered back to her that Nell was away, taking advantage of a friend's Corsican villa while she was still able to fly safely. Flipper, it seemed, just wasn't answering the phone or returning her calls. She knew nothing of his accident.

Finn was brusque. 'You lost his dog. What d'you expect? Leave him alone.'

She could hardly argue. Flipper clearly didn't want to make contact.

Nobody told her that he had spun his car into the Odd that last day they'd spoken, nor that he'd arrived home to the Abbey concussed, with a swollen face covered in blood, a broken nose and chipped front teeth. Only the brothers knew how most of the injuries had been caused. And Finn now basked in the satisfaction of knowing that he had succeeded in warning his brother off his wife, backed up by brother Piers who – mistakenly believing himself to be an arbitrator in an overblown family dispute about a missing dog – had a quiet word with his younger brother a week later:

'You know Finn's temper. Don't cross it. Trudy is a silly fool, but the dog can't be found and she needs to lie low. It all got a bit messy between you two and it's best left alone now. She doesn't want you bothering her, so best off out of it, huh?'

Flipper would have ignored all this had it not been for the ultimate voice of wisdom and moral intercession: his mother.

Dibs cornered her son as he thumped his way down the back stairs from the attic flat one morning, intent on going back into work.

Appearing through one of the side doors from the main house like a ghost emerging round the stair-turn, she made Flipper start back in alarm.

'Darling, I am so worried about you.' She reached out to stroke his hair.

Flipper ducked. His mother rarely made physical gestures, and when she did they were hampered by embarrassment.

'I'm fine,' he muttered.

'Don't get too depressed about this missing dog.'

'I'm not.'

'I know it must seem so unfair, coming so soon after you lost Olive, but—'

'Well, to lose one pet looks like a misfortune, to lose two is carelessness.'

Dibs didn't recognise the quote. 'You mustn't get involved in Finn's marriage, you know.'

He shifted awkwardly, wishing there was enough space on the stairs to brush past her.

'It's a sacred thing,' she went on. 'It doesn't do to meddle.'

'Has Finn put you up to this?'

She shook her head. 'I can see with my own eyes. I am being forced to stand by as one of my son's marriages crashes against the rocks. I cannot witness another.'

'And what makes you think I'm involved?'

'You *are* involved, Phillip darling. You have been for a long time now.' She sighed, wisely not mentioning that she and Jemima had spent many a long morning coffee discussing Trudy's inexplicable ability to attract Cottrell men – Giles, Piers and even Piggy flirted with her – but only Flipper looked at her with barely disguised love. 'She would eat you up and spit you out, you know that.'

'Well luckily for her digestion, I'm not involved. I never have been. She and Finn are welcome to one another.'

'Are you sure?'

'She lost my dog, didn't she?'

He stomped past her and clattered down the last of the stone stairs to the courtyard where the Cottrells all parked their cars. His was a jaunty orange courtesy car from the body shop that was repairing his drowned and dented Audi. On its side in clashing purple was written: 'You bend 'em, we mend 'em'.

Watching from the mullioned stairs window as he drove from the Abbey, Dibs longed to phone Jemima. It was a silly joke Jemima would immediately register, just as she would register her mother-in-law's need for an ear.

But Jemima had been incommunicado for over a week now,

appearing only to collect her children or deliver them home with a flurry of air kisses and thank-you gushing. Dibs had hoped for another mother and daughter-in-law confessional, but she realised that she was being kept 'out of the loop'.

The only person who thought to tell her things was darling Finn – always the most considerate of her sons. He explained that Piers and Jemima were absolutely on course for reconciliation; a matter of days away, he stressed, their rift still thankfully concealed from public view. Equally, Flipper had promised not to pester the married woman he had been bothering again. Dibs knew it was Trudy but loyally said nothing to Finn, aware that he was a proud man who valued discretion. She was grateful to know what was going on, although Finn was too abrupt and unemotional to make a true confidant. She missed her long chats with Jemima. Phoney was no use – all she talked about was the family business going broke, which was a nonsense. It was just going through a bad patch as it had many times before in its long history; Finn had assured her there was nothing to worry about.

Having finally tracked down Trudy by phone to demand a précis of recent events, Liv insisted on dragging her along to the car boot sale the following morning. Car-booting had once been a great passion of hers, before suburban gentrification, children and Martin's snobbishness had led her to withdraw from the early-morning starts.

Trudy hadn't been planning to go along, any pleasure in her personal treasure hunt or hopes of its continuation abandoned. She wanted, instead, to scour the woods again for Mutt.

But Liv refused to back down: 'This will do you good; take your mind off things.'

She was certain that Trudy wasn't telling her the full story. Even though that bubbling, ebullient voice had still managed to break into self-deprecating laughter about the fact that she had pranged her brother-in-law's car and lost his beloved dog, there was a haunting quality to the silences that she left between the laughs which made Liv feel both frustrated and pitying. It was why she had become so insistent about the car boot sale. She needed Trudy to be fun again and to stop her spiralling out of control.

Liv felt like a cat with a bushed tail, desperate to run up and down the curtains. She imagined this must be what Trudy felt like a lot of the time, with all that fizz and energy in need of an explosion. Liv's recently liberated libido was in perpetual motion, her mind wouldn't settle and her desire for a more fulfilling, active, entertaining life – a life more like Trudy's – was overwhelming.

Having overcompensated for an evening's lonely boredom after the children were in bed with too many gin and tonics and too much dancing to the Pigeon Detectives, she decided that she needed to tidy something to calm down her racing mind. Liv had no unknown secret horrors hidden in her drawers, cupboards, wardrobes and filing cabinets. She knew the contents of each, all neatly ordered. She was a fanatical tidier.

In the end she resorted to tidying the contents of her computer – deleting lots of rubbish, creating back-up files and archiving important letters, emails, the kids' downloads, photographs . . .

The latter caused a moment's guilt when faced with herself in lacy La Perla, although thankfully the volume of gin in her bloodstream misted her vision sufficiently to realise that she looked pretty hot. Martin had been quite brusque about her efforts, which had taken her a lot of nerve.

She'd send it to Giles, she decided impulsively. He'd love it.

Unfortunately the level of gin in her bloodstream did her no favours this time, as she located the wrong email address in her neatly ordered contacts file.

How can a car boot sale possibly take my mind off things? Trudy wondered as she brushed her teeth at a quarter to seven the following morning, Liv's engine already idling outside, Radio Two chirruping discreetly from the open windows. I'm following Flipper's last clue to a dead end.

Yet the promise of a connection with him, however small, made her go along with it.

Finn was still asleep. She crept downstairs again, pausing in her study to turn off her computer so that he wouldn't snoop at her work when he got up.

Their marriage was at an all-time low. She could hardly bear to be in the same room as him; her skin crawled with irritation and discomfort whenever he was near. Yesterday, he had told her that he wanted to 'talk', but she knew that meant talk about money – a sure sign that he had run out and run up huge debts again – and she had told him to wait, hardly caring that he had to be at breaking point to raise the topic. As a rule he was so private about money that she had never had a notion how much he earned or how he spent it. Hers was the only income that ever went into the joint account and towards such boring necessities as mortgage, utility bills, taxes and groceries.

She couldn't face the conversation just yet. Even practical everyday realities such as eating, shopping and running the house were at a standstill as she hid behind her work.

She had stayed up all night to avoid joining him in bed but had resolutely avoided the vodka, limiting herself to a modest half-bottle of wine punctuated with mineral water and just three cigarettes. Rather to her surprise, work came as easily as it customarily did in a booze-fuelled trance.

But when she looked back at what she had written, she realised the quality threshold and emotional investment acted in inverse proportion to her sobriety. It was a pack of prettily constructed lies.

Conditioned for over a decade to protect Pete Rafferty's secret, Trudy had tried to gloss over the fateful eighteen-month love affair that had led to a wrecked career, a shattered family and marriage on the rebound. She'd concentrated more on the background: the clubs and bars she'd haunted, the far-flung countries she had jetted through, the labels she'd worn, the celebrity friends she'd had, parties they'd run wild at and some of the more excessive, starry high jinks fuelled by drink and drugs. It was all superficial stuff, beloved of prurient celebrity biography readers, and not a realistic picture of events at all; the truth was that Trudy had been far too much of a workaholic in those early days of success to play the wild star card, and these anecdotes related to just the few rare nights out which had happened over a long stretch of time, now crammed tightly together in one chapter.

Equally, her narration of her love affair with Pete was a scant list of clichés and platitudes that made eighteen months of sexual awakening, of heartbreaking tenderness and the most emotional and turbulent highs and lows in her life, sound like a lost weekend in Brighton. She had carefully not named him directly, nor dropped any real hints as to his identity. Even so, she made him sound like a saint and herself a complete sinner. That wasn't really how it had been. It came across like a fantasy teen photo-story from a nineties annual: all simple, time-trapped vignettes, vintage champagne and designer fashion, without any substance.

Worst of all, her recollections about her father's massive stroke, a death in all but name, were so sentimental and mawkish that she could almost hear him rotating like a mole drill in his eco-friendly grave in the family's favourite Cornish bluebell wood. Thinking about Kit inevitably made her cry, and last night had been no exception as she had written paragraph after paragraph with tears streaming; but in the cold light of day her words were no more moving than a McGonagall eulogy.

Reading it all back that following morning, finger on her computer power button and toothbrush in mouth, Trudy splattered her monitor screen with Colgate.

'Oh, darling Dad – even you would laugh yourself silly reading this,' she mumbled, chewing on the brush as she deleted the lot before hitting the off switch.

Liv was tooting the horn outside now and Trudy was so desperate to run away from life then and life now that she sprinted outside with her toothbrush still poking from her mouth.

Dressed in her yummy mummy uniform of cashmere and suede, Liv looked marvellous, if somewhat unhinged. She had developed a new, schoolmarmy manner which must have come from spending too much time with Jemima.

At the boot fair, Trudy couldn't shake the dark, nostalgic mood. For once, Liv found her less than communicative.

Liv blamed herself. One of the first stalls they had come across was selling old CDs and, on top of a pile, was one of Trudy's. There, pouting winsomely, a cocky, sexy twenty-something Trudy stared up at them.

'Ohmygod, it's you!' Liv shrieked, waving it about like a deranged fan.

'*Drop* it,' Trudy hissed, much as she did if the dogs stole from the table at home.

'Look at your white teeth!'

'Air brushed, or bleached – or both. I smoked even more in those days.'

'You're so raunchy!' Liv was leafing through the sleeve.

'Put it down, Liv – you're attracting attention.'

But Liv insisted on buying it, pointing out that she had never really listened to any of Trudy's stuff.

'No bad thing,' Trudy countered, suddenly under close scrutiny from the stallholder, who had realised who she was.

The morning went downhill from there. That first stallholder, a popular regular who knew many of the others holding pitches there, did a quick ring-around and word spread through the sale that there was a celebrity present. Even though half of those who approached her surely didn't know who she was, Trudy found herself cornered for autographs at every turn, and snapped by mobile phones wherever she went. At least some of the autograph-hunters were honest, pointing out that her signature could fetch a few pounds on eBay – these were all small-time entrepreneurs after all. At least twenty more of her albums surfaced to be signed and even a couple of posters, including that infamous shot of her posing naked on Arty.

Liv blushed when she saw it, resisting the temptation to tell Trudy how beautiful she had been. She was already on thin ice in that department. Instead, she complimented the horse.

'It's Arty.' Trudy looked at the grey mare's young, strong frame covered with painted love hearts – a far cry from her elderly, hairy state now.

'I wouldn't have recognised her.'

'That probably goes for both of us,' Trudy sighed. 'Not quite the old pot-bellied birds we've become. She was just eight or nine there.'

After that, she was distracted by memories, possessing a glazed, faraway look. Liv, who was dying to gossip about Jemima, was furious. Quite against character, Trudy had almost nothing to say on the subject, simply agreeing that yes, Jemima was apparently living with Rory Midwinter, no, her children were not joining them yet, yes Piers did seem to want to patch things up and no, Giles was not involved at all.

This last fact was one Liv needed to discuss in depth with Trudy, who had slandered him so badly in the first place. But Trudy was barely interested enough to engage in the conversation at all.

'Are you sure you saw them together?' Liv grilled her.

'Yeah, yeah it was them,' she agreed as she rummaged half-heartedly through a pile of old hunting prints in search of her treasure.

'But she *must* have been seeing Rory at the same time?'

'Giles may have said something about Jemima using him for a trial run.'

'But that's disgusting!' Liv plundered a bucket of horse whips, pulling out a bone-handled hunting thong with alarming relish.

'It's not that unusual. Men and women both do it – blur the

boundaries between love and friendship, find long term lovers with whom they have no agenda or timetable, develop "fuck buddies" alongside committed relationships.'

'Really?'

She nodded, her head still full of her own memoirs and where they were going next, wondering if she was really still in love with Pete, or if the bitter, loveless years she had endured with Finn had finally rid her of the curse. It didn't register that she too could have blurred those boundaries between love and friendship, or that she could now be in love with somebody else.

Liv was waving the whip around, highly agitated. 'Do lots of people have these 'fu—, fu—,' she couldn't bring herself to say the word aloud in a public place, 'these "buddies"?'

'Well, there are quite a few members of Giles's Cotswold Wives Club, for a start,' Trudy reminded her gently.

Liv disliked the way Trudy highlighted the insignificance of her recent life-changing sexual epiphany and the fact that she was just another notch on Giles's bed-post.

'But it's so calculating – so deliberately hurtful,' she said, quite convincing herself that being spontaneous and unwitting made infidelity less hurtful.

Trudy shrugged. 'I suppose the secret is to make sure it's a mutual agreement and that other lovers don't get jealous.'

'Have you done it then?' Liv was thinking about the come-hither sex siren pouting from the CD sleeves, who was very intimidating compared to the familiar Trudy she knew.

'I've always been a one-man woman, pathetically loyal. Once I fall in love, it takes a hell of a lot to make me fall out again.'

'Like what?'

'Well I'm not wildly keen on perfidy.' She was thinking about her past.

'What's perfidy?'

'Treachery, betrayal; a complete breach of trust.'

'In that case, me neither,' agreed Liv, thinking about Giles and Jemima again.

While not exactly perfidious, a word she planned to use in her email to Martin at some point, thinking it gloriously weighty, the casual way in which they could plot to sleep together for pure sport alarmed her. Was that what she herself had been doing with Giles;

using him as a 'fuck buddy', perhaps even a trial run for something even bigger and better? It made her feel slightly soiled, yet incredibly liberated at the same time. It insinuated that there was even more fun out there – as Jemima was currently enjoying Rory Midwinter – and in its present state, Liv's runaway libido was thrilled at the prospect.

She was less thrilled by how moralistic Trudy seemed today. She was supposed to be the great advocate of naughtiness and infidelity, after all, and here she was revealing herself as a 'pathetically loyal, one-man woman'. Not that her continual bitchiness about marriage to lovely, hunky Finn smacked of a loyal woman in love.

And something even more hypocritical registered in Liv's busy head as she hurried them on to another stall.

'Have you found out who is setting you these clues?'

Trudy said nothing, her mind far away from treasure hunts and clues.

In the end, Liv did all the searching and, after several unsuccessful forays into hunting memorabilia and footwear, she tracked down the 'hunt boot' clue – tucked away on a wonky clothes rail at a stall belonging to a man called Hunt. There was an old scarlet wool hunting jacket with the familiar Vale of the Wolds clashing dark claret lapels that signified it to be a local huntsman of some repute. It was, on closer inspection, also resplendent with eight initialled silver Vale of the Wolds Hunt buttons and had a clue tucked into one pocket, quickly whipped away by the stallholder until the women agreed to buy at a vastly overinflated price.

As Liv pored over the clue, already planning their next adventure, Trudy paid for the jacket with a cheque and folded it over one arm. As she did so, a name-tag caught her eye, neatly sewn alongside the tailor's label by the inside breast pocket: 'Peregrine Cottrell'.

She stopped, letting this register. Piggy hadn't hunted for years; he certainly wouldn't miss one of his jackets – or it could have been passed on to one of his sons.

Buttons. They had joked about butts and buttons the last time they'd seen one another, before she had so cruelly lost his dog, and he had suddenly stopped responding to her messages or texts.

It had to be Flipper.

She felt a wrench of sadness as she walked back to the car alongside Liv, who thought the new clue impossibly romantic:

"'Made by Fedor Ruckert," she read out.
"'And lying together like lovers
Regal connections might be fabricated
Kindred spirits fib the fab stuff
So like a marriage
Pregnant pauses for the childless
Eager for approval
Never realising the twinned agony
Connected to the broken oath
Everlasting is a long sacrament
Repent at leisure; you married in . . .'"

Trudy wasn't interested in the treasure; all she could think about were the heartbreaking clues that the author had spelled out to précis his accurate take on her life, calling her marriage a pregnant pause for the childless, knowing that she had been too eager for approval, for acceptance, to think through what she was doing.

It struck her like an icy wind, covering her entire body in goose bumps and making every hair stand up on end.

She had to end her marriage. She had to leave Finn.

The realisation was so overwhelming, so simple and so obvious.

'Are you all right?' Liv was staring at her.

She nodded, touching her cheeks and finding that they were cold and clammy. Her voice sounded miles away when she forced a reply. 'Just coming down with something, I think.'

'All those cold walks in the woods – and the late night shifts working. You push yourself too hard,' Liv sympathised, opening her car with an electronic peep.

Trudy abandoned thoughts of going up to Broken Back Woods to look for Mutt that day. She had plans to make; she had to plot out how to do this very carefully. She needed to be prepared, to try to keep it as calm, dignified and practical a split as she could manage.

She couldn't wait to get back home and get organised.

Half an hour later, watching Trudy practically throw herself back into Church Cottage with barely a breath of thanks, Liv felt extremely miffed. She had really put herself out to arrange the morning for Trudy, dropping off the children super-early with another school-run mum, scouring the sale for the treasure, trying to cheer her up, buying endless beakers of coffee and bacon sandwiches. She felt that merited considerably more gratitude.

Finn's big Range Rover wasn't in the drive, she noticed idly as she reversed away. So Trudy was now home alone with her secret thoughts while he was out conducting important auctioneering business.

She was hurt that Trudy wouldn't confide in her. Trudy knew all about Giles, after all; Liv felt it only fair for Trudy to return the intimacy and confess the truth. She couldn't help suspecting that Trudy knew full well who was setting her the romantic clues and was indeed already conducting a full-blown affair with him. That made it even more hypocritical of her to bang on about being loyal and faithful.

Liv felt quite sorry for handsome, gallant Finn who sent polite, witty emails trying to help her find a Cornish cottage she didn't want.

As she drove past the Green, she contemplated stopping off to see Otto – and anybody else who might be in situ at River Cottage – but her mood was too dark and her temper too irritable. Instead, she went home and opened a bottle of white wine. Liv had never drunk alone during the day in her life, but a bloody-minded sprite seemed to have taken over her recently.

She put on the Pigeon Detectives' CD and paced around her immaculate kitchen, clutching the glass to her chest. She was behaving just like Trudy she decided. In fact, Trudy was probably drinking wine right now, listening to the same CD, which was her husband's favourite after all, texting her lover to thank him for his clue.

'Hmph!' She thought back to her frustrating morning. Trudy had hardly seemed grateful for the new clue at all. It was Liv who was excited by the fable and mystery of it all, Liv who found the poem impossibly romantic, Liv who couldn't wait to start the search for the spoons. Trudy hadn't been herself for days – not since she'd lost that stupid dog.

'Right now, Liv,' she told herself as she poured another glass of wine, '*you* are more like Trudy than Trudy.'

Liv was the one living life in the fast lane, the yummy mummy calling the shots at last, taking a lover – a 'fuck buddy' – and being thoroughly rock and roll.

Cranking up the volume on the Pigeon Detectives, she danced around her island unit imagining that she was as sultry as the sex bomb who stared out of Trudy's old album covers: a gorgeous creature sprinkled with magical stardust who had found her way to the end of the rainbow and could take her pick of men like Finn Cottrell.

As soon as she was inside Church Cottage, still in her coat, Trudy searched for a piece of paper to write a list. Pulling open one of the drawers of the hall console, she found a great wedge of unopened post springing up to greet her like a jack-in-the-box – all addressed to Finn. It must be junk mail. Finn had always been lazy about recycling, preferring to hide his waste than separate it into the jaunty coloured bins the council provided.

She flipped over an envelope to write on.

Then she froze. This definitely wasn't junk mail. The front made it clear that this was private and confidential and extremely important, despite a three-week-old postmark.

Something compelled her to open it despite knowing Finn would explode if he found out. He guarded his post like a cheetah with its kill, as she had long since discovered to her peril. Squirrelling it away was a classic way of hiding the truth from himself as well as from her.

This afternoon it didn't matter. She was about to leave him. Their marriage was over. She had made up her mind. She would email Johnny with the news, and phone her mother and her closest friends. She would make it irreversible. So what did it matter if she read something that was dated three weeks ago?

When she read the letter the floor seemed to fall away from beneath her.

'Oh shit.' She read and reread, her heart stop-starting randomly in her chest. 'Oh, please no! Oh, Christ. Finn. What have you done?'

That afternoon, Trudy wrote like a demon, ignoring all calls and banning Finn from her study when he returned home.

He had no idea that her life had just turned on its head, spinning like a car in a crash, over and over. He had no idea that their marriage was in the passenger seat and about to be thrown through the shattered windscreen as soon as she'd gained control of the wheel and knew which way was up.

He switched on the television, the volume cranked up deliberately high, and watched back-to-back repeats of *Top Gear* on Bloke TV, complaining loudly that he was hungry.

On the other side of the study door, Trudy's car-crashing life continued to twist, hurtle, collide and smash its way along an unplanned path, decimating everything in her way, including her vows that she would never kiss-and-tell.

She had to plan the end of her marriage. But first, she had to work. She had to get her memoirs written, even if that meant facing her demons head on. It was the only way she could afford to leave Finn. Her guilt wouldn't let her abandon him to a financial crisis, however unconnected her motives from the issue of money. If she was going to be free, she would have to pay for that freedom with the truth.

She would sacrifice Pete for Finn, burn one in the other's image on a huge funeral pyre of emotional purging. She had no idea what she would see when the smoke cleared, but it couldn't be worse than her life now, so she walked willingly into the flame.

It flowed out of her, that first dizzying sensation of falling in love. So like a drug. A first fix.

This was the story her publishers wanted, the chapter they knew they could syndicate all over the world, the first-hand truth behind the damning headlines: how Trudy Dew almost broke up one of the best-loved marriages in show business, forsaking her own dying father for the sake of a man who dropped her like a stone once his press turned bad.

Pete Rafferty. The original wild genius of rock, he was as dangerous, universally recognised and addictive as Marlboro, and just as enduring a brand-name.

Now popularly known as The Rockfather, he was even more legendary than the word-famous band, Mask, with which he had made his mark in the sixties and seventies. All the other band members had died dramatic early deaths – a suicide, a car crash, a drugs overdose and one most famously murdered by a crank stalker – all martyred on the altar of stardom. Not only was he the sole survivor, his marriage to a waif-like sixties icon and rock journalist had famously endured, too. They had raised a family, continued scaling dizzy heights in their individual careers and maintained an extraordinary level of public respect. Together, they had outlived drug addiction, political extremism, kidnapping, death threats and, most dangerous of all, marriage-wrecking temptations of the flesh.

Then Pete Rafferty had met Trudy Dew.

Tears poured down her face as she wrote of her breathless descent into love – her free fall to oblivion. She had lived only for his calls, his voice in her ear, his taste on her lips, his hands on her body. Twice her age and many times more famous, he thought he knew what he was doing. His marriage had withstood his many affairs. But this one was different. This time he fell too. Or so he said.

Obsessive, selfish, damaging, it was a love that in other, sweeter, circumstances might have flourished, but in its imprisoned, secretive context rotted them both to their cores, turned them into the cruellest of liars. At the time there had been no guilt. The passion was too fierce, the blinkered compulsion too driven, and the corruption moving too fast around their boiling bloodstreams. Skin quivered in constant, aroused anticipation, hairs stood up on necks, pulses thrummed like humming bird wings and a heavy electric beat pounded deep in their groins night and day like a war mantra. Their heightened sensations were beyond any narcotic's heavenly effects. Stolen moments felt like years of togetherness. There was no way it could have been sustained.

Hiding such a passionate affair wasn't easy, but Pete had plenty of bolt-holes around the world, and she didn't think to question that he might have used them before in similar circumstances. She was a willing captive in his jet-stream, cut off from reality, living a poisoned fairy tale of love, drugs and rock and roll.

The jet fell straight out of the sky the day they found out that a British tabloid was on to them. It didn't have enough to print, Pete's lawyers told him, but it soon would unless he moved fast.

He told her he loved her, would look after her, would make sure they could be together. He sent her to a friend's ski chalet in Switzerland and flew home to cover the cracks. She never saw him in person again.

Pete Rafferty had a back-up team beyond a manager and a publicist: a band of friends he had known half a lifetime, a wife and children willing to forgive him, a therapist, a drug dealer and a host of 'fuck buddies' to console him when his body craved hers and the master bedroom door remained resolutely locked against him at home.

Trudy had nothing. To her horror, her family couldn't help her.

They were suffering their own grief in which she wasn't ever able to fully participate.

While she had been gallivanting around the world sharing adjoining luxury suites with Pete, hiding away from the paparazzi on yachts and in private villas, letting her career spin away from her and ignoring her family, her father, Kit, had suffered a massive stroke. She was uncontactable. For weeks, while he was in hospital, his life in the balance, her mother and Johnny battled to get word to her.

By the time Trudy found out about her father and made it home, he was in a stable condition but the prognosis was bleak. Much of the damage to his brain caused by the clot was irreversible. He could not walk or talk or feed himself and would regain only limited degrees of these functions at best. He might never communicate with them verbally again. He would certainly need round-the-clock care for the rest of his life.

Her mother insisted on bringing him home, eating up savings and insurance policies, selling equity in their house and relying upon every charity grant and hand-out she could find to care for him away from the system. With a great fortune of her own amassing at the time, Trudy tried to help out, but her mother was fiercely proud, and hurt, needing to punish Trudy's early negligence. Years later, she had told Trudy that it was like living with a ghost, or keeping up the longest wake in history. To her, Kit had died already, had left her the evening that all expression was wiped from his lovely, laugh-lined face by such a massive stroke. But the vigil had lasted years, and Trudy had been excluded by her own actions.

Waking from the dream, coughing out the poisoned slice of apple and realising that a hundred years have passed, the heroic father and monarch is dead, the seven dwarves have seven little gravestones and that while you might look and act just the same, nobody knows you any more; Trudy's life was *Snow White* in tatters, Pete gone and now her father gone too.

Trudy didn't want to sing sad songs any more. The words hurt too much.

But all her songs were sad. It was what she was famous for.

She found she couldn't sing in public at all. Her nerves became crippling. Her record label hired psychotherapists, hypnotherapists and even sports therapists. None could help. Trudy hated herself too much. The public, who still loved her, despite the odds, were at such a complete extreme from her own feelings that she couldn't face them. How dare they love her? She was base and unworthy. She dropped weight like a stone, cut off her hair to an urchin crop and hid behind dark glasses, androgynous and antisocial. It was deemed the new look and thousands followed suit.

She stopped being able to write. Her record label kept on producing the work that she had written previously, but there was no new material. Her next album was a mixture of second rate, overproduced tracks jumbled in with a handful of new songs that were far too personal and angry to be commercial. It struggled to match previous sales.

Yet the public stayed loyal. They wrote, they cheered, they requested 'I Hate Loving You' more than any other ballad in a national radio poll. Her royalties rolled in. She was rich. She lived in a beautiful house in Primrose Hill, she knew film stars and models and musicians. She was beautiful. She wasn't allowed to complain.

When the gossip about her affair with the nation's favourite rock hero husband started to leak out on the internet, she wasn't quite so popular. She became a dinner party joke for those in the know, with word spreading in secret circles, in media clubs and on stand-up stages, then more publicly on panel shows, but nowhere that Pete's lawyers could get at the source and sue it. Her name became synonymous with the dirtiest of backstage passes, wannabe marriage-wrecking and pop diva depravity.

Then Pete Rafferty released a song that guaranteed his exoneration and her condemnation. It was a song of forever love, love beyond the grave, love everlasting – the ultimate love sworn on oath at a marriage. It reinvented his flagging career. Every word cut into Trudy's veins when she listened. Because he had written the song for her when they were together; he'd sung it to her. Now it was a public declaration of his fidelity to his wife. It broke her record for topping the charts. On the video there were tears in his eyes when he sang it.

Trudy wrote to him, even though she knew she shouldn't. She wrote that she was dying without him, that she had to know if he was feeling the same way too. Was the song a secret message?

The letter was never acknowledged, but in a much publicised and rare television interview with Melvyn Bragg that charted his long career, his many addictions, groupies, arrests, obsessive fans and extraordinarily resilient marriage, Pete discussed the recent record and its phenomenal success and said that the cranky fans hadn't gone away.

'At least one girl wrote to me that she thought there was a secret message in the song. It's not that fucking secret. I love my fucking wife. I'll shout it on stage every night when I'm touring. What's secret about that?'

Trudy watched the interview over and over again, punishing herself, remembering his body against hers and that voice in her ear telling her he loved her. She couldn't understand what she had done wrong.

The rejection was spreading its toxin. Her record label's loyalty got shakier. They had a lot of new signings. She wasn't such a safe bet. Times were tough. Budgets had to be spread more thinly.

She started drinking very heavily. She cut lines in her arms. She avoided going out, turned down all invitations, ordered her booze online. When a couple of paparazzi, sniffing a breakdown, started hanging around outside her house, she rang round what few friends she had left and, helped out by their contacts, hired a cottage buried away on an estate in the Cotswolds for the summer.

All the time she was still blinking awake, seeing life for what it really was. If she had woken up from a hundred year slumber then where was the prince whose kiss had broken the curse?

At that moment, along came Finn Cottrell.

She wrote of their love affair now with the dispassionate hindsight of the truly awake.

> I had no idea I was still dreaming my way through life right the way up the aisle and beyond,

she typed furiously, listening as Finn stomped upstairs to get ready for bed, heading into the bathroom for a long pee accompanied by a timpani of farts and then thumping straight to the adjoining bedroom without cleaning his teeth.

> I wish that I were still dreaming now, because admitting that I have woken up at the end of my marriage is too painful a truth to open the curtains to. The curtains fell on my career because I was too afraid to walk on stage and sing it like it really was – the pain that kisses the pleasure, the hurt that embraces the happiness, the way that love beginning fills our hearts but love dying rips our hearts out with twice the force. I feel I can sing that at the top of my voice now, because with all the pleasure and pain and happiness and hurt comes hope. Real hope. Freedom is hope. And I am almost free.

She could hear Finn snoring overhead, sonorous and rhythmic as a clock. Weeping too much to see, she typed,

My marriage is over. At last there is hope.

Not caring if he read her words, Trudy collected her coat and let herself out into the starriest night that had visited the valley in months, intent on walking out on her marriage forever, so caught up in her own legend that she didn't see how ludicrous it was to wander off with no cash, no luggage, no plans – and wearing slippers.

She made it as far as the end of the drive before smacking herself hard on the forehead a couple of times and turning back.

This needed better planning. Making the decision was easy. Doing the deed would be harder. She couldn't leave the horses, or dogs, and certainly not that cat. Finn hated the cat. Plus it was her house. She had paid for it. He had an apartment at his parents' house. He could move there. Her mind was racing with practicalities.

Back in her study, she wrote her ideas and solutions as bullet points on the computer, typing so quickly and determinedly that the letter T on her computer keyboard popped out and landed on her lap, forcing her to stop, breathe and think.

The Memoirs file was still open in her task bar, like a ghost looking down over her. She closed her eyes in horror as the tidal wave of her own hyperbole retreated and reality bit.

She could no more afford to leave Finn than she could afford a new keyboard right now. She hadn't finished the book. She'd barely written sixty thousand words out of a contracted hundred, and she had got no further than 'Sex, Drugs and Rock and Roll' on her publisher's wish list. She hadn't even touched 'Marriage and Happy Ever After'. And, while she knew exactly what was about to happen to one, she had no idea if the other even existed.

Not for the first time that day, she found her mind turning to Flipper and then quickly turning away. She had already dented his car and his pride. That was enough.

This was her solo swansong.

Wearily reaching for her mouse, she clicked on the Memoirs file and then started to type, trying to use words that didn't contain the letter T.

25

Trudy had never been much good at maths, but she did know that owing more money than the value of one's joint assets was a very bad thing. Finn had, it seemed, borrowed against everything and anything: secured loans, unsecured loans, credit cards all taken to their limits, the interest-only mortgage extended to its maximum and – worst of all – huge loans from friends and family. As well as a stack of legal notices warning of forthcoming hearings, there were already court judgments, magistrate's rulings and warrants of execution outstanding; private debt agencies were involved and time was running out fast. Trudy had no idea where to start tackling it.

Her only reaction, perhaps rather deranged, was to keep working as fast as she could by writing night and day, determined to finish her book in a week.

Having now written about her love affair with Pete, a catharsis had taken place, as good as a lengthy spell in therapy. It was as though the scales had fallen from her eyes and she could look back with clarity after years of blindness. She had thought that first great love insurmountable, and yet it seemed entirely physical, short-lived and one-sided now that she looked back on it.

She found she could write more dispassionately about her marriage, although the guilt of ending it still clawed her body like an angry monitor lizard. She tried to be even-handed and honest, blaming her own foolishness and the dreadful, chalk-and-cheese mismatch between herself and Finn for its demise. She would not cast Finn as a demon or humiliate him publicly; that wouldn't be fair.

She doubted he would ever appreciate the irony that this one, last, very public confession might earn enough money to stall the inevitable implosion when his financial house of cards fell down. He would probably never forgive her for bursting the mythical happy bubble of their derailed marriage, the Finn and Trudy Show, days before taking that show off the road.

She wrote without looking at the clock or pausing for food, drink or rest. She wrote of those early 'Prince Charming' days when she'd believed that Finn had awoken her from an enchanted bad-fairy sleep. Inevitably seeing the funny side, because that was her coping mechanism, she recounted tales of rogue builders, gassy horses, her own manic nesting, her eccentrically charming in-laws and Finn's romantic but impractical presents.

It wasn't all bad, she remembered with a well of sentimental regret. It just rotted away from the inside out.

How a decade had crept past baffled Trudy. She felt like J. Alfred Prufrock, except that where he measured out his life in coffee spoons, she was measuring hers in fingers of Smirnoff. As she filled herself with forty per cent proof, the ambition drained out of her.

She'd hardly registered when her record label dropped her; her agent softened the blow so much with talk of taking a creative sabbatical and coming fresh to the market with new material that she was happy to go along with it. The relief at not having to create to order as she once had was colossal. By that point, her self-loathing had become an endless ennui that barely enabled her to work. She filled her days with idle chatter on dog walks, endless internet surfing and emailing, long lonely rides and the self-flagellating torture of knowing that she was wasting time.

She and Finn lurched from house to house and cash crisis to cash crisis, always just managing to keep their heads above water. She left everything financial to him; it was easier to go with the flow. Most of the time she succeeded in putting it out of her head, a sleepwalking child imagining dancing through poppy meadows as it wanders along the central reservation of the M25.

As her career faltered further, Trudy preferred drinking to thinking, and took to it with greater alacrity. Work projects came and went, some fulfilled, others abandoned, but there were enough vestiges of talent to keep the wolf from the door. Out of the public eye and largely forgotten, she did find emoting easier and if she was writing for someone else, the songs sometimes burst out of her like small creatures desperate for fresh air. Powerful, hypnotic, melodies with lyrics that cut through everyday clichés and burned into the head of the listener like a brand. Several bands and singers flew up the charts with her songs to carry them – the winner of a national television talent competition went straight to number one singing her song; cover versions of her old songs were starting to appear.

The money came in fits and starts, although it never lasted long and she dreaded her tax bills which always seemed to be for ten times as much as she expected. When things got really bad, like the three months they had lived off a five-figure overdraft, hiding from creditors, Finn joked about moving to Ireland for the tax breaks and the hunting 'like a proper musician', but Trudy failed to see the funny side. Pete Rafferty lived in a castle in Ireland, now widowed, having lost his sixties icon wife in a much-publicised car crash not long after Trudy married. She half expected to hear from him again as the years rolled by, but he remained as remote as another lifetime. Then the papers were full of his new romance with a leggy model who looked just like a younger version of his late wife. They married in another Irish castle amid much jet-set action and secrecy. Within a year, the new young wife was expecting twins. Pete was quoted as saying that he was the proudest man in the world and felt reborn.

A little more of Trudy died inside.

By then she was raising the subject of children more and more often, usually when drunk. Finn sourly pointed out that they would have to start having sex again first – and that she'd have to sober up. But sobering up meant facing the truth about her botched life, and she couldn't handle that. Being very drunk was the only way that she could face sex with him.

Crazed with frustration, she started making herself sexually available again occasionally, but only when she was ovulating. It didn't work. Month after month the results of the tests were negative. She started to memorise the faces of the check out staff in Tescos so that she could rotate them, knowing her bulk purchases of pregnancy tests and vodka would be a talking point. She even rotated her supermarkets, adding in off-licences and chemists to cover her tracks, paying with cash and throwing out receipts.

But she couldn't fool herself into having a baby. The monthly rejection of a big blue negative sign in the little window and then the big red stain that inevitably followed was more damning than any review or record failing to chart.

Oh what a tangled World Wide Web we weave when first we practise to deceive, she thought as she started a new page, ready to chart the final chapter of her marriage.

The Internet was her ally. She whiled away comforting, nocturnal hours online in search of distraction and daydreams, often while Finn was similarly occupied, in his case involving long odds, the spin of a dice or the turn of a card. Sitting at computers at opposite ends of the house, they held long, lonely virtual vigils through the death throes of married life.

Flipper had moved back permanently to the family fold the previous summer. He had grown up from boy to man, but had brought his adoration back to the family table for laughter and flirtation and more fantasies. He had seen her trapped in her gilded cage for ten years – not quite a hundred years of sleep, but long enough to register that she was wishing her life away.

The Sleeping Beauty was still in her glass casket, delaying the inevitable moment when she must wake up. But now the prince had finally administered the kiss of life.

She knew that she had to speak to Finn. She knew that she had to be clear-headed to do it. Yet on she wrote until her wrists ached, her fingers went numb, T jumped into her lap hourly and her keyboard space bar seized up and needed the crumbs and coffee spills cleaning out from beneath it. Letting her marriage decompose around her for a few more hours, the financial crisis rage on and the outside world go unheeded, she wrote down the last few weeks of her life so far, culminating in the point where she had hurried to the woods to find love, and instead lost Mutt.

That's where the book ended.

In just under a week, hundreds of pages had emerged from her mind, now printed and stacked on her desk, backed up and zip-filed on her computer ready for virtual transit.

She stared at her final words for a long time, dissatisfied and confused, the catharsis of confession having failed her. If it wasn't so saddening and maddening, it would be funny.

Why had she mentioned Flipper's lost mongrel in those closing paragraphs? It was a lousy ending to her book, and she knew the publishers would hate it, the ultimate shaggy dog story. They had assumed that hers was a happy ending – it was what little currency she traded off these days, after all.

Trying not to think about the huge vodka Coke she was craving, she called up her word processor hurriedly.

I no longer love my husband,

she typed, battling tears so that she could see her words.

I'm not sure I ever did love him properly, for what and who he is, simply the safe haven he represented. In the same way, I don't think he loved me as much as my lifestyle, the packaged Trudy Dew product complete with wealth, fame and pretty clothes. He loves designer packaging. He once bought a three-thousand-pound mobile phone just because he liked the way the buttons were laid out. He never used it; he said his fingers were too big. He could never push my buttons either. Poor Finn, with his endless gadgets and toys, like Mr Toad – and I have certainly become insufferably Ratty to him. He deserves to be loved. We all do. Now I am in love again,

she wrote on without thinking,

and I am truly terrified. Love has only ever hurt me, but now I have learned the bitter lesson that not loving enough can be almost equally hurtful. When I wrote "I Hate Loving You" I was just eighteen years old and I had no idea what it really meant – but perhaps it was a premonition. I grew to find love a terrifying place and I hid from it at all costs.

Yet sometimes there is nowhere to hide – especially when love is pursued by one of the best huntsmen around . . .

She stared at the screen, eyes dry now, as she grew emboldened by her confession.

So I am in love,

she typed again, liking the way it looked.

I love a man with all my heart, just as he has loved me with unswerving passion and belief for many years. It may never work out between us – the odds are stacked firmly against it – but knowing that I love him has shaken my foundations so deeply that my safe house is falling down and I can no longer hide here.

By the time you read this, I will be well on my way to freedom. I want to be strong again, to sort out this mess, to find him in clear open space when I have hope and light in my heart, not this black turmoil. I want to be able to sing again, to write music again and enjoy living life. I used to think 'finding yourself' was the oldest joke in the book, but now I get it. There is no map through life; we navigate by our mistakes. I will never stop making those, but I do think it's about time to stop blaming others and to start living again.

She sat back and smiled, lacing her fingers together to loosen them. Much more positive. So what if she sounded like Gerry Halliwell? The public would lap it up.

I LOVE FLIPPER she typed with one finger, then highlighted it, pressed Control C, scrolled down a line and pressed Control V until it covered pages and pages of manuscript. She'd delete it later, but right now, with Finn in the house, it was the closest she could get to shouting to the rooftops.

At the opposite end of the house, Finn had given up trying to monitor Trudy's obsessive activities in her study. He had taken a brief snoop at the early pages of her memoir several weeks ago, but hadn't been able to get more than a few paragraphs into the spurious and over-romanticised schmaltz she had written about her childhood. Her literary style was shocking, even more melodramatic and flowery than her songs, but Trudy was so behind on all her work projects that he could only be grateful *something* was getting done. The sooner she finished it, the sooner they would get some much-needed money.

Instead, he checked a few property websites, convincing himself it was market research for the estate agency arm of the company, although he was largely looking out of Cottrells' geographic area. Perhaps they should look into widening their reach, or better still developing a specialist service to cater for the lucrative second-home market? He'd talk to Piers.

Trudy had been the one to trigger Finn's property website hobby, although his interest had recently taken on a life of its own; he loved nothing more than to hunt for hidden jewels. Finding new projects had always been one of his favourite quests.

Now he'd tracked down a very pretty little granite and cob cottage with exposed beams, inglenook fires, tiny wooden casement windows and a hedged garden leading to a meadow path, all straight out of *Mrs Tiggywinkle*. Even the name was too Cornish cute to be true: Tregawney. He was sure he could charge finder's commission.

Using his mouse wheel to scroll through the open pages on his laptop, he returned to his messages and started typing out a reply to one. It was only when he had almost finished that he spotted a file attachment to the original he hadn't previously noticed. He clicked on it and a picture popped up.

'Blimey!'

Finn studied it with the same objective fascination he felt when valuing rare porcelain.

'There's a piece of skirting board missing there,' he muttered before going carefully back to his reply message and starting to rewrite it, gratefully distracted from financial or Trudy worries.

Piers had advised him that men were better at keeping these things at trouser level, and Finn's trouser level had suddenly experienced a long-awaited interest rise.

26

Rory wasn't really into blindfolding and smacking, but he was besotted enough with Jemima to give them a whirl, and game enough sexually to enter into his new lover's fantasy. Unfortunately, he was not a great actor and his jokey inability to take bondage seriously was frustrating Jemima.

'You're supposed to be chastising me,' she grumbled as he guffawed his way through some low level buttock horsewhipping, Jemima lying over his knee in stockings and suspenders. 'Not shouting, "Come on boy, hup, hup, gallop on."'

'Sorry.' Rory ran the crop along her shapely arse, letting the thong trace the fist-sized hollow beneath her buttocks.

'Mmm, that's better.' She wriggled. 'Now tie me to the bed and tell me off for being such a naughty girl.'

Rory wasn't in the mood for role play. It had been a punishing day, with no help on the yard, several horses lame, and ten lessons to teach. He missed Faith's energy and efficiency around the place. His back and shoulders ached, his throat was hoarse from shouting across the arena and he was dying for a massage from dear, buxom Justine – or at least a hot bath. But Jemima had already taken all the hot water, and she wanted to play.

After years of what she called 'domestic drudgery', Jemima was loving being a scarlet woman and saw no reason to help him out professionally or domestically just so long as she made herself sexually available. Conveniently forgetting that she had relied upon the services of nannies, grooms and housekeepers all of her married life, she complained that Piers had treated her like a plantation owner treated a slave, that he had no time for his own children, that her attempts at building an independent career for herself had been greeted with derision – and that he didn't understand what made her tick sexually.

Nor, regrettably, did Rory.

Jemima, like many a battleaxe, adored to be dominated in bed.

She longed to be turned over, tied to the bedpost, blindfolded and rammed from behind by a big, strong man who wanted to teach her a lesson. She thrilled to the idea of accessories like whips, chains, buckles and gags. She also loved to be girlish and coy, so lace frillies, feather boas and silk scarves featured large alongside smutty talk and teacher's orders. Spelling this out rather defeated the object – she preferred to give out little squeaks of submissive pleasure.

Rory, like many easygoing loafers, liked to make love slowly and with plenty of laughter. The only accessories he favoured were occasional drink stops, a food fight with something yummy like strawberries and cream, a break for *The Archers* and a small spot on the bed where Twitch the Jack Russell could lie in a purely observational role.

He had, of course, entertained the odd fantasy in the past, though nothing too wild or original: two women was a favourite, especially identical twins; nurses were popular after so many riding injuries had landed him in A&E; exes always loomed large in his dreams, along with fantasy figures Anke Olensen-Brakespear and Catherine Deneuve – and, ironically, he had always got very hot under the collar at the thought of being ravaged himself, tied up and taken advantage of by a sexy dominatrix.

Doing the dominating was not his style.

But Jemima did have an extraordinary effect on him that lifted his game and took him to previously unexplored places. That she had sacrificed the safety of her family life for him did wonders for his ego; doubly so when she had brought her best horses to his yard, even if he did have to muck them out every day. To play-act a little in the bedroom was the least he could do. His flagpole was ready to raise the ensign in her honour.

Stifling a yawn, he reached for his white hunting stock and started to wind it around her wrists.

'You are a bad, *bad* girl,' he chided. 'Getting us both into trouble like this. I think I am going to have to punish you . . .'

'How?' she whispered in rapture.

'I will have to spank you,' he said in his best Professor Severus Snape voice.

On cue, Jemima's mobile chimed on the bedside table with a message waiting.

'Bugger – it might be urgent,' she muttered, her hands still tied to the brass bedhead. 'Who is it from?'

Rory checked her In Box. 'Liv Wilson. *"How r u? It seemed ages since—"'*

'Oh, ignore it,' she interrupted briskly. 'Just one of the charity mob. Now, spank me sideways, big boy.'

Rory felt his flagpole drop a little. Mustering enthusiasm, and trying to ignore the fact it was almost seven o'clock, he raised his hand high.

'Little minxes get red botties!'

'Oh, yes, yes!'

Outside, her bike propped against the old chestnut tree, Faith cocked her head as she watched a leg waving around in one of the upstairs windows. From this angle, it was hard to tell if it was male or female, but the sound effects were more squeak than growl.

Trying to remain clinical in her observation, she squinted up through the lowering sun and refused to let her splitting heart get in the way of her hatred of Jemima Cottrell. That hatred had nothing to do with the woman having squeaky, early-evening sex with Rory, she told herself. Nothing to do with Faith being thrown off the yard, losing her trainer and friend, and having to endure pep-talks from her mother about teenage crushes. Her hatred was simple.

Jemima Cottrell was going to break Rory's heart. And that organ was so patched up, Faith wasn't sure it would take another massacre.

A loud snort made her jump out of her skin. She hadn't heard the horse approaching along the thick grass stripe that divided the two gravelly tyre tracks of the bridleway.

It was Flipper Cottrell riding his sister's big bay gelding, Popeye. Faith, who had gone drag hunting with the twins last season and thought they rode like lunatics, shot him a disapproving look from under her baseball cap, expecting him to ride past without acknowledging her, even though he had seen her many times at Rory's yard. The Cottrells were a famously arrogant mob.

But he pulled up and smiled. 'Hi – Fay, isn't it?'

'Faith.' She tried not to blush but failed miserably. He was, despite his bad manners and sullen attitude, impossibly crush-making.

'Rory around?'

'Um – bit busy I think.'

There was a delighted shriek from the open bedroom window and several legs started flailing around beyond the sill.

Flipper looked up. At least one of the legs was wearing a stocking.

'I see.' He remained deadpan. 'Shame. First time I've ridden out since—' He pulled a face. 'First time out in a while. Thought I'd scrounge a drink.'

Faith, who had heard about Flipper's horse dying of colic earlier in the year, didn't know what to say. It was obvious that he needed to talk, and his friend was servicing his sister-in-law. Faith felt sorry for him. She wanted to offer him a measure of the tack room Scotch in a chipped mug, but didn't dare venture on to the yard even with Rory distracted.

'Christ, I need a drink.' He was still staring out across the valley.

'There's a hitching post outside the New Inn,' she pointed out. The village pub – barely a couple of hundred yards across the little green that was known as the Prattle – was famously horsey.

'Yes, good point.' He tightened a rein as Popeye started to crab, eager to move on. 'Care to join me?'

'Me?' she said stupidly. Mousy, teenage Faith with her shapeless body and frumpy hair?

'Yes – you.'

'Thanks.' She grabbed her bike before he had chance to change his mind.

Flipper had no idea why he'd asked her along. He supposed he needed the company; Nell was away, Rory was shagging and his greatest confidante was strictly off limits. Faith seemed a good sort – not really a sister substitute, but close to Rory and eager to please.

As she pedalled alongside, heart racing, Faith realised that this was the first time that she had ever been invited out for a drink by a man – and what a man! She was out with Flipper Cottrell, one of the best looking young studs in the county with a string of broken hearts to his name and a heroic reputation for saving horses' lives.

It didn't matter that he had asked her along much as one would pick up a stray dog found on the side of the road. She *was* his date. And, as Faith walked into the bar of the New Inn with what she imagined were all eyes on her and Flipper, that felt better than anything.

She just hoped word of it got back to Rory.

Flipper chose a very dark corner where they both had their backs to the room. Not knowing what to ask for – she was technically underage for alcohol and didn't even like it much, but wanted to appear cool and grown up – Faith had said to get her anything. He returned with a vodka and Coke. He had a pint.

Faith savoured the moment.

An awkward silence swirled around them like fog.

He drank his pint like a parched Lawrence of Arabia downing lemonade in the British Officers' Club.

Faith did likewise with her vodka Coke.

Saying nothing he went to get two more.

Faith turned to watch him over her shoulder. He was spectacularly handsome. More heavily built than Rory, a good six inches taller and much longer in the leg, he was more of a rugby forward to Rory's fullback, but physically divine for all the difference, his hair as peaty and cavalry neat as Rory's was sandy and wild, his eyes as green and turbulent as Rory's were speckled grey and languid, his mouth as terse and curled as Rory's was wide and smiling.

He was also sporting a fading black eye and a bruised nose, both yellowing with age. At least that gave her an opening gambit.

'Do you play rugby, then?' she asked when he returned with the drinks.

'Not any more.'

Faith slumped into silence once again before inspiration struck. 'Was it a horse? That broke your nose, I mean'

He shook his head. 'I crashed my car a couple of weeks ago.'

'How awful.' Faith swigged some more vodka Coke. 'Rory smashed his car once, d'you remember? He drove it through a hedge and ended upside down in a field of sheep. That was just before he lost his licence.'

He stared into the golden depths of his drink. 'Those were the days – we used to joke that Rory didn't need to fill his car with petrol, it ran off alcohol fumes.'

The vodka had gone straight to Faith's head. She started to babble.

'Rory only drinks because he's lonely,' she explained. 'He has this amazing family, but they don't support him enough – Diana is hardly ever around, and his mother spends all her time making whoopee with my grandfather. He has friends, but he needs an old-fashioned team at the kitchen table. He does such an amazing job, looking after all those horses, teaching people, keeping that place going and competing with no back up and no sponsorship.

'He has so much talent – if it were only recognised, he'd be in the national three day event team. But he always has to sell horses before they make it right to the top, and he can't afford the entry fees and diesel to the big competitions anyway.'

Looking up through his lashes at her tense, pinched little face, Flipper realised that Faith Brakespear was very much in love with Rory. As truly in love as only a teenager can be, with a never-ending supply of energy and hope and compassion.

'My mother says that there isn't a better rider across country in the Cotswolds than Rory, but she's wrong. There isn't a better rider in the whole of the bloody country. He just needs a decent horse. Whitey's great, but he's too old – he's already had a career between flags. Jemima Cottrell has the perfect horse, but she only uses it as blackmail to get Rory to – to—' she had another swig of her drink while Flipper waited patiently '—to roger her,' she finished theatrically. 'She's *disgusting*. Oh!' She suddenly remembered that Jemima was married to Flipper's brother.

'It's OK.' He smiled for the first time, showing his broken tooth. 'I know that's where she's shacked up.'

She nodded, puce with shame.

'But Piers doesn't, so don't spread it about.'

'Of course not,' she promised in a stage whisper. Flipper was absolutely lovely and not at all stand-offish. 'I'm so sorry your horse died,' she blurted out without thinking.

He looked away. But he seemed to understand where she was coming from and nodded in acknowledgement.

'Is that why you always look so sad?'

'No. That's a lot more complicated.'

'Try me,' Faith offered, fighting hiccups.

But having badly needed to talk, Flipper now found he didn't.

'Rory is a very lucky man,' he told her seriously. 'And I hope that one day he realises that fact. Stay true to your dreams and to him, but don't waste all your youth and beauty on him, huh?'

Faith scoffed, redder than ever and far from beautiful.

'I wish somebody loved me as much as you love him,' he said honestly.

'I could try,' she offered, drunken tears of compassion springing to her eyes. How perfect loving Flipper would be if only her heart was free.

He shook his head. 'It doesn't work like that. You love Rory for good. I love somebody the same way.'

'Is she like Rory?'

'A lot prettier, but she certainly drinks too much'

'And she doesn't love you?'

He thought about this for a long time. 'She's got somebody keeping her love prisoner.'

This was possibly the most romantic thing that Faith had ever heard. Her emotions, already heightened, started to bubble over.

'Why don't you busht her out of jail!' she cried, slurring slightly.

He ran a tongue across his broken tooth and barked with laughter, as sexy as a stag calling from a hilltop.

'I've been trying to pick the lock for years. Maybe it's time to use dynamite?'

'Yes!' Faith raised her empty glass.

'Fuck it, let's get drunk.' He headed to the bar.

Already very drunk, and seeing three or four of him dancing around the bar, Faith settled back in her chair and decided that busting love out of jail was the most heroic thing a man could do.

This avowal was revised an hour later when Flipper, realising that she was far too drunk to get home alone, chained her mountain bike to the hitching post and put her up on the saddle of his sister's horse, climbing swiftly up behind her to hold her on with his arms and muscular thighs as he took the reins. Together, they rode into the reddest of summer sunsets dropping behind the far ridge of the valley.

Faith sang dreamily all the way to Oddlode, sobering up enough by the time that they clattered along the road past the railway station that she at least was singing in tune and remembering most of the words to 'I Hate Loving You'. She'd been singing it to the tune of 'Ave Maria' earlier.

Thankfully Anke was at a meeting of the Oddlode Literary Circle discussing *Jane Eyre*, and husband Graham was away on business. The only light came from a high window where Faith's younger half-brother Chad was ensconced in his room playing on his Xbox.

Flipper jumped off and lowered her gently to the gravel drive. Then he kissed her. He was far too drunk to worry about the consequences of his actions. He was even gratified by the enthusiasm with which she kissed him back, by her little grunts and groans, by her cautious then reckless tongue in his mouth and even by the endearing way that she reached up and grabbed his ears to steady herself.

After it all got too messy and squiffy for passion, they both ended up giggling like drains.

'I've had the most unexpectedly enjoyable night,' he said. 'Thank you.'

'Me too,' she replied, pitching sideways into a rose bed for a few steps before making it to the door and falling inside with a happy wave.

It was only as he rode home that Flipper cursed himself for his stupidity – snogging a drunken teenager who, however adorable, had a soul as dark and faithful as his own. It would be a huge inconvenience if she transferred her affections from Rory. He'd slashed enough hearts recently as it was, not least his own.

Having exchanged numbers with her earlier, he now texted her with an apology, still so drunk that thanks to the still unfamiliar phone and its predictive text, when he tried to type 'Hope you're still awake. Was a complete pissed ass, I fear. Kiss big mistake. My gaff. Forget it ever happened! R' it actually came out as 'Gore you're still cycle. Was a complete ripped ass, I dear. Lips big mistake. My iced. Forget it ever happened! R' But he hoped he'd made his point without hurting her feelings.

He rode along the track behind the church, climbing into the field above the village that looked over Church Cottage.

It was almost completely dark now, the yews turned into huge black cliffs of shadows. The light in Trudy's study was on, the blind lowered.

Every cell in his body seemed to stretch itself towards that light, yearning to spur the horse into a gallop and clear every black hedge that separated them.

But Finn's black Range Rover was parked menacingly in the drive. The shark fin, Flipper decided. Beyond it in the paddock, the dark outline of Trudy's mare Tara was framed between two trees gazing across to where she sensed the nocturnal horse and rider; and behind her, totally oblivious, Arty's white coat gleamed in the faint light as she dozed standing up, her face buried in her companion's tail. He remembered Finn, maddened with rage, threatening to inflict some awful deed upon them if Flipper ever went back there, although he doubted his brother would go so far. That was crazy. And anyway, Trudy would blame Finn if her horses got hurt, not Flipper.

Yet he didn't turn back. Something about his brother unnerved him. He could be a very dangerous adversary.

He didn't want to embarrass Trudy again, risk sending her scuttling yet further into her high, impenetrable Rapunzel's tower.

Bust her out of jail, Faith had said.

He started to smile to himself, rolling in his saddle like a cowboy.

'Bust her out of jail!' he whooped, kicking Popeye in the ribs.

Unlike his late sister, Olive, who was as biddable and fleet as a top polo pony, Popeye was a cantankerous soul who had only just come back into work, was sporting a fat belly and a bad temper, and didn't like men. With one almighty effort, he flicked up his back end, propelled Flipper over his head and trotted away to munch on some lush grass nearby.

Staring up at the stars, Flipper guessed he'd had that coming.

The sickle sliver of a new moon was directly overhead.

'I wish for dynamite,' he told the sky. 'Lots and lots of dynamite.'

Liv was frustrated to find both Jemima and now Trudy incommunicado – added to which, Giles had gone on his annual sabbatical to the south of France with a large tent and several of his children.

With her own children home from school for the summer holidays, no yummy mummies with whom to gossip at the gates, nobody with whom to share hacks and shopping trips, she was wretched with boredom. And she was quite certain that both Jemima and Trudy were enjoying clandestine trysts while she was trying to prise her children out from in front of the television, or fight them for some quiet time on the computer to check her emails in private.

She adored spending time with Lily and Jasper, but they resolutely didn't want to bake flapjacks, go for country walks or make handicrafts, and there was only so much Xbox, Sponge Bob Squarepants and pirate ship battles she could take before craving adult company.

Even a visit from the in-laws, normally dreaded, was greeted with great ceremony and a home-baked cake. They complained that the nuts would wreck their dentures, insisted that supper be at teatime, demanded that the light be left on the landing all night and were up and dressed by six thirty each morning wanting to know what the agenda was – but Liv still embraced their stay with delight.

It meant, for one, that she could escape.

Her first port of call was Mark and Spencer's antique shop in Morrell on the Moor. Despite Trudy's lack of interest, Liv was agog to know what the clue from the boot fair led to – and *who* it might ultimately lead to. She felt as though she were trapped in an inverted version of *Cyrano de Bergerac*, pretending to be Trudy as she gathered the treasure and chased the clue-master, all the time falling for the mind of the secret admirer who loved her friend. The fact that she also lusted after the man who was married to her friend made her even more determined to assuage her guilt with a distracting bit of detective work.

The boys, knowing that Liv was a horsewoman, were eager to show off about their latest equestrian feats as tutored by Anke and, latterly, Rory Midwinter.

'Such a lovely man,' Mark enthused. 'An absolute poppet – quite the most patient teacher and a gift to horsemanship. Anke can be a terrible cross-patch.'

'That harridan he's shacked up with at the moment is a pain,' Spencer added. 'Always shouting from the sidelines as though she knows what she's talking about.'

'She *has* ridden around Badminton,' Liv pointed out.

'So, she should stick to shuttlecocks,' Mark bitched. 'Rory's lovely cock is wasted on her.'

'You don't know it's lovely,' Spencer said jealously.

'Bound to be. Matches the rest of him.'

'Not after all that time in the saddle. Your scrotum was like a raw hamburger after that first lesson.'

'Shut up,' he snapped, turning to beam at Liv in embarrassment. 'Tell me, darling, what can we do for you?'

They had just fulfilled her desire for gossip about Jemima and her young beau, but she remembered to ask about Fedor Ruckert.

'Ooooh, I wish we had something of his,' Mark clapped his hands in appreciation of the name. 'But, alas, never beneath this hallowed roof.'

'Who is he?'

'He was one of Fabergé's finest craftsmen,' Spencer told her reverently.

'Did he ever make spoons?'

'Almost certainly.'

'But you don't have anything of that ilk in stock?'

'Try Christie's or Sotheby's,' Mark suggested waspishly. 'And warn your bank manager.'

On her way out, Liv paused to admire an ornate cabinet as big as a car, inlaid with ivory and pearl.

'Beautiful, isn't she?' Spencer glided across to give the piece a stroke. 'Came in yesterday on behalf of a client. Quite exquisite workmanship. You obviously have *great* taste.'

'Imagine it filled with Fabergé,' Mark mused from behind his desk.

Liv could visualise the chest in her minimalist, slate-floored reception hall. Martin would hate it, which was another incentive.

But the price tag quoted a figure that would buy her another horse and a trailer to ferry it around in.

'I'll talk to my husband about it,' she promised. 'He's overseas.' As she reached for the door, she silently added, So I'm about to play with somebody else's husband. She was appalled at herself, but too excited to change her mind. She was after all being very Cotswold Wife – very Trudy. It felt marvellous.

Outside, it was a bright, blustery day, the hanging baskets creaking as they rocked on their chains overhead trailing geraniums, honesty and ivy. Liv took a deep breath of hot, summery air and felt a quiver of happiness. She was thoroughly enjoying adopting this little bit of Trudy's life, chasing her clues and living on her wits. Trudy might blow hot and cold as a friend, but Liv could cope with that; in fact it made her feel better about what she was doing now. Trudy had changed Liv; seeing too much of her was intimidating. What Trudy had done was to open Liv's eyes to new opportunities and make anything seem possible. And by pretending to be Trudy – albeit in a watered down way – those possibilities became realities.

She glanced at her watch. Perfect timing and alibi established. Donning her dark glasses as she turned the corner into the market square, she slipped into the courtyard behind the Corn Exchange, past the upmarket gift shops and the florist, and into the discreet back entrance to the Royalist Hotel.

'Welcome, Mrs Tregawney,' the receptionist greeted her when she introduced herself, 'Mr Tregawney is already in your room – you'll find it on the first floor, up the stairs and to the left. Have you any baggage?'

'Only emotional.' Liv smiled naughtily, feeling more like Trudy than ever.

By contrast, Trudy wasn't feeling herself at all. She had been sober for three days, had run out of cigarettes and not bothered to go out to buy more and she hadn't eaten a thing all day, not even chocolate. She had just printed out and read through everything that she had written, covered it all in red ink marks and was now typing up her corrections at double pace. She had emailed her agent and publisher to warn them to expect the delivery by the end of the week, adding a note to her agent to get the money through as fast as she could.

Two strange men had turned up on the doorstep earlier. Trudy had hidden, unable to face a distraction. They had hung around for ages, then spent a long time examining her battered old sports car before finally admitting defeat, shoving something through the letter box and going away.

She picked up the card. They were bailiffs. They had a court order to repossess goods to the value of several tens of thousand of pounds, including Finn's Range Rover. They would be back tomorrow.

She had no idea where Finn was. She hadn't seen him in hours; or was it days? She was losing sense of time. She wasn't even sure whether their paths had crossed the previous evening or that morning.

She stuck the card to the fridge door, alongside her old GFFA.

'I'm not fit for adultery,' she sighed. 'I never have been.'

In the New Forest, Pheely was getting fitter all the time. The clothes that she had worn on the day of the garden concert fell off her now. Not that she needed to wear clothes – Sven was very relaxed about nudity and his daughters had disappeared to see friends and lovers again, leaving Sven, Pheely, Basil and Hamlet with the place to themselves. With Britten booming from the loudspeakers that were linked in every room, he photographed Pheely while she breastfed, played rough and tumble with Hamlet on the floor like two Graeco-Roman wrestlers, read the papers wearing nothing but his half-moons, carried the grub-pale, plump baby around on a broad, darkly tanned shoulder while Pheely exercised mercilessly on the machines of torture – and made expert love to her while Basil slept peacefully in his hamper. Without a travel cot, and with Basil too long and leggy these days to sleep in his car seat, she and Sven had adapted a huge old Fortnum's hamper with folded blankets. It worked a treat.

'They'll be sending out a search party from Oddlode soon,' she mused one evening as Sven luxuriated in licking each of her toes. 'I really do feel a bit guilty for being away so long.'

'You may go back whenever you choose.'

'But I'll never see you again.'

'That's the deal.'

Pheely looked down at her amazingly flat belly and her curved, silken thighs, so much firmer than they had been a month earlier.

'I'll stay just a little longer. Lose a bit more flab.'

'You are more beautiful when there is more of you.' Sven started kissing his way up her calf.

She could see little dark moles on his tanned, bald head. She wanted to memorise each one of them like stars in the sky.

'I love myself more thinner,' she whispered.

'And that,' he looked up with a movie star white smile, parting her legs as he did so, 'is the point. Only when you love yourself, can you truly love other people.'

Running practised fingers from her navel to her labia, like a pianist spanning several octaves as he prepared for the most intricate of minuets, he gently separated the silken pink curtains and dipped his head to taste his way to that most decadent of delicacies.

Trying and failing to stifle a loud, indulgent groan of pleasure, Pheely closed her eyes as his tongue and lips went to work.

'I love you,' she gasped as shock waves of pleasure started lapping up through her. 'God, I love you.'

There were no words in the Edgehill Suite at the Royalist Hotel, but plenty of action as a large, bullish Roundhead drove home the initiative through the deep gullies of new territory. The pace was determined and measured, the backdrop of four poster and heavy curtains was pure theatre, but the soundtrack was absolutely silent.

Liv held her breath, thoroughly enjoying the pastime, but wondering if she shouldn't perhaps make a noise to cheer him along – a few gasps maybe, or an appreciative moan? It was a shame to let all this activity go unacknowledged, but she still felt inept when it came to adultery, especially with the county set, and was unwilling to be the first to break the silence. If he made a few grunts and groans, she would happily join in, but he was utterly mute.

In fact, he was so quiet that she could even hear the conversations of passers-by on the pavement beneath their window.

One voice rang out clearly above the others: Jemima Cottrell's breathy quack. She appeared to be yapping into a mobile phone.

'No, Pixie darling, I have *no* idea where that bloody chest of Clodhilda's might surface, and I will *not* ask Piers to look out for it in the saleroom – I am keeping contact to a minimum. Tell me, is that dreadful yeti woman still living with you . . . ?

Her voice trailed away.

Quite thrown off her stroke, Liv shifted her hips and lost the Roundhead up one thigh like a fat, blind earthworm appearing from a rose bed.

'Sorry!' she found herself apologising as though she'd just spilled sauce at the dinner table.

Silence resumed as the worm once more went to earth and wriggled most deliciously.

Afterwards, driving home, Liv felt elated by her illicit encounter, which had been every bit as gratifying as she had hoped. Her one niggle, apart from the pounding guilt gland which she was trying to ignore, was that the only word she had uttered throughout the long, masterful hours of lovemaking was 'sorry'.

That wasn't very rock and roll at all.

27

Anke was shocked by how few people remained in the Cottrells' treasure hunt. The most recent clue was admittedly rather obscure – and there had been some bad publicity recently about Piers Cottrell, leading to allegations of a fix – but when she turned up at the early morning viewing of the Collectables Sale at Ibcote Over Foxrush Baptist Church Hall, she found herself alone with half a dozen pensioners and some Japanese tourists who had dashed in out of the rain.

Faith was scuffing her heels behind her mother, complaining that the clue was far too oblique to solve. She had only come along in the vague hope of spotting Flipper who, she imagined, might be obliged to attend family auctions.

Despite a few jokey texts, the exciting new friendship hadn't taken off in quite the direction she had hoped – specifically back to the New Inn for another drink 'date' on Rory's doorstep, perhaps leading to another drunken kiss. Flipper was, she guessed, far too cool to be open friends with a sixteen year old girl, but his private kindness made her feel a debt of gratitude.

'Nonsense – one just has to apply one's mind,' Anke was insisting, eager to solve the clue swiftly because she had promised to be home to help Spencer ride Steve McQueen later.

'Everybody else is getting the solutions off the internet,' Faith pointed out. 'Some do-gooder publishes the lot number and solution, along with the next clue, on an anonymous blog the day after each sale. There'll be thousands of people in on the finish.'

'The fun is taking part,' Anke said piously, fishing out the clue again.

> Picture perfect time travel and Dr Who is there
> He has a stethoscope and a rather haughty air
> He owned at least one treasure and was so very proud
> He caught it all on camera amid unruly crowds

This clue had been written by Finn who, wishing to prove himself superior to both his father and brother in clue-setting, had made it so hard nobody could solve it. Not even – to his satisfaction – his wife, although she claimed to be too busy to concentrate, and had dropped the odd heavy hint about making money in a hurry.

Hosting the auction that day alongside his father, Finn tried not to think about it. He was standing in for Piers, who had sulkily taken himself off to Ireland to look at horses, claiming he would not be humiliated by Jemima's absence a moment longer.

Piggy seemed unperturbed by his daughter-in-law's antics, even though she rolled up daily at the Abbey to visit her children, talk to Dibs and run down Piers. Piggy, if within earshot of the feisty little harridan, just agreed Cottrell men *were* shits. They were famous for it. You got what you asked for. Dibs, trying to play peacemaker, despaired of making progress.

But today, Piggy was more concerned by the dwindling numbers for his company's big media stunt. He blamed the clue.

'What is this rubbish? Dr Who? Is it a Dalek? A Tardis? What?'

'No', Finn explained proudly. 'A former doctor from the area – one who was a keen photographer.'

'Huh? What? Are we selling his camera?'

'No, one of his pictures,' Finn whispered, although there were hardly any members of the public around. 'It ties in with this week's house auction and the next clue which is already in this room, of course. Phoney wrote that one, and it's incredibly obvious. Today, we are selling a postcard featuring the old doctor's house in Oddlode, where there was a surgery up until the fifties. On Wednesday, the house itself goes under the hammer. Do you see?'

'No,' Piggy boomed. 'What has this got to do with Daleks?'

Finn marched him to a table loaded with mixed lots of postcards in boxes, whipping one away from under the nose of a teenager with frizzy hair before stomping through a door marked 'private' that led to a glorified broom cupboard. A moment later he stomped out again and grabbed his father, who was looking around in surprise, wondering where he had gone.

Inside the cupboard, Finn plucked a postcard from the box and waved it under Piggy's nose.

It was a sepia image of an attractive Cotswold stone house, the perfect symmetrical square of windows and door with a chimney at each end, taken on what appeared to be a celebratory day with bunting strung outside and several merry-makers captured in the frame.

'The village fête.' Finn turned it over to reveal another clue discreetly tucked into the plastic dust sleeve:

> '"A child may draw a sky and grass, but somewhere in between
> A chimney smokes, a front path winds and four square
>   windows gleam
> 'Who lives here?' a small voice asks. And as one, they all reply:
> 'Nobody dwells, apart from smells of chloroform and dye.'"

'Ah! Ah! Brilliant!' Piggy barked after he had read it. 'This house is selling on Wednesday, you say?'

'With vacant possession,' Finn said through gritted teeth. 'Phoney wrote the poem.'

'Brilliant! Just the job,' Piggy nodded. 'I must congratulate her. Much better than that pathetic Dalek rubbish.'

With that he exited the Baptist Hall broom cupboard.

It hardly escaped the attention of those few treasure hunters present that father and son Cottrell had holed themselves up with one specific box of postcards.

The lot number and clue were simple to find after that. Even Pixie and Sioux, arriving late in a cloud of cheroot smoke and ferret fumes, managed to work it out before it went under the hammer.

Anke cornered Pixie afterwards. 'Any luck getting your great aunt's chest back from Sexton?'

'Hopeless!' Pixie groaned. 'He's taken the bloody trollop to Spain for a jolly, according to the kids. They're most put out at not being invited along. Sioux and I tried to break into the shag pad while they're away, but the alarm went off and we scarpered.'

'We couldn't see it through the windows, though,' Sioux added.

'Maybe it's upstairs?' Anke suggested.

Pixie shook her head. 'It's too big. You know, I don't think he managed to get it into that house in the first place – there's no entrance big enough. I think he only took it as a gesture of defiance, the stupid oaf.'

'So where is it?'

'Wherever it is,' Pixie sighed, 'he's playing it close to his chest.'

★

Spencer wanted to go for a hack around the village, making Anke very nervous. Steve McQueen the horse was safe enough on the roads, but Spencer was not safe on Steve.

'Perhaps in a few weeks,' she told him.

But Spencer was insistent. He and Mark were in the midst of a domestic tiff, and he had left the shop in high dudgeon, determined to make a point. He wanted to be wild and daredevil and prove that he was the better rider. Last month he had watched the famous Devil's Marsh race and was determined to take part next year. He also wanted to score points by being the first to track down the mystery woman.

By coincidence, the very same afternoon that the woman had visited Mark and Spencer's shop asking about Fedor Ruckert, the couple had been offered a pair of silver Fabergé spoons purportedly traceable to the Imperial family.

Mark was convinced that there was something dodgy going on. The source of the spoons was unexpected but insisted that they were new to the market and that the provenance was genuine. The spoons had been commissioned by the Russian Royal family at the turn of the century as a gift, possibly for a christening of twins or as a wedding present. What's more he wanted a fraction of their value. He was selling them on behalf of a friend, he explained, in strictest confidence. They could not go through a saleroom or one of the larger dealers; he was only offering them to cherry-picked clients that discreet dealers in the area recommended.

While Mark had dithered, Spencer had brazenly announced that they definitely had a buyer lined up.

The potential profit was sensational, he pointed out afterwards. They'd be able to write off the cost of Steve McQueen, and the dreadful oil painting and the mountain of hay that they'd bought at subsequent treasure hunt sales.

'Think of the mark-up, Mark!'

But Mark was down. He was certain the spoons were stolen. Besides which, they had no way of tracing the brunette. She hadn't left a number, and apart from knowing that she lived somewhere in Oddlode, kept a horse, had a very clean green car, a husband who worked overseas and nice shoes, they were stumped.

Spencer was convinced that he and Steve would win the day.

He had already driven around Oddlode a few times looking for the doe-eyed brunette, but couldn't hope to track her down from inside a Golf GTi. Horsey friends had long assured him that from the saddle, he could spy over hedges and into gardens. Today he was on a mission to find her distinctive shiny green car with the bull bars.

Being led along on a rope by Anke riding her old retired dressage horse, Heigi, was not a very dignified experience, but Spencer weathered it nobly, fantasising himself a young nobleman riding through his feudal village. It was actually rather fun this high up in the warm sunshine, listening to the companionable clip-clop of the horses' hooves on tarmac and smiling down at villagers with a cheery hello.

And he certainly had a very good view over hedges and fences. He was appalled by the bad taste statuary and planting he saw, counting at least five cherubs, two gnomes and three clumps of pampas grass in his first three hundred yards.

Then, across the two beech hedges, a small apple orchard and the crenellated roof of a very upmarket garden shed, Spencer spotted a shiny green car. Parked beside it was Mark's red Italian scooter. He let out a shriek.

'Are you all right?' Anke swung round in the saddle.

'We must go up there!' he demanded, pointing at the drive which led up to the exclusive Coppice Court development of barn conversions and mock-Georgian modern Cotswold piles.

'We can't – it's private.'

'Watch me.' Leaning forwards to take the lead rope from his instructor, Spencer yanked at the rein and Steve ambled obligingly left, along the raked gravel strip between neatly trimmed beech and laurel hedges.

The driveway leading to the swanky barn conversion in question was guarded by an impressive pair of electric gates with a CCTV intercom. Almost falling off as he leant down to press the button, Spencer graced Liv with a close-up of Steve's big black nose steaming up her camera with a snort.

Mark was livid to have his pitch queered by his beloved queer pitching up on a horse. It ruined the atmosphere of quiet negotiation that he was trying to achieve: offering Liv an advantageous deal to buy both the Fabergé spoons and the pearl inlaid chest that she had admired.

'What are you doing here?' he hissed at Spencer, trying not to be heard by Liv and her children who were fussing over the horses.

'Testing a new customer interface technique,' Spencer hissed back, forcing a cheery smile at an old couple – presumably grandparents – who were looking at Spencer and Steve in alarm. 'What are *you* doing here?'

'Liv phoned the shop to ask about Sexton Smith's cabinet again. I told her about the spoons and said I'd pop in. Personal service.'

'What cabinet?' asked Anke.

Mark looked up, as though noticing her for the first time.

'Sexton Smith has asked us to sell a side cabinet for him. Beautiful piece. Very exotic.'

Anke resisted pointing out that it might not be his to sell. 'I must pop in and admire it.'

'Oh, do,' gushed Mark, knowing that Anke's husband was very, very rich.

Liv was patting old Heigi. She had been dying to get to know the legendary dressage rider since moving to the area, but apart from her one abortive visit to the bookshop, had never managed to find herself in the same circle. Now, to her delight, Anke was sitting on a horse in her own driveway.

'I am so sorry to barge in.' Anke held out a hand.

'It's quite all right,' Liv shook it, dropping her voice to a whisper. 'You saved me from parting with an awful lot of money. I've always been hopeless under pressure.'

'Mark's terribly pushy,' Anke agreed, glancing across to where the boys were still scrapping. 'You stick to your guns.'

'Thanks.' Liv was deeply relieved, particularly as Mark had only brought photographs of the Ruckert spoons and not the items, meaning she couldn't sneakily look for the next clue.

There was no doubt that the spoons were the latest treasure, but Mark had insisted that the seller would not part with them for less than a thousand pounds – and that was an 'absolute steal'.

Despite her curiosity to reach the end of Trudy's quest, Liv wasn't about to part with that sort of money. Her feelings about the situation were ambivalent, veering between guilt, jealousy and defiant indifference.

'I need to see the spoons before I make up my mind,' she insisted now, grateful to bring the meeting to a close while she had an audience to bolster her. Her in-laws, pointedly shivering on the front step despite the warmth of the day, were clearly piqued that Sunday lunch was delayed. 'I can pop to the shop if that's easier,' she added.

'Very wise.' Anke backed her up. 'I'll come with you, if you like.'

'Would you?' Liv was torn between gratitude and alarm that she wouldn't be able to use the trip as another adulterous alibi.

'Of course. I am very interested in antiques – I shall look at this cabinet while I am there.'

'I'll make arrangements straight away,' Mark promised.

'*We* will make arrangements,' Spencer added.

'Oh, we can all come!' piped Liv's mother-in-law, who was fed up at being left at home to babysit all the time. 'I love bric-à-brac.'

Liv shuddered at the prospect.

Mark shuddered too. 'We don't sell *bric-à-brac*. We sell quality antiques.'

'Oh, call a spade a spade,' Spencer sniped. 'It's mostly bric-à-brac and useless gewgaws.'

At this point, Steve McQueen decided that he had put up with enough standing about in the heat being bothered by flies and small children. With calm determination, he took off at a trot across Liv's immaculate, minimalist lawn and into the shade of a pussy willow, the lowest branch of which swept his rider clean out of the saddle.

As soon as he realised his lover was unhurt, Mark shrieked with unkind laughter. 'Looks like one useless gewgaw just got knocked off by the gee-gee!'

Anke closed her eyes with embarrassment and hoped that the boys would give up riding soon.

28

The promised outing to Mark and Spencer's Fine Antiques ended up as a large group jamboree, consisting of Liv, her children and in-laws, Anke and Faith, and Pixie and Sioux, along with what seemed a small army of Pixie's children.

Remembering Liv from Jemima's yummy mummy lunch, Pixie was immediately friendly, but Liv was too uptight to appreciate her.

Trying to discreetly frisk the box of spoons for clues was not going to be easy. She wished she had cancelled.

Pixie's non-stop chatter was a cover for her own nervousness. She immediately recognised Diana Dors in the shop, warmth bursting through her at seeing her intricately carved and inlaid friend. All she had to do was ensure that everybody else was distracted long enough that they didn't notice her opening the secret compartment and taking out her paperwork. The trouble was, there were *so* many people to distract. Sioux, who had been briefed to do the distracting, was exiled to the pavement because the boys had refused to let her in with her ferrets and a cheroot on the go. She shrugged helplessly through the window.

Pixie groaned. Sioux could be so selfish – the ferret could easily go in the back of the van and the cheroot could go out. She knew she could have relied on Pheely for a magnificent distraction, probably involving Basil and the chaise longue by the far wall covered with tapestry cushions.

She was overcome with regret that she had so neglected her friend since Sioux's arrival. She would remedy that as soon as she got home.

Mark and Spencer were working their two most expensive items to the best of their abilities, Mark showing off every attribute of the huge side cabinet, Spencer waving the spoons around like a QVC presenter trying to flog all the stock of *Today's Special Value* in record time.

Getting increasingly desperate for just a few moments alone

with their allotted targets, both Pixie and Liv started to behave erratically – Pixie urging her children to find something in the shop that they wanted, knowing they'd charge about like bulls in a china shop; Liv urging her in-laws likewise, knowing that they would ask all sorts of unnecessary questions. But the boys would not be swayed.

In the end it was Anke who inadvertently distracted them all by pointing across the road to where a strange scene was taking place beside Cottrells' Morrell-on-the-Moor office.

'Isn't that Finn Cottrell?'

Mark shot to her side. 'Good God. What is he doing?'

'He seems to be lying on top of his car,' Faith muttered.

In the car park, two men with a large flat bed lorry were trying to attach the arms of a lifting winch to the chassis of Finn's Range Rover. He was trying to stop them by splaying himself across the vehicle, shouting and waving his mobile phone around.

'Do you suppose he's parked illegally?' Spencer joined the window front audience, leaving Liv unmarked.

'Hardly – in his own office car park,' Mark sniped.

Torn between the spoons and the sight being described, Liv dithered.

Pixie had no such hesitation. Springing the secret catch, she liberated two folders of family inheritance and stuffed them hurriedly down her shorts before patting her beloved Diana on her magnificent lacquer and marquetry top. 'Thank you, my beauty. I hope we see one another again.'

Liv was still faltering, the spoons ignored, watching the normally dashing figure of Finn Cottrell leaping about like Basil Fawlty.

'I think they're taking his car away,' her mother-in-law said, stating the obvious.

'Maybe it's broken down?'

'They look like bailiffs to me,' Liv's mother-in-law said busily. 'Our neighbours in Tring had everything repossessed. Terrible business.'

'Flashy upstarts,' her husband chipped in. 'All hot-tubs and loud parties – and he refused to trim his hedge. They deserved what they got.'

'Oh dear,' Mark giggled. 'No wonder Finn's so desperate to sell those—'

'Shhh!' Spencer interrupted, glancing around pointedly at Liv.

'Poor bastard. There may be truth in the rumour that his pretty wife snorts all their money up her nose.'

'I heard it was heroin.'

'Have you seen the size of her? She's hardly Amy Winehouse.'

'She has a beautiful voice though.'

'*Did* have. All washed up, poor darling.'

'And now they're broke.'

Both boys crossed their arms in unison as they watched the Range Rover being hauled into position on the truck bed. Beside it, Finn buried his head in his hands and kicked a lamp-post, depositing most of the geranium petals of the hanging basket dangling from it on to his head. He looked like a groom covered in confetti after his bride has run off with the best man.

Moments later, the flat bed was driving away with Finn's sexy black armoured charger on board and the spectacle at the window lost its appeal.

'What do you think?' Mark and Spencer rounded on their targets once more.

'The chest is far too big for me,' Anke apologised. 'Pixie?'

Her friend gave a barely perceptible wink, indicating that it had been a successful mission.

'Me too,' she told the boys. 'Unlike Anke, I'm flat broke – and it seems we're both flat chested, ha ha!'

Liv's father in law fell about, almost losing his top teeth.

'Liv?' Spencer turned hopefully.

'The chest really isn't for me, either,' Liv apologised, reaching for the spoons in their padded velvet box. 'I do want these, though. Martin can buy them for me as recompense for being away.'

'Liv!' her mother-in-law chided. 'You know Martin is working overseas to pay for his children's education.'

'And I will teach them all about Fabergé,' Liv promised.

Back home, the in-laws sulking in front of *Countdown* and her children running riot through the house, Liv locked herself in her bedroom and prised open the velvet box. Hidden beneath the folds of satin was a neatly rolled clue.

> Carter, classy, easy to spot
> Only trouble is everyone will want
> To win them, you must fight

Tell me about it
Rather like I had to fight for you
Except I lost in the end
Like the fool I am
Like the fool you are – a perfect pair
Sacrifice something and you'll win again.

Liv had tears in her eyes. Whoever he was, he was worth fighting for; surely Trudy could see that? She had to get the message across to her somehow.

She'd have to go round to the house, she decided, although the thought that Finn might be there made her balk, especially in the light of what they had just witnessed in Morrell. What if they were fighting about money? In the throes of despair? Packing to leave their repossessed cottage? She would die of embarrassment, not to mention find it impossible to hide her feelings.

As her imagination ran riot, her phone rang.

'Thank God you answered.' The deep voice was hoarse with relief, wildly sexy in its brief burst of emotion. 'I've had a bloody awful day. Can you be at the River Folly in an hour?'

'Isn't that a bit dangerous?' asked Liv, aware that the little Aphrodite temple beside the river track was often overrun with dog walkers and idle teenagers on a summer's evening.

'There's a path on the far side that leads down to the river bank – nobody goes down there. I'll wait for you.' He rang off before Liv could explain that she had in-laws and children to worry about.

But that was what she loved about him: he left no room for fretting. His way was entirely selfish and it made life very straightforward. He was rather like Martin in some ways, only classier, sexier – and forbidden.

She dashed upstairs for a bath, not caring how odd it might appear at four o'clock on a Tuesday. An hour later, she grabbed a bottle of plonk from the wine rack as a prop and told her in-laws that she was going to pop in on a friend in the village.

'What are we supposed to do about tea?' they whinged in horror.

'There's fresh spinach and ricotta tortellini in the fridge and sauces in the larder,' she said airly, already out of earshot by the time her father-in-law retorted that they didn't like foreign muck.

★

At the nursery bungalow, Pixie was leafing through a thick pile of share certificates and bonds, resolving to take the lot to her solicitor the following morning en route to the house sale at which she and Sioux were determined to be the first to find the next clue in the Cottrells' hunt.

'Our fortunes are turning, dear heart,' she told the fattest of her small dogs, who was sniffing at the pile with interest, stubby tail wagging.

Poking out from between two rather grand-looking handwritten documents with wax seals and ribbons on them was a postcard. Pixie pulled it from its hiding place and gaped in recognition. It was Gozo, where she and Sexton had holidayed every year without fail since getting together, staying in a little farmhouse covered in whitewash, geraniums, geckos and oils of stout naked men with equally stout appendages. It was their secret hideaway.

The postcard, of the little fishing village just two kilometres from the farm where they bought their bread and wine, was old and battered, probably dating back to their first visit. Pixie always brought too many. It appeared to contain an unfinished missive. In Sexton's distinctive, spidery hand:

> *My darling one, forgive me. I have made the biggest mistake of my life leaving you. I don't know what to do. I am too ashamed of myself to ask to come back, but I do beg for your forgiveness. I love you. I think that—*

There, the message ended, leaving enough space for an address and stamp.

Pixie raced to show Sioux.

'It must be for me, don't you see?' she gasped. 'He knew about the secret hidey-hole in the cabinet all along, and he knew I'd find it.'

'Bloody long shot fool idea if you ask me,' Sioux huffed, lighting a fresh cheroot. 'Why not just phone you, or write to you here?'

'You don't know Sexton. He's terribly hard on himself, and very withdrawn. He wouldn't want to lose face.'

'He's still shacked up with his dolly bird!' Sioux pointed out bluntly. 'They're sunning their arses in the Med.'

'I'm not so sure.' She fanned herself with the postcard. 'Jacqui certainly is, but I think my boy may be close at hand.'

Sioux hadn't been a top-notch barrister for nothing. It took a matter of moments to turn Pixie's thinking around.

'Sexton left his third wife for you originally, am I right?'

'Second,' she said in a small voice. It remained a guilty corner of her life.

'A classic monkey,' Sioux muttered under her breath. 'Swinging from tree to tree. The wife kicked up quite a fuss, didn't she?'

Pixie nodded. At the time Sexton and Gill had owned and run a very illustrious organic garden centre, far superior to the current little Oddlode veggie, fruit and plant nursery enterprise. Gill had been embittered by his departure; with three children under five and a vast mortgage and overdraft in her name because he was a former bankrupt, nobody could blame her. In fact, the tide of opinion was wholly in her favour and Sexton and Pixie were made to feel like pariahs at the time – terribly humiliating for Pixie, who had always been a popular local figure, and for Sexton who had privately endured a loveless and soul-destroying marriage.

'And you managed to escape from that, am I right?'

'To Gozo, yes,' Pixie sighed, tears in her eyes.

'And you think this postcard dates back to that era?'

'Well, yes. Nothing much there changes, but this shows the old marina before they rebuilt the sea defences. I doubt they've sold these cards for years.'

'So Sexton could have written it on your first visit?' Sioux suggested, going for the jugular.

Pixie's eyes went dull. 'To Gill, you mean?'

'To Gill.' Sioux nodded.

All hope seemed to drain out of her. 'I suppose he could. He could have decided that he had made a mistake even then but, typical Sexton, hated being seen to go back on a decision. The fool. Then he had to wait all these years to get out.'

'Never trust a man.' Sioux puffed on her cheroot. 'Especially not a monkey.'

Pixie took herself and the postcard off to the poly tunnels for a good cry. There, she texted Pheely. *Are you alive? Need you. Sioux getting on my nerves.*

A message came back five minutes later. *At last! The woman's a complete con. Lock up your silver.*

Pixie snorted – she and Sexton had sold all the good silver years ago. But it was true that Sioux hadn't offered a penny in contribution during her stay, just a couple of rabbits for the pot and some weed that had tasted suspiciously like the sort Pheely grew in her greenhouses beside the Lodge.

Another message winged its way through the magical masts from the New Forest.

Sven getting on my nerves, too. He only fancies fat women.

Pixie indulged her schoolgirl cruel streak and texted: *Perhaps I should send Sioux there and you can come home?*

Don't think even my darling Svengali can do much for S. Will come home end week, though. Miss you.

Miss you, too. Pixie realised that the love between friends was as easy to abuse as that between lovers. She had left Pheely as thoughtlessly as Sexton had left her, bounding into the arms of another – in his case, Jacqui, in hers, Sioux.

She looked at the postcard again, refusing to believe that Sexton had written it all those years ago. In that case, how had it got into the cabinet?

On impulse, she sent him a text. *Miss you.*

When, after an hour, she had heard nothing back, she threw her phone into a bed of lamb's lettuce and stomped back into the house.

Sioux was sitting at the kitchen table, working her way through yet another bottle of Sexton's home made cider brandy.

'I think it's time you moved on,' Pixie announced nervously.

'Who have you been talking to?'

'Nobody. I just feel I'd be better on my own for a while. I am truly grateful for your support and it's been marvellous having you—'

'Cut the crap.' Sioux stood up. 'I'll leave first thing. I had hoped to stay until the next Horse Fair, but if you really think you can cope without me . . .'

'I can.'

'And that you'll decipher the rest of those Treasure Hunt clues without me.'

'I will.'

'Then I'll get out of your hair as soon as we've agreed my commission.' She fixed Pixie with her gimlet stare.

'Your commission?'

'Finder's fee for tracking down those papers in the chest.'

'But it was Anke who found the chest.' Pixie didn't care about the money now that she had enough to spare – it was the principle of the matter.

'I *led* her there with my powers,' Sioux was pronouncing theatrically. 'And then I helped you liberate the paperwork.'

'You stood out on the pavement smoking,' Pixie's incredulous laugh rose through an octave of amazement. 'And as far as your "magical powers" go, I have seen no evidence whatsoever. Face it, Sioux,' she fought down the laugh and studied her old friend affectionately, 'you couldn't predict a riot in a revolution.'

It was not the right thing to say. Sioux's face looked thunderous. 'Pay me my commission or I'll take residence in your best greenhouse and demand squatter's rights.'

Sighing, Pixie furled her throbbing brow as she regarded her old friend with a mixture of amused respect and regret. Sioux was an old feral cat and Pixie – who had taken in more than her fair share of strays over the years to love and nurture – knew full well that one could never tame them; once they had grown fat on your hand-outs, if they demanded their freedom with an ungrateful hiss and scratch, it was best to let them go without admonishment.

Pixie went to the drawer in her battered desk and drew out a certificate for some off-shore trust she didn't understand, but which she estimated had to be worth at least a few hundred. Uncapping her pen, she turned it over and signed the back to transfer it as she had seen her father do on many occasions.

'There,' she handed it over, feeling hoodwinked. Sexton would never have let her do it had he been there.

Flipping over the stiff cream certificate, Sioux read her own name above 'Clodhilda Guinness'. She hadn't seen it written down like that in years, although her passport and birth certificate still bore it.

Perhaps it was time to leave, she reflected. Pixie knew far too many of her secrets from the bad old days when she had drunk too much, talked too much and trusted too much. Now she'd turned out to be an ungrateful friend with no appreciation of orphic divination or Wicca spell-casting. If she thought her life was tough, perhaps she needed to be taught a lesson about life's real hard knocks.

'I suppose it'll have to do,' she sniffed, studying Pixie's bold, straightforward signature. 'I expected more of you, Pixie, but of course spoilt little rich girls always revert to type. I'll leave first thing in the morning.' She swept from the room in a cloud of ferret fumes.

Pixie felt as relieved as a lion cub after a large splinter had been drawn from its paw.

Liv reeled back home from the folly at dusk, pink-cheeked from drinking wine on an empty stomach and being ravished beneath a bridge arch. She was also covered in mosquito bites and had very muddy ankles. At least the children would be in bed, she reasoned, and almost certainly her in-laws as well. Liv had installed a television and Sky box in the guest room especially, knowing that it ensured they would take up a hot malt drink to watch an old episode of *Last of the Summer Wine* on UK Gold most evenings. She had secretly disabled the box in the sitting room.

'You can be a very conniving woman, Liv Wilson,' she told herself as she weaved her way along the drive. 'Who would have thought it? Deceiving all these people to get your wicked way.' She stabbed her key at the front door lock a few times, swinging from the handle for balance. 'You really are a scarlet trollop, but my goodness it feels—' she fell through the door – 'wonderful!'

'Here she is!' came her mother-in-law's budgie trill.

'Shit.' Liv squinted groggily ahead.

Beyond the wide acreage of empty hallway, the sitting room lights were on full brightness, not their usual dimmed subtlety. She could see the outlines of her in-laws sitting in their upright fashion on the edge of her leather Laura Ashley settee. The sofa opposite them was just out of sight but she could see a pair of feet poking out from it. Very big feet in Birkenstocks and white socks.

Martin always flew in Birkenstocks.

Her heart took a brief sabbatical as she focused on a large black Samsonite suitcase propped up in the shadows beside the stairs.

The door was still open behind her. She contemplated turning and running.

She reeked of sex, was dishevelled and muddy and too drunk to trust herself.

Martin's shadow loomed around the corner. 'Surprise!'

Liv mustered her most delirious smile. 'Darling. Oh my God. I'm – so – happy . . .'

She burst into tears and fled to the downstairs loo.

Martin turned to his parents with a smug smile. 'Told you she'd do that.'

'Always does,' his mother agreed proudly.

'Remember when I came back from six months in Thailand and she cried so much we had to call NHS Direct?'

'That's love, son.' His father stood up and patted his back, 'Your mother was just the same when I used to go away on insurance business.'

'And he never went further than Preston,' she pointed out fondly.

In the downstairs loo, Liv was frantically douching with Molton Brown handwash and hunks of loo roll. She then hid her muddy ballet pumps in the under-sink cupboard before wobbling around on one leg to rinse her dirty feet in the sink, head-butting the mirror several times. She stuffed her knickers in one shoe, sluiced out her mouth with water and doused herself with Crabtree and Evelyn room spray.

When she finally emerged, Martin had sent his parents up to bed and was propped on a sofa holding two glasses of duty-free champagne.

He'd put on weight, she noticed, and had an unflattering haircut that made him look like Tony Blackburn. He looked out of place in the sitting room – his sitting room, his house that his money had bought but in which he had never lived. She perched beside him, downing her glass in one, gulping as the bubbles rocketed up her nose.

'Atta girl.' He took the flute from her and pulled her up on to his knee, his hand sliding up inside her skirt. 'Have you missed your big bear then?'

'All the time,' she said in the little-girl voice he loved.

His face split into a lascivious smile, revealing spinach between his teeth. He'd obviously indulged in the 'foreign muck' with his parents; he must have been home for hours.

'Where have you been?' he ribbed, eyebrows shooting up as he encountered bare buttock beneath her skirt.

'With Trudy,' she gulped, hoping her nose wasn't growing as fast as his hard-on seemed to be.

'Your pop star friend who has affairs, drinks too much and parties with the A list?' He pinched her buttock teasingly.

She nodded, wishing she hadn't exaggerated quite so much in her emails.

'I hope she hasn't been leading you astray.' His hand slid between her legs.

She shook her head.

'Do you always leave your knickers off when you go to see her?'

'I took them off just now, for you.'

'Atta girl. Time for bed. Big bear has to have jet shag before jet lag.'

It was one of his favourite jokes and had once made Liv fall about in genuine delight. Now she could barely raise a smile.

She followed him upstairs.

'Place looks great,' Martin growled as he admired the bedroom with its feminine drapes and expensive satin cushions from boutique shops. 'Like a tart's boudoir.' Dropping his trousers and Y-fronts, Birkenstocks and socks still in place, he sat back on the bed and patted his lap just below his eager, sprouting red hard-on.

Liv felt bile rising in her throat. Unable to hold it back, she dashed into the en suite and threw up a glass of champagne and two of red plonk into the bidet.

When she finally returned to the bedroom, teeth brushed until her gums bled, Martin was lying on the bed, feet still on the floor, a cacophony of snores erupting from his nose and throat, hard-on wilted to a radish once more.

With a sigh of relief, Liv removed the sandals and trousers and lifted his legs on to the bed.

He opened one sleepy eye and mumbled. 'Still throwing up your food, naughty girl? You shouldn't eat so much in the first place. But at least you are still lovely and trim, huh? Very tasty.' He slipped back into sleep before Liv could ram a Birkenstock in his mouth.

The next morning, Pixie felt as though a thorn had been removed from her side. For a blessed hour, she was liberated. Sioux had left before dawn, even before Pixie, the earliest of risers, had padded her way to the kitchen kettle.

The house felt so much better without her, Pixie realised as she threw open the window and breathed the dewy scent of her lovely, mulchy, fertile land, and it wasn't just because the pong had lessened. There was still a top-note of ferret and cigar, but it seemed brighter inside, less forbidding, easier to move around,

She dressed, checked the tunnels, extracted her phone from the lamb's lettuce and opened the shop, leaving her two teenagers in charge along with old retired Roly from the allotments who was happy to help out in exchange for free plants and seeds.

It was only when she came back inside that she realised the two folders of share certificates and bonds were missing from her desk drawer.

Sioux had taken them. Even as Pixie reached for the phone, she knew that calling the police would be hopeless. She had no proof that the papers were hers in the first place; she never had – in fact she had stolen them from a cabinet in an antique shop just the day before. There was nothing on them to prove ownership; they were as transferable as sterling.

She buried her face in her hands and wailed.

Behind her, a Stanley knife cut through the plastic covering that was patching up the vast hole where the wall and the French windows had once been, slicing it from top to bottom.

Looking round in alarm, Pixie saw a tall figure framed in the jagged slash, his hair several shades whiter than she remembered it, his face youthful in contrast, ruddy and tanned like an Italian farmer's after years in the fields, blue eyes shining as brightly as lapis lazuli. He was wearing a spotted red neckerchief and leather waistcoat like a travelling minstrel.

Sexton stepped inside. 'I miss you too.'

29

Flipper left Popeye pulling on a haynet and returned from the stable yard to the main house, hangover still pulling at his temples. Bypassing the turret entrance that led straight up to his attic annexe, he went to the side of the house – a flat-faced, smooth, classical cheek of its front face compared to the mussed, up mad Gothic slides and ringlets to the rear. There, he let himself into the first door and walked along a side lobby towards the kitchen stairs.

The dawn ride through Gunning Woods had not cleared his head. A late night spent drinking with his wilder friends, the third in a row, had blown his concentration and reactions for the day, but done nothing to ease the pain in his heart or his racing thoughts.

He had no food in the attic, so planned to raid the main house kitchen. His mother was already up, sitting at the table with her laptop. It was an incongruous sight.

'I thought you hated that thing?' Flipper was cheered by the odd spectacle – as unexpected as seeing his father shopping in the Coop, or Piers feeding a small baby.

'I'm actually pretty good,' she countered, hastily blanking the screen to hibernate. 'The only thing I can't work is this wireless whatnot. Can't seem to make it connect away from the library.'

'Let me have a go.'

She held up her hand. 'It's all right – it's working this morning. Finn set it up for me.' She smiled over the screen at him, studying him above her half-moons.

'Finn's here?' Flipper hadn't spotted the Range Rover, which he supposed his brother must have parked at the front. Finn always liked to use the grand entrance and race along the carriage sweep spitting gravel.

'In "his bit" sorting through some things.'

'I thought "Finn's bit" was empty apart from an old sofa bed and a few buckets to catch drips?'

'It's a bit more hospitable than that these days – Uncle Kenneth stayed there last month,' his mother said vaguely, now holding up a laminated Cottrells' treasure hunt clue from a small pile by her computer, all ready for that day's auction. 'Finn popped in on his way to work to collect these. I don't think he's very impressed.'

Flipper recognised the clue that he himself had written: not his greatest imaginative work, but he had been very drunk at the time.

'You look terrible,' his mother observed, not unkindly.

'I had a late night.'

His drinking buddies Tristan and Hamish, fellow vets from the practice and notorious revellers, were very basic in their requirements. Flipper just needed to buy his fair share of drinks, discuss sport and make them laugh. It stopped him sitting at home, eating himself alive with impossible plans to make Trudy run away with him.

His mother had her own theory about why he was drinking too much and sleeping too little.

'It's still her, isn't it? This wretched married woman? The one that you swear isn't your brother's wife.' She sounded unusually irritated, and Flipper wondered if his brother had now said something. But he quickly dismissed the notion. Finn was far too proud to admit that there was so much as a wrinkle in the smooth surface of his cushy marriage, not to mention so protective of their mother than he wouldn't dream of 'bothering' her with such matters.

Flipper found that he couldn't stomach breakfast after all and, kissing his mother on the top of the head, headed back up to the labyrinth of passages that connected the many staircases in the house.

One of the doors to 'Finn's Bit' was ajar as he passed it: an old servants' entrance to an ornate reception room, discreetly hidden in panelling.

Unable to resist, Flipper paused to glance in at the high-ceilinged profusion of plasterwork, stone carvings and panel work.

His eyebrows shot up. The room still looked like a bombsite, with plaster falling, damp wood rotting, ceilings and windows leaking, but now it was filled with expensive-looking antiques, and several oil paintings were stacked against the walls. When he looked closer, Flipper was certain he recognised most of the pieces as being from Church Cottage.

'Hello, Flipper.'

A quiet, cold voice behind him made Flipper jump.

Finn was standing in the corridor, holding a colourful twenties Royal Doulton Chang vase that Flipper had last seen in the snug at Church Cottage: it had been a house-warming present from Trudy's brother and he'd delivered it brimming with chocolates, explaining that he'd brought her a 'vase of Roses'.

'Isn't that Trudy's?'

'Yes.' Finn carried the bowl into the room, placing it carefully on a drop-leaf rosewood table before covering both with a plastic dustsheet.

'Won't that table get damp in here?'

'It won't be here long. I'm just storing some things while we have the beams sandblasted at the cottage. Cheaper than using Big Yellow.'

There was a terse pause, and bile rose in Flipper's throat. 'You're well, are you?'

'As can be expected.' Finn didn't look at him. He hadn't made any contact since throwing him out of Church Cottage with a broken nose, although he'd been one of the first people to hear that his brother had totalled his car in a ditch that same day. He had probably been quietly pleased that the concussion and bruising conveniently camouflaged any sign of the beating.

He longed to ask after Trudy; but his mother's words rang in his ears and the nausea swilled in his mouth.

He just made it to his attic bathroom in time to throw up.

Shivering on the sofa afterwards, he longed for Mutt's solid little hot-water bottle body to comfort him.

When Finn typed up the results of the day's auction of farms, land and dwelling houses later, ready to email through to his web people to post on the Cottrells' site, he reflected that the sale had hardly broken records. In fact the old doctor's house in Oddlode had been withdrawn after failing to make its reserve. The banqueting hall at Eastlode Park Hotel may have been packed prior to the sale, but most of those eagerly leafing through their catalogues had only been there to get the treasure lot number and next clue.

Finn would have liked to make a low offer for the house himself. It would be a fun renovation project to run in tandem with Church Cottage, but he didn't have capital to spare at the moment, and Trudy

– usually good for a big royalty cheque at least twice a year – hadn't been pulling her finger out at all in recent months. Nor was she providing any practical back-up to the house project. She still hadn't found new builders and, although Finn had technically been the one to fire them in the first place, she was better placed to tender projects like this. His only comfort was that the longer they left it, the cheaper they would come. Just as long as they stayed afloat.

The housing market was on a downward turn, paralysed by the squeeze on lending and global recession. It made him twitchy. He had precious little equity left in the cottage, but had always comforted himself with the idea that so much Cottrell family money was tied up in property – backed up with Trudy's hefty income – that they couldn't possibly go broke. Now that all their asset values were plummeting there was no family safety net to rely upon. In addition, Piggy took no real custodial care of the Abbey and its land, allowing the farms to run down to nothing and continually borrowing against everything with no long-term repayment plans.

It was easy for Finn to criticise his father; it had never occurred to him that were in fact uncannily alike. Both thought they were consummate businessmen who might sail close to the wind, but remained completely in control. Both were masters of self-denial.

And in the same way that Piggy had always refused to acknowledge that his wife knew of his infertility (indeed refused to acknowledge it himself), so it had never occurred to Finn that Trudy might realise just how precarious their joint finances were.

He had no idea that she had opened his stashes of post. Since putting them out of his line of sight, he had put them out of his mind.

At the opposite end of the house, Trudy had just finished spell-checking and paginating her memoirs and had emailed the files to her agent, attaching them to a message full of apologies. She was always the same when submitting work, her first urge to hang her head in shame that it wasn't good enough.

She felt far from relieved that her long, sleepless shift at the computer was at an end; she was too beaten up by lack of sleep and mental exhaustion. What she wanted was a huge drink and a bath.

But she knew that Finn was in the house and she couldn't face him just yet. As long as her door was closed, she was reasonably safe.

She switched on her phone and waited for any messages. There was the usual daily one from Liv, but she was too shattered to cope with Liv's paranoia.

She longed to hear from Flipper, hoping against hope that Mutt would turn up at the Abbey and that she would be forgiven. She needed an ally right now, but was frightened of dragging him into the front line of her imminent, life-changing battle. He'd only get caught in the crossfire. Her feelings towards him would be impossible to hide, and she couldn't risk Finn directing his anger at his brother rather than her, inflicting mortal wounds on any future happiness for all three of them. This was her battle and she had to fight it alone. Flipper was always eager to play the white knight on the silver charger, but Trudy knew her husband fought far too dirtily for such gallant displays. Finn would use every modern, computer-aided, satellite-navigated missile at his disposal, and old-fashioned chivalry was no match for that. It was one of the reasons she still had no clear idea how to start setting about lowering the drawbridge and escaping the heavily fortified castle of her marriage.

Now that the cathartic process of writing her life story was at an end, she felt as though she had lost her anchor in a storm. Having fulfilled her moral obligation to bale out their leaky finances by delivering her book, she was free leave Finn, but she hadn't prepared the ground or thought through the practicalities. She was lost at sea; rudderless, anchorless, in full sail and heading towards the rocks. As panic rose in her chest, she reached for her headphones and her electronic keyboard and plugged both into the little mixer attached to her computer. Switching to the music programme, she struck a chord and started to play 'I Hate Loving You' for the first time in almost a year.

'There! I told you!' Faith announced victoriously as she pointed at the computer screen.

The mystery Internet Spoiler had struck again. There was a list of all the Cottrell clues so far, along with an explanation of what auction they referred to, with the lot number and description.

'Is that legal?' Anke read over her daughter's shoulder.

'Must be.' Faith scrolled down. 'Although I can't imagine the auctioneers are very happy about it.'

That day's property auction was already documented with an

explanation of the why lot six, the doctor's house, had been the latest solution. Beneath that, the next verse was posted up:

> A tree should stay a tree
> Unless good carpentry
> Hones its life to be something
> Other than shepherdry

'Flipper wrote that.'

'It's a lot . . . simpler looking than the others,' Anke said.

'He was in a hurry,' Faith defended her new friend. 'Peregrine Cottrell is making each member of the family write one clue, and Flipper forgot it was his turn.'

'What does it refer to?'

'I didn't ask,' she said sanctimoniously. 'But it's in the big general sale on Saturday, so I imagine it's a piece of furniture – the catalogue's already online.' She brought up a new window. 'Here's the Cottrells' site . . . I'll just do a search for . . . hmmm.' She scrolled through the furniture section until her eye was caught by a large Welsh dresser that had been painted in a garish shade of green and covered with stencilled fluffy white sheep. '"Distressed nineteenth-century oak dresser for restoration,"' she read aloud, giggling. '"Distressed" – it looks downright distraught.'

'I think that would be rather attractive in a child's room,' said Anke, who was very fond of folk art.

'Well, there's your lot. So you can go to the fête after all, Cinderella.'

Anke had been in a state all afternoon because the next auction clashed with the village fête, at which she had promised to man the second hand book stall, and at which Graham, her husband, was manfully taking charge of the bouncy castle. They couldn't drop out at this late stage.

'But what about the next clue?' she fretted.

'It'll be on here,' Faith switched back to the anonymous blog. 'Anyway, I can go along to Cottrells and check.'

Anke wasn't sure she liked the idea of letting Faith loose at an auction unchaperoned.

Liv restlessly paced about her kitchen, checking her phone every few minutes. She had to unburden herself to Trudy before she exploded.

Guilt was pressing on guilt inside her like a great wall of remorseful bricks, boxing in her heart and starving it of oxygen.

Martin was with the children in the sitting room, laughing uproariously at some cartoon. He had always adored children's TV and was easy to keep entertained during the summer holidays when he could park himself with the kids and the remote, demanding half hourly deliveries of tea by day, beer after six, and neatly quartered sandwiches with the crusts cut off every two hours. He was difficult to shake off now that he'd begun to settle into a routine, put his feet up and expect waitress service.

He had insisted on accompanying her to the house auction earlier that day, so she couldn't slip away to find Trudy.

She had lost interest in the Cottrells' treasure hunt compared to Trudy's more romantic secret quest and her own desire to unmask the anonymous admirer and play Cupid. But Martin, who had followed the official hunt on the internet from Singapore, was addicted, and certain that he and Liv would win the big cash prize. He took it very seriously, making sure they were amongst the first there and producing a special notebook from his inside pocket, into which he carefully entered the lot number and new clue.

Liv had been on her best behaviour since that awful night when he had reappeared without warning – a trick he'd only tried once before, returning from Dubai to find her with her legs akimbo in front of *Desperate Housewives*, depilating her bikini line and bleaching her upper lip on a self-pampering night.

Tonight, however, Martin's omnipresence was starting to get on her nerves. She'd been summoned to another romantic tryst but she knew she couldn't possibly go without first offering a gift to the gods to ensure her safe passage and absolution.

She did another couple of swift laps around her island unit before opening her tea towel drawer, digging under the many unused novelty tea towels of the Kent coast given to her by her in-laws before finding the velvet comfort of the spoons box.

She crammed it into her shopping bag.

'Just popping to the village store for some eggs!' she trilled.

She ran all the way to Church Cottage.

The lights were on in Trudy's study at one end, the curtains drawn. Liv put the spoons case on the window ledge, glancing over her shoulder. The big yews that hid the churchyard from view were just a few yards behind her. Knocking on the window, she turned and fled into their dark shadows.

Trudy's fingers were alive as they danced across the keyboard, her ears filled with familiar notes. She had forgotten the sheer pleasure in playing from the heart, the way it could lift her spirits.

She didn't hear the tap on the glass behind her, but the dogs, who were crammed in the study with her, started barking witlessly until she was forced to pull the headphones from her ears and investigate.

It was already dusk outside. When she pushed open the ornate arched window, something fell into the flower bed.

There, she found the Fabergé spoons in the velvet box and the clue folded inside. A message had been put in with it, printed in a very theatrical loopy typeface on a textured cream postcard.

Auction on Saturday morning. Please be there.

Even though the style was unfamiliar, it had to be from Flipper. Her heart gave out a loud drum-roll of yearning to see him, even just for a split second. She missed his conversation and his company like a plant misses rain, and knowing that he was still setting her clues was almost worse than enduring his silence.

In the dark just beyond her face, a bat flew past, a strum of flickering black in her peripheral vision, catching her attention and reminding her that she had to stay away from Flipper for his sake. She hastily closed the window and threw the velvet box into a drawer before retreating beneath her headphones again.

This time the melody was unfamiliar, yet she played it without hesitation, repeating the haunting refrain, hearing words in her head that carried through and over the notes with perfect, unforgettable harmony. She played it repeatedly until, reaching for her pen, she started to transcribe what she had heard on staved paper, scribbling crazily, her words, chords and notes illegible to all but herself: not that she would ever forget this song. She wasn't sure she would ever sing it out loud, but it would stay in her head forever.

Finn stood outside the study door, drawn by the dogs' commotion, but hearing her fingers clicking and knowing that he would be berated for disturbing her, he turned away. He slipped out through the front door and walked along the drive, doing a U-turn around the laurels at the end to head along the track to the church. He glanced at his watch. Bang on time. He found punctuality a turn-on.

She slipped out from behind a tall angel tombstone, looking like an angel come to life herself.

'I knew you'd be here,' he murmured, already reaching down for his belt buckle and not noticing that she had pursed her lips for a kiss.

'How could I stay away?' she breathed with a curious half-laugh.

Trudy looked up, the music draining from her fingers. Her ears thrummed with the sound of her own rushing blood. She could no longer hold back the tide, fiddle while Rome burned or put her fingers in her ears and cry 'la la la'. The beautiful song had vanished as quickly as it had appeared.

She opened the wall cupboard that contained the artist's and songwriter's copies of her CDs and records. An Aladdin's cave of Trudy Dew work from every territory in which she had been sold, it was piled high with tens of copies of her German singles releases and Indonesian album, and even some bootlegs that she had picked up on holidays. At the bottom of the cupboard, in a box marked Second Press UK CDs, were her treasures.

She pulled out the box and stooped over it, looking at the gypsy buckles, the first edition of the Primrose Cumming pony book, the battered, framed rubbing of the Purdey engravings – now watermarked and torn, the silver pastel flaking away from the dark paper without its glass protection – and the hunt coat with its Vale of the Wolds buttons gleaming so brightly that she could see her own reflection. To these secret riches she added the velvet case, opening it as she placed it on top of the folded coat and admired the delicate enamel work on the large, heavy Russian sterling spoons, amazed at such infinitesimal detail. What did it all mean?

Sacrifice something and you'll win again, read the last line of the new verse.

The more he laid these clues, the less she felt she knew him. She loved the Flipper who had so often sat at her side, warm and clever and sensual and funny, full of passion and belief and ideas. This Flipper – a distant quiz-master with a clever turn of phrase, sometimes brutal, at other times loving – was rather daunting and alienating.

But all she had right now were the clues. And, like Hansel's trail of breadcrumbs through the trees, she should act on them without delay in case the birds pecked them away before she found the route out of the enchanted forest. Before that could happen, she had to escape the decaying gingerbread cottage of comfort food, sweet dreams and just deserts.

It was time to sacrifice her marriage. From this day forward, she vowed, less than twenty-four hours of married life lay ahead of her.

She sat back down at her computer and wrote an email to her brother.

> *Johnny, my darling.*
>
> *I am going to ask Finn for a separation. It is the only way. My marriage is over, and I cannot bear living like this any longer. I know that I have to be practical – the horses and dogs need caring for so I cannot simply walk out. I will have everything organised by Saturday, and after that I will be free of this wretched sham.*
>
> *Forgive me for telling you this way, but I am too emotional to call you right now – and it has been so long since we have spoken that there are too many platitudes to get through. Can you tell Mum what is going on? I may not be able to speak to her as normal for a while. I will write more soon, I promise, and let you know what is going on.*
>
> *All love, T xxx*

She sent it straight away, committing her heart and her resolve to the deed as she pressed the button and watched the window shrink away.

Tomorrow was going to be a huge, life-changing day. Whatever happened, she was determined that she would be free by its close. Glancing up at the wall calendar, she saw it was Friday the thirteenth.

She then found a clean piece of paper and started to write in long-hand: *How to Leave Finn . . .*

First thing on Friday morning, still sequestered in her study, Trudy heard Finn driving away in her car. She had noticed that his was missing and assumed that it was at the garage undergoing yet another expensive customisation. As always, he used her car without asking, although he complained about its dreadful gearbox, its dirtiness inside and out and the fact that she had yet to get it repaired from her nose-to-nose shunt with the Audi.

It wasn't yet eight o'clock, but the sun was already high in the sky, slicing through the pointed window and providing bright arched spotlights in which the dust danced.

About to turn off her computer, she saw that she had mail and scanned through it, leaping upon a reply from Johnny amid the spam offers of penis enlargements, bored Russian girls and Viagra.

Johnny had kept it simple, writing in the early hours, presumably after one of his clubbing jaunts with Guy. They had always been nocturnal souls. It was a Dew family trait.

> *I am crying with relief as I type this, darling one. I cannot tell you how long I have hoped to hear this. You deserve so much happiness from life. He has given you none.*
> *GOOD LUCK. BE BRAVE. STAY TRUE TO YOURSELF. WE LOVE YOU.*
> *On a practical note, DO NOT leave the house under any circumstances. Throw him out. You paid for the place. He has his family nearby to go to.*
> *Of course, you have us whenever you need us, night or day. We love you, and we are here for you.*
> *Call as soon as you can – even if it is only to cry. Laughter will come so soon.*
> *All our love xxxx*

In a PS, he had included the name and number of a friend who was a top-ranking matrimonial lawyer in London, suggesting that she might not want to hire him just yet, but that he would willingly give advice as a trusted friend.

Trudy was typing a quick thank-you when the broadband connection was suddenly cut. After a bit of plugging and unplugging at phone sockets didn't fix it, she abandoned the enterprise temporarily to go for a much-needed bath, relishing having the house to herself and imagining what it would be like when Finn had gone. The thought was impossible to quantify, like a long-term pain lifting.

The water in the bathroom refused to heat up. Turning on the immersion, she headed back downstairs, trying to ignore the piles of dirty washing and crockery as she went to peer at the boiler for signs of life. It had gone out. Heading outside to check the oil tank – remembering to let out the chickens as she did so – she found that they had completely run out of oil.

It got topped up regularly on account, but she guessed the state of their finances had temporarily stalled that. In an illogical moment of pity, she decided that she couldn't possibly leave Finn without fuel and would need to order more on her private debit card.

She looked up the fuel company's number and tried to dial it, but the landline was dead. No wonder there was no broadband. She wondered if an overhead line had come down somewhere in the village.

But, as if pulled by masochistic marionette strings, she then opened the lower drawers in the hall console on which she was perched. More Pandora's boxes awaited her . . .

The evidence for today's crisis was all there: more final demands, a notice from the phone company that the line would be disconnected on Friday the thirteenth unless the outstanding bill was paid, notices from the oil company that the direct debits for the regular payments on account had been denied along with similar letters from the council, the water company and electricity supplier. Beneath these were unopened joint account statements dating back almost a year. The overdraft was well into five figures, but now the bank had frozen the account. No mortgage payments had been made for months. There were letters proclaiming county court judgements against both Finn and herself, letters from debt agencies and bailiffs, and letters from companies refusing loans that Finn had applied for without her knowing – unsecured loans at ridiculous repayment rates.

Until today, she had foolishly assumed that the huge debts she'd already uncovered were largely personal and that, apart from the overextended mortgages, Finn had left their joint account un-plundered. Now she realised her naivety. They were still two stupid, furry little children's character animals playing at being grown up. In delivering her memoirs before she deserted the house, she'd thought herself nobly squirrelling a fat little stash of nuts high in the branches to safeguard its future through the storms ahead, but her advance would be completely swallowed up in the new overdraft alone. Like an unsatiable beaver, Finn had gnawed right at the base of the tree house so that it was about to crash down, nuts and all.

Trudy knew that the small amount she had as cash on deposit in her private current account was even more of a drop in the ocean, and she desperately needed that drop to cover her most urgent needs over the coming days and weeks. She couldn't mop up any more of Finn's debt, and she wasn't about to try. She was ending the marriage today whether she could afford to or not. It was the only thought that kept her sane.

Upstairs, the immersion had heated the water to lukewarm, enough for a shower that left her feeling at least clean and clearer-headed.

Without a car, she took the best alternative transport she had, tacking up Tara and riding through the village, past the river folly and out on the bridleway towards the Ridgeway.

Otto whickered and Bottom brayed from the River Cottage paddock as she passed. Giles had clearly returned from the Med, his car parked rakishly on the drive, every window thrown open and jazz booming out from the lower ones. Trudy knew that he would offer help and harbour – he was practically the first port of call for bolting wives in the area – but she was unwilling to go there, for fear of being too indebted to him, too vulnerable and needy to play it tough. Johnny was right. She needed to hold firm. But equally, she needed a contingency based on a few close friends being on alert in case things went wrong. Finn had a fierce temper and had come perilously close to hitting her in the past when fighting had been arbitrary in their marriage. She was prepared to stand her ground, but she wasn't going to take a punch.

It would have been simpler to phone Rory and ask if he would be able to take her two horses on livery, but the subject was delicate and she needed riding time to think.

The yard was deserted when she arrived, all the horses turned out and drooping under the shade of trees in the heat, swatting flies from one another's faces with their tails or nibbling withers to ease midge bites.

She could hear shouting from the cottage as soon as she walked through the garden gate.

'You can't do this! I love you!' Rory's voice was hoarse from what had obviously been a long, desperate row. 'I'm *begging* you, Jem!'

'I cannot live like this a single day longer. I miss my children. I miss my home!'

'And that bastard Piers?'

'He's promised to change. He's devoted to his children.'

'But what about me? I love you.'

'You're young. You'll get over it.'

Realising she had chosen the worst possible time, Trudy walked back to the deserted yard, scribbling a note on the back of an old envelope that she found on the desk in the tack room. Knowing that she needed a better plan, and fast, she fetched Tara from the cool stable before riding back out through Upper Springlode and past the New Inn to Broken Back Woods.

Here, she stopped out of habit and listened hard for any sound of Mutt.

Instead, she heard the new song in her head, resounding as clearly as if she was wearing an iPod, every lyric remembered, every note distinct – from the first haunting ones of the intro through verses, the chorus, the middle eight and the coda. It made her shiver, despite the scorching heat of the day. It was amazing; quite possibly the best thing that she had ever written.

Riding back down into the valley in a heat haze, skin prickling as it burned, she looked out across fields bleached golden by the August drought.

She would have to ask Giles if she could use his fields if Finn turned nasty; and that meant asking Liv, too, and confiding in her. She couldn't face either just yet. She needed the comfort of her pre-prepared speech and those lines she had memorised that would liberate her.

But as she passed the Post Office Stores, about to cross the Green towards the church, village gossip Glad Tidings bustled out.

'Trudy dear! You didn't tell us that you and Finn are on the move again.'

'Sorry?'

'The removal men at Church Cottage – loading up all your things . . . I assumed you were on the . . .'

Her voice trailed away as Trudy kicked Tara into action and they thundered across the Green, scattering shirtless boys playing hot games of football.

Two lorries were parked in her drive. One, Cottrells' biggest delivery truck, was being presided over by the familiar stooped figure of the auction house's longest-serving porter, Sid, and two apprentices. The back was closed and they stood guard like jailers. The other lorry, unfamiliar and ominously large, was manned by two broad-shouldered, big-bellied, shaven-haired bailiffs who were busy whizzing up and down the hydraulic ramp with television sets and hifi speakers.

The front door to the house was open and she could see that they had already loaded up the console table with its guilty cargo of bills.

'How did they get in?' she gasped.

Sid shifted his weight awkwardly from foot to foot. 'I'd already opened up when they got here. The boss told me to use the spare set of keys from beneath the potted lavender.'

'Finn sent you here?'

He nodded.

'And them?' She noticed both bailiffs had upper arms wider than their heads.

'They turned up about half an hour ago and started muscling in on the act.'

Trudy looked at the open door. The colour drained from her face as she saw an empty space where her grand piano normally stood.

A surprised Tara was handed to an even more surprised apprentice porter as Trudy rushed inside.

It was as though a swarm of locusts had been through the place in her absence. The downstairs was almost empty – no sofas, chairs, tables, televisions or pictures remained. They had even taken the fridge and freezer complete with their contents. One of the bailiffs gave her a cheery nod as he headed for her study.

'No!' she yelped as she realised that he was taking her computer.

'Now, love, don't kick up a fuss. It's all legally ours now,' said the second bailiff, handing her a wad of paperwork. She snatched her Finn speech and her new song notations from the desk as his colleague unplugged her keyboard and monitor.

Had she known her rights, she would have been able to demand that the computer be left behind because she needed it for work, just as they should leave enough household goods for the occupants of the house to still sleep, eat and live there in relative normality; but the paperwork she was clutching ran into tens of pages and she was too agitated to think straight.

'What's in here?' Bailiff Two was trying the door to the cupboard containing her CDs and her treasure trove.

'Cleaning equipment,' she lied out of self-preservation.

'Why d'you keep it locked?'

'Chemicals – bleach and so forth.'

'Fair enough. Risky for the kiddies. You can keep those – we don't take household goods.' He started collecting her awards and framed photographs from the mantelpiece.

'You can't take those.'

'We can.' He nodded towards the paperwork as he removed the pictures from the silver frames to set aside for her to keep. 'And while we're about it, can you ask the old geezer out there to unload the piano and the other stuff for us? He was trying to make off with it when we got here, so I'm blocking his wagon in till he hands it all over. I've tried explaining that it's ours.'

Relief rushing through her veins, Trudy dashed to where Sid was fanning himself with an auction catalogue and looking awkward as he tried to make a phone call, his youngest apprentice holding Tara nervously at arm's length.

'Why have you loaded my piano in there?' she asked, praying that Finn had organised this so that her most prized possession, at least, would be spared.

Sid, never a man of many words, silently handed her the auction catalogue.

It was on the front cover: her historic Bechstein with its beautiful dark wood and hand-painted panels, one of the finest ever seen. The star of the show.

Flicking through, she found several other familiar items listed – the Regency centre table, the Victorian elmwood teapoy, the William IV dining chairs and the Japanese cabinet among them. She couldn't bear to look further; Finn must have been planning this for months.

'I can't get out of the drive until these buggers shift,' Sid explained. 'And they refuse unless we load everything from here into there.' He jerked his head back and forth as though watching lorry tennis. 'I've been trying to call the boss, but he's not answering.'

'That figures.'

Just then her own phone rang. It was the Cottrells' office line. 'Yes?'

The voice was a familiar drawl. 'Trudy – can we meet for a chat?'

Her blood boiled: 'I think we need to do a bit more than chat about this, don't you?'

'What?'

'How can you let this happen, you bastard!'

'Are you feeling all right m'dear? In a spot of bother?'

She realised that she wasn't talking to Finn at all, but to his father.

'Oh, hi! No, not at all – sorry about that,' she gulped, feigning normality as she watched the bailiffs carrying her dressing table out of the house and across the drive, its drawers sliding open to reveal all her underwear. 'What can I do for you, Piggy?'

'As I say, would like a chat.' He spoke in shorthand as always. 'You free to mix an old man a pre-lunch Scotch?'

Trudy had a vision of fixing Piggy a drink in the house as the bailiffs took the bottle and glasses from her hand.

'We're completely out of malt.'

'Never mind. I'll buy you a drink at the Duck Upstream instead. Say ten minutes?'

Before she could argue, he had rung off.

Her first instinct was that she couldn't possibly leave the house being raided by locusts. Her second was that she badly needed a drink. The Duck Upstream, on the outskirts of Oddlode, was barely two minutes away across the field. She took Tara back from the grateful youth and turned her out with Arty, who was fast asleep under the shadow of the sycamores, totally oblivious of the action. Then she hid her tack in the chicken shed in case they tried to take that.

'What d'you want me to do about the piano and stuff?' Sid called as she made to leave.

'They have no room for it in there.' Trudy pointed to the back of the bailiff's lorry which was now so full that it would never accommodate the dimensions of a grand piano. 'Tell then to come back and get it from the saleroom later if they have to – let Finn deal with it.'

A part of her felt manically liberated by what was going on: it was a brutal, prosaic purging of the soul, scouring the blackened contents of her tainted life with Finn. She hardly cared, yet knew she was probably in a state of denial.

Sending Finn a furious text, she stomped off to meet her father-in-law.

Piggy looked particularly decrepit, despite his handsome, craggy profile. His eyes were bloodshot, skin latticed with broken veins, teeth yellow, hair filled with dry scalpy flakes.

He hardly let her get the vodka and Coke to her lips before he got to the point.

'Thing is, we're in a spot of bother over this prize money. For the treasure hunt y'know?'

'I thought the bank was letting you have it?'

'Well old man Hewitt is as keen as mustard, but we're just experiencing a little hold up clearing the funds in time for the grand finale. Nothing to bother your pretty head about: cash flow, capital movement, taper tax et al. All we want is a very short term loan.'

'From whom?'

'You, m'dear. Always get paid such whopping lump sums – know you have cash like that on deposit. Finn said it would be no problem. In fact I'm sure he'd write me the cheque himself, but I've sent him to Oxford this morning to value a wine cellar.'

Her jaw opened and closed, but no words came out. She shook her head, slowly and determinedly, until Piggy, swigging watered Macallan and blinking at her cheerfully, finally clocked on.

'Why ever not?'

'I don't have it.'

He pushed out a chapped lower lip. 'Fair enough. But you really should let Finn know if you've been dipping into the household funds to buy yourself pretty things, eh?'

Another Macallan later, after some random talk of horse racing and upcoming autumn hunting, he let his guard down somewhat.

'What a pickle! How am I going to lay my hands on fifty thousand pounds by the end of next month?'

Trudy looked at him levelly, knowing that at least she could sort out *his* cash crisis.

'You don't have to.'

'Huh?'

'Just make sure nobody wins the prize. Make the final clue so complicated that no winner comes forward to claim the jackpot.'

'Should get Finn to write the pesky thing then,' he grumbled, not yet getting the point. 'He fancies himself some sort of crossword compiler – thinks the rest of the family aren't up to the job. Keeps complaining the crowds at the sales are too big, even though that's the bloody point of the exercise.'

'Yes, but now you need to reverse the trend so that nobody is left in the competition, don't you see? Let Finn have his way. That way you don't have to find fifty thousand pounds.'

Piggy stared at her for a moment, heavy lidded eyes narrowed to slits.

'Bloody genius!' He reached across the table and gave her a whiskery, malty kiss that tipped her vodka and Coke into her lap.

Trudy shuddered at both the embrace and the iced drink slipping between her thighs.

'I'm glad you married into this family, dear girl!' Piggy sagged back in his chair with a dyspeptic burp. 'You might have gone to seed a bit on the looks front, but your mind's as sharp as ever. I think this calls for champagne.'

Trudy explained that she had to get back home.

The Cottrells' lorry was just coming gingerly out through the cottage gates when she turned on to the church track. Sid wound down the window.

'Still got the piano on board, love. Safe as houses.'

Trudy forced a smile, although she knew her Bechstein's future was as uncertain as her own. There was no point demanding that it be unloaded back into the house. It would have to be sold now anyway. She'd rather see it go than watch it be splintered beneath the wrath of Finn's hammering fists when she told him of her decision. If she needed to run away in a hurry, she could hardly put it in an overnight bag along with her horses, dogs and chickens. Their safety was more important.

'I got through to the boss while you were out,' Sid was shouting over the engine. 'He says the geezers in the other wagon got the wrong end of the stick. These storage companies are all the same – they employ half-wits.'

'Storage companies? Yes! Awful.' Typical Finn to convince the old boy that the bailiffs were from a legitimate removal operation.

'I'm sure the cottage'll look lovely once all that wood's sandblasted. Messy business, I'm told, but worth it. You'll be sorry to see that piano go, though, I'm sure. Pretty thing – holds a lovely tune I should think.'

She nodded, too choked to speak.

Sid gave her a ghost of a wink that said it all. He knew Finn was lying but loyalty to the Cottrell family meant he would never breathe a word to a soul.

The cottage looked as though it had been ransacked. There was barely a piece of decent furniture left, just the dog sofas, the cheap office desks and folding chairs, the built-in cooker, old boot room 'drinks' fridge and scattered detritus of a shared life. The dogs raced around excitedly, thinking that another house move was imminent. Mildred the Bengal cat had taken to her hiding place on top of the fuse cupboard from which she was spitting and growling at anybody who would listen.

Sitting down in the space that her piano had recently occupied, Trudy gazed around her. At least they wouldn't have to worry about dividing up their possessions; the same with the money. The only thing to fight over was the dogs. As Finn had given them all to her as substitute children over the years, she suspected he would be happy to settle for visiting rights, but she wouldn't put it past him to be mulish.

She started to recite her memorised speech, essential if she was going to make him take her seriously. He always accused her of being sentimental, of saying ten words when one would do, of repeating herself. He criticised her songwriting for those same traits, although she pointed out that was why it had been so successful. So she had written a speech he would understand. Simple, restrained, to the point and practical. She could recite it in her sleep. She would not cry. For his sake, she would not cry. She would take a deep breath, keep her voice calm and low and get from beginning to end without breaking down.

'I want a separation, Finn,' she breathed, closing her eyes and pretending that she was sitting on her piano stool, fingers resting on the familiar keys, drawing comfort. 'I no longer love you, and I cannot tolerate our life together any longer. I want you to leave the house – you'll be able to move into the Abbey annexe, so we'll both have somewhere to live while we sort out practical long term solutions. We can discuss more of those details later. Right now, I want you to pack and leave. I need you to understand that this is going to happen and that you cannot talk me out of it . . .'

30

'. . . cannot talk me out of it. I need your cooperation so that we can try to be amicable and grown up and eventually see a way forward,' she said two hours later, fighting to be heard above his shouts of protest. 'I know this will be—'

'You're the one being fucking childish!'

'—incredibly hard on you, but I entreat you to—'

'Hard on me? *Hard* on me? You've gone mad!'

'and – perhaps – this way we can avoid hurting one another any more than—'

'SHUT THE FUCK UP, YOU STUPID BITCH!'

What she had not anticipated in her many rehearsals was that he would refuse to listen, would simply argue straight back at her, blustering and screaming and swearing at top volume.

'I AM NOT GOING ANYWHERE!' he yelled now, sinews bulging in his neck, veins knotted on his temples. 'AND YOU CAN GET THAT INTO YOUR THICK HEAD ONCE AND FOR ALL!'

'You *are* going,' she said firmly, amazed at her calm.

He crossed his arms in front of his chest, suddenly dropping his voice into an angrily controlled whipcrack. 'No I'm not.'

'We are separating.'

'That's up to you, but this is my house and you are my wife. If you want to fuck that up, that's your funeral.'

They were outside in the baking afternoon sun because the garden chairs and table were more comfortable than anything left in the house – and because the sight of it depressed Trudy too much. It wasn't so much the emptiness; it was being trapped in the emptiness with Finn. In her head he had already moved out, so this transitional process was agony.

'You can go to the annexe at the Abbey for now.'

'No. I won't have my family involved.'

'They will have to know – we're separating, Finn. We're splitting up. You can't hide a fact like that.'

'They *don't have to know*,' he repeated in a teeth-gritted undertone. 'My mother had no idea of what's really been going on between Piers and Jemima and that's by far the best thing. Now that they're back together again, she's none the wiser.'

'They're together?' Trudy gulped.

'Jemima went back today. *Ironic*, huh?' he sneered. 'So I suggest you stop playing follow my leader, playing the hysterical wife card, and you and I get on with the *much* more important business of sorting out this financial mess we've found ourselves in.'

'Your financial mess! You've all but bankrupted us.'

'You've hardly helped.'

'I had no *idea* things were this bad!'

He looked at her levelly. 'I know this is what all these histrionics are about, and I do understand, but you have to get a grip and work with me, Trudy. Things aren't that bad – you are due a big payment for delivering your memoirs, aren't you?'

'We're in negative equity on the house, we are overdrawn by tens of thousands, you owe tens of thousands more on credit cards, we have no furniture and you are flogging my piano.' There was a tremor in her voice despite her efforts. 'Things are very, very bad. And yes, I am upset about it – bloody upset about it – but wanting a separation is not about money. Our marriage is *not* just about money.'

He looked at her as if she had said the world was shaped like a mushroom and balanced on the head of a giant octopus.

'You and I want different things, Finn. I can't go any further with you. We can't make this work. I am getting out.'

'And I am staying put.' He had the nerve to smirk.

'Please don't make this any harder than it has to be, Finn,' she tried to reason with him. 'You have a family close at hand who will help you through. You have a house ready for you there. My family are so far away. If I have to leave, we won't be able to try to work this through amicably.'

'Are you saying that you want to go to some sort of marriage counsellor?' He sounded as though she'd suggested he had a mental illness.

'No. I want a separation,' she repeated, 'an amicable separation.'

'No such thing. And you can forget booting me out. I'm not leaving my own house. My family are *not* being dragged through this sordid little domestic tiff, and I am not involving any friends, either.' He got up and walked off.

'You have no friends to involve, remember?' she shouted after him. 'They're all my friends or your family's friends. You're just as hard to like as you are to love!'

Swaggering inside with a dismissive wave of his arm, he made his way through the house to his office, now devoid of all the high-tech gadgetry.

Trudy went to talk to her horses, drawing calm from their hot, sweet-smelling skin, batting flies away as they stood in the lengthening shadows of the big copper beech. She waited for her heart to stop hammering, then she followed Finn inside.

He was sitting in the empty office, staring out across the valley towards the market garden.

'I'm going to leave now,' she told him, a lump as big as a fist appearing in her throat.

He didn't seem to be listening. 'They are back together.' He nodded towards the big, plastic poly-tunnels.

'Are they?' Trudy hardly cared. The girls' lunch where Pixie Guinness had been so funny about failed marriages seemed a lifetime ago.

'You'll come back too.'

'No I won't.'

'We'll go on holiday – the Seychelles again.' He didn't look round. 'I'll book tickets. I'll wine you and dine you, deck you in gorgeous baubles, make you feel beautiful again.'

She swallowed what felt like barbed wire laced around her wind-pipe. 'I don't want what we had. And I don't need expensive romantic demonstrations.'

'Even if they show how much I love you?'

'You deal in gestures and pretence, in acting the part. We can't *talk*, Finn. We never have been able to.'

'So let's try now.'

Staring at his handsome, familiar profile in the certain knowledge that she didn't want to save her marriage, she was drenched with a moment's guilt, as acute as a painful cramp.

'It's too late. It's over. I have to go.'

He said nothing, still staring out at the valley, refusing to let his Cottrell mask slip again.

'I am going to leave the horses here for now,' she said, forced to be practical. The same with the dogs.'

'I'll keep the dogs!' he snapped.

She refused to get into an argument.

'I'll come and check Tara and Arty tomorrow – probably lunchtime if you need to be out of my way. I know there's an auction—'

'I can't possibly be at that!'

'Of course not. Well, I'll come here. We can talk then, maybe, when we've both calmed down.'

'Maybe.' He glared at the window, fingers tapping on his desk, like a headmaster waiting for a naughty pupil to leave his study and go straight to detention.

'I'll see you then.' It was such a dreadful anticlimax.

As she made her way through the door, he called her back.

She knew he could say nothing to change her mind – but saying anything would build a vital bridge across the molten lava streaming between them.

'You're not taking the car are you?' he asked.

The volcano vomited another stream of boiling flames.

'Of course I am.'

'I need it.' As though that settled the matter.

'It's *my* car!'

'*Our* car.'

Trudy bit her lip so hard she heard tissues inside it crunch, but at least it stopped her screaming.

There was an embittered pause.

'So are you leaving it here?' he asked eventually.

'No. I'm leaving you here.'

And so her marriage ended not with a bang but a whimper, in the form of a final spat about the car.

She dashed through the house, diving into her study to grab the bag of clothes and essentials she had managed to cobble together from what little had been left – her emergency survival kit.

At the last moment, she fumbled to unlock the big cupboard and pulled out her box of treasures as well. She was damned if he was going to have them.

With the box buckling under one arm, she raced outside, blew a farewell kiss to her horses, threw her things into the small boot of the car, removed three dogs from the passenger's and back seats to avoid being chased by Finn, and leaped in.

It might not have gone to plan, and the battle was far from won, let alone the war, but the relief was beyond comprehension.

She sang her new song aloud for the first time as she drove to Ibcote under Foxrush. It sounded wonderful. It stopped her crying and almost, almost made her laugh out loud for joy.

The sunset was pure blood orange as she followed the back lane that chased the winding tributaries of the Odd through dark emerald water meadows until it merged with those of the Foxrush in a lacy network of glittering veins. Ibcote's honey stone houses gleamed like treacle sponge puddings in the amazing light as she parked in a little side road as far from the Cottrells' auction offices as possible.

It was the start of the hottest weekend in August and the tourist season was at its peak. Trudy's plans to crash in a B&B soon started to look hopeless as she tramped from guest house to hotel, starting to feel like Mary on Christmas Eve.

'You're in luck – we've had a cancellation.' The magic words came on her twelfth attempt, naturally at the reception desk of one of the most pretentious and overpriced B&Bs in the town, an orgy of camp Chinoiserie and porcelain doll collections named Maison Poupée. It was directly across the road from the Cottrells' salerooms.

Each room was themed, with its own resident doll. Trudy was shown to La Salle de Musique, complete with pictures of harps and violins and a pink-cheeked china doll in a ruffled silk dress draped over a miniature grand in one corner.

'Nice touch.' She smiled.

'Glad you like it. Breakfast at seven thirty.' Her host minced away.

Trudy switched off her phone, already clogged up with text messages from Finn ordering her home.

At last, she had the hot, deep soapy bath that she had been longing for all day. She sang her song out loud, perfecting the tones, the increasing intensity of each refrain, the heart-thumping, toe-twisting, tear-jerking sentimentality which Finn would hate.

Months and months of not sleeping properly, of living a lie, of existing in an upside down nocturnal life, and of going into hiding from someone with whom she had shared a life, seemed to wash away in that bath so that when she let it out, all the tension and anxiety drained away with the tap water,

Still wrapped in her towel, she lay back on the over-swagged four poster with its musical themed net drapes and velvet canopy and was fast asleep before the last of the water had burped down the drain.

Giles, back from holiday, felt sunburned and fat. For the first time ever his hair had been bleached Howard Keel white, not Robert Redford blond, by the sun. His nose was peeling, his ears were beetroot and he had a jellyfish sting on his knee. He had hoped to find England soothingly cool after the Mediterranean heat, but it was even hotter and muggier.

Despite the pain beneath the jellyfish dressings, he jogged around the village, eager to start shedding some holiday flab and check on his female interests. He turned left out of his drive, looping along North Street towards the village heart.

Liv Wilson had her elusive husband in situ at Coppice Court, it seemed – a tall, boring-looking man in fake designer sportswear was mowing the lawn outside the barn conversion, while a barbecue smouldered on the patio.

Giles greeted some familiar faces basking in the evening sun on the Green as they set up marquees and bunting for the village fête. He sliced a path past the duck pond and aimed for the tall Cotswold stone spire.

Trudy's cottage was apparently deserted with no cars outside, but Giles couldn't see much past the rhododendrons and yews from the church track. He looped around the footpath past the neglected Manse and, crossing the lane out of the village, dived along the woodland path that led to the little back alley cottages behind Goose Lane. Ex-wife Pru had the builders in, much to his irritation because he knew he'd be landed with the bill. There was scaffolding and important-looking boards up offering specialist restoration to listed buildings. He jogged on the spot for a moment and peered upwards, suspecting a loft conversion.

Increasingly hot and bothered, he pounded out into Goose Lane and forked left at the lime tree towards the bridleway.

Somebody slim and ravishing was unloading a car outside Pheely's garden gate, long hair coiled up into a Regency topknot of pearl

combs and dark curls, showing off long neck and slender shoulders.
Magnificent breasts spilled from a broiderie anglaise top, shapely legs
rose endlessly from old flip-flops towards tight little velvet hot pants
which showed the highest and firmest of rumps.

Giles's groin tightened involuntarily as his mating instincts kicked
into overdrive.

Then she turned round, overloaded with bags and baby, and he
let out a whoop.

It *was* Pheely.

Letting out a whoop in turn and dropping everything but the baby,
she ran towards him, flip-flops flapping.

'You look beyond divine.' He gathered them both in his arms and
covered them with kisses, saving the longest and most ardent just for
Pheely.

'And you look lovely too,' she said honestly, because to her he was
the most desirable man in the world, knocking every Sven, Brad Pitt
and Orlando Bloom into the kerb.

'What on earth have you done?' He held her at arm's length. 'You
look celestial.'

'I took a leaf out of your book; I had lots and lots of sex.'

'Oh.' He was surprised by the bacon slicer of jealousy that carved
through his body. 'Anybody I know?'

She shook her head. 'A passing fancy. Over now.'

He smiled wide with relief and desire, pulling her close once more.
'Shame to let all that exercise go to waste by falling out of practice.'

'I couldn't agree more.' She rubbed her nose against his, lime green
eyes sparkling.

'I could help you out there. Need some more exercise myself.' He
let his lips trace hers again, Basil fitting snugly between them. 'Been
far too celibate on holiday – teenage kids, you know.'

'I know. They're demanding at any age. Basil is due for his nap
right now.'

'Is he? Shall I help you in with your things?'

'Please do. We can have a drink and catch up.'

'Plan our exercise routine, perhaps?'

'Oh, most definitely. Lots and *lots* of sexercise.'

In a steamy poly-tunnel full of ripening tomato vines, Pixie and
Sexton made love while the serried sprinklers overhead puffed out

spectrum-filled clouds. The misting billows of water made their bodies glisten, their sun-kissed skin squelching deliciously as they made the green oxhearts rattle on their stalks and scarlet miniature plums and cherries rain down like tiny drops from a melting heart.

'Not bad for a pair of oldies, huh?' Pixie gurgled afterwards as they settled back beneath a yellow Ildi with a glorious crop to share a rare Silk Cut. To celebrate getting back together, the couple had decided to give up smoking, except for their favourite post-coital ciggie.

They were now making love twenty times a day.

31

If Friday the thirteenth had been the hottest August day for a decade, then Saturday the fourteenth was set to break all records. Even at dawn, it was as warm as most balmy June days. By the time the doors opened at eight for the morning viewing of the Cottrells' famous summer general sale, the sun was stripping every last drop of moisture from the dusty, drooping petals of the pansies and busy lizzies in the hanging baskets, burning bald pates in the queue, heating buckles on handbags and hats into miniature branding irons and reflecting off the winding Foxrush river so brightly that it resembled a meandering strip of molten steel burning through the sun-bleached fields.

Focus was directed upon two lots in particular. The professionals, who usually disliked Saturday auctions because they clashed with big trading days, were out in force to inspect the art panel Bechstein piano, matched with endless emails and calls from the internet pages and press advertising; it was one of the highest quality instruments of its type to come to the market in years, made in the finest coromandel, hand-painted with cherubs and lovebirds in gilded oblong panels, resounding with notes of heart-stopping clarity and timbre.

The amateur sleuthing general public were out in equal force on the hunt for a painted dresser alluded to in the clue set by Flipper Cottrell and widely published on the internet by the phantom spoiler.

As a consequence, the saleroom was hot, and airless and teeming with bodies, lending it the sweatily competitive atmosphere of an overcrowded Middle Eastern souk.

A few miles away in Oddlode, preparations for the village fête were at fever pitch. The local speciality Aunt Sally game had been erected in pride of place, along with a crockery smashing stand, wet sponge stocks, a grassy skittles alley, and catch the rat in the drainpipe. Stalls of bric-à-brac, books, tombola, cakes, local crafts and plants were being assembled on long, cloth-covered trestle tables. The refreshment tent was already swarming with wasps eager to eye up the cups of squash, sticky cakes, barrels of beer and ice cream freezer. A disjointed voice was checking out the PA system in a 'one-two, one-two' monotone.

The opening – to be performed by a popular local children's author who, having been asked to judge the fancy dress and art competitions, would soon become a local hate figure – was still hours away. The Market Addington Brass Band was booked for the afternoon, a novelty dog show would be judged at three in a 'ring' marked out with straw bales, a tug of war between the Oddlode Inn and the Duck Upstream was taking place after tea, and local Coppice Court newcomer, Martin Wilson, had made a last minute offer of a miniature donkey for rides all afternoon which, due to his forthright manner and slight air of menace, the committee had been unable to refuse.

Trudy watched from the little casement window of La Salle de Musique in the Maison Poupée B&B as more and more people arrived for the auction on the opposite side of the road. She could smell the hot rubber, exhaust fumes and melting tarmac far below as the blisteringly hot High Street experienced exceptional traffic levels with cars driving backwards and forwards in search of parking.

She could hear someone vacuuming the landing outside her door, pointedly banging against the skirting boards. It was a guest house rule written in large, curly faux French print on the back of the door that rooms should be vacated by eleven o'clock at the absolute latest. She looked at her watch. It was five to eleven. She supposed she should have a shower and get dressed. She hadn't been able to face breakfast, but was now ravenously hungry.

After her shower, she ate the pair of miniature shortbread biscuits from her tea and coffee tray, plus all the sugar lumps, before heading downstairs to check out.

'Busy here today,' the receptionist informed her cheerfully. 'There's an auction – have you heard about the treasure hunt? Fifty thousand pounds on offer. Everyone's after it.'

'Not me.' Trudy smiled politely and headed outside into the furnace late-morning heat which beat down from overhead and then bounced back off the pavements for good measure.

She had planned to walk straight to her car and then to drive as far away from the little town as possible.

Instead, as if drawn by an invisible thread, she crossed the road and joined the short queue still waiting to squeeze into the room, catalogues at the ready.

'Serious bidders only!' a hassled voice was calling from the front of the queue. 'Space is severely restricted, so you must register for a bidding number to gain entry – one paddle admits two. No spectators please. Serious bidders only! Bidders must register their details and a credit card number to get a paddle. Serious bidders only!'

In a daze, Trudy handed over her bank debit card and scribbled her details in the book, grateful that the auctioneer's clerk was a temp roped in to help cover the huge crowd, not one of the regular staff. She fished in her overnight bag for a floppy sunhat and her biggest dark glasses, cramming both on in the hope that she'd remain incognito at least long enough to say farewell to her beloved piano.

In the end, she couldn't get close to it for almost half an hour, extending her stay in the sweltering, jam-packed room. It took her far beyond her comfort zone. Piers was on the podium, running the sale, eyes scouring the room for bids. She felt his eye run past her again and again as she squeezed her way towards the Bechstein, like a searchlight crossing a prison yard.

Her heart stopped for a moment as she spotted Jemima just a few feet away, looking very Super-Sloane in a sleeveless blue and white striped cotton shirt and navy shorts, radiating health with her skin tanned caramel and fresh highlights through her blond bob. With the children at her side, she was playing the loyal auctioneer's wife to hype up her return to the fold, watching her husband devotedly as he hammered his way through lot after lot at a breakneck pace.

Trudy managed to get behind Jemima unheeded and, using her cumbersome bag like a battering ram, reached the far side of the hall.

As she closed in on the piano, she could feel tunnel vision threatening as panic mounted. It finally seemed real that this was all happening. Her marriage was over, her piano was being sold. The former had seemed as surreal as the latter last night, even though she had instigated it. Adjusting to the idea was a colossal mind shift, but it was starting to sink in. Grasping the notion that her piano was being sold without her permission was taking longer. She knew that she could object, could throw herself into action right now, point out that Finn had no right to sell it; she had owned it long before they met and married, had treasured it more than anything. It was *hers*.

But she found she could say and do nothing. It was as though something deep within her wanted to turn the piano into a sacrificial offering, a penance for walking out on Finn.

At last she got within touching distance. A large cardboard sign on the top warned people not to touch or attempt to play the instrument without seeking the cooperation of the auction house staff. A piano stool in front of it was being shared by a couple of older ladies, uncomfortably perching a buttock each on the velvet upholstery; it wasn't Trudy's piano stool which had been tailor made by a carpenter friend of her mother's as a Christmas gift. She supposed the bailiffs had taken that.

People looked around in alarm as she let out a funny little groan of regret.

She reached out and felt the cool wood of its curved flank beneath her fingertips.

'Trudy! Hi!'

Trudy let go of the piano as though she'd been caught fondling a stranger.

She hadn't spotted Liv perched on a nearby bench, looking very subdued in a flowered dress and sandals, her short hair combed down flat and her normally spider-lashed, smoky-rimmed doe eyes unmade up, like a teenage girl. She seemed uncomfortable and anxious, as though about to sit a maths exam while suffering toothache and wearing nipple clamps.

Beside her, an impatient-looking man in a baseball cap and a striped canary yellow polo shirt with dark stains under the armpits was staring into the mid-distance, tapping his wristwatch and jerking his knees, unaware that his wife had encountered a friend.

Liv reached out a hand to touch her arm. 'I've been so worried about you. Are you all right?'

'You mean you know?'

'Know what?'

The man in the baseball cap swung round to look at them.

'Ah ha!' He held up a finger, small eyes glittering, mouth forming an unpleasant curl of a smile. 'You must be the infamous – and world famous – Trudy.'

'This is my husband, Martin,' Liv mumbled apologetically as Baseball Cap thrust out a hand as hot and damp as steamed tripe.

Trudy took it reluctantly, too flustered to smile and fake pleasant hellos.

Martin bristled, sensing that he was not the centre of attention, a position he demanded at all times where women were concerned.

'Not that I'm sure I should be extending the hand of friendship,' he said in a nasal whine as he held her fingers in a hot, slithery grip, 'given that you have led my wife astray in recent weeks – and indeed since my return. I hardly see her. I do hope your troubles will be at an end soon. Our wine rack is almost empty and I want my Liv back!'

He was the only one to find his joke amusing or comprehensible.

Trudy had no idea what he was talking about.

Martin, who was under the impression that Trudy was some sort of dipsomaniac depressive, given the number of times his wife had rushed out clutching a bottle of wine in recent days claiming to be going to see her, let the hand drop and looked at his watch again. 'We really have to go, dear. We need to look in on this wretched farm sale on the way home, and then Bottom is needed from one.'

'The donkey,' Liv explained in an undertone as, from the podium, Piers grandly announced a Victorian silver epergne, estimated at five thousand pounds. 'He's being used for the fête.' She shot her husband a withering look.

'We only came here because Liv was determined to see the treasure hunt dresser for herself.' Martin tutted impatiently.

'It won't go under the hammer for ages,' Trudy said. 'The furniture is always in the afternoon.'

'I *do* know,' Martin snapped. 'I have already examined the item and taken a note of the next clue, and I can see what tricks these auctioneer charlatans are up to. We have *seen* the lot number.'

Trudy was too distracted to register his words. This was the last time she'd ever see her piano. She hadn't even played her new song on it.

The hammer fell on the epergne at just over eight thousand.

'Lot twenty-three . . .' Piers boomed, looking down.

'This is it!' Liv squeaked, snatching her hand away as Martin tried to lead her out.

'Lot twenty-three is a pair of sterling silver George III candlesticks by John Carter of London, dated seventeen seventy-one,' Piers drawled, reading from the catalogue. 'Fine pair, these. Stepped, weighted base, beaded rim rising to a fluted column with foliate sconce. Detachable bobeches with scalloped gadrooned rims. I have several bids on commission starting with – one thousand three hundred pounds.' He looked up. 'Who'll bid me fourteen hundred?'

Bidding started immediately, with a regular dealer winking imperceptibly at the back up against the bidders on the auctioneer's book. When the commission bids dropped out at eighteen hundred, the dealer was uncontested. Two clerks on the phones shook their heads as their clients decided not to go higher. Piers looked round the room.

As he raised his hammer, a hyperventilating Liv suddenly elbowed the unsuspecting Trudy so hard that she lurched forwards, knocking one of the older ladies from the piano stool and reaching out to grab at the edge of the keys to stop herself falling.

There was a titter as the piano rang out with a Les Dawson twang.

'Is that a bid?' Piers drawled.

Trudy was transfixed by the familiar keys, touched so many times by her fingertips; touched more often and with more love than she had ever possessed when touching Finn.

Liv elbowed her again, but this time Trudy was steadied by her old friend, her fingers resting on the ridge of wood just in front of the highest octave keys, itching to hear them sing.

Piers was squinting in their direction. 'Did I hear a bid?'

'Say yes!' Liv squeaked.

'What are you playing at?' hissed Martin.

'Yes! Nineteen hundred!' Liv trilled.

'What the fuck are you doing Liv?' He gritted his teeth, smiling with stiff embarrassment at the older woman who had been knocked off the stool and was now clambering to her feet. She and her friend fought their way deeper into the room, leaving the stool empty.

Trudy sank down on it, her fingers running silently along the keys, hypnotised by her adieu.

The dealer had winked again, forcing the bids over two thousand.

'Two thousand one hundred!' Liv squeaked.

'We don't have a paddle,' Martin reminded her through the same gritted smile. 'We haven't registered to bid.'

On cue, the dealer pulled out, deadpan eyes sliding away from Piers' questioning look.

'Going once, going twice – at two thousand one hundred pounds for the last time.' The hammer smacked down.

Liv grabbed Trudy's paddle and held it up victoriously.

Anke arranged the books for the fête stall in serried ranks. Mostly they were trashy paperbacks donated by villagers, along with unwanted gardening and cookery books and, surprisingly, a rather saucy *Kama Sutra* illustrated with drawings of big-bottomed Indian ladies and men in turbans.

She glanced at her watch. Faith had promised to be back in time to help. All she had to do was double-check that the dresser was still the treasure hunt solution, write down the lot number and the next clue and cycle home. She hadn't entirely convinced her mother that looking it up on the internet cheat site was reliable.

The Green was a hive of activity with people rushing everywhere to arrange, berate, encourage, cajole and panic. Everybody was too hot. The refreshment tent was already running out of canned drinks, and the fête had yet to formally open. The smell of the hog roast was all pervasive. Graham's bouncy castle was like a sticky, inflatable crucible.

'Here.' A huge cardboard box was deposited on Anke's table.

She looked up, caught between polite gratitude and anger. Books should have been donated days ago; she had already worked out a price code using little coloured stickers.

It was Finn Cottrell, looking very dashing if a little ragged. Unshaven and wild-eyed, he did not appear his usual dapper self. She rather preferred him like this.

'Thank you.' She smiled, deciding polite was best as she peeked inside. It was crammed full of Trudy Dew CDs. 'Ah! How – kind.' She was officially just selling books, CDs and DVDs coming under the jurisdiction of the White Elephant team, but telling him this seemed like a terrible snub. Not that she was sure trying to flog hundreds of your own CDs, even for charity, was exactly good form.

'Anything that doesn't sell, just give away,' he muttered.

'That is terribly kind. Will we be seeing you both later?'

'I doubt it.' He picked up a book, one of a true crime series that

Anke disapproved of, this edition detailing a Bluebeard character who had murdered no fewer than three wives.

'In that case, can you pass on a message to Trudy?' Anke asked him. 'She left me a voice mail yesterday asking about grass livery. Unfortunately, we can't really take two more, even short term. I'm so sorry, but I already have a friend's horse with ours, plus Faith's stallion that needs separate turnout, and we haven't much land. Have you got something wrong with your fields?'

'Killing fields,' he muttered, leafing through the book.

'I beg your pardon?'

Finn looked up at her again. There was something about him Anke had always found off-putting, unlike the rest of the Cottrell family who were arrogant but essentially harmless. Finn, with his chilly formality and undercurrent of brooding anger, was a different story and very unsettling.

'Our field. The seeds fell on stony ground,' he said cryptically, handing her the book and walking away.

Liv barely had time to issue a dazed Trudy with an apology before Martin dragged her away. Not that Trudy really understood that she had just spent the only money left in her account on a pair of candlesticks. It was there in the back of her mind, like the fact that she had ended her marriage yesterday and had nowhere to live, but her head wouldn't let her go there. She just stared at her piano, craving its comforting sound with every cell in her body.

'I *thought* it was you!' came a familiar stage whisper close by as Piers announced from the podium that they were moving from silverwear to watches and jewellery.

Jemima was right behind her.

'*Why*, pray tell, are you here in disguise buying candlesticks? And *why* are you selling your piano?'

The tears welled as Trudy formed ghost chords over the keys.

'Don't tell me this is something you and Finn are cooking up to transform that pretty cottage of yours?'

Trudy started tracing the patterns of her new song, still unfamiliar with the progress of chords and melody, her left and right hands not quite together.

Jemima was whispering in her ear. 'I'm sure you've heard about my little adventure on the other side of the fence.'

Trudy nodded, running the sequence again, hands coordinated this time.

'I am officially on my *best* behaviour.' She glanced round at Georgia and Bartleby who were sitting beneath a dining table to get away from the crowds, playing with their Top Trumps.

She seemed to think the whole debacle of her recent separation a hugely amusing jape like shimmying down a boarding school drainpipe and going to the pub. Her brief breakout had certainly loosened her up.

'And darling Piers can't do enough for me.' She smiled smugly. 'He was going to take us all to Cheltenham this afternoon, but your bloody husband's man cold has put paid to that.'

So that was Finn's excuse, Trudy registered distractedly as she fingered her way through the complicated middle eight, fingers dancing millimetres above the keys, crossing the ebony and ivory as though she had played the song every day of her adult life. Still in denial, poor Finn. Can't bear to lose face.

'I've left him, Jemima,' she breathed now.

Jemima did not trust her ears.

'We've separated.'

'Seriously?'

She nodded as, on the podium, Piers introduced a lady's antique Cartier watch and made a joke about women not needing watches because there was a clock on the oven.

'When?' Jemima's blue eyes were on stalks as she saw Trudy in a new light.

'Last night.'

Jemima whistled. 'I must say you don't hang about, selling off the joint assets.'

Trudy leaned forwards and rested her forehead on the piano ledge. 'I didn't know Finn was planning to sell this, or any of the rest of our stuff. Most of it was taken away by bailiffs, anyway. He owes hundreds of thousands.'

Jemima's mouth fell open: 'Is that why . . . ?'

Trudy shook her head. 'I've left him because I don't love him, for richer or poorer – or even forsaking all others.'

'You've got someone else!'

Piers was losing his audience as more and more people around the two women at the grand piano were desperately trying to listen in to the *sotto voce* conversation.

'No.' Trudy looked down at the piano keys again. 'I've just got me back. I've stopped forsaking *me*.'

To her surprise a small, soft, warm hand covered hers and she felt a breath as light as a dove's feather on her face as Jemima stretched forwards and kissed her on the cheek. 'God, you're brave. I wish I'd had your guts.'

That was what made Trudy break down. Not leaving Finn and all that was familiar, not her lonely night in a room with a china doll, not even the sight of her piano slipping away from her. It was Jemima, her *bête noire*, a shallow Sloane Ranger who she thought had never understood her, showing pity and warmth and admiration.

Trudy didn't sob and wail and make a scene of histrionic splendour. Her tears were silent as they slid out from beneath her dark glasses. Her shoulders shook, but only slightly. For a moment, all around her carried on regardless: Piers moved on to miscellaneous and collectables, Jemima was forced to crawl off to stop her children killing one another, and across the room Faith Brakespear – who was heading for the main doors – spotted Flipper coming in and bore down on him like her mother crossing a dressage practice arena at extended trot, not caring who got in her way as she dragged him back outside again.

Then Trudy began to play the piano.

She played her new song, that haunting, compelling tune which had echoed in her head and was now emerging from the full, curved body of her beloved Bechstein for the first and last time. She played with all her heart, as she had once played all the time because she had known no other way. A song that had no title and whose words were too personal to sing out loud – they remained in her head. Yet a song of such immense power and soul that all who listened felt they knew it, were captivated and moved, wanted more and more.

On the podium, Piers blustered and joked and fell silent. Even he was forced to listen. It was too good to ignore.

Lost in her music, Trudy played on, tears pouring down her face.

Outside, Faith had dragged Flipper to the shade of a chestnut tree on the corner of the High Street and Sheep Lane. The traffic made it impossible to hear the sounds from the saleroom or realise the stunning sideshow underway.

'Jemima has gone back to your brother, hasn't she?' she demanded.

'God, you're good, Miss Marple.'

'You promised you'd tell me!'

'I only found out about an hour ago.' He looked exhausted, unwashed, stinking of horse and covered in sawdust, with big rings under his eyes. Faith didn't care.

'How's Rory?'

'In a bloody awful state.' He looked down as his mobile rang from a pocket. 'Shit – I'm on call; I must take this.' He fumbled to get it, diving into several wrong pockets.

'The bitch!' Faith was fuming on Rory's behalf.

Flipper was still searching for his mobile. 'No, it's not her – I think he's secretly relieved she's gone. It's Whitey. He's— shit!' He looked at his caller display and answered straight away, turning his back on her, the cliffhanger left dangling between them. 'Yes? What is it? Are the painkillers wearing off?'

Faith hopped from foot to foot, chewing her nails and trying to calm her bolting heart. She was thrilled that Jemima had gone back to her husband but the news that Rory's most precious horse was possibly in danger wiped away any pleasure.

Flipper batted her away as she tugged at his shirt, trying to make him hurry his call and tell her more.

'OK, OK – I'll be with you in ten minutes.' He closed the phone and rubbed his face. 'Shit! I have to go. Shit!' He glanced across at the salerooms. 'I wanted to be in there.'

'For what?'

'The piano.' He chewed his lip anxiously. 'Is Trudy there?'

'Didn't see her. The place is so crowded.'

He started walking back towards his car, double-parked on a nearby pavement.

'What's up with Whitey?' She dashed after him.

'Smashed his chest up trying to jump out of his field, Rory was pissed – passed out after a bottle of Scotch, drowning his sorrows. Left the horse turned out with a couple of ponies that nipped through a gap in the hedge to help themselves to better grass. Whitey started to panic on his own, tried to jump through the gap and got a broken fence post impaled in his chest. Rory found him hours later, waiting patiently in the yard with it still hanging out. He'd lost so much blood the place looked like the Somme.'

Faith started to whimper.

'Is he OK?'

'He was too frail to move so I had to patch him together as best I could running supplies up from the clinic. Quite frankly, if it was any other horse I'd have put a bullet in it, but that horse is like family to Rory – father, mother, wife, lover, child – his only family. Especially now.'

'Where are you going?'

He was in his car, having buzzed down his window to talk to her, the ignition turning.

'To Rory's yard.' The engine caught. 'That was him. Things don't look good. He thinks he's losing him.'

Faith ran round to the passenger's side and wrenched the door open. 'I'm coming too!'

'No!'

'Yes!'

'He doesn't want you there – *believe* me. Not now. Don't be selfish, sweetheart. You'll get in the way.'

'I won't!'

'You can make amends later,' Flipper said more gently. 'Stay away now, for Rory's sake. Now get out.'

She did as she was told.

'I'll phone you with an update as soon as I can, I promise. But you must do me a favour right now. Get back in that sale and watch out for the piano coming up – call me about ten minutes before the lot is due. And call me if Trudy turns up at any point, OK?'

'OK,' she agreed reluctantly.

He smiled – that rare, reassuring inverted rainbow that lit up life. 'You're the best. I'll make sure Rory appreciates that.'

Trudy stopped playing, the last chord echoing around the saleroom like a memory, the crowd rapt and anticipatory, waiting for more, willing the performance not to be at an end.

But Trudy knew she'd said her farewells. She had shared her song with her old friend. That was enough. Leaning forwards, she dropped a light kiss on its painted wooden face board, between the two cherubs that always danced in front of her when she played.

When she stood up, the room erupted into cheers and applause.

For a moment this completely disorientated her. She had been so lost in the madness of the moment, the grief of parting and the enchantment of the new piece that she could have been back at home, late at night in the big reception hall of Church Cottage, lit by candles and the fire with the dogs sprawling on the sofas as she played. But that wasn't home any more.

She could see Jemima clapping wildly nearby, tears streaming down her face. Pixie Guinness was punching a fist in the air and caterwauling for an encore, her newly returned husband whooping along. The antique shop owners from Morrell, Mark and Spencer, were holding one another's hands with tears in their eyes and soppy smiles on their faces. It was that sort of song. People couldn't help themselves. It made them stop still, think and then let emotion take over.

Amazed and gratified, she took a bow, held up her arms to clap her gratitude in return and walked out through the back fire doors which had been opened to let in much-needed air. Ahead of her, beyond the river, stretched the water meadows and their silvery tributaries. Trudy felt as though she was launching out in a small raft, able to steer any course. With the incredible ovation still ringing in her ears, she turned away from the High Street and towards the back lanes to fetch her car.

'That,' Piers' amplified voice faded behind her as he took advantage of the situation, 'was Ms Trudy Dew demonstrating the beautiful Bechstein piano which will be auctioned immediately after the lunch break. Now, Pottery and Porcelain. Lot one hundred and five – a Beswick hunting figure of a girl on a skewbald pony. Who'll start me at fifty?'

When Faith walked back into the saleroom and found Piers fighting to be heard over a crowd that was chattering, laughing and clapping uproariously, she assumed a lot must have sold for a record figure.

She settled against the wall at the rear of the room and stared glumly at her phone.

Immediately beside her, a bearded man was making a frantic call. 'I tell you, it was her, and it was the most bloody amazing thing I've heard in twenty years in the industry. I don't care if it's a weekend, you have to contact her people right now . . . How do I know who her people are? . . . No I can't chase after her – I limp very slowly with a stick, remember? Besides, I have to stay here to buy a piano.'

'You'll be lucky,' Faith muttered under her breath.

'How d'you mean?'

The bearded man had hung up and was looking in her direction. He was wearing very dark glasses and for a moment, seeing his stick and the big, soppy-looking dog panting at his feet, she wondered if he was blind. Then she registered that a greyhound was unlikely to be a trained guide dog and that his cane was an old-fashioned walking stick with a silver handle shaped like a greyhound's head.

'You know something about the piano?' he asked.

Faith was trying to figure out where she had seen him before.

'Just that there's a stupid fool on the end of this phone that will pay any amount of money for it, so you may as well not bother bidding.' She tried to imagine him without the beard.

'What if I said I was in the same frame of mind as him?'

'Then I hope you're very, very rich.' She doubted his salary matched Flipper's income as a vet, backed up by his wealthy family.

Then she changed her mind.

He was much younger than he looked – Faith always associated beards with old men and Islamic terrorists – and much trendier than his scruffy appearance belied. The T-shirt was Blood and Glitter, the faded jeans Nom de Guerre and the Converse trainers were a rare cartoon print that her brother Magnus had spent weeks trying to track down on eBay.

He shifted uncomfortably under her scrutiny.

'I know you!' She exclaimed with sudden recognition.

He let out a frustrated little hiss from between his teeth flashed a nervous public smile and whispered, 'Keep your voice down.'

'You're that bloke who came to learn to ride with Rory.'

The smile faltered, then widened hugely.

'That's right, I'm "that bloke".'

'I remember seeing you. You used to bring all your friends at weekends?'

'That's right.'

'I wondered where you'd got to.' Faith looked at his walking stick. 'Did you have an accident?'

'Didn't Rory say?'

'He never said a thing. He was always a bit shifty about you, to be honest – like you had a big secret or something. I thought you might be his dealer for a bit, but he's more of a Scotch man.'

The man seemed delighted. 'I knew he was a mate. Always felt bad about what happened.'

'What did happen?' Faith was a terrier when it came to defending Rory.

'I cost him a lot of money, I think. He was going to get me a horse. I should've waited, but instead I got my own and,' he looked down and tapped his leg with his stuck, the big grey dog at his feet gazing up at him adoringly, 'well, I'm not going to ride in the Devil's Marsh Cup for a while.'

His accent was strange: slightly Irish, slightly American, slightly public school and slightly cockney. Close up – she had never been allowed to get close to him when he had been with Rory – he was very charismatic and very, very familiar. She wondered if he knew her brother. He looked like a musician, after all; and he wanted a piano.

But when she asked, he said he was a farmer.

'What does a farmer want with an art case Bechstein?'

'I thought I'd play sonatas for the cows.' He grinned, showing very expensive white teeth. 'You really think your friend on the end of the phone there will outbid me?'

'Absolutely.'

'Think you can talk him out of it?'

'Absolutely not.'

32

The children's author, a nervous woman in a creased linen suit with unlikely jet-black hair, opened the Oddlode Village Fête with a stilted speech into a PA system which made her sound like a deranged mynah bird. The Maddington Brass Band struck up the Floral Dance and the Post Office Stores' owner, Joel, was the first in the stocks to be pelted by sponges. Under the shadows of the horse chestnuts, Martin Wilson dragged along a reluctant brown donkey who was braying for his field companion Otto and, never having been ridden in his life, was hugely put out to find a borrowed pony saddle strapped to his back on which small children took turns for a pound a go.

Anke fretted over her bookstall, constantly checking her watch and her mobile, certain that Faith was getting into trouble. She had tried calling several times, but it went through to voice mail. Something was up.

Lurking in the shade of the tea tent with her children and ever-complaining in-laws, Liv was equally fretful. She wished that she had stayed at the auction with Trudy and that – despite the duplicity and danger involved in prying – she had found out more about what was going on. She longed to have seen the secret clue that must have been hidden in one of the candlesticks. It was the only treasure she was interested in.

Meanwhile, Martin was full of vainglory that he had solved the latest official treasure hunt clue from the general auction and saved the day:

Ifor has no engine, nor any true horse power
But he carries more than Jason towards the leafy bower
Shear drops cannot faze him, nor dipping make him cower
As he covers every hurdle he is safer than the Tower

It was a sheep trailer manufactured by Ifor Williams, a part of a dispersal sale for a farm barely two miles from the salerooms. What

Martin had quickly realised with the aid of a local paper, a key detail of which the majority of the crowd at the general auction were oblivious, was that the dispersal sale was taking place that very day. Cunning Piggy Cottrell, following his daughter-in-law's advice, had made a decision late the previous night to insert a last-minute clue to foil the treasure hunters, assisted by Dibs and by Nell, who had arrived home from a spell away in a rare, helpful mood, writing the new poem herself while she waited up to see Flipper.

But Flipper, working through the night to save Rory Midwinter's horse, hadn't come back to the Abbey, and an exhausted Nell had finally dropped off on the day bed in the breakfast room, watched by her indulgent mother who had stayed up until the early hours writing her diary and cherishing the pleasure of having her pregnant daughter home again. Dibs had also rewritten her own carefully crafted clue that was to be diverted from inside the dresser and placed in the sheep trailer at the farm as a result of the last minute swap-around.

That morning, Martin and Liv had been among only half a dozen people to visit the farm auction from the saleroom and take a note of Dibs' much-worked verse before the trailer was sold and taken away.

> "'Chubby fingers press plastic stock into tiny pens,' Martin
>   had read.
> With old felt tip marks branding dead from alive
> Livestock, culled, slaughtered playthings
> Chewed little edifices of farming. Rest in Pieces.'"

'That's terribly sad,' Liv found those four lines far more profound than anything that had come before.

'I know!' Martin had been busy calculating that the next treasure was almost certainly a lot to be auctioned at the specialist toys and models sale in a fortnight's time. 'I might not be here.'

'You won't?' She'd perked up.

'I have to go back to Singapore straight after the Bank Holiday. Drat! You have no hope of getting this without me, and we're so close. There can't be many who worked today's clue out. They're starting to play dirty tricks. That's why you need me. It's business, and I understand business. I'll see if I can swing a few more days' leave, shall I?'

She had smiled weakly.

'Face it, you need me, Liv love.' He'd patted her on the knee. 'You haven't a clue without me.'

On the contrary, Liv understood how to follow clues very well, and Martin was seeking fool's gold compared to her exciting game of luck, chance and daring.

She watched him now, tugging poor Bottom's lead rope, as the little donkey planted his hooves and refused to budge.

He doesn't understand donkeys, she thought – or women. Since returning home, his single most romantic gesture had been putting the en suite loo seat down once. One time out of thirty or more. And he had pointed out the noble sacrifice so that she could say 'thank you'.

In return, he expected to be waited on hand and foot and he never cleared up after himself or uttered a word of appreciation. Her immaculate house had become a bombsite as he emptied out his pockets on every surface, left dirty plates and mugs on top of the dishwasher, hogged the remote controls like miniature battleships on his sofa arm refusing even to record her favourite programmes like *Desperate Housewives*, *Wife Swap* and *Trinny and Susannah* because he thought them 'common'. To add insult to injury, he constantly buttered up his mother and insinuated that Liv failed to match her on all domestic fronts from cooking a Sunday roast to ironing a shirt.

She remembered hacking out with Trudy all those weeks ago in spring, when she had been so excited to have a new friend and had wanted to be just like Trudy with her easy wit, her successful career and gorgeous husband. At the time, Trudy had joked about all the dreadful irritations of married life, listing those very faults that were currently driving Liv demented, along with more personal things that had made Liv blush. Sex became a currency, Trudy quipped – husbands bought it on credit with flattery, favours and alcohol, wives traded it for new clothes, redecoration and nights out. There was always a bit more floating about on holiday because you were splashing out and treating yourselves. When you were broke, his begging and demanding a pay rise got him nowhere, and short-changing him was guaranteed to start a trade embargo. Liv had denied that Martin did any of these things; now she saw it was all true. Trudy had summed him up perfectly, despite never meeting him.

He had huffed up to her now, a confused-looking child still aboard Bottom who was only cooperating because he was being asked to move in the direction of the tea tent.

'You'll have to take over, I can't get the little bugger to go anywhere and they're queuing up for rides. You know about horses.'

'He's a donkey and I told you that he wouldn't want to do it. This was your idea, not mine – ingratiating yourself with Lady Belling.'

'He has to earn his keep.' Martin tried to hand her the rope. 'I'm going to buy Mum, Dad and the kids an ice cream.'

The children started bouncing delightedly at this suggestion and Martin held the rope up for his wife again, indicating that she must take it and not deny her children.

'I'll buy them an ice cream. You carry on.' Liv refused to be bullied.

He gaped. She *never* defied him, apart from the odd secret shopping mission. He could see that blowsy Trudy Dew's influence. The woman was a lazy, man-hating crosspatch.

'Take the donkey dear.' Martin's mother backed up her son. 'You know how to handle him.'

'No I don't!' Liv's voice rose as she faced up to them all. 'I have no idea how to handle him – or the donkey for that matter.' She let out a manic laugh. 'Besides, I have things to do. Martin can carry on with the ride – that was *his* idea. You two can buy ice creams.' She fished a tenner out of her handbag and thrust it at them. 'I am going to see some of my friends in the village. Excuse me.'

'Do you think it's "the change"?' suggested Martin's mother as Liv marched away. 'I went like that in my forties, do you remember, dear?'

'How can I forget?' Martin's father rolled his eyes. 'You were a menace at the golf club. Started suggesting ladies should be allowed in the club rooms, and to play at weekends.'

'Gosh, yes,' she giggled, 'I went quite barmy for a bit. You must have been so ashamed of me.'

'Well, she'll have to get a grip if she expects me to keep working every hour God sends in Singapore to fund this lifestyle.' Martin thought how much easier life was back there, with his Filipino housemaid and Thai masseuse pandering to his beck and call. They'd both become his mistresses and were jolly grateful, too.

He handed the lead rope to his mother, and took the tenner. 'You

have a go, Mum. You're so good with animals. I'll bring you over an
ice cream. Flake Ninety-Nine, or something made of fruit juice for
your figure? Liv's been feeding you too many chocolate biscuits I
see. Beer, Dad?'

He and his father headed into the hot, waspy tea tent with the
children at their heels.

Left holding the donkey, Mrs Wilson smiled nervously, first at the
asinine face in front of her with its suspicious eyes, bald nose and
long, fluffy ears and then at the small child, who was starting to snivel.

'Why are all men like donkeys?'

The child looked blankly back from under an oversized baseball
cap.

'Because they're stubborn old asses.'

It wasn't a good joke, but it cheered her up immensely, and the
child and Bottom chose that moment to cooperate, one emitting a
snotty gurgle of laughter and the other heading back to the shade of
the horse chestnuts.

At the saleroom, during the break for lunch, word had got round
that the clue in the dresser was in fact for an auction that had already
taken place that morning. The crowd was threatening to turn into
an angry mob, tempers frayed by the heat.

Piers was taking the brunt and, with his brusque manner, making
no friends.

'I think you'd better take the children somewhere less crowded,'
he suggested when Jemima and the kids had loyally fought their way
past the protesters and into to his office with salmon and watercress
sandwiches, goat's cheese tarts and a bottle of chilled Chardonnay.
'It might turn ugly here, and they're getting bored.'

'The crowd or the children?'

He smiled, his handsome face lighting up like all the Cottrell men's
when they smiled, in a storm-cloud-to-sunshine transformation.

Their rapprochement was far from straightforward, and much
trust and respect had been lost on both sides in recent weeks, yet
Jemima didn't regret what she had done. She had tolerated an
insufferable marriage before, and getting Piers back into check was
always going to take a drastic gesture. Like a headstrong horse who
had been allowed to get away with bad habits, he was never going
to be a novice ride, but he was rewarding and charming, and they

had a life together with deep roots and a great deal to enjoy. It was worth fighting for.

'I might take the children to the Oddlode fête this afternoon.' She handed him a tart wrapped in a paper napkin covered with pictures of pheasants, a reminder of shooting lunches in happier times.

'Good idea – always a good display there. Be a poppet,' he called as she was leaving, 'and drop off those candlesticks Trudy bought at Church Cottage. After her little performance, I doubt she'll be back for them this afternoon and you know how twitchy the porters get about clearing the room.'

She wondered whether to mention Trudy's confession, but decided against it. Now wasn't the time. People were hammering on the door and demanding an explanation about the treasure hunt.

'Don't let them get to you.' She blew him a kiss.

Piers wiped a pastry crumb from his tie and, ignoring the kerfuffle outside, picked up his phone to call his brother.

'No, I am *not* coming in this afternoon.' Finn sounded thick-voiced and out of sorts.

'I'm not asking you to. I want to know why your wife would purchase a pair of very smart candlesticks in today's sale and then start playing that piano of hers like a demented Richard Clayderman?'

'Is she still there?'

'No – long gone.'

'Fuck.'

'What's happening?'

'Nothing. Have you got the number for Mal Ives?'

'Whatever for?' Mal Ives was a local rogue horse trader who Piers occasionally used if he wanted to get rid of a lame or vicious horse and didn't want it traced back to him, a common course with many of the hunting and eventing dealers like himself who traded on their reputation.

'I said I'd pass it on to a friend in the village.'

'Tell them to count their gold fillings before they open their mouth to crooked Mal,' Piers chuckled, reciting the number. He could hear an engine roaring in the background. 'Where are you? I thought you were sick at home?'

'I was, but Trudy took the fucking car and I need to get – medicine. I'm taking the horsebox.'

Trudy's horsebox was an ancient death trap that hadn't been used for about three years.

'Good luck parking it outside the chemist,' Piers chortled, hanging up.

At this moment a pair of middle-aged treasure hunters in crisp safari shirts burst in through his door. 'Look here, we really do need an explanation. Word is that the next clue has already gone under the hammer.'

'That's right.' Piers looked up from his sandwich.

'That's against the rules!'

'What rules?'

'You cannot release the clues in the wrong order.'

'It was perfectly possible to collect the clue here and then drive on to Gurtoncote Farm in time to locate the next one,' he said, mouth full of sandwich.

'The dresser has yet to be auctioned!'

'So?'

'I demand justice.'

'If you'd like your catalogue cover price refunded, please talk to one of the clerks, but I really think your argument is invalid. If I were to visit a brothel in the morning, for example, I would not feel it necessary to spend all day with the whore waiting for another client to buy her after I had taken my fill. I would take my wife out to lunch and hopefully make love with her too.'

'What sort of a damn fool point is that?'

'A rather valid one, I think you'll find,' Piers waved them towards the door and reached for another sandwich.

Now that Jemima had come to heel, he was set to ring the changes. He had already decided never to dally so close to home again. From now on nannies and grooms were strictly off limits and he would keep his extramarital activities on a purely professional footing.

Faith pounced on her phone every time it rang, but it was always her mother and she was forced to wait for it to divert to voice mail, ignoring the black looks from those around her in the auction room who had got bored of her ring-tone.

In the end she rang Flipper herself, telling him that the piano was about to come up, despite it being a good half an hour away from starring.

'Shit! I can't possibly get away. You'll have to bid for me.'

'How can I? I'm sixteen. I don't have a paddle.'

'I'm a Cottrell. I can break the rules. You *have* to get that piano. Is Trudy there?'

'No sign. How is Whitey?'

'Still with us, amazingly. Christ, he's a fighter.'

'Can you save him?'

'That's what I'm trying to do.' He hung up.

Her bearded friend was still nearby, leaning on his walking stick, greyhound at his feet. He had just bought her a Werner Burri ceramic dish to act as a water bowl.

'Trouble?' he asked kindly.

She shook her head. 'You can forget that piano. He's going to buy it come what may.'

'So am I.'

'Want to bet?' Distress made Faith defiant.

'If you like. Five thousand says I'll win.'

'I don't have that sort of money.'

'You could.'

'How come?'

'We can come to some sort of arrangement here . . .' That husky Irish-American-cockney-toff voice was as hypnotic as it was comforting. She was *certain* she'd heard it before. It was a decidedly odd accent for a farmer, even in metropolitan Oddlode.

'I don't make deals and betray friends,' she sniffed.

'Oh, come on,' he was devastatingly attractive when he turned on the flirtatious charm. 'I bet you can think of something.'

Faith, who had never experienced anything like that level of pure, testosterone sex appeal in her life, was rocked right back on her heels. But she rallied gallantly, thinking about Flipper and his quest to save her beloved Whitey and by implication save her beloved Rory. That was far more important than saving Trudy Dew's ugly, painted piano. 'I know he'll outbid anyone, but he's not bidding. *I* am.'

Two very sexy eyebrows shot up over the top of the dark glasses.

Faith glanced at her watch again, longing to go to Rory's yard, knowing that the piano lot would be ages yet. What did Flipper want with a stupid piano, anyway? Couldn't he just buy the woman flowers like anybody else? Or, if he wanted to be *really* romantic, he could buy her a horse. That's what she'd do if she had money to spend on Rory, along with the new nose and boobs she needed.

'OK, I have a proposal.'

The eyebrows lifted further.

'I'll cut you a deal, but I don't want money.'

'I'm all ears.' He drew her to one side, the greyhound following in their wake.

Five minutes later, as they were shaking hands on the deal, a middle-aged woman in garish Bermuda shorts came rushing up and thrust an auction catalogue and a pen under the bearded man's nose. 'Would you mind? For my daughter. She absolutely *adores* you. We took her to see you at the NEC for her eighteenth. Such fun! Please tell me you're going to release another album?'

Now Faith's eyebrows shot up. She tried to decipher the autograph over the woman's shoulder, but it looked like 'die lonely farty'.

'Who are you?' she demanded.

'You know who I am.' He flashed the white teeth and the testosterone smile. 'I'm that bloke who learned to ride with Rory.' With a modest nod, he waved her farewell, his greyhound crossing its paws at his feet, head cocked elegantly.

Faith raced away to unchain her bicycle from the car-park gates and pedal madly towards Upper Springlode. It was only when she was cycling the last mile towards the yard, dripping in sweat, that she slotted the last jigsaw piece in place.

'OHMYGOD!' She wobbled so much that her bike veered dramatically left and pitched her into a tall clump of willow herb. 'Rafferty!'

She had just been talking to him! She had cut a deal with him. He had been Rory's pupil and she had never even recognised him! How stupid was she?

Liv found Church Cottage strangely, eerily silent. For a moment, she couldn't work it out, and then it dawned on her. No barking. No clucking.

The animals had gone.

Before she had time to think this through, there was a crunch of tyre on gravel behind her.

It was Jemima in her husband's huge 4x4.

Liv looked around in a panic. Jemima could make her feel like the least popular girl at school caught with her knickers down.

But Jemima was all smiles and waves as she leaped from the car, keeping the children child-locked in the rear in their booster seats with the DVD player for distraction. Liv found herself gathered into a hug that smelled of the inevitable Chanel, plus Clarins sun cream and Occitane soap. Glowing with gratitude, Liv was beatified with the gift of the VIP platinum card that was Jemima Cottrell's friendship.

They beamed at one another.

'Trudy here?'

Liv shook her head. 'I'm worried about her.'

'So you know?'

Liv realised there was definitely something to 'know'.

'Yes,' she lied.

'Do you think she means it?'

Liv cleared her throat. 'Oh, absolutely.'

'So do I.' The children started banging on the windows. 'Bugger – I have to get these brats to the bouncy castle and coconut shy; they've been cooped up at the sale all morning. Do you know where Trudy's gone? Will she be coming back here at all?'

Liv licked her lips, totally at sea. 'Yes – yes, I think so.'

'Then you can give her these.' Jemima fetched the candlesticks from the passenger seat. 'I have no idea what she thinks she's doing. One gets ghastly visions of Cluedo and Miss Scarlet in the Ballroom with the candlestick.'

Liv joined in the laughter hollowly as she took the heavy silver.

'Give her my love, won't you? Tell her to call any time. I mean it.'

As she drove off, Liv set the candlesticks down on the garden table and listened to the sounds of fête in the distance, beyond the thick rhododendrons, the allotments and Horseshoe Cottages.

Giles was on the tannoy. She hadn't even known that he was back from his holiday. How quickly she had changed allegiance. It had taken her many years to realise that Martin was not her perfect match, although she had no intention of ending the marriage as long as he remained working overseas; she could cope with him three times a year during school holidays. She couldn't cope with Giles as a lover for more than a few weeks: he was too fickle, too unreliable and, ironically, too closely in touch with his female side. Liv wanted to be the emotional, feminine one; she preferred men to be men – not sexist dinosaurs like Martin, perhaps, but not amateur therapists who could bake Italian bread, give an all-over massage and listened to Katie Melua.

She propped her chin on the closest silver candlestick and then remembered to check for the next clue. It was curled up in the candleholder.

She was reading it when Trudy walked up the drive, having parked her car behind the allotments in case Finn kicked up a fuss about needing it again. She wanted to arrive quietly, not certain of her reception.

The last thing she expected was Liv perched beneath the shade of the tattered parasol, trying to refold the latest clue and stuff it back into the candleholder.

'Be my guest,' she sighed. 'I don't care. Is Finn not here?'

Trudy took a few steps forward to peer cautiously in through the windows of the house, as though frightened she might see a ghost in there.

'"Hard drives make you tired," Liv read in a quivering voice.

> '"Our trip to the Loch left you low
> Now another superhighway beckons
> Over the global black widow's knitting
> Under the hammer of the dark pointed nag
> Recall the first rainy spell we cast
> Embellished with a hallmark
> Born on a slender wrist
> A day, maybe two it lay against your pulse
> You lost your spirit, but never your charms.'"

Trudy turned back to stare at her in shock.

'It's something on eBay,' Liv guessed, eyes raking across the printed lines. 'Black window's knitting is "net" and there's "superhighway", plus "dark-pointed nag" – that's a bay. I like that. I think it might be a bracelet or bangle of some sort because . . .'

'I know what it is.' Trudy steepled her fingers and covered her mouth and nose with them, thumbs under her chin. 'It's a charm bracelet. Years ago, he bought me one in Scotland during a weekend there, and I lost it. We searched the room, the hotel, everywhere, but it never turned up. I was in such a bad mood that weekend; I was going to split up with him, and I think he knew it, but I couldn't pluck up courage, even though I was still in love with somebody else. Six months later, we were married.'

Liv stared at her in confusion.

'It's been Finn setting these clues.' Trudy gave a half laugh, half sob. '*Finn*. Oh, Christ.'

'Your own husband?' Liv croaked in horrified surprise.

She nodded. 'He obviously wrote this one before my computer got taken away, before the bailiffs, before I told him I wanted out.'

'You told him what?' Liv gasped.

But Trudy wasn't listening. 'EBay! He was hiding clues on eBay while the phone line was being disconnected and my bloody computer taken away as payment in kind. There were more court orders out against him than the entire population of Essex and he was hiding clues in two-thousand-pound candlesticks.'

'Do you think he had any idea that you were planning to leave him?'

'*I* had no idea.' She rubbed her face in bewilderment. 'He can't have seen it coming. Laying this trail has been so meticulous; knowing Finn, he planned it for months beforehand, like a military exercise. It's all still out there . . . waiting. Oh, God. All that bloody money he must have spent on top of everything else . . .'

'And now?'

Trudy turned her head away, blinking rapidly. 'What the *hell* did he think he was playing at?'

A great rush of pity and shame drenched her, realising that he had devised all this for her. Why, she wondered – for her entertainment? Or to try to save their marriage in the same way that the treasure hunt was an attempt to save the family company. Both were doomed to failure.

'Maybe he . . .' Liv's voice faltered, petering out because she was finding this almost as hard to take in as Trudy. It went against the neat picture that she had built up in her mind, of Trudy bored in her marriage, bent on adultery, unable to choose a lover from her many suitors until one started setting her clues and aroused her interest to fever pitch.

Two things were wrong. The clues had been set by her own husband, and Trudy's interest had never really been aroused to fever pitch – Liv had been far more excited by the challenge all along, just as she had been more interested in the husband.

A loud, ailing engine approached and a scratching, clouting noise indicated that a high vehicle was being driven at reckless speed beneath the overhanging trees on the church drive. A moment later, it turned into the gateway of Church Cottage.

'Oh, Christ, not the bailiffs again,' Trudy groaned, before recognising the familiar rusted roof of her old horsebox. With an agonised bleat, her eyes swung on towards the paddock and saw that it was empty.

She started to scream.

'What is it?' Liv spotted Finn behind the wheel of the ancient lorry and grabbed the candlesticks and clue, diving behind the empty chicken coop before he could see her.

There, she hid between a pile of tyres and a cement mixer in the shade of a lopsided shed, almost floored by the smell of chicken droppings, bombarded by flies and hardly daring to breathe. Her only escape route would be in full view of Finn who had jumped from the lorry cab and was already shouting at Trudy with terrifying ferocity. Liv was forced to listen to the bitter bile of a dying marriage pouring forth.

'What do you mean "stolen my horses"?' he was raging. 'Don't you *dare* accuse me of that. They are *marital assets*, and I have put them somewhere for safekeeping, along with the dogs.'

'Finn, please don't do this! Tell me where they are.'

'Go to hell! You're the one who walked out.'

'Please let's talk.'

'I'm not interested in talking. I have taken legal advice and I know my rights. I am going to live here, and you have chosen to live apart. If you want access to the house while the legalities are being sorted out, you can contact me through my solicitor and request a date and time.'

'*What?*'

'You heard.'

'My things are still here. I have every right to come to this house.'

'Your personal possessions are in the garage.' He jerked his head in Liv's direction, making her gasp with fright and swallow a fly. 'But I'll remind you that almost everything here is a *marital asset*. I've changed the locks on the house, so you can't get in willy-nilly. I'd ask that you respect my privacy.'

'Please, Finn – I know how much this is hurting you, but—'

'Please leave.'

'Not until you tell me where my horses and dogs are!'

'Suit yourself.' He let himself into the house with a new key and slammed the door behind him.

Dropping to her knees, Trudy sobbed on the parched lawn.

A moment later, a window in the house was wrenched open and Mildred the cat was ejected through it, hissing and wailing furiously.

'You can take this fucking creature with you. Save me dumping it in Broken Back Woods – I gather that's the place to get rid of manky old strays.'

Liv was forced to emerge from her hiding place to help Trudy catch the terrified cat, who had immediately managed to get stuck in a tiny gap in the stable roof overhang. Still spluttering from the dead fly, and now covered with cat scratches, Liv was convinced that Finn must be watching them from the house, intent on revenge. She just wanted to run away as fast as possible. Being this involved was beyond treacherous. More than ever, she determined not to let her own marriage break up.

'Is there anything I can do?' she asked Trudy, hoping the answer would be no.

Trudy had no money and nowhere to stay. She needed to find her horses and dogs. She needed legal advice. She needed a tent and a camping stove. More than anything, her immediate need was for an armour-plated cat box. Hanging on to Mildred was like trying to hug a flail strimmer.

'No – nothing,' she told Liv, no hand free for the candlesticks her friend was grasping like an Olympic torch bearer. 'Keep them.'

'Absolutely not. They're worth a fortune.'

Trudy supposed she couldn't afford to make any more noble sacrifices; losing her piano was her biggest deposit on freedom. 'OK, but you'll have to carry them to the car.' She imagined trying to barter with a hotel owner for a room in exchange for George III silverware.

'Of course, Liv trotted after her, 'but what about the eBay clue?'

'Do what you like with it. I don't want his romantic gestures any more. I just want a divorce.'

In Ibcote under Foxrush, the hammer went down on the Bechstein art case piano at twenty seven thousand pounds, bought by a bearded man with a greyhound who limped straight to the reception desk and paid with cash.

Piers wiped his sweating brow with a creased handkerchief. The commission would buy a very smart new ladies' hunter for Jemima. She deserved a treat.

Just ten minutes later, the hideously decorated dresser, which was actually a good Victorian oak example under all the bright emulsion and bouncing sheep, sold for just two hundred to an overexcited Mark and Spencer, who still harboured the misconception that buying the treasure lots would increase their chances of securing the big prize.

Piggy arrived in time to see it go, with Dibs hovering five paces behind him so he could talk business.

'Think we've whittled down the field?'

'Undoubtedly,' Piers assured him, relieved that he had switched off the microphone when his father approached the podium.

'Good, good – keep up the good work.' Piggy patted his arm. 'Glad you're back on form again, too. Nice girl, Jemima. You two deserve to make a go of things.'

'Thanks.'

Piggy nodded formally and moved away, raising his panama to one or two of the regular dealers in the room.

It was as close to an intimate father–son chat as they ever came.

33

Trudy stood in Broken Back Woods, craning for the slightest sound that could be horse or dog. Nothing. Just wood pigeons and rooks calling lazily on the hottest of afternoons.

She sat on a fallen tree trunk and looked up at the broken canopy overhead, light dancing through the leaves. The confrontation with Finn had been appalling; he was like a stranger, an enemy to whom she wasn't allowed to show compassion. Twenty-four hours ago they had shared a life and a house and a marriage. Now they were unwelcome outsiders in one another's space.

She froze at the sound of what might be hoof falls, but it was just a woodpecker testing a nearby tree.

Trudy got her phone from her pocket and wondered where on earth Finn would take the horses and dogs. Her first thought was the Abbey.

Nell answered.

'No, Finn's not been here at all. Nobody's here apart from me and Aunt Grania. D'you want to come and cheer me up? *Please*, Tru. I've been so bored since I got back – Mum spent all last night trying to persuade me to let her raise the baby so that I don't ruin my marriage prospects. I mean, what century was she born in?'

Trudy apologised and rang off, realising how life changing all this was. The Cottrell family, for all their monstrous qualities, had become so much a part of her life, more woven into the fabric of day to day existence than her own family, that breaking free would be agony.

She texted Johnny with an update, playing down the homeless and broke aspect. She knew she could drive to London to stay with him at the drop of a hat, but she would never do that with the dogs and her horses still missing.

She blamed herself. She had been too wrapped up in her own immediacy to plan properly. She should have done what Johnny had advised her to and stayed put demanding that Finn be the one to leave. But like her beloved Tara and Arty, she was a creature of flight and fear. Panic gripped her as she imagined the terrible places they could be in now: wandering loose alongside main roads, travelling in the back of a dark cattle truck to an abattoir, or abandoned on wasteland, targets for the sort of lawless gangs of bored youths that shot cats with air rifles and burned puppies alive.

Of course, she knew who she had to call to find a missing horse. He had the best contacts through his work, and he might even be able to get his brother to tell the truth for the sake of animal welfare. Take it out on Trudy, but not innocent animals. Yes, Trudy is a silly bitch and a tease, but the horses have done nothing.

The trouble was, the moment she heard his voice, she started to cry – and that was just listening to his outgoing voice mail message. She rang the number three times and each time she just sobbed and sobbed, pressing cancel before the beep.

Flipper left Rory with Whitey for a moment and hustled Faith into the tack room. 'I am going to try to persuade Rory to get his head down for a few hours while I go home and shower. You keep an eye on Whitey and call me the moment you see any change. Do *not* try to talk to Rory. He can't take it.'

Faith glowered, but she nodded nonetheless. When she had first arrived, wobbling tearfully into the yard on her bicycle, Rory – too demented with detoxifying, self-loathing stress to think straight – had told her to get lost. But Faith was tenacious and brave as well as besotted, and Flipper could see that she was good to have around. In truth, he and Rory both needed her right now.

It was easier to get Rory to rest than he had anticipated. He was almost asleep beside his horse in the thick bedding that they had banked up round the patient. Flipper could almost have scooped him up like a toddler and carried him into the house to tuck him up. He was tempted to employ a barrow, but in the end Rory walked meekly alongside him to the cottage and curled up on the sofa beneath a blanket with Twitch coiled into the hollow of his belly.

'Thank you for saving him.'

'Not out of the woods yet.'

'We're close – I can feel it. It means everything. I know you went through it with Olive. You lost that time. This time we'll win.'

Flipper nodded, ignoring the knot in his belly. It didn't feel like a day to trust to luck changing.

Back on the yard, he tracked down Faith. 'Thank you.'

'I had to be here.'

'I meant for the piano. How much did we get it for?'

When she told him that she hadn't been able to buy it, he exploded.

Faith had never seen anything like it. The Cottrells had legendary tempers but Flipper, who had a longer fuse than the rest of the family put together, rarely ever demonstrated his. When it was ignited, it was nuclear.

Thankfully, it was also short lived and the aftermath was gentlemanly penitence as he issued Faith with a wholehearted apology and a hug.

'It was too much to ask,' he told the top of her head, which was tucked tightly into his chest and shaking along with the rest of her body, like a chastised dog suddenly forgiven its transgression. 'I'm sorry. I shouldn't have shouted at you, but I so desperately wanted to buy her piano back for her. Now I have no dynamite.'

'Could have fooled me,' she mumbled into his armpit. 'You're pretty explosive when you get going.

He kissed the frizzy hair that smelled of fly repellent and hay. 'Look after Whitey. Call me if you're worried.'

'Will do.' She straightened up with a rare smile, fighting the urge to boast about just who she had been talking to that day and what she had done for Rory. It was hardly appropriate.

Suspecting his untrustworthy luck was truly in freefall, Flipper decided to wash and nap before he caused mass calamity in the Lodes Valley.

But when he got home, he was greeted with his first glorious tonic of many that afternoon. Nell was home, playing cards with Aunt Grania in the shade of the terrace.

He hugged her and the bump as tightly as he dared, breathing in her comforting presence.

'I'm fine – great, it's all good,' she answered his barrage of questions. 'The baby's doing well. Milo and I are getting on famously. He says he will never leave his wife for me, and I say I will never leave my child for him, but we agree that we are madly in love and always will be.'

'How very complicated.'

'I think it's perfect symmetry. You should try it with Trudy – might change her mind about you.'

He ignored this, grateful that Aunt Grania had gone to fix herself a fresh drink.

'I'm going to move into a little house in West London after the baby's born.'

'Paid for with what?'

'Milo will pay. He needs a London base, after all. Of course, I'll live here, too – not with you in the annexe, natch, but I'm definitely not moving into the main house. Mummy is *far* too overbearing with babies. I thought I'd ask Finn and Trudy to let me use their bit as they're never there. You know, I think something's awry with them,' she said, watching his face closely.

'Yes?'

'Even more than usual, I mean. She called earlier – sounded *very* odd.'

'Yes?' A muscle ticked in his cheek.

Having been away from the Abbey for so long recently, Nell had let her twin radar slip. She had heard about his accident, but he looked as though he was still behind the wheel as the car crashed.

'I thought you might be involved.'

'Haven't seen them in weeks.'

'You do realise you're covered in blood?'

'Uh huh.'

'And have a broken nose?'

'I had noticed that.' He went inside to recharge his phone, rubbing the back of his neck where it had stiffened up. He hadn't slept in thirty six hours.

Nell followed him, folding her hands over her bump in a very matronly way. 'I'm surprised at you, Flips. I thought you had more balls.'

Before he could reply, his phone came back to life now that it was plugged in and started to list the messages and missed calls.

'I've been looking for dynamite.' He started to scroll through them.

'Dynamite?' She sat down on a nearby chair to relieve her swollen ankles.

'Blow open the jail,' he explained. 'Hard to get hold of round here.'

He suddenly became animated as he saw the list of missed calls and pressed call-back, waving her silent.

Nell waited.

'It's Flipper. You called earl— shh, shh. Calm down, sweetheart. I'm going to help. Are you all – what's the – has something—' He couldn't get past the barrage of tears. 'Where are you? Shhh. Please tell me where you are. Shit!' The line had clearly gone dead. He tried again, but the call went through to voice mail.

'It's me again. I'm coming to the cottage. It's OK, I'll find you.'

'Who was that?' demanded Nell, although she was pretty certain she knew.

'I have to go. Shit, I have no fucking dynamite.' He was breathless with fear and exhilaration.

Nell caught his shirt tail in her hand, dragging him to a halt. 'What's going on?'

'I don't know,' he said, pulling her and her chair along with him towards the terrace as he started heading for the carriage drive, 'but I think she's walked out, or at least she's trying to. She's in a terrible state. Christ knows what the bastard's doing to her.'

'Flipper, wait!'

'Sorry.' Remembering she was pregnant, he prised her hand from his shirt and straightened her chair.

'Good luck.' She reached up and wiped the dried blood from his face. 'You *do* have dynamite, you have *you*.'

He sprinted towards his car.

'Oh – has he gone?' Aunt Grania came back out on to the terrace from her private apartment rooms, having located an industrial-strength margarita and a sunhat to cover her dyed Titian hair which was turning an unpleasant shade of copper in the sun. 'I was going to suggest we make up a bridge four with Bournemouth.' Bournemouth was her speckle-bellied yellow Labrador, named after her last ever dirty weekend with a long-term married lover who had keeled over on the golf course with a heart attack the following week. The puppy had been Grania's solace. He was now ancient, creaky and half-blind, but made a wonderful bridge dummy.

'I think he's galloping into the sunset to save a maiden in distress.' Nell joined her outside.

'Oh, how foolish,' Grania tutted, settling back on the rickety wooden bench. 'Giles has spent a lifetime doing that, and he never wins the girl at the end of the movie.'

In Oddlode, the fête was winding up and Giles was making the final thank-yous on the PA system. He had enjoyed a day of locally made cider to keep his larynx cool in the heat. The fancy dress and art competitions had been judged by the children's author who was duly universally loathed as a result; the dog show had passed with just two fights, a live canine sex show and a bloody ear – the judge's – and the tug of war had been won by the Lodes Inn in a complete walkover, followed by a ceremonial dunking for the losers in the duck pond – for which they were entirely grateful. Wet sponges, wellies and crockery had been hurled; raffle tickets had been bought in strips, the tombola spun and prizes claimed; cakes, bric-à-brac and plants purchased; the rat had been splatted, skittles felled and the Aunt Sally lowered. And throughout Giles had kept up his affable, informative banter.

Anke had sold a table top of books and was hurriedly gathering the unwanted dregs into cardboard boxes ready to hunt for the errant Faith. Graham was standing by while the bouncy castle deflated.

The last portions from the hog roast were being distributed amongst the small crowd that remained, along with cider. The ice creams had sold out hours ago, as had all cold soft drinks. As a consequence, the crowds were merrier than usual. In their midst, looking amazing in a short, clinging red dress and flip-flops, her dark corkscrew hair tumbling over her shoulders and her face full of laughter, was Pheely. Dilly, a similar vision with tumbling golden locks tickling baby Basil in his rucksack, stood beside her mother with Magnus, Anke's oldest son, holding her hand. They, like the others, were revelling in Pheely's infectious *joie de vivre*.

Over the tannoy, Giles cleared his throat.

'I'd just like to say one final thing before we declare this, a vintage year among Oddlode fêtes, over. I feel my own fête is hanging in the balance somewhat . . .'

The crowd groaned.

'. . . and I have a *very* important question to ask, on which my every happiness and future well-being depends.'

'Bloody hell.' Graham caught his wife's eye.

Pheely had stopped laughing. Dilly reached across and patted her mother's arm. Giles was prone to embarrassing practical jokes when pissed.

'A question for Ophelia Gently.' Giles's voice crackled across the Village Green, amplified enough to be heard in the Lodes Inn beer garden, in the allotments, in the playground and in Church Cottage's garden where Finn was building a bonfire out of all Trudy's clothes and books.

'Ophelia Gently, my love, my life – will you do me the very great honour of becoming my wife?'

Emerging from the sweltering tent in which the PA system was housed, Giles – resplendent in white shirt and beige shorts, his sunburn aglow behind the aviator dark glasses – walked up to Pheely and went down on one knee, holding up an open ring box containing a whopper of a diamond cast between two emeralds as sparkling green as her eyes.

Pheely, who had waited almost forty years for a marriage proposal of any kind, had not seen this one coming. And, as proposals went, it was a pretty high goal. In her childhood dreams, she had always faltered slightly before accepting with a ravishing smile and great dignity and then sinking into a long, delicious embrace.

In reality, she screamed. She screamed so loudly that Giles tipped over in shock, Basil started crying, two dogs ran away and several members of the crowd covered their ears.

'Yes, yes, yes, yes PLEASE!' she screamed, shrieking delightedly as she ran around the Green, issuing out a Red Indian war cry and waving her arms in the air.

'Bloody hell!' Graham said again as he admired the way her magnificent chest bounced about as she ran round the duck pond. 'I don't remember you doing that.'

'Hmm?' Anke was trying to call Faith again.

'How quickly it all goes downhill after those first heady days of courtship,' he sighed. 'Before they know it, they'll have successfully tuned one another out of audible recognition. Perhaps I should warn them?'

Giles and Pheely were united at last and kissing now, to a round of applause.

'Warn them about what?' Anke muttered, not looking up from her phone.

'Exactly.' Graham pulled her close. 'Now let's go and find that daughter of yours, who has even more to learn about life and love. I think we both know where we'll track her down.'

Anke leaned against him gratefully as they walked towards their lengthening shadows, both looking around as a dusty silver Audi came screeching round the corner from the ridge road and, in a spectacular handbrake turn involving burnt rubber and a cloud of dirt, belted up the church track with gravel spitting behind it.

'New vicar?' wondered Graham.

34

Unable to make sense of a word Trudy had been saying, Flipper had driven straight to Church Cottage.

There, he found Finn presiding over a menacing-looking bonfire that roared and crackled like the entrance to hell. Wearing thick gauntlets, no shirt and ancient denim shorts, his eyes hidden behind dark glasses and his feet encased in huge protective boots, he looked like a gay pin up.

'Jesus!' Flipper stepped back from the wall of heat that greeted him. Finn was standing just two feet away, almost within the flames themselves, ripping pages from a big sketchpad and feeding them in, though most dropped short of target because his big gloves made it impossible to grip.

'Jesus!' Finn stared at his brother in equal alarm, taking in the drying blood on his shirt and trousers.

'What the fuck have you done to her?' Flipper yelled.

'And who have you murdered?'

'Come away from there,' Flipper moved back further, his eyebrows about to be flambéed.

While Finn pointedly ignored him and detached the last pages of sketches from the coiled spine of the pad, Flipper stooped to pick up a stray sheet and found it was a nude charcoal of a woman, executed in just a few skilful strokes, but still instantly recognisable. There, lying back and smiling, legs wide open, was Trudy.

Flipper felt his throat, chest and groin tighten, run through with the twin blades of desire and jealousy.

'Did you do this?'

'Christ no – some musician she was shagging in the nineties. She was quite a slut before she met me.'

Flipper felt ready to deck him.

'Quite a slut after she married me, too, it seems.' Finn snatched the drawing away and studied it. 'I should have kept these to sell –

worth a packet to rock-and-roll memorabilia types. The artist is a famous bastard; you used to be mad about them. This is a Rockfather original.' He identified Mask, a band so familiar it was like name-dropping a household brand. Their lead singer, Pete Rafferty, was almost as famous worldwide as the Queen.

For a second Flipper was caught out, so thrown was he by the revelation.

'Of course her pulling power has diminished somewhat since those heady days,' Finn snarled, crumpling the drawing. 'She has to make do with close members of her husband's family now – cousins, brothers – probably after Father, I shouldn't wonder.'

Before he could stop himself, Flipper's fist flew out and cracked into his brother's jaw.

Quite who came off worse was debatable. Caught off balance, Finn reeled back, tripped over a box of books and pitched into a flower bed. Flipper span round, trying not to howl, burying his throbbing hand in his opposite armpit, the knuckles decimated.

'OK – you've made your point.' Finn straightened up, feeling his jaw, which was barely scuffed. 'You've come here to gloat but you can fuck off now. Just remember, she won't stick around. Ask yourself what she wants with a dull country vet half her age? You're even less exciting than me. We just look alike and sound alike, so it makes the transition easier.'

Flipper glared at him. 'Where is she?'

'Surely you know?'

Flipper shook his head.

'Christ.' Finn started to laugh, a brittle, dry sound totally without humour. 'She must have gone off with Giles after all.'

Flipper hammered on the River Cottage door for five minutes without answer. He knew that Giles was in there: all the windows were open, there was music playing and he could definitely hear laughter.

Marching round the side of the house, he found the French windows open and, above the music, he could distinguish shrieks and cries coming from upstairs. It sounded like a woman under attack – Trudy! He knew his cousin of old. Giles might have a reputation for being a safe haven for unhappily married women who had finally decided to make a run for it, but he expected to claim bodily pleasure as recompense.

Flipper ran up the stairs two at a time, his blood boiling. When he tracked down the noise to the bedroom, he found Giles, stark naked and lobster red apart from the whitest of buttocks, pummelling away aboard a magnificent vessel. Pale, creamy thighs tumbled to either side of his pumping, muscular hips, breasts as plump as Galia melons juddered happily beneath his chest as he held her arms above her head, her wrists pinned to the pillows across which long curls of oaky brown hair spilled like ink.

It certainly wasn't Trudy. And whoever it was, she was shrieking and wailing with pleasure, not pain. Giles was grunting like a warthog. They were both so carried away that they didn't seen him.

Flipper backed away hurriedly, and took the stairs practically in one leap.

He tried calling Trudy from his mobile, but there was no answer. On the driveway, he found his car blocked in by a shiny 4x4 from which Liv Wilson was extracting a large chain and padlock along with a big sign warning off horse thieves.

'I'm protecting Otto,' she explained. 'You can't trust anyone round here.'

Flipper couldn't be bothered with distractions.

'Do you know where Trudy is?'

The big eyes blinked in consternation. 'He took her horses away – her dogs and chickens too. He won't tell her where they are.'

'Shit! Why?'

'She left him,' she said, amazed that he didn't know. 'He's changed the locks. He told her he'd see her in hell and take her for every penny,' she embellished, 'but I don't think she cares. They're up to their ears in debt – everything's been repossessed, the house will be too, soon.'

'You're kidding?'

She shook her head. 'I think Finn's gone a bit mad with the stress of it all. He's been setting her this weird trail of clues with poems – like the treasure hunt. She thought it was a secret admirer. I think that's what's got to him. She told me that she was in love with someone else when she married him.'

'Where is she now, Liv? Where?'

'I don't know,' she said in a small voice, riddled with guilt that she hadn't been a better friend. She had spent all afternoon on eBay, ignoring her family's demands, before being struck by an illogical panic that Finn might take Otto as revenge against her, too. This sent her to the local agricultural shop for the gate chain.

'You must have some idea,' Flipper pressed her, taking her shoulders in his hands.

Looking up at his face, thinking how unlike Finn's it was for all the physical similarities – the eyes bigger and more expressive, the mouth fuller, the chin and jaw less broad and dominant – Liv wondered what it must feel like to have two such beautiful men in love with you. All she had was unromantic Martin, taking her for granted.

'I think Finn said something about dumping strays in a wood,' she remembered.

The heat radiating from the lane that ran alongside Broken Back Woods was blistering. Sitting high on the ridge to the west of the woodland, it had been cooking in bright sunlight since mid morning, its wide verges burned down to resemble oat stubble rather than their usual lush green pelts, its tarmac dancing with mirages and sticky with melting asphalt, the sky above a uniform strip of cerulean blue.

At first, Flipper thought that Trudy had crashed her car. It was parked nose-first in a ditch, its passenger side pressed right up against the trunk of a huge oak. Swathed in the heavy shadows cast by the lip of the wood, it looked even more battered and rusty than usual, the canvas roof ripped and the front still partially caved in from its encounter with his Audi.

When he heard desperate wails coming from inside, he broke into a run, stumbling across the verge and down into the ditch.

Two spotted cat forelegs were dangling from the open driver's window as Mildred desperately tried to escape, yowling plaintively.

Trudy had purposely parked in the only available shade for the sake of the cat, Flipper realised, pitching her car into a ditch in order to do so. The fat Bengal cat, far from looking overheated and lethargic, was bushed out like an Afro hairdo and had clearly been taking out her frustration on the car interior. The leather seats were lacerated with scratches, the stuffing oozing out, the roof full of rips, an AA atlas shredded and a bowl of water had been upturned and splattered everywhere. The miniature leopard had attempted to clamber out through three inches of open window and, elbows jammed in, was stuck.

He managed to manoeuvre the cat's legs gently back into the car, much to her ungrateful irritation, and pulled the window up a fraction so that she wouldn't get stuck again. She could probably make it through the holes she had scratched in the roof without a great deal of effort, but he hoped she'd stay put for now, safe in the shade beneath the canopy of trees.

As he climbed over the nearest gate into the woods, ignoring the PRIVATE – KEEP OUT signs, he felt icy cold, despite the hammering heat of the day. The woods were cooler than anywhere he had been for hours, making his teeth chatter and his sweaty shirt stick to his skin with a cold, clammy grip.

He started calling her name as he searched, running along the wide forestry tracks that cross-crossed one another, swivelling his head left to right to check each path and avenue.

When she called back, he turned again and again, disorientated, her voice like a woodland ghost.

'I'm here. In the tree.'

It hadn't occurred to him to look up.

She was about twenty feet above his head, straddling a high branch that jutted from an ancient beech.

'So your cat is in the driving seat and you have climbed a tree?'

'Something like that.' She started to cry.

His overwhelming urge was to rush to comfort her, but she was dangling inaccessibly above him.

'Are you stuck?'

'No.' She wiped her eyes with her forearm and dabbed her nose on her hand. 'Sorry – I'll stop crying. So stupid. I climbed up here to get a better view.'

'What can you see?'

'Smoke. Is Church Cottage on fire?'

'No – it's just a bonfire.'

'Is Finn OK?'

'Depends how you define OK,' he called up. 'He's in defiant mood, shall we say.'

'I've left him.' Her voice shook.

'So I gather.'

'He's done something with the animals.'

'I heard.'

'I thought they'd be here.'

'They're not?'

'Not unless they've all gone wherever Mutt is.' She started to sob again, wobbling alarmingly.

'Stay there. I'm coming up.'

Flipper was a brave individual as a rule. He rode like a cavalryman, drove like a rally champion, faced huge, frightened animals with calm expertise, and he had always been a daredevil, into off-piste skiing, diving, contact sports and extreme challenges. But he had no real head for heights. Flying he could just about tolerate – similarly chair lifts and cable cars if stoked up, but free climbing was against every instinct.

Getting to Trudy took more energy and effort than he had appreciated. The fingers on his right hand were swollen and numb from punching Finn, some of the branches were perilously narrow and weak and, once he got there, still drenched in icy sweat but exhausted, breathless and terrified, there was barely enough room for him to perch beside her.

'I'm not sure the branch will take our weight,' Trudy sniffed as it creaked alarmingly beneath them.

'Shut up,' he snapped, rendered fierce because he was frightened – of her and of the situation.

'Have you got a tissue?' she asked, her face a mess of tears and running nose, speckled with bark flakes, dust and leaf fragments. To Flipper, she had never looked more beautiful.

He shook his head, still gripping on to the branch for dear life. 'I've come to rescue you.' At this moment the branch let out a groan and seemed to drop by a few inches. He lurched forwards instinctively and grabbed for the trunk, his arms now around her, her snotty face in his chest.

'You're soaking.' She realised.

'I've been running.'

'And you're covered in blood!'

'I was treating an injured horse and I haven't had time to change.'

'I shouldn't have called you. I didn't know what to do about the horses. I still don't.'

'You did the right thing – I'll put feelers out straight away. They won't be far away. Same with the dogs.' He risked taking a hand from the trunk to stroke her cheek, but lost balance and had to grip her shoulder.

'My hero.' She put her hand over his to steady him.

They wobbled together for a moment, Finn terrified and Trudy in the sort of altered state that felt no fear, her eyes scanning the woods for movement, still certain her horses were there somewhere.

'Why didn't you tell me you were going to leave him?'

'Sorry – I haven't had the announcement cards printed yet.'

'This is *me*, Trudy.'

There was a long pause and she stared at her hands, cut and scratched from climbing.

'I was worried that you might decide not to buy after you sampled the goods.'

'What?'

'Sorry, I shouldn't have said that. We should never have gone there in the first place. We can't ever happen. It's all wrong.'

'Why?'

'You're like a little brother to me.'

'A little brother who loves you in a wholly inappropriate, incestuous way. Sorry, but I won't *do* little brother. If you don't want me, then that's fine. Just admit it. It has nothing to do with some sort of fucking Partridge Family fantasy you've got going on there.'

She stared at the top of a nearby oak in which a jay was calling across to them with repeated rasping cries, telling them to shut up.

'I want to look after you'. He said hoarsely. 'I won't let you out of my sight.'

Her amber eyes glittered, tearful and fearful. 'I prefer to be on my own sometimes – in the loo, for example.'

'Except the loo. Special dispensation.'

She shook her head. The jokey patter couldn't deflect from the truth at hand. 'How could "we" work? Where would we go? To your flat in the Abbey? I'm sure the family would love that. I need to learn to look after myself first. Then maybe we try this thing out for size, not throw ourselves together as I run away from the burning pile of my marriage.'

'Literally.'

'Exactly. I'm still asphyxiated right now, Flips. I couldn't breathe with Finn. I felt so trapped for so long, so shut down and unable to access myself, my life as it used to be, my confidence and lust for life. Lust for anything.'

'Lust for me.'

'I think we can safely say that exists.' The jay, still shouting, was joined by two nuthatches, tweeting with comedy shrills. 'But I am so raw – too raw to risk losing myself, before I've even found the silly cow again. I don't expect you to wait.'

'I've waited a decade. What's a bit longer?' He watched her warily. 'I'm too like him, aren't I? You don't want to love me because you think I'm like him!'

'No, of course not.'

'I'm his brother. I look a bit like him, I sound like him, I was brought up in the same small world as him: same family, education, class, holidays, Christmases and whole damn shooting match. But I am *not* like him, Trudy – *nothing* like him, apart from a close DNA match. He's like Father – pig-headed and shallow and self-seeking. He thinks he knows it all, always has. He's sexist and old fashioned and a cruel bastard at times. I am not like that.'

'I know.' She tried to soothe him. The branch was swaying about alarmingly as he punched at the trunk over her head.

'I'm more like Mother,' he went on. 'I have her quietness sometimes, and her patience, but not her goodness.'

'You *are* good.'

'Not good enough for you, though, huh?'

Trudy listened to the birds and to a distant aeroplane. The sun was dropping fast towards the horizon, a red fireball refusing to relinquish its fierce hold on the hottest day of the year. High up in the tree, a breeze made Flipper shiver as it dried the icy sweat. A muscle was leaping in his cheek and his eyes blazed furiously as he watched her, indignant and passionate and misunderstood, six metres above terra firma.

'You are not like Finn,' she agreed, looking at the way his lips curled in two arched longbows – a far kinder, more welcoming shape than Finn's, from which he uttered cheering support and funny anecdotes, not criticisms and orders. 'You are nothing like Finn. Nothing like Piggy.'

Even dangling from a weak branch twenty feet in the air, battered and bruised as he was, Flipper felt his veins pump and leap in response to the way she was looking at him. He was acutely aware of her body against his, her quick breaths and warmth. He could almost feel her heartbeat slamming as fast as his.

His mouth touched hers and for a split second the electric charge was so powerful they both jumped, making the leaves around them tremble.

'Trudy and Flipper sitting in a tree, k – i – s – s – i – n – gee,' she muttered.

'Shut up.'

Flipper kissed her and for a moment Trudy could forget everything. It felt right and good and too powerful to fight, the best thing to have happened in a lifetime, the most truthful, honest and downright sexy thing that she could wish for. She kissed him back and she was flying, tree or no tree, high above the world.

'I love you.' He said breathlessly. 'I love you with all my heart.'

The kiss became deeper, moving from tenderness to passion in a series of angry, hungry bites. His tongue slithering against hers was firm and muscular and made her greedily want more of him inside her. She wanted him all to herself, she loved him totally and selfishly, and that wasn't big sisterly at all – that was all-encompassing infatuation.

'Christ, I love you too,' she gasped, unable to deny it a moment longer. 'I love you, I love you, I love you.'

Passion became all-out carnal appetite as they body-slammed one another twenty feet in the air, limbs tangling, mouths seeking out skin.

Trudy knew that they shouldn't do this, that she needed time, that she needed space, that they needed a safety net – and that above all she needed to tell him a truth that could change his life far beyond her and this and now. But as her hands found their way inside his shirt and discovered that his cold, icy chill of fear had been replaced by the hottest, smoothest of eager skin which leapt at her touch, she abandoned shame and guilt and morals for self.

Flipper had lost his fear of heights. He was happy to slide down the evolutionary scale and become an ape once more despite his lack of matching balance. In fact, had they not been up in a tree, nothing would have stopped him and Trudy getting down and dirty right there and then, but a sense of self-preservation just about overrode their mutual greed.

Eventually they pulled apart, hands tangled in one another's hair and clothes, their branch now a place of comfort and protection rather than a knife edge of fear.

'I have somewhere for us to go.' He kissed her face, tasting salt and tree bark. 'Not the Abbey. Somewhere else. A cottage. I'll take you there. It's safe. Finn doesn't know about it.'

'I'm not sure—'

He touched her mouth with his finger. 'No pressure. It's a place to stay. You need to find a way through this. "Us" doesn't have to happen yet.'

'Us *is* happening.' Her lips slipped around his finger and they both felt as though they were falling from the tree with stomach-dropping anticipation.

He ran the wet finger along her bottom lip and then kissed her damp mouth, tenderly this time. 'I love you.'

Getting back down the tree was considerably harder than getting up. The woods seemed on fire with the blazing red sunset now, the birds all starting to chatter and call excitedly, the tree that had been their safe haven tricking them with breaking branches and loose bark.

By the time she reached the bottom, breathless and scratched, blood rushing in her ears and heart battering its way around her ribcage, Trudy had made up her mind to tell him. She couldn't wait until he took her to this 'cottage'; there they would make love, she knew it, and after that it would be impossible to say, would feel like a betrayal made too late. If she was to ruin everything, better to do it now while she was still falling.

He had his hands round her waist from helping her jump the three feet between the lowest branch and the ground. He'd deliberately pulled her down too fast so that she'd landed half on top of him, legs round his hips, chest ledged against his, their mouths level. His kiss pushed her expertly back up against the broad tree trunk and his hips suspended her around him, legs falling into position like two pistols in holsters.

Trudy remembered Flipper's reputation for alfresco sex. The temptation to abandon herself to the moment was almost over-whelming, but she found enough willpower to struggle away.

'Flipper, I have to tell you something.'

'Whatever it is,' he chased her with kisses, 'I don't care.'

'It's important.'

'I don't care. So you have three nipples, you still believe in Santa Claus, you have a sexually transmitted disease, you killed my dog after all, you have a split personality – I still don't care. We'll work round it.'

She ducked her head away. 'It involves Nell, too.'

'Nell?'

At last she had his attention.

'Oh, Christ, Flipper – I should have told you as soon as I found out,' the lump leapt to her throat, tears to her eyes, her belly churning nauseously as she prepared to crash the day-dream into the mountain-side. 'It's Giles – he told me that he's your father.'

He cleared his throat, eyes shining with amusement, totally dis-believing.

'Giles Horton is your and Nell's father.' She repeated.

To her amazement, he ran his tongue over his upper teeth, nodded and said 'Good.'

'Good?'

'Yes, good. If it's true – and the man might be a complete charlatan, but this is too wild an accusation to be without at least a germ of truth – then it makes a lot of sense. I have never understood how I could possibly be related to Piggy and nor has Nell. Admittedly, Giles isn't a great improvement, but he's better looking and a lot funnier. Nell will be thrilled. Especially by the idea that Mother has a wicked streak after all.'

'You're not bothered?'

'Not unduly.' He reached out and stroked her cheek. 'Only that it worried you so much telling me.'

'I thought you'd freak out.'

'I'm not like Finn.' He reached up to take a leaf from her hair. 'Although I am slightly alarmed that Giles told you this great secret. It sounds horribly like pillow talk.'

She shook her head. 'He was drunk – very, very drunk. I was having a go at him for having an affair with a friend of mine who's pretty fragile and he started banging on about you and the fact that you are in love with me.'

'Giles said that?'

'He's worried about you. He thinks I'll break your heart.'

'And will you?'

'Only if you break mine.'

'I'd better mend it first.' He led her to her car, from which angry yowls indicated that, far from escaping, Mildred had clawed her way beneath the passenger seat and was now trapped there.

Flipper had to pull the sports car from the ditch using a rope on his tow bar before he could lead the way the short distance to his great secret. It was barely a mile beyond Broken Back Woods, on the Foxrush side of the valley

Trudy followed almost blindly as the Audi threaded its way along a narrow, high-banked lane to a gate nearly hidden in a high hedge. Flipper got out and opened it, only just scraping his car through the tight opening. Trudy followed and jumped out to close the gate, wondering why on earth they had just driven into a big cornfield with a narrow track through its centre that appeared to lead to a small, distant wood. She suddenly had a vision of an old barn with a camping stove and a bucket to wash in. That would be very Flipper.

But he was already driving on again, waving at her to follow into the red shot-silk skyline.

Trudy's suspension trampolined her head up and down against the canvas roof of the car. Beneath the passenger seat, Mildred complained vocally.

They drove round the outskirts of the wood from wheat to maize, the track narrowing into a tunnel so that branches scraped the cars one side and maize stems the other. Then there was another gate, a lopsided wooden five barred one which Flipper hauled open with some difficulty to reveal a sea of ancient meadow.

The track almost disappeared at this point, the bottoms of the cars flattening tall grasses as they bumped and bounced across this small, hidden ocean of green, dotted with big yellow evening primrose flowers – about two acres in all, shaded by tall, banked hedges of field maples, hornbeam and ancient beeches and fed by a natural spring bubbling up at its highest point to form a fast-running, deep-sided stream that itself had encouraged more beeches and willows to grow along its banks. Hardly touched by the drought, or indeed by man for many years before this summer, it was a Hardyesque vision of pastoral bliss. And in one corner, shaded by the tallest beech and a row of poplars, was a stone cottage, jewelled by the sunset, deep-set windows sparkling topaz in the dimpled copper walls, sagging roof like the thickest gold chain.

They parked outside and, with the engines cut, there was total silence. Even Mildred, crawling out from beneath the car seat, looked suitably pacified by the occasion.

'Is this yours?' Trudy asked as they climbed from their cars.

Flipper shook his head. 'Aunt Grania's. She rents it to me for peanuts and in exchange I look after it and keep the secret.'

'The secret?'

'Imagine what the family would do if they found out about this? Flog it as quickly as they could. It's a gold mine. Grania is far too sociable and inept to live here – it's a real antisocial, practical sod's paradise.'

'And you're the antisocial, practical sod?'

'I thought I was, but when I got the job at the clinic and set about moving back to the area, I realised I wanted to be with the family. I figured Nell needed me.'

'So how come you still have this?'

'I couldn't let it go. This place is for sharing, and so I lived in hope.' He cast her an awkward look. 'It was bought for Grania as a bolthole by her very rich, married lover and she's kept it as a memento mori. She won't let Piggy get his hands on it, nor Giles who would just use it as a shag pad. Nobody knows it's here apart from the estate that owns the surrounding land and the odd poacher – plus my resident fox.'

'Fox?'

'You'll see.' He reached in his pocket for a set of keys and let them in through a thick front door that was painted a jaunty shade of yellow.

The cottage might appear trapped in time, but inside it was surprisingly modern with electricity and water.

'It has a generator and a bore hole,' Flipper explained. 'All mod cons. I painted it myself last summer, so it's pretty liveable, although it lacks a few home comforts.'

'Like furniture?'

It was true. Apart from an old range and kitchen sink, two folding chairs, an upside down crate acting as a table and – rather incongruously – a large stool made out of an elephant's foot, there was nothing downstairs. Upstairs was just a single camp bed and a folding stool.

'I'm sorry. I would have kitted it out, but you didn't give me any warning.'

'Church Cottage ended up looking very Zen like this,' she said with a shrug. 'It was the first time I actually liked it there, ironically. Having lived in building sites crammed with inappropriate furniture and gadgetry for ten years, it's an unexpected relief to be able to walk across a room in a straight line.'

'I wanted to buy your piano back and have it here when you first saw the place.'

She shook her head, choked at the thought that he would do that for her. 'It belongs to another life now. I was like Grania, I guess – I kept this ridiculous, impractical gift as a *memento mori*. Better that it finds someone who cherishes it. I just covered it with drinks rings.'

His eyes drank her in, still not believing she was there.

'Did Pete Rafferty give it to you?'

'You know about him?'

'Finn told me.'

She nodded. 'Pete Rafferty gave it to me. Now it – and he – are totally out of my life.'

'And Finn?'

'Finn might take longer, but he'll move on. We'll move on.'

'Why did you marry him if you were in love with someone else at the time?'

'Did he tell you that too?'

'Were you?'

'I don't know. I thought so. I was infatuated, obsessed. When it ended, I fell apart; Finn was the glue that held me together, but I didn't love him as much as I should have done.'

'Wrong sort of glue – botch job. I should know. I'm an auctioneer's son – *step*son,' he corrected himself wryly. 'Bad gluing devalues an object.'

'Did marrying Finn devalue me then?'

He nodded earnestly. 'Only an expert could spot the quality hidden there. But now that you have fallen apart again, you are too priceless to let near an open market. You need expert restoration.'

She laughed at his corny analogy.

'Do you still love Rafferty?' he cut her laughter short.

'God, no. I think my idea of love shifted. All that passion was too much to handle; he was older, he knew that it couldn't last, but I was too immature to accept it. Equally what I sought from Finn – security, lifestyle, co-dependency, reliability – was no basis for lasting love, not without the children I'd imagined we would have. Our life was so static and acquisitive, it just created frustration and ennui. The only enduring love I've ever found is family love. My mother, my brother. Your family, too, in their way.'

'Maybe I *should* want to be your little brother then?'

She looked at him levelly. 'You're more than that.'

'I want to be more,' he said finally, not taking his eyes from hers, a clear six feet dividing them, yet less than a hand-span between the echo of their thumping hearts. 'You are the family I want to grow from here on – lover, mother, wife, sister, aunt – I want to know you in every guise. I want us to be surrounded with children and cousins and uncles and aunts and grandparents and step-everything. But I want to have you all to myself, too. My Trudy. My only love.'

She bit her lip, letting this sink in, her heart skipping with joy.

'Our love, laughter, conversation, common passions and furious debates taking us into batty old age together?'

'Something very like that.'

'I'll grow old and batty first,' she reminded him.

'Naturally. You are the love of my life.' He smiled easily, mocking her now with their routine banter. 'You will *always* come first.'

'I'll hold you to that.'

'I'm sorry this isn't a rock star's palace.' Flipper kicked a skirting board, remembering Finn's jibe that, as a lowly country vet, he could offer her nothing.

'This is heaven's embroidered cloths,' she sighed, almost suffocated by a delicious sense of heart's ease as she looked at the high colour in his cheeks, the romantic stance, black sweep of hair, broad shoulders and curled brows, all set against a backdrop of puritan, rustic white – her Byron hidden in a byre. '*You* are heaven's embroidered cloths.'

'Makes up for the lack of carpets.' He raised an eyebrow, the claret red streaks on his tanned cheeks darkening. They were together, for the first time ever, alone in a bedroom with just a single camp bed and a folding stool.

Trudy shook her head, too blown away by the place, the situation, to carry on the repartee.

'I have a visiting fox,' Flipper was saying, trying to fill the vortex with normality. 'He must get in through the broken cat flap in the back door. Grania used to bring her Persians here when visiting from London, although what they thought of the place God only knows. I think they fought their way out and called a cab to Kensington. I keep meaning to mend it.' He bounded back downstairs, leaving Trudy to follow with just a cursory glance into a bathroom fitted with a claw foot bath, and a second empty bedroom with a tiny, deep-silled window at knee height.

At the foot of the stairs, Flipper was pointing out a cat-flap sized hole covered with a piece of old carpet nailed on to stop the draught coming in.

'He must get in here and then he mooches about knocking things over, leaving paw prints and the odd crap.'

'I didn't think foxes were very keen on breaking and entering?'

'They're not usually, but I think this must be a wise old dog fox. It's certainly not a badger.'

'Feral cat?'

'Can't climb. I left some food here a few weeks ago by mistake, just some biscuits by a mug of coffee on the floor, and some old sandwiches up on the kitchen cupboard there,' he nodded towards a high fitted cupboard beside the sink. 'When I got back, the biscuits had gone and the coffee had been knocked over with little fox prints running everywhere, but the sandwiches were untouched.'

Trudy was sitting on the stairs, leaning against the banisters, watching him as he talked. He slid the bolt of the back door and opened it, revealing a view through an archway formed by two bowed beech trunks that stretched as far as the eye could see, north across the Foxrush valley to an infinite mist of darkening mackerel sky and striped fields.

'Wow.'

'Wow.' But he wasn't looking at the view. 'You're really here.'

'I'm really here.'

'In Grandma's house.'

'Grandma? Oh, Christ—' She covered her mouth as she realised what he was saying. Aunt Grania, Giles's mother, was his grandmother.

'In Grandma's house with the big, bad wolf,' he finished.

'Oh, my.' She peeked out at him from over her hand. Then she stopped herself. 'You need to tell Nell, you know.'

'Later. I need to talk to my mother, as well, explain to her what I know. It's too big a secret to hide.'

'And your father? I mean, Giles – and Piggy too, of course—'

'In time, perhaps. Giles, certainly – not Piggy. Not yet. It would finish him off.' He stood up and held out an arm. 'Right now I am going to take you outside to tour your garden and rescue a car from a cat.'

The last streaks of red were fading out of the sky. Dew damp grass brushed their legs and an owl hooted them on round the boundary of the little meadow. They jumped the deep brook and laughed as they landed flat on their faces on the opposite side.

Flipper rolled her over and kissed her as she lay on the steep bank, grass tickling her ears and throat. His body moved over hers and she felt as though she was melting down into the ground, a liquid pool of molten excitement. Then he kissed his way down with exquisite leisure, along her throat to her collarbone, fingers liberating her breasts so that he could kiss her nipples, running his tongue around them until they tightened into tiny pips of joy. On he kissed, button by loosened button to her navel, dipping into it to taste the salty well, making her belly quiver like jelly. Any self-consciousness had disappeared, drowned in the hot honey of lust.

He eased off her denims and knickers with such consummate skill she barely knew they had gone until she felt his breath light on her pubic hair, kisses stretching down along one hollow dip between belly and thigh and then along the other, breath warming and quickening as he parted her legs and pressed his mouth lightly to the point of her creased hollow, dipping his tongue between the soft folds to draw out her clitoris and roll it with the lightest, slipperiest of flicks into a intense pinpoint of pleasure as focused as the brightest star overhead.

She climaxed so quickly, she barely had time to gasp. There was no great theatrical cry for more, no panting demands that it never end – none of the fakery that she was so accustomed to through her marriage, before sex was abandoned totally. Instead, she gasped, felt a swoosh of all-over nerve-tingling heat and came with a great shudder of delight.

'Wow.'

'Wow,' Flipper agreed, rolling back to lie beside her and admire the stars.

'What about you?' She propped herself on one elbow.

'I can wait.' He looked up at her with such devotion she was wiped away by love. 'I'm filthy and covered in blood, and have to wash before I get too carried away to care. It gets better, I promise. First, I have to go and buy some food. I'm starving.'

'Me, too.'

'And I have to buy condoms,' he pointed out.

'Practical.' She pursed her lips, trying not to be too thrown by his pragmatism.

'I want us to have children.' He rose alongside her, eyes inches from hers and burning with meaning. 'Christ, I want a clutch of us running around. Just not yet.'

'Of course not,' she agreed, turning away to hide her stupid tears

'Hey, shh – it's OK. Forget the condoms. We'll make babies right here, right now.' He kissed her ear.

'No, please let's not.' She laughed as she did up her buttons with fumbling fingers. 'It's just what you said. About wanting us to have children. It's – I can't explain – Finn decided against children after we married, and I just gave up hope of ever getting the chance to try, and now . . .'

'Christ, I'm rushing you.' He held her tightly. 'Lovers – parents – grandparents, whatever . We'll be whatever. Just not little brother and big sister.'

'Never that,' she agreed, turning to kiss him. 'Never again.'

They kissed for what felt like hours, until the owl bored of cheering and hooted away, until they became ungainly and greedy and grabbing, the urge to lock their bodies together in the ultimate embrace too much to bear so that they were forced to scramble upright, stomachs roaring from lust and hunger.

They continued the tour hand in hand, moonlit now.

He was just explaining that the only place he could ever get mobile reception was in this highest corner of the field behind the spring source when, on cue, both their phones started tweeting and shrilling in pockets.

'Let's ignore them.' He gathered her in his arms.

Kissing him was to switch off the lights on real life and find a quiet, dim corner in which to be utterly, hopelessly selfish. It was heaven.

They gathered Mildred from the car, where she was now quite happily curled up asleep on the back seat, and deposited her in the house, where she shot upstairs and took refuge beneath the claw-footed bath.

Downstairs, they lit two cheap white candles from the kitchen cupboard and wedged them into the silver George III candlesticks, setting one on the upturned crate, the other on a windowsill.

'Most of us pack a change of clothes, not silverware, when we run away from home,' Flipper pointed out, opening a three quarter full bottle of malt that he had found in the cupboard with the candles and dispensing hefty glugs into a chipped mug and a small cut glass jug. 'I had another mug, but the fox smashed it,' he explained.

She took the jug and they touched rims before letting the pungent, bittersweet whisky scour their throats with its mohair warmth.

'I did pack clothes, too.' She gazed into the little, twitching flame that divided them. 'So have you ever run away?'

'Lots of times as a kid. The secret is getting beyond the end of the drive.'

'Well, yours was a very, very long drive.'

He stared down at his hands, a middle finger leaping involuntarily.

'You must go. Get food. Talk to Nell – and your mother,' she said wisely, her voice hoarse because she didn't want him to go at all. 'Come back.'

He nodded.

At the door, they kissed as though he was going away to sea.

When his car engine faded away, she picked up his mug from the makeshift table, hugging it to her chest and then draining the dregs for comfort.

Somehow, she knew he wouldn't be back that night. Hunger had deserted her, anyway, and tiredness swamped her. She blew out the candles and clambered up to the camp bed. Still fully dressed, she got into the sleeping bag that was thrown across it. Its lining smelled of him. Within seconds, she was asleep.

35

She woke in the early hours of the morning, minutes before the first steely talons of dawn were set to claw their way over the distant Gunning Woods. It was utterly black. Outside, the resident owl was still calling. She thought she heard a fox barking too, and something else moving about – was it outside or in?

Suddenly there was an almighty howl and something ran across the room, skittering as it slammed on the brakes to make the corner, screeching again and leaping right across her in one bound.

Disorientated and terrified, Trudy reached for what she thought was a torch and found herself clutching her own shoe. She felt around for her phone, but its little screen gave out next to no light and there was no signal to phone for help.

The creature was cowering in the corner now, hissing and growling, its silhouette huge.

'Mildred!' Trudy gasped in recognition. 'What is it?'

The cat carried on hissing in the direction of the door.

Straining her ears past the sound, Trudy heart a crash from below, a scuttle and a snort, like a nose being blown.

She froze. It hadn't even occurred to her to lock the cottage door; now she felt vulnerable and terribly afraid. She didn't know where the light switches were. She didn't even have a have a candlestick to defend herself with; they were both downstairs.

She sat up slowly and eased her feet on to the bare boards, standing up as quietly as she could. Tiptoeing through the door, she hovered at the top of the stairs, waiting for her eyes to adjust to the dark.

There was another snort and sniff downstairs, followed by a clatter of something being kicked over.

Still holding her shoe in her hand, she crept down, wincing at every creak of board. She could just about see a panel of light switches ahead of her in the little lobby and knew that she could hit them before bursting into the kitchen. It was her best chance. If it was Finn, she'd hammer him over the head with a size six mule and run for it.

She gritted her teeth, hit the lights, let out a banshee wail, raised her mule and lunged.

With a terrified yelp, the little creature she had disturbed fled behind the crate – but not before Trudy had taken in its dimensions, colouring and familiar ratfink face.

'Mutt?'

He stayed put, in hiding.

'Mutt?' She tamed her voice to sound more cajoling.

He crept out from behind the crate, ropy tail waving nervously between his legs, head pressed subserviently towards the ground.

Thin, frightened and almost feral after so many weeks living rough, the little dog was beyond gratified to find himself gathered into a hug and showered with kisses, then tummy-tickled and ear scratched. He was just skeleton and scruff, covered with fleas and scratches, but otherwise intact.

'I'm sorry I haven't any food, baby,' Trudy told him as she carried him upstairs.

Mutt was just as happy to spend a few hours pressed up against a warm human being in a sleeping bag, safe and secure for the first time in weeks.

The feeling was mutual.

Only Mildred remained singularly unimpressed, stealing back to the safety of the claw-foot bath which, a full sized leopard to her Lilliputian one, protected her with its sturdy bulk.

Later that morning, Flipper arrived on horse back, bearing a full breakfast of miraculously unbroken eggs, bacon, huge field mushroom, home grown tomatoes from the Abbey hothouses and freshly baked bread from his mother. He let Popeye loose in the small corrugated barn beside the cottage and carried his booty into the house to find Trudy washing Mutt in the claw foot bath.

Their reunion was rapturous, soapy and noisy – as was Flipper and Trudy's.

The breakfast was a greedy feast for all three, ravenous after too long without a decent meal, not caring that they had to cook it all in one small, crusty saucepan and a grill tray that appeared to have been used to wash paintbrushes, then share it from a fruit bowl using a soup spoon and a carving fork. It didn't matter. They were sharing breakfast as they had so often before, a ritual finally shared entirely alone in their new, loved-up bubble.

'I talked to my mother all night,' Flipper told her as they forked up rashers of bacon. 'Christ, there's a story. We've agreed to tell Nell the basics for now – Mother thinks her hormones are too volatile to take more. She's going to talk to her as soon as she can.'

'And Giles?'

'He can wait.' He rubbed his face tiredly, yawns ripping through him. 'I told my mother about us.'

'Christ! What did she say?'

'Let's say it's the first time I've ever heard her swear. Finn hasn't said a thing, of course.'

'Oh, God.'

'He'll be fine. Rory seems to think he might have been seeking . . . a distraction of his own recently.' He cleared his throat, uncertain whether he'd be hitting a raw nerve.

'Oh yes?' It was raw, but Trudy refused to let on how raw just yet. 'And how does Rory know?'

'I popped in to see him on the way back here. His best horse took a hammering the day before yesterday, but it's pulling through. He's going to call everyone he knows to try and trace your horses – I've already asked the girls at the clinic to send out emails and print some posters. Finn is completely tight-lipped, of course, though Mother called him, and then Rory tried. He just told one to mind her own business, the other to fuck off.'

'Oh. God.' Trudy gagged on a mushroom. 'He's falling apart.'

'As I say, perhaps not – Rory says he definitely saw Finn in the Mill Race Inn at Lower Ditting with a mystery woman a couple of weeks ago.'

'Really?'

'For sure. Rory was there with Jemima, who was so paranoid that she refused to even let him go to the loo in case they were recognised by one of her mates – although, God knows, the Mill Race is in the middle of nowhere and everyone who drinks there is related to one another. But he swears it was Finn, and he wasn't with you.'

'Plainly.'

'Jealous?'

'Furious,' she fumed. 'He thinks I've been shagging away from home for bloody months.' She thought about the secret treasure hunt clues which she had imagined to be teasing suggestions of adultery, but were in fact accusations. 'And I haven't. He, meanwhile, has.'

'A meal does not necessarily indicate an affair.' He speared a tomato with the carving fork, wondering why in hell he was playing devil's advocate. 'Look at us – we haven't even slept together yet.'

The 'yet' hung tantalisingly in the air like an echo.

Trudy was shaking her head. 'Finn's a tightwad. He wouldn't buy a woman dinner unless he thought he was getting a shag out of it.'

Flipper snorted and held up the little red sphere. 'I have a similar attitude to breakfast.'

'You do?' She spooned up her fried egg in one.

'Especially where free range eggs are concerned.'

'In that case, I hope you bought condoms so that no free eggs are fertilised?'

'You know, I didn't. My mother went to such a lot of effort last night to remind me that I am a good Catholic, I didn't have the heart.'

She put down her spoon. 'Then we must refrain.'

He shook his head, a tomato pip on his lip.

'Yes we must.'

Still he shook his head.

'We must. There is only a single camp bed for a start.'

She reached out a finger to wipe away the pip and he snatched her wrist, pulling her across the makeshift table towards him.

Seconds later, Mutt was enjoying the feast alone, tipped all over the floor, while Flipper carried Trudy outside, both laughing and kissing and Trudy protesting that she was too heavy.

The sun was high, but swathed in mist; the meadow still dewy and cool as a crisp mattress. There, Trudy and Flipper rolled blissfully through the grasses together, creating a crop circle that even Reg Presley would have difficulty explaining as they made whoopee with complete disregard for their families past, present or future. They were family now. That was all that counted.

36

Nell woke with her first contraction in the early hours of the morning on the day of the Cottrells' specialist toy and models sale. Only her parents were in the house and, assuming them both to still be in bed asleep, Nell pottered around the apartment she usually shared with Flipper, checking her hospital bag and running a bath to soothe the cramps.

She felt surprisingly calm, sipping a raspberry leaf tea in the bath and listening to an all-night radio show. She was looking forward to meeting her baby; late pregnancy had become uncomfortable and limiting. Life was about to begin – literally.

She texted Milo, who was at his home in Amsterdam with his wife, so calling him was a complete no-no, and then she texted Magnus to let him know their baby was imminent.

Starting to feel excited, she decided to get dressed and head for the Abbey's main kitchen for some of the lemon drizzle cake she had seen her mother baking the previous afternoon. The midwife had told her to try to store some slow release energy food early in labour.

Stopping on the back stairs to breathe her way through a short, mild contraction, she glanced out of the little mullioned window and saw a light spilling on to the courtyard below from the library. Somebody was up.

It was Dibs, sitting at the high-tech laptop Finn had bought her for her sixty-fifth birthday and which, as far as most of the family knew, she never touched. Everyone assumed she was too frightened although she had occasionally played Solitaire with it.

Not looking round from typing with one finger when Nell walked in, she reached a hand up over her shoulder and her daughter moved across the room to take it, standing behind her and reading.

Nell's eyes widened.

'*You're* the phantom blogger!'

'Don't sound so surprised. I once got an A grade in matriculation

I'll have you know. It's quite easy to master this little contraption. I borrowed a book about it from the library.'

'But you've been publishing all the treasure hunt clues and answers on the internet!'

'It seemed only fair. Your father is a terrible cheat, so I knew he'd try to bend the rules somehow, and it's not as though I'm really changing anything. There can only be one winner.'

'Daddy doesn't want there to be a winner at all, does he?'

'Now that would be a very unchristian thing to assume.'

Nell stared at her with new-found admiration. Her mother, always an avid diary-keeper, note taker and letter writer was also, it seemed, a clandestine blogger in order to remain moral arbiter of the Cottrell clan.

She winced as another cramp sliced through her.

Dibs touched her daughter's belly. 'Have you called the midwife?'

'Not yet.' Nell perched on the library steps. 'It will be hours before I need to go to the unit.'

'Very wise.' Dibs switched off her computer, the next day's clue ready to go live at the press of a button. 'I'll make us a cup of tea.'

'And lemon cake?'

'Oh, I gave that to Finn. I'll bake another.'

'But it's three in the morning,' Nell pointed out.

'I often bake in the early hours.' Dibs stood up and held out her hand. 'It's the perfect time. When I went into labour with Finn, it was just after midnight and I baked two lots of scones, some soda bread and a porter cake to keep your father going while I was in hospital.'

'What about when Flipper and I were born?'

'I was too busy thanking God.'

Nell threaded her arm round her waist as they walked towards the kitchen. 'You're not too mad at Flipper, are you? About Trudy?'

Dibs managed to shake her head with a faint smile. 'He knows his heart better than any of us. I just hope to God she makes him happier than she made Finn.'

'I think it'll all work out. Look at me. I'm happy and I'm hardly conventional. Sometimes marriage isn't the answer to a happy ever after, you know. This,' she patted her belly, 'is going to make my life completely different and bring so much love into my life. *All* our lives.'

'You are a good soul, although may the Lord forgive you your wilfulness.'

They walked into the huge kitchen with its comforting warmth and sweet cooking smells.

Nell turned to face her in the half light. 'I know Magnus and I aren't together as you would have liked, but he will be a wonderful father. This baby has the *best* genes. He is an incredible man.'

Dibs nodded, stifling a curious sob in her throat. 'I *do* understand. I should have given you the chance to know your father in the way that this baby will have. Your father is an incredible man.'

Nell sniggered. 'C'mon Mum – we both know he's a pig-headed old despot.'

'No, *your* father.' Dibs took her hand, her mournful, mountain hare eyes shining brightly. 'I am going to tell you something, my darling girl, because it is time and I think you should find out before your own child is born. It is very important that you know the truth . . .'

At almost exactly the same moment as the hammer fell on the penultimate lot in the Cottrells' treasure hunt, Piggy barking out the paddle number to his assistant and reaching into his blazer pocket for his hip flask, Nell gave birth to a baby daughter.

Bald, blue-eyed and very red-faced, Giselle Caoimhe Cottrell-Olensen was placed on her mother's stomach, still sticky and wet with the umbilical attached, and her father at her side.

Her grandmothers, called back across the road to the Maddington Maternity Hospital from where they had been banished to the pub by the midwives, were ecstatic to greet the little bundle, now cleaned up, swaddled in a white blanket and sporting a pink beanie on her bald head.

'She should have a name beginning with a "P",' Dibs fretted while Anke took pictures with her mobile phone and started texting them to friends and family.

'Jemima didn't give her brats P names,' Nell pointed out.

'True,' Dibs smiled. 'Lord, but she's gorgeous!'

'Just like her mum,' Magnus grinned.

'And her father,' Anke said proudly, inadvertently sending a photograph of Giselle latching on to the breast for the first time to her farrier.

'And her grandparents.' Nell beamed from Anke to her mother and she and Dibs exchanged a look of private, contented understanding.

At the toy and model sale, Faith flipped open her phone and regarded the photograph of her new niece without much interest. Babies really weren't her thing, and Magnus's love life was too messy to celebrate.

She was in a furious bad mood. Rory was still behaving as though she didn't exist and if she went near him, he snapped her head off or was just too drunk to notice her.

She longed to be at the yard now, but her mother had sent her auction clue-hunting again while she sat in vigil for this boring baby to be born. Now she had to wait in a long queue to get out of the saleroom. The field had certainly thinned – Faith suspected that very few knew about the obscure blog, and those left in the hunt were getting shifty and competitive, no longer sharing tips and camaraderie as they had in the initial stages.

In front of her, Liv Wilson and her husband were having a badly disguised scrap behind fixed smiles; Faith recognised Liv and her shy, nervous children from several riding lessons with Rory, and remembered that she had bought the Gentlys' tricky roan, although she had never seen her riding it. That appeared to be the crux of the argument.

'We should just have done and sell it,' he was saying. 'It costs a fortune to keep and you never use it.'

'*He* is not a machine,' Liv said through gritted teeth. 'Unlike that hugely expensive motorbike that's been gathering dust in the garage for three years.'

'That's my pride and joy!'

'And Otto is mine.'

'Well, you are going to have to move him at least.'

'Why?'

'I don't trust that oily bastard, Giles Hornton.'

'He's just got engaged for Christ's sake.'

'From what I hear that will make no difference. You have no idea what men like him are like. The horse must be moved before I fly.'

'But you're leaving in less than forty-eight hours!'

'Not if the horse hasn't moved,' he said petulantly. 'With my job at stake, on your head be it.'

'All right! As soon as we get home, I'll phone Rory Midwinter about livery.'

'I wouldn't bother if I were you.' Faith didn't look up from forwarding the photograph of Giselle to Rory, who loved babies and might, she hoped, be enchanted from his stupor. 'He's letting everything go to pot up there. Lives for the bottle. Odds are he'll be in rehab by the end of September.'

Liv elbowed her husband hastily from the building, the children trailing along behind.

'Who was that?'

'Faith Brakespear. Not quite all there. I'm sure Rory will be fine to take Otto.'

'And Bottom?' the children whined as they were wedged into booster seats.

'Him, too,' she promised, already planning to move the horse and donkey back as soon as Martin had flown to Singapore.

She was getting quite good at deceiving him without feeling that familiar vice grip of guilt. In fact, having her own secrets was one of the few things that had really cheered her up during his long leave from Singapore. Some secrets were far too dangerous to keep up while he was at home, but others – like Trudy's private treasure hunt – were far better than his domineering handling of the main Cottrell event.

Having tracked down the charm bracelet on eBay, being sold on a Buy-it-Now at a vastly overinflated price, Liv had waited for the post each morning like a child at Christmas. Eventually, when the little parcel arrived, she'd signed for it with a shaking hand in case any of her family came to investigate the doorbell. Then, unable to wait, she'd dashed straight into the downstairs loo and ripped into the Jiffy bag and bubble wrap, barely glancing at the charm bracelet before locating the next clue and unfolding it:

> He likes to brag about his wealth
> Or so it seems in print
> Rags to some, but I'm a snob
> Never made a mint.
>
> Tradition is my bag, you see
> Old-fashioned sort, that's basically me
> Not terribly keen on adultery
> Encountered somewhat painfully.

Come on, we'll keep it classified
Hold your horses and Miller's Guide
Open lips and legs for fulsome kisses
Atop the mounted king that stole my missus

Divorce or die on the toss of a coin
Says the married tart led by the groin.

Liv could hardly pretend that this was romantic; in fact, there was a definite implicit threat. Yet she was rendered breathless by its poignancy and hurt anger; it sent a frisson of excitement through her as she read down the first letters of each line – *Hornton Echo* Ads – and realised that she had to scour the local paper.

Having been delayed by Martin's military trip to the toy and model sale, she was now finally free to get back to the real hunt.

As soon as they all got back home, she left Martin checking the cricket scores with his father, and grabbed the kids with offers of ice cream.

Liv was in and out of the village shop like a whirlwind, taking her newspaper and an ice cream on to the Green to settle on a bench in front of the duck pond, shaded by one of the horse chestnuts. The children, equally relieved to be free from their father for a few minutes, giggled as the ducks ate their crumbled Cornetto cones while Liv flipped the pages.

There, in the midst of classified adverts for outgrown children's bikes, unwanted three-piece suites and stolen iPods was a small ad in a section of its own – Rare Coins – which stood out as completely incongruous, boasting a rare hammered silver Charles I crown featuring the king on a horse, and dated 1645. It had to be the one.

She dialled the number from her mobile, worried that it would be Finn himself who picked up the phone. But it was an elderly sounding man in Market Addington who explained that he wanted a thousand pounds for the coin.

Liv balked. She had no money left in her personal account and Martin had suddenly become very twitchy about the joint account, arranging for the bank's text service to SMS him the balance daily along with the last three transactions. He said that it was because she had 'lost control' of the family budget and become too 'high maintenance' like her yummy mummy friends. As always, he was trying to regiment her.

She had credit cards, but she doubted the old man would take those, and getting cash out on them was hugely expensive. She would have to ask Martin.

He was at home in the study, checking through an itemised phone bill.

'Whose number is this?' He pointed at one that came up repeatedly.

'Oh – Trudy's; I mean, Church Cottage.'

'I see. And this one?'

'Her mobile.'

'So if I call it, she'll answer?'

'More likely Finn,' she said quickly, wishing she had used her mobile rather than the home phone. 'He kept her phone when he changed the locks and burned her clothes and everything. He might think you are having an affair with her and come round and beat you up.' She was delighted at her quick-minded deflection from the lie.

'Dreadful business, divorce. Makes perfectly normal human beings behave like small children. That's why we will never do it.' He made it sound as though he was railing against an antisocial pastime like lighting bonfires at weekends or hogging the motorway's centre lane.

'Of course not.' She shook her head furiously, relief coursing through her.

'We are made of sterner stuff; we took *our* vows seriously: "to have and to hold from this day forward . . . till death us do part".'

'Exactly, um . . . Martin darling, I need a little bit of extra money.'

'For what?' He didn't look up, finger tracing the itemised bill past Jemima's number and – embarrassingly – premium rate talking horoscopes and her favourite tarot reading line.

Her mind raced. What could she say it was for? Botox? Colonic irrigation? Unwanted hair removal?

It wasn't as though they were budgeting; Martin was earning a fortune in Singapore – even after covering the mortgage, household costs, school fees, a generous allowance for Liv and his own living expenses, he was left with thousands to play with each month. He was just tight-fisted, as he always had been, expecting her to beg for any money.

Remembering what Trudy had said about sex becoming currency in a marriage, she felt her sinews tighten and her resolve harden.

'OK, if you must know, I want to go on a Perfect Wife course,' she improvised suddenly. 'One of the other mothers from school has started running them – she's an ex model.' She knew he'd love that. To Martin models were a breed apart, like professional sportsmen.

'Oh yes?'

'You learn everything from cordon bleu cookery to keep fit to keeping the children quiet to sexual tips. It's all to make your husband's life bliss. Apparently they're all the rage in London – a reaction to so many years of political correctness and domestic equality. Some women *prefer* being good wives. I thought I'd take the course while you're away again.'

Martin thought this a perfectly marvellous idea, and quite plausible. 'To whom do I write the cheque?'

'She needs cash,' she explained apologetically. 'She is being the perfect wife and keeping this from her husband to spare his feelings – he's run into a spot of bother financially and she wants to help him out without him knowing.'

'It's not Trudy is it?'

'God, no.'

'Good.' He started texting his bank. 'She strikes me as a completely *im*perfect wife. What a nightmare! That poor sod she married is probably better off without her.'

'Quite,' Liv agreed with more feeling than she had intended.

But Martin was too distracted by his new banking text service to notice. 'There – money transferred into the joint, poppet. You just have to withdraw it.'

'Oh, thank you!' She pressed a kiss to the top of his head, noticing that his hair was thinning so much there it was like a threadbare carpet.

He pulled her on to his lap, hands straight up her skirt. 'I meanwhile have *no* intention of withdrawing.'

'What about the children – your parents.'

'Lock the door.' He tugged eagerly at her knickers.

'It doesn't have a lock.'

He glowered angrily at the lock-free glass door and then slid her off his knee and waved her away, picking up the phone bill once again and squinting at it, far too vain to wear his reading glasses. 'Mother's right – you never phone her. Her and Dad's number's not even listed among Friends and Family.'

'They're always here,' Liv pointed out. 'I don't need to call them.'

She escaped to the bedroom and arranged to meet the man who was selling the coin that afternoon at a quiet tea room in Market Addington.

'Yes, I'll bring the money,' she assured him.

Listening at the door, Martin realised the awful truth of the situation.

He was not so thick-skinned that he hadn't realised something was awry at home, although it had taken a lecture from his mother to convince him that Liv might be unhappy with more than just the soft furnishings and the clay soil in her flowerbeds. Martin's mother suspected an overactive thyroid like her friend, Shirley, but Martin was doubtful. Liv, always nervy and sensitive, was like a Catherine wheel that had come loose from its anchor, letting off too many sparks to pin down. He knew she was hiding something, and now he had proof.

The one-sided phone call said it all. His wife was being blackmailed.

At River Cottage, Pheely and Giles had just made love on the banks of the Odd. Alas, unlike other lovers who had recently indulged in alfresco waterside unions, theirs had not been without incident. They'd been bitten to death by midges, one of Giles's favourite crocodile skin loafers had fallen into the river, and they'd been leered at by a random walker taking an illegal short cut from the bridleway to the trout farm along the far bank.

But it was still with great pleasure and sated appetites that they lay back and stared up at two puffy white clouds crossing by overhead.

'Looks like a butterfly chasing a caterpillar,' sighed Pheely, who had loved *Truly, Madly, Deeply*: 'Like the eternal quest to chase youthfulness.'

'Looks like a large pair of breasts to me – and that one's a big willy.'

She turned her head to kiss his ear. He was always so refreshingly straightforward. His juvenile delight in things was a constant reminder that one didn't need to chase youthfulness if one refused to grow up.

'How would you feel about my being a grandfather?' he asked suddenly, not sounding remotely young at heart.

'Christ, not Georgina?' The oldest of his teenage daughters was barely sixteen, the same age that Pheely had been when getting pregnant with Dilly.

'No.'

'One of the younger ones?' She was shocked.

'I'm talking abstract concept for now.'

Pheely realised she had misjudged him. Just because he chose to be childish, it didn't mean he wasn't capable of deep thought.

'I'd call you "Grandpa" a lot and make cheap jokes about Zimmer frames, of course,' she told him earnestly.

'Thought so.'

'But of course, in conceptual terms, I am just as likely to become a grandmother,' she reminded him, turning so their noses touched and they had to blink hard to focus on one another's eyes at such close range. 'Dilly can't wait to have children, and she's almost a stepmother; Magnus is about to become a father, after all.'

'Already has,' Giles murmured and then, deciding that there was no point keeping this momentous secret from his future wife, he told her about the twins. It was make or break. He wasn't sure that she would understand why he had acted the way he had, and why he could never fully extinguish the torch he had carried for Dibs for a quarter of a century.

Pheely took his face in her hands and kissed him tenderly. 'You know all about Dilly's father. He still haunts my heart, just as Dibs does yours. They'll always be a part of our lives even though we can't ever get together for family days out to Legoland. We are not so very different, you and I. *All* our "love children" were born of a very great love. And we're going to be very, very happy together.'

He ignored the midges as he kissed her back.

'Grandpa Horton.'

'Step-Granny Gently.'

'I never thought I'd say it, but I'm looking forward to having a stack of grandchildren around the place.'

'We'll have to open up the Lodge then.' She was excited at the prospect of reoccupying her father's long-neglected and beautiful house.

'Absolutely,' he agreed. 'We're a family now. We need a family home – not your scruffy little flea pit or my bachelor pad.'

Overhead the butterfly and the caterpillar joined together and mutated into a swan that Giles would probably say looked more like a gogo dancer.

'Of course we'll have to get ramps and stairlifts installed,' she mused.

'Why on earth would you want to do that to a beautiful old house like the Lodge?'

'For you, Grandpa,' she said and then shrieked with laughter as, with an outraged wail, Giles jumped on her. Laughing and tussling, they rolled down the bank, taking themselves, a picnic hamper and the second crocodile loafer into the Odd with a loud splash and a squawk of terrified moorhen.

Pixie was thrilled to learn that Pheely and Giles were engaged, although she privately suspected the betrothal wouldn't last as long as Harvest supper. She and Sexton were on full steam at the market gardens as so many fruit and veggie crops ripened simultaneously, so they had no time to dwell on the matter. The few precious minutes that weren't taken up with work or children were spent trying to track down Sioux.

'She won't have gone far,' Pixie assured him. 'She arrived with the Spring Horse Fair and she'll leave with the autumn one. That's her style, especially now she's older. She prefers to travel in a crowd; it's easier to hide. Besides, she wants a crack at this treasure hunt money – we solved all the clues before she buggered off. The grand finale's set to be at the fair, isn't it?'

'So where does a fifty-something woman with pet ferrets and a serious cigar habit lie low for three weeks in the meantime?'

'The weather's great, there's rich pickings in the fields and unguarded Cotswold gardens. She's out there.' Pixie straightened from pulling up beetroots and nodded at the horizon. 'She's a wily old fox. We'll never find her.'

'Not without a pack of hounds and a horn.'

'Still illegal, remember?'

'But you say she'll be at the Horse Fair?'

'I'd stake my fortune on it if she hadn't stolen the lot. We'll catch her there.'

'How?'

'Good question.'

Sexton placed his broad, bronzed forearms over his faded denim knees as he squatted amongst some Swiss chard, and squinted up at her through the sun, his dark eyes glimmering. 'I'll think of something.'

That was the wonderful thing about Sexton, Pixie reflected gratefully. Whereas other men might say such things as a chest-beating way of buying time because their minds were a blank, she knew that Sexton, part gypsy himself, and an only partially reformed rake, meant quite the opposite. He already had a plethora of ideas to catch Sioux. He just had to whittle them down to find one that wasn't so entirely illegal and life-threatening that Pixie would sanction it.

She loved having him back: for his solidity, his practicality, his earthy sensuality and his outrageous sense of humour. Their children were equally overjoyed to be reunited.

She forgave him without any difficulty. Having been unfaithful to three husbands and numerous lovers over the years, Pixie knew how easy it was to stray, to get caught up in a spiral that span your head too fast to think straight, to run away rather than face the consequences and then, sometimes, to regret one's actions but to be too fearful of rejection to risk any attempt at reconciliation.

Since he had come home, they'd stayed up talking night after night, however heavy their limbs and stiff their joints. They both felt they understood what had gone wrong: Pixie, while not the first to stray physically, had been the first to disengage from the things that kept the relationship working, things she herself had once initiated to lure Sexton in from the fields. They were both mercurial types whose lively minds sought constant distraction and stimulation, even if their bodies were exhausted from working seventy-hour weeks on the smallholding. Increasingly wrapped up with her friends and family and a new passion for crime thrillers, she had neglected to notice that Sexton had started to climb the walls during the long dark evenings of the previous winter. He felt she was rejecting him, felt cold-shouldered and unwanted. Soon, their weekly cinema or theatre trips had been forfeited for Ian Rankin; their foodie love for cooking complicated Indian meals together had been abandoned in the wake of Patricia Cornwell; their long summer evening walks had been shelved while a James Patterson was on the go; their shared bath, massage and early-to-bed night of naughtiness was replaced by early nights with Kathy Reichs; and all the time she was sloping out to meet up with Pheely and Anke, or spending hours on the phone to daughter Julia, cousin Jemima and other further-flung family with whom she was gradually seeking rapprochement after so long cast as the black sheep.

Pixie's infidelity was not sexual, but was a distinct and tangible transfer of affection from Sexton to other amusements, just as Pheely had felt her friend's allegiance switch suddenly to Sioux. It was a pattern that had repeated itself throughout her life.

'We won't let it happen again,' she'd promised Sexton the previous evening.

Now, her eyes sparkled as a thought occurred to her.

'Who needs detective novels when one can do it for real?' She waved her root harvesting knife in the air. 'We're on the trail of an arch villain – like Inspector Lynley and Havers.' She was a great fan of Elizabeth George novels. 'We'll stop at nothing to apprehend the perpetrator! Sioux Denim is in our sights!'

Liv slipped into the tea shop just before three. Apart from a couple of pensioners sharing a pot of Assam and a cream horn, the place was deserted. She settled by the window, enabling her to see anybody approaching along the little alley that led from the antique arcade beneath the historic stilted roundhouse out on to Market Addington's large thoroughfare.

But the man appeared through the back of the tea shop like the shopkeeper in *Mr Ben*. He settled beside Liv without greeting and drew a folded silk handkerchief from his shirt pocket, unwrapping it to reveal a small, ancient silver coin.

Liv gave the coin a cursory inspection. The focus of her attention was the familiar cream square of folded paper that she could see inside the furls of the silk.

She sat back as a pot of Lady Grey and a scone were delivered to their table, complete with delicate china cup and saucer, jug, jam and butter dishes and clotted cream in a tiny bowl.

The thought of parting with a thousand pounds for the coin she didn't want was an act of lunacy to solve a quest that was becoming increasingly enslaving. Yet she was far too involved to walk away. Handing over the money was easy, like passing a bus ticket to a conductor. She'd done it and was pouring her cup of tea before she had a chance to question the deed. The man went back out the way he came in – she couldn't have picked him out of a police line up to save her life – and her fingers itched to read the clue. But she savoured the moment, milking her tea and buttering her scone first, the clue tucked temptingly under her saucer.

Which was when Martin ran down the alley and burst into the café like a cop crashing in on a heist, looking surprised to find her on her own.

'Where is he?'

'Who?'

'The man you are meeting here. The blackmailer.'

'I'm not meeting anyone,' she said calmly. She felt icily in control. 'Care to join me?' She drew her cup closer to make space across the table, palming the folded clue and sliding it on to her lap.

'I heard you on the phone arranging an assignation.'

'My friend who runs the courses.' Liv sipped her tea as he stood at her table, starting to look foolish. 'We just met up briefly so that I could pay her the money.'

'I didn't see her.'

'Where were you?'

'Under the covered archway out there.'

'Did you follow me here?'

'I borrowed Dad's car.'

'The Picanto?'

'Yes.'

His father's little gold Korean Noddy car was the butt of Martin's utter contempt and he'd claimed many times he would not be seen dead in it. This desperate drive to save her was a feat of heroism and sacrifice. She looked at him in wonder.

'Why?'

He dropped his voice to a low hiss, as though frightened the pensioners would lip read. 'You're being blackmailed. You have a guilty secret – an affair, is it?'

'No, I'm *not* being blackmailed and I'm *not* having an affair,' she said firmly and, as of that moment, completely truthfully. She was no longer having an affair. For a week she had agonised about whether it was on or off in the light of recent events, waiting for a call, a sign, a decision. But now she felt empowered as she made the decision herself. 'Martin, I'm not having an affair. I'm having a cream tea, which might make me fat, but it's definitely not extramarital sex – as you can see.'

'Don't be disgusting.'

'There is nothing disgusting about making love.'

'Will you shut up,' he hissed, turning beetroot. He looked alarmingly like his mother, from whom he had no doubt learned that all talk of sex was 'disgusting' however smutty one's mind – and Martin's mind could be supremely smutty. Liv had long guessed that he kept a mistress overseas – she had amassed enough evidence to damn him for a lifetime – but she worked on an out of sight out of mind policy, which had proved effective over the years. Moving to the Cotswolds and meeting Trudy, she had assumed it would be just as simple to turn the tables. But she hadn't allowed for her own sensitivity.

Looking across at Martin now, Liv realised that she had misjudged her infidelities. She had not wanted to exchange Martin for anybody, merely to entertain herself in his absence. Her affairs had been an attempt to step into somebody else's shoes for while; she had always loved shoes.

Martin was undoubtedly a selfish lover and a thoughtless husband, but at least he provided well financially, had given her two beautiful children, had the courtesy to live halfway across the world and although he didn't go in for romantic gestures and epic quests, he let her live her life in relative freedom and peace, if occasional boredom.

She had lately found herself in a tryst with a man who was equally selfish and spoiled, but who lacked even Martin's qualities. All he'd wanted from her was sex, and even then his desire was more competitive than physical – claiming his wife's friend for himself. Looking back, she realised theirs had been silent, shameful, rushed acts that were curiously solitary for all their shared fluids. She had wanted so much more than he was willing to give. For pure adulterous pleasure, Giles had been far more fun, even if he was far too closely in touch with his female side for Liv's liking. A hundred satisfied Cotswold wives couldn't be wrong.

For marriage, Martin was her one true love.

'You really promise you're not hiding some terrible secret?' he asked now, looking vulnerable.

'Of course not. I am going to be the Perfect Wife, remember?' She meant it. Just so long as he lived in Singapore for most of the year, it would be very easy to be perfect. He was equally perfect at that distance. Theirs was a perfect marriage.

She felt more self-confident than she had in years. She hadn't realised just how much being married to someone as dominant and forthright as Martin had stripped away her personality and self-belief. His job was her salvation; and, having resented it so much when she first arrived in Oddlode, she now found herself eternally grateful that he had been redirected to Singapore. In his company, she was content to keep the status quo and play the model wife. In private, she could be Liv again. Not a naughty Cotswold adulteress, a yummy mummy, or a wild child like Trudy, but Liv – who loved chocolate, shoes and trashy television, who was a loyal friend, had an immaculately tidy house, rode for the thrill even though it scared her, and who might occasionally take a lover in just the same way. More than anything, she was a fulfilled mother who loved her children devotedly, but was now as confident and carefree in the big, wide world as she was in their company. She felt could live again.

'Liv and let live,' she said out loud now, reaching across the table for his hand. 'Martin, I have no "disgusting" secrets to share apart from these cream teas in Maddington and a stash of Green and Black bars behind the recipe books in the kitchen.'

He looked very boyish and uncertain. 'What if I don't believe you?'

'You have to trust me. Like I trust you.'

Martin thought briefly about his two mistresses in Singapore, who would grant any sexual favour, together or separately, and who were gloriously 'disgusting' whenever he demanded. In many ways they were perfect companions, yet they held no influence over him in the way Liv did with her gentle, neurotic neediness, her big brown doe eyes and her amazing body like that of a leggy teenager. She had mothered his children, pandered to his demanding parents, kept his castle as immaculate as he liked it and the home fires burning for his occasional returns. Her innocence was a huge turn on for him, especially when interspersed with the more high-end sexual skills he could acquire elsewhere. He wanted to preserve that purity at all costs.

'I don't want you to be friends with Trudy Dew any more,' he said tetchily.

'We're neighbours – I have to be civil to her.'

'No more than a passing hello. I insist. She's a bad influence.'

Realising that she would have to agree to keep the peace right now, she swallowed. 'In that case, I'll need to see her just one more time.'

'I absolutely forbid it.'

'I have something of hers I must return – it's valuable.'

'Can't we have it couriered?'

She shook her head. 'It will only take a few minutes.'

'We'll go together.'

'I don't know where she's gone yet.'

'We'll start with the husband.'

'No! Let me do this my way, Martin. *I* insist. I'll call her later. Not here.' She would have to go through with it at least temporarily, but she was damned if she'd let him dictate terms.

She scrunched up the clue and threw it into her handbag, hardly caring if it fell on the floor now.

'Let's go home,' she stood up.

'Is that a tip?' He disapproved of tipping.

The Charles I crown was still lying on the flowered tablecloth.

'You're right. Very mean of me.' Liv rebelliously replaced it with a pound coin from her purse.

As they walked along the shaded cobbles towards the sunny buzz of activity beyond the arch, something occurred to Martin. 'I thought you said Finn had kept Trudy's mobile? How can you call her?'

'She's always had a second phone. One he didn't know about.' She improvised, using the actions of a character in a racy bonkbuster she was currently reading.

Martin thought of the second mobile that he had been using all week to exchange hot texts and receive X-rated photos of his mistresses.

'You definitely must steer clear of that woman,' he said firmly, hooking an arm round her shoulder and steering her into the town centre. 'Now, if you don't mind, I'd prefer it if you drive my parents' car back. I find the seat position very uncomfortable.'

Martin might have done anything to save his marriage half an hour ago, but driving a Kia Picanto was beyond the call now that he believed his wife was loyal and simply indulging her sweet tooth. He pinched her bottom discreetly as they crossed the square. 'I must say I'm looking forward to coming back to this slim, exercised, sex expert Perfect Wife you're going into training to become.'

She gave him a weak smile. Right now, the Perfect Wife couldn't wait to pack him back to Singapore in a few hours' time, then return to their perfect house and wave off her perfect in-laws, kiss her perfect children goodnight and have a perfectly huge gin and tonic.

Propped on a fenced rail on her own, Faith was reading the final clue to the Cottrells' treasure hunt, the only one that she'd found to be of any real interest. She was convinced that the ultimate treasure was a lot at the Autumn Horse Fair:

> See the twinkle in her eye,
> She once was rather grand.
> Carrying a side saddle,
> Or driving down the Strand
>
> She could have trooped the colour
> Or won Badminton in style
> She might have played High Polo
> Or raced the Rolling Mile
>
> Ignore cow hocks and pigeon toes
> She was a beauty in her day
> True horses come in every shape
> And the very best are grey.

It made her think of Whitey, the 'could have been' horse, now recovering from his horrific accident. He had, at least, made it through the worst of the trauma, although Rory remained wary of infection and checked him obsessively. He was bandaged up, trussed like an Egyptian mummy horse around the chest and shoulders; Rory said he reminded him ludicrously of a pasty, flat-chested girl in a boob tube.

Faith, who was paranoid about her flat-chested pastiness, had taken this personally and Rory, in an unusually belligerent frame of mind because he was heartbroken about Jemima pushing off and worried sick about his horse, had done nothing to spare her feelings. He had been so drunk on the yard in recent days that he made potentially lethal errors like forgetting to tighten girths for children's lessons, putting total novices on advanced horses and on one occasion mixing feeds with unsoaked linseed and beet, a combination that could prove fatal if fed to horses. Of all his cock-ups, Faith found this last one unforgivable. He could compromise a human life, but not an equine one.

Today, she was at snapping point. His unpaid, unthanked helper who had loyally turned up on her bicycle morning after morning to muck out his horses while he staggered about too hungover – or still too drunk – to be of any use was running out of patience and, unbeknown to Faith, her short fuse was seconds from burning through.

She went to the tack room to show him the clue. There, she overheard him on the phone, begging Justine to come back:

'I was such a shit to you,' he wailed, voice cracking with emotion. 'Forgive me, Tin Tin. I was infatuated, crazed – I had a crush on her when I was a kid and couldn't get my head round the fact she wanted me. It was a stupid, selfish fantasy . . . Yes, yes, I know,' he groaned. 'Christ, I hate myself for hurting you. You are so beautiful. You have the most beautiful face, the most beautiful body – your breasts are my dream come true.'

Faith winced, mentally recalculating the share of the winnings that she was going to apportion to buying him a new horse, so that the change she had left for a boob op and nose job would buy her the very best.

In the office, Rory started laughing, clearly well on his way to being forgiven. Faith was hardly surprised, although she was incredibly disappointed in Rory. Justine had always been a pushover, an easy stand-by for when he was too drunk or lazy to make an effort, which was all the time these days. Justine was the female equivalent of junk food. Faith, as unpaid staff and biggest Rory fan, felt that it was her right and hers alone to fill this role. If she could turn herself into a female burger with all the trimmings, she would.

'Yes, quite,' he carried on winning Justine over, voice as husky as a tiger purr. 'I really did have a crush on her, when I was a teenager. She was a big eventing star, then – short-listed for the Olympics. Imagine how you'd feel if Robbie Williams or Justin Timberlake turned up and said he couldn't live without you? . . . OK, if Dillon Rafferty turned up at your house, then . . . Exactly! You'd have dumped me like a shot . . . What? Christ!' he started to laugh even more. 'It is *not* like me offering myself to Faith. That's a repulsive idea.'

Faith stiffened.

Rendered garrulous by a dash of whisky in his coffee and a cooing Justine to massage to his ego once more, Rory hooked his booted feet up on to his cluttered desk.

'Faith comes here for the horses – not me . . . Bollocks! You're kidding? . . . OK, OK, maybe she *thinks* she fancies me, but she's barely past puberty. Face it, I smell of horse, have a mane like a horse, run like a horse because the metal in my leg makes me lame – I even snort like a horse when I laugh, you've said so yourself. To Faith, I'm a transitional object: part horse, part man. It happens all the time with female kids I teach. The thought of taking advantage of that is nauseating. It'd make me feel like some sort of pervert child molester – and, in darling Faith's case, a homo child-molester because she looks like a boy.'

Faith found tears speared through her lashes and blurred her vision.

At this point, Rory grew hysterical, protesting that he was *not* queer and had no secret fantasies about shagging Ronald McDonald.

Faith wanted to stab Justine through the heart for planting the thought in his head. It had been a bullying nickname that had plagued her at her last school in Essex, but since the family had moved to the Cotswolds and she had started having her hair highlighted, she though she'd shaken off the Big Mac taunt.

The one-sided conversation had got more whispered now, teasing and sexual as Rory started egging Justine to come and see him that afternoon, telling her he couldn't survive without her another day, saying how much he missed her soft, smooth-skinned curves after Jemima's bony creases.

'I want you to let me smear baby oil over your tits and ass like I did before,' he growled huskily. 'Make you all slippery and welcoming. Christ, I've gone stiff just thinking about it. How soon can you get here? . . . Noooo – tell them you're sick, Justine – Tin Tin, please, for me, for Roreeee . . . OK, OK, let's have phone sex – hang on – I'll just close the door in case Faith— shit! I've spilled my coffee!'

Faith managed to get to the feed room by the time he rushed past, reeking of spilled coffee, and grabbed the hose from the standpipe in the stables aisle to wash his crotch.

Faith passed no comment, silently mixing up Whitey's mid-afternoon snack in which they hid his painkillers.

'I might cancel my lessons this afternoon.' Despite his breeches being black around the crotch as though he had wet himself, he looked so beautiful and tragic with his flopping hair, his heavy-lidded eyes and his curling mouth that her heart flipped over.

'You said you'd teach me this afternoon.' She'd hacked Rio the four miles from home that morning and had spent all lunchtime grooming him, cleaning her tack and prepping her bandages especially. It was weeks since he'd seen her ride and she had been practising endlessly at home to impress him.

'I can do that any time.' He waved a dismissive hand. 'Could you call the other clients and let them know I'm busy?'

'Doing what?'

'I have a friend coming round.'

So Justine had caved in. She nodded and reached for the feed scoop in the barley rings.

'What are you doing?' he asked, his tone suddenly changing.

'Mixing Whitey's snack.'

'Well, stop – I do that. I told you.'

'I thought—' She was horrified to find his face a mask of anger.

'You're not paid to think.'

'I'm not paid.'

'*I* am looking after Whitey,' he went on, ignoring her. '*Nobody* else goes near him, d'you understand? Certainly not a goofy kid.'

'But after you mixed the feeds up wrong and—'

'I did *not*. I was going to soak them.' He snatched the feed bucket from her hand and tipped its contents into the waste pile, although it was mixed exactly to the list on the wall that Flipper had left. 'You're always interfering.'

Something in Faith ignited, and her anger, a family legend, erupted with full force – a red-blooded, red-haired anger that was ruthlessly Boudicca, brutally female, and in no part Ronald McDonald.

'Perhaps if I'd interfered the other day, Whitey wouldn't have lost half his blood out there while you lay in a drunken stupor missing your married lover,' she howled. 'Perhaps if I had interfered more, you'd keep your clients longer than a few weeks instead of frightening them all away because you are too pissed to care if they stay on or fall off. Perhaps if I'd interfered your horses would be fit and well instead of injured and miserable. Perhaps if I'd interfered more, you'd be a nicer human being instead of a prime idiot – a selfish shit – a—' her mind had raced for a suitably damning, wake-up-and-smell-the-coffee insult. Not the 'C' word. That was too much. What? What?—'

instead of being a total and utter . . . BERK!' she yelled, satisfied enough to turn on her heel and shove her way past him, running as fast as she could from the yard, along his drive and across the Prattle towards the bridleway, Broken Back Woods and the short cut home.

It was only when she was back in her room, her boiling head starting to cool, that she realised she'd left her horse behind.

Lying on her bed, staring blindly at the printed clue about the grey horse once more, she couldn't stop crying. It was hopeless. She wanted to call him and leave a message to apologise and ask whether he could look after Rio until the morning, but even looking at her phone made her break down.

Her mother was fretting downstairs, baking biscuits to try to cheer her up as if she was a little kid. Faith hoped they weren't gingerbread men with curly red icing hairdos – a favourite in her teenybopper days.

When she heard the hooves on the drive, she assumed it was her mother taking a break from baking to ride Steve McQueen around the block. She had grown fond of the old black horse recently and was hugely upset that Mark and Spencer, already boring of equestrianism as a pastime, had decided to sell him at the Autumn Horse Fair.

But the hooves were dancing and stamping in a decidedly un-Steve way. Then a voice called out her name.

Peering down through the ivy that had almost grown over her window, Faith saw Rory sitting on Rio: her great love and her stallion, a beautifully matched pair, guaranteed to make her heart fly.

'Forgive me, Faith,' he called up, his voice cracking as it had when she overheard him speaking with Justine earlier. 'I take you for granted. I am a total shit to you. A twat in fact. You are right. I AM A BERK!' He punched his chest with his fist.

Faith giggled.

Far below and out of sight, she heard her mother at the kitchen door asking Rory if he'd mind editing his language because Chad had two school friends around to watch the latest *Pirates of the Caribbean* DVD.

Mumbling apologies, Rory turned puce.

'I had no idea I wasn't paying you!' he called up to Faith again. 'I am a – a fool. I abused our friendship, and I want to repay you. Please come and work for me again, for money, real money, and coffee breaks and lessons and proper lunch hours. Everything!' He waved an expansive arm, looking like a noble highwayman on a shimmering midnight-black steed that could outrace any coach and four.

'You can't afford to pay me.' Heart swelling, she watched her most beloved four-legs dance beneath her treasured two.

'I'll do anything to get you back,' Rory entreated. 'You are the best worker I've ever had – the best rider, the best around horses, the best damned kid I know.' This time the crack in his voice was so genuine it split her oversized heart in two. He must have put off Justine to come here, she realised. *I may be a kid who looks like a boy, but I count above junk-food sex.*

'Name your price,' he called, 'Anything I have is yours!'

'Take Rio back on your yard. School him for me,' she called down.

'Are you sure? That sounds more of a treat for me. Can't I offer you any more?'

Only your heart, Faith thought silently.

Why hadn't she thought of it before? Rio would be the perfect horse for him. The stallion was really too strong for her, and too talented at jumping to be restricted to pure dressage this early in his career. He could be a top event horse – four star, international, Olympic. He had the talent and, matched with Rory, they could find the dream ticket.

'I want nothing more,' she called, her own voice cracking. 'Except perhaps your help to find a horse.'

'You want another horse?'

'A grey mare at the Horse Fair.'

'Whatever for?'

'You know what pony mad kids like me are like, Rory. We can't resist a happy ending. I thought she'd make a nice girlfriend for Whitey in his retirement.'

'Now that,' Rory whooped, 'is *bloody* romantic.'

37

Flipper tracked down Trudy to the cottage bedroom where she was making up a mattress on the floor.

'Where did that come from?'

'I sold the candlesticks and bought it from a shop in Cheltenham. They come ready rolled so you can drive them home in your car.'

'You fitted that in your Alfa?'

'I put the roof down and stuck to thirty.'

'We don't need a mattress – we have the meadow.'

'What if it rains?' She laughed. 'Besides, we can't sleep together comfortably on a camp bed, especially now we have the dogs here. I fell off three times last night.'

Mutt had been joined by Trudy's unruly pack, rescued from a local RSPCA centre, where they had apparently been left anonymously, tied to the reception door by their leads.

'I didn't even make it on to the bed in the first place,' Flipper conceded, and then remembered the urgency of his news.

'Tara's turned up – entered into an auction in Herefordshire. A vet mate of mine spotted her freeze brand and called straight away. I talked to the auctioneer who pulled her and she's now out at grass with the vet's pointers until I arrange transport.'

A sob of relief choked Trudy as one of the final swords was pulled from between her ribs. 'And Arty?'

He shook his head. 'No sign. The auctioneer reckoned Tara came with a job lot from a local pikey dealer, so chances are she changed hands three or four times in as many days before that. It's how they operate. Arty must be going to sale the same way, probably in another part of the country entirely – we have people looking everywhere. There's every chance we'll find her.'

'And there's every chance she's already gone for meat,' Trudy said realistically, thinking of her doe-eyed old campaigner, as white as a dove and as redundant in horse terms as an ancient lawnmower in a car saleroom.

Flipper said nothing. It was too true to deny.

'Church Cottage is being repossessed by the bank today,' she sighed, trying not to remember Arty under the sycamore tree there.

'Did Finn call you?'

'God, no, the bank did. They've left lots of messages, but I can only get them when I walk up the meadow or head out to buy a mattress. It's bliss.'

'Will they make you bankrupt?'

She shook her head. 'This clears the worst of the joint debts – of course I am still partly liable for Finn's huge personal debts as his spouse, but he'll avoid bankruptcy if possible. He's far too proud. He'll want to put as much of a positive spin on it as he can. You know Finn. All show.'

'Where's he planning to go now?' Flipper asked.

'Guess?'

'He wouldn't. They're practically bankrupt themselves. He'll tip them right over the edge.'

'Just watch him.'

Naturally, Dibs welcomed Finn home as a prodigal son, not questioning his motives for returning except to blame that harlot Trudy. Her poor sons! First Piers with Jemima, now Finn and, of course, poor Flipper caught up in the trollop's skirts to await his tough lesson in life.

She cooked Finn a veritable feast for his return: langoustines dripping with herb and garlic butter; rare, wafer-thin slices from a carpaccio loin of beef drizzled with a sharp reduction of vintage Merlot, honey and Dijon that seared the tongue as fast as it sweetened and drenched it, then the stickiest of gooey toffee puddings with a frothy, creamy custard that seemed to curl round every taste bud like a purring kitten.

Piggy – less enthusiastic about his son's return than his wife – raised no objection for now; the food was too good to forfeit.

The following morning, Finn awoke to find that a bath had been run for him and an ironed shirt laid out along with clean underwear, a suit and tie and even a matching handkerchief.

Downstairs, there was a full Irish breakfast, a crisp copy of the *Daily Telegraph* and a cup of real coffee made with cream.

He had returned to civilisation after years in the wilderness. Watching his mother preparing a batch of fluffy smoked salmon sandwiches for his lunch (he hadn't yet broken it to her that he wasn't going to go in to the Cottrells' office that day), he wondered why he had stayed away so long. He should have come back years ago, to the most perfect woman he had ever known. Nobody could match up to her. He had foolishly married Trudy because she was so different, so wild and undomesticated and seemingly free-spirited, offering a world of sexual excess, financial rewards and high-flying kudos that he couldn't resist. But she had let him down – she had wanted to buy into his life, sequestered in rural seclusion, but without offering the skills to merit such a position. She couldn't be bothered to cook, wash, clean or take an interest in his life. She had grown spoiled and lazy. His mother would never let herself down like that.

Recently, aware that his marriage was faltering, Finn had looked around for alternatives. He had searched the internet for Thai and Eastern European brides, contemplated a stay in Ireland to look for a younger, sweeter model. But Trudy still captivated him more than he cared to admit. Her very indifference to him had always been his downfall, a mystery he longed to solve. The more he tried to entice her – buying her gifts, lavishing attention and even devising a romantic quest to rekindle her interest – the less impressed she was. Very recently, he'd started to think the unthinkable: to doubt her fidelity. The romantic quest had become a battleground as he sought answers to questions he could barely bring himself to consider, let alone ask out loud.

Instead of answers, he had found a woman who had come closer to fulfilling his mother's living legacy than any other. Yet, far from wanting to trade in Trudy for her, or run her as a mistress, the encounter had simply made him realise he wanted the maternal original back. He had been genuinely frightened in recent weeks to see his lifestyle accessories slip through his fingers one by one; his car, his gadgets, his antiques, his art, his house, his wife. A mistress was too high maintenance. He just needed his mum.

And today, as if to compound his sense of self-discovery, his mistress called on him, the big doe eyes anxious, the long thin fingers interlaced and wringing fretfully. He tried to let her down gently, but her tears said it all. She would never find another like him. She had tasted the nectar of love – they both had – but theirs were two complicated lives that could not be tangled. He had to eradicate mess from his life, clip its edges, and present it for public consumption once again.

He took her for a walk in the Abbey grounds, steering her deliberately towards the Italian garden with the topiary and mosaic beds that were at least navigably well maintained thanks to a television company that had used it as the setting for a *Midsomer Murders* the previous year.

'This place is staggering,' she gasped.

'One gets used to it,' he said airily, sitting her on a rickety bench and telling her that his life was too traumatised for a relationship right now, especially a complicated one involving husbands, children and his own marriage wobble. He would have liked to suggest that occasional recreational sex would be fine, but he was too well brought up to suggest it directly, and too inexperienced an adulterer to know how to phrase the idea more subtly.

And so she cried a little, patted his arm, kissed his hand – a touching gesture for a Catholic, Finn always found – and answered his prayers.

'My husband goes overseas again tomorrow,' she said, 'and after that, I am always there if you need me. I hated being so out of touch when you were going through such a bad time, but he is such a jealous man. If you ever need to talk, just call.'

The open ended arrangement was fine by Finn. He knew what she meant by 'talk'. Trudy had been just the same. She meant sex. He was not a particularly carnal man, but it suited his ego to know that it was available on tap.

'I have felt so sorry for you.' She squeezed his hand.

This suited him less. He hated women crying and hated being the object of pity even more.

'I am very happy with the way things have worked out.'

'Good.' She traced the tips of his fingers. 'I'm glad. You seem in a happier place.'

'I am.' He looked around the misty, sun-milky garden and realised he meant it.

After she had gone he went to his laptop, thankfully kept with him the day the bailiffs had called at Church Cottage, and deleted the files on which he'd planned and stored his quest for Trudy.

It hadn't turned out as he'd hoped, but in a way the project had still brought him much gratification, not least because his was the last laugh and that was a point scored off Trudy. She'd always claimed to find his sense of humour juvenile. He'd also had the last word – a space they had continually battled to occupy when they had been together. Unaware that it was Liv, and not Trudy, who had solved most of the clues and whose imagination he had captured enough to keep the trail alive, his sense of gratification and atonement was acute. His clever poems spoke volumes more than her flowery, over-sentimental songs, after all. He felt he had made his point well and, in the circumstances, it was a vindicated slur on her weakness, her duplicity and dishonour. He'd expected more of her.

'Wasn't that Jemima's friend from Oddlode?' Dibs asked when he went back inside. She never forgot a face. 'Liz is it, or Lynn?'

'Liv,' Finn confirmed. 'She's a friend of Trudy's too.'

'Oh?'

'Trying to bridge the gap, I think,' he sighed. 'But it's gone too far. I don't want her back.'

'You're better off without her. You were very unhappy, the pair of you. You've put up with enough, Finn darling,' Dibs was eager to keep her favourite son at home in the wake of the others detaching themselves so much.

'I have,' Finn agreed. 'Can I smell cake?'

'Coffee and walnut.' She cuffed his arm. 'Your favourite.'

He hugged her tight in a sudden, impulse move that almost knocked her flying.

'I love you, Mum,' he croaked.

It was the first time Finn had told her that in a quarter of a century.

'I love you too, son.' This was it. Love had come home again.

> So we come to the end
> Of a long, loving battle
> Weary and spent
> In stasis and without transport
> No longer travelling together
> Going nowhere fast
> End this as it started, my love
> Rolling, rolling, rolling . . .

Trudy read the verse quickly, eyes dashing ahead of her mind so that she made no sense of it at first.

'It's full circle,' Liv pointed out, 'SOWINGER – that's what the first letters spell. Just like the very first clue at the gypsy fair.'

'I never found it.'

'I did.'

'But I . . . *you* found it?'

'Yes – then I left it in the Cottrells' marquee.'

'Finn must have brought it home,' Trudy remembered. 'He was there when I found it on the door – gave me a terrible scare.'

They had met at the New Inn in Upper Springlode, a favourite of clandestine adulterers thanks to the many little nooks and crannies in both the ancient pub and its vast garden which overlooked the Odd Valley. Tucked away in a natural cubbyhole created by two fat spruces, the women nobly drained a bottle of iced Orvieto in the name of honour and honesty.

'I kept the hunt going – you kept losing interest,' Liv went on.

'Speaks volumes when you consider who was setting the clues and hiding the treasure, which ironically cost you and me a small fortune to assemble. No wonder I lost interest. I've never liked shopping much.'

'I love shopping,' Liv confessed.

'Quite.'

'But he must love you to have done all this.'

Trudy shook her head. 'Funny how you can say "I love you" to one another for years before realising that, actually, you have entirely different concepts of "love". Finn always wanted to control me, to "better" me. He wanted to find my Achilles heel, trip me up, show me up and then play Pygmalion to my ignorance.'

'I was the one who kept his hopes alive.' Liv grimaced with shame. 'I collected all the clues that you didn't.'

Trudy twisted her glass stem in her hands. 'You found him interesting.'

'I found you both interesting. My life was – *is* so boring.'

Trudy picked up the Charles I coin, looking at the crude depiction of a king on a horse. 'Well, maybe you'll find this interesting. Have you counted up the treasure and realised what it amounts to?'

Liv looked at the coin, racking her brains, trying to connect coins with buckles, a book, hens, candlesticks and spoons. 'A fairy tale?'

Trudy shook her head. 'No fairy tale. No happy ending.' She held the coin up in the sun so that it reflected down on her face like a dancing sprite. 'Finn set me – *us* – a challenge to gather together thirty pieces of silver.'

Liv's jaw dropped as the clues started to add up.

'Two silver buckles, a copy of *Silver Snaffles*, a rubbing of a pair of engraved silver shotgun side-plates – does that count as one or two? – eight silver hunt buttons, half a dozen silver Wyandottes, two silver spoons, two silver candlesticks, five silver charms, a silver coin . . .' She counted on her fingers. 'Twenty-eight? Twenty-nine?'

'And a final treasure at the Fair.'

'Making thirty.'

'Thirty pieces of silver for betrayal.' Trudy nodded, placing the coin back on the table.

'Betrayal?'

'He thought I was having an affair. He thought I was sleeping with Giles. I have never slept with Giles.'

'I have,' Liv said in a small voice.

'I know. And you slept with Finn.'

'I—'

Trudy covered Liv's hand with her own, warm and strong. 'Rest assured, my indignity at this stage is far outweighed by my relief that this hell is all at an end. I am positively tangoing around on the moral upper ground, here, thirty pieces of silver or no. I was *never* unfaithful to Finn, at least until the day I walked out on him. He was unfaithful to me.'

'Only because I threw myself at him.'

Trudy waved her hands. 'No details. I prefer we stay friends.'

'Martin doesn't want us to stay friends at all,' Liv admitted.

'And will you honour and obey?'

'Not if you'll forgive me.'

Trudy carefully moved the wine and two glasses to one side and reached across to cup her friend's face in her hands, 'What's to forgive? It happened just as I predicted. You became a bored Cotswold wife. You took up riding and then took up adultery. Welcome to my world.'

Liv watched her uncertainly. 'Except that you never actually committed adultery.'

'I have now.' She couldn't stop smiling broadly as she thought about Flipper. 'I am still technically married, although not for much longer.'

'You're the one who found freedom.' Liv breathed, admiration mixing with envy.

'For thirty pieces of silver and an ever-guilty heart.'

'I can't pay that price,' Liv realised, with sudden insight, 'not with the children – the house – the family.'

Trudy nodded in understanding. 'I feel like a phoenix emerging from ashes; but to do that, one has to be prepared to burn in hell first. Pixie told me that. It's not for everyone.'

'You found love.'

'I found a love I never knew I was looking for. It was there all along.'

Liv took her friend's hand. 'Will you come with me to the Horse Fair?'

'Why?'

'I want to find the final treasure.'

'To which treasure hunt?

'The love hunt!' Liv laughed suddenly. 'The ultimate treasure.'

38

The smell of autumn was in the air at the Horse Fair. Apple trees and bramble hedges were heavy with fruit, the leaves were starting to turn, bonfire smoke drifted through the misty, early morning valley and there was even a tang of frost to the north, although it was only late September.

Hundreds of travellers had been arriving all week and camping up on verges and commons around the Lodes. Now they began to pack up their sites and congregate towards Morrell on the Moor for the big event.

The autumn fair traditionally had a different feel from that of spring. The frantic matchmaking and flirting was replaced by the celebration of weddings and births; the horses were fatter and healthier after a summer of grass; the pace was steadier and the mood more mellow.

But Sioux Denim was feeling far from mellow as she ate a breakfast of berries along with a pint of milk that she had stolen from a doorstep in Upper Springlode. She was aware that her recent behaviour had not been within very reasonable bounds.

She stroked one of the ferrets absent-mindedly as she chewed on her victuals. Having moved around the valley for the first fortnight that she found herself free-ranging once more, she had then stumbled upon a boarded up house in a thick, wooded garden set well back from the lane on the outskirts of the village. It was an extraordinary place, built in the style of a French chateau on a miniature scale. At first she had assumed it was fire damaged or condemned, but when she had investigated further, pulling off one of the window boards and peering in, she'd found the place fully furnished and in extremely good order, although it clearly hadn't been occupied for years, with expensive, if dated, furniture including comfortable, dry beds. All the utilities were switched off, of course, but there was a spring-fed well in the garden that provided clean drinking water, and she had built a small cooking fire away from the house so as not to alert the locals.

She was sad to leave the place today, although she knew her guardianship could only last a brief spell. The house had a certain lonely eccentricity that they shared. But it was time to move on, taking her guilt and her ferrets with her.

She had taken Pixie's bank bonds on a whim, in a moment of pique, not thinking of the consequences. She'd grown so accustomed to living on her wits and taking what she could through life that the notion of repaying hospitality and honouring friendship had become suspended along the way. In hindsight, she regretted the move. The bonds were no real use to her; their value was far too high to trade in without questions being asked, plus she had no need for such amounts. She'd acted out of anger that Pixie – always such a meek little thing – had so suddenly and decisively to asked her to leave, like a ranger throwing her out of a park or a farmer moving her on from an illegal camp site. Sioux, who felt she had been a great help and support, had hot-headedly decided that if this was the way she was rewarded, she would share the hurt. Now, repenting at leisure, she knew she had to make amends. She had been on the road too long.

She could simply post back the bonds, but that was too predictable. She prided herself on her originality. She was certain that Pixie would be at the fair later; it was the big showdown for the treasure hunt, after all. She had a plan. She knew a way of making herself irresistible to Pixie, like catmint for a cat, and that way, she was certain, she could give her the bonds back without losing face.

But first, she had to adopt a disguise. All week, she had busied herself collecting essential items from washing lines around the village, along with useful drapes, curtains and throws from the fake French house, and even the trim from a lampshade. She always carried a needle and thread in her backpack, heavy duty stuff more suitable for mending leatherwork, but functional just the same. Over the past few evenings she had fashioned herself quite a fetching outfit. She doubted even her own mother would recognise her in it.

Trudy and Flipper made love in a bright pool of sunlight that streamed in though the curtainless windows of their hideaway cottage, their noisy, new-found pleasure in one another's bodies easily blotting out the growls, howls and scrapes of the dogs at the back door. With the bed-hogging pack inside, the mattress was far too crowded and rowdy for anything more lively than a sleepy kiss, and so they were regularly banished. Flipper had even bought a new lockable cat flap to stop the smaller ones creeping back in. He and Trudy liked being very lively indeed. This morning, they had been lively since just before six and were both sated, exhausted, happily sweaty and – in Flipper's case – horribly late for work.

'Bugger! I must dash.' He chased round the room for his clothes, dressing so fast that he kept falling over.

Batting away a bumble bee that had flown in through the window to investigate, Trudy watched him indulgently.

'I wish you wouldn't go to this bloody Fair today,' he grumbled as he dashed into the bathroom.

'I told you, I gave my word to Liv,' she called after him. 'I promise to avoid your family at all costs.'

'I don't care about *them*.' He came back in, toothbrush poking from his mouth, electric razor whirring at his chin. 'You can go right up to every member of the family and hold your head up high. You are the woman I love and they will accept that. That's not why I'm worried.'

'Finn won't have a go at me.'

'I know – he won't risk a public display, but I just don't like to think of you there without me.'

'I've got Liv.'

'With respect, that's rather like saying you're going into battle with a small penknife and a mosquito swat.' Flipper liked Liv, but her nerviness, which trebled when he was around, made him uncomfortable.

'I'll try to get away as soon as this op is through.' He buckled his watch and leaned down to give her a long, cool, stomach-dissolving kiss that tasted of Colgate. 'It won't be before midday.'

'I'll see you there, and I promise I'll keep out of trouble until then.'

'It's bound to be a bloody bun fight. Apparently Dad's got himself a safe full of readies with two big bouncers to guard over it. Very Ray Winstone.'

'Where did he get the cash from in the end?'

'God knows – but I don't think it'll be the main attraction today.'

'Why on earth not?'

'I have something far more show-stopping planned,' he was already bounding down the stairs.

'Wait! Whoa there! What?' she called, scrabbling after him.

Before she could reach the top of the stairs, however, she was flattened by dogs surging up ecstatically to jump on the bed. A moment later, she heard his car engine start.

She rushed to the window, but the Audi was already halfway along the track through the overgrown meadow, which was dancing with thistledown, seeds, autumn insects and the last few butterflies, its long blond grasses covered with little indentations where they she and Flipper made love in the past few days.

Wailing in frustration, she stomped through to the bathroom and found that he had written 'I Love You' in toothpaste on the mirror.

Rory followed Faith as she dashed around the official lots at the Horse Fair in search of the grey mare in the poem. The trouble was, there were several grey mares entered in the sale, all of whom could fit the description.

'Even if we dismiss the ponies and driving cobs, there are five grey mares listed all over the age of eight,' Faith moaned plaintively. 'The clue is useless.'

'How old is the oldest?'

'Thirteen.'

'Well, it has to be her – the poem says that she's old, doesn't it?'

They went to look at lot forty-six, a grey hunter of unknown breeding standing just over sixteen hands. With her long, Roman nose, ewe neck and hollow back, it was impossible to imagine that she had ever been a 'beauty'.

Several other treasure hunters were inspecting her, clearly thinking the same thing. The mare eyed them all with a weary lack of interest, having been bought and sold so many times in her life that she was accustomed to critical ringside appraisal; she was always taken for granted, overworked and undervalued.

Faith knew how she felt.

Piggy Cottrell was satisfied that nobody would win the big cash prize thanks to his stroke of genius; making the final clue so vague that it could be any one of a number of lots was magnificent. This way,

Cottrells' could claim that the correct lot was, in fact, one that nobody had guessed. As well as finding a small legion of grey mares to confuse the public, his money was doubly safeguarded: the standby winning lot or 'treasure' was a late entry – unlisted in the catalogue and waiting in a quiet corner to go through the ring so fast nobody would spot her until it was too late.

Grania had composed the final clue, insisting on being involved like everyone else in the family. At first, Piggy had been miffed, but now he saw this as another stroke of genius: his dear, gin-soaked sister had concocted a verse of splendid ambiguity.

The safe containing the cash was on display beside the auctioneer's rostrum, its combination a closely guarded secret known only to Piggy and, in theory, the winner. Upon presenting a catalogue for each participating auction, marked with the correct lot number, competitors would have just one go at opening it – the winning number being a sum of all those lot numbers from the clues.

Inside was fifty thousand pounds in fifty-pound notes, borrowed amid great stress and cajoling from Phoney's city trader husband Henry, who needed it back first thing on Monday to balance his books.

'Of *course* you'll get it back, old boy.' Piggy patted Henry on the back now, not noticing that the stocky prop forward of a man was as pale as a consumptive waif. 'This thing'll go like clockwork, you'll see.'

Liv knew exactly where to find the Sowinger's pitch in the little courtyard, where the painted Romany caravan was parked as it had been in spring, advertising fortune telling with Marie-Rose.

Trudy followed her anxiously

An old woman stood in the shadow of the caravan door, draped in layers of brightly patterned fabric like an exotic tent, her hair covered with a finely striped red scarf trimmed with golden coins, her weathered face obscured by a fine layer of organza, and her eyes concealed behind tiny, circular dark glasses like two blackened pennies.

'Palm reading? Fortune?' She beckoned them forwards.

Liv pointed at the basket of buckles and combs, just where it had been last time.

Shrugging, the woman stepped back in the shadows.

'What are we actually looking for?' Trudy asked as Liv started rooting through the buckles and horse brasses.

'Something silver, obviously.'

'It could be anything.'

'Here!' she drew out a little silver comb, the spine of which featured a high relief depiction of a gypsy caravan and vanner cob, so badly cast that it looked more like Santa's sleigh being pulled by a mutant reindeer. 'Rolling, rolling, rolling.'

'Are you sure?'

'It's closure.' Liv insisted, calling up to the woman. 'How much d'you want for this?'

'Tenner.' She didn't even look at it.

Liv pulled the money from her purse and handed it over.

'Aren't you going to wrap it?' Last time another clue had been hidden in the paper bag.

'Packaging is the bane of modern living,' the woman cussed somewhat unexpectedly. 'Think of your carbon footprint.'

Liv and Trudy backed away, chastened, to the busy Corn Market.

'I think that's it.' Liv handed her the comb, disappointed by the anticlimax of the situation. 'Your secret hunt is over.'

Trudy looked at the little silver object. 'Give it to your daughter. You and I need a stiff drink.'

'I thought it would be something a bit more dramatic,' Liv confided as they made their way to the cluster of catering stands for a spiced cider.

'Like what? An effigy of me full of silver daggers?'

'God, no! Just something more significant. A silver horse, maybe?'

'He stole one of those from me, remember?' Trudy muttered. 'He's hardly likely to try to sell it back. Although . . .' She sucked her lower lip and stared intently at Liv. 'You know, you might just be on to something.'

'I am?'

'By God, yes! Finn's sense of humour is famously unevolved. Think of a six-year-old: toilet jokes and cracker jokes. His all-time favourite was one he learned as a child about a horse that's had its tail stolen, leaving the police "combing the scene". Arty has practically no tail, she rubs most of it off in summer with sweet-itch, and Tara nibbles off the rest. *Comb* – don't you see? It's not a solution. It's another clue!'

An unwitting Watson to Trudy's Holmes, Liv smiled, not understanding what she had said, but very gratified to be of help.

Anke found a good spot at the ringside and waited for Steve McQueen to come in, although his lot number was still a long way off. Since the horse was not worth a good deal she had set a modest limit and planned to stick to it. It disappointed her that Mark and Spencer had not accepted her private offer, but the boys were quite adamant that the Friesian should go back the way he came, and seemed to think his value had rocketed since their original purchase.

When she studied the catalogue, Anke suspected they might be right. The little sods had put in that the horse had been schooled all summer by 'Olympic Dressage Star Anke Olensen-Brakespear' and was now a 'push-button schoolmaster ride'. She'd have to treble her budget.

'I've found her,' Sexton reported back to Pixie, who was happily propping up the spiced cider bar watching Liv and Trudy quizzing the man in charge about horses with no tails.

'Really? The grey mare?' she hiccuped, imagining what she would do with fifty thousand pounds.

'No – I've found Sioux.' He tried and failed to remove the beaker from her hand, knowing that Pixie was always hopeless after a drink, and that at least fifty thousand pounds worth of bonds and shares was at stake if they didn't act fast.

Standing close enough to overhear, Trudy was instantly on alert. '*What* grey mare?'

But Sexton was already dragging Pixie away, mulled cider spilling everywhere.

'The last clue to the treasure hunt,' she called over her shoulder. 'Trouble is there are tens of the things here . . .' She disappeared round a corner.

'Did you know about this?' Trudy turned to Liv, the sweet cider suddenly curdling in her stomach.

Liv fished the official final clue from her pocket and handed it over. 'Martin didn't want to fly back to Singapore without telling me exactly what to look for – but I think even he would be hard pushed. It's like looking for a needle in a haystack.'

'Don't you see, it's Arty? It *has* to be.' She raced towards the horse pens, so blinded by hope and panic that she crashed straight into someone coming the other way.

'Steady!' drawled a familiar voice.

'Sorry – I—'

It was Finn. Tall, tight-lipped and poker-faced.

At her son's side, Dibs was the bastion of propriety and frosty civility. 'Trudy, my dear. Are you well?'

'Fine thank you, Dibs. And you both?' she managed to croak.

'Very well, thank you.'

'Finn?'

'Fine.' He nodded brusquely, giving nothing away.

'Good!' Glancing around anxiously, Trudy realised that Liv had disappeared.

Nodding like a plastic dog on a parcel shelf, she turned to leave and then executed a balletic three-hundred-and-sixty-degree turn to stare up at Finn. 'Is Arty here? Please tell me.' Her voice shook. 'I understand how hurt you were, how much you wanted to punish me by taking them away, but you know how much she means to me. If she's here, please say.'

'I have no idea what you're talking about.' His face a mask of haughty disinterest, he took his mother's arm and they walked away like a pair of Regency toffs on a promenade.

Not bothering to find Liv, she ran to the horse pens and searched along them, dismissing one after the other. Pixie was right: there was a surfeit of grey mares, but none of them was Arty.

She raced past the trade stands and Portaloos and into the field where caravans and horseboxes were parked in long lines, most of them with a horse or two tethered nearby to sell unofficially. These horses weren't entered in the sale and were on the whole a much sorrier lot, thinner and wormier – mostly vanners and mountain ponies, but with some miscellaneous types of questionable origin thrown in. Nothing remotely resembled Arty. Trudy wanted to howl with frustration. She was certain that the mare was here. It would be just Finn's style.

She leaned on a post and rail fence at the very bottom of the big field and pressed her hot face into the crook of her elbow, fighting tears. Seeing Finn again had compounded a strange, unnerving day. Flipper might make nothing of being seen together by his family and friends at such a key Cottrells' event, but to Trudy it was crucifixion. She wished she hadn't let Liv persuade her to come, yet there had been an overwhelming pull that would have brought her here anyway, and it wasn't the 'closure' Liv kept talking about like an American shrink, or the 'balls' Flipper insisted they should show along with whatever *coup de grâce* he had planned. It was something else, and Trudy was certain it had to do with Arty.

'She's here,' she breathed, straightening up. 'I know she's here.'

Despite a stitch raking her side and lungs like burst balloons, she ran back up the hill towards the sales ring.

Skulking around the inner perimeter of the beer tent, trying not to inhale the noxious fumes of spilled cider, stout and cigarette ash, Liv felt relief at having avoided any contact with Finn.

Seeing him just now, alongside Trudy, he was a figure of such cold detachment that their intimacy seemed wholly one-sided, and shedding a tear at their recent farewell irked her. She had no idea what she had seen in him or how she could have felt such passion for him. She wished she'd dumped him by text, although she suspected that he'd already withdrawn interest before she formalised the deal; he hadn't made any effort to contact her, after all. Affairs were terrible things, she was finding. The swift disenchantment was just too traumatic, and in such a socially incestuous area as the Cotswolds, one's skeletons spilled from cupboards faster than leaves falling from trees.

At that moment she backed clumsily into Giles and Pheely, conspicuously drinking champagne and cooing.

Pheely couldn't resist flashing her huge diamond and emeralds under Liv's nose.

'Isn't it just *scrumptious*?' she gushed, every inch of her left side glued to Giles. She looked ravishing, dressed like a gypsy bride – all tumbling hair and lace. 'We thought we'd marry on Valentine's Day next year. It falls on a Saturday.'

'As long as it doesn't clash with an England match in the Six Nations.' Giles nuzzled her ear, shooting Liv an amused look over the top of his fiancée's head.

He still had the roving twinkle in his blue eyes, she realised. Oh, poor Pheely.

But then, she thought, surely love – however transitory – is worth celebrating? And Pheely was relishing a bursting, fruitful cornucopia of love right now. Liv would dance on the rooftops if she were in the same position.

'Congratulations! I'm so thrilled for you.'

Quite against character given her normally reserved demeanour, she stepped forward and hugged them both.

In Gypsy Marie-Rose's caravan, Pixie could not take the situation seriously, despite Sexton's military briefing on the way there. In the near dark of the wooden house on wheels – a startling contrast to the bright autumnal sunshine outside – the broad-shouldered gypsy, who bore a whiff of cheroot about her, was gazing at Pixie's small, weathered palms and grunting thoughtfully.

'You know there's a sauce named after you, don't you?' Pixie babbled, filling the rather tense silence that had descended upon them since she'd crossed her palms with silver. 'Delicious with prawns.'

'I see great fortune,' the gypsy told her in a thick accent that was Eastern European via Kent in a bad Cold War spy movie.

'Oh, yes?'

'Yes. Much money. You rich lady. Very soon.'

'And whereabouts might I find all this money?'

'It is in a peg bag shaped like a big pair of knickers.'

'Yeah, *right*!'

'I speak no lie. You find it straight away. Outside.' She jerked her shawled head in the direction of the door, beaded fringes jangling.

'Who d'you think you are, Mystic Meg?' For a moment, Pixie had quite forgotten what Sexton had told her about avoiding confrontation, and was ready to tug the chiffon scarf from Sioux's lower face.

'You have a secret you cannot tell your lover.'

'Hmph.'

'You shared your bed with another man while you awaited his return.'

Pixie froze. She hadn't breathed a word about her roll in the hay with Rory the previous spring, not even to Pheely – and certainly not to Sioux.

'You know that your lover will be very jealous if he finds out. He may not understand, even though he was with another woman.'

'Yes, well, he can be quite hot-tempered.' Pixie hoped that the gypsy wagon's wooden walls were sound-proof.

'He will never know,' the fortune-teller reassured her, pressing a nicotine-stained thumb into Pixie's heart line and peering at it myopically. 'You will remain happy together until you are very, very old.'

'We will?'

'The young man who was your lover will become very famous. He has a great fortune and much love ahead of him. You helped him on his way,'

'Bully for him.' She felt slightly affronted that Rory's destiny was hijacking her reading. She was taking the old gypsy seriously now; she'd always longed to have her palm read.

'He has a long journey ahead of him, but he has a guardian angel at his side.'

'Great – I'll tell him next time I bump into him,' she said pointedly. 'And me?'

'You have a great fortune hidden in the big pants.'

'Not that again!'

'Go and look, and you will have long life surrounded by love.'

Breathing in undertones of ferret and cheroot, Pixie stared at her in silence, still amazed by the Rory revelation.

'I am sorry. I can say no more than that.' Whether she was signalling that the reading was at an end, or simply apologising for her actions, was uncertain.

Pulling herself together, Pixie replied, 'I hope you have a long life surrounded by love, too.'

The woman dipped her head in a nod of acknowledgement.

Outside, Sexton was making a rigorous search of the panniers on the side of the caravan.

'What are you doing back out here?' he hissed. 'I said fifteen minutes, then if I've had no joy out here, I'll come in and read the riot act.'

Pixie saw the small collection of novelty peg bags lined up for sale. Most were lacy and flowery concoctions, some indeed shaped like knickers and basques. She selected the biggest pair; unattractive, French bloomers with 'Pegging Out' embroidered on the crotch, and drew out a fat roll of papers, which she waved victoriously.

'How on earth did you get her to fess up?'

'I didn't.' Pixie put her arm round his waist and started leading him away without a backward glance. 'She read it in my palm. D'you know, I'm not sure that *is* Sioux in there. She's much fatter and older, and has a completely different nose . . .'

In the beer tent, Jemima flapped up to Liv, Pheely and Giles like an overexcited goose – a vision in off-white cashmere, pearls and cream chinos, again playing the auctioneer's wife to perfection.

'There you are, Liv,' she squawked, sounding like a head girl gathering stray upper fourths. Remembering her manners, she nodded politely at Giles and Pheely. 'I understand congratulations are in order for you two.' Without actually congratulating them, she turned back to Liv. 'Have you seen Trudy? I've been looking everywhere.'

'Is she here?' Liv feigned.

'Of course she is – you two arrived together in your car hours ago. Now where is she? Flipper's just turned up and I think he might make a spectacle of himself.'

'Surely not?' Pheely was agog. 'He's so dashing and composed.'

'The silly idiot's had some dreadful pash on Trudy since childhood. Of course she's completely exploiting it now that she's homeless. The family are up in arms, apart from wretched Nell who seems to think it's marvellous. I've promised Piers I'll take a firm grip on them both.'

It was the second time in half an hour that Liv behaved against type.

'You will not!' she fumed, waving her glass at Jemima. 'The two of them are *absolutely* in love, and there is nothing wrong with that – Christ knows, we all wish we could have what they have sometimes. You ran off with Rory Midwinter when you were "homeless", after all, and while that might not have worked out, this may well. Keep your beak out. Let them celebrate their love, just like Giles and Pheely.' She raised her glass to them.

Giles and Pheely raised their glasses back.

Jemima looked as though she was about to cry.

'Oh, have a glass of bubbly.' Pheely sent Giles to the bar for another glass.

'What about the family?' she quacked in a small voice.

'Stuff the family,' Liv said brightly. 'You are with friends now. We're a lot more fun and a lot more forgiving.'

Jemima, queen of the far-from-fun, far-from-forgiving Cotswold yummy mummies, looked from Pheely to Liv in slowly awakening surprise. Social one-upmanship was a lonely pastime compared to a yacht full of friendship, launched with champagne and bonhomie. Perhaps her renegade cousin had a point after all with her happy clichés like: 'You can't choose your family but you can choose your friends.'

On cue, Pixie herself joined them with that scruffy chap of hers in tow who, like Piers, had recently come back to heel, promising to keep his trousers buckled. As Pixie and Pheely gleefully fell on one another's shoulders, exchanging news and merriment in the shorthand of genuinely old friends, Jemima started to feel part of a true gang. She even kissed scruffy Sexton on the cheek, having never offered more than a cold, formal handshake in the past, although she had secretly always found him dishy in a David Essex sort of a way. He smelled pleasant – Equipage by Hermes, she recognised.

When Giles returned from the bar with more champagne, she raised her brimming glass alongside theirs and toasted the happy couple. Just like everyone else, she didn't imagine the engagement would last for more than five minutes, but she was suddenly hugely grateful to be able to rejoice in it while it did. Having told all her girlfriends that the only reason Giles had proposed was because Pheely had lost so much weight, Jemima realised that it didn't really matter just so long as they were both this radiantly happy. The spark between Pheely and Giles was as welcoming as a roaring hearth. And the pleasure of new, true friends was equally heart-warming.

Finn accompanied his mother round to the edge of the sales ring with his head held high, a young country squire mingling with the serfs. He was already filling out thanks to magnificent home cooking, the waistband of his gold cords a little tight, the lower buttons of his tattersall shirt gaping slightly, but well hidden by a moleskin waistcoat and Barbour, matched with a silk cravat and flat cap.

Dibs looked magnificent in a fur-trimmed jacket with a tightly belted waist and tailored camel trousers that showed she hadn't put on an ounce of weight in forty-five years, the grey stripe in her hair hidden beneath a jaunty brown trilby trimmed with a feather.

They were the height of aloof detachment, in a world of their own, relieved to be united, mutually supportive and deeply, unconditionally in love.

Their self-contained cool was not even shaken when Flipper noisily took to the rostrum halfway through the horse auction and announced a last minute addition to the sale.

Finn and Dibs exchanged knowing looks, accustomed to the youngest Cottrell's wilfulness.

At the ringside, Rory turned to Faith, 'What's he doing up there? He's never sold a lot in his life.'

'If you don't mind bearing with me for a few minutes,' Flipper was announcing over the speakers, 'I have a very unusual lot to sell.'

The crowd eyed him suspiciously, a few rowdy revellers already heckling for him to get off.

'I've heard it said that there's a tradition at these fairs – not exercised for many years, some say not in living memory – which is as solemn and binding a ritual as any religious oath.'

The crowd took more interest, starting to listen.

'I don't want to mock your traditions or make light of them. I am absolutely sincere. It is very important that my family understand the depths of my feelings on one matter, and if you will bear with me, I think this is the most honest way to show them – *all* my family.' He looked across to Trudy as she arrived at the ringside, her face bright pink from running.

'*All* my family,' he repeated and he knew she understood. Taking a deep breath, he addressed the crowd. 'As such, I'd like to invoke a blood auction.'

There were gasps among the older travellers.

'What's he talking about?' Faith asked Rory.

'God knows. I think it must be an old Romany tradition.'

'Not Romanichal, son.' An old woman with a wizened face the colour of toffee turned to them both. 'It came from Minceirs – Irish travelling folk, they say. Used to auction their hearts and souls here as a form of betrothal.'

'Bloody hell,' Rory gulped, gaping up at the podium. 'D'you suppose he's thought this through?'

'That,' Faith breathed, 'is the most romantic thing I have ever heard in my life.'

'You're *always* saying that,' he scoffed.

'*You're* always saying it, too.'

'Am I?'

Faith's heart missed a beat. Surely he had to realise that this was a key moment, an instant of electric connection that they would look back on in years to come and say, 'That was when I started to see it,' an early champagne bubble rushing to the surface to pop the cork of love?

'Yes, we're *both* a pair of hopeless romantics, aren't we?' she hammered home the point with an elated smile.

But Rory wasn't listening. He was watching his old friend, gormless with incredulity.

To loud cheers, Flipper leaned down over the mike and, still staring straight at Trudy, asked somebody to bid for his heart and his soul.

A few jokers shouted out random, low figures, but were angrily hushed by those around them.

Dragging her eyes away from Flipper, Trudy glanced at his brother on the opposite side of the sales ring. His face was blank. She didn't want to humiliate him, yet to say nothing would be to humiliate Flipper.

For a moment her head swam with the pressure of the situation, the thumping heartbeat in her ears deafening her, the sight of Flipper, so brave and defiant and handsome, tearing at her heartstrings. He had put his neck on the line to show he loved her. It was her turn. It was about time she actually earned her thirty pieces of silver.

She thrust her arm in the air, shouting two, three, four times to be heard over the shrieking hubbub of the crowd.

'I bid!' she shouted. 'I bid! I BID!'

'What do you bid?' the crowd around her goaded.

Trudy didn't know the rules. She had never heard of a blood auction. She knew it couldn't be money – and blood was a bit macabre. So she bid the only thing she had to offer willingly and freely.

'I bid my heart and soul for his!'

By the sound of cheers and screams around her, she knew this was the right answer. And looking across at Flipper, at his shining eyes and mile wide smile, she was left in no doubt that it was the best thing she had ever bought in her life.

Then without warning, she found herself hoisted up high on to the shoulders of a stranger and spirited along at breakneck speed to be united with Flipper beside the podium.

Twenty yards away, Finn let go of his mother's arm and slipped open his mobile phone.

'Whoever you're calling, don't.' She touched his forearm with her kid-gloved hand, her voice a low, soothing Irish peal. 'You can't fight this, son. None of us can fight it.'

'I'm not trying to fight it,' he snapped, pressing a speed dial and talking rapidly into the little silver shell. 'Send the additional lots through the sales ring now – immediately. Nobody'll fucking notice.'

The crowd was gathering round Trudy and Flipper, congratulating them, cheering and shaking hands and trying to remember the last blood auction. They were drawn into its jostling heart and plied with goodwill wishes, gifts and skiffs of cider.

Amid the chaotic distraction, Piers climbed back to the podium, turned the microphone down to low and spoke rapidly. 'OK – moving on to lot one hundred and ninety-three B, not listed in your catalogue. Aged broodmare, thought thoroughbred, no warranty. Who'll bid me a hundred?'

Blinking in confusion having been hurriedly unloaded from a horsebox in the Co-op car park, Arty tripped over her own big feet and gazed in alarm with her half-blind eyes.

Finn was right. Nobody gave more than a passing glance to the long-backed, sway-bellied old bird with her terrible lumpy legs and her raggedy stump of a tail, eaten by field companion Tara. She had dropped a lot of weight in the short time since her serene life of leisure had been so rudely interrupted and was tucked up and ribby, resembling a fleabitten grey toast rack propped on knobbly Twiglets, with an over big, long-eared head out the front. She was also dyed a very unlikely shade of dirty buff, like a camel.

'Fifty, then?' Piers looked at the meat men, but they were busy lighting fags and talking about the blood auction.

From the furthest corner of the ring, a notorious travelling horse dealer known as Shadrack the Butcher winked at Piers.

Faith elbowed Rory hard. 'Bid on this one.'

'What?'

'Bid.'

'You are *kidding*? That's bloody glue. And it's not even grey.'

'Bid as though your life depended on it. If you buy it, you'll ride Rio round Badminton one day.' She belted towards the podium, counting on her fingers as she ran. A second later she dashed back and grabbed the catalogue from his hands, 'What's eight hundred and twelve plus a hundred and ninety three?'

Adding up had always been Rory's party piece. 'One thousand and eight.'

'Thanks. Now, *bid*.' She ran again.

Watching her go, admiring her pert bottom, Rory suddenly realised his mistake. 'One thousand and five!' he yelled. 'Faith, it's ONE THOUSAND AND FIVE!'

'Is that a bid?' Piers asked from the podium, having been about to lower his hammer.

'Er – bollocks,' Rory muttered, thinking about Badminton and bottoms.

'Yes or no?' Piers held the hammer aloft, eager to get the horse out of the ring.

Rory nodded again. 'Yes. Yes.'

One glance at Shadrack's shaking head and Piers slammed his hammer into the podium. Then he jumped as a hand pulled at his sleeve. Faith thrust her collection of marked catalogues at him. 'I'd like to try a combination in the safe.'

Piers glanced across at Finn. 'Later – the sale's still on.'

Finn hastily steered his mother away from the action, intent on distancing himself from any responsibility if blame was likely to be apportioned.

'I want to try a combination,' Faith insisted. 'It says nothing in the rules about waiting until after the auction, it just says the first to successfully open it will get the money.'

'My father is going to oversee the safe opening,' Piers hissed. 'He's still in the hospitality tent with clients.'

'Then get him out.' Faith sounded alarmingly like her mother.

The thoroughly overexcited crowd, listening in over the loudspeakers, started cat-calling for action.

'Ladies and gentleman – we have a young lady here who thinks she's won the Cottrells' treasure hunt!' Piers tried to get them on side, jerking his head urgently at one of the ring stewards to fetch Piggy.

★

Trudy surfaced from a hundred delicious kisses with Flipper in time to see Arty being led away from the ring. She was thin, confused, lame and a weird colour, but it was unmistakably Arty.

'Stop!' She raced towards the man leading her. 'Who bought this horse?'

'Shadrack the Butcher, I think,' said the handler, a hired-in cattle market porter who hadn't been taking much notice.

'No!' Trudy took the lead rein from him.

Arty, suddenly recognising a familiar voice and smell, let out a furious whicker of appreciation and turned, almost flattening her mistress as her big, short-sighted head swung into her like a great, buff quintain spun by a direct lance strike.

'Oy! You can't do that!'

'Point Shadrack out to me.'

Dragging a delighted Arty behind her, Flipper at their side, the porter in hot pursuit, Trudy bore down on Shadrack, who was far more interested in what was going on at the podium.

He waved her away, pointing in the direction of the opposite side of the ring, where a tall man was apparently exchanging heated words with a slim, straight-backed woman in a feather-trimmed trilby.

Trudy stopped in her tracks. 'It's Finn. Finn bought her back.'

Flipper narrowed his eyes and turned to the auction handler, who was demanding the horse back. He gave him twenty quid and told him to bugger off.

'What about the bloke what bought her?'

'Tell him it was a mistake. She's been withdrawn from sale.'

Red faced from too much champagne drunk too quickly, Piggy lurched up the steps a few minutes later, convinced that the safe would not open. There was no way anybody could have guessed at the lot; certainly not a slip of a girl like this.

Hands shaking, Faith tried the combination on the dial, its clicks matching her racing heart as she span it this way and that.

With a reassuring creak, like the jaws of a slumbering lioness opening to show her tongue, the safe swung open, revealing a stack of crisp, red fifty pound notes bound in paper sleeves.

The crowd roared.

The local press photographers surged forwards for a shot.

Piggy clutched on to the rails of the rostrum with a white knuckled hand.

Faith looked at the cash and thought about her future nose and boob jobs, and of earning Rory's unswerving, undying love. Next year, she was determined, there would be another blood auction, and this time it would be Rory offering her his heart and soul.

On cue, he appeared at her feet, looking up over the raised platform to announce that the horse he'd just bought had been stolen. 'What do I do?'

Faith beamed. 'We can start by offering a reward – look, I just won all this.'

'You did?' It was a testament to Rory's character that he was far more worried about the missing horse. 'Well done. Do you think I should tell the police? They're just over there.'

Faith scanned the Fair from her elevated position.

Making their way towards a distant field gate were a couple with a strange-coloured horse. She was riding bareback, her chest resting along the horse's neck, and he was leading, his hand on her thigh. They were deep in conversation, laughing and smiling.

Faith shook her head. 'Leave it. We can buy Whitey a much better companion now – I saw the sweetest little spotted pony among the lorries earlier.'

Rory started to register the size of the pile of cash in the safe. 'Did you really win all that?'

'Yup.'

'Bloody hell, will you marry me?'

'Yup.' She knew that it would take a lot more than that – but it was a good start.

'Well that's blown it,' Piers muttered to his father as he helped him off the podium and steered him back towards the Cottrells' marquee for essential brandy and privacy away from the press. His assistant conducted the sale in his absence. 'I thought Henry needed that money back tomorrow?'

'Small technicality.' Piggy waved a dismissive hand. 'He knew the risks. Always a slim chance somebody would crack the code. Girl's obviously one of those ruddy child geniuses.'

'What are we going to do, Pa?' Piers parked him at the family table and noticed that his mother was sitting there already looking very pale and expectant.

I don't know.' Piggy rubbed his face, suddenly defeated. 'I don't bloody know.'

Salvation came from a very unexpected direction.

'Finn is fetching the money to pay Henry back,' Dibs announced across the table in a low voice.

'Finn?' Piers laughed hollowly. 'Finn doesn't have a bean!'

'He has over seventy thousand pounds sterling,' she told them. 'He's been selling off bits and bobs for months, stockpiling cash, knowing that he was about to lose it all. It's at the Abbey. I've sent him home for it. He knows what to do; this is family, after all.' She would never betray the fury, threats and blackmail she'd had to employ to make Finn agree to hand over the money that she had found in his sock drawer that week.

'Those must have been some bits and bobs!' Piers whistled.

She shrugged. 'The original manuscript for "I Hate Loving You", the Bechstein, the Lautrec sketches, the *Goblet of Fire* first edition – you should know, you auctioned most of them.'

'But those were all Trudy's things,' Piers pointed out. 'Surely she got to keep the proceeds?'

'She did not.' Dibs lifted her chin defiantly, sounding very Irish and very indomitable. 'Sure, she's not even noticed they're gone. She's got something of far, far greater value, after all: the hearts of two of my sons. And I think fifty thousand pounds in cash is a small price to pay for that, don't you?'

Across the table, Piggy was staring at his wife in astonished rapture. 'You are a wonderful, *wonderful* woman Deibhile Cottrell.'

'That I am, Peregrine Cottrell,' she agreed with a curt nod. 'That I am.'

It was the tenderest moment that had passed between them in many years, and both the couple and their eldest son now looked away in embarrassment, brought up to loathe public displays of affection.

The first purchase on which Faith spent some of her winnings, much to her mother's disapproval, was an evil-tempered spotted pony riddled with worms; the second was a familiar black Friesian who sold for twice his true value because he had been briefly schooled by an Olympic gold medallist.

'Please change his name from Steve McQueen,' she begged Anke, who quite uncharacteristically burst into noisy tears of gratitude.

'He was called Undertaker before,' she remembered between sniffs and hugs.

'God, no.'

'There's a wonderful Dutch gypsy guitarist called Lollo Meier,' Anke went on. 'Perhaps that would be fitting?'

Faith, who had been about to suggest she call the horse Blackie, shut up. She thought Lollo was a type of lettuce but what did she know? She had more pressing concerns.

Abandoning her mother, she raced through the streets of Morrell, ducking past the increasingly drunken crowd, trying to avoid recognition because she had already been mobbed for handouts and was getting quite scared of the attention.

The old Romany caravan was preparing to leave, its pots and peg bags and baskets of wares gathered inside, a smart black and white vanner with vast feathers and a forelock that covered its entire face harnessed between the stays.

'I'm closed for business,' the old woman barked when Faith found her packing away the last of her loose possessions inside. 'Seek your fortune elsewhere, kid.'

'I want *you* to tell me.'

'I know nothing.'

'I'll give you a hundred pounds!' Faith edged further inside amongst the clutter.

The old woman looked around, the heavy, coin-fringed shawls and tiny pebble dark glasses making her look all the more sinister.

She cackled, a throaty, sixty-a-day laugh with an echo of the death rattle about it. 'You'll never make your fortune giving away money like that.'

'It's not my financial fortune I'm interested in.'

The woman sighed, glancing at an old cuckoo clock on the wall.

'OK – sit down.'

She fished in her skirts for a box of matches to light a paraffin lamp swinging from a hook overhead.

'It's all right,' she reassured Faith as she took hold of the young girl's shaking hands. 'I speak as I see, and death rarely visits these eyes.' Her accent seemed to have thickened dramatically as she peered at the fine lines running across Faith's palms.

Half an hour later, after a far more detailed analysis than she could have dreamed of, Faith emerged beaming from the caravan.

Even more gratifying, Rory was pacing around outside looking pale-faced.

'There you are!' he cried in relief. 'I was about to come in – I thought you were going to be stolen away by the gypsies.'

'Don't be silly.' She stomped along beside him, hands thrust in her jeans pockets, staring at her feet as usual, but with a rare smile on her lips.

'So what did she say?'

'Can't tell you. Bad luck.'

'Give me a clue at least?'

'She says mine will be a very, very happy ending.'

'She predicted your death?' He was horrified.

'*Ending*, Rory – it's a totally different thing. It marks a new beginning. Like the end of an era hails a new one.'

'Oh, right.' He scratched his head, deciding it must be something to do with her A levels. 'Great. Happy ending. Great. I look forward to that.'

'Me, too,' she said as she beamed at her feet, thinking of huge breasts and tiny noses and love ever after. 'Me, too.'

'Nice sunset.' He nodded towards a blood orange sun balancing on the horizon like a vast beach ball.

'Beautiful.'

'That sun is so *round*.'

'Mmm.'

'I must phone Justine.' He grabbed his mobile. 'I promised we'd meet for a drink tonight and she'll be so excited to hear your good news.'

Faith turned as a caravan rattled towards them with a rhythmic strike of shod hooves and clatter and jangle of pots and pans. From beneath many heavy shawls, a hand waved at her as it passed. A ferret was sitting on the driver's shoulder, sniffing the air.

'Happy endings start with the most unlikely beginnings,' she reminded herself as she waved back and tried not to listen as Rory made his call.

Despite the sunset, there was a tang of frost in the air. Spotting something gleaming amongst the scattered leaves underfoot, Faith stooped and picked up what turned out to be a tinny little silver coin;

the sort that came from a gypsy's shawl. It might be lucky, she decided, pocketing it for Rory; her own luck had been so good that day it seemed selfish to hog it all.

'That's a shame.' Rory was flipping closed his phone. 'Justine has to work tonight and can't meet for that drink after all.'

Faith smirked and patted her jeans pocket.

EPILOGUE

'We're going to be terribly, terribly late,' Trudy gasped as Flipper rolled her over to straddle him and, clutching her knees with his hands, raised himself up on to his elbows so that he could kiss her protests away.

Laughing and tasting his tongue, Trudy angled herself better so that she could feel him sliding further up inside her, a perfect weight of hard muscle and taut, silken skin surging rhythmically against her delicate, slithering and delighted nerve endings. She matched his tempo as she worked her hips over his, gathering speed and hearing him gasp in pleasure, knowing that he couldn't hold back much longer.

Nor did she want him to; nor could she hold back, as they both started to groan more loudly – yelping and laughing and kissing and calling out one another's names as they reached for that amazing pinnacle they had now scaled together so many times.

Accustomed to living in such utter isolation in their hidden cottage, the couple had become even noisier over the months since they'd started exploring one another's bodies. They were both happy screamers, loving the sound as they egged one another on, the involuntary gasps, moans and whoops, the staccato breaths and instinctive cries of ecstasy.

Today, in a plush central London hotel paid for by Trudy's publishers, they were grateful for modern sound-proofing, but even the best insulated partition walls couldn't quite mask their joy as they climaxed loudly and proudly before collapsing into a sticky heap of post-coital love on the bed, cooled by the open window that let in a bite of February breeze along with the drone of traffic.

Outside their door, hovering in the corridor, a nervous publishing publicist decided to give it five more minutes. When Trudy hadn't answered her phone upon the third summonsing call, the publicist had been sent up to check on her – the launch party for *Dew Drops* was well underway in the private suite of rooms downstairs, and its missing star was due to stage a very special performance in just under half an hour, and then be swept away with a group of VIP booksellers and press for dinner in the hotel's three-Michelin-starred restaurant.

Inside the bedroom suite, dashing to the bathroom for a quick shower together, Trudy and Flipper found the hotel's luxury spa miniatures of body washes, oils and soaps far too distracting as they applied them to one another's skin, entranced by the slipperiness they rendered there and by the textural beauty it wrought over their bodies. With only the claw-footed bath at home, they rarely ever washed one another standing up and this was an irresistibly stimulating novelty. Turning Trudy round, Flipper soaped her back and then reached forwards to her breasts, letting the slithering foam run through his fingers as they circled her nipples, his lips starting to taste her wet throat.

She could feel him hardening again between her buttocks as he pushed her forwards, letting her rest her palms on the cool marble ahead of her, his own hands slithering along the hot rivulets of foam that ran from her breasts across her belly, dipping into the hollow of her navel and then frothing between her legs. Sinking his fingers through her soft pubic hair, their tips feeling through the bubbling water and soft furls for her clitoris, he loved the way she spasmed against him with an involuntary jerk of pleasure as he traced its hard, eager little tip.

Bending further forwards, she opened her legs and gasped with delight as he found his way deep inside her once again.

'Oh, Christ I love you!' she cried as he started to thrust with that familiar, thrilling speed, her back arcing against him; their wet, oiled bodies sliding together blissfully.

They were, as Trudy had pointed out, going to be terribly, terribly late.

Downstairs, the party was in full flow.

Trudy's mother, Rosie, who along with husband Jim was enjoying a rare week away from Dorset staying with Johnny and his lover in Battersea, were charming a journalist from a glossy magazine.

'I had no idea what she had been going through when her father had his stroke,' Rosie confessed. 'She never breathed a word about her love affair or the unhappiness when it ended. Such a dreadful man, I hear. He was one of *my* pin-ups as a young woman, can you believe? Her father and I saw Mask play the Isle of Wight Festival in nineteen seventy, before she was born.'

The journalist, who'd had her discreet Dictaphone confiscated at the door, was making obvious notes on her wrists, but Rosie was happy to be quoted defending her daughter.

'Poor Trudy was barely more than a child when she found the limelight, and terribly naïve. She was so beautiful and full of life, she was bound to fall prey to dreadful exploitation. We should have protected her more. When her misguided love affair with that ghastly old roué ended, we were terribly harsh on her, I think – blaming her for not being there for her father. If only we had known. But that is so typical of Trudy. She never admitted how unhappy she was when she was married, either, so we all assumed she was having too much fun to bother with us. It's so sad we couldn't see past that.'

To coincide with publication, a national newspaper had been serialising the story of Trudy's affair with Pete Rafferty all week. Despite crawling all over it with a magnifying glass, his incredibly aggressive lawyers had been unable to find anything defamatory that wasn't factual. His heroic husband image had consequently been badly tarnished, especially when several other erstwhile lovers had suddenly come out of the woodwork to sell their stories alongside Trudy's confession. It now transpired he had at least one love child in each of the five continents, leading the tabloids to nick-name him Old Father Time Zone.

Trudy's guilt and shame at spilling the beans on their affair after so many years' silence was at least partially appeased by the discovery that her heart had been only one of many that he'd shattered; although secretly she felt aggrieved that what she had imagined so exclusive a love, so extreme and passionate and true, was just a routine affair for Pete.

When a letter from him had arrived that morning, she'd consoled herself that perhaps she *had* been different, if only because she was the one to blow the lid on the 'nice guy Rafferty' myth. It was unsigned, but she recognised the spidery handwriting with a sharp sensation like an electric shock even after all these years. It simply said:

So much for loyalty. I hope you rot in hell.

That finally cauterised the tiny fragment of her heart that she had kept aside as a shrine to him. He had never shown any loyalty to *her* over the years, for all his erstwhile proclamations of love. He had just abandoned her and then hidden behind the same high walls of property, people and power that he used to hide from the press and public.

Flipper had hugged her tightly and kissed away her tears of guilt and self-loathing as he always did, although there were far fewer tears these days and far more fits of uncontrollable shared laughter. Sometimes she went weeks without finding a single thing to blame herself for. That fact in itself gave her something to be self-critical about, at least, as she feared egomania had taken hold. And she was not averse to some very petty self-entertainment . . .

While driving up to London that afternoon, Trudy had insisted that she and Flipper divert to Maddington where she'd bought a pair of ugly silver plate candlesticks and eight tatty silver bottle stops from a little antique shop.

'What d'you want those for?'

'To replace the missing bits,' she had explained, opening the boot of the car to reveal a large box containing all the 'treasure' that she and Liv had collected when pursuing Finn's angry, sanctimonious clues the previous summer and which she had retained, never really knowing what to do with them. When she added the new purchases to make up for the missing candlesticks, the bantams, the book and Arty – all of which were far too precious to pass on – there were thirty pieces of silver nestling tightly together in amongst bubble wrap, all of which she sealed up and carried to the Post Office to send to Pete Rafferty. It was time to pass the blame. She might have just betrayed him with a kiss-and-tell, but he had committed the true treachery all those years ago.

It was petty but it felt good, and she very much doubted Pete would bat an eye before giving it all to a charity auction where it would fetch ten times its market value because it had come from him. So at least some justice would be restored. It was, as Liv was fond of saying in a lilting rhyme, a 'very Trudy Dew thing to do'.

The counter staff at the Post Office had asked for her autograph and told her they'd always thought it sad she'd retired from the spotlight so early. Now they knew why, they thought she was very brave to speak up about it.

Trudy was amazed by the public support and approbation. She hadn't expected so many people to be on her side, particularly women. The letters of support were already pouring in. Of course there were plenty of diehard Pete fans who thought she was lower than plankton, but most were blokeish musos who couldn't care less about his private life and in fact rather approved of the fact that old squeaky-clean 'Rockfather' Pete Rafferty had turned out to have slipped one to a few groupies over the years.

At least his iconic first wife was no longer alive to witness the prurient public revelations of her husband's habitual betrayal. And their grown up children had both seen enough of Pete's duplicity close up over more recent years to remain unsurprised by this not unexpected turn of events, although the press had been doorstepping them all week and speculating like mad about their reactions to this latest dent in Daddy's rock god halo. Both kids already patently disapproved of their father's second marriage to ex model Indigo, a rampant self-publicist and obsessive adopter of Third World babies. Pete's oldest daughter, the society shoe designer, Cat, had purportedly not spoken to her father in six months. Her brother Dillon, who was universally known to have a volatile relationship with his father, had not been seen in his company for over a year. Equally famous in his own right, Dillon had been having press troubles of his own this week to compound a long spell of hounding by the red-tops. Rumours already abounded of family feuds and paternal jealousy, of Pete's crazed behaviour upon finding his press cuttings to be half those of his son, his record sales a quarter and his female fan base barely a twentieth. Just that morning a new rumour of father–son rivalry had scorched through the headlines – one that involved Dillon and Trudy.

The latest story was that the two Cotswold residents, who lived barely ten miles from one another, were in cahoots. Far from denying this, Dillon had cheerfully admitted that they were friends when cornered by a stringer outside his organic farm shop near Morrell on the Moor that morning – this revelation all the more shocking because it was the first time in months he'd been photographed smiling. But he was now about to make an even more public affirmation. He was set to shock the already overexcited media tonight by walking into Trudy's launch party.

Scruffy, unprepossessing and shy, nobody recognised him at first. He was a reclusive Cotswolds farmer these days, after all, not the

big-entrance, lifelong career rock star with personal videographer
and double-figure entourage like his age-defying father. In many ways
Dillon's shaky past paralleled Trudy's. His more recent celebrated
career had also been cut short, although in his case by prolonged
spells in and out of rehab to try to control his drug taking, followed
later by the collapse of his own marriage to the Anglophile American
movie star, Fawn Johnston. The resulting breakdown and career hiatus
had led to a long-awaited third album, a car crash of self-indulgent,
self-loathing tracks – one of the first 'free' albums offered for
download on the internet. Even gratis, nobody had wanted it.

Now, after several years in the wilderness, Dillon Rafferty had
pulled himself together. He'd acquired a seriously good reputation
as a foodie and farmer, was an *Observer* columnist and regular
television and radio spokesperson for good quality produce. And he
was reputed to be poised to relaunch his singing career.

Although he'd recently shaved the Grizzly Adams beard he'd been
sporting for eight months, plus had a half-decent haircut thanks to
some weekending friends holding him down in a kitchen chair while
the former stylist amongst them reduced the mop to a modish flop,
he was still hiding most of his considerable light under a bushel of
stubble, country clothing and lack of condition. He was in the midst
of a sea change in anticipation of resuming his recording career,
eating healthily, working out at the gym most days, sleeping regularly,
but he was still a long way off. He was carrying a little too much
weight, facial hair and tweed to highlight the few remaining vital signs
of his once active sex-symbol life – the devastating white smile,
legendary blue eyes, rare designer Converse boots and Nom de
Guerre jeans. He still walked with a pronounced limp from his riding
accident a year earlier, although the crutches had long gone to be
replaced with a discreet stick with a handle shaped like a greyhound.

He made a beeline for Rory Midwinter who, conveniently
positioned by the bar, was drinking himself steadily and cheerfully
to oblivion. Recently dumped by Justine Jones, who had swapped
allegiance to her smarmy boss Lloyd Fenniweather with such rapidity
that Rory suspected the two relationships had overlapped by quite
some margin, he was in a surprisingly ebullient mood.

'I get a mention in Trudy's book!' he was thrilled to boast, picking
up the copy he'd purloined from the display by the door and turning
to a late chapter. '. . . "which was when I turned to the brilliant young

event rider and coach Rory Midwinter for help and found my confidence turned around again in just weeks . . ." Typical of Trudy to give me a plug – I hardly did much, just lunged her on an old cob of mine to get her confidence back in after a nasty fall.'

'You are the William Fox-Pitt to her Madonna,' Dillon laughed. 'It should be your new marketing campaign: "riding coach to the stars". Just don't mention my accident.'

'Quite.' Rory eyed him ruefully. 'Madge broke an arm under Fox-Pitt's tutelage, didn't she? I'm so grateful you never sued me.'

'How could I? I fell off *my* horse on *my* land totally ignoring everything you had taught me.' He shrugged. 'Besides, it did me a favour – although I could have done without the pain. Got me back into music again.'

'Seriously?'

'Seriously. It's why I'm here.'

'So you're not planning to launch some dastardly revenge plot against Trudy for playing kiss and tell with your father?'

Unaccustomed to such directness, Dillon took a sharp, sardonic breath. 'I hardly think that's necessary, do you?'

Rory, whose own father had possessed a similar reputation to Pete Rafferty's new-found love rat label, albeit on a local scale, handed him a glass of champagne from a nearby tray with a complicit nod.

'So, if you don't mind my asking, what are you doing here?' He knew how private Dillon was and was amazed that he would chose a public outing this week of all weeks, to this party of all parties. 'I have to admit I'm pretty baffled why *I'm* here. I assumed there'd be a stack of Oddlode locals invited along, but I hardly know a soul. Trudy's in-laws are pretty thin on the ground.'

Apart from Nell Cottrell and Liv Wilson, there was barely a Lodes Valley stalwart in sight, the dark and super-fashionable media haunt being largely peopled with press, high-end book trade VIPs, like Sharon Gurney and Gaynor Allan, and celebrities that Trudy had reluctantly but obediently dredged from her more celebrated days to attract newsprint.

'I gather the family disapproves of her defection from one brother to another?' Dillon asked.

'Somewhat.' Rory raised an eyebrow. 'It's very *Legends of the Fall*. But I think they disapprove more of Trudy spilling the beans about her private life and Finn's financial cock-ups in particular. She's actually pretty kind about him in the book – we all know what a shit he can be – but to the Cottrells breathing a word outside the family is tantamount to heresy.'

'I heard Cottrells' is in crisis?' He put the champagne glass to one side, too polite to remind Rory that he was teetotal.

'Exactly! You can't open a copy of the *Cotswolds Weekly News* without a double-page spread on the state of the family firm, and that's nothing to do with darling Trudy.'

'Will they go under d'you think?' To a Cotswolds local, it was the same as a Londoner faced with losing Christie's, Sotheby's, Winkworths and Foxtons all rolled into one.

'Far from it,' Rory confided. He had got the low-down from Justine just before her defection to estate agent Lloyd. 'The company has just been bought by their rivals Seatons for an absolute mint, added to which, Piggy Cottrell has been flogging everything the family owns for the past six months and is rolling in filthy lucre like his proverbial namesake right now.' He dropped his voice to a conspiratorial hush. 'I've just heard that he's sold the Abbey for millions to some secret celeb.'

'Ah – yes, I know about that.' Dillon cleared his throat.

Rory's sleepy grey eyes widened. 'Don't tell me, *you* . . .'

He shook his head. 'God, no. Far too pricey for me. I'm a humble farmer, remember? Actually,' it was his turn to glance over his shoulder to check nobody was listening, 'keep this to yourself, but it's my father . . .'

'You *are* kidding, right?'

Dillon shook his head. 'He's always loved the area.'

'What about the neighbours?'

'They'll never see him – he'll helicopter in and out and never step past his estate walls, just like he does all his houses.' He knew that Pete was equally unlikely to pop into his son's farm shop for some organic cream and a chat. There was such bad blood between them right now that Dillon longed to scupper his father's plans to land on his own doorstep. He had no intention of leaking the story directly to the press, but by telling locals like Rory, he hoped that it would find its own way out.

'But surely, after everything that Trudy has said he won't want to live within a hundred miles of her?'

'You don't know my father,' Dillon sighed. 'He swims with sharks, flies too close to the sun and baits tigers for fun. That's his nature.'

'Oh, Christ! Don't tell Trudy.'

'She already knows. She's cool.' Dillon reached for a glass of cranberry juice from a passing tray.

'So you two really *are* good mates?' Rory fished.

'We've got close recently.'

'Must be very close to defy "He Who Swims With Sharks",' he whistled. Darling Trudy is more of a dolphin. I guess that's why she lives with a man called Flipper.'

Dillon had forgotten what entertaining company Rory was, and how much he'd enjoyed his time riding in Upper Springlode. He was glad he'd finally got an excuse to spend some more time with him, and not just this evening.

'But that still doesn't explain why *I'm* here at this party.'

Dillon smiled at Rory. 'I asked Trudy to invite you.'

'*You* did?'

'Last year, I was at an auction to bid for the Bechstein piano. I've wanted an art case one for years. My father has three; I learned to play on one of them. Of course, I had no idea he'd once owned this one, too – and had given it to Trudy Dew.'

Rory, half cut and thoroughly overexcited that Kylie Minogue had just arrived, was not listening properly.

'Trudy was at the auction – I didn't recognise her at first. But when she sat down and started playing at this piano . . . phew! It was electrifying. I've heard a lot of the greatest rock artists unplugged, but that was amongst the best ever moments in my life. She was playing some new material she'd just written – an amazing piece. I knew straight away that it was something really special. But then she left before I could introduce myself.'

Rory knew the feeling. Kylie, who hadn't taken off her coat and was surrounded by admirers, looked as though she was only staying for one drink and a supportive photo call before heading on.

'Trudy was distraught to see the piano sold,' Dillon went on. 'And Flipper had been determined to buy it for her at whatever price. He had a scout planted at the sale to outbid any rivals, but she and I did a deal before it went under the hammer. It turns out the only reason I could get away with buying it that day was that Flipper himself was saving your horse's life at the time.'

'Whitey,' Rory remembered with a wince. His old star campaigner, now retired, still bore the scars of that awful day. He was all ears now that his favourite horse was involved in the story. 'I had no idea – Flipper never said.'

'I tried to give Trudy back the piano when I found out that her husband had sold it without her permission,' Dillon explained. 'I even tried to trade it for the song she'd played that day, but she sensibly knew that was worth a hell of a lot more. And she said the piano had bad memories. So I just bought the song in the end.'

'And did you get the song for a song?'

Dillon shook his head. 'It cost a bloody fortune. My record company came in with me to make her an offer she couldn't refuse.'

'Lucky Trudy.'

'Lucky me.'

'Lucky Finn,' purred a voice behind them as Nell reached for a champagne flute from the bar.

Six months after the birth of her daughter Giselle, who was happily spending the night with Anke in Oddlode, Nell was more radiant, whip-slim, olive-skinned and sensual than ever. Motherhood had given her a sense of well-being and serenity that she had never possessed before. She had recently dyed her cropped hair light blond in honour of her birth father and the pale honey and brioche streaks complemented her turquoise green eyes absurdly well. Wearing a figure-hugging white cashmere dress and with a single, fat black Tahitian pearl suspended from matching ribbon tied around her long, slim neck, she was by far the most stunning creature in the room.

'Lucky *Finn*?' Rory queried.

'My brother.' She swapped his empty glass for a full one and kissed him hello on the cheek. 'Tall, sulky bloke. Crap with money.'

'I know – but what's this song of Trudy's to him?' Rory asked, failing to notice that Dillon, to whom Nell had yet to be introduced, was dumbstruck with admiration.

'He gets half of everything Trudy earns right now.'

'Surely not?'

'According to his lawyers. They're still married, after all, and he won't accept her divorce petition for unreasonable behaviour so is counter-suing her for adultery. He's after every penny – even her future earnings. He claims he "inspired" this song. It's all set to be nastier than Macca and Mucca.'

'Christ – poor darling.'

'She seems remarkably unbothered, I think love is all she needs right now, as the song says. Hi, I'm Nell.' She reached out a hand to Dillon, who was still gazing at her with rapt appreciation.

'I know. I'm Dillon.'

'I know.' She smiled right into his eyes, making him quiver to the soles of his shoes.

On the opposite side of the room, Trudy and Flipper finally arrived at the party to whoops of delighted welcome.

Radiant in a long, clinging slither of smoky caramel silk that showed off her astounding figure, Trudy looked every inch the star.

'Christ. She's had some work done, hasn't she?' whispered one of the tabloid gossip columnists. 'We're talking *industrial* liposuction.'

'Apparently not,' replied her companion from a weekly trash mag. 'She claims it's all good old-fashioned *love*.'

'Love does *not* Botox a face like that.'

But love had smoothed away the worry lines that had etched Trudy's pretty face. Now no longer drinking a bottle of vodka a night or smoking a packet of Marlboro, her skin glowed and her hair was a glossy fountain of curls. She looked absolutely wonderful, bursting with health and happiness and – unbeknown to anybody including herself – harbouring the very first few hours of conception.

With Flipper at her side – handsome, courteous yet charmingly irreverent, deeply proud and yet baffled enough by proceedings to highlight their absurdity – she was a sunbeam that lit up the room in ricochets of golden light as she circulated, apologising for her lateness, thanking those who had come, remembering names and faces with enchanting assuredness. She was the Trudy that many remembered from years earlier, before the crippling self-doubt and self-hatred had made her want to hide herself away and only put on a performance once in a blue moon.

And tonight was going to be a performance she would never forget. She was at her most captivating and charismatic, making everybody in her company feel like the guest of honour; yet all the time she would rather have been upstairs alone with Flipper making love. That knowledge, his love, their happiness and her own absolute ease with the world around her meant that she finally had the confidence to sing in public again.

And that was the reason that Dillon Rafferty was there; the one, true guest of honour.

The relieved publicist stepped up to the microphone and tapped for attention, hushing the babbling crowd to introduce the star turn.

'I think all of us agree that Trudy has written an amazing book, made all the more astonishing when you read the circumstances in which it was written. Witty, wise, in turns howlingly funny and desperately sad, *Dew Drops* is as truthful and poignant as it is inspirational. To those of us who grew up with Trudy Dew's beautiful, soulful voice ringing in our ears in the nineties, tonight is very special indeed. In fact, I can now reveal that tonight is going to be mind-blowing, because Trudy is going to sing again.'

Whoops and claps resounded around the room.

'There's more!' The publicist hushed them again, taking a deep breath to introduce one of her all-time pin-ups.

Tonight, she explained, for the first and the last time, Trudy Dew was going to duet with the legendary Dillon Rafferty on a song that she had written just before changing her life forever.

She stepped back to free the stage and the crowd cheered ecstatically. Trudy clung to Flipper's side for a moment, gripped with the familiar paralysis of fear.

He dropped his mouth to her ear to breathe, 'Remember its original title. Just think of its title as you step up there.'

She snorted with unexpected laughter, her shoulders relaxing.

Almost a year ago, Flipper had bet his soul that she would take a lover. At the time, she had been too unhappy to remember what falling in love, what being in love and what making love felt like. She hadn't written a love song in years. Then she had lost her bet. She had taken the only lover she wanted to have for the rest of her life, and they had traded souls at the horse fair to prove it.

This song had burst out of her as spontaneously as tears and laughter. It was the song that she was most proud of, one that had seemed to spring from her fingertips, her nerve endings leaping involuntarily without input from her mind. It was a song written from her soul.

Now, as she girded her loins to perform, she remembered proudly announcing its title the first time she'd prepared to play it to him, on the sit-up-and-beg pianoforte they'd installed in their hideaway cottage.

'Our souls!' she had told him adoringly, saying it aloud for the first time. 'The song's entitled "Our Souls".'

Flipper had fallen off his chair laughing.

When Dillon Rafferty had bought the song, they had finally settled upon the less ambiguous, simple title 'Two Souls' that made them laugh less, but kept the record label happy. And the record label was very, very happy indeed. They were so confident of a massive global hit that they had paid more money for this song than any other in their history.

Dillon and his record company jointly owned all the rights, and it was set to be their knockout punch in a long-awaited fight back. In a fortnight, Dillon would disappear into a studio for several weeks to record 'Two Souls' along with a dozen other new tracks for the album that would make or break his relaunch. All predictions were that he would come back bigger and better than ever before.

Trudy had no intention of relaunching her own singing career. This book release was the only launch into uncharted water she had planned for a long time. She was happily docked in port with Flipper and wanted nothing more than to compose. Tonight was all about singing for her friends and family, singing for her lover, and singing for the joy of it.

The small crowd, banned from bringing any sort of recording equipment into the party including mobile phones, suddenly realised what they were going to witness as Trudy settled at a piano in one corner and the familiar, much-idolised figure of Dillon Rafferty strapped a guitar to his chest, checking the tuning with quick deft strokes of strings and pegs before limping to his mike. There, fixing them with those blue, blue eyes and smiling that devastating, pure testosterone white smile, he said simply, 'Trudy.'

'My publishers originally asked me to make a short speech tonight,' Trudy's husky voice told everyone across the loudspeakers, silencing the chattering room into hushed anticipation. 'But I am lousy at public speaking and so, apart from thanking all of them – and all of *you* – from the bottom of my heart, I think it kindest to shut up and sing instead. My friend Dillon here has generously agreed to help me out on that front. I think you'll find this sums up what the book's all about better than anything.'

To great whoops, she struck a chord. To even louder cheers, Dillon struck a chord. Then, to absolute silence, they began to sing.

Rory found himself standing between the Cottrell twins. Always a bit of a sentimentalist, and very, very drunk, he soon had tears streaming down his face and a lump the size of a small house brick in his throat. It was one hell of a song. The achingly familiar, beautiful voices of the duo on stage complemented one another perfectly, and it was a one-off performance of a lifetime. Soon the song would be associated just with Dillon's world-famous voice, he would claim it for his own and, with the help of slick production and mixing techniques, it would stand up to a million repetitions on airwaves, iPods, stereos, in shops, clubs and bars around the globe. But tonight, it still belonged to Trudy.

Searching in his jacket pockets, Rory blindly pulled out a stray exercise bandage he'd stuffed in there while checking the yard that morning, and mopped his tears on it. The familiar smell of horses in such an unlikely spot made the twins turn as Rory loudly blew his nose and stuffed the bandage back with a sentimental sniff.

Catching her brother's eye over Rory's head, Nell smiled. He was so proud of Trudy, so at ease with her, so madly in love. She had never seen him this happy.

Rory slapped his old friend on the back after the song had ended, his words barely audible above the cheering and whistling and demanding for encores all around them.

'She is bloody talented.'

'I know.' Flipper caught Trudy's eye across the room and mouthed, 'I love you.' Beaming, she mouthed it back before once more disappearing behind a wall of journalists and well-wishers.

He turned back to Rory. 'I've always known how talented she is, even when she no longer believed it. Like you're a talented bugger – you just drink too much and think too little of yourself. It's a good job somebody loves you.'

'And who's that?'

'Us, of course.' Flipper gave him a reproachful look. 'Your friends. We're looking out for you.'

'Is that why I'm here?' Rory reached for yet another brace of drinks as a waiter clinked past with a tray. 'To bolster my ego? Because an introduction to Kylie would definitely help on that front . . .'

'Don't push your luck – you were balloted in like a true eventer. Trudy wanted to invite the whole of Oddlode tonight, she even suggested having the book launch party in the valley, but her publishers insisted it had to be very London, very media and almost entirely "undiluted" with irrelevant country folk.'

'They said that?'

'Not in as many words, but it was . . . implied.' He raised a cynical eyebrow. 'Anyway, it was Dillon Rafferty who insisted that your name be added to the list.'

'So he said.' Rory was perplexed.

As Flipper rejoined Trudy for the power dinner, Rory sought out his erstwhile pupil, who was leaning on his stick in a corner, mobbed by eager gossip columnists, features writers and diarists, all desperate for a scoop.

Dillon waved him over.

'I'd like to introduce you all to Rory Midwinter,' he slapped him affably on the back. I have this man to thank for the fact that I heard that beautiful song in the first place, and bought the piano on which it was played. The song, as you know, is all about the strength of true love – the guardian angel of our souls if you like; the sort of unswerving love that looks after those lucky enough to find it throughout their life, whatever gets thrown at them. And this man is one of the very lucky ones.'

'I am?' Rory looked baffled.

'He is,' Dillon insisted. 'His guardian angel was there the day of the auction, when Trudy Dew played one last time on her piano – although his angel didn't hear a single note of that magical song. She was far too busy looking out for Rory, here. She and I did a deal: she let me buy the piano, even though she knew another wanted it at any cost. In return, I promised her that I would help Rory with his career.'

Rory was struggling to keep up.

'He's one of the most talented riders in the country,' Dillon told the assembled press. 'And I already owed him big time because I brought him a lot of business for a while and then, through my own stupidity, I wrecked that for him. So today is payback.' He reached into his pocket. 'Here you go, mate. You are now officially sponsored by Oddford Organics. And if my new album goes platinum, I'll treble that.' The big, white smile lit up his face.

Rory found a piece of paper thrust into his hand. Unfolding it, he saw a cheque for more money than he had ever dreamed possible in his cash-strapped sporting career.

'Is this a wind up?'

Dillon shook his head. Then, reminding himself of his duty to the foodie campaign, added in an undertone. 'You'll have to feed the horses all organic products, of course. It doesn't look good otherwise.'

'Trudy asked you to do this for me?'

'Not Trudy. I told you, this was your personal angel. Someone so madly in love with you they'd trade their soul for you, you lucky sod.'

'Just give me a name!' Rory pleaded, frantically thinking through possibilities – surely not Justine? Pixie, his Pussy Galore? Jemima? His ex, Dilly? Nell, the first love of his life, even? Who? 'Who was it? *Who*, Dillon?'

'That's confidential. I have made a solemn vow that I can only reveal her name if you win the eventing Grand Slam.'

'Ha bloody ha.' That meant winning the three biggest and toughest horse trials in succession, Kentucky, Badminton and Burghley – a triple crown only ever achieved once in history. 'I have more chance of scoring with Kylie tonight. And, lovely as she is, she wouldn't trade her soul for me. Please tell me who it is?'

'You have to be patient and win your new sponsor a few cups first,' Dillon told him, blue eyes caught by something on the far side of the room. 'Flipper had to wait ten years for Trudy and watch in agony as she spiralled downhill, but the time wasn't right for him to do a thing about it until recently and he knew it. That's life.'

Rory huffed in frustration, 'It's all right for you. You have to fight off women like Kylie with your walking stick.'

'Not quite,' Dillon corrected him, 'certainly not for a very long time. Like Trudy, I married the wrong person and paid the consequences. It knocks you sideways.' He didn't take his eyes from the blonde in the white dress who was smiling at him across a sea of heads. 'But I keep on looking everywhere I go. Never give up the hunt,' he rapped his walking stick vehemently on the floor. However trapped you may feel, or lonely, or desperate because you cannot make someone love you, never give up hope. Never give up the hunt, Rory.'

'I'll remember that.' Rory was staring cross-eyed at the cheque once more. 'Thank you, Dillon. Thank you from the bottom of my heart. I won't let you down. I'll clean up my act and focus one hundred per cent on the horses. That's a promise. First thing tomorrow I'll—'

But when he looked up, Dillon had gone.

Desperate to share his good news, Rory went in search of other Oddlode faces in the room. But Trudy and Flipper had moved on to their dinner and Nell had disappeared, too.

He was left with Liv Wilson, who was looking surprisingly glamorous in a smart nip-waisted navy blue suede skirt suit and with lots of dark, smoky make-up painted round her huge, doe eyes.

'Hi, Liv – fantastic boots.'

From that moment forward, he was guaranteed Liv's total undying gratitude, first because he'd noticed her new footwear – three hundred pounds from Thomas Wylde that afternoon, even in the sale – and second because she had been trying to seem fascinated by a display of modern art photographs for over half an hour now, too shy to strike up a conversation with a single soul there. She wanted to hug her saviour and cover him with kisses like a dog rescued from a car boot.

'There's nobody from the village here,' she lamented.

'Tell me about it.' Rory, who thought she looked rather like Isabella Rossellini in *Blue Velvet*, kissed her on both cheeks, perilously close to the mouth. 'Don't tell me they've only invited you to tease you about your secret admirer, too?'

'What?' Liv felt dreadful, having nagged Trudy endlessly to invite her tonight, only to find that she was hating every minute. She had thought, when Trudy insisted there was practically nobody from the village circle going, that she was just spinning her a line as an excuse. Now she could see that Trudy had been telling the truth. Having bragged about her invitation to Martin via email all month, she felt a fool. Even star-spotting had done nothing to lift her mood. But seeing Rory certainly did.

'Let's drink champagne together and laugh at the natives.' Rory threaded an arm through hers and led her towards the bar. As he did so, a tiny bell rang in the back of his mind.

'Tell me,' he asked as he parked Liv on a bar stool and beckoned for more free champagne, 'were you at that auction where Trudy played the piano?'

'Yes, but I didn't hear her play.'

'You didn't?'

She shook her head, explaining how Martin had bossily dragged

her away to the farm dispersal sale and the village fête in Oddlode.
It seemed a lifetime ago. 'The song is beautiful, isn't it? I can't get it
out of my head.'

'Me neither.'

Rory noticed a delicate froth of white lace bra peeping out from
beneath the sharp collars of her jacket and he smiled wider than
ever. In his top ten Bond Girl fantasies, along with front-runners
Honey Ryder and Pussy Galore, he had always been rather keen on
Plenty O'Toole who had picked Bond up in a casino in *Diamonds
Are Forever* and lured him back to her hotel room to seduce him –
although the baddies popping up and throwing her out of the window
into the swimming pool had been a bit of a passion killer.

'Are you staying in the hotel tonight?' he asked. She was much
sultrier than Kylie.

'Yes. I'm meeting some girlfriends for lunch tomorrow. My in-
laws are looking after the children.'

'How thrilling. I'm staying here, too. Do you happen to know if
there's a swimming pool?'

'Oh, it's lovely.' She nodded enthusiastically, having managed
twenty lengths of backstroke that afternoon. 'And there's a gym and
a spa – there's even a casino.'

'Really?' Rory filled up her champagne flute.

In a small Italian coffee house just around the block from the famous
hotel, Dillon and Nell had given the press the slip and were blowing
the steam from two espressos.

'Do you mind my bringing you here?' he asked.

She shook her head, although she would have killed for another
glass of champagne, perhaps in one of the many private members'
clubs in the area, to all of which he was bound to belong or would
be readily admitted because he was so famous.

He was pulling nervously at his cuffs. 'I find it hard – all the noise
and attention, plus alcohol everywhere.'

Nell stayed very cool, as she knew she must. His accent was strange
– part London cockney, part Irish burr and part transatlantic, it was
hard to place.

'I have a daughter,' she announced suddenly. 'She's six months
old.'

'I have two.' He stared at his bitten nails. 'Three and five.'

'And I have a married lover.'

'Ah . . . I don't have one of those.'

'Really? You absolutely must, you know – they're all the rage in the Cotswolds. *Everybody* has one.'

'Are you married?'

She shook her head, looking up at him through her lashes. 'Only one of you has to be married.'

That big, beautiful testosterone smile spread through his hollow, stubbled cheeks. 'In that case, I'm glad I'm not divorced yet.'

Upstairs in the hotel, Flipper and Trudy were back in their bedroom suite, breathless from running down long hotel corridors.

'Is this what they call inter course?' he gasped, dropping his trousers with practised speed as soon as they were through the door.

'We only have five minutes.' She pulled his shirt over his head with the cufflinks still attached so that he was left looking like Houdini in an unravelling straitjacket. 'They'll get restless if we're any longer.'

They had both sneaked away from the big, corporate table in the Michelin starred restaurant under the pretext of checking Mutt, who was staying in their room under special dispensation because, unlike Trudy's pack, he could not be trusted overnight in kennels.

But Mutt, sprawling on a huge leather sofa in front of the television, happily watching meer cats on the National Geographic channel, went completely unchecked as the couple hastily and happily slotted together against the back of their hotel room door and began a fast, furious race towards pleasure.

'D'you think we'll always be like this?' Trudy laughed between kisses as he hooked her thighs higher on his hips and slid her right up to his hilt.

'Night and day for the rest of our lives,' he said ambitiously, pressing his forehead to her shoulder and starting to issue those familiar cries and bellows of joy that heralded a rapid fire climax.

Breathing in the sweet smell of his hair, hardly able to remember a time when she'd thought it impossible to enjoy sex again, Trudy felt her body succumb to rapture as she squeaked and moaned frenziedly along, too.

On the other side of the door, dashing along the corridor to fetch his wallet from his own room, Rory, who had just discovered that

Liv had never played a roulette table in her life and was dying to spend some time in the casino, paused to listen by one of the exclusive suites.

The moans and groans coming from inside were inspiring.

He raised an impressed eyebrow. Loud sex was sensationally rock and roll and un-PC in this age of strictly enforced noise abatement, Asbos and reduced urban pollution. He guessed it had to be someone from the country.

Unfolding the cheque from his pocket one more time to reassure himself that he'd not dreamed it, he wondered whether the groaners were Dillon Rafferty and his latest quarry.

As far as Rory knew, he was the first professional rider to be sponsored by a glamorous rock star – even if it did rather unglamorously mean that he'd have to name his horses after a range of organic cheeses. Working with Dillon was bound to be great fun. He couldn't wait to see Faith's face when he told her tomorrow. But first he had Plenty O'Toole to entertain.

'Never give up the hunt,' he murmured, kissing the cheque and saluting the shaking door with his best James Bond brio. 'Never give up the hunt.'